Maven of Mayhem Series Omnibus

Mila Sin

Copyright © 2021 Mila Sin

All rights reserved

The characters and events portrayed in this book are fictitious. Any similarity to actual persons, living or dead, is coincidental and not intended by the author.

No part of this book may be reproduced, stored in a retrieval system, or transmitted in any form or by any means, electronic, mechanical, photocopying, recording, or otherwise, without express written permission of the publisher.

Dedication:

This book is dedicated to you, dear reader, who chose to take a chance on a new author. Thank you for helping make my dream a reality.

Content Warning

Content warning:
This book has explicit moments, from murder (described graphically) to sex (also described graphically). There is also a short flashback of childhood trauma in Chapter 12 from Rogue's point of view that can be skipped if it's upsetting. I've italicized the section so you know where you can restart reading. There is also forced prostitution (not of the main character) mentioned throughout the book.

The Secrets We Keep

Chapter One

Rogue

Great, blood on my shoes again. Just fucking perfect. I knew these old boots were on their last legs, but I hoped to get one more kill with them.

I kick out a leg like a deranged ballet dancer, flinging some off against the stained concrete to my right. Leaving blood spatter doesn't particularly matter when most of the dark alleyway is painted crimson with my recent mark.

That's right. Mark.

Mark the mark.

I fucking love it when someone's name lines up with their descriptor. Like a jerkwad CEO named Dick. Or a hairstylist named Bob.

In my case, I'm an overpaid assassin called Rogue.

It's always better to hire a professional than an amateur thug who would sell you out for the right price. So, if you don't want your murder-for-hire plot exposed, be ready to pay well for a professional.

My adoptive father, King, holds the reins to my mayhem by hoarding my secrets like a dragon hoards its gold. He pays well for my services too.

He dubbed me "Rogue" when I was a kid, and no one in my line of work or lackluster personal life has called me by my given name since I was seven years old.

My parents gave me the name Ivy Montgomery, and it died along with them.

The cool autumn breeze brushes against my sweaty forehead as I circle the lifeless body of Mark. My heart races with adrenaline as I quickly pack away my knives and discard my blood-soaked shirt into a plastic bag in my backpack. Behind a nearby dumpster, I strip off my stained clothes and change into a clean set, carefully avoiding any curious onlookers at this early hour. After wiping down the soles of my boots, I cautiously step around the crime scene, ensuring that no trace of my presence remains for the authorities to find. I strategically chose this alleyway for its lack of security cameras—except for the one pointed at an unimportant delivery entrance fifteen feet away.

Rifling through the bag, I find a sweatshirt. I slip it over my head and pull the hood up to conceal my face and hair. My black jeans have bloodstains, but the inky black denim hides it well. It's not my usual style, but it's perfect for blending in and avoiding detection by security cameras.

As I walk out onto the street, I adjust my posture to mimic that of a homeless person. Hunched over, with my backpack slung low on my back, I shuffle along with my head down. No one pays attention to those living on the streets, making it easy for me to slip away unnoticed after committing my bloody crime.

It's a sad reflection of our society's disregard for the impoverished, but it works in my favor as I make my escape.

I hoof it a few blocks to reach my designated safe house. I pull the key from inside my boot, untie it from the laces, and slide it into the lock. A soft click, and I'm in.

Ah, home sweet, safe house away from home.

I trudge through the bland living room and head to the kitchen. Grabbing the standard burner phone that my organization stocks every safe house with, I video call King.

"How's Mark?" he asks in greeting. I hear some soft murmurs on the other end and assume I've woken him and his flavor of the week. She doesn't seem like a morning person. Too bad.

The screen blurs as King removes himself from his bed. A flash of blonde hair fanned over golden sheets is visible on the corner of the screen just before a door clicks shut, and I look into King's serious eyes.

"Dead," I reply with a casual shrug of my shoulders. I wasn't supposed to off Mark immediately, but I have my reasons. King's salt-and-pepper hair falls to his forehead as he laughs. His defined black brow arches, and his dark eyes narrow at me. I can feel the scrutiny through the screen.

King's parents were from Istanbul and immigrated to California when he was a child. He has an olive complexion, and a constant five o'clock shadow gives him a 'devil may care' look to the casual observer. But it's the little tics that tell you you're in danger—the tiny twitch at the right corner of his mouth, a slight flaring of the nostrils—all signs I learned to look out for early on.

"You've got blood on your neck, daughter. Wash it off and get here for tonight's meeting."

Thankful that King left the bedroom, I send a silent prayer of gratitude to any deity listening that the woman he has in his home isn't listening. If she'd heard us, King would kill her for simply being in the wrong place as he said the wrong thing. And he wouldn't have a care in the world about it —he taught me my trade, after all. He's a wicked man who does despicable things. A testimonial of my childhood would see him in prison for multiple life sentences.

"Yes, King," I reply before hanging up.

King, the leader of The Gambit, is one of the most feared men in the state—dreaded not only by his legions of flunkies but officials and politicians as well. He's got most of California under his thumb, and his reach is growing. Only Los Angeles and the most southern cities in the state remain free from his grip.

I hear Oregon and Washington are on the docket for the next takeover. He'd prefer to focus north than deal with the pushback in the south. The Rattlesnakes, another gang on our coast, run the north, but King thinks they're ripe for the picking with their new leadership.

King is the man who raised me after my parents passed away when I was seven. I don't even know his real name. He's always just been "King" to me. His previous life was covered up so efficiently when he ascended to the leadership role of The Gambit that even I couldn't find anything.

The Gambit is a well-organized, statewide gang based in El Castillo, California, involved in drugs, gun-running, blackmail, and general mayhem. You want chaos? We deliver. I fucking hate the organization. But I'm almost done.

Three more years of this shit, and I'm free. My contract with King binds me to this life until I reach twenty-seven, the age we agreed upon after a fierce negotiation when I started working for The Gambit at sixteen. If I don't follow through, the consequences will be swift and deadly.

When I was new to this role, he compiled evidence of my crimes, no matter how careful I'd been. I've seen the files, and they haunt my dreams. Since then, I've learned to cover my tracks and never do the job when King expects me to, but it doesn't erase the footage he already has. One toe out of line, and he'll sink me, using the cops he has on his payroll. In the event of his death, the evidence goes to the authorities. More than that, the sole person I love in this world will suffer.

I once dreamed of having an everyday life and connecting with a nice guy to settle down with. I'd love to find someone I can build a life with. Maybe sit around and get fat while binge-watching Netflix shows. You know, normal. But alas, my job is murder. That harsh fact tends to creep into the fantasy as well. Who wants to come home to that?

I can just imagine it now.

Hi, honey! How was your day? Oh, super, I killed four people for a gang lord and had to bleach a crime scene because one guy was too wiggly, and my knife got stuck in his neck. The blood spray was epic. Want to order pizza? I'm feeling pepperoni.

Give me a break. My relationships have been shallow, superficial, or one-night-only situations, with less entanglement and less risk. I'm not arming anyone else with the ability to get me arrested or killed. That kind of trust doesn't exist.

Heading down the narrow hallway to the shower, I strip off the weapons still strapped to my body, toss the clothes into the incinerator, and stuff my favorite boots into plastic bags to take home and clean in hopes of using them again.

Evidence is bad. DNA evidence is worse.

I've been the head assassin for The Gambit for nearly five years. Before this role, I was one of many on tap. Now, I run the select group, using their assets to the best of my abilities and giving them the jobs they're best suited for.

Before I could even read properly, King started my training, but he only forced me into The Gambit once I graduated high school at sixteen. I worked my ass off double-time as a homeschooled kid because I couldn't fathom another two years of looking at math equations when it all looked like hieroglyphics to me. If I had known what my graduation present would be, I'd have endured trigonometry with a smile on my face and joy in my heart.

Most daughters of well-to-do, super-rich guys get a car for their sweet sixteen or graduation. I got a contract for a hit.

The Secrets We Keep

King strong-armed me into this line of work. He's my guardian, and so he threatened to cut off all financial, housing, and general support if I turned him down. He's also the leader of a motherfucking gang. I couldn't say no; I'd be dead, and so would my sister.

In the shower, scrubbing with whatever no-name brand soap they keep stocked here, I think over my morning and make sure I did everything correctly. I rarely do, but I'd rather be safe than in jail or dead.

I followed Mark the mark from his home. He lived in a modest apartment on the third floor with no security. He went to the coffee shop on the corner while eying the new bakery that opened across the street. He enjoyed a latte and a croissant, his Tuesday usual, and headed to his convenience shop early to do inventory. I feigned a stumble in front of him as he made his way to his shop.

Why was Mark a mark? He owns one of the businesses that pay protection fees to The Gambit and decided to record his last encounter with one of King's enforcers.

The tape held nothing too damning, but he managed to pass it along to one of the only cops in that precinct not under our thumb. Mark knew he was dead as soon as he hit record on his phone.

Adding to Mark's sins, he's been accused of rape twice and beat his last girlfriend to a bloody pulp. As soon as he was brought up as a target, I knew this job would be mine.

I try not to kill *only* for the benefit of the organization. My bread and butter are the men who prey on those weaker than themselves. Everyone else gets divided among the other assassins.

His kill didn't need to be so bloody. It could have been a simple knife to either side of the ribs, slipping between to puncture the lungs, but no. Mark has a type, and when I feigned a trip in front of him, he thought I was actually a damsel in distress who needed a big strong man to save me. One hand snug around my waist and the other clamped on my wrist made him feel confident as he pulled me into the alley.

I took much joy in pulling my knives from their hiding spots and may have stabbed a little too hard. If you do it carefully, there's minimal bleeding with maximum damage. But if you get stab-happy like I did, it makes one hell of a mess.

One knife made it to his lung as planned, the other to his kidney. Oops.

If nothing else, it looks like a mugging gone wrong. I even lifted Mark's wallet and cell phone, which I dumped into the river on my way to the safe house.

The last piece of this puzzle includes getting a cop on the inside to misplace the video evidence Mark handed in without raising too many suspicions. I know just the guy and make a mental note to cash in a favor from him.

After the shower and my trip down memory lane, I kill the water and step out to do a once-over in the mirror.

My face is clean and bare, with a light smattering of freckles across my nose and green eyes that look too jaded for my age peek out from under my lashes. A button nose and full lips make up the rest of my face. Pretty, but unremarkable.

My body is a different story. I'm tall, coming in at five foot ten. I have a nice figure, more hourglass than anything else, with a full bust and wide hips. Tattoos cover the entire right side of my body, including my limbs, while the left is clear of any markings aside from the rune scars on my lower stomach. The stark contrast is only emphasized by the dark line of division running down my torso from neck to clit and up my spine, disappearing into my hair.

Half dark, half light.

I dry and set my hair into my usual pin-up style and add my war paint in the form of winged eyeliner and a bold red lip. I wrap my bandana under my mane and tie it atop my head, making the bow jaunty and playful.

Gathering the other go-bag I stashed before work, I pull out a red and black polka dot halter dress with a flared skirt. Black peep-toe stilettos are the last addition. That's more like it.

I enjoy dressing in rockabilly styles—a bit of flair for breaking up the monotony of everyone wearing carbon copies of jeans and T-shirts.

My boots, knives, and guns go into the bag I'm taking with me, and I toss the one with trace evidence into the incinerator with the rest of the bloody clothes. I text Rosa with the cleaning crew that she can scrub the place down, toss the burner phone into the incinerator, and close the front door when the sound of flames consuming the evidence reaches my ears.

Chapter Two

Rogue

Ten hours later, I'm sitting at a conference table in Rook Industries' conference room after regular business hours. The Gambit runs this corporation to maintain its legal operations and launder money from its less-than-legal ones.

The legal side is a venture capital firm with various companies throughout California. I'm a member of the seven-person board along with King and five other higher-ups.

The syndicate was formed in El Castillo and has preserved the city as the base of operations for nearly fifty years.

King leads the board as the chairman of our organization, CEO of Rook, and general thorn in my side.

There's Mr. Hiroto Tanaka, the COO of Rook Industries. He worked his way up the company ladder, and only when he reached the highest management tier did he learn the whole company was a front for the criminal empire. At that point, he had two girls at Ivy League schools and needed the salary his position was awarded. I found out later that King guaranteed that something would happen to his daughters if he tried to jump ship.

Leo Horvat, an all-around prick, is our "weapons acquisition expert"—a title he gave himself. He's in charge of getting shipments of weapons and running them up and down the state or to allies in neighboring territories. Horvat has been around since I was ten, and he enjoyed helping King teach me to be a killer. His lessons were, in a word, monstrous.

Mrs. Elise Batten is a no-nonsense woman who spends her days about town with the other old biddies. She took her first husband's spot on the board after he passed twenty years ago. She ran his life anyway, and the connections those two forged in high society and the political sphere are incomparable. Batten is responsible for swaying the upper crust under our thumbs by lending an air of civility. She uses husband number one's old Rolodex and her fancy soirees to do some real damage. She's got a habit of outliving her husbands and inheriting their fortunes. I'm almost positive she killed numbers two through four, but I haven't found concrete evidence yet.

Nina Wilson is a thirty-seven-year-old Stanford MBA grad whose dad had terrible debts. She is a whiz with Excel and acts as our financial overlord. Wilson didn't want to be on the board, but it was a way to keep her father alive and a roof over her parents' heads. She organizes the bribes, facilitates money laundering, and gets our employees paid legally with dirty cash. Nina also set up an offshore account for herself and has been skimming money off the top since joining us. But on a positive note, she did get us all on a fantastic healthcare plan.

Lastly, Enrique De La Cruz runs drugs for us. The drug shipments come in, he allocates it to the dealers and gets a healthy cut from the sales. De La Cruz is charming as hell when it suits him. I've seen him help an old lady cross the street just to watch him kill one of his dealers not fifteen minutes later because he was forty bucks under his expected count.

This is a group anyone would be stupid to mess with. There are dirty cops and government officials on our payroll, and we've got the backing of the surrounding criminal enterprises due to a treaty the neighboring gangs agreed upon five years ago.

On the table for discussion tonight is the destruction of that pesky video evidence, a route the gun runners are using, and punishment for selling our drugs to kids.

The last one is due to an initiative I started when I witnessed a kid overdosing while doing recon for a hit a couple of years ago. The memory still gives me chills.

I framed the strategy as intelligent business. Sell to adults, keep the product pure, and they'll return. Kids scare easily when one of their friends overdoses. They all stop hitting drugs out of fear, leading to tanking sales. It is, perhaps, a fool's hope that kids wise the fuck up and not do drugs in the first place.

Most of the time, I hate what the organization does. At least they no longer sell to minors, and the guns are kept within The Gambit or run out of state to allies. We compensate the politicians and civil servants well to keep the heat off our backs. All while paving the way for possible expansion without too much bloodshed.

"For the last time," I hear a gruff voice bluster, "we should be selling to whoever has the cash, regardless of their age. Not punishing our dealers who are busting their asses out there making us money."

Here we go, I internally gripe while fighting off the urge to roll my eyes during a board meeting. I pull the curved knife from a slot between my stiletto heel and the sole of my shoe. Jabbing the knife into the dark wood before me, I level a glare at De La Cruz. "No."

One word and a gesture convey my profound disagreement with his statement. Considering all the information I've gathered over the years, few people in this room would counter me. But every once in a while, someone gets bold.

Enrique continues with reduced menace in his voice, regarding the knife with trepidation. The purple flower he always wears in his lapel is damn near shaking. I love making him nervous. "We're losing out on a valuable corner of the market. It's only a matter of time until a rival group moves in, and we're left with our thumbs up our asses."

I pull my knife from the table in front of me with a saccharine smile, launching it at the board behind Enrique's head. It embeds in the wall and quivers with the strength of my throw.

King huffs out a sigh and rises from his chair. He moves over to the corkboard while buttoning the jacket of his charcoal three-piece suit. Everyone notes his exasperation. Enrique has been tiptoeing over the line more than he should lately, and he fucking knows it. He's on thin ice, and this is the hill he wants to die on.

King yanks out the knife and follows the graphs on the board with the tip of the sharp blade. The charts and projections aren't entitled "DRUGS!" but are deliberately mislabeled with profits from other businesses under our umbrella—a preventative measure if things fall into the wrong hands. "Rogue is right."

I smile sweetly at Enrique while garnering head nods from the remaining four board members not involved in our spat. His charm is losing its shine while his bald head gains it with all the stress sweating he's doing.

If I tilt my head just right, I can see the reflection of the overhead lighting bouncing off his shiny skull.

Elise Batten, the aging socialite dressed in a Chanel pantsuit and dripping in pearls, pipes in, "Sales are up without that nasty side effect of kids overdosing and scaring their friends. It also results in fewer questions from the authorities or that daft governor. It may not be the rise you want immediately, Enrique, but it is steadily climbing, and we've had no significant drops in the two years since Rogue championed this move. If someone moves into the state to 'corner the market,' as you say, we kill them. Simple, like last time."

I choke on a laugh, smothering it with a cough instead of breaking into hysterics. Damn. This woman always manages to shock me. For an old hag who looks like she's on her way to a tea party with the motherfucking Queen, she shoots straight and puts Enrique in his place effortlessly. The air quotes she uses to mimic him make my dark heart smile. I hope I'm as badass as her when I get older.

Murmurs of agreement rise from the members around the table. Good, that should keep Enrique quiet for the rest of the week. Hopefully, knowing he doesn't have others in his corner to back him might keep him from spewing more bullshit. I'm surprised Horvat isn't supporting him. Those two degenerates stick together like pages in a porn magazine.

King walks around the table while flipping my knife in his hand. Each member he passes shrinks a fraction in their seat—except Elise, who sits taller. King's aura is unhappy as it presses down on all of us. Tension radiates from Enrique as the shadow passes over him. King approaches me, leans over my shoulder, and gently places the knife in my waiting palm.

He pats a hand on my bicep, where there's an old scar from a bullet wound. His thumb digs into the exit wound as a camouflaged warning to follow his command. "Rogue, my darling daughter, will handle any dealers you can't rein in. Give us their details, and we'll see it done."

I tip my head to the rest of the room in agreement while twirling my knife in my left hand, knowing there will be at least five new names on my list by the end of the day. Enrique runs the dealers, and King will pressure him for names as soon as possible. The slightest twitch under our leader's right eye alerts me that he's seething.

King starts the new topic of gun-running, and I zone out. I won't be required on this topic unless I'm sent after someone who tries to fuck us over. Most of the time, the dumbshit who tries to up the bribe cost just needs a good scare to fall back in line. Our routes are secured and bribed to high heaven; I rarely need to ensure understanding.

I watch as Horvat and Nina Wilson, the definite brains of that duo, discuss the running across state lines.

Wilson organizes our guys and the shipments with eerie precision. She pulls out a tablet from her designer bag to run through the routes they're using, measures they've secured, and a slew of contingency plans as Horvat blathers on about the caliber of weapon they're shipping.

I can appreciate the dedication and organization that go into our deliveries. Then again, Nina's Stanford education and subsequent MBA degree should be standard. What better way to use those brains than to earn more money than God and keep her dad alive?

The meeting took an hour, and we wrapped everything up with a discussion about the tape Mark sent in. By lunchtime, I'd handled that with a simple text. Officer Sails had confirmed the destruction and followed up with a message begging me to lose his number when the deal was done. Fair enough.

As everyone stretches in their seats, Enrique takes the opportunity to slide a page toward me. I flip it over when I stand, finding names to add to the assassins' list. Every dealer has been warned, and it is Enrique's lack of discipline to thank for their upcoming demise. I hope the guilt eats him alive. Then, I hope King decides Enrique isn't worth the risk anymore. I'll start digging into the dealers' lives tonight before doling out the assignments to my team. Maybe there's one or two just for me.

We trickle from the meeting room, and Mr. Tanaka bows in my direction as we approach the elevator foyer. I reciprocate the gesture, and he smiles warmly at me. He's always been a man of few words, but Tanaka runs the business well, and the employees are satisfied. He has also worked to increase the diversity in legitimate higher management positions because he noticed he was the only person of Asian descent in an executive position.

"If you have time next week, can we set up a meeting?" he asks without emotion.

Curious about what it could be about, I nod. "I'll check my schedule, and we'll make it work."

He smiles again and takes off down the hall toward his office—no doubt heading back to work to earn his keep.

Horvat catches up with me at the elevator. Great. Thirty-five floors with this sweaty pig. He's thirty-eight, medium build, beady-eyed, and shifty as hell. He always tries to get under my skin, but he doesn't seem to realize that without holding him in high regard, there's not much he can say that will genuinely bother me.

"After you, *draga*," he intones, lifting a hand to direct me into the elevator ahead of him.

I don't hide the cringe as I enter the elevator and stab the button for the lobby, willing the whole damn box to plummet to the earth so I can get out of here.

I fucking hate Rook. The Gambit. The members of the board. This life. I mentally chant *You're almost out, you're almost out* ten times in an attempt to keep myself from just saying fuck it and going on a rampage in this snake pit.

As Horvat's blathering washes over me with nary a reaction, I let my mind drift to my exit plan to keep my meditative state. Unfortunately, snippets from my past sneak in, ruining my zen place. This man standing next to me has done horrific things, both before joining The Gambit and in the name of the organization. My stomach holds the rune he held me down for as King etched it into my skin.

I may play the dutiful foster daughter to King, but I've got some qualms. All the fucking qualms. Cut off from external influences, my adolescence was spent with King or a nanny, and I was homeschooled to avoid the real world.

I was relentlessly trained and beaten to within an inch of my life to learn from my mistakes. This whole shit show is going up in flames when my deal is up. He trained me to be merciless while calling me "daughter" the whole time.

Finally reaching the lobby, I stomp out of the elevator, leaving Horvat in my dust.

I gleefully threatened him about a year ago by sneaking into his family home the night he returned from his honeymoon. I held a knife to his carotid while his new wife slept soundly in the next room.

Only a week after the wedding and already sleeping in separate rooms? That doesn't bode well for the longevity of that relationship. His wakeup was less than graceful, and he nicked himself on my knife when he jolted.

Seeing that small scar on his neck always makes me smile.

Chapter Three

Noah

The flashing blue and red lights are getting so goddamn annoying. There are three squad cars, a coroner's van, me, and a slew of morbid passers-by, hoping to see something grotesque.

A few detectives are conversing while looking over the area, and a crime scene tech is taking photos of the dead shop owner and yelling at his intern to stop stepping in evidence.

Incompetence and jockeying for promotions like these assholes is why I'm glad I work in the private sector. However, what my four-man team and I are working on now is anything but Annex Security sanctioned. They'd be pretty pissed off if they found out what we were up to while under contract.

Our squad was formed nearly five years ago, and someone thought I—Noah Tate, curmudgeon on a good day and a mute, scowling bundle of sunshine on a bad—was an excellent fit to lead our group. Maybe it's because I'm ex-military and was conditioned to follow orders. I had my doubts about leading a civilian security team at first. But together, Lucas McCreary, Han Shin, Jacob Waters, and I have the top spot in our company because we are obedient and work together seamlessly. At least, we were mindlessly obedient until a couple of years ago when we started digging into the orders and discovered some alarming truths.

"Victim Mark Sandoval, forty-four. Found this morning by a cleaner tossing garbage into the dumpster from the restaurant's back door. Beaten, obvious broken wrist, four broken ribs, and stab wounds to the right lung and left kidney. The force of impact and bruising indicate a male assailant around six feet tall. Time of death was between five and six this morning." I listen as the detective and technician go back and forth over details, seeing my opportunity while they try to prove themselves to each other. Douches.

I walk around the foot traffic crowding the alleyway and dart inside the restaurant. The manager sees me in my expensive suit, and I pull out a counterfeit badge claiming I'm a detective. "I'm here to take all the recordings you have from the camera facing the alley," I state authoritatively. Fake it till you make it, right?

The balding man looks nervous but complies with the order. "Yes, sir. One of the other officers already told me to load the footage onto a drive and have it ready for the detective. It's in the office; I'll go grab it."

Well, that was easy.

Gotta love procedural cop shows. They taught me everything I need to know for this type of grab. A beat cop does the preliminary canvassing first, and the detective comes to collect significant evidence if it isn't readily available.

I try not to let the relief show on my face. It was a gamble that the owner had already finished loading the video since the officer who came by only visited about twenty minutes ago.

The military provided me with a different form of education. Their brand of knowledge came from running a tight ship and emulating authority. Not to mention running missions and keeping upper management abreast of our work. These days, my team reports to me while I run things and liaise with our management at Annex. I hate the liaising part.

Sometimes, the guys complain that I'm too serious and can't relax. But after four years of JROTC, then four of ROTC in college, ending with my four-year contract in a leadership role in the Army, relaxation doesn't enter my realm of thinking very often.

The nervous man disappears into the back to get the tapes, and I tap my foot impatiently. I only have a little time before someone comes in here, and I'm witnessed stealing evidence.

A few seconds later, he returns and hands over the USB. I grip it tightly and hope it has the information I want. "We're grateful for your cooperation. The police department thanks you."

He grumbles that the city's crime rates are bad for business, but I'm already turning and weaving through the tables to get to the front entrance. The back exit is not an option, with the corpse a few feet from the door.

I'm five feet from the door when it swings inward. The bells above jangle merrily, and I tip my head politely to the real detective working the case. He nods back distractedly while letting me pass. The door is just closing behind me when I hear him ask for the tapes. Oh fuck, time to book it.

Thumbing out a text to Lucas, the teammate on assignment with me today, I break into a jog, confirm the thumb drive collection, tell him to get the truck started, and meet me at pickup point C. We mapped the area before I split off from him and came up with a few options.

I pick up the pace after turning a corner to get lost before the detective tracks me down. Thank God Han makes me do so much cardio. Must never mention I'm grateful, or he'll make me do more.

"Hey! Stop!" The shout comes from behind me as the detective starts gaining speed. We're both running flat out now, but I'm faster. Snaking through obstacles in an alley between shops and jumping over disgusting stains on the floor, I make it to a chain-link fence and start to haul my ass up.

Detective Douchecanoe reaches the fence as my second leg swings over the top. I launch myself off, do a tuck and roll, and hobble a few paces to the mouth of the alley where Lucas has the truck idling. I dive into the bed of the truck, and a moment later, the tires squeal as he hits the gas and speeds off. I risk a last look and see the detective doing his best to catch up on foot.

Sending him a one-finger salute, I lie down in the truck bed and grip the handles we added for situations like this. It's a mere few minutes before we're cruising at high speeds on the freeway, headed across town to our base.

———

Lucas drives us through the opening in the fence—unlocking it via the app on our phones—and into the parking area of our converted warehouse. He opens the window at the back of the cab and pops his head through. He sees me squinting into the sunlight and totally at ease. "You didn't get shot, did you?"

It's a valid question. It's not often Lucas sees me calm enough just to lounge around. I must be bleeding out if I'm this relaxed. He didn't have any time to check on me before speeding off. He just shouted something unintelligible, and I banged on the truck's cab in response. "Nah, man, I'm good. This is Rogue. I know it."

Rogue Assassin. Okay, so maybe "Assassin" isn't his last name, but fuck if I know what it is. We've seen his work periodically and want him on our side. We've heard the name whispered like a boogeyman for the genuinely vile but haven't managed to locate him in the two years we've been actively looking.

We did some research into the people he's killed. Nearly all of them were black souls, having done truly ignoble deeds, deserving of some vigilante justice. But, the only problem is, we can't fucking find him. Hopefully, today will get us one step closer.

The truth is, we need Rogue. He is the only one on the board of The Gambit with a hint of integrity. Our organizations have been working together for a while now, using each other's skill sets to gain more control in the criminal world. He'd be a helpful connection because of his discerning nature regarding his hits. No one in that organization has morals based on the rumors we've heard and their grip on the state. But we're operating on the theory that he just might and wants to be rid of his bosses.

We signed up for this job to do good and protect those who need it. Over the last few years, those opportunities have dried up and been replaced with shady assignments we've done our best to avoid.

There were a couple of relocations, identity changes, and other ways to avoid completing the kill orders handed down to us. We've managed to keep ourselves and some of our former targets from being discovered.

"You said that about the last killer we chased down. It ended up being a really pissed-off housewife who knew how to wield a boning knife," Lucas grouses. He's getting sick of the run-around, too. This hitman has managed to evade us for an embarrassingly long amount of time.

"Yeah, but she taught us how to filet a fish by the end of our first meeting. Worth it." I laugh, thinking about Mrs. Morganson, and make a mental note to text her later. She became our "den mother," as she likes to say. Like we're her cubs. Her knife-and-gun-carrying, spying, murdering, all-around asshole cubs.

I hop out of the truck as Lucas emerges from the cab. He shakes out his dark red hair and leaves it as a mess. It must be a younger trend. I keep my dark locks neat and tidy. Although, that's a holdover from my army days.

Lucas extends a tanned hand for a fist bump, and I reluctantly give in. We did good work today, though the gesture feels an odd way to celebrate

The Secrets We Keep

it. He tosses an arm over my shoulder in camaraderie, and I laugh at his happy-go-lucky attitude.

Lucas brings a lightheartedness our team desperately needs in our daily work, while I often lend a bit of gravity to situations—intentionally or otherwise.

We reach the steel door to the warehouse, and I shrug Lucas's arm off of me. He keys in the code on the panel while one of our guys inside checks the CCTV feed we use around the warehouse perimeter. The door starts rolling to the right, opening up to the anteroom.

The warehouse was Jacob's find. He's our information expert, for lack of a better term. He knows far too much about every subject, and what he doesn't know, he finds out. Tattooed from head to toe, his usual business attire throws people for a loop when they meet him. His English accent helps him get shit done because everyone is a sucker for his posh enunciation.

A couple of years ago, he went through a real estate phase, resulting in this empty shell that he converted into our base of operations. He got it for a steal, and we've got enough money socked away between the four of us that it barely made a dent. The contractors working on it thought it would be a start-up space. We have server rooms, but they're full of security feeds and secrets people wish would stay buried.

Lucas pushes through the frosted glass doors into the heart of the base. It's wide open, with exposed ductwork, desks, and a lounge area spread throughout the space. The perimeter of the bottom floor houses our meeting room and the kitchen, and to the back is our gym and Jacob's computer room. Glass walls to divide those spaces make the warehouse feel spacious and open rather than blocked off and disjointed.

Upstairs are our private rooms, bathrooms, and two guest rooms, which we've used in the past to hide someone before relocating them out of Annex's reach. We brought them here blindfolded and often cuffed so they couldn't poke around or find our location.

I can see Han doing a set of curls in front of the mirrors at the back of the gym. The weight drops to the ground with a loud thud as he sees us in the mirror's reflection. He spins and pushes his way through the gym's glass doors. Working out while others are on a mission is Han's distraction method. It keeps him from focusing too much on what could go wrong.

He approaches us, pushing his sweaty hair off his face. He pulls out the shirt he has tucked into the back of his workout shorts and tosses it on before he reaches us, his brows raised in question.

"Jacob!" Lucas yells toward the second level as he lopes up the stairs to the catwalk. Loud music comes from his room, so the door must be open. The rooms themselves are soundproofed for this exact reason. Jacob likes his music far too loud for the rest of us.

I hear them arguing before I see them. Lucas loves to get under Jacob's skin about everything. Jacob likes to ignore Lucas until his lack of attention drives him insane. They're worse than siblings; they're unlikely friends.

After turning off the music, Jacob leads the way out of his room. He adjusts his black-framed glasses on his nose and rolls up the sleeves of his dress shirt. He always looks like he's attending a board meeting, but the tattoos lining his jaw and reaching his toes say otherwise.

They descend the stairs to start processing the video I've returned with. Jacob's tattooed fingers rest on Lucas's shoulder as he steers him to the tech room, giving him a hearty shove when he tries to take Jacob's fancy white gaming chair. He's weirdly protective of that thing.

Lucas seizes the opportunity to veer off to the coffee machine we put in here—despite Jacob being a tea drinker through and through—and prepares himself a cup. Han and I follow in after them, and I see Han's hands wringing with leftover nerves he worked up while waiting for us to return earlier.

We cluster around the back of Jacob's chair while staring up at the five monitors Jacob has surrounding him. He pops in the USB and gets the footage cued up to play on the three central monitors.

Lucas rounds the desk to join us with a cup of coffee in a mug that reads: *You do realize one day I'll snap, right?*

Fitting. Jovially, he chimes in, "Here we go, boys. Let's find us a Rogue."

Chapter Four

Rogue

A WEEK AFTER THE ROOK MEETING, I'M WATCHING ONE OF OUR dealers grasping at his neck as his poisoned beer mug smashes to the floor in a local dive bar. His eyes are wide and wheeling around in his skull when they land on me. I send him a flirty wink and shift my body to keep him in my peripherals.

His buddies are panicking. One is doing the Heimlich, the second is just staring blankly, and the third is yelling at the guy who's slowly losing his airway and breaking out in hives. Yeah, that'll help.

Counting down from ten, I hold my breath until his body hits the table with a loud bang. "Another One Bites the Dust" by Queen continues to pump out of the speakers during the ordeal. He's down. I exhale and nod at the jukebox in the corner that I queued up with appropriate death songs.

Enrique will get the word out that the same will happen to anyone caught selling our drugs to minors; they report to him at the end of the day, and we all know King won't bother dealing with the underlings despite his humble beginnings. Word will get out, and no one will want to end up poisoned in a bar, shitting their pants in front of their friends. It's not a very dignified way to go.

See? Finesse.

The bar picks up again, business as usual, and the guys haul their dead friend out of the bar. He'll probably end up in the river tonight. Good riddance. This isn't the neighborhood to die in if you expect a moment of silence or the cops called.

I pay for my drink and slip out the door after waiting half an hour for the usual bar rhythm to pick up again. Once some girl starts yelling at her boyfriend for checking out her friend, I know the patrons have moved on from tonight's earlier entertainment.

Walking out into the crisp night air, I feel the wind play through my loose tendrils of hair. It's curled and hanging down my back in soft waves, complimenting my black dress. My vintage-style black T-strap heels click across the pavement as I strut toward my car.

It's not safe for women to walk in this area alone in the dark. Unless you're a scarier monster than those who go bump in the night around here. Boo, motherfuckers.

The city of El Castillo is known for both its incredible wealth and its incredible poverty. If you walk ten minutes in any direction, you will find the houses shifting from mansions to shacks, apartment high-rises to crumbling duplexes.

I fucking love this city, but there's no middle. There are the haves and the have-nots, the rich and the poor. The middle class died out or moved away more than twenty years ago.

My black 1957 Chevy Bel Air is in the parking garage where I left it. Keys in my hand already, I unlock the door and slide in, dropping my clutch on the bench seat. I'm looking forward to an evening with a bottle of wine and Vikings on Netflix. A prickle of awareness tickles my neck a second before I hear a soft exhale. I'm not alone.

Lucas

Having been on a stakeout for the past few hours, my body is tired, and my mind is mush. I followed who I assume is Rogue's girlfriend as she left the apartment building in the car we tracked from the alleyway kill. We haven't been able to get into the building to find him, but when I saw the car leave, I knew it was a chance for us to get some information from his partner.

The door opens, and just as I'm about to announce myself from the backseat, she slides in and tosses a small bag onto the seat next to her. The scent of lemons and lavender momentarily stuns me.

Moving faster than I've seen in a long time, the woman spins in place, using the front seat as a springboard, and launches herself into the backseat.

There's a butterfly knife pressed to my neck. Where the fuck did she pull that from?

"Hey, Buttercup. Want to put that down?" I try to sweet-talk the stranger into releasing me. She presses the blade a bit harder against my neck. There's a sharp sting suddenly poking my groin, and I realize she's got a second knife pressed to my dick.

Not a great first meeting.

It's in that moment, fear for my dick obviously distracting me, that I realize this is possibly Rogue. I followed the car from the apartment building we've been staking out since we tracked the hitman. Damn, hitwoman. I caught a quick look at who was driving and wasn't sure whether to follow, but we observed the same car on the cams, so I took a risk.

I trailed the car to this parking garage and watched her leave on foot. I parked one level above and waited beside the vehicle for her return. I needed to see if I could get some information from her about her husband or boyfriend or whatever.

I just wanted to chat and see if we could set up a meeting with him, not get a knife to the cock. It turns out that either this woman is Rogue or he has trained her. The steady hands and stern look on her face make me pretty damn confident this is Rogue.

She lifts a sculpted brow at me, pausing for my explanation as to why I'm waiting for her. In her car. In a shitty neighborhood. In the dark. Yeah, I can see how I messed up here.

"Who the fuck are you?" she asks. Oh, fuck. Her voice is raspy and like being wrapped in a warm blanket on a cold, snowy night—a cup of tea with honey in one of my unique, witty mugs on a sore throat. Somehow, I've become a poet for this woman, and we've only exchanged a handful of words.

"Lu—Lucas," I push past my lips quietly. My breath makes her black, wavy hair float around her ears. "I'm with Annex Security."

She stares into my eyes, showing a brief glimmer of recognition at my employer's name, but never once reduces the pressure on the blades she wields. "And why are you in my car?"

I create a bit of distance between us so I can at least pretend to maintain some dignity during this awkward-as-fuck surprise meeting.

"It got cold." I've got to admit she does not look amused. Fuck, that's my whole personality! What am I supposed to do? Act serious? Pfft, that's not my style. But alas, desperate times.

"I was waiting next to the passenger side door, but it got cold out there. I kind of broke in." It may be early autumn, but the evening chill gets to me. "Our team finally tracked you down, and we want a meeting with you to hire you. We know you work for The Gambit, and we'd like to offer you an alternative." It was a fifty-fifty shot that she's Rogue, and with the knives digging into me, I'd say it's more like ninety-ten now.

"Get out." She flips the blades closed and stuffs them down the sides of her top into the outsides of her cleavage. At least the knife mystery is solved.

As she swings her legs to the side to prepare to step out of the backseat, I grab her wrist firmly but gently enough not to cause any pain. Yep, I'm now nearly one hundred percent confident that this is Rogue after watching her stash weapons like it's second nature.

"Please, let me explain. We've been looking for you for years. Years. We finally caught a break, and you. You need us as much as we need you. If we can catch you, who says the dirty cops in this town can't as well? We have a proposal for you."

She pauses. Her eyes flick down to my hand on her wrist, then out the windows—no doubt looking for witnesses to my upcoming murder. I have a feeling she's already got it planned out in her head. "How did you find me?"

"Agree to a meeting with our team, and we'll tell you. If you work with us, we'll correct the mistake. If you don't, well, at least you'll know what happened and how to avoid it in the future."

"Fair point. Three days. Where?"

No nonsense, huh? Okay, I can roll with that. After all, Noah is my commander. The dude wouldn't know hilarity if it stuck its dick up his ass and tickled his balls with a feather duster while calling him Norma Jean.

Doing my best imitation of Noah, I reply gruffly, "Fine. Tuesday, three o'clock, I'll text you an address twenty minutes before. Security reasons, you understand."

Okay, I may have taken it too far—the woman's looking at me like I've lost my damn mind. I feel like my Noah voice might have been overkill. She nods and exits the car—the conversation apparently over.

"Aren't you going to ask how we'll get your phone number?"

"If you want me to work for you, you'll have to impress me. Call this attempt number one."

"No way," I object. "Number one was identifying you. Two was finding you. This will be attempt number three!"

"Sad it takes you three attempts." She smirks at that as she spins, placing her heels on the parking garage concrete. She lifts out of the seat with more grace than Mrs. Morganson, our adoptive mama bear, when baking treats for us in her kitchen.

I'm done. Rogue's amazing. I love her. Can I keep her?

I scramble to exit the car after her, trailing her like a lost puppy begging for scraps. Her ass is perfect in her black dress. It hits her knees with a slit running high up her thighs in the back, and her hair tumbles down her back like an inky waterfall. Up at the top, she's got these swirls in her hair. She's rocking this retro look, and I am here for it.

She turns her head to glance at me over her shoulder as she climbs into the driver's seat. Her red lips tip up in a slight smile; she winks, and I grin. "See you Tuesday, Buttercup."

WATCHING ROGUE DRIVE OFF IN HER VINTAGE CAR WHILE STANDING in the chilly-as-fuck parking garage, I can't help but thank God for Jacob and his freaky-ass computer skills. He finally managed to track down Rogue yesterday because of a new cheap security camera across the street from her alleyway kill that had only been installed the day before.

Noah got his hands on the restaurant's security tape, but it didn't show us jack shit. The cops, who probably got a backup copy from the restaurant owner, won't find her with just that.

She kept her back to the camera and used the dumpster to hide while she shed her shirt and threw on a hoodie. The angle was all wrong, too. With her height, she could be anyone. Male or female.

Dear Leader, aka Noah, is still complaining about his wash-out hair dye and sanding down the truck's paint color so it couldn't be identified by the detective from the crime scene. He was pissed that all his effort didn't equal answers via the recording.

We knew the kill was Rogue's because Mark Sandoval had a deal with them for protection. We got word from a colleague that there was some new evidence against The Gambit from Mark. When a mugging was reported near his shop, Noah and I rushed out to see if we could gain some intel.

After Noah got the footage and we drove back to the warehouse, we saw there wasn't enough to go on. But there was enough to see which direction she turned when she left the alley. A new bakery is opening on the corner, and Jacob hacked their feed, backtracking enough to follow her movements before wiping their server.

After that, wide-panned street cams helped us get a glimpse at the sidewalks as Rogue walked by. A camera showed her hooded figure from the back, quickly patting the hood of an old car as she passed before she disappeared from the cameras.

Thirty minutes later, the car was gone. The angle of the camera didn't give us a view of who got in and drove off because the damn trees on that street need to be trimmed—I've already put in a complaint with the city—but we were able to follow it to an apartment building near the city center. The tinted windows and low roof covering of the car prevented us from getting a good look at who was inside as it made its way downtown.

We've been taking shifts and watching the garage to see if it leaves. We don't know Rogue's real name and about thirty apartments in the building are owned by Rook Industries, The Gambit's legal front. We couldn't exactly go around door-to-door asking who the assassin in the building was.

She drives a distinctive car—a beast of a car. Han did a happy dance when he saw it on the traffic cam. He started rambling about the merits of Chevrolet versus Ford and Pontiac. We all zone out when he does that. Mech and Tech—aka Han and Jacob—tend to get a little overzealous about their areas of expertise.

Han has a love for all things mechanical. He customizes our weapons, enjoys blowing shit up, and fixes up our cars. He also claims he has fixed our bodies since becoming our resident nutritionist and trainer. We love him, but all hate him with the fire of a thousand suns on cardio day.

Speaking of Han, he's waiting for me around the corner. We decided to keep comms open on my end; he was silent but could listen in and provide backup if needed. The group text agreed to have only one of us approach her. I look the most harmless.

Jacob helpfully pointed out that if we outnumber her, she may not react well. In our line of work, you follow that gut feeling, and he's never one to underestimate a woman. If she felt threatened, she may have screamed, attacked, or done any number of things, resulting in no meeting. And after Noah described the alleyway, I'm delighted she didn't attack.

Han has a contemplative look as he props himself up against the facade of the parking structure. His body looks relaxed, but I can see he's fixated on something because his scarred brow is creased, and he's worrying his bottom lip with his teeth. I rarely see him in an uproar, so it instantly has me on alert. He shakes his head almost as if he's disagreeing with himself. I hear him mutter, "Ivy," and the headshaking continues. His head pops up when I scrape my shoe on the floor to alert him of my approach.

The Secrets We Keep

"Wait till I tell the guys it takes you three tries to please a woman." He howls with laughter, the earlier look clouding his face wiped away. I let it go because Han usually needs to process things independently before bringing them to us.

Despite his face's transitions in the last couple of minutes, his body looks relaxed. He's leaner than Noah and Jacob, but we're pretty similar in body mass, while I stand just a few inches taller. His Korean features and toned body make him hard to miss when we do our missions because both men and women tend to notice him. I blame his fucking perfect skin, and no matter how well I follow his routine, mine doesn't look that good.

At first glance, you would think it easy to beat him to a pulp. Standing alone in the dark in a dangerous city, he doesn't give off the vibe of a threat. You would be wrong. When he stands to his full height and squares his shoulders, his prior fight experience shines through.

Han grew up around here and has a reputation for building explosives. A memory that lives on in the local replastered high school gym. Han blew a hole in it the day they announced square dancing would be a PE requirement starting the following week. I can see his reasoning.

"Shut up, dude! I hate that you could hear that. You didn't hear the desperation in my voice, did you? I'm pretty sure if she hadn't had a knife pointed at my cock, I would have proposed."

Han's face takes on a hard edge, and he kicks off the wall. "She looked hot as hell walking into the parking garage. And also really, really familiar. Did she pull the gun on her thigh too, or just the knives?"

"How the hell did you know she had knives? And why didn't you move in if you knew she was strapped?"

"I figured she would be if she were Rogue's girlfriend. But with how quickly she pulled those knives and got one over on you, we need to up your training. You were woefully underprepared for her to flip the tables on you. I can't believe we've been looking for a guy. How did we end up on that theory again?"

"You knew she would likely be packing weapons and didn't say anything? Dude, come on! And it was because of those few whispers that it was a man, not to mention the height we guessed on the video. She's tall."

He rolls his eyes at my dramatics, and I wonder where he could know her from. "I could hear you; you were fine, but her voice was harder to hear. I'm guessing she had a hand near your throat where you stuck the microphone. You did well catching her attention with her slip-up. She'll want to correct it. Maybe adding an additional wardrobe change in a busy store on the way back to a safe house would do it. No one expects killers to be gorgeous women in skirts and heels."

I could hear the admiration in his tone when talking about her work ethic. You didn't rise from the streets like Han did without some impressive determination and ambition. He recognizes that drive in others and fosters it when he catches glimpses of it in us.

We take a second to look around and realize we're alone besides a homeless man nearby and the sounds of bar patrons having a good time. Han takes off for the SUV parked down the road, and I start backing up toward the parking structure to hop on my motorcycle.

I see Han cross the street and head for the homeless man. He always gives what he can, and since we're earning decent money now, we all chip in. It's become a collective habit.

Han approaches the man, who looks recently homeless, and hands over a crisp twenty from his pocket. I can't hear what he's saying from here, but it's usually something like, "Please take this, get some food or a place to sleep for the night. Stay safe."

The man avoids eye contact with Han but bobs his head just the same. His dirty hand snakes out from an overly large jacket and takes the cash. Han knows the money he hands over sometimes goes to drugs or booze, but he also knows what it's like to be homeless and reliant on the pity of strangers. He never mentions the good deeds he does because he's been exactly where these people are. He's just paying it forward when and how he can.

His family lost everything when El Castillo lost its middle class. Their quaint family market was doing well with the area's residents until convenience stores took over and supplied food for the more impoverished communities. Simultaneously, the rich got groceries from the fancy boutique markets or had their chefs buy and prepare their food.

They lived on the streets from the time Han was about seven until twelve. Five years of bouncing from shelter to shelter left a mark on him. He learned to fight for his place in this world, and when his family managed to get an apartment, he earned money in the ring—contributing to the rent the only way he could. His parents now have a modest apartment a few hours away and are enjoying the quiet retirement that their son funds.

Han continues and heads to the other parking lot a few streets over. I return to the dark garage and head up the stairs for my bike. We're due back at HQ, and we have to let the others know about the meeting in three days.

Chapter Five

Rogue

Now that Netflix and wine are canceled due to nerves, I'm all out of sorts. I have a ritual, damn it! A routine! Kill and chill.

I pad through my shoebox apartment, looking for anything to take the edge off. I can't believe I've been found. Worse than that, caught and identified. Half the reason I agreed to the meeting is to gauge how much Annex knows about me. The other half is to find out how the fuck the team caught me.

Rogue is an alias, but it's the only thing I go by. Only legal documents have "Ivy Montgomery" listed, and my apartment is registered as a corporate apartment through one of Rook Industries' subsidiaries. More than half the apartments in this building have a Rook employee living in it, either from the legal or illegal side. I doubt the Annex agents would knock on doors like Girl Scouts to find me.

To be safe, I did a shit-ton of evasive driving on my way home in the event I had a tail. I even went as far as to leave my gorgeous car at one of The Gambit's chop shop garages and Ubered home. Axle, the head mechanic there, knows to keep Black Beauty safe and sound until I return.

The Bel Air is my goddamned pride and joy. I bought her when I was seventeen and had squirreled away enough money for a rebuild. I did it myself after a lot of manual readings, watching YouTube videos, and getting help from Axle. I named her Black Beauty because I adore the freedom she represents while knowing I'm stuck in El Castillo and my role a bit longer.

Tomorrow, I'll be switching cars again. Please, God, don't let me end up with a minivan like last year when all the sedans and coupes had already been lent out. It was not a good look for me. Then again, it's better to be safe and alive than dead in my Beauty because she sticks out like a sore thumb. A pretty one, but still.

I reflect on my encounter with the redhead and replay the conversation to see if I've missed any critical information. He said he was with an Annex Security team. That company is highly criticized for lacking female employees, so it's unexpected that one of their teams wants to talk shop with me. I need to know how they found me. That's my motivation. If anything, L... Shit, what was his name? I'm going with Lance. If anything Lance said is right, it's that if they can find me, the police might also have a shot at it.

To be honest, I also have this burning need to know why his demeanor changed so suddenly. He was playful and charming, with his amber eyes sparkling one minute and sounding like he was choking the next. Odd one, that guy. Pretty, but odd.

He's attractive; I'll give him that. His dark, reddish-brown hair was styled to one side, the top long and the sides short. He had freckles across the bridge of his nose. His eyes flared wide when he felt the poke of the knife in his groin. He filled the space in the back seat well with his tall frame.

Under other circumstances, I'd have had him flat on his back in seconds.

Too bad he was creeping in my car and thought Rogue was a man based on the look in his eyes when he felt my blades. Better to keep suspicion off of me, a woman, I guess. I can't really blame him; not too many people know my gender, and general murder statistics for women indicate most assassins would be men.

I'll research the company in the morning when I've rested and can come at this with a clear mind. I text Enrique to let him know I got one of his dealers tonight and make my way to my bedroom. The rest will be taken care of by the end of the month.

Everything in this apartment has been carefully selected to suit my needs. There's just enough space for my minimal belongings. That's what I want people to think if they catch a peek inside. I also have the apartment

The Secrets We Keep

directly below mine on the third floor. I connected the two with a concealed drop-down ladder.

My home consists of a living room and kitchen, connected with a small counter dividing the spaces. The living room has a closet on the back wall where I keep some dresses, coats, and shoes. The bottom is covered by a rug that hides a trap door leading to the ladder. A small hallway connects my bedroom and a small bathroom. It's all I need, but not all I want. One day, when I'm out of this mess, I'll build my dream home and fill it with things that bring me joy—Marie Kondo style.

The apartment below my living space, which I have aptly named the Bat Cave, has all of my work tools—guns, knives, poisons, tarps, cleanup supplies, and a computer setup that would rival even Mrs. Wakowski's son's gaming shrine in apartment 4H.

Harold Wakowski can kick my ass in first-person shooter games, but he's my little bitch when it comes to every other game. Real-life shooting is very different from video game shooting. Go figure.

I set my phone on the charger, strip down to my thong, and flop into bed. With my nightly routine thrown out the proverbial window, I almost forgot that I must meet up with King for our yearly visit to my parents' graves tomorrow.

We've always gone together on the anniversary, and even though sometimes I hate our tradition, it oddly comforts me to know I'm not the only one visiting their tombstones, even if I wish the company were better.

AFTER A FITFUL NIGHT OF REST, INCLUDING MANY DREAMS ABOUT being chased down and thrown in prison, I decided to get back to my routine so I could head into this meeting armed with more than just weapons. Seven in the morning sounds like an excellent time for an information dive.

Annex Security is a firm that works primarily for more prominent corporations looking to shore up their defenses online and in person. After reading their website and testimonials, I've got their party line. I'm sure they do more than just defense and personal security. Espionage and assassinations seem like a good bet. They may not tout it, but it makes the most sense.

This is not your run-of-the-mill security firm. Their website is too carefully curated; the pictures too posed. Plus, the things I found on the dark web point to heaps of shady business practices in recent years.

Having finished my preliminary research, I clean up my apartment and switch from work mode to video game time. I need to unwind a bit before getting ready to meet King.

After kicking Harold Wakowski's teenage ass in video games for an hour and cursing more than a sailor would, I decide it's probably high time I move my ass.

I choose a white dress with cap sleeves and a flared skirt. Paired with yellow heels, I look fresh despite my fitful sleep. Mom always said black was too sad for funerals and grave visits when we should celebrate the time we had with those we've lost. I try to keep that in mind any time I visit them.

I pop my hair into victory rolls up top, scoop the rest into a yellow bandana, and tie it behind the rolls on my head. If I do say so myself, I make the retro vibe look good.

While my job requires lots of black or dark colors and coverage, I enjoy dressing like the woman I am when I'm not wiping up blood from a hit. I'm sick of living in this duality. Mentally, I tick another day off the countdown until I'm free of the contract.

My phone lets out a ping on the nightstand with an incoming text. I expect it's King letting me know he's here with the car, so my surprise is understandable when I see an unknown number. The only people with this number are the board members and other hitmen.

It occurs to me that Lance, Luke, Logan, Lars, or whatever the fuck his name was, said he would text. I've taken to calling him Red in my head. And we're not due to meet until Tuesday.

Unknown: *Hey, Buttercup. Whatcha doing?*

Unbelievable. It's not even about the meeting, but the little nickname confirms it's Red.

Me: *Going out. What do you want?*

Being bitchy to someone who sneaks up on me in my car and makes me ditch it at a garage sounds like the proper reaction. I. Miss. My. Car!

Red: *Where are you going?*

Me: *Out. Let's skip the whole meeting thing, and you just tell me how you found me. We both know I'm going to say no anyway.*

Red: *But then how will I convince you to spend time with me again? Want to have dinner with me tonight?*

Me: *Not a chance, Red.*

I make an undignified snort as I realize I called him his nickname because I can't be bothered to remember his real name. Predictably, he gets way too excited.

Red: *Oooh, I have a nickname already. And you're Buttercup. So basically, we'll be getting married and giving adorable crotch goblins nicknames in no time. I can't wait. :wink emoji:*

My eyes roll so hard; I swear I can see into the past. I text King that I'll be waiting on the sidewalk for him, power off the phone before Red can continue texting me, and head downstairs. There's a crappy little bodega on the ground floor with excellent shitty coffee. A decent place to wait while avoiding preposterous text messages.

———

KING SHOWS UP IN A FANCY BLACK TOWN CAR as I drain the last dregs of my cheap coffee. I open the back door and slide into the seat next to him. It's tradition for us to visit together every anniversary of my parents' deaths. As usual, his driver pulls out into traffic before King bothers to look up from his phone to acknowledge my presence.

"Good afternoon, daughter," he greets after the car reaches cruising speed, lifting his eyes to make contact with mine. We haven't spoken since the meeting last week. Not uncommon, but today especially, it makes me long for a bit more human interaction in my life.

Harold, the little gamer boy, can't be my sole source of verbal sparring. Hell, we swear like sailors—on leave with scurvy while getting stabbed—at each other, and he's like fifteen, max. I need some damn friends.

"King," I respond. We've never been overly loquacious with each other. I remember being a regular, chatty child and being told to be seen and not heard more often than I got responses to my natural curiosity. After a while, I just learned to keep quiet rather than continue to face disappointment in conversation.

"How many years has it been now?" he asks, despite likely knowing the answer.

My bitchy self can't bear to feed into it, and I respond with, "Too many." It's been seventeen years, asshole.

He hums and scrolls on his phone while I stare out the window. Watching the people merrily go on about their day, like it isn't a reminder of one of the worst of my life, drives me up the fucking wall. I know everyone has those moments in their past they wish they could forget and move on from. But fuck it. I need a mental health day, not an afternoon with King.

As we make the drive, I let my mind wander. On this day, when I was seven, I was herded away by a social worker and dropped in a group home, while my sister was sent to another because she was so young. My parents had no relationship with their families because of their involvement in The Gambit. I ended up staying in the group home for a few days until King pulled some majorly illegal strings and got me into his care. It was all fine for a month; then, things took a drastic turn for the worse, and life became a struggle to survive.

I preferred the group home.

I tune back into reality as we go down the boulevard toward the old graveyard. It's one of the oldest in El Castillo, and a time-worn Catholic church has stood sentinel for over a hundred years. As we approach the massive building, I see the spire looming over the stately homes on either side. It brings a sense of calm knowing my parents are resting in a beautiful, old, haunting cemetery behind an immense church. It means kids are less likely to try to sneak over the wrought iron fencing while looking for thrills in a spooky cemetery.

The driver leaves us off to the church's left so we can take the side entrance through a slightly rusted gate. As I always do, I'll go through the church on my way out to leave a donation.

King follows me, seemingly lost in thought, as we weave through the old gravestones toward the newer ones in the back. Brothers, sisters, parents, children—all surround my parents' graves as obstacles to reach my lost relatives.

We approach the angel statue hovering over the Montgomery graves, and I look up into her weeping face—the angel the King selected, bought, and installed to stand guard.

King remains behind me, next to one of the old oak trees, so I can have a few minutes alone to say hello and goodbye, I love you, and I hate you for leaving me, all at once. I proceed with my internal diatribe, both thanking them for my mostly uneventful childhood with them and cursing them for dying because I ended up with the sadistic asshole behind me.

It's kind of sad to think I preferred the life with my drug-addled parents over the one King gave me. But honestly, I'd take some passed-out parents over his brand of torture any day. The only regret I have about that time in my life is not doing more to get them off drugs.

What could a seven-year-old do? Hell, I flushed their stash more than once. I called the emergency number when I saw the dealer approaching the house. They ended up dying from overdoses one night when they took things too far.

I can only be thankful I was at my friend's house down the street when it happened. Her mom walked me back when my own was late for pickup. She opened the door and found my parents on the couch. She ushered me outside before I could see them and waited with me until the police came.

After a couple of minutes of letting me ponder my parents' lives, King makes his way forward. With a sigh, like this is taxing for him, he raises his head and places his hand on my father's gravestone. "Hey, old friend." Dad and King were at the same rank within The Gambit syndicate when Dad died. They were making their way up the ladder together.

I often wonder if Dad were still alive, would he be in King's position now, leading us all? Or would he be handling his own branch of the organization like the other board members? Like I do? Corralling hitmen is not something I think he saw for my future.

My day consists of assessing risks and sleights against the organization. I assign either a hit or destruction order. I dole out the names to the other hitmen or save the degenerates to take care of on my own.

King glances to the left at my mother's stone and sighs heavily. "Sweet Marie." He always has a pet name for her. She was his childhood best friend. They grew up in the same shitty apartment building and saw way too many things young eyes should have been shielded from.

She met my dad through King when they were in their teens, and as they say, the rest is history. One unexpected pregnancy led to marriage, which led to further entrenchment in The Gambit to keep a roof over our heads, eventually leading to their demise. All to keep us safe and secure.

He continues with his usual, "We miss you, life isn't the same," blah, blah, blah. It's the same every time, and it's starting to get old. Part of me is thankful to have someone with me today; I just wish it was anyone but him.

We say a final goodbye and turn to head back to the church. The fees for keeping my parents here are exorbitant, but it's worth it. I think they'd have liked the peaceful nature of this place.

We reach the old wooden doors to the side of the church, and I see the flicker of a red dot on the door before me—laser sight. Time seems to slow as I whirl, snaking King's arm as he reaches a hand out for the brass handle.

I twirl like the ballerina I certainly am not, ducking as I maneuver us behind the hedge lining the stone church. About a foot of space between the bushes and the church's stone exterior gives us just enough room to squeeze between and follow the path to the corner of the building. King catches on quickly and pulls his ever-present phone from his pocket to alert his driver, I'm sure.

When we've turned the corner of the church, King whispers almost silently, "Daniel is down."

Fuck. That's our way out.

I peek around the corner quickly, recalling the beam's origin, and peer into the distance for the glint of metal in the sunlight. For a moment, I thought the old oak tree by the graves shielded us. But I quickly realized that no sniper worth his salt would set up the gun to aim at us while the oak could give us cover.

The church steps were meant to be the kill spot. It means they know we go to donate each visit. They planned to get King or me there, on the steps, instead of by the graves. How long has this asshole been watching us?

I don't see the tell-tale metallic shine, and I don't plan to investigate right now. Extraction is the name of the game. I lead King around to the other side of the church. The building now stands between the sniper and us. Unless they anticipate our move to get to the street, we should be okay making it to a cab.

Who knows if the hit is for King or me? We have multiple hits out on us, but we don't know who today's intended target is. It doesn't matter who goes out to hail a cab. Either way, it's a fifty-fifty shot, but King is the organization's head these days.

His safety is item one of my job description, and I'd never keep my reputation or my head if he got shot while in my company. Not to mention, all the evidence he's been holding about my kills will go straight to the authorities. He has the best security I could muster up for his guard when he's not with me. I'm not letting some asshole ruin my life because he's pissed at King.

I raise a hand behind me, palm facing King, to tell him to hold. I glance back to see him respond with a "message received" signal. One of the most helpful things King taught me was tactical hand signals. They work well in these types of situations.

I see the light turning green up the street as I slip through the hole in the gate. I pop off the sidewalk curb to flag down a passing taxi, and it screeches to a stop, far too close to my body for comfort. A pretty girl in a white dress calls a lot of attention; add in the screeching tires, and we're sitting ducks if the sniper manages to anticipate our exit and pick us off in broad daylight.

The Secrets We Keep

I pull the back door open as King hauls ass off the curb and throws himself inside. A shot rings out and pings off the taxi door. I carelessly launch my body in after King and yank the door closed behind me.

The driver is understandably pissed off. He starts yelling as he takes off, but make no mistake, he doesn't forget to start the meter. He's threatening lawsuits and complaining about the damage to his car while careening down the road.

"Slow the fuck down; you're drawing too much attention to us," I snap when he pauses to draw a breath, no doubt to gear up for another screaming tirade. His foot eases off the gas, and we return to a regular speed. "Thank you," I say with a forced smile.

"What the fuck is happening? My mom told me if I came to America, I would get shot. She was right. Fuck! I'll never hear the end of this!"

While I find it hilarious that he's worried about proving his mom right, I feel the need to reassure this poor young man so he doesn't spiral and crush us all into a blazing heap on the side of the road.

"We're fine. We aren't being followed. Please take us to the Rook Industries building on West Eighth Street. We'll happily pay you for the ride, the damage, and include a generous tip if you keep this experience to yourself. Even from your mom."

King rolls his eyes at me. He's always said I'm too soft for this line of work. I disagree. I think that softness lets me hold on to my humanity in this life. Too much darkness with no light is what leads to men like King. Men who torture. Men who harm. Men who think they rule the dark when, instead, they're only temporarily holding on until someone sets things right again. Or, you know, someone worse comes along.

The cab makes its way to Rook Industries' headquarters at a more reasonable speed. The illuminated sign hovering atop the skyscraper, as if it were the fucking Bat-Signal for The Gambit members, spins gently. The building boasts top-tier security for everything housed within the structure. I should know; I was contracted to try to breach it multiple times. Security was shored up each time I could break in, physically or electronically.

I only told them some of the access points. A girl's gotta keep her options open.

King continues typing on his phone, likely updating his personal security team about the shots taken at him and sending someone to collect Daniel, dead or alive. King often skips the bodyguards when he's alone with me because he knows I'll do my best to keep him breathing while he's got both my past and future in his slippery hands.

The cabbie pulls to the curb, and I slip a few crisp hundred dollar bills from my purse to cover the ride and buy his silence. The driver's eyes widen when he sees the money, and he thanks me profusely. He made good time, so I grab a card from the holder screwed to the Plexiglas divider. I glide out, and King follows.

"Do we have any other business?" King inquires distractedly. I mean, I've got to give it to the guy. Getting shot at, avoiding a sniper, and nearly getting hit by that bullet doesn't seem to have fucked up his day. How many other people could slide back into business as usual?

When I've paused a beat too long, he lifts his gaze and arches one of those bushy brows at me. "No, sir."

"Good. Assign a team to figure out who shot today and eliminate whoever it is. Then, continue with the dealers. I have a new name for the main list but finish the rule-breakers first. Their name has already been sent to you in the secure channel."

Orders received, I nod and lead King to the building entrance, where he'll be shadowed by his security once inside. The whole time, I've got my eyes peeled for signs of another threat at our legitimate site.

Nothing out of place, I spin on my heel and head to the taxi rank to grab a ride home. Our former cabbie is still sitting there, but to avoid the risk of adding more trauma to his already overly eventful day, I make my way down the busy street and decide to take the subway.

Fewer snipers underground, I find.

Chapter Six

Jacob

It's motherfucking Tuesday.

When Lucas texted us from the parking garage that Rogue was, in fact, a woman, we all realized what shitheads we'd been by assuming she was a *he*. Not that a woman can't do the work we've seen, but it's been a trip to wrap my head around the gender reveal. I mean, a few of the bodies she's left behind would make even some of the most iron-nerved killers uneasy.

Not to mention, various terrified assholes over the years have described the elusive Rogue as a man. I have a feeling there's some planted false information floating around to keep suspicion off her back.

Lucas detailed their encounter as we sat in the meeting room a few nights ago. His voice got wistful at some points, and it's part of the reason I'm anxious today. Lucas doesn't take a lot of stuff seriously aside from his job, but his voice was reverent as he detailed how she had a knife aimed at his cock. Only Lucas would find that a turn-on. Maybe this wasn't such a good idea.

Han was quiet for most of the meeting, but he peppered Lucas with questions about her appearance once the critical shit was dealt with. When Lucas started describing her "moss-colored green eyes," we sighed collectively, and Han punched him up before he could create a sonnet in her honor.

Han's expression grew melancholy as time passed, and he withdrew for the rest of the evening. I cornered him about it later on, and he just shrugged and said that she reminded him of someone he used to know when he heard her speak over the comms and saw her face from the side as she drove away.

He doesn't share much from the dark days of his past, but it's easy to see that's where his mind went. His face always takes on a harsh edge when that era gets dragged up.

It's seven in the morning on the day of the meeting. Han and I are working out as we always do this time of day. Noah and Lucas are likely still sleeping, but unlike most tech nerds I know, I function best during the early morning and only pull late-night hacking sessions when absolutely necessary.

I live my life by a strict routine. Wake up at six, work out first thing with Han, shower, eat breakfast, hack shit, spy on douchebags, eat lunch at one, assess risks, do fieldwork if needed, have dinner, read, and sleep at ten.

Life on the dark net is chaotic, and my schedule's rigidity helps keep me focused and reminds me to take necessary breaks when I'm in a deep dive.

Today, however, we've got a meeting. The timing isn't ideal for my schedule, so I've been a bit anxious the past few days as we've been preparing. Han lands a punch to my ribs that has me grunting in pain. I let myself get distracted; I earned that bruise.

"Jake, man, get your head out of your ass. So, you had to switch fieldwork with risk assessment on the itinerary today. Does that fuck up your toilet schedule too?"

Wanker. I swing as he leans just out of reach, my punch glancing off his jaw. He comes back hard, but I get him pinned to the mat in four moves with sheer force of will. "Gotcha."

"Dumbass English bastard. Get your fat ass off of me!" Han's still struggling under my body weight with my arm around his neck in a chokehold. He reluctantly pats my forearm to tap out, and I roll off him, landing next to him on my back. We're both twenty-seven, but the drills he's put us through this morning have us panting like we're seventy.

Han groans, rubbing at the red spot forming on his upper thigh. I could have been gentler in taking him down, but that's why he's the best trainer we've ever worked with. He pushes and won't accept anything less than your best.

He shoves up to his knees and extends a hand to me. I clasp it, and he helps to haul me into a sitting position. Han's been one of my best friends for years now. I'm closer to him than the others. I think part of it comes from some of our shared past experiences.

We had wildly different childhoods, but some themes remained the same. Our families loved us unconditionally, but money was tight. While my family never ended up on the street like Han's did, we struggled for too many years. To help out, Han and I both did things we aren't proud of.

I learned to hack using ancient computers at my local library in England. Coding and hacking came effortlessly to me, and I used that skill to earn money for my family and a scholarship to Caltech.

I moved to California and worked my ass off to earn my degree. Between classes, I worked to help my parents keep the house and provide for my younger sisters, Blair and Anna. Annex noticed my skills, and with the pay they offered, I couldn't turn down the job.

Mum and Dad found proper work, and my sisters are doing well in their university courses. We keep up with each other, but eventually, I'd like to be closer geographically.

Han and I bonded over those familial relationships and doing what it takes to help your family survive. Honestly, all of us on the team have had pretty shitty cards dealt. They just vary on the shitty spectrum.

Lucas and Noah tend to take the lead on most of our jobs, so Han and I end up hanging back and supporting. I work on all aspects of the tech while Han supplies and manages our weapons and any incendiary devices. This arrangement gives us a lot of time together, and we wound up becoming best friends.

It works out especially well for us because of our personalities. I need a schedule and a plan, and Han needs to care for someone. When I end up in a deep dive online and lose track, he's always there to pull me away and get me back to where I should be.

Lucas is different. He's friends with everyone. You can't spend more than twenty minutes in his company without laughing your ass off.

Noah runs our team with a level of patience I've never seen before. He's calm and collected, while the rest of us are happy to leave the management to him. We just happen to cause arbitrary chaos for our Dear Leader, if only to see that little vein pulse on his forehead.

The whoosh of the automatic door sounds, and I peek to the side to see Noah striding into the gym dressed in his usual black sweats and a white t-shirt. "Guys, move it. We've got to run through the strategy one more time before Rogue gets here."

Han groans, and his body topples to the side. Laughing and still struggling to breathe, we stand on shaky legs after our workout and follow Noah to the doors.

We reach the central part of the warehouse, and I nearly ram into Lucas, who's coming out of the kitchen in his boxers and holding a mug that says: *If you say 'gullible' really slowly, it sounds like 'orange.'*

I narrowly avoid his shoulder as we turn the corner. He just laughs, shakes his head, and continues scratching his ass as he makes his way to the lounge.

IT'S HALF-PAST TWO IN THE AFTERNOON, AND LUCAS HAS JUST SENT A text telling us he's in position. He sent the dummy location to Rogue since she'd expect him to make contact, not one of us. Lucas is waiting for her at the fake address to escort her here.

We wouldn't put it past her to be wearing a wire or carrying weapons, but here, we can control the situation. We have no interest in pissing her off, but we don't want her to know exactly where we are, just in case.

Lucas follows up with a screenshot of her response.

Buttercup: *On my way.*

Oh shit, he's already given her a cutesy nickname. I doubt it's one she likes. Our elusive hitwoman is anything but cutesy. I've only heard about her from Lucas, and coupled with my observations of her work, she doesn't seem the type. We want her to work with us, not have Lucas drooling after her like an obsessive stalker.

It takes nearly thirty minutes, but as I watch the monitors, I see Lucas and Rogue arguing in the car. He's half-leaned over the armrest to angle his body toward her in the backseat as he carelessly navigates the parking area.

Once parked, he rounds the car and helps Rogue out. Her blindfold prevents her from knowing where she is, but I can see their body language through the screen. She's pissed.

Lucas does a final pat down once she's steady on her feet. How in God's name is she steady in four-inch heels and a blindfold?

He finishes, signals a thumbs up to the camera positioned on the corner of the building, and I release the bolt on the front door from my computer station. Han and Noah stand ready to meet them and show her in while I do a final check that they weren't followed.

I hear the door slide open, and loud voices immediately fill the silence that previously permeated every square foot while we waited. "How on earth could you think Batman is better than Superman?" Lucas shouts with far too much exasperation. "He doesn't even have any superpowers!"

She sighs like she'd already explained this repeatedly, and knowing Lucas, she probably has. "That's what makes him better. No freaky alien powers. Just motivation and money."

Lucas pulls at his auburn hair and growls as if he can't believe the audacity of this woman. "I'm taking her back. This will never work," he jokes. His hand lands on her wrist as if he's going to lead her outside, but she spins quickly. Yanking his hand roughly behind his back, he falls to his knees as she suddenly pushes him down until he's on his stomach, her sharp heel pressing him to the floor.

Noah reaches behind Rogue's head and unties her blindfold. It slips down her face until she's blinking her eyes against the sudden light, and a breath catches in my chest. Holy shit.

She has hair like a vintage pinup model, a black fitted top, and ripped jeans with those damn stilettos that make her legs look impossibly long. Tattoos of everything from flowers to faces to Sailor Jerry-themed artwork cover half of her body from her neck down to the glimpses of skin I can see through the holes in her jeans on her right leg.

My brain stutters before I push up from my chair to introduce myself. Rogue looks around the open warehouse, from the lounge area to the catwalk and bedrooms upstairs.

Lucas lets out a pained groan, reminding her of his predicament, and she straightens and dusts her hands off on her jeans. Today is not the day for us. We've all been taken down today in one way or another, except Noah.

Although, with the look in his eye, his take-down was metaphorical. He's doing his best not to be obvious, but I see him looking at her face for a second too long. His gaze flicks down her body, and his brow quirks as he trails the tattoos dripping down to her fingers.

"Ivy?" Han's voice rasps out in disbelief. Her head whips to Han, who's standing next to Noah.

"Han?" she sputters out as she looks at him in amazement. A few seconds pass as she studies his face, then scans him from head to toe. "Holy shit, it is you!"

She leaps off the ground, and in a flash, she's got her arms wrapped around Han's neck and her legs around his waist. They're engaged in a fierce hug. I see his face peeking out from her mane of black hair, and his eyes are scrunched tight as he squeezes her around the waist.

How the fuck do these two know each other?

From my office, I can see them whispering in each other's ears and grins on their faces as Han slowly spins her in a circle. Bloody Christ, her smile is dangerous. He twirls her with more zeal, and she lets out a laugh that reaches my ears.

I make my way across the expansive bottom floor of the warehouse, past the lounge area, and rock up in front of them.

"Gorgeous," Han starts, "this is Jacob Waters." He leans in and whispers to Rogue, "He'll make you wet."

With a smack to the back of his head, I take over for Han before he can butcher the introduction more than he already has. I extend my hand. Even though she's half facing the wrong direction and still hanging onto Han, she gracefully sticks her hand out to shake mine with only the slightest mocking smile on her lips. "Jacob. Tech."

Smooth move, dipshit.

She puts her warm, dry hand in mine, and her deep and raspy voice floats out, "Rogue. Don't let this asshole teach you it's okay to call me Ivy. He knew me a long time ago." She laughs with her warning, and I immediately see why Han likes this girl. Her laughter is infectious as it fills the vast space of the warehouse.

My tongue is caught in my throat, but Han doesn't give me a moment to fix my response as he gently puts her back on her feet to introduce her to the others. Han takes her tattooed hand when she withdraws it from mine.

He pauses as he bends over her knuckles and kisses them. "Hi, Gorgeous. I'm floored to see you again, but we need a new introduction. I'm Han. I'm responsible for mechanics, weaponry, and health. What knife did you use in the alley?"

"Mechanics, weaponry, and health?" she repeats, evading the knife question and taking her hand back. "I didn't think those went together."

Han smirks at her and turns to Noah, who is still silently laughing at Lucas getting his ass handed to him by our blindfolded guest. "That big guy is Noah. He runs our unit and hands out assignments. Don't let on that you know, but he prefers the fieldwork to the bureaucratic nonsense."

Noah nods and says a hello, giving her hand a firm, brief shake. He then offers Han a solid punch in the bicep for outing his little secret. He's nervous about this meeting because we need her to work with us if we have any chance of dismantling both our organization and hers.

Han continues as he rubs his arm. "You've met Lucas, who has already informed us you're getting married this spring. Best wishes and congratulations. Although, with how you took him down, I'd say the relationship is on the rocks."

Lucas puffs out a breath of ire, but Rogue smiles at their antics, her eyes sparkling. He takes a moment to add, "I run infiltrations, extractions, and dispatches." Right, dispatches... another word for assassinations. How our resident funny man manages to be solemn enough for hits is still a mystery I'm working on solving.

Regaining my composure from the shock of our recruit being a fucking goddess, I turn my body and wave my arm out, indicating we should move. "This way, please. We'll sit in the conference room to discuss our proposal."

Everyone makes their way through the living and working space. Rogue's eyes swivel as she takes in the exits and access points. No point. This place is battened down tight.

As he veers toward the kitchen on the other side of the space, Lucas calls out, "Buttercup, what would you like to drink?"

"Surprise me," she answers with a wink. Oh, for the love of the Queen, he's already got her flirting back.

He grins his megawatt smile and heads into the kitchen to start the drinks. We enter the room and find seats around the sizeable, brushed steel table. I've already uploaded our data and footage to the laptop in the corner to show how we found her. A deal's a deal.

After a torturous few minutes of silence filled with little looks between Rogue and Han, Lucas comes strolling in with six mugs on a tray—one for each of us guys and two for Rogue.

He hands me my usual mug of Earl Grey tea with a sugar lump and a milk splash. The cup says: *What doesn't kill you... disappoints me.* Lucas has a bit of an obsession with ridiculous drinkware. He's got about a hundred mugs he uses and forces you to use depending on your mood.

Noah has a cup of black coffee in a mug that reads: *Surely not everyone was kung-fu fighting,* and Han has a pink mug filled with a latte that pronounces: *Someone out there loves you. Not me. I think you're a cunt.*

She's going to think we're insane. It wasn't until Noah floated her name as an option that we upped our game to find her after witnessing the havoc she's capable of leaving behind. She's particular about her kills, and we need someone with a hint of morality, or the partnership will never work.

I watch as Rogue eyes the remaining three mugs. "Which is mine?"

Lucas gingerly lifts two of the mugs and places them in front of her with a weird flourish that I bet he wishes he could take back, grabs his own, and flops down into his seat. He starts drinking his sugar with a splash of coffee with a Superman logo on the cup. He winks at Rogue when she eyes it.

I can't take it; I need to know. "So, how do you two know each other?"

Han quirks a brow at Rogue, and she gives a little nod. "Ivy, I mean... Rogue and I used to fight at the same ring when we were younger. Her stage name back then was Gorgeous." He turns to her before continuing, "We ran into one another on Fight Nights, probably once a month or so, and got to know each other pretty well. It's been years, and I haven't seen her since... Anyway, it's not important. She's good for the team. I trust her."

Lucas impatiently clears his throat and gestures to the tray. He's apparently feeling a little miffed that the attention was stolen from his hard work. "I didn't want you to have to choose, Buttercup. Variety is the spice of life. There's Earl Grey tea like Jacob has and a latte like Han's. There's sugar on the tray."

One mug has two giant X marks, and the other says: *In my defense, I was left unsupervised.* She doesn't move to drink them but raises her eyes to Noah. "So, what do you want? How did you find me? And most importantly"—she pauses for dramatic effect—"who has my knife?"

Noah

And most importantly, who has my knife? Really? That's the most important thing? Not where am I? Who are you? Are you going to kill me? Why is my old sparring buddy with you? Girl's got some fucking ovaries of steel.

"We want to bring you onto our team. We're unhappy with management and plan to restructure. We need you for another plan involving The Gambit, but that's a lower priority at the moment. Jacob will explain how we found you after you hear our proposal, and your knife is in my pocket." Her thumb silently drums on the tabletop. It's the only indication she is not okay with the current whereabouts of the dagger. "You'll get it back at the end of our meeting."

I look around at my team and take a deep breath. "Our company has been corrupted, as most are over time. The three who sit on the board take on some work, but the majority going out to teams at our level has been taking out rivals who have done nothing more than set up a shop in competition with our agency. I'm all for capitalism, not because you kill the damn competitors but because your service or product is better.

"We've kept an eye on the execs and noticed a crossover with dealings The Gambit worked on. Yes, it's our job to take orders, beef up security for companies, and do the odd kill or extraction, but lately, we've been sent after rival security firms. 'Wipeout' was the order."

I don't mention the amount of blood we have on our hands. But if there's anyone who would either understand or not judge us for our sins, I think it's this stunning woman sitting at our table. Our orders were fucking senseless and not what we're about. We were used in a capacity that doesn't sit well with us.

Jacob chimes in, "You work for The Gambit. Now, doing our research, we know you're brilliant and could have gone to college. Based on our findings, your parents had connections to The Gambit. We can only assume you were brought into the world more concretely after they died." Rogue swings her eyes to his. He notices the hard edge her face took on when he mentioned her parents, and he meets her gaze unflinchingly.

I've got to jump in before she well and truly hates us without fully hearing our pitch, or she'll never agree. From the corner of my eye, I swear I see Jacob's mouth form "dipshit" as he internally chastises himself for his blunder. "He means to say that we understand your long-standing connection to the organization, but we would like you to consider working with us. Not our agency, but our team specifically. Our company is working with The Gambit on some shady shit, and we can only speculate that you don't want to be with them forever."

Rogue only cocks her head while reaching for one of the mugs and takes a sip of her tea. I see an almost imperceptible smirk at the corner of Jacob's mouth. No one else drinks it regularly on our team, but that will change if she joins us.

Her eyes narrow, and her lips part as she thinks through the information we've given her. "You're not worried about me sharing this little plan with my boss, which means either you've poisoned my drink or you're confident I'll join you. Which is it?"

Han takes a turn answering her question. "We aren't confident you'll join us, but we are hopeful. Your skills are some of the best we've seen, and it's taken us years to find you. I honestly can't believe I've known who you are all this time. You're uniquely positioned to be on the board, but you pull on the reins enough not to do all their bidding without remorse. When Jacob finally caught your trail, I thought he'd die of excitement." Rogue snorts into her mug and shakes her hand to remove the excess tea. Jacob does not look pleased. Han and Lucas are grinning like loons, and I stifle my laugh.

"Next question," she poses, "how did you find me?"

I nod my head at Lucas. "Buttercup, we figured out which killings were yours and which were done by hacks. We noticed a pattern that most connected with The Gambit, but to be honest, who in this fucking state doesn't? We have a contact in the police department who alerted us of some new evidence. He told us who brought it in, and we kept our ear to the ground, hoping it would be you to strike and not another of the hitmen in your crew."

Rogue sits patiently for the ax to fall. She wants to correct the slip-up that got her caught.

"Noah grabbed the security footage from the alley camera, but it didn't show us much. We used the new bakery's camera to get your direction, and from there, we used traffic cams to watch as you walked to a residential area. Don't worry. We erased the footage so the cops can't do the same.

"As you passed a car, you patted it. We couldn't see you enter the vehicle, but we managed to track that to an apartment building. We took turns staking out the building until you left for the bar the other night. From there, it was just a matter of slipping into your backseat." Motherfucker dares to wink at her; I hope and pray she isn't offended by his bravado.

"There was a fucking leaf on my car. That's what led you to me? Me brushing it off? Unbelievable."

Jacob takes a moment to load up the video footage he compiled, along with the list of Rook Industries' subsidiaries and their leasing agreements with the building owner.

Rogue nods like all of this makes sense, then shocks the hell out of us with her follow-up question, "Okay, so who took a shot at me the other day?"

Chapter Seven

Rogue

Mother. Fuck.

Who the hell is giving out Gambit information? Going as far as to tell people my next possible mark paints that person as a pretty target. My hand instinctively reaches for the knife in my thigh holster—a reflex that always happens when I'm feeling particularly stabby—only to remember the damn thing is still in Noah's pocket.

The shock on their faces after I asked who shot at me is almost comical. I mean, I know I shouldn't be drinking the tea they provided because, hello, poison. But, then again, why not kill me in the car on the way here? It would have been much less complicated. I had a feeling they weren't my mystery shooters, but it's nice to have that confirmed with their slack-jawed, wide-eyed stares.

"Someone shot at you?" Lucas roars at a decibel I'm not entirely comfortable with. His red hair has flopped over his forehead due to the sheer number of times he raked his hand through it since my earlier question. It was already in disarray from the Batman versus Superman debate. I think I'm going to make him lose his hair early.

"Yep. At the cemetery, when I was visiting my parents' graves. The day after, I was surprised in my car. I take it that it wasn't you guys?" I choke down a chuckle as I watch them sputter in outrage.

Han finally says, "Gorgeous, you'd have gotten away if you weren't up against us; you're good." I think he's done speaking, but then he opens his mouth and proves me wrong. "I'd never let them shoot my—"

"Fair enough." I cut him off before he could utter something too revealing about our time together all those years ago. The last thing I want is everyone knowing we slept together back when I was eighteen and that I ghosted him like an asshole. From his reaction when I first got here, I'm hoping he doesn't harbor too much ill will toward me.

Look, it's not something I'm proud of. But it was necessary. Han would have been dead if King had found out I was seeing someone regularly and that I had told him my real name instead of sticking with Rogue as he'd commanded.

When we were younger, Han's kindness had all my defenses dropping, and I let my name slip when he asked. For a girl who hadn't been offered an ounce of decency in ten years, it was a breath of fresh air amidst the heap of shit I'd been wading through.

Han smiles his boy-next-door grin at me, likely walking down memory lane. The last night I saw him, we had sex, and that little smirk now gracing his face tells me his trip through yesteryear has just landed there.

The confidence in the shooting ability he alluded to makes me want to see what he's working with, skills-wise. The naughty smirk ghosting across his lips as he remembers us fucking in the locker room makes me want to throw my mug at him.

I raise a finger to tell them I need a moment and stand from my chair. I head out of the meeting room and go to the lounge smack-dab in the middle of the warehouse. I need a moment to think. I also need a moment to get past the guilt I've always carried around after disappearing on one of the only friends I'd ever had. And I'd like to do that without four big dudes staring at me.

Thinking back, a smile flits across my face too. I started fighting in the rings when I was seventeen. It was after my first few kills, and I needed to keep my body limber between jobs. It was an excellent way to get out my rage and frustration at the whole damn world. Han was a few years older than me and showed up to Fight Night every week.

He wasn't undefeated back then, but his record had started tilting more into the win column than loss. He fought with an intoxicating mix of fury and desperation. His opponents rarely stood a chance if they were of equal size. He eventually learned to use his leaner body as an advantage and

The Secrets We Keep

became lightning-fast. It was beautiful to watch him take down his challengers. Admittedly, he's filled out since back then, and I'd bet on him every time now.

I was a bit star-struck when he finished a match and joined me in the locker room. I'd seen him fight a few times before, and his skill was becoming unparalleled.

One day, nearly six months after I first saw him fight, he just plopped down next to me in the communal locker room and introduced himself like he hadn't just kicked the shit out of some gang banger that easily had fifty pounds on him.

We chatted every time I made it to the fights, and a small, tentative friendship grew. I had just turned eighteen, still had my natural blonde hair, no tattoos, and was always dressed in sweats and a tank top. It's no wonder Han was shocked to see me today. I don't even recognize myself in the mirror sometimes.

I look nothing like I did back then. My hair is long now and dyed black, and I've got more tattoos than I can count, covering every inch of the right side of my body. Once I moved away from King, my body filled out more.

King was always rigid about my weight and how it affected my training. My body is healthy and toned, and I finally have my natural curves and valleys after all the deprivation and damn near killing myself on his regimen.

In any case, I'm glad Han is here and safe. He seems to enjoy his work with Noah, Lucas, and Jacob. Honestly, if he trusts them, I do too. It's time to remember their names if I'm considering working with them. It would be awkward as fuck to continually say, "Hey you."

Weighing my options here, I run through what I know. King is using my sister Sage to keep me on a leash. I get her back when I fulfill my side of our bargain if I don't get killed first, that is. These guys don't seem to know about that, and Sage has been hidden away for so long; I doubt they'd ever figure it out unless I told them. I'll keep that close to the vest until I'm sure I can trust them.

The guys used a connection with the police to find me. Someone is leaking information, and that can't continue. Looks like I'm adding a new name to my list—not to kill...probably. I mean, unless they're a shithead and an abusive asshole like Mark was. I'll just scare them a bit.

They're looking to take their board down. Who that is is the next unknown. I doubt the guys will tell me everything right away. Seems like they're planning to do it on a need-to-know basis until the time is right, but fuck that. I want to know what I'm walking into here. They also want to take The Gambit down because of the connection to their board. That can't happen until I get Sage out and the evidence King has on me. They couldn't make a move on The Gambit without an inside man. Woman. Me. Shit. They're going to get me killed, aren't they?

But I'm in if they can promise to help me get Sage away from King and back with me. Between their skills and mine, we'll be a force to be reckoned with.

I stop my pacing and flop down onto the most comfortable leather couch I've ever rested my pert ass upon. I sigh and think through everything once more for good measure.

I hear movement to my left and decide to have a little fun. Quick as I can, I whip the tiny knife out of the heel of my stiletto, as I did in the boardroom of Rook Industries, and chuck it in the direction of the noise. I aim a bit wide so I don't kill anyone today. It wasn't on the agenda, after all. I swing my gaze to the left and see Noah with his arms crossed and a none-too-pleased expression on his face.

"I thought you got all her weapons," he growls at Lucas, who is crouched behind him. Wimp.

"I thought so, too. I mean, I took seven weapons away, and you have the knife she pitched a fit about in your pocket. Where'd that one come from, Buttercup?"

"Wouldn't you like to know?" I ask in my sweetest tone possible. Lucas just nods repeatedly while his eyes glaze over. No doubt remembering where I stashed my knives when we first met in the parking garage. Tits, nature's built-in distractions.

Jacob strolls out of the meeting room, casual as fuck, and yanks my knife out of the wall. He approaches me and hands it back, hilt-first, like a gentleman. Lucas scoffs and starts to open his mouth to argue. Jacob simply holds up one of his tattooed hands to halt Lucas's upcoming tirade. "If she wanted to hit you, she would have. You've seen her work."

Satisfied that I'm regarded as an equal in an incredibly male-dominated profession, not to mention clubhouse—I mean, warehouse—I slip the knife back into the base of the stiletto. Han pokes his head out of the room, checking the coast is clear of flying projectiles. "Gorgeous, please don't kill my team."

I roll my eyes at his use of my old fight name. The first time I showed up to fight, the emcee asked my name, and I told him it was Rogue. They already had a fighter with that name; it was some big, burly dude from a local motorcycle club. The emcee snapped his fingers and called me Gorgeous, and that was that. Fight name established.

I didn't care enough to argue it. I just needed to vent my aggression, and the damn name stuck. "You may as well sit down to hear my terms."

Lucas whoops like a freshman co-ed on spring break in Florida, hopping over the back of the couch to sit far too close to me. Jacob takes one of the armchairs while Noah takes the other. Han lowers to my other side while placing my half-drunk tea on the coffee table. He, too, relaxes back on the couch, but with a respectable amount of space between us, unlike the red-headed barnacle on my other side, who is staring at me way too close for comfort.

"One, I will continue to do my work for The Gambit, and the motherfucker who sold me out will be mine to deal with. No exceptions. Mine. I probably won't kill him."

Jacob snorts as he laughs. "Love, you can't kill our guy. He's a good one and on our side."

"I figured something like that; that's why I said 'probably.' But I reserve the right to scare the guy a little." I playfully wink, and Jacob chuckles at my crazy. I take a deep breath before continuing. Item two will clinch the deal if they agree.

"Two, you will help me get someone out of The Gambit and safe. I'll provide details, and we'll make a move when the time is right." Everyone nods, but curious glances bounce between the guys.

"Is it your boyfriend?" Lucas asks with all the tact of a wrecking ball.

I laugh and shake my head.

"And three, you will immediately bring me into the fold on all intel related to your cause. I need to be as informed as humanly possible. I don't plan to risk my life so you can all have cushy corner offices." No one nods. No one says anything for a second.

"Ivy," Han starts after glancing at Noah, who tilts his head at him in encouragement, "it's not about offices or a bigger salary. It's because they're sending us after people who don't deserve to die. Our kill orders went from a few times yearly to over thirty in twelve months.

"We don't claim to be in a position to judge others, but if their worst crimes were setting up rival security agencies, we have a problem with that. We didn't know they were all connected with other firms until it was too late. But from then on, we started finding ways to circumvent orders. We were played, fed false intel from management, and used in a way we are not, and never will be, okay with."

His tone is full of remorse and a hint of self-loathing while Lucas's head hangs low. I can tell they're like me. They only eliminate with just cause. Hell, it's half the reason I don't mind being an assassin for The Gambit.

Most of the time, my marks are those who break The Gambit's rules and sell to kids or double-cross in a way that hurts innocents. The few eliminations I've done that I disagreed with still grate on my soul in a way I know they'll never cease.

Jacob picks up where Han left off, "From what we've gathered, your kills are only the scum of the earth variety. You only deal with extreme cases or those who break some of the rules of The Gambit. We agree with rules like the blanket order prohibiting selling to minors. But they're not just sending you and the other hitmen after the big offenders, are they?"

I catch his drift rather quickly. They're standing up for what they believe in. They're fighting for what is right and against what is most certainly a betrayal of trust and human decency.

This British tattooed tech nerd is talking me into joining them, isn't he? I study his light blue eyes shielded by black-frame glasses, dark brown hair in a gentleman's cut, broad shoulders covered by a white button-up shirt, and long legs in black slacks. He sits with poise, and the concern on his brow only endears him to me further.

He's repulsed by what they've done, and they're working to correct their wrongs. His elbows rest on his knees as he leans forward, his hands twisting together as he waits for my response. Those tattoos covering his forearms and neck have me internally drooling.

I touch my fingers just below my lip to make sure it is, in fact, internal drool. It's been way too long since I've had sex if just the look of this guy has my body heating. But honestly, I'm more impressed with how he could hack the street cams than anything else.

Picking up the tea Han brought from the table, I shake my head in response to Jacob's earlier question, then raise the mug to finish my beverage. I glance at the bottom of the cup and see the words printed: *You've just been poisoned.*

It's a joke, right? Right?

I calmly place the cup on the coffee table between the seats and shift my body to look at Lucas to my left. "You wanna explain the cup?"

He looks at the mug with the two innocuous X marks and chuckles nervously. "It was a joke, Buttercup." He looks at Noah across the seating area and points a finger accusingly. "He used the one I had all picked out for you this morning! It was perfect."

"The one that said—" Noah starts.

"Dude! Don't spoil it; she'll use it next time," Lucas grumbles.

"Anyway," Jacob starts to get us back on track, "we agree to your terms. So, when can you move in?"

I'm sorry, what?

Chapter Eight

Han

After a tense conversation about having Ivy live with us, we agreed that she would stay at her apartment until we were ready to move on one of our organizations. With that concession, we agreed that one of us would stay with her to keep her in the loop better.

Because of our history, I jumped at the chance to spend some one-on-one time with her. Time has been especially good to her. A few years ago, when she was eighteen and I was twenty-one, I saw her fight and was immediately enamored. She was meticulous in the ring, a testament to years of training.

It's why I pushed myself to get better. Ivy inspired me to learn some new tricks when I saw her take down a guy who weighed triple what she did back then. Her speed and quick thinking had me working on some new moves within a week.

It took me the better part of five seemingly endless months to work up the courage to introduce myself.

Ivy wasn't a regular like I was, showing up every damn week. But when she did enter the ring, I was sure to watch. The night I plopped down next to her in the changing room, I was nervous as hell but tried to play it off like I wasn't sweating bullets.

We established an easy friendship and talked about fighting, our shared love of cars, and the movies we enjoyed. We never got into anything heavy. I never pushed for more information from her because I could see those little tells that alluded to painful past experiences.

A few months into our unexpected friendship, I had still been calling her "Gorgeous," and she called me by mine, "Boom." It was a horrid nickname that stuck from my childhood on the streets into my fighting career, all because I was willing to take the hits and wait out my opponent before striking back.

God, I fucking hate that name. Ivy finally told me her real name when I mentioned how ridiculous it was that we were still going by our given monikers. She said the name, and panic swam in her eyes as a declaration poured from her mouth so quickly that I almost didn't understand all the words running together. *"You can never call me that outside of the two of us. In fact, just forget it altogether. Just stick with Gorgeous. It's safer that way."*

I know now she was protecting me from her identity. I'm slightly miffed that she didn't trust me to know her as Rogue. But seeing the line of work she's in, I get it. I followed her orders and called her Gorgeous because I couldn't bear to see the fear in her eyes again. The only time I used her given name was in my head, except for that last night.

I had just finished a fight in the ring, and Ivy was near the door to the changing rooms. She had watched me take down Fury, a drug dealer from the east side. We entered the rooms together, and Ivy pulled a medkit from her bag to wrap up my hands. She and I usually took care of each other after our fights.

Her hands were tender, gentle even. After watching her fight for all those months before getting to know her, this soft side always surprised me. She was a genuinely kind and enchanting person. With our hands linked together, I took a chance and leaned in for a kiss. I still remember her sigh and replayed it in my head for months afterward, clinging to the memory of that night.

We made out like fiends before she started pulling on the waistband of my shorts and slipped her hand inside. Now, I wasn't new to sex, but Ivy was a bit younger than me. I didn't know her experience. She moved confidently, and when I questioned her if this was really what she wanted, she all but blurted out the word "yes" and climbed into my lap.

Our time together was drawn out and sweet after those months of buildup. I had a crush before even speaking to Ivy, and after seeing who she was outside the ring, I was smitten.

We fucked slow and gentle at first, then hard and fast when she demanded it. I'd been afraid she was inexperienced and tried to take it slow. But after she threatened to finish the job herself if I didn't pick up the pace, I figured she knew what she was doing.

When I came, I cried her name out into the empty room, and she froze. We came down from our highs, and she started packing up. I asked if I could see her again outside of the fights, and she said she was busy during the week but would see me at the next Fight Night. I hoped it wasn't a brush-off, but I knew she was gone when she didn't show up to that one, the next, or the next.

I've had a lot of time since then to ponder her rejection, and it always came back to me using her name and the first time she warned me off of it. I should have kept her name in my head, but it felt like the most natural thing in the world to call out the name of the girl I had inadvertently tumbled into love with.

Drawing myself out of the past, I look to my right and see Ivy sitting next to me in the newly painted truck on our way back to her place.

Noah wants to ensure she doesn't spill the beans to The Gambit about our intended targets, but I know she won't. He's cautious about trusting anyone outside the team and with good reason. We're about to engage in a deadly game.

"You drew the short straw, huh?" she asks. Like hanging out is going to be a burden to me.

"Nah, Gorgeous. I won the rock-paper-scissors tournament." I laugh. It's been the way we settle things for years. I'm convinced Noah usually wins through sheer force of will, but today was my lucky day. At least for this.

I did not win this morning when we decided who got the last cinnamon bun Mrs. Morganson baked for us yesterday. Somehow, one out of two dozen survived twenty-four hours, only for Noah to shove the whole thing in his mouth victoriously when his scissors won the battle.

She straight-up giggles behind her hand. I could listen to that sound forever.

Ivy puts out this vibe that she's the biggest, baddest thing in the room, or truck as it were, and then this chime of laughter comes out of her. I have a feeling she's a study in contradictions, and I love a good enigma.

We make our way through the afternoon traffic, and she tries to give me directions, but I remind her we've been staking out her building. A blush rises on her cheeks, and I find it fucking adorable.

I spot parking along the street and glance up at the surrounding buildings. Everything in this neighborhood is relatively modern, and every building on the block has security. Ivy chose her apartment well.

I still can't believe she agreed to have one of us with her. She seems to do everything on her own. She never looks to the others around her for reactions; she just focuses on doing her own thing.

Her only stipulation to the new arrangement was that we couldn't come with her for the Gambit assignments. We agreed because the less her associates see of us, the better.

We know she can take care of herself within her organization. She's done it all alone this far, and we'd be assholes to think she couldn't do it without us just because she's suddenly part of our team.

Only a dumbass would try to change this creature currently strutting up the street ahead of me, hypnotizing me with the sway of her full hips.

I barely stifle the groan inching its way up my throat as I imagine my hands on her ass as she bounces on my cock. We never did get to that position that night all those years ago.

Ivy reaches a big green awning, and the doorman sees her and nearly strains a muscle trying to open the door for her as quickly as possible.

"Good afternoon, miss," he greets.

"Hi, Jim. This is Han; he'll be here for a bit," she says sweetly—a complete one-eighty to the badass persona she portrayed at our warehouse.

I nod and tack on, "Hello, Jim."

He runs his gaze up and down my body, finally landing back on my face. "Hello, welcome to the building." He turns to Ivy. "There's been a delivery for you, miss. It's on the desk with Hugo."

"Thanks, Jim. No flirting with Han. See you later." She walks through the door to the lobby desk staffed by an enormous attendant.

Fifty bucks says Hugo isn't just in charge of deliveries. He looks like a security guy. The guns in the harness around his shoulder and under his jacket clued me in. If you know where to look, they create a ripple of fabric.

He simply nods to Ivy and hands her a large manila envelope with tape and a signature across the flap.

She murmurs her thanks, and we make our way to the open elevator on the ground level and take it up to the fourth floor. Her reflection in the mirrored elevator doors shows no emotion except a slight furrow on her brow.

She taps one foot in a slow rhythm as we ascend her building. Not nervously or impatiently, just as something to pass the time. "Just so you're aware, both Jim and Hugo are mine. King brought them in, but they're loyal to me."

We reach her floor, and she exits and turns to the right as I try to figure out how she might have swayed two of King's men to her side.

According to the number and letter combinations, this floor has ten apartments. The apartments must be smaller to fit this many on one level. She warned us there wasn't much space at her place, and she wasn't lying.

She unlocks the door with a small set of keys from her front pocket and steps through. She holds the door wide, allowing me entrance. I look around as she closes the door and locks it up.

It really is a small space: a living room with a black couch and green armchair, a record player on top of a bookshelf overfilled with too many spines to count, a small kitchenette, and a hallway that looks like it leads to a bathroom and single bedroom.

It's small but quirky. I don't see a television anywhere, but that's fine. While Ivy's out working, I'll be on my laptop or dive into her little library. Jacob would love this, and he's always trying to get me to read more than just recipes and manuals.

Ivy joins me at the edge of her living room and waves an arm, encompassing the entire room with a flick of her wrist. "Welcome. You're sleeping on the couch." She thinks that's going to make me change my mind about staying. Ha, I've slept in smaller and worse places.

"Sounds good, Gorgeous. What are we doing tonight?" I breeze over the couch comment. She doesn't know I spent a chunk of my youth living on the street, but she does know I was at those fights, and people who go there don't have many options.

"I've got a hit tonight, so I need dinner early. You can pick where we order from. Menus are in the drawer next to the sink." She continues talking, taking off down the hall to what I assume is her bedroom with the envelope still in her hands. The door closes once she's inside, and I go to the kitchenette to choose our dinner.

Rogue

Ugh, houseguests seriously cramp my style, even if they are the first guy I had real feelings for, and gave me my first non-self-induced orgasm.

I don't have a strict routine for my off time, but you can bet your ass that as soon as I walk in the door to my home, I whip my bra off faster than a stripper at a millionaire's bachelor party. There's even a hook next to the key holder that I use to hang it on.

Bras are the devil; underwire, an addendum to Eve's original sin punishment. Straps that dig into shoulders while supporting big tits are the worst.

I whip my bra across my tiny bedroom and reach for a sports bra lying on my bed. I spend the next few minutes giving myself a stern talking to when I conjure up the image of Han in my bed, naked and glorious, as he fucks me into next week. God, he's grown up.

He may not have been my first, but the memories of us coming together after months of teases and light touches always make me smile. He was incredible and let me forget about my job, life, and responsibilities for a little while. I came to crave those fights like a person with an addiction. Not for the violence, no. It was a craving for the sweet man who fought like he had nothing to lose but spoke as though he had everything to give.

I spent half the car ride trying not to sniff his delicious scent. He smells like cologne, and I'm a sucker for the expensive stuff. Combine that with the windows down, fresh air swirling around us, and sunshine beating down on the truck, and I was a few minutes away from seeing if he was still as good as I remember.

My biggest regret is not seeing him after. I know it was best for his safety, but God, it hurt to do that to him. I can only imagine how he felt when I never showed up again.

Han's the type of guy who would understand, and I'm thankful he hasn't cornered me about it yet, but with the big "Rogue" reveal, I'm sure he's started putting the pieces together.

I'm already dreading that conversation because I know it's coming, not because of how Han will react, but because of my shame and guilt, which I don't want to relive.

"I'm torn between sushi and burgers!" Han shouts from the living room, breaking me out of my daydream.

After tossing on a sports bra and tank top, I peek out the door to see him standing at the end of the short hallway with a menu in either hand. "Burgers," I reply with a shrug because I have a feeling if he can't decide between two entirely different types of food, he will take forever to decide on his sushi order. My local place has a lot of stuff on the menu.

"Burgers it is," he declares as he holds up the winning menu. He starts perusing their offers as I shut the door and finish changing from jeans into yoga pants and adding a long-sleeved navy Henley shirt.

I open the door again and pass through the hallway to make my way to the living room. "Ready?" I ask.

He nods and points to a veggie burger. "This and the sweet potato fries. Oh! And a milkshake. But I want all three flavors. A Neopolitan shake if they do that."

"So healthy until you got to the shake." I laugh as Han gets a twinkle in his eye, no doubt dreaming of the shake.

"It's about balance. I like junk food and regular burgers like everyone else. But if that's all I ate, I'd be fucking huge; you know that doesn't work in our business."

"Amen, Boom. I'll get the same," I laugh as I surreptitiously check out his physique from the opposite side of the couch while his head is tipped back, asking God for a new nickname.

He's a few inches taller than me but not imposing, leaner than the other guys, and toned as hell. The muscles he's added on over the years are excellent additions. His black sweats hang from his hips, and a gray t-shirt is tight across his chest yet loose around his middle. A few tattoos cover his upper arms, trailing up and under his shirt sleeves. There goes the internal drooling thing again.

He catches me looking and shoots me a quick wink after cocking his scarred brow in my direction. I'd nearly forgotten about the fight when he got that scar. Some preppy kid wanted to slum it with the rest of us and joined a Fight Night. Han caught an elbow to the brow when the kid started flailing around. The ring was stained red for weeks, but at least he didn't catch that flying elbow directly to the eye.

I avert my wandering gaze and make my way to the kitchen, hiding the embarrassment splashed across my face. I grab my phone from the small counter, where I'd dropped it earlier, and place our orders on a takeout delivery app.

While we wait for the food, we shoot the breeze about weapons. Han decides my knives are practical but waxes poetic about guns and their mechanics. I have a feeling he'll never be swayed to my side—the right side—of the argument that knives are better.

Around eight, after dinner has been eaten and cleaned up, I grab a duffle bag and tell Han I'm heading out. He waves me off from his spot on the couch while his nose is buried in one of my smutty books, and *Stranger Things* plays on his laptop in the background.

He doesn't need much entertainment as a houseguest, thankfully. But it's good to know I'll be able to go back to my routine of kill and chill when the job is done.

We avoided talk of the past, and I didn't want to tell him I had developed intense feelings for him. I've tried to block out the moment I disappeared on him for years, but I know that confrontation is coming. Over dinner, we spoke about superficial things like we did at the beginning of our friendship.

I grab my keys from the hook and lock the door on my way out. I take the stairs down to the level below my apartment, and after checking to see the hallway is empty, I use my key to access my Bat Cave. There's no need for Han or the guys to know about my supply room just yet or that its access point is next to Han in the living room.

I used my current privacy to check out the envelope I had stashed in the duffle. It's from King; a new player is moving in on our turf. A full-size photo shows a man in his mid-forties with sandy brown hair and glasses that look like they came from the nineties. For all intents and purposes, he looks like an accountant.

I read up on the details forwarded along with the photo. Neil Carter moved from Oregon to just north of San Francisco to try and establish a foothold. He's gathering numbers and offering a protection ring in the city. Either he doesn't know or doesn't care that California is The Gambit's territory. I make a mental note to spend some time researching later. Tonight, I've got a dealer to take out.

After choosing a butterfly knife, my favorite hunting blade, and a gun for backup in case everything goes to absolute shit, I head out into the night and make my way to a dive bar across town.

I find the dealer, but everything does, in fact, go to absolute shit.

Chapter Nine

Noah

About half an hour ago, Han called Jacob with some grim news. The three of us grabbed our shit when the usually unflappable Brit went tearing through the warehouse, shouting to grab a patch-up bag and move our asses.

Jacob said Han wasn't in danger, alleviating some of our worries, but then made it ramp back up again by saying that Rogue was bleeding.

We just found her and finally secured an in with The Gambit. There's no way our plans will work without her. We load up in the blacked-out SUV we keep gassed up for emergencies and make our way to the apartment.

Rogue apparently told the doorman to expect us when she returned, and the gangly man opened the door for us, telling us where to find her. The elevator ride takes longer than I'd like because Lucas hits a few extra buttons in his haste, causing us to stop at every floor between the lobby and Rogue's level. It would have been faster just to take the stairs.

In the moment that I'm shaking my head at his antics, I see a tiny smear of blood on the floor. I grab an alcohol pad from the medical bag I'm carrying and wipe up the small mess.

When the doors finally open on the fourth floor, Jacob leads the charge to Rogue's apartment and bangs on the door. There's a bit of blood on the doorknob, so I grab another wipe and clean it up in the few seconds we're stuck in the hall. After seeing what's happening inside, we will bleach the door and the elevator floor.

Han flings the door open and has blood all over his arms and shirt. "What the bloody fuck happened, man?" Jacob's voice reaches that same volume it did in the warehouse when he catches sight of our bloodstained teammate.

"Jake, relax. It's Rogue's. She came in right before I called you about half an hour ago, stumbling and clutching her stomach. There was blood all over her arms, and I tried to help. She told me to fuck off very loudly, reminding me she's been on her own for a while now, and pushed me out of the way. She grabbed a bottle of whiskey and locked herself in the bathroom. She's barely speaking to me through the door other than to growl at me to, you guessed it, 'fuck off,'" he ends on a sarcastic note, but the worry on his face is hard to miss.

Deciding enough is enough, I take the bag off my shoulder and charge down the hallway to the closed door that must be the bathroom. The sound of water running and grunts of pain get louder as I get closer.

"Rogue, open the door, please." I try to be pleasant first because whatever Han has been doing hasn't worked.

"Noah? Fuck off." Well, at least she's consistent, even in her state—stubborn woman.

"Not happening. Open the door. I've got a medkit, and Han says you're bleeding. Let's get you patched up," I state firmly, realizing that *nice* isn't going to get me anywhere with her right now. Leaving no room for argument usually works with the guys; I hope it has the same effect on our newest team member.

I hear a groan and a click as the pocket door moves to the right. When it cracks open, I hear a pained sound as I slide the door the rest of the way.

Rogue is sitting in a tiny bathtub with a needle and thread in one hand while the other returns to her middle to hold an angry-looking slash closed over the untattooed portion of her stomach on her left side. The faucet for the sink is still running, and water carelessly runs over her knives. Somehow, she thought to start cleaning her blades before sewing her abdomen shut.

I don't know why I'm surprised; she has the strangest priorities.

I blanch and turn back to the guys hovering at the end of the hall, looking each one in the eye respectively as I give them their directions. "The bathroom is too small for all of us. I'll get to work on helping Rogue.

Han, clean yourself up in the kitchen. Lucas, mop up the blood in the apartment and bleach the elevator floor and her doorknob. Jacob, find new clothes for her to wear."

The guys quickly nod, ready to do anything to help. They hustle down the hall to get to work while I turn and take in the scene of our newest recruit gutted like a fish. It doesn't look too deep, but she needs those stitches.

"What, no orders for me, Captain Atom?" she jokes, then groans as her laugh causes her pain. She clutches her stomach and winces. Who the fuck is Captain Atom?

"Your orders are to keep holding that slice closed while I finish up the sewing and to stop telling people to fuck off." As I step through the door, I swear I hear one last raspy 'fuck off' tumble from her lips in a whisper. Yep, stubborn.

I kneel between the sink and the toilet to face Rogue in the tub. Her teeth are clamped together, and I see she's done a pretty decent job of closing the wound, but there are still a few stitches needed. Her eyes are a bit glassy, and it has me worried she's going to pass out any minute.

"Hey, Trouble. Hang in there; blood loss is no fun." I position her left hand on the wound to keep pinching as I pull on some gloves and pull out a sterilized needle from my medkit. Her entire supply has seemingly spilled onto the ground, and there's equipment strewn about the postage-stamp-sized bathroom.

Jacob drops off a water bottle for Rogue and makes his way to her bedroom to find her clothes. She gulps it greedily as I clean the remaining open part of the wound and tell her to brace herself. She pulls a face of steely determination and keeps pinching the damage in stoic silence as I run the needle through her skin to stitch her back together.

I avoid crushing all the supplies underfoot, and she looks up at me with those big green eyes. "Hi, Captain Atom. Thanks for stitching me up. Since you're here and probably know what you're doing, I'm just gonna chill for a second." Her voice gets a bit slurred, and I remember Han mentioning she grabbed a bottle of whiskey.

I'm just getting the last few stitches in when her hand loses its strength and flops to the side against the porcelain tub. I look at her face and see her eyes are closed. I think the worst has happened, that she's lost too much blood when she suddenly lets out a light snore. At that moment, I see the nearly half-empty whiskey bottle cradled in her colorful right arm like a baby.

I finish up the job, and Jacob offers to take over. He's got some clothes for Rogue bundled in his arm. My back is killing me from being hunched over the tub, and I gratefully take him up on his offer. Part of me wants to help get her settled and situated, but I'm not the only one concerned.

I stand and see my shirtsleeves have blood on them, and there's blood above my wrists where the gloves didn't cover me. I let Jacob take over and make my way to the kitchen.

Han is anxiously wringing his hands, and his head snaps up. "How is she?" he asks with gut-wrenching concern.

"She's sleeping it off. The cut wasn't too deep, but it needed stitches. She did a bang-up job on her own. She could have finished by herself, but I'm glad you called us. When she saw I was handling it, she took the opportunity to pass out after calling me Captain Atom. Who is that? And how full was that whiskey bottle Rogue grabbed?"

"No clue who that is. As for the whiskey, it was new. I heard the seal break as our dear teammate unscrewed it on the way down the hall. Why?"

I laugh as I shake my head. "Because it's half-empty now. We'll have to watch out for infection and a hangover in the morning."

Han starts laughing, and it spreads to me as well. He's relieved she's okay. Hell, we all are. Lucas walks in the front door with a flower bouquet and a slushie straw in his mouth. "What?" he asks around the straw.

Han buckles over and laughs again. This is a weird night. I never expected gaining another team member would cause this much upheaval. But I have to admit, aside from the blood, it's been an adventure.

I clean off at the kitchen sink and toss my bloodied shirt in the laundry with Han's clothes while he's asking Lucas about Captain Atom.

He's a DC comic book character, and according to Lucas, he fits me perfectly, and he's pissed he didn't think of it first.

Jacob comes down the hall, having moved Rogue to her room. "She's out like a light, man. I cleaned her up, and she came round enough to get dressed, but she refused to wear pants. Something about a woman's right to choose."

Lucas and Han both perk up at the mention of her sass, and I am confident those two will make a move on Rogue sooner rather than later. They know my stance on this. If it doesn't fuck up the team and doesn't hurt anyone, go for it. Han and Jacob were both into a girl they met once and instead of letting her come between them, they let her *come* between them.

I have to trust my team to make the right decisions for themselves, but I'll step in if I see the potential for disaster or our plans are jeopardized. I tell the guys I'll stay in Rogue's room tonight, heading off any argument, or God forbid, a rock-paper-scissors tournament, by ordering them around and setting up a watch schedule.

Rogue

Warmth surrounds me as I wake to the sounds of the neighbors whisper-fighting about God knows what. I can't make out the topic, but I swear I hear the words coffee, tea, and panties. Huh, weird.

Wait. I shouldn't hear whispers through walls.

I decide I must be dreaming and tuck into my warm nest of blankets. The scent of cedar reaches my nose. Mmm, it smells like a warm and toasty sauna in a snowy mountain retreat, like ignoring the raging storm that surrounds you just to take a calming breath. I wish all dreams were this cozy.

I feel prickles under my hand and explore the expanse before me. A soft laugh stops my wandering appendage.

I open a bleary eye to see light streaming through the gap in the curtains. It's too bright for me to see anything just yet. It's all just shapes and blobs of color at this point. I move to sit up when pain rolls across my stomach, and the blanket on top of my thighs tightens. It takes me a moment to realize that blankets don't move voluntarily.

"Lie back down, Rogue, please." Blankets don't have voices either. The 'please' catches my attention. I turn my head to see Noah lying next to me, shirtless. He's above the covers next to me while I'm cocooned inside, my hand resting on his pec. That I just fucking caressed. Great. His big hand rests on my thighs over the comforter, his touch gentle but firm. He won't let me get up, and the painful reminder of my stomach agrees with him.

He's got a look of concern in his dark eyes, and his stubbled, sharp jaw ticks back and forth. I doubt he's slept since they arrived, and since I feel a little groggy, it must have been a fair few hours. This isn't my first experience with blood loss, but I'm feeling pretty okay, other than the sting of pain and a pounding headache. I know those will pass soon too.

The whispering that isn't coming from the neighbors but originates from outside my door continues, and I can only assume it's the other three musketeers. "Guys, come in," I croak out as Noah slides his massive form further up the bed to rest his back against the headboard while keeping one hand on my thigh—like he knows I'll try to bolt as soon as he lets go.

Lucas is the first to barrel through the door, and his face relaxes when he sees I'm alive and functioning. His eyes drop to Noah's hand on my thigh over the blanket, and I witness a bit of color bloom on his freckled cheeks.

I prop myself up on my elbows with a bit of a wince that I hope no one notices. The hand-to-thigh contact remains.

"Buttercup! Good, you're finally awake. What do you want to eat? I was going to make you tea again, but I can't find your stash."

Jacob is the next through the door as he crowds Lucas further into the room without giving me a moment to answer. "Morning, Love. Why do you have a hidden trap door in your closet?" Shit, he found the entrance to the Bat Cave.

Han is the last to complete our clown car scenario, and he pauses next to Jacob as he looks around the room. His eyes skate over Noah's proximity to me, returning his gaze to my face after a moment. "Hey, Gorgeous, you're a little pale, but you look alright. Did you take the antibiotics we procured?"

I look at my bedside table, and sure enough, there's a bottle of water and a packet of pills with a note under it. The message reads: *Buttercup, take one every twelve hours until you finish the pack. Yes, you must take every single pill.* Damn Lucas, being all considerate.

I hate taking medicine and struggle not to gag every time, but it's the right thing to do. Who knows what touched that blade before it penetrated my skin? I'll wait until I'm alone to take one so they don't see the faces I make when swallowing the chalky tablets.

Noah takes a moment to whisper in my ear, "Trouble, if you want them to leave you alone, answer their questions, or send them to go do something." He chuckles at the shiver I failed to repress as his breath danced across my sensitive ear. I lift my eyes to the slight crease between his eyebrows that furrow as his eyes crinkle with mirth.

He's got just the barest hint of laugh lines and wrinkles on his weathered face. It makes sense; he looks to be around thirty-five or so. He'll be a silver fox for sure in another decade or two.

I clear my throat and immediately notice my disgusting whiskey breath as my senses come back online. "Good morning, boys. Lucas, yes, there's extra tea in the cupboard behind the sugar. Jacob, that is absolutely none of your business; stop snooping. Han, thank you. I'm feeling better, but you should always tell a girl that she looks ravishing in the morning. Noah, get your giant paw off me. I need the bathroom."

Lucas's eyes ping between Noah and me like he's watching a tennis ball crossing the court in a Grand Slam match. His voice is a hushed whisper. "Good God, there are two of them."

The Secrets We Keep

They're shuffling out of the bedroom, talking about a football game, of all things. Jacob peels off, comes around to my side of the bed, and uncovers me to help me up. It's a bit breezy, so I have a feeling I know what I'll find if I look down. Risking it, I glance at my bottom half. Sure enough, I'm in only panties and a tank top someone maneuvered me into last night. More curiously, I'm clean from all the blood I lost.

I figure I'm in the clear since Jacob is a professional, and I'm a few stitches away from playing jump rope with my own intestines, but when I look up, I notice a tinge of color high on Jacob's stunning cheekbones. He coughs to redirect my attention.

"I cleaned you off last night in the tub with a couple of the wash rags I found under the sink. Noah had finished stitching you up and needed to wash off in the kitchen. You roused enough for a few minutes to take over changing your clothes but refused to put sweats on."

Makes sense. I hate wearing anything more than panties to bed, and even in my delirious and drunk state, I managed to mostly hold fast to those preferences—atta girl. The camisole was an excellent concession to make, though—tipsy and anemic brain for the win.

"Thank you, and sorry if I flashed you at some point. What a way to make an impression on my new super-secret spy colleague." I try adding some humor to the mix to disperse my embarrassment.

He laughs loudly—and fuck me, are those dimples?— and regains some of his composure. "No, Love. You didn't flash me. Also, 'super-secret spy colleague' is an excellent way to refer to our teammates. We'll need to get shirts made. Team bonding exercises are still the norm, are they not? Brilliant, we could have a corporate retreat! I've always wanted to go to the Caribbean."

Okay, now it's my turn to redden a bit. Jacob sounds, well, to be honest, this man sounds sexy as fuck whenever he opens his mouth. I wonder if he'll consider just speaking to me for days on end with his delicious accent. My internal drooling may be external at this point. There's no stopping it; it was inevitable. Rest in peace dignity. "Good to know. I'll look into getting some shirts. Pink okay with you?"

Jacob smiles and reaches out one of his tattooed hands to take mine. I move to stand, and immediate pain and nausea wash over me. I'm sure I must be turning a lovely shade of green. Looking at my face this morning must be like staring into a kaleidoscope between the blushing and blanching.

Suddenly, strong arms hook under my knees and around my lower back as I'm hoisted into the air and cradled like I'm made of glass. Jacob is a pretty big guy, but as far as techies go, I haven't known many with the upper body strength it takes to lift a size ten woman. Yet here I am, floating through my bedroom door like a goddamn fairy, gently being put on my feet in the bathroom.

Jacob leans in after I've steadied myself on the sink and cups my face with his hands. His thumb trails across my cheek, and he whispers, "I'm glad you're okay, super-secret spy colleague." His gaze flicks to my lips briefly, and I'm almost sure I imagined it.

He spins with a soft groan, heading down the hall to join the others. I need a second. Okay, a few seconds. My equilibrium is off balance in both the best and worst ways.

How did I go from completely and utterly alone to suddenly having burgers and leisurely conversations with one guy, waking up next to another, and sweet caresses from a tattooed god? Not to mention Lucas, who has apparently already planned our upcoming nuptials. My head is swimming.

I'm used to my life being mine, with no interference from others, but a small part of me must admit it was nice to wake up and have support. No one admonished me for my dangerous encounter last night. They only showed concern for my well-being and rallied around me. Is this what a dedicated and loyal team looks like?

Jacob, Noah, Han, Lucas

"She's moving in."
"Jinx!"
"Ah, fuck."
"Double jinx!"

Chapter Ten

Lucas

GREAT, WE'RE STUCK IN A FOUR-WAY DOUBLE JINX. AND NO, YOU dirty bird, it's not a sex thing. At least we stopped playing prison rules, where you have to hold your breath along with not speaking until someone says your name. Noah made us stop playing that way after I passed out for the fourth time. Or was it the fifth? Whatever. I can now hold my breath as long as some professional divers. I'm going to call that a win.

When Jacob returned to the living room after helping Rogue to the bathroom, we all blurted out, "She's moving in." Then followed it with, "Jinx." A profanity followed from all of us, thus resulting in a double jinx. Someone has to say our name twice for any of us to be able to speak.

There are very few things in this world I take seriously. My job, team, superheroes, rock-paper-scissors tournaments, and jinx are basically it. When Buttercup comes hobbling down the hall in sweats and a tank, Noah lifts his head to offer assistance, and as his mouth is opening, I sock him in the gut. No speaking!

He doubles over and wheezes while Rogue gapes at the sight. "Uh, hey guys, what's going on?"

No one speaks. All eyes are glued to Rogue imploringly. I don't think she knows what we want. She probably didn't hear us jinx each other from down the hall. In fact, she looks guilty for some reason.

"Okay, I guess the silent treatment is fair after going out on an assignment and getting cut, then coming home and telling a few of you to fuck off. The profanity may have been excessive. It wasn't my first cut, and it very likely won't be my last. I know how to deal with it, and I won't have my independence taken away just because I've joined forces with you guys. I will not be one to toe the line and respond to everything with a 'yes, sir.' That's not who I am, and if you think I'll change that to work with you, you've all got another thing coming."

As she takes a breath to continue with her speech, which I am in awe of —hell yeah, girl, stand your ground—when the sound of a phone making a call rings out in the apartment. After two more rings, it finally connects. Rogue looks like she's going to blow a gasket as Han lifts the phone flat on his palm to the middle of our huddled group. "Han! Han, darling, is that you?"

"Hi, Mama Bear. Are we still on for this weekend?" Han answers. She said his name twice, so the motherfucker is free to speak as the rest of us silently curse him for his ingenuity.

"Yes, of course, darling. I'll see you on Sunday. I'm making pot roast unless you have any other requests. Such a good boy. The others don't call as much as you do." Her loud voice rings clearly with admonishment in the apartment as Rogue continues her impression of a mime, trying to figure out how to convey 'what is happening?' The arm-waving is a particularly nice touch.

"That sounds wonderful, Mrs. M. Can we bring a friend?" Han is positively glowing with glee. And I must admit, imagining Mrs. Morganson meeting Rogue has me chuckling—silently, of course. Noah will be looking for a reason to hit me back harder than I hit him.

"Certainly. Is it a lady friend?" Mrs. M asks with excitement.

"Why, yes, it is, Mrs. M. You'll love her. See you soon! Bye." Han pushes a button on his phone and looks at Rogue.

"Hiya, Gorgeous. These idiots are banned from speaking unless you say their name twice. We can chat without being interrupted. Also, we're having dinner with Mrs. M on Sunday. You don't have any food allergies, do you?"

Rogue looks to us silent idiots, kicking ourselves for not thinking of calling Mrs. M first. She bursts out laughing and immediately clutches her stomach with a grimace. Jacob darts toward her and helps guide her to the couch so she can catch her breath. His hand lingers in hers, and he looks reluctant to pull away as he settles himself on the arm of the couch.

Well, well, well. Someone else is looking to get punched today.

Color returns to her face, and she chokes out in disbelief, "Did you four double-jinx each other?" I knew she was brilliant. I beam. Noah and Jacob shake their heads like they can't believe they got caught having fun, and Han just laughs because he can.

Han, the self-appointed current spokesman of the group, does the honor of explaining our current situation. "We think you should move in so we can monitor your injury and help get you back on your feet. It was a unanimous and simultaneous conversation. Also, where did we land on the allergy thing? Yay? Nay?" Rogue's eyebrows shoot up.

"Nay. You all wound up in a silent standoff because you each think I should move into your clubhouse?"

I hold up a finger and retrieve my phone from my back pocket. I type out: *It's not a clubhouse. It's a warehouse. You can bunk with me. Wink.*

"Lucas," Han snorts, eyeing my message from beside Rogue. "Typing 'wink' doesn't have the same effect. You're right in front of her; you could have just actually winked."

I wink.

She sighs.

Noah, predictably, rolls his eyes.

And yet, the big softy plays along with my game and keeps his mouth shut. He loves it; I'm a hundred percent certain of that. Okay, more like sixty percent.

"Okay," Rogue draws out the word as she thinks. She's probably trying to figure out how to tell the others she's bunking with me tactfully. "To be clear, you have no problem with how I handled last night. You all just want me to move in until I recover. Have I got that right?"

"Well, sort of," Han corrects. "We still want you to move in for the duration of our partnership, as we discussed yesterday. As mentioned, taking out our board and The Gambit will take time, and we can more easily coordinate from the same location."

Rogue still looks dubious, but we're wearing her down.

I fall to my knees and prostrate myself across the tiny living room's black rug to show my desperation, and I'm not above begging to make sure my Buttercup is safe.

Yep, she's mine. Jacob can suck it. I met her first. I mean, aside from Han.

Remembering Noah's hand on her thigh has me making a mental note to let him know she's mine, too. We might as well include Han in the memo, or he'll feel left out.

"Lucas!" she begs, and I see my opportunity. I stay down and ignore her. As Han's objection starts to come out, she tries again, "Lucas! Get up. There's probably still blood on the floor."

Sweet, sweet victory.

My head pops up. "Why, Buttercup, what kind of cleaning job do you think I did? I got everything while Noah was watching over you, and those two took a nap." I gesture to Han and Jacob. "God, it feels good to speak again! It's been ages!"

Han lets out a groan at my regained speech ability. Rogue's eyes roll even more dramatically than Noah's did that time I swaggered into the warehouse wearing nothing but a leather miniskirt and five-inch neon green platform heels—a story for another time—when she realizes her mistake of saying my name twice.

She glances around and takes in the clean apartment. I even popped into the bodega downstairs last night to get her a little bouquet for her tiny-ass kitchen. I swear her eyes sparkle when she leans around Jacob to see them. I mean, I was in the elevator, bleaching it anyway. I needed some fresh air after repeatedly riding up and down with those fumes damn near choking me. I'm going to go ahead and blame the chemical-laced air for my decision on the white roses over the red ones. And the Kit-Kat bar. And the slushie. Cleaning makes me hungry.

"Red, did you buy me flowers?" she asks, looking down at me. I nod my head, unsure if I did okay in this situation. I can't tell by her expression, and honestly, it's a toss-up if she wants to knee me in the balls or hug me. I hope it's the hug.

"No one's ever bought me flowers before." I did damn good. I beam at her when she smiles softly at me. I'm buying her more. I'm mentally arranging bouquets, thinking of color schemes while the others move on.

"Damn it, Gorgeous! Jinx is the only time Lucas stops talking. We also used to stop breathing when jinxed, but Boss Man here," Han gestures to Noah, "pulled the plug on that when Lucas passed out for the eighth time." Okay, so I passed out a couple more times than the four I initially thought.

I hold my tongue. I can be quiet.

I lied. I can't hold it much longer. It's like I'm still jinxed. Must. Prove. Han. Wrong.

"Noah, Noah!" I shout, my breath heaving out of me with the restraint I clearly just showed. I don't even know why I un-jinxed him. I just needed to say something, anything.

Still silent and sitting on the arm of the couch, Jacob just throws his arms up in the air in exasperation. Sucker.

"Rogue, please grab a bag and stay with us for a few days while you heal. Let's call it a trial run, and we'll be helpful," Noah says, ever logical, ever calm.

Finally, she relents with a small nod.

After directing us around her apartment to gather the things she'll need for about a week, she asks for a few moments alone to finish security. We reluctantly agree to meet her at the SUV since it will be better for Rogue to lie down in the backseat to keep from pulling on her stitches.

About ten minutes later, she comes down with an additional bag. We took the one with her clothes and toiletries and loaded it up. I guess she forgot some stuff. Jacob, still silent, of course, offers to take the bag for her. She hands over the bag, which drops about a foot when he adjusts to the unexpected weight.

He moves to the back to load it into the car's trunk when whatever is inside clangs and rattles as he sets it down next to her other bag. It has to be weapons—lots and lots of weapons—or cookware, but that's not as likely.

Rogue

After a smooth ride to the clubhouse in the backseat and a cautious Noah driving, I'm starting to feel okay. Han and Jacob drove the truck back while Lucas rode with us.

Noah assured me, no less than four times, that I would not need to split my private space with anyone. I think he's nervous Lucas is going to scare me off. They have a couple of unused bedrooms on the upper floor of the clubhouse. Lucas just wanted to share because, well, he wanted to share.

As I stand in my temporary room in their clubhouse, I realize I'm starting to feel relaxed—more than I have in quite a while.

I can hear Han teasing Jacob about his inability to speak. Jacob is not responding, but the sound of a thud tells me he's retaliating in bodily harm.

Lucas is singing songs from *The Sound of Music* in the lounge area downstairs, gesticulating with his arms wildly while his headphones are plugged in, so it sounds especially dreadful.

If the smells are any indication, Noah is in the kitchen making mouth-watering Thai food for lunch.

I look around my new, neutral-hued abode. There's a queen-size bed in the center of the far wall, a back-lit window that doesn't look outside on the wall to the right of the bed, and the left side has a decent-sized wardrobe that is far too big for the meager possessions I brought. I'll have to find a place to stash my weapons around the building; something should always be accessible.

Still in my sweats and feeling gross, I grab the hem of my tank top and lift it to check my stitches and bandages in the mirror next to the wardrobe. I hear a shuffle from the direction of the door behind me and turn to see who came to visit.

Han stands in the open doorway, and his eyes are on my mid-section. He steps into the room and reaches out to me, then his hand falls, rethinking his move to touch me without invitation. Han probably remembers that time one of the bouncers grabbed my ass unexpectedly. He hit the concrete beautifully.

"Can I change your bandage?"

"I can do it. It's no problem. Just point me in the direction of the bathroom."

"Ivy, we're here to help you with this. It may not have happened because of your work with us, but we're all on the same team now. We look out for each other," he says like it's the most obvious thing in the world. My jaw clenches upon hearing the use of my name.

He extends his hand again, and I place mine in his after relaxing my face. His fingers curl around, giving a little tug, and I approach him. He turns, leading the way to a bathroom between my room and another shut door on the opposite side.

We enter, and I see this is a regularly used room, unlike the guest room I'm staying in. Towels are haphazardly flung over the towel bars, and water droplets are still clinging to the large glass partition separating the enormous shower from the rest of the bathroom. My tiny bathroom could fit in this room four times over.

There's a double sink and vanity, cabinets under the basins, a large tub, a giant shower, and a toilet cubicle, so there's privacy if the bathroom is being shared. Dark gray tiles cover the walls, and the black ceramic tiles underfoot are heated. Yup, I'm going to need to use this shower setup soon.

Han guides me over to a stone bench, which is also fucking warmed, next to the shower, and encourages me to sit with a hand on my shoulder. He crosses the room and reaches into the cabinet between the two sinks.

He pulls out a box and starts rifling through it, finding some gauze and medical tape.

He kneels between my spread thighs and positions himself in front of me to redress the wound. "Lift," he says as he opens the packaging for the gauze. I take a moment to steel myself against another's touch.

Having someone touch me always requires a beat to reassure myself I am not back with King, who used his hands to harm, not heal. I flip the hem of my tank top, folding it in half just under my breasts, and my stomach is exposed.

Han places the instruments to my left on the bench with the packaging removed. He gently pulls the tape from my skin to remove the old bandage. It's only a little bloody. Noah must have done a bang-up job stitching me last night.

Calm and steady breaths ghost across my skin, and I repress a slight shiver. Once the last of the old tape is removed, Han uses a cotton puff soaked in a cleaning and antibacterial agent to swab the area clean again. His concentration on the task puts me at ease. He isn't looking for a weak spot in my shield. He's just helping. I remind myself of that a couple of times during his ministrations.

Like this, I can study his features while he's focused elsewhere. His black hair, a few inches longer than he kept it when we were younger, falls across his brow. His almond-shaped eyes are an alluring deep brown up close instead of black like they seem from afar. I remember the first time he spoke to me; I nearly fell into the depths when we looked each other in the eye the first time we were truly face to face. His skin is sun-kissed, and his bottom lip is fuller than his top, making a slight pout when his features are relaxed.

He's matured and grown into a man instead of the skin and bones he was a few years ago. The span of his chest, the width of his shoulders. All of it is a seemingly hand-mixed cocktail that calls to my baser desires.

As my gaze continues down to his broad shoulders and trim waist, he clears his throat softly. My eyes snap up to his. He's looking into my eyes, and immediately, I know I've been caught studying him. Again. The corner of his lips tip up on one side. "Ivy."

His hands have finished bandaging me and are resting on the swells of my hips.

"Why did I never see you again after that night?" Han asks in a soft, imploring voice. He doesn't sound angry, but I know he needs an answer.

The conversation I've been dreading since I saw his face yesterday has finally come.

I hang my head as the old guilt and shame wash over me. I feel heat spreading up my neck and into my cheeks. I'm embarrassed that I lost control and gave in to our attraction back then, but I don't regret what we did. I regret never telling him how much he meant to me. I regret letting him slip through my fingers—the one light in my life of darkness.

"It wasn't safe. I worked for King directly back then. If he had found out about you, he wouldn't have hesitated to put a bullet through your skull. I don't regret us—our friendship, our night together. But I was in an impossible situation, and I let myself risk you. I couldn't face you afterward to tell you to forget about me. I didn't want to see the hurt in your eyes or the disgust at what I did... do for a living. I'm so sorry."

"Ivy, my Ivy, I would have understood. I don't like the way it happened, but I get it. You were trying to protect me."

I nod my head as some of the blush dissipates. How is this man, this brutal fighter I once knew, always this kind? This forgiving? When I ask him these questions swirling in my head, he just shrugs and replies that the world is an unforgiving place, and if he can balance the scales a bit, he's happy to do it.

"Thank you, Han," I breathe softly as the sensation of his hands on my body starts invading every thought in my brain. His face is closer to mine than it was a few seconds ago.

His hands start inching their way up my waist, skating along my ribs until they reach the part my shirt is covering while his thumbs find and caress the sensitive underside of my breasts.

"Han, we—" I stammer as his head tilts to mine. My hands are gripping his white shirt. I have a split second of confusion before I realize that I pulled him to me with my clenched grip on his clothing. What if he wasn't leaning in for a kiss?

My concern is suddenly washed away in a sea of lust when Han's lips connect to mine, and he takes charge. That full bottom lip feels as pillowy as I remember. My breath has stalled in my lungs. Han's mouth moves over mine like it's all that exists in this world.

The kiss is achingly sweet, gentle but firm, likely in deference to my current wounded state. His tongue sweeps into my mouth, and I swear I lose all sense of time. Our mouths move together for more minutes than I can count. I nip at his bottom lip, insisting I'm not wholly injured, when there's a soft knock at the door.

The Secrets We Keep

Han reluctantly pulls away after a playful bite, and I raise a hand to my lips. They're puffy and likely flushed after our interlude.

He sits back on his heels and pulls the folded half of my shirt from my heaving chest back over my stomach, covering me from whoever is outside the door. My nipples are evident after the arousal Han stoked in me. Well, there's no hiding those.

"Come in," Han raises his voice to be heard through the cracked door.

Jacob pushes the door open, and his eyes snag on Han between my legs, my nipples saluting everyone in the vicinity, and our kiss-swollen lips.

His eyes flash with heat for a second before he removes his glasses and cleans them with the hem of his shirt as if he wants a second to gather his thoughts. He places them back across the bridge of his nose, then mimes lifting a fork to his mouth and eating. Han howls with laughter and looks at me. "Oh shit, he's still jinxed!"

"Should I unjinx him?" I ask, looking at this manicured English man as he follows such a childish game's rules. Jacob just shrugs one of his shoulders as his usually ice-cold eyes continue to burn with fire.

"Leave him be for a bit so I can interrogate him quickly." Han looks to Jacob. Uh-oh. "Jake, do you have a problem with what happened here?"

Jacob shakes his head.

"Do you like Rogue?" A nod follows this question, and I appreciate him not using my given name as freely with the others.

"Rogue, any interest in the English bastard here?" My turn to nod. "And me?" Another embarrassed nod from me. This is an odd way to figure out who likes whom.

"I don't do the commitment thing. You know how it is in our line of work; I don't squash attraction when it's there," I blurt with only the smallest waver in my voice.

Jacob's head snaps up at that, and he gives me a scowl I'd expect from stern-faced Noah rather than him. He motions for Han to unzip his lips, but Han just shakes his head, giving me a look that tells me I should leave him jinxed. Jacob sighs and continues to stand there, propping up the door frame.

Maybe he's got an issue with my reluctance to commit. I'm not sticking around after my contract is up; why bother with putting down roots? Maybe he thinks I'm trashy for liking more than one of them. Surprise, dude. I also think Lucas is pretty damn adorable. And Noah's stoicism makes me want to figure out what makes him tick.

As if Han can hear the thoughts in my head, he puts his finger under my chin to raise my head the fraction I let it drop. "Rogue, whatever you've got brewing right now, let it go. I promise you, no one here is judging you for your choices. They are your choices." I take a deep breath to start a response, but he keeps going.

"I used this wonderful jinx situation we currently find ourselves in to ask him other questions in the truck on the way here. We're both interested in you and want to get to know you. You're smart, kick-ass, and a strong woman. He and I have similar tastes in women, and after you and I spent some time together last night over burgers, I knew I wanted to know you more. Specifically, who you are now. He feels the same." Jacob nods from the doorway as Han delivers his speech.

"I'm simply asking if you'd like to spend some time and get to know each of us. No jealousy. Your mind, your body, your choice."

It may be Han's easy understanding and acceptance of my preferences, but I genuinely consider getting to know these guys on a more personal level. I was just complaining that my only company lately is a pubescent teen who regularly kicks my ass at Call of Duty.

Jacob is sexy as hell in his buttoned-up shirts, but I see the tattoos they cover. There's a bit of a challenge in him, and I like his meticulous nature. He seems interesting, and anyone who gets down with a good cup of tea is aces in my book.

Han is a sweetheart through and through. I laughed my ass off while eating burgers with him last night as he regaled me with stories of his misspent youth getting into trouble. He alluded to some troubling times that led to him fighting in the ring, but it made him more attentive to others' needs instead of hardening him to the world.

After I've taken a few minutes to consider Han's proposal while he and Jacob focused their attention on me, I nod enthusiastically as a small smile plays across my lips. How often will I encounter multiple men willing to bend to my wants without jealousy becoming a factor? "I'm in."

Jacob flashes a smile and knocks his fist on the doorframe twice as he backs out of the room. God, he's pretty when he grins. Han extends his hand once again and helps me up. I stop in my room, and after a quick wardrobe change to hide my persistently pebbled nipples, we head downstairs to have some lunch with the others.

Chapter Eleven

Jacob

I'm still banned from speaking. We all sat around the big table in the kitchen and ate Noah's pad thai, stuffing our faces so thoroughly I doubt we'll want dinner later. That bloke can fucking cook.

Once a month or so, he becomes fervent and learns new dishes to add to his repertoire. As the rules dictate, I kept quiet during the meal, as did the rest of the team, as we stuffed our faces with food.

Han's hand kept finding reasons to touch Rogue subtly. Walking into the bathroom earlier, I could almost taste the lust in the air. It took me a moment to rein in my excitement about the idea that Rogue was into us. I wonder if she's into the others at all. This is going to be an engaging conversation if it comes up. I suddenly felt glad I couldn't speak yet.

I didn't expect to feel disappointed when she said she didn't commit. I enjoy being in a relationship, caring for someone, and owning them—body and soul. After knowing them for less than twenty-four hours, I didn't expect to find myself this engrossed by someone.

Hell, I met this girl yesterday, and I can already imagine all the delicious fun we could get up to. I felt my body slump as the words came from her mouth that she didn't imagine a future for herself because of our work.

She has more than a platonic history with Han; that was clear when she arrived yesterday. He affirmed that notion while we were in the truck on our way back here. With her physical confirmation of it in the bathroom earlier, a part of me prickles with jealousy.

I can't help but be curious if she's interested in us separately. Or together? Han and I have shared women in the past. He wasn't wrong when he said we tend to go for the same type.

It's only something we've ever done twice, but imagining all three of us in bed has me readjusting my slacks. Han, of course, catches my movement and shoots a quick grin at me across the table.

I know our carefree time of eating good food and drinking cold beer ends as the mood turns more serious now that our baser needs have been met.

"Jacob, Jacob," Noah says on the tail end of a sigh, releasing me from my silence.

"Bloody finally!" I shout at the top of my lungs because I fucking can. "It's been four hours, and you dickheads were too fucking careful. Han only said 'Jake' once earlier in the bathroom, and you assholes banned nicknames last year."

Rogue's cheeks color as she likely thinks back to what we'd been discussing only an hour ago in the loo.

"Pft, four hours is nothing! Remember when you guys didn't say my name for three days? Three goddamned days?" Lucas jumps in. "You got it easy, dude."

"It was so quiet." Noah reminisces wistfully with a twinkle in his eye. "But now, we need all of us to be able to speak. Rogue, do you want to go over what happened last night? How did you get hurt?"

I've been running through scenarios in my head all day, at least when it wasn't full of a gorgeous rockabilly girl, and planning ways to get back at these guys for leaving me jinxed all goddamned morning.

"It was a setup." Rogue mumbles. A sound of concern escapes Lucas's lips, and my hand flexes into a fist on the table next to my beer as my thoughts find corroboration in her statement. "It's the only explanation. I've got my list of dealers to hit for selling to kids. The only others with the full list are King and Enrique; he's the board member who manages the dealers.

"I arrived at the hole-in-the-wall bar that particular dealer hangs out at and sells from. He was there with his buddies, and I waited until most of the patrons were deep in their cups or high as fuck, and I followed him to the bathroom. When I walked in, it was wall-to-wall with other dealers."

Imagining our Rogue going against multiple attackers has my protective instincts on high alert. She can handle herself. She's sitting across the table from me. She's been doing this for years. But those odds would be hard to overcome for anyone. Expertly trained or not.

"How many were there, and how many did you take down, Buttercup? Do we need to do any cleanup?" Lucas, our experienced dispatcher, knows that if anyone is left, it will only become more dangerous.

"There were six of them; they're all down."

Silence follows her statement. She took on six guys in a surprise ambush. Thank Christ, she only got the cut on her stomach instead of a worse fate.

Noah moves his hands from his lap and spreads his fingers on the tabletop. I swear I hear a low growl in his throat. He has a history of being double-crossed, and knowing that Rogue was on the receiving end of that must grate his nerves.

I've only seen him do the move with his hands when he's upset with our organization's management. It's his go-to reaction.

Annex Security will get its comeuppance soon, but we may have to move on The Gambit earlier, especially if they're gunning for our newest recruit.

"Okay, Trouble. We will need to review your intel on The Gambit and its organizational structure in the next few days. We'll review our board's info tomorrow and see how to remove members. The fewer threats on any side, the better."

Noah's announcement echoes my thoughts, reminding me why he's a good leader. He is good at reprioritizing when something changes and is flexible as long as the job gets done.

"While we're all here," I start, "where did the bag of weapons come from, Love?" I did a tiny bit of snooping in her apartment as I gathered clothes for her to change into after she was sewn up and didn't find any weapons. I didn't mean to snoop, but I had to dig through her stuff to find clothes that wouldn't put pressure on her stomach. Her closets were bare of any guns or knives but full of sexy retro garments.

A laugh bubbles out of Rogue. "Yeah, about that. You know that hidden door you found? It leads to the apartment underneath mine. It's full of work stuff." She looks at Lucas before continuing, "It's my Bat Cave."

"You have a motherfucking Bat Cave!? No wonder you like stupid Batman so much!"

The room erupts in laughter as Lucas mumbles about having recruited Bat Girl. I hear him mutter, "But how will we raise the children? Oh, sweet

Jesus, have mercy." His head hangs, continually shaking back and forth in despair.

Noah clears his throat and gets Rogue's attention back. "Trouble, you're sure the room is locked while you're here?"

"Yep. I did it up the way I would for an out-of-town job. It's impenetrable." A twinkle in her eye makes me think anyone who tries will regret it after the fact.

Following an afternoon nap that threw another wrench into my perfectly organized schedule, I found Rogue sprawled out on the lounge couch with a box of Wheat Thins wedged between her side and the sofa. I suddenly find myself not craving that structure as I look to our assassin. She represents a shakeup in our day-to-day, and I'm excited about it.

"Couldn't sleep anymore?" she asks as I approach. I don't see anyone else around.

"Nah, I rested on your tiny, uncomfortable couch last night, and even though I'm knackered, it didn't feel very restful these last few hours."

She nods like she agrees as I move to the end of the couch. I lift her feet and slide under her blanket-wrapped legs. "I think I slept enough last night, so I wasn't too tired."

I hum in agreement and look around the warehouse. I see some updates I'd like to make in the next few months, especially if we're all going to be sequestered here for a while. Is there something Rogue would like to add?

The music coming from the sound system is low. It's linked to the phone on the table and playing "Glass Piano" by Kathleen. The song is simultaneously chaotic and mellow—a perfect metaphor for how she seems to be feeling now.

It's soothing to sit in relative silence. We're between assignments now, and we all relish the rare quiet when we have the opportunity. The space is vast and open; we usually hear each other working across the building unless we're in the soundproofed rooms.

For now, I plan to enjoy adjusting to a new person in our space. Her scarlet-painted toenails wiggle on my lap to point out they've come uncovered. I grab and squeeze the arches of her feet, making her laugh, before pulling the blanket over them.

She spends the next hour answering my questions about her Bat Cave. We have a weapons room, and my tech setup is in its own nook next to the gym. I can't help but admire her innovation in getting the flat below hers for storage. No one would know a thing if they didn't think to lift the small rug covering the hatch in the small closet in her living room. It could be anything under there to the uninformed.

Rogue sighs and stops eating her crackers long enough to bring up the bathroom conversation from earlier. "So, the... uh... non-monogamous thing is really okay with you? I mean, you and Han are teammates. I'm attracted to both of you, but the last thing I want to do is cause issues within the group. The takedowns have to be our priority."

"Rogue, Love, we are okay with it. There has to be a certain level of communication between us, but we can all do what we like individually. You don't have to worry about keeping things even or whatever. Just do what feels right; if something feels wrong, say it. And the takedowns will be our priority. You know how it is with some of these jobs, stages of non-stop planning, scheming, and chaos only to be followed by vast periods of inactivity. We'll have time to explore this without compromising the missions."

I don't know if now is the time to tell her we've been in situations like this before, but if honesty is the name of the game, it would be prudent to get it all out there at once. I take a deep breath and hope for the best.

"Han and I have shared women in the past. He was spot on when he said we tend to go for the same type of woman. I like more submissive types, but we both look for someone to take care of. If you're feeling unsure or awkward, just tell us. We don't have to do anything together if you don't want to. You're running this ship. Direct us where you want us to go."

Han and I have talked about this at length in the past. We never wanted to make someone choose, but in the end, they did it anyway. We always figured it would drive us apart, but our friendship has always been one of respect for each other. So, we never put that type of pressure on the women we dated.

We only have a couple of months together if our plans come to fruition, and she was right when she brought up the nature of our work. There are no guarantees. We live for today and the hope of a tomorrow.

Rogue's hand, now free of her snacks but still sprinkled with cracker dust, reaches for mine. I lace my fingers through hers as she sits calmly and processes.

Rogue

I'm having trouble wrapping my head around being with two guys in the same time frame, let alone simultaneously.

I appreciate Jacob's laying out how he and Han have operated in the past. His saying it plainly makes it seem logical, and his gorgeous accent makes it almost sound entirely normal.

What is it about an English accent that makes you trust in everything they say? Tom Hardy could tell me it is perfectly acceptable to stick metal objects into an outlet, and I'd gleefully dump out the silverware drawer.

Speaking of Han, I see him padding barefoot down the steps to join us in the lounge. Jacob lifts his head and follows my line of sight. His lips tip up in a smirk, and he extends the hand not resting on my leg to Han.

Han reaches us and claps Jacob's hand in one of those weird, intricate bro shakes. He leans in and plants a quick kiss on the top of my head. Damn butterflies start swirling around in my stomach at the casual affection.

"What are you guys talking about?" he asks.

Jacob, the tactful bastard that he is, replies for us with a smug grin, "Relationships."

I snort a laugh, which eventually turns into full-blown howling from all three of us.

"Gorgeous, we really should get you to lie down on a fully flat surface. Propping up on the arm of the couch like that might pull a stitch. Jacob, help me out here."

With that, Jacob delicately pulls the blanket off of me, and Han grabs the box of snacks, nearly having his hand bit when he does so. My snacks. Mine.

He tuts in my direction and places them on the low coffee table. Strong, tattooed arms snake under my knees and around my waist from the back of the couch, lifting me easily, just as they did at my apartment. Jacob carries me as Han starts flipping off the lights of the main living area.

Jacob ascends the stairs and passes my room to take me to another. I'm still marveling at the ingenuity it took to mold this old abandoned structure into a base of operations and a home.

"Where are we going?" I ask as we pass the bathroom, swiveling my head over his shoulder to look back at my open door.

"We're watching a film in my room. The bed is bigger and more

The Secrets We Keep

comfortable; you can stretch out. We'll hang with you but won't crowd you too much." Bossy bastard.

Oh, shit. We're going to Jacob's room. Bedroom. Bed. This is the worst fucking time for an injury. Especially with all that talk of "sharing" still fresh in my mind.

I'm feeling better; I really am. This thing will be healed up in no time. I've clearly gone without sex for too long if I'm leveraging my health for nooky.

Han, who catches a glimpse of my face, chuckles lightly. "Don't worry, Gorgeous. We won't take advantage of you while you're still healing." Dammit. There goes that fantasy for the moment. Any chance to change their minds?

Han steps around us as Jacob slows to open a large black door. Inside the room nearly twice the size of mine down the hall, I see a massive bed taking up the entire back wall. It's like a California King on crack. Jacob strides in and places me softly in the middle of the cloud-like mattress. Heaven. This is heaven. Even if this stupid knife cut kills me, I'll happily die in this spot.

Jacob stands to his full height and starts unbuttoning his cufflinks and shirt one by one as he turns and makes his way to a door, which I assume is the closet. Han pulls himself onto the bed next to me, and we turn to each other as the closet door closes with Jacob inside. We both start laughing, realizing we're both staring after him.

I look curiously at Han, who just shrugs his shoulders and winks. I have an inkling he's got some unaddressed feelings for Jacob, lust being the apparent one, but it's not my place to bring it up.

If he wants to talk it out, I'm here. We haven't talked about sexual preferences, but with the kiss in the bathroom still playing on a loop in my head, I know he's into me, at least.

Han is already in comfortable workout shorts and a tank top. The armholes are cut low enough that I can see muscle bumps along his ribs. I don't know the names of those, but I like calling them "riblets" in my head.

I'm still in the yoga tights and an old band tee I threw on after Han cleaned me up in the bathroom. I didn't think nipples pointing at everyone through lunch was a cultured way to ingratiate myself into the team dynamic. Although, maybe it would have been perfect, seeing as these two and Lucas seem to like me well enough.

As Han starts rummaging in the nightstand drawer on his side of the bed, Jacob comes out, typing away on his phone, dressed in gray sweats, and that's it. Gray motherfucking sweatpants. He has to be doing this on purpose. Doesn't he know those things are like catnip to us? Pair that with an entirely tattooed torso and a built man, and we're fucking done. Cue drool. Again. External this time, to be precise.

Han pops back up from his pilfering with a remote and points at the ceiling. Sure enough, there's a projector and a few metal rings hanging from anchors up there.

Huh, what are those for?

Han eventually finds the settings he wants on the device and cues up a movie from his phone. Figures Jacob would have everything hooked up to Bluetooth. Tech guys, man.

As I regulate my breathing and thoughts while sandwiched between two delectable men, the guys bicker back and forth before deciding on *Batman Returns*. Han blames me for all the Batman talk recently. I'll happily take the shade he's throwing my way. Batman is awesome.

The projector is positioned to display on the wall. Thankfully, I don't need to lift my head for a decent view. Is that? Yep, it sure is. Jacob's pillows smell like lavender. Yep, heaven.

We make it through the film's first twenty minutes, bantering back and forth about what moves would work in real life and what is pure Hollywood. Han discusses the Batmobile's merits, while Jacob compliments Bruce Wayne's technology setup. I focus on the fighting. It's nice we all have our niches.

After a particularly spirited debate about Alfred's origins, which Jacob wins, he slides his arm under my head for support after noticing I'd started rubbing at it. The neck strain had begun in all the talking, excitement, and turning my head from one side to the other to argue with the guys.

So warm. I feel muscles rolling and flexing in the arm under my head and turn toward Han to see Jacob's fingers playing with the loose hair on that side of my head. I'm grateful they included me in what appears to be a wind-down routine they sometimes do. I guess everyone has their version of "kill and chill."

Han catches me looking and breaks his concentration from the movie. "Hi, Gorgeous," he purrs, turning his body so that Jacob's hand is pressed between the side of his face and the pillow.

"Hi," I smile and whisper back. Han's dark eyes search mine for a beat before he leans in and presses his mouth to mine. My eyes flutter closed, and I lose myself in his kiss as our mouths explore. Lost to sensation, I startle when I feel movement against my back. A warm hand settles on my hip from behind.

Rough fingertips play with the inch of bare skin between my tights and my loose shirt.

Jacob's arm under my head is tense as it holds Han and me during our embrace. I feel the fingers on my hip nudge my top up as he traces the lotus tattoo running up my side. It reaches just under my breast, and oh, how I hope he keeps going.

There's no discomfort from my injury as Han and Jacob explore. They are painstakingly careful not to move my body too much, and I desperately wish this stupid cut didn't effectively bench me.

I would relish the opportunity to kill the fucker who gutted me all over again. Unfortunately, I have to settle for just the one time.

Han breaks the kiss and, with a finger on my chin, turns my head to the other side to see Jacob. He's damn near panting, and his eyes are hooded from watching us. He discarded his glasses at some point, and now that I can see his eyes without their usual shield, the color lends itself more to gray than blue. "Bloody hell, you're a dream, Love. May I?" he asks in a throaty whisper.

"You'd better," I quip back. Jacob's hand releases its hold on my side and reaches for my face. Likes submissives, my round ass.

He cradles my cheek and pulls me to him with more force than Han showed earlier. I get the feeling Jacob is dominant in all aspects of his life. Here's hoping the bedroom is one of them.

Han's hand mirrors Jacob's earlier exploration under my shirt but on the other side of my body. He's careful to avoid the cut he's close to but raises my shirt with deft moves to uncover my breasts. His mouth descends just as Jacob's reaches mine.

The first touch of Jacob's lips to mine ignites something in me. His lips are lush yet unyielding. He directs the kiss, allowing me to let go and follow his lead. Han's tongue circles my left nipple, and I let out a groan as he flicks it repeatedly and sends sensations firing up and down my rapacious body.

My panties are drenched at the sensation of both of them playing with me. My breath is short, and my hand snakes between my body and Jacob's. My fingers slide over the divots between his abs as I make my way south.

I may not be well enough to have full-on sex right now, but I sure as hell don't want to stop at making out. I break away from Jacob's all-consuming kiss to judge his reaction to my wandering hand, but his hand palms the back of my head and pulls me back to him, effectively redirecting my attention.

Han hovers over my body, supporting himself on his elbows, his lips having reached my other nipple, and then he pulls. An unholy moan lets out, and I wrap my left arm around his body to anchor my fingers in his hair, keeping him where he is. I feel his smile against my breast as I inadvertently try to smother him with my tits. His hardness against my hip starts to grind, and I feel the scorching heat radiating off of him.

Jacob stops my hand from further exploration, directs it to Han's head, and ends our kiss with a bite to my lower lip, soothed with a flick of his tongue. I'm now clasping Han to my breast completely as Jacob slides his big body down the bed, dragging his fingertips in a feather-light touch and driving me mad the whole way.

Han takes all of my attention momentarily until I feel my tights being peeled down my legs, and I lift my hips to assist. Jacob kneels between my knees and rests back on his heels as he looks us over. All previous discomfort in my neck is seemingly forgotten as I crane my head forward to see the tattooed God between my thighs.

"Lose it," Jacob demands as he teases the hem of Han's shirt. Han whips off his offending garment, exposing the tattoos that pass from his biceps to just under his collarbones, spanning his chest, then goes right back into position. Jacob's gaze never wavers as he looks me over. He sees the dark line dividing my body and runs a finger along it from my navel to my panties. I mumble out some combination of "please, yes, and oh my God" in an incoherent stream of gibberish.

Jacob's finger reaches the edge of my thong, and he hooks a finger and yanks. Hard. The delicate fabric ripping makes Han lift and turn his head. He does a double-take when he sees how low the tattoos go. "Are you truly half tattooed?"

Jacob nods distractedly, like I do, as he uses his thumbs to spread me before him like a buffet. One hand stays at the juncture of my hip, and the other disappears under my ass. His fingers grip me hard enough to leave bruises as he keeps me from squirming and pulling on my cut. His head disappears behind Han's body, still hovering across my torso, as he lowers himself.

Han drags his tongue along the line trailing up my sternum, and after reaching my chin where it ends, he slides to the side to nibble my ear and look down my body to Jacob. Looks like we're both ready for the show. Jacob looks up at me from between my thighs and lets out a panty-melting

The Secrets We Keep

grin. Well, it would be if I still had my panties. My pussy is fucking dripping at this point, and I'm pretty sure I'd be embarrassed if I still had the brain capacity for that.

Jacob shoots me a wink as he lowers himself, slowly running his tongue from my opening to my clit, and my body bows off the bed in response. He dives in and laps at me like it's his last meal. Twisting, flicking, plunging into my pussy as my Brit powerfully works me over. I can't keep a single thought in my head as he performs his magic.

Han has his hand down his shorts, working his length while watching Jacob worship my body. He gets frustrated at the restricted movement and whips them off faster than I can follow. His cock is throbbing as he grips and pulls at his length in a corkscrew motion, paying particular attention to the head. Mental note taken for future rendezvous.

Han's free hand crosses under my thigh, and he finds my greedy pussy, driving two fingers in while Jacob focuses his tongue on my clit. His movements pick up pace as my writhing increases. I try to reach for Han, but Jacob's hands clamp down on my thighs.

"Be. Still." His growled words have me gasping and surrendering to his will.

My orgasm is building, and in my mind, I can see myself approaching the precipice. I'm quickly losing the battle between Jacob's tongue and Han's fingers, struggling to hang on a bit longer to enjoy the dual sensations. Han's head dips to my breast, and as his fingers curl, he bites down on my nipple, and I explode.

Han reattaches his lips to my sensitive peak after giving me a small reprieve, using my languid moment to add another finger into me, setting a punishing pace as Jacob works my swollen clit like he's taken a MasterClass in the art of cunnilingus. At the same time, his hand reaches up to pinch my neglected nipple. I break again just as Han's fingers find my G-spot once more while Jacob draws hard on my throbbing clit.

I break into a million pieces and have no hope of ever reassembling.

A moment later, Han spills across his taut stomach, and Jacob continues, leaving small bites along my inner thigh, guiding me down from my high. I pick my head up and look lustily at Jacob. "Your turn," I tell our Brit.

Han pulls his fingers from me and, while looking me in the eye, dips them into his mouth and sucks. He groans in ecstasy at the taste as I try to remember how to breathe, then nudges Jacob back until he's standing at the edge of the bed. Jacob pulls the waistband of his sweatpants over his prominent erection and kicks them off to the side.

Yep, heaven. The cozy bed, the renewed old flame at my side who, despite everything, forgave me for my shitty move in the past, and this gorgeous man smirking down at me with his pierced monster cock.

He crawls up the bed, and Han positions him to straddle my chest, careful to avoid any pressure on my stomach. Jacob's hand reaches out until he's supporting himself on the wall behind the bed. His chest flexes with restraint. Han sits back and looks at the two of us with lust burning in his eyes.

I use the moment to put my hands on Jacob's chest and run my nails lightly across the vast planes of his chest, noticing the goosebumps that pop up every time I trail across his nipples. I look down to see Jacob's free hand wrapped around his very rigid, very pierced cock. There's gotta be at least four piercings on that thing. My eyes go wide, and I can hardly stand to look away.

Han winks at me as he lowers his head into my line of sight and runs his tongue along my collarbone. "Have you done this before?" he asks with a sly grin. I shake my head because I can't seem to form coherent thoughts as my eyes trail over Jacob's cock.

The piercings glint in the dim light of the still-running movie and shift with the minuscule thrusts he can't seem to help. My hands glide down his stomach and wrap around his dick. The accessories are new for me, but, good lord, they are sexy.

Han pulls away from my neck and reaches into the bedside table again, his hand coming out with a bottle of lube. He checks Jacob still isn't near my injury and drizzles a dollop between my breasts, massaging it between the valley.

Jacob seizes the moment and rubs his cock between my breasts gently at first. I push them together to create a channel, and he groans at the pressure wrapping around his cock. I may have never done this personally, but I know how to work a porn site. The pillow supports my head enough, and when Han sees what I'm thinking, he props another one under my neck. I'm unsure how the piercings will factor into this, but I'm desperate to try.

I open, and with each forward thrust, Jacob's dick surges into my mouth. This angle shouldn't fuck with my delicate gag reflex, but my lips are stretched wide, and in my head, I'm thinking how to best swallow him down later. The piercings are new to me and require more research. It's not wholly uncomfortable but will take some getting used to.

His pace picks up, and I look into his tempestuous eyes as his moves become increasingly erratic.

"Fuck, yes, Love. You feel perfect. I love your smart mouth wrapped around me." I glow under his encouragement, loving how the words come out in a staccato rhythm with his vehement thrusts. Knowing I'm making this rigid man lose his control is the ultimate power trip.

The look in my eyes must set him off because seconds later, he's warning me he's going to come, and I do nothing to adjust my position, my intention clear. I want this organized man out of control and jetting his cum down my throat. Unable to hold back. Unleashed.

A moment later, he lets out another strangled curse as he leans forward, slamming both hands onto the wall behind us and powers into my mouth. I swallow him down as much as I can, and his breathing quickens, then stops entirely as his back arches, and he comes with a long groan.

Han sits back with a satisfied smirk, enjoying the show, and Jacob struggles to control his breathing. He flops to my free side, runs his hand along my hip, and murmurs, "Good girl."

He alights my hand with a kiss, and I link my free one with Han's. The three of us sneak out of the room and head to the bathroom to do it again.

By the time my head hits the lavender-scented pillow again an hour later, I'm sated, cleaned, bandaged, and wrapped in four arms that shield me through the night.

Chapter Twelve

Rogue

I'M IN THE CONCRETE ROOM IN KING'S PENTHOUSE APARTMENT. HE WAS *promoted to The Gambit's leader six months ago and takes my education seriously. He plans for me to join their ranks.*

As he told me last week, his intention is for me to be a hitwoman for the crew. He doesn't like the candidates he has in his employment and wants to shape the perfect weapon—a weapon that only answers to him.

I miss my parents and my sister, Sage. I miss our walks in the park, camping trips at the beach, and board games on Sunday mornings.

I keep those thoughts to myself as I practice with the butterfly knife he put in my hand about an hour ago, focusing on not cutting myself as I whip it out of my pocket. I do a few of the flipping maneuvers he showed me earlier. I nick my finger as it flails out of control.

"Again, daughter."

Every time he calls me daughter, I feel a fissure of anger for my parents. They surely didn't want me with King. Who would? But for him to use that term for me makes me rage inside my tiny body. I know I can't end him yet, but one day, I will.

I wipe the blood on my jeans and try again. And again. And again. I have to master this soon. Last year, when he showed me how to use the switchblade, he got frustrated after a few hours, and I ended up with it embedded in my calf. It went deep enough to connect with bone.

The private doctor The Gambit employs stitched me up, gave me some physical therapy exercises, and that was it. Once she was gone, King had me on my hands and knees, cleaning up both the vomit and blood that escaped me after I was knifed.

The knife continues to spin in my hand as I learn how to wield this new blade. I will get this. I will not end up stabbed again. At least the stabbing last year was better than the waterboarding six months ago.

King says he's teaching me to take the pain I will eventually unleash on others. He claims, as my adoptive dad, he's training me in the family business and helping me through my grief. I don't want anything to do with this crap.

I'm eleven, and while my first two years with King were more manageable, they worsened as he rose in the ranks. He mostly stuck me with nannies and tutors when I moved into his place. He has started paying more attention to me as he's become more powerful. Lucky me.

I think he wants to use me for the rest of my life.

He separated us sisters, using our visits to head off any disobedience. Sage is all that's left of my old life, and I desperately want to see her.

I know she's safe. I saw her a few months ago, and the woman caring for her seemed pretty nice, if not a little strict.

Anything is better than having her here under the same roof as this man. One of the Montgomery girls is more than enough. I couldn't take it if I had to watch her endure this same freak show. King says he has other plans for her future. Mine is settled.

I whirl the blade around my hand again and again until the motions begin to form muscle memory. It's getting better—more fluid. Maybe I'll learn it this time without having to "learn my lesson" from King. As my confidence grows, I start adding the new moves he demonstrated to me earlier, and I get the spinning into a movement I like for my small hand.

It slips just as I give it a final spin to open the blade and fully join the two handles.

I watch in abject horror as it sails out of my hand and toward King, standing a mere three feet from me in the training room. The blade flies toward him, and he just barely moves out of the way so it doesn't impale his chest. The knife cuts into his light gray suit jacket lapel as it flares from his body in his evasive move.

Silence echoes out in the room as he looks from his ruined suit jacket to me with menace in his eyes. I feel my stomach sink in fear.

The Secrets We Keep

He pulls the gun from his shoulder holster in one smooth motion and fires a single shot into my right arm—my knife hand.

"I'm ashamed of you, Rogue. My daughter is better than this." It's the last thing I hear before the internal screaming starts. It would be far, far worse if I let my cries out.

Pain radiates from my body, and I drop to my knees. One day, I'll get this right, and he won't have a reason to punish me.

Sage and I will be together again, and I will be fine. We will be fine.

―――

I jolt awake after my memory in nightmare form and open my eyes in panic. Jacob and Han warm and shelter me on both sides. We fell asleep together after fooling around again in the early morning hours.

Han rewrapped my stitches and said they were healing well. The cut isn't too deep, and the pain is manageable after everything I endured in my adolescence. But I don't want to share those bleak years of my past with them, so I keep from rustling the covers.

Han is lightly snoring on my left, with one arm tucked under his head for support. The other rests on my hip, just below the bandage. Jacob is on my right.

His usual perfectly coiffed hair is mussed with a slight wave as it spills over the pillow. His left arm is under my neck, and he's fully snaked around me with his right hand over my breast. It's hard to tell where his tattoos end and mine begin when we're skin-to-skin like this.

He looks younger when he sleeps and isn't entirely put together. I wonder how old he is. He's twenty-five at least, but he's usually dressed professionally, which ages him a bit.

I look past Jacob to see the clock on the nightstand. It's only seven in the morning, but I'm wide awake after my nightmare.

There's suddenly pounding on the door. Both Jacob and Han spring out of bed and land on either side in a crouch.

I'm not the only one trained to react to a threat by using my body in a fight, despite Han's insistence that guns are the way to go. Wait, is that? Yep, he's got a gun in his hand. The nightstand on his side has a drawer cracked open. Damn, he's quick.

The pounding continues, and the door flings open. Lucas comes striding in and looks at Jacob, who's blocking me from the "intruder."

"Buttercup isn't in her room. Her bed doesn't look slept in, and I can't find her anywhere. I've been calling out for her all over this damn place, but if she's in one of the soundproofed rooms, she won't hear me. Come on, we have to go find her."

Jacob relaxed his pose as Lucas was speaking and shifted to the right. It's then that Lucas sees me lying naked on the bed, doing a piss-poor job of covering myself with my arms since the guys flung the covers off. The two pillows on either side of me still have indentations where the guys rested their heads. He's putting two and two together, and I see his face fall.

"Oh. Uhm, I see you're okay. I was worried for a bit." He turns toward the door, and his posture deflates. "Okay, I'll go."

"Lucas, wait," I call out, but he's already striding through the door and down the catwalk. The look on his usually joyous face has me feeling like shit. But I made no promises. I agreed to nothing with him, with any of them.

Is he funny? Absolutely. Am I attracted to the redhead? Completely. But I know not to wait for what little happiness I find. If everything can be taken from me, and a swift death is the best I can hope for in my line of work, I will not delay gratification in my anticipated short life.

"Aw, shit." Han sighs. "I'll go talk to him."

"No, no, it should come from me," I reply. I know Red's been flirty, and maybe this is something we should have addressed before we fooled around.

I've made a mistake here. Not doing what we did last night, but by not speaking to Lucas after Han and Jacob shared their affections in the bathroom yesterday.

If this ends up being nothing else in the long term—and, honestly, how can it?—it will at least be a learning opportunity for me. I've never had to juggle men before. I don't anticipate I will again in the future wherever I end up, but I can always learn some humility.

I sit up carefully, glad to feel the pain is not as bothersome as yesterday. I make my way off the bed, using Jacob's hand as an anchor to lift myself to a standing position. Han collects my clothes from the floor and kneels in front of me. He tosses the shirt onto the bed and holds up my tights, helping me guide a foot in while keeping my hands on his shoulders for balance.

Jacob grabs the shirt and helps me to slip into it. I can't remember the last time someone helped me dress; it feels comforting and childish. Having to grow up quickly, I forgot what it's like to have someone do something for me without expecting something awful in return. Thanks, King.

I leave those two with a lingering kiss for each other and go downstairs to the kitchen. Walking in has me suppressing a gasp. There is flour everywhere. I mean fucking everywhere.

Somehow, it even reached the top edges of the higher cabinets. A towering stack of burned pancakes rests next to the stove, and a decent-looking pile sits in the middle of the granite island. Syrup, sprinkles, butter in a dish that looks like someone tried to carve a flower into, but the petals are all dying, and a single white rose. I know precisely who attempted to cook today.

The smell of coffee is damn tempting, but I have to find Lucas, the master chef, first. As I turn to leave the kitchen, I see him peeking up from the couch in the lounge.

"Red, did you do all this?" I call out to him. His head nods, but he doesn't meet my eyes.

"Get your ass over here. I need help. I'm injured." Okay, I know I can do most of my own shit even if I've been shot and have multiple limbs in casts, but he doesn't. I'm hoping his chivalry won't let him leave me hanging here. We need this tension broken.

Sure enough, he pops up, vaults over the back of the couch, and rushes over to me. "Are you okay? What can I do?" Guilt at using my injury to get him to speak to me feels like a shitty thing to do. King used to manipulate me and still does, and I vow to myself that I won't do something like that again. It's time for some honesty.

"Lucas, I need a mug, please. You can give me the one Noah used the other day—the one you wanted me to use." I'm kind of curious about his mug collection, and he seemed overly pissed at Noah for using the one he picked out for me.

A small smile tips his lips, and I see some of his natural demeanor reenter his eyes as his laugh escapes. "You got it, Buttercup."

As he's rifling through the cabinet next to the fridge, I take note of his mussed hair. It looks like he was running his hands through it repeatedly, and yep, I'm definitely going to make this one bald by the end of our partnership.

"Here it is!" Red exclaims. He spins around and holds it to me with a broad smile, letting me read it. *Once in a while, someone amazing comes along. Here I am.* The side without lettering has a sloth in a yellow polka-dot bikini. I was not prepared for this.

Imagining Noah drinking his black coffee with that stern look on his face while this girly lettering faces outward, has me snorting at the mental image. Lucas gets that playful look in his eye again, and all feels right in the world. "You just imagined Noah in this bikini, didn't you?" Lucas laughs out, and I join him with a giggle.

I gesture to the breakfast spread, "Red, did you do all this for me?" The kitchen's state makes it apparent that he's not usually the one cooking, but his efforts make me feel warm and fuzzy. He is so sweet, and I'm afraid I'd break him with the darkness creeping along the edges of my soul.

He hems and haws for a second before finally answering, "Yes, fine. I made this for you. I don't know how to cook, but I followed one of those stupid recipe videos online. They go too fast; I had to rewind and pause like twenty times, and that's hard to do when pouring shit into a measuring cup. Why don't they just write it out?" Oh, honey. There are usually instructions in the video description, but I'll show him another time. Let's keep that little nugget of truth for later.

"I know. Those videos suck. But these look good," I motion to the stack in the middle of the island. "Can I have a plate so I can try?"

"Yes! Of course. I had one, and it's pretty good. It's nothing compared to the food Mrs. M makes, but she's like significantly older than me and has had way more time to practice. I'll get there." He defends his cooking skills, and I love that the enigmatic Mrs. M acts as a surrogate mother to them. Han told me a bit about her over burgers at my place.

Lucas hands me a plate and some silverware. I load up a pancake with one of the weird butter flower petals and pour on some syrup.

"Coffee or tea?"

"Coffee, please. Always coffee first thing in the morning. One spoon of sugar and a bit of milk." I love that first caffeine jolt in the morning. Anything after that, it's tea. The last thing I need to be is a hitwoman with caffeine jitters, making mistakes because my hands won't stop shaking.

He prepares my cup as I cut into the pancake. I put the small piece into my mouth and chew. The flavor that hits my tongue is... well, it's awful. It tastes like baking powder.

I think someone switched the teaspoon with the tablespoons—plural. At least they're fluffy.

I pretend it's incredible and make yummy noises because he went through the trouble of cooking for me, and I force myself to take another bite. I can do this. At least, I think I can.

Lucas opens and closes his mouth a few times. He was gearing up to ask about what he saw upstairs, no doubt. I swallow the appalling pancake, settle my fork and knife on the plate, and wait patiently for him to broach the subject.

If I approach it first, I don't think it will go as well. Red will likely want to steer the conversation, and if he has questions, he can ask.

After a moment, he finally probes the subject. "So, you, Han, and Jacob?"

I thoughtfully chew my piece of disgusting pancake for a few seconds and swallow it down. "Yes. But we aren't committing to anything. They know how I feel about monogamy, and you know our jobs don't often lend to making plans."

He considers this for a few seemingly endless minutes while I pray he won't judge me for jumping into bed with two of his teammates.

"Okay. I won't lie and say I'm not jealous as hell, but a little competition never hurt anyone. Will you go out with me next week?"

Er, what? First of all, I'm praying this is just another example of Lucas putting his foot in his mouth and not his true meaning. Second, I am not something to be won. I feel a sting from the competition comment. My immediate reaction is that he thinks I'm some kind of trophy and, with all my baggage, I definitely am not.

"Red, I will go out with you on one condition. You drop the competitive aspect and are not asking me out in some kind of bid to steal me away from the others. I am my own person and will decide who I spend time with without some kind of sick childhood toy complex at play."

His jaw, which was steadily dropping as I spoke, snaps closed. "I did not mean it like that. I just meant it pushes people to do better when there is competition. I don't plan to win you; I plan to woo you." He emphasizes the last bit with a waggle of his eyebrows.

Oh, my jaded heart just did a little thump thingy inside my rib cage.

"Deal, as long as you don't try to take away my autonomy. I will not be with any of you if it jeopardizes our goals."

"Deal." His hand reaches across the countertop, and we shake on it over the melting butter flower.

With that settled, I relax against the back of the stool I'm perched on and sip my coffee as I attempt to return to the land of the living. Getting gutted and rounding the bases with a couple of hot security guys really takes it out of you. Who knew?

Noah strides into the kitchen a few minutes later and snags a pancake without a plate. He takes a bite and makes a sound that's a cross between a groan and a retch as he whirls and spits it into the sink. "Who the fuck messed up pancakes? It's like five ingredients."

A laugh bursts from my lips, and Lucas looks from me to Noah, trying to figure out who's lying to him.

Lucas

After my fabulous-ish breakfast, Han and Jacob join Buttercup, Noah, and me in the meeting room to run through our plan for the first Annex board member. The guys are sweaty from the gym, and I see Rogue's eyes trailing across their bodies.

I'm more than a little jealous, but I meant what I said. I see Buttercup's point about not making promises we aren't in any position to keep. I'll take a page from her book and live for the moment. And I want her at this moment. Not just her body, which, fuck yes, but I want to know what makes her, her. I want to know fucking everything.

Noah and I spoke last night and decided to let Rogue tell us about The Gambit members once she feels up to it. Between the new team, getting stabbed, a likely hangover, and moving in, it seemed prudent to let her settle before holding an unending meeting about her board. However, after learning about her ability to bounce back this morning, it wouldn't be a problem for her to walk us through it.

The whiteboard in the glass-walled room holds three names printed in Noah's neat handwriting: Richard Blake, Mara Hendrix, and Patton Cross, more formally known as the board members of Annex security.

Dear Leader, aka Noah, sits at the head of the table and runs this meeting. He has to inform Rogue of what these three are capable of, and we need to devise a plan together. I know we've all had ideas, but it doesn't feel right to pull her in as a team member and then dictate the entire operation.

Noah may lead us, but we work as a democracy.

"Richard Blake is our weapons and combat-specific board member. He deals in arms and equipping businesses and companies with security teams. Blake is highly skilled in both areas but doesn't train regularly now that he's approaching fifty. He's enjoying the wealth of being one of the top dogs and now delegates more than he participates.

"He has a weakness for high-end prostitutes and coke. We think his extracurricular activities initially linked our board to your organization." He directs the last statement to Rogue, informing her of the connection. She nods, obviously having put two and two together.

"Mara Hendrix worked her way up from the technology sector and now sits in the seat vacated a few years ago by her father when he retired. She didn't follow the nepotism route, exactly. She worked from the bottom up, and her skills are unparalleled," Jacob explains. He's more than a little miffed that he hasn't been able to crack some of her code, which prevents us from looking into her digital life. He's frequently working on it when he's not focused on a job.

Han takes up the baton to give up the details on our last member. "Patton Cross is from El Castillo and has been on the board since Annex Security's inception. He's deeply connected to this community. He deals with politicians and CEOs to sell our teams and services to them.

"He's clean, as far as we can tell. Way too clean for someone in our line of work. We're still trying to figure out his weakness, but I have a feeling it'll relate to being from this area."

"I remember hearing my parents talk about him. He was thought to be responsible for hundreds of deaths over the years, but they could never pin anything on him, right? That kind of description sticks in a young kid's mind," Rogue muses.

"Right," I confirm. "So even though Cross's reputation has been reformed and rewritten over the last twenty years, some still remember when he was running the streets. We've been looking for informants from that era, but they're not keen to speak up when they hear his name."

Noah directs the conversation back to the board member on whom we've got the most intel. "Blake should be our first to deal with. We don't have to strike them all hard and fast. The time it takes to fill the seat when a member is removed should give us some breathing room between removals."

Buttercup pipes up with a slightly unsure look on her face, "So, hookers and blow sound like something I can help with. I can get the product from a dealer if you can set up a meeting. There's a hotel near the Annex Security building that doesn't ask too many questions. I say we use proximity, prostitution, and product to lure him."

"And the prostitute?" Jacob asks with an unfamiliar edge to his voice. Uh-oh, someone's not happy.

"Me."

The four of us start talking over each other with various objections and reasons why she shouldn't do this, especially while injured.

"Shut up!" she shouts at us.

"I'm not saying we go today, but we set shit up today. Jacob, can you find out his schedule?" He nods in assent. "Good. Han, grab a burner phone. You look similar to one of our dealers who works with the professional crowd. You'll set up the meeting and be with me in the hotel room. Noah, you book a reservation when Jacob and Han find a date that works. You can be in a room down the hall for backup. I will absolutely be the bait and offered as a reward for his loyal business."

I have to admit, it's fucking genius. But there's something, or should I say someone, missing. "Uh, Buttercup, since you're taking point on this, what am I doing?"

"You, Red, will be working maintenance or something with access to the rooms at the hotel. Better brush up that resume to get a new job."

I like that—an extra set of eyes and ears in the vicinity when all of this goes down. I nod. Plus, it gives us someone on the ground after the fact to make sure no one sees or hears anything. The hospitality industry is teeming with gossip.

Jacob chimes in with a more straightforward solution, "I'll just add it to their system that he's coming in as a transfer from one of their other properties. You'll start this week to get the lay of the land before the meeting. You can even set up a few bugs so we can be sure to hear what's going on while Rogue and Han are with Blake."

"What's the goal here? Kill or ship off?" Rogue asks without hesitation in her voice, as if she's offering wine choices. I know it's her job to kill, but damn. That sounded a little cold, even to me, a fellow hitman.

Noah decides for all of us. "Blackmail and ship out. If his habits get out, the board of Annex will kill him themselves to maintain their pristine image. We get you guys to coax him into admitting his addiction problem and stepping out on his wife and use that as leverage. I'd rather not kill anyone."

Decisions made, we break before we gather blueprints, the burner, and the cocaine—what a shopping list.

At Jacob's usual lunchtime, the alarms start alerting us someone is at the warehouse gate. I spin to the monitor, and a huge smile overtakes my face. Working makes me hungry. Mama Bear is here, and she likely brought food. I enter the code to open the gates, and she drives her old station wagon into the lot. I sprint for the door, pull it open, and leap into the sunlight as I hear Rogue ask someone what's happening.

Mrs. Morganson parks next to the SUV and starts to remove her driving gloves. Motherfucking driving gloves. I wish I could be that cool. I

The Secrets We Keep

reach for her door handle and pull it open as I bow with a flourish. Sure enough, the smell of Italian food comes wafting out of the car. My mouth starts watering. I have no shame when it comes to her food—none.

"Lucas, dearest! I know we had plans in two days, but I figured you boys could use some food."

I love this woman. Can she adopt me even though I'm nearly thirty?

"We can always use your food, Mrs. M." Hashtag truth.

I help her out of the car and head to the hatch for the trunk. There are three catering-sized containers, and the smell of tomato sauce and melted cheese smacks me in the face. I don't even care what's in here. I'm eating all of it.

"Well, well, who's this?" Mrs. M asks as she looks back at the warehouse, shielding her eyes from the sun.

I see Rogue standing in the open doorway in her ripped black jeans and a white button-down shirt that is way too big on her. I think it's Jacob's, and a little stab of jealousy pings in my stomach. I want her in my shirts. Her face is free of makeup, and her green eyes are alight as she looks at me and Mrs. M across the small parking lot.

"Hi, let me help. I'm Rogue, and you must be the amazing Mrs. Morganson the boys won't stop talking about. You must tell me how you got them to worship at your feet the way they do." She ends with a laugh, and Mrs. M joins her with her small chuckle. From talk of killing to showering little old ladies with compliments. All in a day's work.

"Oh dear, I think you and I will get along just fine." Mrs. M slithers an arm through the crook of Rogue's elbow, and the two of them walk back to the warehouse as Rogue looks back at me and lifts a shoulder. She wanted to help carry, but Mrs. M has other plans. Interrogation ones, no doubt.

Han lopes out to the station wagon and helps me bring all the food. We settle it on the kitchen island as we all grab stools for seating. Jacob snags the plates, Noah works on the drinks and silverware, and I start uncovering dishes because patience has never been a virtue of mine. Working up an appetite while cooking breakfast has left me a little hangry.

Mama Bear and Rogue are chatting about knives on the couch. I guess Mrs. M shared the story of how we were looking for The Gambit's white knight assassin, and the homicide of her husband made us think it was Rogue for a moment with how she handled the knife.

We finally caught up with her, and after hearing why she did what she did, we couldn't turn her in. Her husband had it coming with his abuse of our mama bear.

We checked up on her repeatedly over a few months, which eventually turned into monthly dinners, and now, as you can see, food delivery when she misses us. We look to her for advice our parents can't give, and she sees us for who we are, not just our jobs.

"Hey, Killer! Come help me up." See? She calls me Killer. She's cool with it because she's one too.

I head to the lounge and let her use my arms as leverage to stand. She uses the opportunity to wind her arms around my waist in a side hug and leads us to the kitchen. "I like her," Mrs. M whispers. "She told me she's going to give me one of her switchblades because I've always wanted one."

I laugh at what they've bonded over. "Yeah, Mama Bear, we do too." I wink, and she catches my meaning. She just scoffs and hums.

"Rogue," she calls out, "my boys being good to you?"

"Yes, ma'am," she answers with a shy smile.

"Good." She nods with confidence. "Then let's eat. I didn't spend all morning making lasagna as a ruse to meet this new 'friend' Han mentioned, just to sit around on my wrinkly ass while it gets cold. Dig in."

We happily do as we're told. Mama Bear has spoken.

Chapter Thirteen

Han

A WEEK AFTER OUR PLAN TOOK SHAPE, WE HAD CONFIRMATION THAT Blake would meet us at the Eastwick Hotel at seven tonight. Lucas has been working on their maintenance team for four days now. Noah made the reservations for two rooms as soon as Blake confirmed, and I forwarded the room number to the man.

Ivy is currently wearing a short black dress and heels that lace up her calves. Her hair is curled in enthralling waves. Deep purple lipstick stains her lips, and her makeup is almost garish after seeing her barefaced and natural for the last week.

She's been running herself into the ground lately, working on things for The Gambit and setting up this Blake meeting. She spent time looking over the data Jacob was able to pull, though it wasn't much. She barricaded herself in the tech room to do some additional research on someone King wanted her to deal with.

We could look at what she was doing, but Jacob trusts her, and I do as well. It's not our business until she decides to involve us.

Noah and Jacob spent the week setting up a path for Blake to follow when we get the evidence on him.

Lucas has been laying the groundwork here at the hotel, including adding some bugs to the room we booked today.

And me? I've been living on cloud nine at having Ivy back in my life. And in the spirit of helping, I've been dropping by the Annex building to grab some things.

Ivy told Jacob and me about Lucas asking her out, and, to be honest, we both knew it was coming. He's not one to chase after any girl, but Ivy isn't just anyone, is she? She's sweet, she kicks ass in the ring, and she has already brought Jacob and me to our knees. We assured her that there was no issue for us. If she's happy, we're happy.

Speaking of Jacob, Ivy totally caught me checking him out. First, in the bedroom when we had our movie night when she moved in with us, then again two days ago when we were working out.

Yeah, I tend more toward women than men, but damn, he's hot as fuck. You'd have to be dead not to find that man sexy as hell. Even dead, it'd probably be fifty-fifty.

I've never acted on my attraction since he's my best friend. We've been with women together but never done anything on our own. I've caught a glance or two over the years that made me wonder if he was having any of the same thoughts about me, but nothing has ever come of it, so I've put that little crush to rest.

Somehow, having Ivy with us is reigniting some of those feelings. The way she submits under his dominating words and his soft touches has me wondering what would happen if he turned those attentions to both of us.

Ivy and I haven't had much time together like we did the other night because the plan took shape quickly. There was just no opportunity between preparing for this, her being away for a few days to deal with two more dealers and a board meeting of her own.

A few stolen kisses and a quick stint in the warehouse's weapons room have left me wanting much more. But the best parts of our moments were catching up on each other's lives and spending time together.

Thankfully, her recent hits were uneventful, and she returned to us without a new scratch.

"Ready, Gorgeous?" I ask as I lead her into the hotel lobby. We're thirty minutes early to set up and wait for Blake.

"Ready," she confirms shortly.

Her face firmed up in the car, and she started answering monosyllabically, the same way she used to before a fight in the ring all those years ago. Everyone has their way of gearing up for a mission, and this is hers. Conserve energy, focus, and pay attention to surroundings. It's always been her habit, but I only glimpsed it as a fighter, not a partner in crime.

We grab the key at the reception desk and head to the elevators. We're up on the fourteenth floor because someone of Blake's standing would think anything lower wasn't worth his time.

Ivy grabbed some cocaine from a dealer she dispatched a few days ago. Her stitches are almost due to come out, and since the cut wasn't too deep, she's been able to join us in the gym and regain some of the movement she lost.

Watching her train has been a study of discovery. I always knew she was a badass when we were younger, but her dedication to her training, even while injured, has me in awe. We used training sessions to reminisce about those old fight days, showing each other moves to take down bigger opponents. Jacob was our unsuspecting victim, and he played the part with a smile as we took turns bringing him to the mat.

We have earpieces in, and comms are working. The guys come through loud and clear from their positions. Jacob is in a van parked near the hotel's service entrance near the kitchen, and Noah and Lucas, having just finished his shift, are already in a room three doors down from us. Close enough to help if anything goes wrong.

Ivy sits calmly in the suite's living room while I park my ass on the desk chair. The bedroom and the living room are wired, thanks to Lucas's access. She says she has some ideas to entice Blake into talking about his extracurriculars.

The whole point is to get enough evidence on tape to use as blackmail to have Blake resign and quit the country for good. Neither the company nor his wife will want him after this is compiled, and the company would rather kill him than have a loose end.

Ivy agreed with Annex's position, especially since he ordered hits to line his pockets with cash by eliminating corporate competition, but we're keeping that option as a last resort.

As the clock ticks past seven, there's a brusque knock on the door. Showtime. One last check-in with the team, and I walk to the door to let Blake in.

I'm dressed in nice slacks and a black button-down shirt. I look like an office manager having a goth phase. It's not my look, but it's what The Gambit dealers are made to wear when meeting high-value clients.

"Mr. Blake." I move my body to allow him into the room. We discussed the idea that he might recognize me from employee files, but we're counting on his racism to have ignored me within Annex.

"Wang, thanks for the invite." Yep. It looks like Jacob was right about this asshole—no recognition in his eyes whatsoever. Lucas got to pick my alias because I lost a bet last week that he couldn't finish everything Mrs. M brought us to eat.

He could. And he did. And I think Ivy is no longer interested in the human garbage disposal.

Richard Blake is a mid-fifties ex-boxer who used his skills to make money by training recruits at Annex before he was brought up the ladder. His hair is blond but fading to gray, and his stomach has begun to bloat due to inactivity. The buttons on his suit are starting to do some heavy lifting, trying to keep the jacket closed.

I usher him into the room, and he looks over to the couch and raises a brow. "Why is this one brunette? I always have a blonde," he sneers at her. Sex workers are people too, asshole.

"She's our absolute best," I try to recover smoothly. The management sends her as a thank you. I assure you, she is incredible." I send a secret wink to Ivy, and I can tell she's doing her utmost not to roll her eyes in the company of our guest.

"Stand up, girl," he orders her like a ruler over a peasant.

Ivy stands and does a spin, allowing him to check out her body. I clench my fists and resist the urge to simultaneously punch this dickweed or block her from his line of sight. I, unfortunately, settle for neither. The plan has to take priority here. Completing her spin, she strolls over to Blake, grabs his silk tie between her hands, runs one up to the collar, and yanks.

He falls to his knees instantly. "She'll do," he chokes out. Huh, I wonder how she knew he liked a domme. It must be one of the things she found out when she was researching him. I place the small block of cocaine on the desk and sit on the couch, crossing one ankle over my knee. Blake peers at me, probably wondering why I'm not leaving.

Ivy sternly answers the unasked question in his eyes, "There are two rooms, and I am not allowed to be without an escort. No matter who is buying, I'm too valuable to the company to take the risk."

"Yes, ma'am," he drops his head and acknowledges Ivy's position here, submitting completely.

"Tell me what you want, Blake," she purrs and starts the veiled interrogation to get the necessary information.

"I want to be dominated. I want to be made to beg. I want to fuck you and earn your praises, ma'am."

"And do you want your coke before or after you fuck me?" she asks, referencing the drugs we brought along. Annex likely won't care about hookers, but they've got a strict no-drugs policy that even management can't override.

"Before, during, after... whatever you want, ma'am. My last bump was this morning in the office. I need more. Please."

Bingo.

I hear Noah's voice in my ear, confirming that they've got the evidence on the recording.

Blake takes a moment to lift his head to mine, breaking his surprising sub position. "She may not be Sage, my usual, but I have a feeling we'll get along just fine. She always makes me wait to take a hit until after I fuck her raw."

It's brief, but it's there in spades. Rage flickers across Ivy's face, her eyes narrow to slits, and I see her hand tremor. She speaks to him before I can tell him his exit plan.

"Crawl to the bathroom, pet." Her tone is no longer merely dominant; it's so icy that it gives me chills. A calm mask has replaced the emotion that flitted across her face moments ago. She moves her hand behind her body, indicating I should wait. For what? We have the evidence.

"Yes, ma'am." Blake does an embarrassing crawl toward the door on the other side of the living room, his slightly pudgy belly hanging low, reaching for the floor. His breaths are coming in heavy gasps, and he's getting off on her orders. He crosses the threshold of the door and kneels just inside.

She raises a heeled foot and places it on his chest, pushing him down until he's lying on the tiled floor. Is this another thing he's into? He raises a hand to touch her foot, but she stops him by moving the foot from his chest and slamming it into his hand. Her stiletto digging into his open palm.

"Listen here, you little shit. You will never see Sage again. You will never think of her again. Most importantly, you will never touch her again." Ivy is seething as she spits the words at him in a low voice. I think it's part of her dominatrix routine until I see Blake reach for his weapon, a knife, with his unpinned hand.

She sees the move and withdraws her blade from her corset top. She drops down to her knees, straddling Blake's body. In seconds, his arms are pinned between her legs and his torso. Blake tries to use his body weight to buck her off.

Oh, shit. Why is Ivy suddenly on him? We have the evidence to blackmail him to hell and back. Everyone knows how Annex would react if word got out that one of their board members was fucking hookers instead of his wife and doing coke at work.

He may be older these days, but he's been trained by the best, and those moves are hard to forget, even after aging out of duty. He lifts a leg high enough to plant his foot on the floor to gain leverage. He bucks her off, and she rolls into a crouch.

Blake is just getting to his knees, and they slice at each other, attacking with fervency. I watch from the bathroom door and wait for an opportunity to get him from behind, but he never lets Ivy turn him. I don't want to get in the way and trip her up by barging in. I see his arm as he rears it back and lets it loose right over her previous injury. She doesn't go down but starts to favor her right side.

Her hands pull away, and his grin is sickening. "I guess I got lucky with that hit. You're good, I'll give you that. You didn't show any indication you were already injured. Who are you?" he asks as he grabs Ivy in a chokehold in front of his body, shielding himself from the gun I've pulled from my waist.

"Rogue." His eyes widen at her name, and he digs the knife harder into her neck. He recognizes her name.

The knife starts cutting into the skin just under her jaw, and I don't have the patience to watch her escape. I know she can, but I don't think my nerves can take it. Neither can the guys if the shouting in my ears is any indication—damn comms.

I see the opening and fire without a second thought. Ivy had her head angled away from the shot, even as it pushed the knife further into the skin of her throat like she knew I'd take it without hesitating and didn't want to waste time.

Silence follows on the previously non-stop comms, and I hear a door down the hall bang open. A beep and a click have Lucas barging into the room with weapons drawn. He sees Ivy in a crouch on the floor in the bathroom, moving away from Blake's now unmoving body.

She must have known it would end this way. Having him move to the bathroom just made cleaning up a hell of a lot easier.

Lucas barrels into the bathroom, knocking me out of the way, holsters his guns, and picks her up, carrying her into the main room without a word.

Noah comes in seconds later, a phone to his ear. He ushers Lucas, who is still holding Ivy, out of the hotel room, instructs him to take her home, and heads to me. "I called a cleanup crew not connected to Annex, and Jacob has a heads-up that the two of them are headed down there now. Let's finish here, then get home to check on our girl."

Rogue

Lucas carries me into the service elevator at the end of the hall, despite my protests that I can walk, and we're into the back hallway and crossing through the kitchens in no time on our way to Jacob.

Lucas hasn't said anything this whole time except to murmur curses about Han taking a reckless shot. He didn't act recklessly. I saw he had an angle, so I tilted my neck to let him take a shot. I would expect any competent deadeye to do the same.

Han's marksman skills reconfirm they weren't responsible for that attempt at the cemetery a few weeks ago. He wouldn't need a laser to focus on his target. He's fucking poetry in motion with a weapon.

Lucas slides open the van door with one hand while keeping me steady with the other. Jacob meets my eyes over his shoulder, and I offer a small smile. I'm fine. I do not need to be coddled, but Lucas needs to feel helpful. I can live with this.

Once we're in the van, Jacob takes off leisurely down the road to avoid drawing attention. The last thing we want is to be pulled over for speeding while I may be dripping a bit of blood from my wound. I'm sure I have chunks of Blake in my hair, but I can do nothing about that now. Lucas hasn't noticed it quite yet.

I undeniably ruined my panties while watching Han take down Blake with a single shot. I need to fuck him. Soon. We've fooled around, but he and Jacob have been overly cautious about my stitches. We've all been busy as hell too, and it's seriously making me crazy—too much sexiness in such close proximity. I may die from their teasing touches—not to mention Red's attentiveness and general exuberant manner. Sometimes, he makes me laugh so hard that I thought I would pull a stitch this week.

Lucas continues not to speak. Jacob continues to flit glances uneasily in the rearview mirror at us. I keep my mouth shut, refusing to lash out about handling myself without all this worry clouding around us.

I owe them an explanation for why I moved on Blake despite having the evidence we needed to make him go far away. The "Sage" he was talking about is my sister. His description of fucking her raw had me seething. I've never encountered someone who knows her in her professional capacity.

She was forced into the escort business while I was involuntarily recruited to the hitman game. King not only split us up, but he also pushed us into inescapable positions where we'll be lucky if our souls make it out intact after all the shit we've seen working for the criminal syndicate. I need to tell them, but not right now. I'm still calming the prickling nerves under my skin; I don't want to lash out at these two in the car.

Jacob drops us at the warehouse and heads back to the hotel to help clean up. Lucas ushers me inside as his face remains thundered. "Red, honey. Talk." I plant my feet and refuse to move further while he radiates this much anger.

"You," he starts, taking a shaky breath before continuing, "you got hurt again. That asshole hit you, then cut you," he whispers as he tilts my chin up to see the small cut. I felt it in the van; it's not too bad.

"Red, I'm fine." He starts to shake his head in refusal. "No. Look at me, Lucas. I am fine. I have been hurt worse, and I had multiple ways to get out of his hold. Han had the opportunity first and shot." If our positions were reversed, I would have done the same as Han. I would act the same way Lucas is now if anything similar happened to him. Frustration that I wasn't there, stewing about what could have gone differently if I had been. I get it. And talking about how I've been dulled to pain over the years is going to open up a can of worms that can never be repacked.

Most importantly, he needs to know that I am perfectly okay right now and that there was no alternate outcome. I need to tell him something.

"I know the plan was to get recordings, but he brought up my sister, and I snapped. Knowing that cock-sucking, coke-snorting miscreant had my sister as his 'favorite' had me seeing red, Red. I'd rather not talk about it tonight, but I'd like to discuss it with all of you. She's the one I was talking about when I laid out my terms to work with you. She needs out. I'll walk you through everything I know, but I can't do it tonight, Lucas. Please don't ask me to. I never let emotion cloud my judgment, especially on a mission; this was my fuck up. Do not take that onto your shoulders."

Lucas just looks at me and sweeps me into his arms again, "I need to hold you for a bit. You can't get killed before I can woo you, Buttercup. Our date keeps getting postponed, and I'm pissed as hell about it. We'll discuss your sister in the morning with everyone. Stay with me tonight; I want to be sure you're okay. Also, you need a shower. You've got blood in your hair."

I laugh because this is the Lucas I know. This person changes direction so fast in conversation that you give yourself whiplash just trying to keep up.

We reach the large bathroom I share with Han and Jacob, and he lets me down onto those blessedly warm tiles underfoot. I strip off my dress, unbuckle the weapons holsters on my thighs and from under my breasts, and walk over to the vanity mirror while Lucas watches me.

I wash all the makeup off my face, giving Lucas a decent view of my ass in a red lace thong as I bend forward to rinse off the cleanser. When I dry my face with a towel and make sure I don't look like a raccoon, my eyes meet his in the mirror. He's staring at me. But not at my ass or my body. He's staring at my face.

"Buttercup," he sighs. "I'm glad you're okay. What do you need?"

I think about it for a second and take stock of my body. It's in one piece. The stitches leaked a little, but nothing too perilous. My neck looks fine in the mirror now that it's cleaned up. What I need most right now is to get out this excess adrenaline. Usually, I play video games or work out, but tonight, I want Lucas. I need his wit, banter, hard body, and sweet words in my ear.

"You," I state simply, never breaking eye contact.

In three strides, he crosses the bathroom and spins me. I look up into his sun-kissed face as he cups mine with his big hands. His lips come crashing down on mine, and I feel myself returning to normality with his touches.

His kiss is unexpected. As much as he acts like a goofball, always joking and laughing, I can see there's much more to him now. His kiss is possessive, desperate, searing, and soul-searching.

I kiss him back with a zeal I've rarely experienced. I need him tonight. I need him badly; I think if I'm denied, I'll cry. I never cry.

I bind my hands around his neck, and he slips his hands behind me and onto my ass. He stoops, and his hands move to the back of my thighs. I hang onto his neck as he wraps my legs around his waist. Between our unending kisses, I lift the hem of his shirt, and he helps me take it off.

The air changes temperature, and when I open my eyes, I see we've moved out of the bathroom. We're on the walkway and headed to Red's room across the small, bridge-like crossing connecting to the other side of the clubhouse's second level. I cling a little tighter at seeing the drop below us.

Lucas turns to the left and kicks in a door. This must be his room. I've tried to stay away from the others' quarters except when Jacob invites me into his room for movies and making out. I know I'm new and all up in their space. I don't want to step on any toes while I'm bunking here. I quickly look around and immediately wish I had come in here earlier.

There are shelves of comic books covering an entire wall. No wonder we had those silly arguments about superheroes. I'm dragging a chair in here later and reading these. I love these quirky aspects of Lucas that he slowly unveils to me.

He crosses his room and flings me onto the bed. The playful look in his eye is gone, and he is all predator right now.

"Are you sure, Buttercup?" he asks, removing his jeans and boots. Left standing in his electric blue boxer briefs, he almost looks afraid of my answer, as if I've changed my mind.

I tilt my knees open, and he sees my drenched panties and nipples, once again, saluting from within the confines of this stupid-ass lace bra. I loved this bra when I put it on earlier, but now the lace's scrape on my sensitive nipples only makes me feel more insane by the second.

"Words, Buttercup. Words."

"Ye—" My word is cut off as he launches at me. One moment, he's standing at the foot of the bed; the next, I'm being hauled on top of him as he lies back with my leg flung over his hip.

I instantly start to rock on his growing ridge that has nestled itself under my cunt. His hands reach under my arms, braced on his chest for stability, and he runs a hand up my spine. He catches my bra strap and unclasps it smoothly. His hands trace up to my shoulders, and he takes the straps in his fingertips and glides them down my arms with sure movements, tossing both it and my tucked-away phone to the floor. His touch sends sparks up and down my body with shocks of electricity as he resettles them on my hips.

His eyes finally move from my face to take in my body. His mouth opens with a groan as he watches my body move over his. My hips roll in an unending wave, making my breasts sway near his face.

He reaches his body up, supporting himself on one elbow, and takes one of my nipples into his mouth. He rolls it with his tongue, using his teeth to set me on edge. My moving hips start to stutter at the pleasure his mouth provides, paired with the constant friction on my pussy. His other hand wraps around my hip to palm my ass. He encourages me to keep going as he grips me.

I drag his face to mine, and our mouths move together as if they were always meant to. He lifts one leg under me and uses the momentum to roll us to the side, and he wedges himself between my legs.

He runs a hand down my side before slipping it into my panties, finding me drenched.

"Rogue, you are goddamn soaked," he croaks out in a hoarse voice. His fingers play with me way too gently, driving me utterly crazy. I've been treated like glass too often this past week and a half. I can't take it anymore.

"Fuck me, Lucas. Please," I cry out into the vast room. No one is here to listen to our sounds, so I don't hold back.

His pupils are blown as he pulls my panties to one side. He slips down his boxer briefs a bit to free himself and lines up his cock with my pussy. "Condom!" I shout before he can plunge into me.

"On it, sorry." I almost didn't remember, either. I've got an IUD, but without knowing each other's history and no promises of commitment, I'd rather be safe. Getting caught up in the moment is no excuse for people our age. That shit's for teenagers who act recklessly.

He reaches into a drawer, takes a moment to shed his boxers, rips the packet open, slides on the condom, and gets back to where he was before. I use the same move he did earlier and flip us until I'm on top. I have a feeling he'll try to be gentle, and I don't need it or want it like that right now.

I raise my hips and sink onto his cock. His head immediately bows back, and he groans. "Fuck, Buttercup. Fuck. You feel so good," he calls out as his hips start to move on their own accord. "So tight." I move my hips with increasing speed, and my clit grinds on his pubic bone with every forward motion. It's been ages since I last had full-on sex. Foreplay and oral have been incredible with Han and Jacob, but there's nothing like a big dick pounding away at you. It's an overwhelming sensation for me as my body struggles to accommodate his size.

Lucas starts to move in erratic pumps. His upper body rears up suddenly, and I fall onto my back with the momentum as a squeak I am not proud of slips out. My Red moves over me and starts driving into me with reckless abandon.

My orgasm came hot and fast; I didn't have a chance in hell to see it coming. The way he went from taking it to giving it has me panting and writhing underneath him. What woman doesn't want to give up control in bed now and then? We run shit all damn day; sometimes, it's nice just to let go.

He continues to move in and out of me as I come down from my high. His thrusts into me are rough, but the slow slide he does, dragging himself out of me, has me feeling every ridge.

"One," he counts out as my senses return to my body. Oh, hell yes, he's going for more.

He pushes into me and starts to grind with each connection. The pressure is too much. My toes are curling, and my breaths are short. I realize my fingers are digging into his back, and my short nails are clinging onto him for dear life. The only sounds in the room are Lucas and I groaning in satisfaction and the slaps of our bodies coming together with force.

This. This is how I need to be fucked.

Often.

Daily.

Forever.

Red's hand reaches between us as he massages my clit. His moves are becoming increasingly ragged as he finds his finish line. He pinches my clit and bites down on my nipple. I come so hard I see nothing but white light, then bursts of color. I feel his lips on mine and his pulsing cock as he comes in me.

"Two," the cocky motherfucker sighs.

After a few minutes of quiet, he mumbles into my neck as he traces the mermaid tattoo on my ribs, "Buttercup, I can't take it when you get hurt. I need you to be safe." He's still settled over me, careful to keep his weight from crushing me.

"Red, you know our job. I can't promise you that, but I can promise not to add to risky situations." I concede. I think back to earlier, and at that moment, I realize I would've had the same mindset if our roles had been reversed. I would want some reassurance. I take a moment to offer him the same.

He pulls out of me, and when our bones don't feel like jelly, we head to the bathroom to clean up. We fall into his bed and sleep the night away, tucked together.

―――

Hours later, I roll to the side and see Lucas isn't in bed anymore. I grab my phone from the bra material on the floor. It was tucked in there last night.

One benefit of big tits is our bras can hold a ton of shit when we don't want to carry a purse. My weapons are probably still in the bathroom where I stripped them off last night.

It's already a bit after nine o'clock, but after Lucas and I rode out our adrenaline, it makes sense we crashed hard. I bet he's already in the gym and getting shit done. I feel a bit lazy today and want to lay in this bed and read comics.

I see I have a missed call from King, and I walk to the door to ensure it's closed and locked. I don't want him hearing the guys if one of them wanders in. As I learned from Jacob last week, the rooms are soundproofed, but if someone comes in here, I won't be able to silence them immediately. I press his name on my contact list and lift the phone to my ear.

"Rogue," he answers, "I haven't seen you in a while. I see you're moving down the dealer list. Have you made a move on Neil Carter yet?"

"No, not yet. I'll head to San Francisco in a day or two to monitor the situation and see who he's got with him. We don't want a hydra situation—to kill one and have three pop up in his place."

"Good. Go now. Neil is a priority. Get the info, and get it done. I'm tired of hearing about his exploits up there. Northern California is our territory."

"Will do," I answer, knowing he'll threaten Sage if I don't toe the line. He hangs up, and I toss the phone onto the bed.

I've known King has her working with the local prostitutes. She's stunning. Of course, he'd want to cash in on that. He's holding me over her head the same way he's doing to me with her. But this is the first time I've met someone who knows her in that capacity. Blake had to die.

My promise to Lucas to explain everything just took a backseat to keeping King away from Sage. I have to tell the guys about her, and we need to sit down to go through The Gambit's board members.

We've got the Annex members taking up wall space in the war room—aka meeting room. I'm just renaming shit all over the clubhouse at this point. 'Clubhouse' is my favorite thus far—but it's time to cover all our bases. Blake took our attention this week, but they need to know everything when I return from San Francisco.

I put on a pair of sweats and one of Red's discarded shirts that still smells like him for my journey across the clubhouse to my room. I know Lucas, Han, and Jacob wouldn't mind catching a glimpse of me naked, but I'm trying to be respectful of Noah. He's been great since I joined the team.

He's stoic, but I enjoy watching him confidently lead his team. It must take a lot to keep the other three in line, and with the little glimpses of his military background, I don't think there's anyone better suited to his job.

It doesn't hurt that he's built like a tree, and despite my choice of men in the vicinity, I find myself studying his face a little too often. Bad Rogue.

I make it to my room, stuff a backpack with a week's worth of clothes and weapons, and shuffle off for a shower. Did I mention how amazing these bathrooms are? I revel in the warm water and the ache between my thighs. Damn. Lucas surprised me in the best way possible last night.

Thoughts swirling around, I make it to my room when my phone pings with a calendar reminder. Ah, shit. I was supposed to have a meeting with Tanaka today. He wanted to talk to me about something but wouldn't say it over text. I told him I needed to postpone because of work and tossed the phone into the bag.

Lucas meets me at the bottom of the stairs and looks at the backpack slung over my shoulder. "Buttercup, where are you going?" he asks as he leans in to kiss me good morning.

"Huh?" I ask when we break the kiss. I don't remember the question. His tongue playing with mine just reawakened my previously sated libido, and I'm having some trouble forming thoughts at the moment.

He laughs at my response. He slowly enunciates each word, "I said, 'Where. Are. You. Going?'"

He gets a quick jab to the spleen for his joke. "I have to head to San Francisco to gather some information. It should be a pretty quick trip, and I hope to be back in a couple of days."

"And you have to leave now?" he asks as he pulls me close, grinding his growing erection into my lower stomach.

"Regretfully, yes," I groan when my brain threatens to shut off again. "I know the guys need to know about Sage, but do you think you can let me do it when I get back?" I ask carefully. I don't intend to withhold information, but I've heard how people speak about sex workers, and I don't want anyone to have a biased opinion about my sister. It's not like she chose her profession; it wouldn't be fair to be judged on something you have no control over.

"Deal. But you'll fill us in on everything when you get back."

"Deal." I seal my promise with a kiss and head for the door. Lucas walks me to the car and opens the door for me. He kisses my lips passionately before guiding me into the Bel Air I brought back from the garage the other day.

"Be safe, Buttercup. And check in often. Oh, and your stitches are due to come out. Call us when you pull them out so we can make sure you're okay. Please?"

How can I say no to that face? "I will, Red. See you soon."

"See you."

He closes my door, and I crank the engine, heading out of the compound. It's a two-hour drive to San Francisco, and I think of Lucas the whole way.

Chapter Fourteen

Noah

I'vE BEEN CALLED INTO THE PRIMARY ANNEX SECURITY BUILDING A week after we dispatched Blake. The first thought that crossed my mind when they announced the meeting was that they knew we took him out. But now, as I see the other team leaders in the waiting room on the top floor, I know it's a top-tier meeting. I'm sure he'll be mentioned, but our odds of not being singled out seem good with everyone in attendance.

As I wait in the building's executive floor lobby, I review what has happened since Rogue joined us. The day after she moved in, I heard Lucas and Rogue in the kitchen when she told him she was with Han and Jacob, too.

A little pang of jealousy hit my gut that my guys were finding happiness while I focused on work, but I kept myself hidden to the side of the kitchen so I wouldn't interrupt their talk. Lucas showed far more maturity than I expected from him. He simply let the information in, then confidently threw his hat in the ring.

His attitude has significantly improved over the last week since we dealt with Blake. He was downcast when Han, Jacob, and I returned from our morning tasks and found him sitting on the couch without Rogue. He told us she had to go to San Francisco to chase a lead for The Gambit. He said she had some information for us but made him promise that she would be the one to share it.

It's had us on pins and needles all week, but Lucas would spill the beans if it were something threatening. Han tried asking him if she explained why she went after Blake when we had the blackmail recordings in hand, but he just said it's something she needs to share with the group and that her reasoning is sound.

Over the last week, we buckled down and made sure Blake's false trail looked like he had left the country and our tracks were covered.

After Rogue texted that she had arrived safe and sound in her rented apartment in San Francisco, Lucas went to the gym with a big-ass grin and more enthusiasm in his training than I've seen from him in a long while.

He usually does his shit, occasionally listens to Han on how to improve, and stops as soon as he's completed his workout. That day, he was lifting weights with a smile, running on the treadmill with a spring in his step, and had his phone in his hand all day, waiting for more texts.

The next day, I made her promise to text the group chat with periodic updates so I wouldn't have to watch Lucas go crazy with worry when he didn't hear from her for more than a few hours. Sleep, apparently, shouldn't come between texts.

Her stitches were due to come out a few days after she left, and she called us via video chat to see the wound. She's done stitch removal like this on her own before, and her steady hand as she pulled the thread from her body impressed me. Once she was thread-free, proving yet again what a badass she is, we were told a bit about who she's been following up there.

She explained that Neil Carter had set up shop with a protection ring and was taking liberties in Gambit territory.

She rented an apartment near his home and is doing some recon. He's got two mistresses that she knows of and a ton of bodyguards, but so far, there's been no connection to other players in the area. She thinks he's working with The Rattlesnakes, who control the Pacific Northwest territory. They have a treaty with The Gambit and surrounding organizations, but tensions have consistently run high between them.

She's been there five days and is due back today. The guys have been antsy since she texted the group chat this morning, saying she was coming home. It gave me a little flutter when she referred to the warehouse as 'home.' I didn't expect that reaction, but there it was, all the same. I don't know what to make of that.

We're all on edge when she's away, as I would be with any teammate

The Secrets We Keep

operating solo. But, as Jacob reminds us, she can handle herself. We don't need to worry. She's been mindful about texting the group, so we know she's okay. But her little thumbs-up emojis are driving me insane because they include no relevant information.

That little jealous pang starts to build. I think Rogue is incredible. She's obviously been through a lot, yet her demeanor is always sweet and kind when not dispatching low-lives. My life has been missing that sweetness for the last couple of years.

I had a wife until three years ago, and while I can't see myself forming a deep attachment again, I miss having someone to lean on. My wife didn't know my job's true nature; she just thought I ran a few companies' security teams. I had to keep much of my life hidden from her, and I know now that I shut down and stopped connecting because I couldn't share everything with her. I understand a lot of that is on me. We were doomed from the start.

She became resentful of the long hours, days, and weeks away on assignment, as anyone would. She later claimed that those resentments led to her cheating. I only found out way after the fact when Callie, the daughter we had been excited for, made her entrance into the world and needed surgery and a blood transfusion. They asked for ours since it might be easier for her body to accept.

Mine didn't match. At all. It led to a paternity test, which showed that sweet angel wasn't mine.

The build-up of those nine months was suddenly crumbling down around me, and I was lost. I divorced Sheila and let her keep our house. I didn't want to drag anything out for the sake of Callie's stability.

Sheila and William, the father of Callie, ended up getting together full-time, and I moved into the warehouse permanently.

I am not built for a woman who has multiple partners. My past has tainted that option for me. I love my team, and I wish them all the best. As much as I like Rogue and find her fascinating and sexy, I can't see myself ever giving someone that level of trust again.

The receptionist for the top floor walks to the waiting area to gather us and lead us to the conference room. We all take seats around the table and leave three free for the board members—despite them only needing two. But no one else knows that.

Patton Cross and Mara Hendrix walk in and sit in their cushy chairs. Mara looks around the room, nods acknowledgment to all of us, and starts the meeting. She's wearing a smart pantsuit, and her red-orange hair is swept into a severe bun at the base of her neck. She looks more like a librarian than an information technology specialist. Cross is wearing his usual black suit and tie with his shiny shoes on display as he sprawls out in the chair, crossing one leg over the other.

"Good afternoon, team leaders. We called you in to let you know we are missing Richard Blake." I feign a look of surprise to match the other five leaders in the room when Mara makes the announcement. "He was last seen a week ago here in his office. We received a letter of resignation from his personal stationery, and there was mention of wrongdoings in his personal life." Thank God for Han breaking into Blake's office the day before the meeting with him and swiping some of that letterhead.

We mailed it to the company the following day from his neighborhood so the post office's printed code would match. Blake was notoriously terrible at technology. He used pen and paper for most things and then handed everything to his secretary to type up and digitalize. A letter would have been expected as opposed to an email.

When Jacob returned from dropping off Lucas and Rogue, he removed evidence of our spying from the hotel room. Lucas continued working at the hotel for a few more days to ensure the room was cleaned up and returned to its proper state.

He's been keeping his ear to the ground if any workers noticed one of the maid's carts missing. We had to move the body somehow, and this was the best way for our cleanup team to get it downstairs through the service halls.

"While we want three of our teams to search for Blake, we have other assignments for the remaining three of you." A reasonable reaction, but why are they looking for Blake if he 'resigned'? We set up a trail that shows him flying to the Balkans.

The six of us nod in agreement and wait for the assignments to be handed out.

Patton takes up the conversation, "Teams one, two, and three: you're on finding Blake. Teams four, five, and six: you are to divide what's on the agenda in the shared folder and complete it. Adhere to the dates on the files, and you'll get your bonuses."

A shared folder on the main servers has assignments sorted by priority. The bonuses for handling those assignments paid for our warehouse and the renovations. It's no mere pocket change.

Naturally, we're Alpha Team One, so we'll be able to handle the Blake thing and guide the other teams to our false trail. We discussed the possibility of a search, and when it is something high-profile and needs discretion, one of the top three teams usually handles it. It's rare for three teams to be assigned one task. Blake, being a board member, must buy him some extra manpower.

After Mara releases us, we leaders turn to each other and start divvying up the work. As we divide and conquer, the frosted glass door swings inward, and an older Hispanic man dressed in a nice suit with a flower in his lapel walks in.

"Ah, gentlemen, this is Enrique De la Cruz. He's here to assist the first three teams with their search. He is a friend of Blake's and doesn't believe he would just disappear without contact. Use him in your investigation, please."

As we speak with him about his concerns, my phone vibrates in my pocket. I slip it out, covertly scanning the screen under the table.

Trouble: *Hey, Captain Atom. I'm just going to call you Captain from now on, k? What do you want for dinner?*

The text takes me by surprise, and I repress a grin that she's thinking of me while she's got the other three at her beck and call. Her little nickname for me has stuck; even Lucas has tried using it on me once or twice over the past week. That got shut down quickly. I don't mind when Rogue does it, but it's weird coming from him.

Me: *Surprise me, Trouble.* :winky emoji:

Ah, shit, now I'm using emojis like Lucas. What is happening to me?

Jacob

Rogue got home around half past four from her recon in San Francisco. As soon as I saw her in the Bel Air on the security monitor, I buzzed her into the parking area and unlocked the front door before she had even reached for her phone to use the app I installed.

When she got out and moved around to the trunk, I called for the guys, and we all went out to help bring stuff in. She still had to carry some of it, despite Lucas insisting he could take all of it. What is it about grocery bags that make you want to drag them all in at once?

She dropped her bag off to the side and led us into the kitchen, where she taught Han and Lucas how to make tamales and empanadas while I continued sifting through data.

As the food was cooking, she took the opportunity to put away her stuff and check in with each of us. She also gave me a proper snog, and if that's how she likes to be welcomed back, I'll gladly oblige every time.

I love spending time with her and seeing her soft side, one-on-one and in our group setting. She settled into the team naturally, as if she had always been here. Even Noah seems to be softening to her, and he's suspicious of everyone. I mean, hell, to keep our location a secret, we don't even get pizza delivered here. The only person to come here is Mrs. M, and she still won't tell us how she found us. She just rocked up to the gate in her Shaggin' Wagon and called me to demand I open the door. Yet, as soon as Rogue agreed to work with us, he got on board without issue.

Last week, I was admittedly a bit down when Rogue said she didn't do relationships. I am a relationship guy. I'm the best fucking boyfriend ever. But I'll take our non-commitment arrangement over nothing at all.

While Rogue was away, I replayed my moments with her repeatedly. I swear I can still smell her on my pillow, even after washing my sheets. And I may or may not have snuggled up with that pillow when I awoke over the last few days.

Remembering sharing her with Han has my cock hardening, and I've given up trying to repress it at this point. Working together, bringing her to the brink over and over again, only to watch her scream out her ecstasy, has become my go-to in the shower when I want to get myself off.

Three days ago, I was sparring with Han, and his hand wrapped around my arm, setting off the memory unexpectedly. I had to excuse myself to have a wank before he caught a glimpse of my hard-on.

By the time I was pumping my cock with my head thrown back as the water beat down on me, the image had changed to me fucking Han, who had Rogue impaled by his dick while under him as she chanted both our names. Something about the three of us just works for me.

It was out of the blue, hot as fuck, and only something I'd briefly considered in the past.

Han and I have been friends for a while, but I've always found him attractive. How does one bring that up without it being awkward as hell if he doesn't have the same interest in me? I thought I'd seen something in his eye over the years, but I've never been sure if it was just me reading into things.

Being with Rogue and Han a few weeks ago has beckoned the notion to the forefront of my mind again. I know it's something I'll have to bring up with them at some point, but what if it's all in my head?

Noah makes it back from the meeting at Annex around eight o'clock.

Rogue is just finishing up dinner while Lucas nurses a burn he got as he was trying to help. Since she left for upstate, he's been peppering everyone with questions for date night ideas to "woo" Rogue. He called us all useless and turned to Mrs. M for help instead.

Dinner ready, table set and all team members accounted for, we all gather around the island to tuck into the food that smells goddamned heavenly. Noah starts going over what we've been assigned to at Annex since that takes some priority, and it will be noted if we wait to start pretending to look.

We knew they could put someone on finding Blake, so good that we set up a false trail. It leads him to Montenegro, and we can track the other teams' progress on the slim chance we missed something.

When Noah reaches the part about this Enrique guy showing up at the meeting, Rogue drops her fork.

"Buttercup, what is it?" Lucas asks with concern. He instantly moves to stand behind her, and his hands reach around her midsection.

"Red, I'm not choking. Do not Heimlich me."

"Then, what's up?" asks Han.

"Enrique De La Cruz? What did he look like?" she directs to Noah. Her expression has gone from carefree to stoic in an instant.

"About six foot one, Hispanic, bald-headed, dark skin, wearing a pinstripe suit with—"

"With a purple flower on the lapel?" she finishes for Noah. He nods his head.

"Oh, fuck. De La Cruz is on the board of The Gambit, and he just walked into your offices? There's our connection."

"What?!" Noah and Han sputter at the same time.

"Jinx!" Rogue shouts victoriously, punching her fist into the air.

Lucas beams with pride and leans forward to kiss Rogue on her crown from where he's still standing behind her. "That's my girl," he whispers in her ear. Raising his voice, he continues as Noah and Han both glare at him. Wrong time to be jinxed. Rogue shrugs and shovels another bite of tamale into her mouth.

"Jacob, you and Buttercup hit the web to see if you can find out exactly how deeply these two are connected. Dear Leader, you correspond with the other teams to see where they're starting their Blake search. Offer to work together and steer their investigations. Mech, you're on deck tonight to do the dishes and clean the warehouse. I'll run point today since, you know, Dear Leader can't." He ends his instructions with a grin, no doubt loving that he holds some power now.

He's careful not to use their names. It isn't a double jinx; only one utterance of their name, and they'll be able to speak again. Lucas takes this game way too seriously. We indulge him because he's our family, and it makes him happy.

I love Lucas like a damn brother and would take a bullet for the bastard, but the last time he wasn't jinxed while the rest of us were, he took the opportunity to do some genuinely awful pranks. I do not want to relive those. Han still cowers in fear every time he hears a whipped cream dispenser.

"Han, Noah," I sigh, releasing them from their silence after only a few minutes. "Lucas made a good plan. Let's get to it."

They agree and get to work after sticking their dishes in the dishwasher as Lucas grumbles about his power being stripped.

Han starts gathering the pots and serving plates to scrub up while Noah heads to the meeting room, and we veer off to my office. We agreed to meet up again when Han finished his task. Rogue can walk us through The Gambit and all the information she can grab from the servers.

Now that the two organizations are clearly working together, we need all the intel we can get. And we need it soon. Pulling all the info shouldn't be an issue, but it's a lot. It'll take some time to download. We'll work side by side as we dive in and unpick it all.

I lead Rogue to my computer setup in my glass-walled office, giving her my gamer chair to use while I pull over an uncomfortable office chair from the meeting room.

No one, and I mean no one, sits in my chair. Unless, of course, it's a gorgeous girl with raven hair that makes my dick hard by just walking by.

We each have a keyboard and get to work. I already hacked most of Blake's stuff when we made him disappear, and there wasn't a lot since he hated technology. Still, we didn't see any link to this Enrique guy, so I'll recheck everything now that we know exactly who we're looking for a connection with.

Rogue works for about half an hour on The Gambit member's side while I go through Blake's shit with a fine-tooth comb. She uses a back entrance to The Gambit servers.

When she sees me focusing on her work instead of my own, she lifts a shoulder and says, "I hid a back door in the HR files to easily maneuver from the legal side to the illegal without raising too many red flags."

The Secrets We Keep

I'm impressed. Rogue used someone named Tanaka as a gateway between Rook Industries and The Gambit. He's the CEO of Rook, so no one will be looking through his file too much—bloody brilliant hiding spot.

She gets in, finds what she's looking for, and starts a data dump onto one of our hard drives. The spinning wheel and loading bar tell us it'll take an hour or so. She uses the time to lean on my shoulder and watches me work as I skim through Blake's info.

After ten minutes of mindless code, I feel her lips on my neck over my crown tattoo. Her kisses are soft, but then she uses her tongue to lick a line from my shirt collar to my ear. I lose focus entirely and swivel in my chair to face her.

Her hands run up my pecs and settle on my shoulders. She launches herself at me, and because this shitty chair doesn't have armrests, she's able to straddle me immediately.

This is the best chair ever made.

Her hands continue mapping my chest, and she brings them to my front to undo the buttons on my shirt. "Jacob, I need you."

Oh, thank the Queen. We've been too busy for anything between the injury, hits on dealers, Blake, and her trip to do anything other than make out before exhaustion runs us over. We haven't had sex, but the way Lucas asked if we had while Rogue was away makes me think they had. Lucky bugger.

I growl low in my throat as the rest of my shirt is ripped apart, buttons flying in all directions. Rogue lowers her head and kisses me desperately.

She unbuckles my black leather belt and undoes my trousers. I lift high enough to assist in pulling them down to my thighs, and she drops between my legs. Her tongue trails down my stomach as she makes her way to my straining black boxer briefs.

Her nails scrape lightly over my nipples, and I shiver. They continue south until she has them hooked into my waistband. She pulls my underwear down to join my pants in a tangle near my knees and leans forward. I fist a hand in her hair and direct her where I need her most.

"Suck my cock, Love," I groan out in a tone that brooks no argument.

Her tongue traces my dick, and she flicks the piercings as she goes by them.

She asked about them last week, and I told her they're called a Jacob's Ladder. She snorted and said it worked, given that my name is Jacob. Apparently, she has a thing about apt names.

I also have a Prince Albert piercing, which feels incredible with each lick and stroke of her tongue. The pull of the metal, the heat of her mouth, the caress of her tongue... When she grips the base with her hand and opens her mouth to direct me in, I almost lose my shit like a teenager getting his first blowie.

She teases me with small strokes before sucking me down. She reaches about halfway before coming back up again. Rogue continues her descent, going further each time she bobs her head until her gag reflex kicks in at about the three-quarter mark.

Her lips are stretched wide to fit me in, and her cherry red lipstick has smeared all over my cock. It's an image I'll carry with me forever. Despite her determination to take me to the hilt, I don't want her to hurt herself. I'm a bit bigger than most, and I know the piercings cause a bit of a hindrance with oral if you're not used to them.

I'm getting close to coming, but I'd rather come in her hot pussy than her mouth. I haven't had her to myself like this, and I'm determined to pleasure her, not just take what I want. I'm a man desperate and on edge.

Clenching my jaw to keep myself in control, I order her up.

Hooking my hands under her arms, I haul her up and into my lap. Her skirt settles over us as she grinds herself on my dick, and I hike it up to her waist. I fist the crotch of her panties and pull, ripping yet another pair in my enthusiasm. Whoops.

I'll need to buy her more if I keep doing this to the few pairs she brought from home.

Before my mind can take off in the direction of Rogue modeling lacy lingerie for me privately, she settles on my lap, and she's so wet she takes me partway into her pussy. She instantly locks up as my cock is engulfed in her heat, and I struggle to maintain a clear head while every instinct in my body is demanding I push into her with everything I've got.

"Are you STD-free?" she asks, wigging out that we didn't put a condom on and smacking a hand to her forehead in a real-life, honest-to-God facepalm.

"Yes, I tested a month ago and haven't had sex since. Birth control?"

"IUD, but we need a condom," she responds quickly. Agreed. Surprise babies and super-secret spy colleagues probably don't mix.

I nudge her off of me, and despite her whimpers of protest, she complies because she knows the condom is vital.

Grabbing the hem of her sweater top, I pull it over her head and watch as her tits spill out of the top of her bra. Is that her mobile in there? I pull out the phone and toss it onto the chair behind me. The white lace is losing the battle with her full tits; I pull the cups under, resisting the urge to motorboat the fuck out of her.

Skirt still rucked up around her waist, I spin her around and push her forward onto the desk in front of us until her tits are flush against the glass tabletop. She lets out a whimper at the cool temperature but stays where I've positioned her. I whip my belt from my trousers' loops and fashion a quick knot with her hands through either side. I pull to tighten it, and her hands rest above her ass, locked together.

"Okay, Love?" I ask to be sure. I don't know her preferences, but I can tell she's tired of being wrapped in cotton wool by us.

"Yes, Jacob. Fuck me." She ends her demand with a groan as my hand tightens around the length of the belt. Her breath fogs the monitor in front of her. I snag my wallet, now hanging from my back pocket, and grab the condom out of it as quickly as possible. I hold the foil pack in front of her face. She grips a corner with her teeth, and I pull the packet away so it opens. Teamwork makes the damn dream work. Rolling it on, I feel my hands shaking in anticipation.

I slide my condom-covered cock up and down her slit a few times, coating my dick in her juices, then line up and push inside her. I slide in effortlessly despite my size, and it feels like coming home. I hold the tail end of the belt so her arms are taut behind her, and I lean back to get a different angle. Her moan that breaks free is glorious, and I feel like a man unchained as I pound into her from behind. My hand reaches around to find her clit, and I start rubbing slow, taunting circles.

She shouts out a curse, and my name is ripped from her throat as she comes. Her body begins to quiver below mine. I release the knot on her hands, her palms slamming the desk on either side of her head.

She starts pushing back into me after I give her a moment to recover. She tries to take control and top from the bottom. "Oh, no, Love. I'm in charge here. Keep that arse up and stay still." My accent isn't the only thing that grows thicker with each stroke inside her.

"Jacob, keep talking," she pants out. A smug smile takes over my face, and my hand grips her hip hard enough to leave fingerprint bruises on her delicate skin as I keep her steady. My other hand draws up just to come back down and deliver a slap to her round ass that has the color pinking nicely.

She squeezes my dick and lets out a moan as my hand connects again, this time to soothe away the sting. I feel her walls clenching as I continue thrusting into her, and when it seems they can't get any tighter, she comes with such a roar and a vise grip on my cock that I can't help but follow.

"Good girl," I murmur and leave a trail of kisses up her back and over her shoulder until I reach her ear, biting on the lobe. A shiver overtakes her body, and a tightening around my dick has me already thinking about round two.

As she steadies, I spin and haul her into my arms, collapsing onto the chair with her astride me. I hear clapping coming from nearby and turn my head. Rogue follows my direction, and we both look out into the central area of the warehouse through the glass wall to see Noah, Han, and Lucas awarding us a standing ovation.

I worry about how Rogue will react to our audience, but she just drops her head back and laughs.

Chapter Fifteen

Rogue

I'm still coming down from my orgasm, nestled into Jacob's warm body, when I hear the clapping. Jacob whips his head to the side, and I follow suit. There, in the middle of the goddamned clubhouse, are Han, Lucas, and Noah, applauding us and smiling through the glass walls. Glass. Fucking. Walls. Oops.

I tip my head back and laugh because what else is there to do? They've all seen what just happened. I can only be thankful Jacob's tattooed back must have blocked a lot of their view of me. I'm confident in my skin. I love my body for helping me survive, but that doesn't necessarily mean I want to be seen getting railed by my sexy Brit.

Especially by Noah.

He's been accommodating, if not a bit distant since I've been on the team, and I see how hard he works at keeping the other three hooligans in line. He's pretty austere, but I see him joking around and volleying playful insults back and forth with Lucas during their downtime, so I know there's some humor under his unshakable facade. I just don't want to add more to his plate.

Seeing his new recruit getting fucked can't have been high on his priority list.

I see a twinkle in Lucas's eye from here. He leans to his left toward

Han, and I watch his lips move to form the words "standing O against the wall later" on the tail end of a whisper. Han, my darling Han, socks Lucas in the stomach and walks away with a laugh. I don't know whether to be excited for that later or uneasy that they're discussing fucking me this openly with each other. I decide to let it go. We all know the score among the four of us.

What surprises me is the flash of emotion in Noah's eyes when he hears Lucas's quip. As he turns toward Jacob and me, the sentiment remains, but his eyes fill with fire.

Lucas and Noah disperse, so Jacob and I take the opportunity to race upstairs and get cleaned up for the meeting. After a quick shower and a change into some leggings and one of Lucas's Deadpool shirts I find in my drawer, I make my way downstairs and into the war room.

Lucas's eyes zero in on the shirt, and a proud grin overtakes his face. He hops up from the couch to meet me at the foot of the stairs. "I wanted you to wear my shirts too. I hope it's okay that I snuck a few in your dresser while you were gone." He has a vulnerable look in his eye, and I wrap my arms around him in a big hug.

I tilt my head up and whisper, "I love it. The Merc with a Mouth and I are kindred spirits. It smells like you."

Lucas groans, and I'm instantly reminded of him grinding into me in this spot just before I left for San Francisco. No! Bad Rogue. No time. I can't hop off one dick and onto another, can I? No, seriously. Can I? Ugh, no.

This talk has to happen. I made Lucas promise to let me tell the guys about my sister, and that conversation needs to transpire now.

I cup his cheek and guide him in for a kiss that gets far too heated, far too quickly. I break the kiss, panting again, "Let's go, Red. I've got a secret to share."

Settling in our usual seats, I kick us off with a quick rundown of The Gambit's board members. The data I collected is ready; we'll sort and go through everything in the morning, as it's already nearing midnight. After naming everyone in the top tier, I write their names on the whiteboard we use for strategy.

"Finally," I start, "I have something to share about why I killed Blake and my second condition of working with you." I look around nervously and make eye contact with each of the men.

I think I shatter their brains with the information that follows. "The girl you will help me remove from The Gambit is my sister, Sage. She has been helping me gather information from the organization's escorts."

The guys are collectively frozen as the information soaks in. Han is the first to speak. "So, when Blake mentioned his favorite prostitute... that's why you snapped?" I just nod at his question. My eyes are downcast, and I'm somewhat afraid of their reaction. I don't want them to look down on her for the job she was forced into.

"She and I have been separated since we were kids. She was sent away. I don't know where. We were only allowed to see each other once in a while, as she was two when she was taken away and raised elsewhere. She was used as my reward when I did something right and vice versa. While I run the organization's hits, she is the bargaining chip over my head. She and I have a way of communicating when we do see each other, but we have to be cautious because King either comes with or monitors from afar."

Noah swears under his breath, and I see the slight tremor in his hand resting on the table. This barely controlled rage is not something I've ever seen from him, but I know what the beginning signs of a man-trum look like.

I reach across the table and gather up his big hand in mine. He raises his head and meets my eyes. Tears well in mine and fall as his thumb gently wipes one away. "No one knows about her relation to me except King," I explain.

I neglect to mention that King chose to raise me. I've dropped one bomb today, and to be completely honest, I'm terrified of how they'll look at me when they know a monster has raised me. That tidbit will keep for one more day. I can't take another big reveal today.

Tomorrow.

"Buttercup, we'll figure out how to get her away from The Gambit. We will find her. We will get her out of there and here with us," Lucas vows somberly in a tone I've never heard from him.

While the guys recover from the revelation, I shake off my tears and explain how my sister and I communicate. I should be able to see her as soon as the last dealer is handled, so we'll discuss what information I need to pass on to her.

When the clock ticks over to half-past two and we've got a decent plan in place, we call it a night and plan to dig through the information we have on The Gambit members in the morning. I'm emotionally wrung out after sharing my most guarded secret. All I want to do is curl up in a ball and sleep for a week.

We all stand to stretch and make our way to our beds. Jacob grabs my hand as we climb the stairs, and I look over my shoulder to see Han and Lucas following. No words are spoken as we enter Jacob's room, and we all crawl into bed together. Jacob is on my right, Han is on my left, and Lucas is halfway up my body, resting between my legs with his head on my stomach.

I drift off quickly after my long day, or rather, week, surrounded by hard bodies and soft touches, all the while thinking about how it is both terrifying and relieving to have shared my secret, thus sharing the burden.

IT'S BEEN NEARLY A MONTH SINCE I MOVED INTO THE GUYS' clubhouse—aka warehouse—and two weeks since I unveiled my sister, and yet, I don't want to leave. They want me to stay until this whole thing is wrapped up, but part of me worries that I'm taking advantage of their hospitality. Every time I bring it up, it gets shot down immediately.

Things are going well thus far. We're working on angles for the remaining two Annex board members. With all the data I was able to sift out of the servers for The Gambit, we've been putting together a decent framework of how we can start to manage my board members as well. I just wish there weren't nine million players to deal with.

I've finished the list of dealers Enrique provided me with, and thankfully, there were no more incidents. I changed tactics for each dealer, so I haven't been caught unaware like I was in that shitty bathroom when that dickhead dealer brought his five friends with him to his execution.

The final one I went after was in hiding. It took me nearly a week to ferret the last dealer out, but when one has a nicotine addiction, you just have to watch long enough for them to step out to buy a pack of smokes at the corner store.

There are only a finite number of places in the city with a don't-ask-don't-tell, cash-only policy to rent from. Dealers don't tend to have many friends to count on for a sofa to crash on, so they mostly hide at shitty motels.

With my work for The Gambit winding down, my only focus for them is Neil Carter.

I found him in the Castro District in San Francisco last month. He had set up shop in a three-unit house and conducted most of his business downtown in the Tenderloin.

His routine was easy to follow, but after observing him, it's clear he isn't the main one in charge. He may be running the streets and taking over some territory, but someone is backing him.

I'm working on the details, but I need to go back up and find a way in. The info I gathered has been passed along to King, along with the completed list of dealers, and it earned me an hour with Sage in Santa Barbara, a city three hours from El Castillo on the coast.

I reached the address King texted me five minutes before the appointed time, nerves fluttering in my stomach. Parking Black Beauty on one of the small beach streets, I got out and made my way to a tiny white cottage with a teal fence, texting the guys that I'd arrived.

Sage doesn't live here; I don't know where she lives. This house is one of The Gambit's properties. King has wired this place to hell and back with cameras, microphones, and enough men loyal to him that even I might have difficulty taking all of them down. All of these measures serve to prevent Sage or me from sharing too many personal details.

I go through the small gate in the fence and walk up the stone path to the front door. Before I can knock, Sage yanks the door open and pulls me into her arms. She's five years younger than me, making her only two when our parents passed and we were separated. I don't know much about her childhood, but I'm thankful she didn't grow up with King as a surrogate father, and I can only pray hers was better than mine.

We were kept apart except when I did well with King's lessons. So, we only saw each other once every six months until I graduated and started work for The Gambit. I started doing more difficult hits, and King rewarded me with more frequent visits to a preteen Sage. It's an abnormal feeling—being simultaneously thankful for the gift of seeing her and murderous at the man who tore her away from me.

Seeing her now has me freezing on the spot. She's thin. Way too thin. Her long blonde hair is slightly matted, and I can see her makeup smudged on her face. She's been working as one of the escorts and subtly trying to gain information for me. At the beginning and end of our meetings, our hugs are our chances to slip notes to each other without the King's men catching on to read later.

Our visits are short, stilted, and never dive deeper than surface shit. King watches our meetings via live stream for any overshares using the cameras in the houses where he sets up our rendezvous. He has replayed our conversations and beaten me nearly to death for speaking about running away together one day. I only made that mistake once.

The notes started about four years ago. I could share more, offer assurances that we'll be out of this mess soon, and give encouragement to keep hanging on. Sage's letters back have been sweet and quirky. She's got a sarcastic attitude, and she's brilliant.

Doing this shit must be taking her will to live more than mine. I don't mind taking down disgusting men; she, unfortunately, has to fuck them.

I use the hug her bony arms engulf me in to slip the note into the pocket of her dress. It's a loose sundress, and I keep my movements small and settle my hands on her narrow hips to tell her it's done.

The team and I discussed what to include in this note and what we needed to find out. If Sage has any information or can gather some, it would help us immensely. We're looking for credible gossip about the board, places they frequent, and escorts they use. We need a way to get to them that doesn't include walking into Rook Industries armed to the teeth and opening fire where someone else could get hurt.

We pass the time quietly, sharing mundane details of our lives and asking about recent experiences, all while being monitored. When Sage brings up my dating life, my face flushes, and I pretend to sneeze, hoping King doesn't notice it on one of the video feeds.

I do not need him to know I'm seeing someone—make that *someones*. Plural. I've had lovers in the past, but they were out of the picture so fast he wouldn't even need to bother checking on them. The only one that could have been a problem for King was Han.

I tried to keep him as far away from King's radar as possible. I only showed at the Fight Nights sporadically, then, of course, dropping off the face of the earth there at the end.

These guys might cause a more visceral reaction to our cohabitation and general scheming.

After an hour, King texts me to say time's up, and we say goodbye. With our parting hug, she slips a note into the back of my corset top. I always have an open back for our visits so she can easily stuff notes inside. I don't even bother checking them until I reach home in case I'm being followed on the drive.

My note to her is coded, as hers is to me. I gave her a cipher key a few years ago that translated letters and ubiquitous words into shapes and small doodles. She memorized and destroyed it; that way, Sage could claim she was doodling if anyone came upon a letter either of us wrote.

The Secrets We Keep

I arrive at the clubhouse after stopping off at my apartment. I hope I lost any possible tails. As a bonus, I got to grab some more underwear. Jacob keeps ruining mine.

Lucas meets me at the front gate. He stands there with a grin as the steel gate slides along the tracks to open. It's rolling along at a glacial pace, and his grin is starting to look forced.

He's regretting his decision to smile that big from the beginning. Finally, it's wide enough for me to drive in, and he meets me at my newly designated parking spot, opening the door for me.

"Why, thank you, kind sir," I mock as he tips an imaginary cap.

He leans in for a kiss, and I return it gladly. "We're meeting with everyone quickly, then if you feel up to it, I'd like to take you out like we talked about. Sorry it kept getting delayed, what with all the killing and spying."

My pulse picks up pace, and I find myself nodding quickly. "Yes! That sounds perfect. What are we doing?"

"Ah, ah, Buttercup. You'll have to wait and see." He leads me to the door and straight across to the war room. We do all of our diabolical planning here, so the name fits nicely.

Before I step in, I veer off to the downstairs bathroom quickly, holding up one finger to indicate I'll just be a moment. I was so rushed to get back here that I didn't pee or read the note at my apartment, so I take the opportunity to do both quickly.

After reading the code on Sage's note, my brain was melting, and I knew I needed to keep my nerves until I could broach the topic. I wash my hands and refold the letter. Placing it into the front of my top, I turn the handle and school my face. I still need a few minutes to process, but the guys have to know what King's up to.

When I enter the war room, Noah and Jacob are chatting about Mara Hendrix, the next Annex member on our list. Han is standing in front of the board, looking at The Gambit's members' information. He's tracing lines to and from the few photos we collected to memorize the connections and specialties.

Tanaka, Batten, and King had images drifting around the web, but the others have kept a low profile, so we agreed I'd snap some photos at the next board meeting. Their employee files didn't even have pictures.

We don't want anyone to be caught off guard like we were when De La Cruz walked into Annex a few weeks ago at Noah's meeting.

Jacob is the first to notice me come in, and he leans over in his chair to plant a sultry kiss on my lips. Han follows suit and goes in with more passion than I'd expect in front of Noah and his other teammates. I'd really, really like to spend some time with Han soon.

There's a ton of nerves on my end regarding Han. Yeah, we've done everything except have sex since we've reconnected, but I'm almost afraid the real-life thing won't live up to the memory I've clung to for so long.

We've been working out every morning that I'm not out on the job, and watching his muscles flex and bunch has me changing my panties far too regularly. I'll need to buy stock in Agent Provocateur between him and Jacob. Or fuck, if they keep getting ripped, I'm just going to Target. Five-dollar panties rip just as well as two-hundred-dollar ones, right?

Noah nods his head to welcome me back, but I swear I see a slight blush on his cheeks under his short beard. "How was Sage?"

"Good, thanks. A little thinner than I'd like, but overall okay." The note is burning a hole in my corset, and I'm amped to tell the guys what Sage managed to discover and why King's followers are so loyal to him.

"Something to consider as we move forward: The escorts involved with The Gambit are not there willingly. At least, a lot of them aren't." My declaration hangs in the air while their views of my organization drop to an impossibly low level. And here I thought they were as low as could be already.

I pull the note out of my pocket and unfold it. Noah swipes up the letter and attempts to read it with a furrow in his brow. I gave them the list of symbols last week, but it takes time to decipher if you need to get used to it. "What does all of this mean?"

I broke it down for him by going through the code Sage and I use. "She says she's met about fifty different girls at various events over the past few months, all managed by the same company—the same one she works for that The Gambit controls. She isn't allowed private contact with others, but she subtly chatted with them at functions.

"You know how her freedom is dependent on me and my work? Well, she thinks the others are the same. The Gambit is using their members' loved ones to keep them in line. The people they take as leverage are cut off from the world, forced into prostitution or other avenues, and abide for fear of retribution."

A cloud of rage fills the room as I look at the stony glances in each of their eyes. It's a theory Sage and I have been working on for a few years now, and at a recent party, she was able to talk to a lot of the other girls while their "dates" were playing poker. The girls who were brave enough to speak up said they were in a similar situation to Sage. I'm going to fucking murder King.

Lucas

"Another One Bites the Dust" is playing repeatedly in my head after seeing Noah's stunned reaction to Buttercup's revelations earlier this afternoon. He was angry for the women in this situation, but he was even more enraged on behalf of Rogue. She's been doing all this alone to get her sister out.

I throw in some hip action as the words go round and round while carrying the basket to the truck. Freddie Mercury was too good for this world.

It's about five o'clock now, and the sun should be setting soon. It's mid-October, and the weather has a stranglehold on the last vestiges of warmth. Rogue follows me to the truck and laughs at my antics. She doesn't know why I'm thrusting because she can't hear the song in my head but enjoys it all the same.

We load up and head out to the coast. I started planning a theme park, a gun range, or even mini-golfing for our date, but thanks to some input and the picnic basket from Mama Bear, I was reined in a bit.

Mrs. M suggested doing something Buttercup wouldn't expect—showing her my softer side and getting to know each other. I know she isn't looking for commitment, but we've already slept together and don't know much about each other besides work. Like I said before, I want to know everything.

We cruise for about thirty minutes while arguing over radio stations until we finally crest the last hill and reach the shore. I pull into a spot along the sand and run around the truck to help her out. She climbs out gently and pulls me in for a sweet kiss. She's so soft and nurturing when she isn't killing people.

I hook the basket in one arm and pull the backpack over the other, slinging it over my back. I use that arm to tuck around Rogue's waist and lead her to the surf. We stop about ten feet from the water's edge, and I pull out the blankets and set us up. Her curiosity gets the better of her, and I catch her peeking into the basket.

The sun is just starting to fade, but the weather's nice enough that we shouldn't get too cold. I've got backup blankets in case. Rogue pulls out the bottle of wine, salad, bread, and Fettuccine Alfredo that Mrs. M packed for us in little plastic tubs.

She lets out a groan when she sees the creamy pasta, and it makes me do a double-take, my brain conjuring images of us fucking here and now on the blanket in the sand. Not now, dude! I chastise my dick. Our date kept getting pushed back with everything we're handling, and I don't want to ruin it.

"So," she starts as she pulls the lids off the dishes happily, "what made you choose this for our date? I was expecting the unexpected from what I know about you. And in a way, I guess I wasn't wrong."

Point to Mrs. M for the suggestion.

"We end up in wild situations all the time, Buttercup. It'd be nice to relax for once.

After we clink our wine glasses, she makes a thoughtful noise and starts in on her food. We eat in peace as the sun sinks over the water. The sky plays in pinks and oranges before slowly fading to purple and indigo. It really is the perfect evening to watch the sunset.

After we are stuffed to the brim, I suddenly stand up and strip off my shirt. I hop on one foot, trying to pull one of my boots off, as Rogue laughs at me. "What are you doing?" she cries as I lose my balance and fall back into the sand.

"We're going swimming. Get naked!" I cry out.

She does not, in fact, get naked.

But she does take off her dress, and in her bra and panties, she grabs my hand and hauls us to the water. She carefully dips her toes into the receding surf, and before she can protest that it's too cold, I pull her into my arms and drag her into the water with me.

She's climbing me like a monkey to avoid the frigid temperatures, but I don't relent. Finally, when I'm at mid-chest, and she's sitting on my shoulders like a kid at a carnival, I flop forward, and she has no choice but to fall in with me.

She comes up sputtering and spits water into my eye. Mascara runs down her face; I swear she's never looked more beautiful.

We splash and play until the sun is gone, and she looks around like she's waiting for nocturnal sea monsters to wrap a tentacle around her leg and drag her under. I take her hand and guide her back to the safety of the sand, and we flop down on the blankets with towels wrapped around us.

Between sips of wine, she starts us off, "So, tell me about what you do when you're not in dangerous situations. I've seen the comic books, but that can't keep you busy constantly."

"You're right. It's a hobby I love, but I enjoy the artwork more than anything else. I planned to be a cartoonist or an animator before entering Annex."

My small confession has her eyes widening. I bite the bullet before she gets stuck on that little kernel of information. I want to be open and honest and be myself for the first time in a long time.

"I was orphaned when I was ten. My parents were in a car accident and didn't survive the impact. I didn't have any other family, so I was put in foster care. I still had almost eight years before I aged out, and I was bumped around a lot in that first year. My parents' deaths were torturous to get through, and I was a sad fuck most of the time. I got lucky with a lot of the families I was sent to, but some of the other kids were dicks. I had to learn to stick up for myself, which eventually led me to Annex.

"My artwork and sketchbooks were ripped to shreds sometimes, and the rage that came with that made me stop drawing. I couldn't stand to see all of my hard work in pieces scattered across the floor every few months."

"Lucas." She puts a hand on my forearm in both regret for what happened and encouragement to continue. Her eyes glisten with sympathy, but thankfully not pity, as she hears the pain in my voice.

"Like I said, most couples that took me in were fine; it could have been infinitely worse. But I got tired of moving around. I learned early on that if I was fun and made jokes, I stuck around longer. Being a brooding artist is not good for kids who want to get adopted. Too many mood swings." I shrug my shoulders at the last part.

She takes a deep breath and gives me more of her backstory. "You know my parents died when I was young. It was a drug overdose. We had our good and bad days as a family, but I never hated them more than when King took me in. That's why I'm part of The Gambit. He hired tutors and nannies to raise me, cut me off from Sage, and 'trained' me to be his assassin." Her finger quotes around the word trained raise more questions, but I know now isn't the time to push.

I brush a tear from her cheek and tuck her head into my shoulder.

Raised by King? We knew she was orphaned but didn't find out where she ended up after. We assumed it was a relative embedded somewhere within The Gambit, but knowing it was King, the fucking leader? Shit.

I agree to yet another promise that she'll be the one to tell the guys. She follows through on her commitments, and I know she won't keep it from them for long now that I know.

I'm totally the Buttercup whisperer. I need to make a mug that says that.

Our hands weave together, and we sit to watch the color bleed from the sky, comfortable in our shared connection.

Two orphans who've found each other.

Alone, together.

Chapter Sixteen

Rogue

After another phone call with King the morning after my date with Lucas, I push my way through the glass doors—bright and way too fucking early—and into the upper offices of Rook Industries. He's been asking after me, and the last thing I want to do is give him a reason to suspect anything. I'm coming for him. I'm coming for the whole damn board.

I've got to stop answering his calls first thing in the morning. They never lead to anything good.

I nod to a couple of the receptionists and don't bother to wait long enough for them to alert anyone I'm here. They should know better than to try to slow me down by now, anyway. I hear the whispers behind me, and a smirk graces my lips.

I may dress like a girly girl, but I'll still kick ass and keep my manicure perfect.

King is in his office on the phone. Surprise, surprise. He hangs up when he sees me through the glass and settles the phone face-down on the sprawling oak desk before him as I enter.

"Rogue, come sit," he says as he gestures to the club chairs opposite the desk.

He doesn't even do any work on the damn desk. He just likes the feeling of superiority when he does his job from here. All he does is direct people from his phone, and he could do that shit anywhere—pompous prick.

His office chair puts him a couple of inches taller than me, and I see his smug satisfaction when he looks down at me.

"King," I say as I settle in, my flared skirt folding around my thighs and covering me as I cross my legs. My black pumps sparkle a bit in this god-awful fluorescent lighting. The skull and crossbones on the heel look particularly menacing. Damn, I love these shoes.

"Daughter. Where are you on Neil Carter?" He's eerily calm. I know when he's calm, he's most dangerous.

"I was up in San Francisco last time we spoke, and I've been tracking him and his whereabouts. I'm heading back up to do some more recon this week. I'll figure out who he's working with and take him out."

"Very good," he says as he leans back in his padded chair. "Do I need to remind you of what happens if this isn't wrapped up soon?" he asks, and my hackles rise.

"No, King," I answer demurely and try to keep my annoyance out of my tone.

"One other thing, Rogue. You will see Sage once this next week as a reward for your work with the dealers, but then you won't see her for a little while. She will be otherwise engaged. However, I'll make her available when you settle this Neil business. I tried sending word to your apartment, but you've been 'unavailable.' Anything I should know about?"

My hands grip the armrests of the chair. The pressure turns my knuckles white, and I'm sure my nails leave divots in the brown leather. King cannot know I've been staying with the guys; he can't know about the guys, period.

"I understand about Sage, King. No, there's nothing to know. Like I said, I've been back and forth on the Neil thing and rooting out that last dealer. Finding which motel he was holed up in required a few stakeouts." At least that wasn't a lie. Shit. I'll need to spend some time at my apartment and ensure Jim and Hugo are still on Team Rogue.

His phone starts to ring, and he holds up a finger to indicate I wait, and I refrain from fidgeting while he answers. "Yes, send him in."

I quirk an eyebrow and wonder who he'd invite into our meeting, which, in all honesty, could have been handled over the damn phone. He gets off on the power he has to order me around—dragging me in for useless meetings, keeping Sage from me, and being a general killjoy.

Ah, the little things.

The door pushes open, and Enrique walks in. He's wearing one of his pinstripe suits, a white shirt, and that stupid small purple flower in the lapel. What now?

Enrique walks to my chair's twin and folds his big frame into the seat. He finally looks at me and greets me with a sneer. I respond in kind.

We've never seen eye to eye, and he blames me for the loss of income and immediate cash influx he would gain from selling to minors across the state. I'll happily take the blame for that small mercy I afforded the general population.

"Rogue," he greets, "I see from your periodic messages that you've handled all the dealers on my list."

"It was a walk in the park. Got any more for me?" I ask with a smile.

King just tips his head back and laughs. "Bloodthirsty, isn't she, De La Cruz? That's why she's my favorite." I resist the urge to give in to the bile creeping up my throat. Being this man's anything is not a position I want to be in.

King may be upset with me over one thing or another, but he never shows it in front of another board member. Perceived unity is how he keeps his flunkies in line, and Enrique is one of the flunkies. He rode King's coattails up from the bottom.

Enrique levels his eyes at me, then runs his gaze from my head to my toes and winks lasciviously when they return to my face. I fight the all-over body shiver trying to escape. I won't give him the satisfaction. I just blink my eyes from him to King. I know who holds power in this room, and it isn't the man with a flower on his jacket.

"Enrique says those are all the dealers he found selling to minors, but he had five others go missing. Any ideas of what happened to them?"

Ah, yes, the dickhead who invited his friends to his own funeral and gave me a new scar to add to my already full inventory. "I killed them when they sided with the dealer I was there for," I say casually.

"King, she can't just go around killing my guys. It takes time to train them and get them to sell as much product as possible," Enrique complains.

King's eyes flash in rage as he looks at the drug lord. "They wanted to take down Rogue. How did they know my daughter was coming, Enrique?"

This is a question I've been grappling with since the incident. Enrique must have warned some of them. Not all, obviously. Most were easy to dispatch, but the dickhead from the bathroom and the last guy on the list were a bit more challenging to track down and take care of. How did the last guy know to run?

Enrique shifts his eyes from me to King with an edgy look. "I didn't say anything," he protests too loudly.

"Rogue," King whispers, drawing my attention back from Enrique's protests. He's an idiot if he doesn't hear the barely concealed rage in King's voice. "You may go. Continue with the plan."

I nod and excuse myself from the room. I do not want to be there when King rips into Enrique. Literally or figuratively.

I exit the room, and the door swings shut behind me. I hear a crash from within the office and fight my instinct to turn around.

If Enrique had anything to do with those dealers cornering me and slicing me open, King would kill him. He laid a claim on me when he adopted me, and he takes threats to my life seriously. He may have been the worst adoptive father ever, but he's protective in his own way.

I start making my way to the elevator in the lobby when I hear Mr. Tanaka finishing up a conversation with someone. I slow my steps because seeing him and paying him my respects is always a treat. I keep postponing that meeting with him, and I feel pretty shitty about it. He handles a lot for the organization, and anyone with the patience to deal with King daily deserves my respect.

He finishes speaking with a glamorous Indian woman in a tailored dress, and she turns on her heel after giving him a grateful smile. Tanaka returns it, bids her a good day, and wishes her son feels better soon.

He turns just as I come within easy speaking distance. "Rogue, good to see you." He bows, and I return it with a warm smile.

"Mr. Tanaka, always a joy. It makes visiting this office entirely worth it."

He chuckles and stretches out an arm to indicate we move to his office. The space is well-used, worn-in, and inviting. He makes me a cup of tea, and I know he always keeps Darjeeling on hand for me because it's my favorite.

"How are you, Rogue? I only saw you once in the last month at that godawful meeting. You never come to visit me anymore." He pouts, and I can't contain the laugh that bursts from my lips. He plays the dad card well for a fifty-something corporate guy I only met because of our connection to the criminal world.

"Oh, Mr. Tanaka, does your wife know you've adopted me?" I gasp in mock horror, raising a hand to my chest. "Does King?"

We share a laugh, and his face turns serious for a moment. "Speaking of adoption, when was the last time you went to visit your parents' graves?" he asks, and I'm taken aback a bit. We never talk about my past. It's only known within the board that King adopted me when my parents died. No mention of graves or plots. For all anyone knows, they're in an urn on my mantle or buried somewhere on the East Coast.

"Uhm, about a month ago or so, why?" I ask curiously.

"Just wondering. I love those old cemeteries. Did you know if you move the plaque at the back of some statues or headstones, there's a small space inside?" Tanaka muses cryptically.

I don't know what direction this is going, but when he winks, I know he's giving me a clue. To what? I have no idea, but I will need to figure it out.

If he knew about the graves and the statue over them, could he have been the one to take a shot at me the last time I was there? If he's leading me there, will there be another attempt on my life?

"Interesting," I respond dryly. "I'm heading out of town, but maybe I'll check it out when I return."

No way in hell am I waiting that long to figure out what he's hinting at.

I SCAN THE AREA WHEN I STEP OUT OF THE UBER AND LOOK FOR ANY indication of weapons before setting foot into the cemetery. I may still be jittery after my last visit here. I paid the guy an extra fifty bucks to get me here in record time; Tanaka wouldn't expect me so soon in case I can't trust his intentions. He's always seemed like a good guy, but what if that isn't true?

I work my way through the locked gate and step into the graveyard. There isn't anyone visiting at one o'clock in the afternoon on a weekday.

The path is clear. New flowers sit on some graves, but the cemetery looks the same as it always does. I reach the old oak tree and peer around it toward where the shots were fired last time—no sign of anything.

I pick my way along the path and have yet to make a sound by the time I reach the back of the angel statue. I drop to my knees and find a small metal backing at the base. I dig my nails in and try to pry it up. It's been secured with screws; this is a job for the multi-tool I keep on my keychain. Once I've popped off three of them, I swing the plaque up as it hinges on the last screw.

Inside the small space is a key. It's old and looks like one of those keys to a treasure chest. I have absolutely no idea what this could be for until I see a small folded piece of paper tucked into the back of the cubby.

I pull it out, make sure nothing else is hiding in there while praying no spiders are lurking in the dark corners, and replace the screws I'm holding between my lips. Have you ever assembled Ikea furniture? That shit sucks when you misplace a screw. I've learned my lesson.

Cubby covered up, I use the cover that the angel statue provides to unfold the note and see the church name at the top of the page and *Father Andrews*.

There really is no time like the present, is there?

I stick to the tree line as much as I can, key clutched in my hand, and make my way to the church. They keep the main area open for mid-day worshippers, but it's risky without knowing who's inside.

Tanaka could have set all this up so I could meet my end. He doesn't seem like the type, but then again, neither do I if I'm off the clock.

Trusting my instincts, I approach the door and decide to go for it. I have my weapons if I need them, but it'll be hell to fight in a dress if I have to.

The large door I saw the glowing laser mark on last time is unlocked. I walk on the ornate tiles, and my heels announce my presence.

I spy a man leaving the confessional booth, so I know there's at least one person working in this church. I wait for the priest to exit and make my way across the tiles.

"Father," I respectfully nod to him before continuing, "I'm looking for Father Andrews. Do you know if he's available?"

"I am Father Andrews, child. You must be Rogue."

My head spins momentarily, and I try to place this man in my mind. I've never met him before, yet he knows who I am. What has Tanaka done?

I call Jacob on my way home and tell him to open the gate in a minute. I don't want the driver dropping me precisely at the clubhouse, so I have him leave me at a local apartment building, hauling ass the rest of the way home while keeping to the shadows.

As I approach, I see the gate open enough to slip through, then start to shut as soon as I'm through the gap. Noah is at the front door waiting for me.

"Rogue, what's going on?" he demands authoritatively. His worry is evident, but all I see is the possibility of comfort in his arms.

I've got tears streaming down my face and launch myself into his chest when I get close enough. So much for never crying, huh? The stiffness in his body only lasts a few seconds before his arms wind around me and hold me to him. "Hey, Trouble, take your time."

His voice soothes me, and I think of this man who has kept his team together for nearly five years. Lucas knows parts of my story that the other guys don't, but I have to share everything. I promised Lucas at the beach last night that I would.

It looks like that time has arrived. Especially if what's in the file Father Andrew handed over is accurate.

Noah carries me, legs dangling, into the main living space. He calls out for the others to join us, and I hear more than a few concerned and curious comments from around the clubhouse. Noah doesn't respond; he just lowers me onto the couch. Han claims one side and Jacob the other. Lucas is crouched in front of me, having bumped Noah out of the way. I look up to our team leader with gratitude in my still-watery eyes and take a deep breath.

"Lucas knows some of this, but the rest of you don't because I can't keep my mouth shut around him. So I'm just going to blurt all of this out because you need to know, and I trust each of you."

Taking a deep breath, I let the air and the secrets out all at once.

"When I was orphaned at seven, King took me in and raised me. He grew up with my mom and worked with my dad. I didn't know him before that, but the man adopted me anyway. He had custody of Sage too, but she was raised elsewhere, as you know. He trained me and made me into the hitwoman I am."

Lucas nods. He knew the bit about King raising me after our talk last night on the beach but not the why. Jacob, Han, and Noah watch me as I collect my thoughts. I grit my teeth and make my way through the next part.

"I ran into Tanaka, who has been trying to get us together for a while now to meet. Things kept coming up for us, so we postponed countless times. He said something about the cemetery that gave me a lead I had to follow."

Noah grumbles something about "Rogue going rogue," and a smile finally breaks free. It gives me the courage to go on.

"I caught an Uber there as quickly as possible, and sure enough, in the hidey-hole behind the angel over my parents' graves, there was a key and a note that said, Father Andrews. I went into the church and found him. He led me to one of the offices and into a room with boxes affixed to the wall. They looked like the safety deposit boxes at the bank in various sizes.

"The key had a number on it. I found the box it corresponded to and opened it. Inside was a copy of a police file I'd never seen." The faces of the men I've come to depend on are frozen as they wait for the big reveal.

"I was always told it was an overdose—that one too many injections in a short period killed my parents—and with their history, I never questioned the story." I take a deep breath, knowing the cloying scent of drugs is just in my imagination.

"The file in the box said that the amount of drugs in their system was small. Not nearly enough to have caused an overdose, according to the tox screen. No, they died because someone was in our house and slit their throats while on the couch. They were murdered while I was at my friend's house, and Sage was sleeping down the hall."

Chapter Seventeen

Han

AFTER ANSWERING QUESTION AFTER QUESTION ABOUT THE CHURCH, the police file, and her general mental health at the moment, I see Ivy fading fast. It's only early afternoon; I can't imagine how she'll go on the rest of the day. This girl needs a damn nap.

I look to Jacob and raise my brows, hoping he'll take the hint and shoo everyone out of here or keep them busy so I can take care of our girl.

"Han, why are your eyebrows dancing?" Lucas asks, with all the tact of... well, Lucas.

I sigh. My efforts have been in vain. "Guys, I'm going to take Gorgeous upstairs for some quiet. Go check the validity of the police report."

Jacob shoots me a playful wink, and I try not to let it get to me. Since Ivy entered our little bubble, keeping thoughts of him out of my head has been pretty damn futile. Not to mention, seeing him fucking our girl in his office has been playing on a constant loop in my head. It's like I'm being Rick Rolled and can't—or don't want to—escape.

"Come on, Gorgeous. Let's take a nap." I drag Ivy from the couch, leading her up the stairs to my room for some peace. I should probably lead her to her room, but I want to hold her, and she looks like she could use the silent support.

"That... Fuck, that sounds kinda good," she admits as she trails behind me and into my room. She's been in here a couple of times over the past month and always comments on how she wants to mess up my organized space a little bit just to screw with me. I've been distracting her from the idea with making out and foreplay. But at this point, if it makes her feel better, I'd give her a damn sledgehammer to get the job done.

"Let's go. Hop in; it's nap time. You had a shit day. Hit reset, and when you wake up, it'll be better," I coax and hope she'll take my advice to try and sleep it off. I know when she's keyed up, she overworks herself, and I am not above stealing a set of handcuffs from Jake or Noah. There's a time for overworking yourself, but emotional turmoil sometimes just needs a cry and a good fucking nap.

"And there's no way I can convince you to work out right now?" she asks despite knowing the answer.

"Nope. Sleep."

Finally, she relents. Ivy isn't an overly sensitive person, but between the revelation that her sister has been kept from her, King being her adoptive dad, and now finding out her parents had been murdered, anyone would be a swirling vortex of emotion.

I get her tucked in, and she curls up against my side. Her head rests on my chest above my heart, and her leg is thrown over mine.

The tranquil sigh she lets out just before she drifts off tells me I made the right call. No one should have to go through the emotional wringer on their own. With that thought and a silent vow to support this woman through anything, I let myself fall into unconsciousness with Ivy.

I don't know what dream I've been having, but when I feel the warmth of a mouth descend on my cock, I groan and arch into it. Light scratches of short nails make their way down my bare chest, and clarity enters my mind. Ivy.

I lift my head and see the most gorgeous girl I've ever known going to town on my cock.

Am I dreaming?

As her hands descend and wrap tightly around the base, I realize I am most assuredly not asleep. Fuck, she's good at this.

She lifts her eyes to mine and sends a saucy wink before refocusing on her self-appointed task.

"Gorgeous, get up here," I beg. Ivy sucks and pumps for a few torturous seconds longer before I feel the pop as she releases me.

"Did you know you have a boyfriend dick?" she asks.

"A boyfriend dick?" I ask. Because that's what it sounded like she said, but I have no fucking clue what it means.

"You know, it's the perfect size. Not a monster cock, which is awesome, but it can be painful in some positions. It's not small or thin, so I'll never have to ask the dreaded question, 'Is it in?' It's just... fucking perfect," she ends with a moan as she eyes my dick while pumping in the same rhythm she had with her mouth. Did she just compare my cock to the beds in that Goldilocks story?

She distracts me by kissing her way up my chest until she reaches my mouth. Her hands thread through my hair, and I can't help the groan that escapes my throat. Boyfriend dick, huh? As her pussy settles over my naked cock, and I feel the slick desire between us, I decide I'll fucking take it. She obviously likes it.

"Han?" she breathes out when she breaks the kiss.

I open my eyes and look into her gorgeous greens. "Hmm?"

"Fuck me." The way her teeth catch her lip on the first part of that command has me snapping to attention to do her bidding. After weeks of keeping things pretty PG-13 and dying to do more, I quickly bend to her will.

I waste no time in rolling her to the side and reaching into my bedside table for a condom. She laughs at my haste while making a hurry-up gesture with her hand. Suited up, it takes no time before I drive into her. No longer hindered by her injury, I settle my weight over her slightly while keeping the majority on my forearms next to her head.

Her moans spur me on to go faster and harder. Her hands are tangled up in my hair and then down my back. The memory of the first time we were together slams into my mind. She had her hands in my short hair then too. She grips my strands, and the pulling feels blissful when coupled with her heat around my cock.

I feel her legs wrap around my waist; she hooks her ankles and digs her heels into my ass, and before long, she's clamping around my boyfriend dick and riding out an orgasm with a look of rapture on her face. I continue thrusting slowly, guiding her back down, and when she opens her eyes, I see unshed tears in the corners.

"Ivy," I start, but she raises an arm, telling me to ignore the wetness in her eyes—an impossible task. I move in close and trail kisses up and down her jaw, nibbling that place between her neck and her shoulder that she loves.

"It's just unbelievable that we've managed to find each other again," she whispers into my neck. "All those years between then and now, I never forgot you. I'm so fucking sorry for how I ended things back then."

I pull back and look into her eyes. "You don't seem like you had a whole lot of options. And while I wish I had been with you since then, I know you did it to keep me safe. There's nothing to forgive, Ivy. I'd also do nearly anything for the people I love."

Instead of letting that bomb hang in the air for too long, I drag her over with me until we're lying on our sides, looking into each other's eyes as we fuck slowly and lazily until the afternoon fades into evening.

Ivy spent time in my bed three nights out of five this week. After the initial revelation and reaction to her parents' murder, she dusted her hands off and got to work.

She had explained to us how Tanaka got her the file, and while we're all harboring different degrees of wariness, she trusts it. I might too, if it implicated the bastard who hurt her throughout her adolescence. It makes sense now why she was reluctant to join us and why she sometimes shies away from touch.

I'd like to get my hands on King and throttle him. Ivy gets first dibs, though. I'll be there to back her up if she wants or needs it. She's earned the right to mete out the punishment independently, but as I like to remind her, even Batman had Robin and Alfred for support.

After a few days of non-stop research and digging into the police records, Jake finally verified that the digital files she'd seen in the past were falsified. The ones Tanaka led her to were the correct and legal ones. I got to confirm this by slipping into the old records storage room at the police station using the contact that led us to Ivy back in September. I seriously owe that guy.

Between all of the research and Ivy's insider knowledge, we've outlined a basic framework of what we're dealing with regarding her side of our fucked-up equation.

Out of the six members other than Ivy, she's got some decent, and sometimes downright chilling, evidence on four of them. Only Batten and Tanaka have managed to remain squeaky clean, at least on paper. My girl has her suspicions about Batten's husbands, but the only crime she could envision Tanaka doing is fucking up his taxes somehow.

Earlier today, six days after the cemetery, she was understandably still caught up in her head. She wanted to get out some of the excess stress, and we ended up boxing for over an hour. Her motion range has recovered well after her injury, and she's tough to keep up with. Her training in her youth turned her into a machine when it comes to working out.

When I asked her about it, she just said that if she slacked off, King punished her. She showed me the scars I'd seen on her abdomen and explained them a bit.

They're a series of runes. King literally carved them into her while she had to lie still. If she moved, he dug deeper. For the ones she couldn't handle, he had one of his colleagues, Horvat, hold her down while he dug in with the knife.

The symbol she pointed out to me is called an Algiz. It looks like a capital letter Y with the center extended between the valley above. King told her it represents strength, protection, and family. If only she had any of that while he was carving her up.

After our workout, she asked if she could hang out with me. I think she's been feeling a bit embarrassed about what was revealed, and she feels duped by the only person she knew as a child. I'd be looking for any kind of connection too.

I ushered her upstairs and into the bathroom, where we could get cleaned up. After getting clean, then dirty, then clean again, we head toward my room to tuck in for the evening. On my way out the door, I notice the bruise forming on my side from her right hook. Girl's got some reach.

We climb into bed, and she takes up her usual post, curling herself into my side as we sink into the mattress. She doesn't seem to be getting comfortable as she usually does and looking down, I can just make out a soft furrow on her brow.

Something's up, and with the number of times I've just seen her open and close her mouth, she doesn't know how to bring up whatever's plaguing her mind. Her index finger draws delicate patterns on my chest in a fidgeting manner. We've discussed King, her parents, and her sister at length today, so something else is bugging her.

"Ivy, what's swirling around up there in your head? I promise getting it out will be better than letting it stew."

She huffs out a breath like she's steeling herself. She closes her eyes, and in a soft voice I've rarely heard from her, she asks what's been on her mind. "You and Jacob? Is that something I'm getting between?"

I sigh. I knew this was coming. I've been caught looking a few times, and I struggle to find the words to say I find them both incredibly attractive, sexy, and alluring, and I'm pretty sure I've been in love with Ivy since I was twenty-one and first spoke to her. I do not want to fuck this up, yet I know a part of me will regret not at least attempting to talk to Jacob about all this.

"It's nothing I've ever acted on, but I won't lie and say I haven't thought about it. We've certainly never talked about it.

"I'm bi, and Jake knows that. We've shared women in the past but never done anything on our own. He's one of my best friends, and it in no way changes how I feel about you. I just... Fuck, Ivy. I don't know. His mind and his body are just so damn sexy; I swear sometimes my own brain turns to mush," I end on a groan and flop on my side to the mattress.

At my final admission, she lets out a laugh and clutches her middle as she collapses next to me. After a moment, her tone turns serious. "Han, honey, I believe you when you say it's separate from what you feel for me. You don't have to stress about that. We agreed to no commitment, remember? What bothers me is that you're having feelings and hiding them. If you ever want to go for it, even if it's while I'm still here, you have my full support. I never want you to hide who you are. I think I would feel differently if it was someone outside of one of us, but it's Jacob, you know? Do you know if he feels the same?"

That's the big question, isn't it? Do I risk our friendship and easy working relationship, hoping he's thought of me in that way too? Or do I bury it?

Knowing Ivy is understanding and not pushing me in either direction gives me the sounding board I seemingly need. I sit up and prop myself against the headboard, wringing my hands together.

"I doubt he feels the same. But, when the three of us were in bed together, I saw something in his eye I'd only glimpsed once or twice in the past. Then there was that wink the night you came home after the cemetery. Fuuuuuuck, we're going to have to talk about this, aren't we?" The groaning continues as I drop my head into my hands. I'm usually the first one to talk about situations, but the vulnerability and fear of rejection have me reliving some of the dark days of my youth. I keep my face schooled so Ivy doesn't see how much this might hurt me, but she's right. I can't bury my head in the sand and never talk about it.

Ivy chortles next to me but lays a hand reassuringly on my chest. "Even if he doesn't feel the same, I'll be here to back you up. But fuck, I'm rooting for you guys."

We move on to safer topics. My childhood insecurities don't stay buried in my mind because I let a few stories slip as we talk about growing up. Our talks about our stunted youth lead to me telling Ivy about my family's failed store and our stint as homeless. She's seen all of us periodically giving money to those in need but didn't know our reasoning is more personal than moral.

We laugh about my "alleged" destruction of the school gym. Ivy fights for breath as she makes her way through the story of the first time a guy asked her out when she was sixteen, admitting she basically ran in the other direction, citing improper teenage socialization in her formative years.

We fall asleep with Ivy draped across my body and my arms around her waist, keeping her anchored to me. I don't remember ever having slept this well, and I know it isn't because of the exhaustion that usually overtakes me after a grueling workout. It is all because of the girl who was wrapped up in my arms all night.

I'm woken in the morning by Jacob's warm, dry hand brushing my arm. I'm half convinced that I'm dreaming of the tattooed hand drifting over my forearm.

He squats down next to the bed on my side and lures me into a state of consciousness. I have a little worry in my mind about how he will react to Rogue and me finally connecting like this over the last week, but he only looks over my shoulder at her peaceful face and smiles.

"We've got something on Mara. Let's go."

That's how I find myself in the car at five-thirty on a Sunday morning with Lucas and Jacob, half-asleep, while we watch Mara Hendrix for the day.

Four fucking days later, and we're still pulling shifts watching this woman. Today, Lucas, Jake, and I decided to stake out Mara together and use the downtime to discuss Ivy.

She and Noah went up to San Francisco to stake out her Gambit assignment, Neil Carter. She gave us some info on him the last time she was up there doing recon and said it looked to be an easy job. King has informed her that he's the priority at the moment.

Noah didn't feel great sending her on her own again, so he tagged along. He insisted it be him because if it were any of the rest of us, he said we might get distracted.

Instead, all three of us are distracted by thoughts of Ivy as we camp out in the van outside of Mara's apartment building. Jacob finally cracked her phone and has been tracking her movements via GPS. She should be leaving for her therapist in about an hour, but sometimes, she goes early for coffee.

My thoughts turn back to Ivy to settle what I want to say before we all start composing sonnets in her honor. But let's be honest, Lucas's would probably be a limerick ending with something that rhymes with "Nantucket."

I love that she gets Lucas and his need for jokes. He confided in us that he shared his past with her, and she basically told him on the ride back from their date that Lucas should just be who he is. No jokes required. She just wants him—silly or serious, goofy or stern.

Jacob is half in love with her, and it has been startling to see the difference in him when she is around. He's calmer, and I haven't seen him stick to his usually inflexible schedule since she showed up.

The sharing aspect has yet to come up again, neither with Ivy nor Jacob. It's an awkward conversation to start, and we've been overly focused on getting all the information we can on the boards. I don't know if it was a one-time thing or if we're all on board to do it again, but Ivy will likely avoid the topic until Jacob and I have the talk I've been dreading since she brought it up.

Lucas starts us off in only a way Lucas can, "Rogue is fuck-hot, and I'm not giving her up."

Well, this is going to go well.

"Luke," Jacob sighs and shakes his head. "No one is asking you to give her up. Do we all agree not to put that kind of pressure on each other?"

Lucas and I nod. Leave it to Jacob to break things down into digestible pieces for us to follow along. "Do you have feelings for her, or is it just a fling for you?"

"Feelings," Lucas and I reply at the same time. No one jinxes anyone, and we all look around suspiciously, waiting to see who will be a dick and ruin our talk.

"This conversation is too important to have someone unable to speak," I state.

"Okay, so we all like her. She's not looking for commitment, but we know feelings are there, and we're all good with sharing." Jacob and I nod. "Does anyone know where Noah stands on this?" Lucas asks us.

"Nah, man. But did you see how quickly he volunteered to go up north with our girl?" Jacob asks.

Lucas and I nod, both sporting matching evil grins on our faces.

"He's not going to give in no matter his attraction to her. Sheila messed him up good."

"I think it's crazy that this amazing woman slashed her way into our lives, and fuck, if I don't want her to stay," Lucas muses. "Noah's going to give in. Are we okay with adding a fourth to this merry band of bastards?"

I think on it for a moment before answering, "I'm okay with it, but let's lay off and let him come to his own conclusion. This might be a moot conversation, after all. What was it he said after he and Sheila divorced?"

Jacob laughs and recites the answer, word for word, like I knew he would, "*Even the devil himself does not know where the women sharpen their knives.*"

Those trust issues are going to be a bitch to get over.

"Uhm," Lucas starts, "I promise to leave him alone from now on. I may have already sent a text."

Jacob groans and rubs his hand on the back of his neck in frustration. Most of the time, Lucas's quips and little barbs are fun. I don't think Noah will see it that way this time.

We watch Mara's sleek Tesla pull out of her building's parking garage and head to her therapist's office. This is going to be a long day of watching her again. Lucas had too much coffee and has already started bouncing in his seat while singing "Black Magic Woman."

Chapter Eighteen

Rogue

It's been six goddamned days, and Noah and I are still camped out in an Airbnb across the way from the apartment Neil Carter owns. It's the same one I rented last time I came up to do my stakeout. The good thing about this neighborhood is that the bay windows are one of the homes' appeals. We've got a decent lookout spot into the apartment across the street.

Noah and I talk logistics, message with the guys in the group chat, and keep a lookout at all times. The air has been thick with tension for the last few days after Lucas insinuated something was going on with Noah and me in a joking text. Since then, Noah has made it his mission to stay as distant from me as possible.

I've got three amazing men waiting for me back at home, and I'm in no way going to push my company onto someone who clearly doesn't want it. I never even thought I'd find one guy I like as much as those three dickheads back at the clubhouse.

Noah can keep his distance all he wants. But my brain keeps whispering about figuring out why he's reluctant to let people close, why he cares so deeply for his team but is equally distrustful of anyone else.

Noah has been pretty tight-lipped since the text and scowls more than usual—shocking that it is possible to increase the scowling. Gruff, bearded, and yes, sexy as hell. Bad Rogue.

I have to chastise myself more often than I'd like to admit. I think I'm just a little dick drunk, and since having slept with all three of my sexy guys back home, I'm going through withdrawals. That has to be it.

Turning my attention back to the window, I monitor the comings and goings of Neil's building. I haven't noticed other couples or families going into or out of the building; I deduce he's the only one living there.

The building is privately owned, so I can only check records to find the original owner's name, Claudette Shuman.

From what I can see, she has a few properties and manages those. Nothing of importance has popped up. I'm keeping tabs on her and, in the meantime, assuming she doesn't know she's renting to a drug runner.

Neil isn't the top dog, but he has enough security for me to know he's important.

I see a few of the beefed-up security dudes guide Neil to the blacked-out Escalade idling at the curb—time to move. I call for Noah, who's taking a nap down the hall in one of the two small bedrooms, and tell him it's time to go. He comes out, already dressed and ready to leave. I guess that's one good thing about working with other professionals. They're always prepared.

Noah adjusts the back of his shirt, likely covering up the gun tucked into the waistband of his dark jeans. My eyes trail down his body, noting the shoulder holster as he slips a worn leather bomber jacket on. My stare catches on the fit of his jeans, and good lord, have mercy, those thighs flex under each step.

See? Dick drunk.

Noah palms the keys to the rental car and opens the front door. I follow him out and lock up. We wait until the car across the way pulls away from the curb before hopping into the silver sedan we rented.

Noah trails a few car lengths behind the Escalade. I've got my phone out so we can follow if they get out of sight. I took a run the other day and slipped one of my tracking devices under the bumper as I stopped to tie my shoe.

The security guys were too busy staring at my tits in a sports bra to even notice my wandering left hand.

We continue straight on the road when they take a left into Chinatown. I've got the tracker going, and we'll catch up with them when they've slowed down. Tracking is essential, but even more so, is seeing if we can find out who he's meeting with or working for.

After about ten minutes of driving parallel to them on another boulevard, we see them turning into a building on the phone. As we get closer, I see the sign for a parking structure. We follow in, keeping an eye out for the Escalade. As we reach the final floor before the roof, I ask Noah to park near the stairs.

We park and hop out. I climb the stairs first to peek my head over the railing at the top, level with the pavement. Noah's head pops up next to mine. His voice is low, his eyes rounded. "What the fuck?"

I see Neil speaking to a woman wearing a dark green fitted dress, her orange-red hair streaming down her back. She's speaking harshly with him, and I can see from his tense shoulders he's trying not to snap back and defend himself from her verbal barbs. "What is it?" I ask Noah.

"That's Mara Hendrix," he says in an incredulous tone. Mara? As in the same woman the guys are currently watching? Oh, shit. I didn't recognize her without the glasses, the severe bun, and her usual pantsuit outfit.

But if she's here, who are the guys staking out?

They've been watching her the entire time we've been here. We get continual updates from them in the group chat that nothing is happening. She's going to her meetings and back home—no signs of anything suspicious, and certainly no drives up to San Francisco. They would have alerted us to that.

I pull out my phone and see a text in the group chat. Maybe Mara did come up here, and the guys tried to warn us, but I missed it in all the rush to follow Neil. My phone has been on silent mode since we left the rental house. The guys would have alerted us way before that if she had started the two-hour trek north. I open the group chat just in case and see that Lucas has asked me to intervene in an argument he's having with Han and Jacob about which superhero is better, Arrow or The Flash.

I roll my eyes and resist the grin trying to overtake my face. At least they're keeping it in the DC universe. I love Marvel as well, but DC is my jam. I stow my phone and plan to give my two cents after this Mara thing is cleared up.

We hang around for the fifteen minutes it takes for them to finish their meeting, and Mara hands Neil a thick envelope that looks like it's bursting at the seams.

Once they pile into their cars, we wait until they drive down the ramp to circle down to the exit, keeping our legs tucked up, hoping they don't glimpse us lingering on the metal staircase.

As soon as they're out of sight, Noah raises his phone to his ear, no doubt calling the guys to figure out what the hell is going on. "Do you have eyes on Hendrix?" he asks in a tone that nearly chills me to the bone. He's fucking pissed.

He puts the phone on speaker, and we listen as Jacob responds, "Unfortunately, yes, this is boring as shit. She just walked into the Annex building two minutes ago. Why, what's up?"

"Any chance she could be a body double? A decoy?" Noah asks quickly.

"No way, man. We've had eyes on her since before you left. Plus, I'm remotely tracking her phone, and you know we techies never give our devices to other people. Why? What the hell happened?" Jacob probes after Noah finishes scoffing at his confidence that the Mara they see is, in fact, Mara.

I decide to cut to the chase before Noah can bluster some more. "Jacob, we just saw Mara meeting with my target here in San Francisco. She wasn't wearing the pantsuit, and her hair and makeup were different, but Noah is confident it's Mara. After getting a decent look at her, I have to agree. We have a problem."

Noah jumps in, "We'll stick around here for a few more days, see if we can get another chance to see Mara two-point-oh. Neil deferred to her authority, and she handed off a package. I'm thinking she's running shit up here."

With it agreed upon to keep Mara One and Mara Two in our sights if we can find her again, Noah and I get in the car and head to the apartment. Neil's Escalade is headed across town and in the direction of one of his mistresses.

He'll likely spend an hour or two there before returning to our shared neighborhood. I'll keep an eye on the tracking app so we'll know when he's back. Nothing like a good fuck after being yelled at by your boss, I guess.

After a few days, Noah and I saw neither hide nor hair of Mara Two. I text our group chat that we're leaving in the morning to head home.

Lucas celebrates this news by sending me dick pic after dick pic.

Jacob sends a sweet text telling me he can't wait to hold me and then punish me for leaving him for so long.

Han follows that with honeyed words that make my heart flutter just a little bit.

I can't fucking wait to get back.

Han hasn't mentioned the comment about "also doing anything for the people I love." So, I'm sure as shit not bringing it up.

Did I love him back then? Do I still? My only somewhat healthy example of love was my parents, and it's been so long that I don't even really remember what that felt like. I love Sage but in a different way. I'm going to have to spend some time mulling this over when we're not juggling fifteen balls in the fucking air.

Noah is still running point for the team regarding the "disappearance" of Blake and has a team leader meeting in two days. The guys are obviously not working on that with any urgency, but they send along details from their "investigation" to the other teams.

As we watch out the window and wait for any other signs of Neil getting up to no good, we spend the time getting to know each other a bit. After the whole Mara reveal, Noah let go of the earlier tension, and we settled in for our stakeout. I learned he grew up on the East Coast and enrolled in JROTC in high school to help pay for college. He finished his degree while involved in ROTC and moved on to a leadership role in the Army.

Knowing that information now, I think back over the last month, and so many things make more sense now.

Noah is firm with his team but leads them with precision, which I would expect from a former Army officer. He was recruited for Annex during his last year in the military when he showed an aptitude for infiltrations and reconnaissance. He's been with Annex since he was twenty-five, about ten years now. His team was formed about five years ago when the others were put into a unit, and they've climbed the ranks quickly.

They're now Alpha Team One.

He's quiet about his personal life, but it's really none of my business. He's not one of my "harem," as Lucas has taken to calling himself and the other two. I mean, he's not wrong.

After a few hours of chatting about this and that, his phone rings. When he gets a look at who's calling, a vicious curse leaves his lips, and he lets out a groan before lifting the phone to his ear and answering, "Sheila."

I don't hear the other side of the conversation, but between the set of

Noah's jaw and the furrow between his brows that he gets when he's upset, I can assume it's not a welcomed call. "Sheila, I told you, leave me out of it. You made your choices. You agreed only to call me in an emergency."

I wonder who Sheila is and what she's done to elicit this kind of reaction to the team's usually level-headed leader.

Whoever she is, I want to rip her fingernails out one by one when I see a light sheen of sweat break out on Noah's tanned brow from his anger. I don't know why I'm having this visceral reaction to someone I don't know, but Noah is on my team. He shouldn't be dealing with this shit.

I stick my hand out, pop Noah under the elbow of the arm, cradling the phone, and watch it go sailing through the air.

The move unexpected; Noah looks at me in shock as I pluck the phone out of the air and put it up to my ear. A woman is crying on the other end of the line about how she misses Noah and wants him back.

"Ahem," I cut in without remorse, "Noah asked you only to call in an emergency. Desperation for his cock is not an emergency. Please refrain from calling again in the future, or we'll be forced to move on to extreme measures." My voice is dripping with disdain and honey at the same time, a skill I've honed over the years.

Her voice cut out immediately after she heard me start. It now picks back up with a vengeance, demanding to know who I am and why I'm with "her" Noah. I pull the phone from my ear before this woman's vulgar words reach into my brain to scramble it around and hang up.

Noah looks at me like I've lost my mind for a second before he tips his head back and lets out a huge laugh. I've never seen him laugh like this. It's not just his mouth opening wide and the sparkle in his eye. I swear his whole face glows. I guess he's okay with the way I handled things.

He's still laughing as I place the phone in his hand and try not to stare at this glorious man in front of me. The screen lights up with Sheila calling back, and he silences it as he stuffs it into his pocket.

"Thank you, Trouble. That was my wife." Cue the sound of a record scratch.

Chapter Nineteen

Noah

"Okay, Noah. Next time, be more clear. 'That was my wife' makes it sound like she still is. 'That was my ex-wife' is the better way to say that so you don't give anyone else an aneurysm."

Rogue has been peppering me with questions about Sheila since she called last night. Up until last night, when the call came through, we'd kept things pretty superficial when we talked. I'm reining in my inclination to bark out that it's none of her business because she's not really asking anything that any curious person wouldn't. It's not a dig for information on me to use at a later date; it's just natural inquisitiveness. We're only about an hour from home, and I'm going insane. She clearly wants to know everything but has been respectful enough to let me get it out in my own time.

"Sorry, Trouble. EX-WIFE!" I shout in the cramped confines of the rental car. She laughs her head off, and the sound helps heal some of the wounds Sheila wrenched open last night.

"What a duplicitous woman," she comments with acid dripping from her tone. "Why would she think she could get away with cheating on a security dude? Doesn't she know the information you have access to? Even if you hadn't figured it out right after Callie's birth, she had to know it was only a matter of time."

I nod. We've already discussed this, but Rogue can't get her head around Sheila's attempt to pass Callie off as mine. Her eyes softened when I told her the crushing devastation I'd felt when I found out she wasn't mine. I didn't mention that I still had a college fund set aside for her.

It's not her fault her mother royally screwed up. No kid should have to suffer for their parent's mistakes. In my own way, I think it's my version of an apology that I won't be a father to her as she grows up. I know I bear no responsibility, but my gut wouldn't let me just walk away without helping in some way.

As we get closer to the warehouse, taking a circuitous route to avoid The Gambit's well-known stomping grounds, Rogue pulls her phone out and texts the group chat, asking where the others are.

I see the text on my phone in the cup holder, and Lucas responds with a string of ridiculous emojis and a few words, saying that he's on his way home with Jacob while Han stays behind to keep his eyes on Mara. When did emojis become the norm for the team's group text? Likely, the same instant this fascinating creature, fiddling with the radio, showed up.

We get to the gate, and I unlock it with the disguised app on my phone. Jacob really is a genius. I've got to give him more credit when I see him. No one would assume the stock market app on my phone is really the way into our compound.

I drive across the concrete and park the car as Rogue bounces on her seat. Looking over at her as she stares at the warehouse entrance, I can both see and feel her excitement, and that jealousy hits again.

She's eager to see the boys. It must be nice to have someone looking forward to welcoming you home.

We hop out of the car and move to the trunk to grab our bags. Just then, the SUV comes through the fencing, and Rogue's smile hits me like a ton of bricks as she looks over my shoulder to the yawning gate. Her lips are stretched wide, teeth gleaming in the sun, and a sparkle in her eye. Yeah, I'm a jealous and covetous bastard.

Jacob pulls the car in, parks at an unusual angle in his haste, and flings the door open. She runs to his side of the vehicle as he steps out and throws herself into his arms. Her legs wrap around his waist, and he holds her close as he whispers in her ear. His hand playfully connects with her ass in a soft slap. A movement on the other side of the car has me making eye contact with Lucas. He lifts a brow inquisitively and smirks.

He's figured out that I've got some feelings for Rogue, but he's kind enough not to put me on blast in front of the others. Again. I'm sure he'll seek me out later for a quick and painful chat.

Jacob sets Rogue down as Lucas comes close. With a soft hand, he leans in, cups her jaw, and gives her a passionate kiss.

I turn my head to avoid raging out in envy. I pick up the bag Rogue dropped on the ground and start making my way to the front door with Jacob in tow.

"We need a debrief with everyone so we can go over what we saw and how the hell Mara can be in two places at once."

Jacob nods and pulls his phone out to check Mara's schedule, finding that she doesn't have anything of relevance later that afternoon. Han will take a break to join us, and we can work everything out.

Lucas and Rogue trail in after us, and she takes a deep breath when she enters the warehouse. "I'm so glad to be home," she says as she shucks off her jacket and scans the place with a critical eye—no doubt looking for any disturbances.

There are takeout containers on the lounge area's table, along with empty bottles of beer. The meeting room has pages strewn everywhere, and the projector is still on, showing the four photos of the board members of The Gambit that we could find.

Turns out not all of them like being photographed. Even the employee files didn't have photos of all the members. We quickly got one of Batten, Tanaka, and King from the Rook Industry servers. Rogue got one of Nina Wilson from the Harvard alum pages. Horvat and De La Cruz are still proving to be tough to find photos of, but between Rogue and I, Lucas was able to draw some sketches of their faces, so we have some point of reference.

The guys have been watching Mara in shifts, and no one had enough time to clean the place up before we got back. Sometimes, it's like living in a frat house, but we're good about cleaning up after ourselves. It's not like we can have cleaners come in. We don't give this address to anyone, and plus, there are weapons fucking everywhere. I hope Rogue doesn't judge the guys too harshly, but as she returns from the kitchen with a garbage bag, she just starts grabbing the trash and tossing it in.

Lucas makes a move to help her, and she just shakes her head and asks, "Red, honey, when was the last time you slept?" He scratches his head, and I see the dark circles under his eyes that indicate it's been a while. Rogue is pretty perceptive, and I love that he has someone other than me looking out for him.

"Uhm, two... no, three days ago. But you're here now; I've got my second wind." He tries to talk himself into spending some time with her, but she just crosses her arms over her chest and widens her stance. She's willing to throw down and flex her influence just to get him back on track. She lifts an arm and points to his room on the second floor.

"Go. Sleep. I'll join you in fifteen minutes. I've got to move around a bit after sitting in the car."

He accepts her orders but looks petulant about it.

Jacob sees that he's about to receive the same treatment, so he raises his palms in surrender and climbs the stairs on the opposite side of the building to reach his own room. She sighs with contentment, and my jaw hangs open.

"Trouble, we're keeping you around with those powers you wield." She looks at me with questions in her eyes before I continue, "I always have trouble getting those two to take care of themselves. Han helps, and Jacob's scheduling usually keeps him on track, but he seems to have thrown the whole damn routine out the window since you arrived."

I see her face fall as if I'm blaming her, but really, I'm thankful someone has pulled him out of his need for control. A bit is fair, but too much, and it becomes a problem. I'm quick to assure her it's a good thing.

"He would never go for a rest in the middle of the day before you came. I can't tell you how many times we've had arguments about him needing to sleep or leave things for the next day. Magic, baby. Pure magic just happened."

She giggles, fucking giggles, and I aim a soft smile in her direction. "I'll help you get this cleaned up, then you can join Lucas. We'll have the meeting when Han gets home."

"Deal," she agrees.

WHILE ROGUE IS RESTING OR RESTING WITH LUCAS, I TAKE THE FEW hours we have to head over to Mrs. M's place. My skin is itchy thinking of her with him while we're all in close quarters after having had her to myself the past week.

I need to get out of the house before I do something stupid and throw my hat into the ring. I haven't had any one-on-one time with Mama Bear in a few weeks, and with all the shit spinning in my head, I think I need a chat.

She has this way of cutting through all the bullshit with her snarky attitude and clearing things up. I've got more than a few feelings for and about

Rogue, but the nature of her relationships with my other teammates makes me a little hesitant to initiate anything. Especially with how I was burned before.

I reach her small townhouse and pull into the drive behind her ancient station wagon. We offered to buy her a newer car, and she just laughed in our faces. "But where will I seduce my new beau if not in the back of my Shaggin' Wagon before our dinner date?" she asked, and I swear all four of us simultaneously threw up in our mouths.

Climbing the steps quickly, I knock on her door. It swings open, and I am immediately whacked in the face with the scent of beef stew. Oh, hell yes. Mrs. M makes the best food, and I know she always makes enough for the neighborhood when she cooks.

"Noah, dearest! Come in, come in." She yanks on my arm until I'm stumbling over the threshold and trying my best to get my boots off.

Last time, she just dragged me through the house and then yelled at me for leaving dirt on the carpet. It's happened a few times, actually. I don't like being reprimanded by the person who caused the problem in the first place. Not that she's ever agreed with my reasoning that it was her fault.

I get the boots off with one hand as the other is still in her clutches. She drags me down the hall to the kitchen, where she forcibly shoves me onto a stool and puts a plate of stew, Irish soda bread, and potatoes in front of me.

It's only eleven in the morning, but fuck it; I'd eat this morning, noon, and night if I could. "Spit it out."

I'm momentarily confused if she means the food or whatever's bothering me. I swallow the mouthful and dive in.

"I have some... conflicting feelings about Rogue." Mrs. M takes a moment to put her spoon down gently on her own plate and looks up at me from across the kitchen island.

"Noah, sweetheart, no shit."

Leave it to Mrs. M to see through me. "She's genuine and kind. But she can also take a man down in two seconds flat. She took Han to the mat last week in an impressive move I've never seen anyone pull off. She's loyal and hard-working, and she handles the team effortlessly."

"She's different; I'll give you that. She's also doing the dirty with your three team members. Oh, don't look at me like that. It's obvious the others are enamored with her. How do you feel about that?" she asks with sincerity in her tone. She knows about Sheila and Callie, the baggage that I now carry around.

"Honestly, I don't know. I caught myself admiring Rogue's ability to handle them earlier today. It's nice that someone else is looking out for them. My trust in her is growing, but what if something happens and she leaves? I don't know if I can start something, knowing she doesn't adhere to the usual relationship dynamics. I love the guys; they're like family, but dating someone who's dating other people? Can it even be considered dating if we're keeping to the warehouse to avoid being seen? I don't know how to do that. Not after Sheila."

"Even if they're people you trust with your life? Noah, the others are your family. Rogue fits into that. I see the way the others care for her. I also see the way you care for her but are way too stubborn to admit. Your eyes give you away, sweetheart."

I think about it like I have for weeks now. None of the guys would try to monopolize her, would they? Jacob and his need for control instantly pop into my mind. He's been entirely flexible since Rogue has been around. Maybe she's loosening him up from that rigidity. Han and Lucas are always relaxed, so I don't think they'd do anything to try to keep her to themselves. What if they do? Could I handle being left in the cold with the other three as the one she chooses rides off into the sunset with her?

"Look, Noah. I'm not saying to jump in one hundred percent right off the bat. But what does your instinct tell you? I know better than to ask what your heart says; you muted that bastard years ago."

"Instinct says she's good for me, us, the team. But fuck, if I'm not terrified."

Mrs. M laughs at me, and it warms my soul a bit. It makes all our problems seem trivial when she can just laugh them away.

"Just talk to the girl. Then, talk to your team. Make sure you're not stepping on any toes. For the love of God, do you know how many fewer romance novels there would be in the world if people just figured out that communication is the key? All that angst for nothing. Finish your food, and go home, Drama Queen."

Serious talk over, we move on to lighter topics, and she asks if Rogue has any new knives she can play with.

I swear, this woman is going to put me in an early grave.

Rogue

After a not-too-restful rest with Red, in which he had me up against the wall as he drove into me and did indeed give me that standing O he said he would, we pad down the stairs when we get a text from Han saying he's on his way home.

My hair is still in a nest atop my head, and my thighs have a delicious ache between them. Not super professional for our meeting, but I've been away for too long, and I simply couldn't help myself.

I shoved one of Lucas's shirts over my head and pulled my jeans up. I've taken to wearing the guys' clothes around the clubhouse, and I fucking love it. The scent of them lingering on my skin afterward is its own version of heaven.

Jacob walks down the other set of stairs and meets us in the middle of the bottom floor. He scoops me into his arms and kisses me until I don't know which way is up and which is down. Lucas clears his throat, and I pull away to shoot him a little grin over my shoulder. My hands are wrapped around the back of Jacob's neck, and I refuse to let go just yet.

His glasses are slightly askew, and he laughs as he tries to remove my hands, but he is met with resistance. God, he's sexy. Do we really need to have a meeting now?

With that thought, the front door opens, and Noah makes his way in. He looks at the three of us, and his eyes shoot to the floor in front of him. Noah knows about all of us. We haven't kept anything a secret, obviously, but I've never seen this reaction from Noah when catching sight of us being affectionate. Hell, he was with the others as they applauded Jacob and me for our tech room performance.

He stalks to the war room, and Jacob sets me on my bare feet to follow. Lucas grabs some drinks for us as we settle into the chairs around the table. He surprises me a few minutes later with a mug that reads *Murder, Mayhem, and Marshmallows* in a font that drips with blood filled with white hot chocolate. I don't even care that the weather is only slightly crisp in early autumn; it's perfect. He's just started off the hot chocolate season well before winter arrives, and I am here to support his campaign.

Han joins us half an hour later, and we dive in. Noah and I go over what we saw in San Francisco. A whole lot of nothing followed by a considerable something.

The guys detail their shadowing of Mara and insist it was her. Noah still thinks that she hired out a body double to continue business as usual here in town.

We move on to what The Gambit has been up to since I've been gone. I've got to reach out to King today to tell him what I learned on my trip.

I really don't want to kill Neil yet, seeing as he hasn't done anything to indicate he's deserving of my knife other than running a protection racket. He honestly doesn't even look like the type to run with a gang. He's too clean-cut, too dull. But I know better than most that appearances can be deceiving.

Jacob promised to check him out after I told him my thoughts on his demeanor. I did a deep dive, but I can't deny that Jacob is better at it than I am. He seems to be able to get into anything designed to keep people out. Mara's network is exhibit A.

We're wrapping up our meeting and, frustratingly, getting nowhere. We agree to keep eyes on Mara, especially in light of the development that she's working with Neil Carter.

King wants Neil and whoever he answers to dead. If that's Mara, it works out well to remove her. But we still have questions about how she's wrapped up in this. There are too many connections between the Annex and The Gambit.

Chapter Twenty

Jacob

IT TAKES A WHILE BEFORE WE ALL FINISH UP WHAT WE'VE BEEN working on since our meeting in the afternoon to discuss the Mara situation. Hell, Noah is still out meeting with one of the other team leaders, and he left immediately after our debriefing. It's been a couple hours already, but if anything wasn't going our way, he'd send a text to let us know.

Han has been working in the weapons room, cleaning, sorting, and taking inventory. You know, the fun stuff. My eyes involuntarily drift over to him when I'm not focused on the monitor during a download, and the way his biceps bunch and flex as he maintains our weapons with that serious look on his face has me doing a double-take.

Lucas went out to continue trailing Mara until she retired to her home for the evening. He was out for an hour and posted one of his contacts, who was not employed by Annex, outside the door if she took off at any point during the night.

I've been doing a thorough investigation into Mara's digital footprint, but it's been slow-going because of how meticulous she is. No doubt she's set up traps along the way to keep hackers out.

A lot of this job is of the "hurry up and wait" variety. When something is urgent, it's fucking life or death. When we're doing recon, sometimes it takes days for something to pop. The cycle can be a bit of a drag on the nervous system.

Thoughts of both her and Han keep invading my mind as I mine data. It's distracting as all hell. Rogue trusts us, and we trust her implicitly. It's those considerations that first clue me in that I'm falling, and I'm falling fast for this girl. She is strong, independent, fucking deadly, and yet caring and supportive in our day-to-day.

Rogue comes down the stairs with a determined stride, and I see her through the walls of my office. Every time I see those transparent partitions now, I think of Rogue and I fucking on my workstation while the others watch from the other side of the glass. A smile brightens my face when I think of the applause we garnered and Rogue's boisterous laugh.

Amidst all the shit raining down on us, I'm glad we find pleasure in the little things.

The only thing is, earlier, I saw her grabbing a clean mug from Lucas's cabinet and bringing it up to her room. It's not the theft that bothers me. It's the reasoning I suspect behind it. I think she's stealing shit to take back with her when this is all over. It breaks my heart a bit that she might not see a future with us—neither romantically nor as a team.

Rogue finds Han in the weapons room and drags him out to the lounge. Lucas, who is in the gym running on the treadmill, is next. She hauls him over, and he pulls out his earbuds with a thank you.

Everyone in this warehouse, except Han, hates cardio and is always thankful for a break. I join them without Rogue needing to get me because it's clear she's about to head my way next.

"Love, what's going on?" I ask, concern lacing my tone. We should have Noah here if it's vital, so I pull my phone from my pocket, ready to dial out.

"We are hanging out. All together. Captain texted me that he was on his way home. There's been too much going on, and we all feel like shit because we're not sleeping. So, having said that, tonight we are playing board games, eating the pizza that Noah's picking up, and going the fuck to bed."

The three of us look at each other and grin maniacally. We haven't had a game night in forever, and that shit gets competitive. But she's right. We've been running ourselves into the ground.

Rogue spins to turn on the small Bluetooth speaker and loads up a Spotify list on the community tablet called "Walk Like a Badass." I take a look at the list, and it's perfect—heavy beats, easy to sing along, a bit eclectic; it suits us.

Noah gets home soon after we pull a selection of board games from Lucas's room and set up our pickings on the floor next to the lounge area's low table. Noah drops the pizzas on the table, and we all crowd around, ready to inhale the cheesy goodness. Han hops up and grabs a few six-packs of beer from the fridge. With Lucas's exclamation of "fuck plates!" we all just grab a slice and dig in.

We chat about nothing but which game to play. No work, no threats, no weird body doubles. Just an argument about whether Scattergories is a better choice than Monopoly.

With a three-to-two vote, Scattergories takes the cake. The rest of the games are shoved under the couch, and we gather around the coffee table.

Pizza devoured, we clear the table and huddle around it with our notepads. Rogue gleefully tosses the die with letters on it. It rolls until it lands on S, and we flip our category cards.

The game involves only listing things from the categories that start with the letter on the die. Double points if it's a ubiquitous double name or phrase and both words begin with the letter. Rogue proves this in the first round by gaining points in the candy category with "sour skittles."

Han and Noah highlight the cancelation of points rule that if two or more players have the same word for the same category, they earn nothing. They both had Snickers.

You have to be creative and know who you're playing against.

Of course, those two would pick Snickers. Noah has a stash of the candy bars hidden in one of the kitchen drawers that Han regularly raids. Health nut, my arse.

The game goes on for a few hours, and by the end, we're all a bit drunk.

Lucas has reverted to finding all words with an innuendo.

Han and Noah are surprisingly similar in their thought processes and end up canceling out more points with each other than gaining them.

I capitalize on my British upbringing and use words for products that aren't common in the States.

Rogue's score hovers around the middle, using her extensive knowledge of all things retro to pull obscure words from her memory.

Rogue and Noah both laugh freely as they try to figure out what I've written, and I notice Noah paying a bit more attention to Rogue. His eyes linger when she tips her head back to drink her beer from the bottle, and he's open with his casual touches when they win points. I wonder if he's thinking of making a move.

While he's generous with his small advances, I'm doing my best to avoid looking at Han. Not because he's done anything wrong. No, it's because, with my inhibitions lowered after a few beers, I'm afraid I'll get caught staring at him. Rogue seems to notice this and elbows my ribs suggestively until I'm hunched over laughing.

I haven't been as covert as I should have been. I look to my left, where Rogue sits, and she waggles her brows for a second, shooting a quick look over to Han, who moans as he bites into the last slice of pizza he pilfered from the boxes behind him.

I raise a brow to silently ask what the hell she's talking about. She just shrugs a shoulder and nods her head in encouragement. Is she...? Yeah, I'm pretty sure she just gave the go-ahead to ogle one of her other lovers.

Later, Lucas points out that Rogue has a nickname from each of us. Noah calls her Trouble, Lucas calls her Buttercup, and Han calls her Gorgeous. I'm the only one without an obvious nickname for her.

I've been calling her "Love," but apparently, all British people use that; therefore, it isn't unique enough. Lucas starts throwing out suggestions like "Ro-Ro" or "Raven" for her hair color.

She nearly rolls backward laughing when she tries to mimic my voice and intones, "Ro-Ro."

"Alright, Tipsy. How's that for a nickname? Let's get you to bed before you topple over and take down the furniture."

Rogue tries to squirm away playfully, but I'm too quick. I spring to my feet and scoop her into my arms. Her body is relaxed and melts against my chest.

I start up the stairs as she calls "goodnight" back to the guys in the lounge. The others start picking up the mess, and I know Han will likely join us in a bit.

Lucas had her all to himself this afternoon, and I have a feeling Han feels just as deprived as I do of her company.

I stop off at the bathroom for her, and we get ready for bed. She walks out ahead of me, and instead of turning to her room, she automatically turns in the direction of mine.

When she wasn't away in San Francisco these last few weeks, she was sleeping in one of our beds. I love when she curls up next to me and snuggles in for the night. More than that, I love waking up with her wrapped around me and coaxing her back into the land of the living with wandering hands and deep kisses.

By the time we reach the room, Han has finished up downstairs and meets us at the door. We both look at her a little unsurely. We haven't seriously discussed the dynamic of all of us. She's been with both Han and me individually recently, but aside from that first night we fooled around, we haven't been in this situation. Add to the fact that she silently called me out on my Han-ogling earlier, and I'm decidedly in uncharted territory.

She rolls her eyes, pushes the door open to my room, and grabs both of our hands, dragging us in with her. When she reaches the bed, she basically flops forward and wiggles her way up the bed to the pillows. Han and I make our way to her sides as she lifts the blankets to get inside.

Han pulls her, anchoring her back to his chest, and I turn on my side to look at them. Just as her head hits the pillow, she lets out a huge yawn, and I see her fading into oblivion. "Goodnight, Tipsy," I murmur.

She puckers her lips for a kiss, and I oblige. She's relaxed as she lets out a little sigh and settles into Han. He looks at me as he kisses Rogue's neck. His eyes hold mine as he whispers, "Good night, Jacob."

My hand finds its way to Rogue's hip and connects with Han's hand, where it's settled on the lace of her underwear. His hand trembles slightly as he lifts it and laces our fingers together, laying them down again on Rogue's body. Something settles in my chest, and I murmur a goodnight as my eyes drift shut.

Rogue

I wake in stages, wrapped in someone's arms, and contentment I haven't felt in a long-ass time fills my body. Last night was perfect. We needed a damn break, and without someone to force it on these guys, I don't know that they'd ever take one.

Pizza, beer, games. The recipe for a good time. Not having had many friends in my life, I had to draw on memories of my parents and our old traditions. But instead of apple juice like back then, I substituted it with beer. I wholeheartedly approve of this change.

There was a marked change in Noah last night. I've never seen him that carefree. He let loose and played the game with a competitive streak I haven't noticed in him before.

I caught his eyes drifting over my face and body as we played games and drank too much beer. Taking stock without cracking an eyelid, I feel that I'm still wearing my black loose tank top and white bralette that peeks out, but I lost my pants at some point. I must have crashed without even getting adequately undressed.

I reluctantly crack an eyelid to investigate the heavy weight pressing on my side. I spy two hands linked and resting on my hip. One tattooed and one bare. Jacob and Han.

After a bit more wiggling into the soft mattress, I feel one of the hands tighten on my stomach. A shift of someone's hips, and there's a hardness grinding into my ass. I fully open my eyes. Facing away from my snuggler, I see Jacob asleep and breathing deeply in front of me.

"Good morning, Han," I softly say to the man holding me from behind. I don't want to wake Jacob earlier than necessary. According to Lucas's texts, Jacob has been staring at his screens day and night lately. He needs sleep much more than the rest of us. His schedule has gone entirely out of whack, and he's pulling odd shifts.

Han responds by nipping the skin between my shoulder and neck, following the sting with a swipe of his tongue. "Morning, Gorgeous. Feeling better today?" he asks.

"Yeah, I think we all needed a break. I want to come at things with a clear head today. I think last night helped give me a reset. What about you?"

"Agreed. When do you want to start today? Could I persuade you to put it off for a couple of hours?"

Smooth-talking motherfucker. "Hmmm." I hum in agreement, letting my eyes drift closed as his mouth moves up my neck to that small patch of skin under my ear. I push my hips back into his, and he reciprocates by grinding harder. Fuck, I need him. I need Jacob too.

Since the first night we spent together, I've been more than a little curious about sharing. Han and Jacob haven't mentioned it since that initial conversation, but it's something I am fully on board with.

I don't want to make things uncomfortable for them, but I've briefly spoken with Han about his feelings for Jacob, and after seeing Jacob's small glances at Han during our game last night, I know they're not one-sided.

This is something they'll need to work out and discuss on their own. I don't want to keep those two apart or be the glue holding them together. If it's something Han and Jacob want to explore, it's entirely up to them. Separate from, and yet somehow woven into what we already have.

I really hope they talk soon. Their covert glances give me anxiety, knowing they're both interested but reluctant because of a fear of rejection.

As Han's hands trail down my body, my eyes drift closed. His fingers find their way into my panties, and I let out a soft gasp.

My eyes snap open to check I haven't woken Jacob, only to find him watching my face with a look of unadulterated desire on his face. The only light, a small lamp in the corner, casts shadows across his expression and makes his stare all the more penetrating. He looks down at my body and follows Han's arm to where it has slipped under the blankets.

Han is circling my clit with insistent fingers, lavishing my neck with his skilled tongue, and grinding into my still panty-covered ass. My skin feels flushed, but it's nothing compared to when Jacob leans in to shift my tank top and bralette to the side. My nipple now exposed, he circles his tongue around it and lets his right hand drift down my body to join Han's.

He passes Han and my clit as he strokes his fingers through my wetness, then pushes two fingers into my pussy. I groan in ecstasy as the dual sensations roll through me.

It takes only a few minutes of their unwavering attention before I'm coming. The attention these two pay me makes me feel powerful.

Wanted.

Cherished.

Loved.

Han withdraws his hand from my clit and drags off my shirt and bralette as Jacob pulls my panties down and tosses them toward the closet.

Jacob pins my lower body to the mattress. I'm still on my side facing him, and he pulls my left leg up over his shoulder, and in an instant, I'm bared to him. His tongue takes over for Han on my clit as his fingers continue pumping slowly in me, curling every once in a while to send shivers running through my body.

Han pulls away from my back for a second and returns after rustling in a drawer for something. I feel his fingers run up my thighs as he gets closer to my heat. "Is this okay?" he asks as he finds his way to my ass.

I nod in desperation. "Yes!" I hoarsely whisper out just as Han's finger reaches my ass. Jacob's tongue is driving me crazy, and if I don't get one of them inside of me soon, I'm going to kick them both out, grab one of the toys I saw in Jacob's nightstand drawer a few weeks ago, and do this myself.

Han drips some lube onto his fingers and teases me for a moment before pushing one in. I moan in a voice I barely recognize. He strokes a few times as Jacob does the same to my dripping pussy.

After a few minutes of pure torture, Han withdraws and pushes another finger in, scissoring to prepare me for more.

Just the thought of both of them in me simultaneously has me clamping down and coming like a freight train. My body writhes and quivers uncontrollably. I've lost complete control of my elevated thigh as it tremors against Jacob's body.

I hastily remove the leg from over my Brit's shoulder so I don't end up with a cramp and ruin this whole damn experience.

Jacob flips to his back, rolls on a condom, and pulls me on top of him. His hands steady my hips as I settle over him. With a fucking hot show of upper body strength, he pulls me up and drops me down onto his gloriously hard dick. I'm still recovering from my last orgasm, and it's a tight fit for his monster cock.

I ride him as Han moves his way behind me. His hands circle my breasts, and he plays with my nipples in ways I feel in my clit. I want him too. I want them both at the same time, and I love that they've done this before. There's no awkward shuffling around, figuring out angles, or stilted movements. They work together flawlessly.

I've had anal before, but I've never had two men at once. I'm a little nervous about it, but mostly, I'm excited. I feel no shame, neither in the taboo nor uncertainty. I know these two will take care of me, watch out for me, and, most importantly, never push me for something I'm not willing to give.

Han presses a hand on my upper back to lean me forward over Jacob, who slows his thrusting. Moving just enough to keep me on edge.

I feel Han settle his knees on either side of us and move in close. "Ready, Gorgeous?" he asks me in a worshipful tone.

"Yes, Han. Fuck me," I beg as I try to push back onto him. I feel a slight hesitation and look at Jacob in time to see him nod as he takes in the scene in front of him. His eyes are aglow with want, and it's not just aimed at me.

Han's slicked-up cock runs its way up and down my cleft before settling at my hole and slowly pushing in. My breath is coming in shallow pants, and I feel deliciously full; the breath I had in my lungs is forced out.

Jacob commands Han with a single word. "Move."

And good God, does Han move. They alternate their thrusts, so I'm always full, and feeling the two of them stroke the thin wall between channels is pure bliss. Every time he withdraws, Han moans, likely feeling Jacob's piercings as they slide in and out of me.

"Han, how does our girl feel?" Jacob waits for the answer with bated breath.

"Good. So good. Gorgeous, you're perfect. Your ass is gripping me so goddamn tight."

"Hear that, Love? You've got him on the edge. Are you there too? I feel your pussy fluttering around my cock. Do you want to come?"

The Secrets We Keep

I attempt coherent thoughts and words, but only a strangled sound escapes my lips.

"Come." Jacob's order is clearly for both Han and me, and with the tone of his voice, the sensations I'm lost, and the fact that my nerves are frayed beyond repair, it's impossible to deny what he commands.

I close my eyes and come with a scream as the sensation overwhelms me.

Han releases a groan as he pulls out and comes all over my ass. He flops onto the bed next to us with a blissful look on his face. His hand runs down Jacob's chest and abdomen on its way to where we're joined.

He uses his deft fingers to rub maddening circles on my clit as Jacob holds my hips in a bruising grip and lifts me so I'm hovering over him as my knees struggle to find purchase on the mattress.

I place my hands on Jacob's chest and look into his blown pupils. He's using his legs for leverage as he takes over and pushes up into me hard and fast. My tits are bouncing, and there's cum dripping from my ass and onto Jacob's powerful thighs.

He lifts one last time, and I lean back as he comes with me a final time, Han's hand still cocooned between us.

Panting breaths are all I can hear for a moment until there's a rhythmic sound coming from near the door. My face is smashed on Jacob's chest, and I drag it to the other side and look to the door.

Lucas is standing there, his cock in his hand, and he's pumping away.

He must have caught the end of our little show to have been able to slip in unnoticed. His eyes are burning as they trail my body, still on top of Jacob's, as his cock softens inside of me.

Although, it's not as soft as it was a few moments ago. Interesting. Exhibitionism with Jacob sounds fun.

I raise my head and crook my finger at him. He steps up to the bed as I open my mouth. He feeds me his cock, and I finish him off in record time, smiling as I swallow down his cum. He cups my jaw and leans in for a bruising kiss.

Jacob shoves him away, and Lucas just laughs. He shrugs his shoulders unashamedly and just says, "I came to see if you guys wanted breakfast. I didn't expect to walk onto a porn set. Buttercup, that was hot as fuck."

He takes me up in his arms and walks me to the bathroom with a determined gait.

I look back at Han and Jacob over Lucas's shoulder just before we leave the room, and I see them with linked hands. Han leans into Jacob, and they share a tender, tentative kiss. My heart does a little happy dance inside my chest.

Lucas

After Buttercup and I washed off in the bathroom while I basically held her up in the shower, we made our way downstairs. She demanded coffee, so we headed to the kitchen. I plopped her on the island and spent ten minutes just standing between her thighs, sharing sweet morning kisses over coffee.

Walking into Jacob's room earlier, I hadn't expected to see them fucking like that in the low-lit room. I initially went in early to wake Buttercup for breakfast so I could steal some time with her.

Seeing her riding Jacob while Han recovered next to them was something I never knew I wanted to see. My teammates are like my brothers, and I would have thought it would be awkward. But, no. It was anything but.

The look of bliss on Jacob's face as Rogue's head lifted to the ceiling in rapture is an image I'll never forget. Cum was dripping down her ass; Han's doing, I'll bet.

I couldn't help myself. The next thing I knew, my hand was in my briefs, and my jeans were sliding down my legs. Pulling on my cock was instinctual. That was better than any dirty video I'd ever seen.

When Buttercup collapsed and turned her head in my direction, I almost wept. She motioned me closer and took me into her mouth. Finishing way too quickly, I couldn't help but steal her away to lavish her with kisses and small touches in the shower.

She's now sipping on her morning coffee and shooting coy grins in my direction. Her mug today is perfect for her. It reads: *Go ahead, underestimate me. That'll be fun. Talk about poignant.*

This girl walked into our lives, and none of us saw her affecting us the way she has. Even last night was a welcomed surprise. Getting everyone to stop doing shit, to just relax, has already had its benefits. I slept like the dead last night.

We take our time talking about what we're doing today before we have our team meeting this morning. Buttercup grabs a yogurt from the fridge and settles on one of the stools at the island. Slowly, the other guys join us and stock up on their breakfast of choice.

We take everything we need and head across the warehouse to the 'war room,' as our girl insists on calling it.

It's catching on. I heard Jacob use it last week without noticing. Little changes are slipping in around here, and I love it.

Chapter Twenty-One

Noah

It's been a couple of weeks since Rogue and I returned from our stakeout in San Francisco. I've seen more bare asses in our warehouse than tits on spring break. Between doing research and formulating plans, Rogue and the guys are fucking everywhere and anywhere.

Apparently, Jacob's got a bit of an exhibitionist streak; and fucking Lucas is a voyeur. How, oh how, did I end up with these idiots?

I'm more than a little vexed that I haven't found a way to approach Rogue despite my talk with Mama Bear. I've been ruminating on it more than I'd like to admit, but I manage to keep my head in the game and continue misleading the other two Alpha Teams we're supposed to be working with.

Somehow, amidst all the envy, research, and fucking, we find the time to develop a rough plan to get Sage away from King. It's something we've been talking circles around for the better part of the week without a solution in sight. As autumn ticks by with Halloween right around the corner, it's been too long since Rogue saw her sister, and she's getting edgier and edgier.

Before any of that can happen, Rogue is due to take care of Neil Carter in San Francisco. After we returned from up north, Rogue contacted King and told him Neil was working for someone. She hasn't divulged information related to Mara on the Annex board, but King demanded that she get back up there and "deal with" him and anyone else he's working with.

After an insane amount of digging from both Jacob and Rogue, we can safely say that not only is Neil Carter charging businesses for protection, but he is definitely a part of The Rattlesnakes, the syndicate based north of The Gambit's territory.

He's encroaching and basically shitting all over the treaty the surrounding gangs all signed. He's clearly operating under the orders of Mara Two, whom we've finally managed to track down.

It took Jacob damn near the whole week to work out that Mara has a younger sister named Claudette. When Jacob announced his findings, Rogue hopped up out of the stool she'd been sitting on and told us a woman named Claudette owned Neil's accommodation in San Francisco. Once Jacob was able to pull up a photo from the Hendrix sisters' teenage years, it became crystal clear the woman who met with Neil and provided his accommodation was one and the same.

All mention of Claudette has been wiped from Annex information servers; no doubt the majority of cleaning house was Mara's doing.

Claudette's rap sheet is non-existent, but if she's in charge of Neil and working with the Pacific Northwest's biggest syndicate, there has to be something to find. Jacob's scouring the web for the next few days while the rest of us use our other methods to find out more.

Rogue and Han headed up to San Francisco yesterday with plans to either put a bullet in Neil Carter now that we have something to go on or, hopefully, meet up with him and Claudette and come to some kind of agreement to join forces to remove King.

If everything goes according to plan, King will think Neil is dead and that Rogue is making moves to take out his superiors; all the while, we'll work with them on the real objective: dismantle The Gambit.

I hated sending the two of them up there on their own, but the rest of us couldn't be spared with the ongoing investigation into Blake's disappearance.

Rogue has been jittery as hell about Sage, but I get where she's coming from. It's hard to fathom having that one connection to your old life and watching it dangle in the breeze on the whim of a psychopath. That's the best moniker I can think to call the asshole. Rogue told us a bit about her upbringing with King, and it makes me want to stab the motherfucker in the eye.

Han and Rogue arrived in San Francisco yesterday, booking the same

Airbnb we rented when she and I were up there. The rest of us are basically sitting with our thumbs up our asses because we don't feel like we're contributing.

Rogue continues to send updates via thumbs-up emojis, and Lucas likes to remind me that I'm going to pull my hair out if I keep tugging on it in frustration. I'm older, so he reckons mine will fall out first.

The three of us who remain behind are still trailing Mara, dealing with the other alpha teams, and keeping things running. Jacob took point on organizing all this shit because he has a gift for breaking it down and ordering us around. If I didn't already know how much he hates all the red tape I have to deal with, I'd be worried for my job.

Once Han and Rogue handle Claudette, Neil, and their associates, they'll be back here until she gets word from King for another assignment.

Hopefully, he'll want to do some digging before sending her back up there to get the big players. Now that we have a name to pass him, he'll undoubtedly start working on a plan to either bring her into the fold or dispatch her.

My phone starts pinging with text messages in our group chat.

Trouble: :thumbs-up emoji:

Han: *What she means to say is: "It's done. We have an agreement with the Rattlesnakes. Han is an amazing sniper, and it appears that Neil is 'dead.' We're already in the car on the way home."*

Trouble: :thumbs-up emoji:

Lucas: :crying laughing emoji:

Jacob: *Children, all of you.*

Noah: *Good work. Get home safe.*

Lucas: *Oooh, he never tells us to get home safe. He just implies it. Buttercup, I think you have another contender for your affections.*

Jacob: *Leave him alone. He's being nice.*

Trouble: :thumbs-up emoji:

A pathetic part of me wonders if she's thumbs-upping the possibility of me having feelings for her. We haven't talked about it. I don't even know how to approach the subject. We share looks often, and the night we played Scattergories, I noticed her eyes on me almost as much as mine were on her.

Mrs. M was right. I have to get my head out of my ass and just talk to her. I'd like to ask her out on a date, but how does one initiate something new while that person is also with your best friends and teammates? Added to that, we're fielding psychopaths on one side and the board of a security company with unlimited means on the other.

Maybe when some more of this clears up, I'll finally pluck up the courage to see if it's something she might be into.

Maybe. Probably. Fuck, I'm a wimp.

Rogue

Han and I got back a few days ago from San Francisco, and after a lovely reunion with my guys back at the clubhouse, we sat down to talk about what happened up north.

Once Han and I had the keys to the Airbnb, I put on my dark gray fitted dress and black heels; then I marched my ass over to Neil's house after doing a bit of spying to make sure he was home.

The security guards tried to stop me, but when I politely said that I'd like to save their boss's life and had information, I was promptly led inside. They didn't even frisk me for weapons. Fucking amateurs. Just because a girl looks harmless doesn't mean she is.

Han was on the roof of our building in a sniper's nest with a good vantage point into Neil's place, and I had enough weapons and ammo to take down everyone in that building twice over.

I was led to Neil's office—which overlooked the street, giving Han a clear shot if anything came up—and I promptly sat down in one of his swanky chairs facing his modern art piece of a desk. All chrome and glass with paperwork fucking everywhere.

Before spilling any details, I swept the room for bugs with the device Jacob handed to me with a dominating kiss before leaving. Neil's security team was outside, so the coast was as clear as it was going to get. I explained that I wanted King gone and The Gambit dismantled.

I laid out the facts and told him I was working with The Gambit as their main assassin, and there was a hit out on him. He had no trouble believing me after he made the mistake of scoffing at me, and in response, I threw a knife I had tucked up in my cleavage at a poster of the Foo Fighters and hit Dave Grohl between the eyes. Poor Dave. It did, however, take a bit more convincing to get him to agree to my plan.

Neil held his own pretty well during our negotiations. He dialed Claudette in and filled her in on what was going on. Talking out details only took one short hour, but she was quick to agree when she heard my motivations—without mentioning Sage by name, of course.

Seems like King hasn't made friends with The Rattlesnakes. Especially since he has plans to move our operation up the coast and into their territory. Neil was a little more reluctant when it came to our strategy of putting a bullet into his Kevlar vest in a busy area, but he ended up going along with it on Claudette's orders.

He was a shockingly good actor, and the blood capsule between his teeth popped at the most opportune moment with tourists taking photos at the wharf—not to mention the fake blood packed under the Kevlar vest that pooled around him when he went down.

Anyone would have been convinced of his demise. At least Claudette had an in with the coroner and got Neil packed up and driven away to a safe house to avoid being seen strolling the streets while we worked out a plan.

He was featured on the news as being murdered, so naturally, King was happy with my results and promised a visit with Sage shortly. On a call just before our Oscar-worthy performance, I told him about Neil working for someone and followed up with a bit of info.

With Claudette's input, I gave up a fake name and some vague details that she and I came up with together during our phone call with Neil in his office.

She and I have an agreement to get together over the next couple of days to continue ironing out details and coming up with a more thorough plan while the guys take a backseat in our meeting.

They know I'll be the one running between, so I'm taking point on this. We need to see if she's working with Mara at all or if she's cut ties.

Look at me, working with people. I never thought I'd see the day.

I'M IN THE MIDDLE OF A SEX AND MARVEL MOVIE MARATHON WITH Lucas when my phone lets out an annoying ping. I nearly say fuck it and ignore it, but the name snags my attention from the bedside table.

It's a text from Tanaka, and my blood boils all over again as I think about the information he passed to me through the graveyard and priest.

Reluctantly untangling my limbs after we both finish this round with satisfied groans and *Guardians of the Galaxy* playing on the flat screen, I roll to my side and pick up the phone as Lucas big spoons the crap out of me.

Tanaka's text is a bit shady, asking if we can meet. He's led me this far with the truth of my parents' murder, so I'm inclined to agree. I switched to a burner phone to continue the conversation, and we arranged to meet at my apartment in a couple of hours.

Lucas does that thing with his tongue, and I lose track of time until the alarm on my phone lets me know it's time to go. I grab Han and Noah on my way out the door, and we ride over to my stale apartment in the blacked-out SUV.

Scaling the fire escape more quickly than I would have given them credit for, the guys meet me at my bedroom window after going through the lobby and doing a quick evaluation of Jim and Hugo.

They both mentioned King sending some people around to drop things off for me, but they swear that they always just told the messengers that I was unavailable.

I know I've still got their loyalty, and King has no reason to doubt them, as the footage of Neil getting shot at the wharf proves I've been spending some time up there.

I met Jim when he started here. Hugo was one of the hitmen I corralled for The Gambit, but he wanted out. I helped him move to the quieter side of things and got him moved to the building as security. When Jim and Hugo met, I swear the sparks were flying. I got the building manager to align their schedules years ago, and they've been dating ever since.

I make my way upstairs and let the guys in, and after a heated kiss from Han and an awkward look from Noah, I set them up in the living room closet. I'm feeling a bit rushed after hauling ass over here, but I feel good knowing I've got two of my guys watching my back.

Tanaka arrives a few minutes before the agreed-upon time, and I quickly usher him inside. The guys have the trapdoor open; they're poised on the ladder with weapons in their grips. I didn't want to leave them in my bedroom or bathroom, as that would be too far if Tanaka suddenly turned on me. The closet is slightly open, so Tanaka can see in and not suspect anyone else is here, but it gives better acoustics for the guys lying in wait.

He enters my apartment and removes his shoes before giving me a small bow. I mirror him, as I always have, and gesture to the couch. He flops down in the most unprofessional display I've ever seen from him.

"Rogue, I got a call from Father Andrews, and he told me you picked up the files. Have you not looked at the information?" he asks in a tone that a parent might use for an errant child.

"I've read it. I'm still processing, and I've been away taking care of something up north," I reply with more than a bit of steel in my voice. He drops a bomb like that and just expects me to do what? Thank him? Confide in him? Not happening.

"I found this information about a year ago. It was on one of the old servers. I've been combing the police records from back then, and it was all buried. King is reckless. He's manipulative. But most importantly, he's going to end you when your contract is up."

These are all things I know, but I don't let that information slip. "Why do you care, Mr. Tanaka?" I ask. "You have a top job in the organization; your sector does good work. Why is this important to you?"

"Rogue, there are some members of the board who wish to make a move against King. We want you on our side." Oh, fuck.

"Are the files real? Or are you fabricating things to get me on your team?" He doesn't need the files to sway me to his side, even if they've been verified. My parents are dead and gone; only Sage is left, and I can't even see her or speak to her when I want. That right there is more than enough of a reason for me to want him dead. Once I figure out where exactly she is, of course.

Han worked his magic to get into the police records room and pulled the original files. A few months after King took me in, the digital ones had been altered in the system, preventing Jacob from accessing the original files. They were stuffed in a box in one of the police's storage areas, but thankfully, they weren't well guarded, and Han was able to grab them.

"They're real alright. I know you want King gone too. Your mask is good at the meetings, but you're a good person, and I see the light dim in your eyes every time he gives you a new name. You fought to ban the sales of drugs to minors. Your job may be handling the other hitmen, but I've noticed a pattern in your kills. You only kill those who earn it."

"Who else is backing you?" I redirect the conversation, ferreting out more information before letting him know I'm in.

"Elise Batten and Nina Wilson." The socialite and the organized MBA grad. Add Tanaka and me, and we make up the majority of the board. King, Horvat, and De La Cruz won't be happy about this.

Fuck their happiness.

Leo Horvat, the Croatian bastard, has stepped on too many toes in his short tenure, and I definitely owe him for his assistance in helping King carve up my stomach. Enrique De La Cruz is pushing to sell to minors, and I can't get behind that, no matter what. I have the overwhelming suspicion he told his dealers to be on the lookout for me. After the bathroom beatdown, that suspicion is extreme. King must suspect the same thing, or he wouldn't have laid into Enrique in his office. King deserves to be taken down more than anyone else I've ever met.

The sheer volume of carnage he's left in his wake on the way to the top is horrific. I know the guys are listening from the closet. My head tries to turn in that direction instinctively, but I keep my reflexes in check as I was taught.

Tanaka looks imploringly into my eyes. I know he needs me for this, and I'm going to say yes. But there's one factor he hasn't discussed yet. "What happens when King is removed? Who runs this shitshow?"

"We're working on a plan to dismantle. We have a party interested in taking over, but we have many stipulations if we go that route. I'd rather raze it all to the ground, but who's to say someone worse wouldn't pick up where King leaves off?"

The same questions have run in my mind for years. I spend a few seconds wondering if The Rattlesnakes would be better or worse than The Gambit in sunny California.

I mull this over, along with other possible scenarios, as Tanaka sits on the edge of the couch with his forearms resting on his knees. He hasn't sat back to get comfortable the entire time he's been here. He's on pins and needles, waiting for my response.

"I'm in," I say. But I make sure that my warning that comes on the tail of my acceptance brooks no room for misunderstanding. "But if you fuck me over in this, Tanaka, I'll end you."

A sad smile takes over his face as he replies, "I know, Rogue." He takes a deep breath before starting again, "There's something else I need to discuss with you. It was us at the cemetery that took a shot at King. Well, technically, at the taxi door, not King." My fingers that were steadily drumming on my thigh fall still.

Well, with fifty-fifty odds, I'm still glad no one was aiming for me.

"Who exactly took the shot?" I ask. I can't imagine any of the three on our side of the fence picking up sniping as a hobby.

"Elise. She got a little impatient and wanted to act."

No fucking way. The sixty-something-year-old socialite took sniper lessons? Waited for us to reach the cemetery, then tried to kill King? I've got to hear this story someday.

Seeing the disbelief on my face, he continues, "Elise apologizes if she scared you. Her eyesight isn't quite what it once was, so she had to use the laser to target."

I think I've permanently dislocated my jaw as it hangs open. Wait, wait.

Did Batten not need the laser in the past? How long has she been taking shots at people? I think it's time I take her up on her invitation to "lunch." She fucking uses it as a verb like the socialite I thought she was. Or is? Fuck if I know anymore. I'm questioning everything.

Realization washes over me as I run through the consequences if Elise's shot had been successful. I have no way of contacting Sage without King, and all of the evidence he's collected on me would be released. Fuck.

They can't kill King until I settle those matters now that I'm apparently not waiting until the end of my contract to make a move.

"Mr. Tanaka, you've given me a lot to think about. I'm in, but I need some time to deal with King. I'll keep you posted on my progress, and please let Elise know I'm not mad at her for almost shooting me, but she cannot get impatient again. King has something of mine I need to get back before she shoots him. She can also reimburse me for the cab driver's repairs." I end with a chuckle, hoping the good faith I've garnered until now with Tanaka helps make this unlikely team-up possible.

He laughs at that, agrees to keep Elise in line, and bids his farewells. We make a plan to use burner phones for all communication from here on out. He writes down his own burner's number and leaves it on a takeout menu on my counter. I usher him out, and when the door closes behind him, I lean back against it.

The whole conversation took less than an hour and a half. Still, we've got four board members agreeing on a restructuring of the company and a heads-up about Elise's extracurricular activities.

I hear some rustling in the closet and slide the door open, letting the guys climb out into the living room. Noah is the first one through and grabs me in his arms. He's holding me tightly in a hug and speaking softly in my ear, "You handled that well, Trouble. Are you okay? He doesn't know about Sage, does he?"

"No. King wouldn't let it slip that he's harboring not just one but two unwilling women. Tanaka doesn't know, but Elise might. She's been around a long time."

Everything wrapped up, the guys and I grab some stuff and head back to the clubhouse to let the others know what's going on. I can't believe that of all the shit in my life, an errant socialite might have been the one to end my reign as the Maven of Mayhem in El Castillo.

Not happening. I'll die before I let Sage slip through my fingers.

Chapter Twenty-Two

Jacob

Han: *We've just finished up, and we're coming home now.* :winky emoji:

Han's message to me alleviates the worries I've been fixated on for the last two hours. Ever since they left for Rogue's place, I feel like I've been on pins and needles. What if something had happened? We only just found her, and I'd really like to not lose her.

Add in the fact that Han and I are in a weird, unfamiliar place at the moment, and I've got more stress than I usually like to deal with.

After we had our threesome with Rogue and Lucas was carrying her out of the room, Han leaned in and kissed me. It was... amazing. But things are weird now. Not long after, he and Rogue headed up north, and now things are just flapping in the wind. Unresolved. I hate that.

After Noah, Han, and Rogue return from the Tanaka meeting, I see triumph and defeat swirling in each of their eyes. The war room has become the place we spend the most time lately, and as they make their way inside, I grab Lucas from the kitchen and follow them through the doorway.

I snag Rogue's elbow before she joins them and give her a soft kiss on her forehead. I don't like the look in her eyes and don't want to add to her stress. I guide her into her seat and find my own after another small kiss on the crown of her head.

Rogue explains what's been happening and gives us more insight into the players we're dealing with. She trusts the information that Tanaka gave, and we're able to cut down on the number of board members of The Gambit that we have to deal with. I'm grateful it takes some things off our plate. Bloody Christ, it's a full plate.

As Rogue tells us about the unveiled mystery sniper, I find myself laughing along with the other guys. I don't think anyone saw Elise Batten, a high-society enthusiast, as the shooter. Don't get me wrong, Rogue proves you can be a woman and do fucking anything, but Elise is so proper it just doesn't gel.

"Does Annex know you guys live here?" she asks apprehensively. "As we start making moves, I'd like to keep this place under wraps."

"No," I answer with confidence that's slightly waning in light of the new information and the lengths to which her board members will go. "We each maintain a home elsewhere that we visit weekly to keep up appearances. We're careful not to let anyone know we live here, but there's always a chance we could be followed at some point."

Noah picks up the conversation where I leave off. "We've given no obvious reason to be followed or questioned. We've only been working together a little while, and I haven't noticed anyone tailing us. Have any of you?"

We all shake our heads, but the thought takes root. What if someone sees us? We'll either have to start using the tunnels to get in and out at another access point or pack up and move to one of the safehouses. And the damn tunnels only work if we haven't been followed up until now.

Lucas, who has been doodling as we speak, perks up with another question, "Buttercup, what was the plan to get Sage away from King before?"

She shrugs her shoulders and sighs. "I always assumed I'd work for him until I fulfilled my contract. He would likely let me see Sage then if only as a ruse to kill me, but I had an exit plan in place that included getting the fuck out of the country and as far away as we could with new identities. I've already got the documents ready using another girl for the photo, but she looks enough like Sage, and with some Photoshop, it's passable."

Lucas clearly doesn't like that answer. "So, is that still your intent now? To just leave?"

I admit, my hackles are up as well. I can't stand the thought of Rogue just taking off to some unknown locale and never seeing her again. She's one of us now. Where she goes, we go.

She clenches her fists and looks around the table, finally ending on Noah. "I don't know. Do I want to stay here? Yes. But is Sage more important than anything? Absolutely, unequivocally, yes. Her life has been traumatic. She was brought up only God knows where, forced into prostitution, with her safety and mine hanging over our heads at all times. I will not get her back only to shove her into a life she hates. Hiding and cowering while a man we despise walks among us mere mortals like a god among men.

"No. I'm getting her away and into a safe city where she'll be free to do what she wants as long as it doesn't put her at risk."

Han pipes up for the first time as he looks at Lucas, "I think I know what your mind has cooked up, but we need to be sure. Not to mention overly prepared."

Lucas nods his head. It's the most serious I've seen him in all the years we've known each other. He turns his head to Rogue with a slight grimace on his face. "We need Tanaka to request Sage from King."

Han is shaking his head in the corner of my eye and just whispers, "I knew it."

At once, her face changes entirely. I see a rage in her eyes that wasn't there moments ago. The flush on her face rises, and the tremors she's been keeping on lock finally overtake her hands. She seethes in a voice entirely too calm to be anything but deadly, "Tanaka needs to do what, now?"

"Just to get her with him, he won't do anything to her if you make this a stipulation for joining him like you did with us. He wants to make a move on King, and this will expedite his timeline. We can run an extraction to get her away from King. Tanaka can take a hit to the head, a convincing one, and say that she escaped."

I mull the plan over from a logistics standpoint. It's got some decent merit. If we plan it at the correct location, we can be in and out in under ten minutes. It falls on Tanaka to be a decent actor. King would start a manhunt for her to keep Rogue under his thumb. We could hide her in a safe house until we deal with King.

Noah seems to be letting the idea take hold, but he asks the question that should have come up first, "Do you trust Tanaka with the information? He doesn't know you have a sibling, right? Would it be passing the reins of control from one man to the next?"

Rogue's face starts to lose the flush it had before as she ponders over the idea. "Tanaka has always been a kind man to me. I honestly wouldn't have expected him to have the balls to come to me regarding taking King down. I don't know if I can trust him with Sage. If he can conspire to take down an empire, hanging on to leverage should be no problem for him."

After a moment, she continues, "If, and that's a big fucking 'if,' we do this, we don't tell him who she is to me."

Plan forming, we sit back as Rogue makes her obligatory call to King to let him know some of the details she and Claudette cooked up together about Neil's boss. She's been calling in updates once a day to space out the information and make it seem like she's working on that diligently. She leaves her phone on speaker and dials out. It rings twice before it's answered. There's no greeting, which has Rogue looking inquisitively at the phone.

"King?" Rogue prompts.

"Ivy," comes a tear-soaked woman's voice.

"Sage! What the fuck?! KING!" she shouts at the phone. A man chuckling is heard, and the woman's shuddering sounds become fainter as footsteps echo when he moves away.

"Relax, Rogue. Your precious Sage is safe. You haven't given me a reason to harm her, have you?" he asks, his voice—pure venom.

"Touch her, and I will kill you, King. Contract or no contract. Put her back wherever you've been stashing her, and if one hair on her head is harmed, there will be no mercy."

"Little Rogue, how you underestimate me." His voice sends chills down my spine. I've never met the man, but we've stared at his picture long enough for me to envision his manic smile and raised brows.

"Let. Her. Go." Her command comes out without a tremble, and I am overwhelmingly proud she's standing up to the man who abused and tortured her for most of her life.

"Not just yet, darling daughter. You owe me Neil's boss. You seem to have gathered enough intel to start the hunt. I expect that to be done immediately. Until then, I'll be keeping Sage here with me as some extra motivation." Rogue's eyes are closed, and as each blow hits, her lids twitch.

"Get to it, Rogue. And get to it quickly. Sage has been asking for you. I'd hate to think what would happen if you fail." Rogue's breathing picks up its pace, and she shields her mouth, hoping he doesn't hear how his threats affect her. "Did you know she has a birthmark on the juncture of her thigh and her pussy?" he asks amusingly, and I nearly snatch the phone then and there to deliver my own threats.

King knows how to push Rogue's buttons when it comes to her sister.

The greatest threats he could use are to kill her outright or use her and then kill her. The result is still the same. A broken Rogue and a dead innocent.

"Don't you fucking dare," she seethes.

King is quiet for a moment; he doesn't seem to be used to her talking back. But this is her trigger. Her weak spot. And he holds the fucking trump card.

We have to get Sage. I have to get her out of this mess immediately.

"You will not touch her. I'll get it done, and I'll figure out who he's working for and kill them for you. It's going to take some time, but you will not touch her."

She hangs up the phone before he can respond. None of us want to hear the threats, the leverage, the vile, depraved things that are sure to come out of his mouth. I want him dead. I want him gone. I want him bloodied and broken as I watch the woman I'm falling in love with drive her knife into his heart and feel the life flow out of him.

Rogue

One moment, I'm listening to King insinuate that he slept with my sister and the next, I'm watching my phone crash into the glass wall of the war room. In what I can only describe as a rage blackout, I shove out of my seat and head to my room.

I pull off the dress I'd been wearing and rummage around my duffle bag until I find a pair of black jeans with some stretch in them, a tank top, and pull on my shitkicker combat boots that I desperately need to replace. I'm going to fucking kill King one day. But unfortunately, today is not that day.

He's got Sage with him, and he'll be anticipating a move against him personally, but I'm not going to give him the satisfaction of being right. I've got a plan forming in my head, and I'm nearly ready to execute it. I'm just missing a couple of weapons.

I finish up strapping on the shoulder holster for the guns and shrug a leather jacket over it all. Just as I'm leaving the guest room, I see the guys down in the clubhouse's central section, huddled up and speaking in hushed tones.

I make my way to Jacob's room and pull out the hunting knife I stashed behind his dresser. I head to Han's and grab the gun I stuck in his closet behind his suits. I figured he's always working out or on a job, so the gun wouldn't be disturbed back there.

I march along the catwalk to the staircase and make my way down. Two out of four are watching me as they continue to discuss.

Lucas sees me head into the kitchen and come out with a gun being tucked into my shoulder holster's left side. That one was in the bag of muesli no one wanted to eat.

Last but not least, I approach them in the lounge area and drop to my knees. Flipping onto my back, I shimmy my way under the coffee table to grab the knives I taped under the bottom shelf while everyone was sleeping and stick one in my boot and the other at my hip in its sheath. I'm fucking ready to go to war, and these assholes are still standing around.

I stand up, face them, and immediately see the resolve in their gaze. My guys are going to try and stop me, aren't they?

"Rogue, we're heading out with you. What's your plan?" Noah surprises me by backing me. I look at the others, but their faces are just as resolute.

My plan involves going to Horvat. That dumbfuck has been backing King for years without question. He votes through any initiative put forward.

I don't know what or who King has on him or if he even has any leverage at all. Maybe Horvat is just a sick fuck? But he chose the wrong side when he held down my skinny thirteen-year-old arms while King carved up my skin. Then the asshole had the audacity to ogle me through my teenage years.

"Grab your shit. We're taking out one of King's allies. Without the support of some of the others on the board, he'll be weakened. I can't hit him while he's still got Sage, but I can take out one of his backers and cut him off at the knees. It's not the kill shot I want at the moment, but it's fucking something. And I have to do something."

Han nods and heads to the weapons room. The guys are all dressed casually, so they don't need the wardrobe change that I did, but they're taking it seriously and arming themselves to the teeth.

If I got to choose who to go after on the board, I'd select Horvat every time. His crimes back in Croatia were deplorable, and with the bureaucratic red tape and frustratingly glacial court process, he was able to get away with more than anyone should. This is going to be a pleasure.

It's that thought which has me pausing for just a second, hovering over the door jamb to the clubhouse.

The guys have seen my work after I'm done, but they've never seen this side of me live and in person. Is it weird that I enjoy my work sometimes?

Will they see me in action and recoil? I hope to hell not because I'm not changing my mind about this, and it's fucking go time.

Armed up, we head out to the parking area. Han and Jacob climb in the truck while Noah, Lucas, and I take the SUV. Our car leads the way as I snap directions at Noah in the driver's seat. He drives carefully and skillfully, but he's white-knuckling it on the steering wheel.

The tension in the car is palpable as we leave the industrial district and head into the suburbs. It's mid-afternoon, so there's a good chance Horvat won't be home, but I'm more than happy to lie in wait. I heard his wife works as a hairstylist, so her hours are a bit of an unknown factor, but if worse comes to worst, I'll tie her up and stick her in the garage.

We reach the wide streets of his neighborhood, and I tell Noah to slow down. I direct him to park a few houses down, hiding us in plain view. Jacob and Han take the truck farther down the street and park on the other side to have a getaway facing both directions.

I take a look around the neighborhood. There aren't any kids playing in the street, the lawns are meticulous, and the landscaping makes everything seem normal. Gag.

All's quiet. It's only three o'clock in the afternoon; I guess most people are still at work. Good, fewer potential witnesses. Jacob calls Noah, and he puts the phone on speaker. "Which house is it?" he asks.

"The tan one with the green door on our side of the street. Three houses east of the one you're parked across the street from. Number 462."

"Got it." I hear him typing on a laptop he must have snagged from the house when we left. He keeps going for a few minutes until he finally says, "He's Croatian, right? I'm picking up Modrić as one of the networks in the area."

"That's him," I confirm with a smug grin.

No lie, Luka Modrić is an incredible soccer player, but it made finding the network stupid easy. Get him, Jacob.

The typing continues until he triumphantly sighs into the phone. "Okay, I've scoped the place with the internal cameras and shut his network down. No one seems to be home. His electrical and camera feed were wired up because he's got a 'smart house,' which is really dumb, but I sent a notice to the alarm company that it's scheduled. The internal cameras are off and not sending a feed to the servers.

"Rogue, have you visited this man before? I've never seen someone with this level of security who wasn't in politics or leading a nation." A giggle escapes my lips.

"I may have visited him once before and left him a tiny souvenir." I laugh as I remember the scar on his neck. I feel smug that he beefed up his security because the idea of me coming back scares him.

But people who link up everything to their networks are just asking for trouble if they don't have a backup in place. It's not like he would have asked me for my advice when picking out his new system. "Are we good to go?"

"All set," he confirms. "We'll head around the back." I see him and Han exit the truck and make their way down the side street. They're going to have to hop a fence or two, but it's less suspicious if there are only a few of us seen at the front door.

Noah, Lucas, and I pile out of the car and make our way up the street. Lucas starts talking about the weather, and with our wardrobe, we just look like we're out for a walk in case we're spotted.

We reach the front door, and I bend down to look like I'm tying my shoe while the others block me from any peeping neighborhood busybodies.

I pull out the lock picking kit I have stashed in my pocket and get to work. With the security alarms on hiatus, it should be a quick job to get in.

I hear the tumblers click into place, and I turn the knob. The door swings inward, and we're greeted with silence.

I release my breath, and Lucas extends a hand to help me up. We walk into the foyer, and Noah makes his way toward the back of the house to let the others into the home. I push the door closed behind me as Lucas cases the place to make sure we're alone.

God, I barely looked around here the last time I visited. It reeks of new money. There are little glass figurines on the mantle; the artwork is all modern prints with rose gold accents. Gen-Zers.

I know his wife is young, but this just confirms it.

Lucas finishes his exploration of the bottom floor and heads upstairs on silent feet. Noah, Han, and Jacob join me in the living room, staying out of sight from the untreated front windows.

A knocking sound on the banister has me turning to see Lucas grinning from the landing on the stairs. "All clear."

We move to the kitchen to wait for Horvat to come home. The backyard is well shielded by trees, reducing the chance of a neighbor seeing us in here. Jacob pulls his phone from his pocket and restarts the electricity and network. "We want him to think everything is normal when he comes home. I looped the camera footage from the ten minutes before I disabled it,

The Secrets We Keep

so we won't be seen." My tattooed, sexy nerd explains his incredible work with a shrug. "Plus, the longer it's offline, the more chance he has to check the app and see things are down."

We all sit around the kitchen. Waiting, watching.

Lucas spends the time snacking on a bag of Cheetos he found in the pantry. Gotta love his devil-may-care attitude in moments like this. My bloodlust continues to rage, but I can't exactly do anything about it until Horvat gets home.

Noah opens the fridge but quickly shuts it with his face scrunched up. The smell finally reaches me, and I have to suppress a gag.

Well, that explains why he always smells like sauerkraut. His fridge reeks like it's fucking stocked with fermented cabbage.

Han coughs out, "Make a note to never open that thing again. Phew, gross."

Everyone chuckles for a moment and then gets back to waiting around. We have to wait a couple of hours, and we pass the time by mostly just sitting around and running through some scenarios. We've all got our orders.

A beep sounds in the house moments before keys slide into the lock on the front door. Horvat.

We stay where we are in this part of the house, out of sight from the front door, and I swear, no one moves a muscle as we wait for him to make his way inside. Jacob and Han originally sat on one of the couches but now silently stand near the hallway's opening; he'll need to walk down it to access this area. Once he makes his way over here, we'll have him surrounded with no escape except the backdoor, which I see Noah slightly shift toward.

The door shuts, and I hear him drop his keys on the table by the front door. He groans as he walks through the house, heading toward us in the kitchen. No doubt to eat more of that disgusting cabbage in the fridge.

He finally emerges from the hall. Jacob and Han are standing at the ready, just out of view, and once Horvat clears the opening, Jacob shifts, his body blocking it. Horvat's eyes wander to the kitchen just as his access out of here is cut off.

His eyes land on me, sitting on the island counter with my legs swinging back and forth merrily. I'm fucking pumped for this.

"Good afternoon, Horvat." I wink at him just to piss him off. I need a fight, and I'm hoping he'll provide.

"Jebem ti, what the fuck are you doing in my house again?!" he roars. I love it when his little Croatian curses come out.

"I'm here for information. These are my colleagues," I raise my arm to gesture to the men surrounding him. He turns to look back at the front door and sees Jacob's wide frame blocking his escape. Han stands to Jacob's right, blocking the living room as his hand casually holds a gun at his side. Noah's linebacker body barricades the door to the backyard, and Lucas, my darling Lucas, waves his Cheeto-dusted fingers at Horvat from the other side of the kitchen island.

The tremor that started in his hand starts working its way up his body. He knows he's vastly outnumbered, and his last chance is to spill. "What do you want to know?"

"What's King plotting these days? I know he trusts you and Enrique for the dubious shit he doesn't want to tell me about. Spill it. Now."

"He's been working with Enrique more than me lately. I'm just working on running the guns." He lifts his hands in a placating gesture that rakes across my nerves. He's been privy to a lot of information over the years and used that to further his reach.

Part of me is reluctant to make a move on Horvat, but my gut tells me it's the right thing to do. My instincts are rarely wrong, and over the years, I've learned to trust them. "Let's take a walk, Horvat."

He looks around at the guys once again, his head swiveling to and fro. He knows the odds are against him, and before he can even get his arm close to the waistband of his pants, Han has him in a headlock with his arm pulled taut, poised to break it. We all know a gun grab when we see one.

Now closest to Horvat, Jacob slips the gun from where he was trying to grab it, checks the safety is still on, and tosses it to Lucas, who immediately covers it in orange dust from his hands. He makes a joke about "dusting for prints," but I'm too caught up in getting some answers.

One by one, we all make our way down the hall to reach the office on the bottom floor, frog-marching an irate Horvat in the middle of the group. Han handed off our prisoner to Noah and stayed near the door to look out for the wife.

If she comes home early, we made a plan to keep her trussed up in the garage until it's all over. I don't plan to kill her.

The only shitty thing she's done is have lousy taste in men. And let's be honest, we're all guilty of that one at some point. Although knowing Horvat's winning personality, there's a distinct possibility she's not invested in this relationship.

We walk into the office, and I motion to Jacob to take the seat behind the desk. He swivels the laptop toward Horvat when the password prompt pops up. "I could do this myself, but why don't you save us some time, hmm?" His British accent makes him sound like an impatient motherfucker. I love it.

Horvat tilts over the computer to type his way in, and I hear him mutter "Limey bastard" under his breath.

I pull my hunting knife from my hip and jam it through Horvat's hand, where it was resting peacefully on the desk. Lucas and Jacob don't react, but I see Noah's eyebrow cock as if impressed. He watches the knife wobble a bit at the handle because of how hard I struck.

Curses fall from Horvat's lips as he trembles, trying not to move his hand despite the natural instinct to curl his arm into his body to protect it. The knife embedded deep enough into the wood below that I know he's not going anywhere any time soon.

The adrenaline might give him enough strength to pull it out with the other hand, but with the way he's shaking and turning a nasty shade of green, I doubt he'll even try.

Jacob barely pays attention to us as he sifts through files on Horvat's computer. Code goes flashing by, and I recognize the patterns enough to know he's checking data for calls and electronic communications. Satisfied he's found something, he pulls a USB from his pocket and loads it into the port.

"Okay, Horvat. I know you're probably hoping to get out of this alive, but King has been pissing me off. I happen to know why you got locked up back in Croatia, so I feel justified in doing this. You really thought bribing your way out of it was going to erase everything?"

He looks at me, now sweating and his jowls wobbling, like I'm the devil incarnate. Well, maybe he's got a point. "Doesn't take much to access data in your small hometown. Three girls brave enough to step forward and accuse you of stalking, molestation, and rape who disappeared before trial? Ring any bells? So, you can either tell me what you know, and I'll make it quick, or drag it out, and you'll end up begging for death in a few days when I'm done with you. What'll it be?"

No one moves. No one speaks. Jacob even stops typing to hear his answer. Finally, he sings like a damn canary, "King is planning to cut down the board to the three of us. Himself, Enrique, and me. Tanaka will still run Rook but will not have a say on our side of things. Wilson is getting antsy and wants to move on anyway. Elise isn't necessary because King has enough ins with the upper crust, so she's not needed anymore. He was reluctant to cut you out and claimed he could keep you on your leash. What a load of shit."

He glares at both my guys and me with barely concealed rage, and I so very badly want to nail his other hand to the desk with the knife in my boot.

"He's working on the threat in San Francisco now. He said you killed Carter but haven't dealt with his boss yet. He said he'd get you to do it. I don't know how he planned to accomplish that. I didn't ask. That's it." He puffs up his chest and looks me in the eye.

"A deal's a deal, Rogue. Kill me, and make it quick." Noah lifts his gun with the silencer on the barrel. He's facing Horvat, whose back is against the wall. A shot rings out, but it's not Horvat who goes down. It's Noah.

I see blood blooming on the right side of Noah's chest where the bullet exited. I drop down to my knees to break his fall as he sinks like a bag of rocks. Lucas pulls a gun and swings his arm out wide in the direction of the source of the shot. Jacob pulls the computer down with him to the floor behind the desk, and I hear Han barreling through the house to get to us.

Lucas fires off a shot, and I see part of the closet door get blown off. Han dives into the room and sees Noah and me on the floor. He uses his body to shield us as he starts pulling Noah out into the living room. I help to carry his legs out, and once he's clear, I grab a gun from my shoulder holster and raise it to enter the room. Lucas is partially hidden behind a bookshelf when the person in the closet places the pistol on the floor and slides it out in surrender.

Horvat is cursing up a storm in Croatian, completely fine. Well, other than the knife in his hand. I raise my gun and fire off two shots—two to the chest, one to the head for good measure.

I duck and roll to the desk and wrap around the other side. I aim at the closet and order whoever is inside to open the door and step out. The whole thing takes less than a few minutes, but it sounds like the aftermath of an explosion when all gunfire ceases. My ears are ringing, my mind is in turmoil, and all I can think about is getting the rest of the guys out safely.

Lucas carefully makes his way over to the accordion doors of the closet. He finds a woman slumped over, fighting tears and looking at us with equal parts fear and relief. The gun she was using is still at the entrance to the closet. Lucas kicks it away and pulls the woman into his arms. This must be the wife.

"I'm so... s- sorry." She wails. "I wanted to shoot him." Her arm flings out in the direction of Horvat, and I see she nearly had the angle to shoot her husband. "I wanted to kill him." She's a babbling mess and clings to Lucas's neck as he hoists her into his arms.

Lucas checked the house, so I don't know where she was while he did a search or why she was packing a gun, but I'll definitely get some more info out of this woman later when Noah isn't in dire straits.

Lucas leads the charge out of the room with the woman in his arms. Jacob and I follow. The room looks like a war zone, but it will make the narrative of a burglary more plausible.

Jacob has the laptop in his hands, and before I have to see Noah bleeding out, I rush upstairs and grab a bunch of the wife's jewelry, but there isn't any. Only Horvat's got the expensive shit. It's better to make this look like a robbery than a murder.

I make it downstairs with a small bag of pricey watches in my hand and round the corner. Han and Jacob are waiting, Noah slung between their bodies, supported on either side by reaching an arm over each shoulder.

"Hi, Trouble. Did you get me something pretty?" Noah rasps out, eyeing the open bag hanging from the crook of my elbow.

"Sure did, Captain. Let's get you patched up." I fight the concern in my voice, and tears threaten to fall. I can't look at him. It's my fault he's in this mess in the first place.

I bolt out of the house and make my way to the SUV. Lucas left the keys in it if we needed a quick getaway, thank God.

I start it up and get the SUV as close to the house as possible, lightly scratching Horvat's flashy BMW on my way past. Fuck him.

The guys get the back door open as I put the car in park and move to the back seat, where they lay Noah down. His head is on my lap, and he looks up at me with those golden eyes. I feel the first tear streak down my face.

I don't know who's driving or who else is in the car with us. I don't care. As long as someone gets us the fuck out of here before Noah bleeds out. He continues looking up at me, and when I think he's going to pass out or go into shock, he raises his left arm and crooks his fingers, indicating for me to move closer.

I do, and he surprises me. "Have dinner with me if I live through this?" he asks.

This man. This gorgeous, selfless, stoic man who has charmed me with his dependability, dazzled me with his rare wit as we kept watch through the windows in San Francisco, and brought all of us together without asking for anything for himself.

His breathing is labored, the blood still pouring from the wound as I keep it packed with his shirt and my trembling hands. We're flying through the streets on our way to get help, and his breathing becomes thready.

"Yes. Just fucking live."

A broken wail of agony escapes my lips as he exhales his final breath.

Bonus Scene

Bonus Scene

Lucas -Three months before meeting Rogue and the scene that caused Noah to roll his eyes so hard, they almost got stuck in his head, as referenced in chapter 10

There are way too many guys here tonight. The club is a veritable sausage fest. I've been moving my ass on the dance floor for nearly an hour now and only bumped and ground with two women so far. And one or two guys, but I'll take any dance partner at this point.

What is the point of the bouncer at the club's entrance if not to keep the numbers more balanced? As I move my booty to whatever's popular at the moment, I make eye contact with a girl who looks as if she'd rather be anywhere else than with her friends out celebrating a bachelorette party.

She seems sweet. Mousey-brown hair piled up on her head, presumably to keep the heat off her neck as the temperature in the club skyrockets.

She lets out a laugh and looks down to the floor after catching my inquisitive look. It's an absolute smorgasbord here for a single girl in her twenties. She could have the pick of the bunch, but she seems content to keep fending off advances and hanging out near their booth in the VIP section.

Since I'm not feeling this either, I decide to make my way over and chill

Bonus Scene

with someone who isn't looking to drag someone home tonight. I just finished a job and thought this would be an excellent way to let off some steam by shaking my ass. Instead, I'm bumping into dudes left and right as they hunt for their next conquest.

I weave my way between the dancers, waving a hand before my face as if that would dissipate the desperation filling the air—no such luck.

I finally emerge on the other side and stop in front of her table. "Hey, I'm Lucas, and I'm not looking to get laid tonight. Want to hang out?"

Her soft brown eyes widen in shock, and one side of her lips tip up in a smile. "Lena, and sure. Although, that could be a line engineered to make me lower my defenses. Is it a line, Lucas?"

"Absolutely not. Watching all of the guys doing laps around the bar and dance floor has made me ashamed of my gender. Not feeling the vibe, what with my fellow compatriots making all of us look like assholes." My assurance seems to hit the spot, and she waves a hand at the empty side of the booth as she laughs. I slide in and relax against the plush seat.

"That's true. I've got a boyfriend and was dragged to this party kicking and screaming by my cousin, the bride-to-be. I know it's tradition and all, but woof. This is just sad."

We chat for a bit as the other girls from her group come and go. Turns out she's been in a relationship for five years, is incredibly happy, and doesn't like other guys pressing in on her while she dances. She's self-confident, assured, and happy just to hang out. If I didn't have respect for other people's relationships, she'd be just my type. I like the bold yet sweet type. Meh, maybe one day.

As we sit and drink beers in the booth, we get to talking about insane scenarios we could get up to if we were the other gender. To prove my point that I could pick up any guy in this sweaty club, I came up with my most genius plan ever.

"Then let me try, but let's make it a challenge." I poke my head under the table, intending to check out what she's wearing, and she slaps my arm just as my head dips below. "Jesus, Lena! I just wanted to see what you were wearing. Okay. I have an idea."

"And it involves looking under the table when your companion has a miniskirt on?!" She laughs.

"Ooh, that'll be perfect. You're tall, right? What size shoe do you wear?" I ask. We're nearly the same height while sitting, similar build since I've always been slimmer around the waist, but my shoulders will never fit into her top.

"Uh, size ten. That's super random. Why?" Lena asks warily.

"We're going to switch clothes. You won't get hit on wearing a Superman t-shirt and baggy jeans with sneakers. Granted, you'll be swimming in the shoes a bit, but consider walking a new challenge. And I, my darling, will pick up a guy wearing your skirt and heels. We got a plan?"

"Oh, fuck. Okay, this is gonna be good. Can I record it?" she asks.

"Yep! Let's do this."

We make our way to the bathrooms and grab two stalls after waiting in the godforsaken line for ten minutes. She's been picking out guys for me to hit on in my new outfit, and they're all the biggest, beefiest motherfuckers in the place.

Once inside, we both strip down in our respective stalls and pass the clothes over the dividers to get dressed in our new outfits. I laid toilet paper on the floor before handing over my sneakers, being a gentleman, so she doesn't run the risk of bare feet on a public restroom floor.

Once dressed, I run my hands down the skirt that's just a bit too tight and make sure my feet are steady in the neon green heels. This may have been a bad idea.

"Ready?" Lena asks from the sink area outside of my closed stall door.

"Ready!" I shout.

I unlatch the door and take a few unsteady steps as I emerge. I fling my arms out and call into the cavernous bathroom, "I have arrived!"

Women washing their hands and reapplying makeup laugh and cheer at my antics. I catch sight of myself in the mirror and choke. I'm now towering in height with the added inches the heels provide and all legs as the miniskirt only hits me at high-thigh, barely covering my cock and balls. My chest is bare, and I look absurd.

Lena pulls a lipstick from her bag and motions me forward. She smears it over my lips and does this weird smush and pop thing with her own, waving her hand impatiently. "You're supposed to do that now, Lucas." I follow her instructions, feeling the others in the bathroom watching me with glee in their eyes, but I accomplish my task.

Lena is swimming in my clothes but looks much more at ease than she did before.

"Alright, Lena, let's do this thing!" I declare. The girls in the bathroom whoop and cheer as I saunter my way to the door, yanking it open and swaying my hips with each step in the too-tight shoes and snug skirt, only tripping once.

I lead the way onto the dancefloor and immediately start looking for

Bonus Scene

possible targets. I move with the music, using my insane height in these shoes to scope out the possibilities. Lena, who is still beside me, points out a man I've seen a few times tonight, working his way around the room and not having much luck.

I nod my head, unable to speak over the booming music from the speakers. I do a side shuffle to get closer to him, and while he's facing away from me, I run my fingertips down his back, catching his attention. He turns with a smile on his face that quickly disappears as he finds my bare chest at the height he'd usually find a woman's face. His face turns into a scowl when he finally reaches my face.

"What the fuck." I barely hear him say over the music.

"Let's dance!" I shout, grabbing his hand and pulling him deeper into the crowd. He laughs, and after being shot down repeatedly through the night, he's probably just looking for some fun in any form at this point. He joins in after a few stilting movements, and we start a dance-off.

The crowd makes a ring around us, and after a few minutes, more people join in. I spy Lena on the side of the circle, laughing her ass off. I'm glad I helped make her night more fun, but honestly, engaging in these little challenges and inane antics has helped me feel more like myself after the mission.

Lena and I spent an hour on the dancefloor with the other club-goers before we headed back to the VIP table she and her girls had. A few of them are slumped in the booth, having drunk too much. We start hauling them up to get them back in the limousine with the bride-to-be.

"This was really fun, Lucas. Thanks for not being a creep," Luna says once we've got the last of the girls in the limo and are standing out in the warm June air.

"You got it. Oh, your clothes!" I exclaim, realizing I'm still in the ridiculous outfit, which has grown surprisingly comfortable in the last hour.

"Keep 'em!" she shouts as she jumps into the limo after her friends, and it speeds off. My clothes obviously go with them, and I realize I'll have to Uber home in this. This is better.

Seeing Noah's face when I get home in this outfit is sooo going to be worth it.

Afterword

Hey, there. Are you okay? No? Not yet? I get it. You can hate me for a bit. Hopefully, Noah will be okay. I mean, he did stop breathing... so I guess

Bonus Scene

we'll see. I can't wait to see how Rogue and her guys handle King and his fucked-up fiefdom. See you in book two...

The Sacrifices We Make

Content

Content warning:
This book has explicit moments, from murder (described graphically) to sex (also described graphically). There is also a short flashback of childhood trauma in Chapter 15 from Rogue's point of view that can be skipped if it's upsetting. I've italicized the section so you know where you can restart reading. There is also forced prostitution (not of the main character) mentioned throughout the book.

Prologue

Lucas

As I stare across my room in the renovated clubhouse, despair threatens to overwhelm me. It takes a lot to get me into this state of mind; this bone-deep, aching sense of loss is not a feeling I particularly relish.

Funerals always bring out the worst in me.

I haven't felt this melancholy in a long time. It's bringing back those old ghosts I thought I'd long since laid to rest. The similarities between his death and my parents' are startling. One moment here, the next, gone. It's almost as if fate enjoys fucking with me because he took his final breath in a car as well.

I hear a knock on the door and reluctantly stand from my unmade bed. My shoes snick across the polished concrete floor of my room, and I swing the door wide. There, in all her rockabilly glory, is my Buttercup.

"Hey, Red. You doing okay?" Her raspy voice is a balm on the scars that threaten to reopen whenever I let my mind wander.

"Yeah," I choke out in a voice I don't recognize and stop to clear my throat. "Yeah, yes. I'm fine."

"Nah, you're not. But that's okay." She reassures me with ease and folds me into her arms to lend me the comfort and strength I desperately need today. I inhale her familiar lemon and lavender scent, and my nerves settle.

"Do we need to pick anything up on the way, or are we headed straight to the cemetery?" I ask as a way to distract myself. One foot in front of the other; that's how I get through today.

"We're good to go. Han and Jacob are waiting downstairs for us. Can you just grab the flag?"

I grab the carefully folded American flag from my dresser and follow Buttercup from the room. She takes my hand and places a soft kiss on the knuckles. After he died, we spent some time talking about how it mirrored my childhood loss. The withdrawal into myself is not something I expected, but Buttercup is always there, trying to pull me back to the light.

She pointed out that I may have some abandonment issues, and we've been talking things out. Buttercup has experienced loss firsthand and still manages to maintain her level head like it's nobody's business.

I peer over the railing as we descend the steps to see Jacob and Han resting on the couch. Their tailor-made black suits, matched to my own, paint a gloomy picture with somber expressions on their faces. Generally, at this point, I'd make a joke—something stupid and entirely inappropriate, like asking, "Who died?"

Not today. Not this past week. Probably not for a little while.

"Han ordered us an Uber, so we don't have to worry about driving if we drink too much after the funeral. We've got this, man," Jacob tells me.

He's handled everything from the flowers to the reception, and with Buttercup's input, he even got a plot in the cemetery where her parents are buried. That way, we can visit everyone at the same time.

My girl keeps hold of my hand but leans in to kiss Jacob and Han in succession, no doubt in gratitude for thinking of the small details while she babysat my sorry ass. I feel my face stiffen into a grimace and consciously try to relax while I'm with the others.

Jacob grabs the bouquet of white lilies resting on the low table in the lounge and leads us out the door. We walk down the block and wait for the Uber at an intersection because we can't let anyone know where we live, even for a funeral. Noah wouldn't want that.

We pile into the black town car when it arrives and cross El Castillo to Saint Ignatius church. The very same one Buttercup visited to get information on her parents. The place where she narrowly avoided being shot by one of her board members as they aimed a bullet to take out King. Now, the graveyard there will also house one of our own.

Despite the locale's more recent memories, Buttercup described the graveyard's serenity with a soft and reverent tone, and I could instantly see the appeal. It's a large stone church with a well-maintained cemetery and,

The Sacrifices We Make

most importantly, availability. She showed us some photos online, and we knew it had to be the place. Mrs. M was in complete agreement, and we'll meet her there for the service.

Even though there's a definite chill in the air now that we're deep into autumn, my body feels too warm in the cramped car. The scent of lilies dredges up even more memories of my parents, and I distract myself by playing with the window controls.

Open. Closed. Open. Closed.

Is it going to be an open casket or closed?

Buttercup's head settling on my shoulder helps redirect my thoughts to the present. She's wedged between Han and me in the backseat as Jacob sits up in front with the driver. Her white dress is fitted and falls to her calves with a small slit running modestly up the back. She paired it with a grey wool coat, blush pink heels, and a matching headscarf wrapped around her wavy hair. The tattoos visible on her right leg are vivid against her outfit's soft, muted colors, and it suits her impeccably.

Our ties match her heels—another detail Jacob took care of—and we look like a macabre group headed to prom with our matching garb. I think it's adorable in a sick and twisted way.

We round the last corner and pull up to the church. Buttercup slides out after Han and links an arm with him as she reaches back for my hand. She's been my life raft this week, and she refuses to let me sink.

Jacob opens the gate and ushers us through, and the four of us make our way to the small lawn for the ceremony. The coffin rests above the grave, and the priest waits behind a small podium. Mrs. M is already seated in one of the few chairs gathered, dressed all in black with a veil covering her face.

She notices us approaching and tears her gaze away from the coffin. "Hello, boys. Rogue, honey, come sit by me." She pulls Buttercup onto the seat next to her while we take the three seats behind them. Why they needed to make two rows is beyond me. There are only a few of us attending this thing.

We settle in as the priest begins his speech.

He reads from Ecclesiastes in the Bible first, reminding us there is a season for every activity under heaven; a time to be born and a time to die.

When he moves on from scripture and reaches the military career our dear friend was so proud of, I feel a hand clamp down on my shoulder.

The priest looks up from his Bible, and Noah apologizes as he slides into the seat next to Mrs. M, holding her purse on his lap. She must have forgotten it in the car.

I have to admit, the matching pink tie looks good on him.

Noah drove her over here when she called him in a panic an hour before the funeral was set to begin. She couldn't bear to look at the Shaggin' Wagon, let alone drive it. After all, her boyfriend Archie died in it last week.

Yup. He had a heart attack while helping the Wagon live up to its name.

Chapter One

Rogue

Wow, that's some impressive blood spray.

I step back, pulling my knife from Governor Reyes's neck. I use my forearm to wipe my face free of the gore and end up smearing it and making it worse instead of cleaning it off. Great.

Why am I killing a prominent political figure?

The official reason is that he asked for more bribe money than he was worth from The Gambit. My reason is more personal.

I chose to do this job myself because of his proposal and the subsequent passing of a bill undercutting funding for veterans while funneling the money into the PAC's interests, thus ensuring another four years with this asshole. No, thanks.

The other reason was that his wife cowers in fear whenever he lifts his hand when the cameras aren't around. It doesn't take a genius to figure out there's abuse happening there if you know where to look.

I've been working on Reyes for nearly a month; I took my time with this one. King wanted recon first regarding where the bribe money was going and why he wanted more. To the best of my knowledge, Reyes just wanted more to keep stockpiling it for the day he left office. I sent in Giacomo—aka G—to lay the groundwork.

G is one of the hitmen in the crew I run for The Gambit. With his intimidating demeanor and athletic physique, he was easy to plant in the governor's security crew.

I started working on his placement when King gave me the orders to take Reyes out. It took a bit of time and some exceptionally well-crafted credentials, but within a matter of days, I had G doing recon for me from inside the residence.

We were lucky there was an opening in the security team.

I mean, luck didn't have much to do with it. It was more like I randomly picked someone from the Governor's team and made it seem like the guard and his wife had won a sweepstakes prize, sending them on a three-month holiday to Spain. All paid for by The Gambit, of course. I expensed it.

G called me a week ago to say that the wife was covering up bruises on her arms with long sleeves, and he thought I'd want to handle this one on my own. I hadn't known that little detail when this started, but I was sure glad to know it now. Gotta love the chain of command.

I had initially planned to do this somewhere public and embarrassing. In such a way as to tarnish his legacy for his crimes against his wife and the general populace, but I figured the quicker the wife was rid of her shitbag husband, the better.

King called Reyes to agree to the increase, which had him chomping at the bit to get the cash as soon as possible. A day later, I followed up and arranged an in-person meeting with Reyes to deliver the money bag. It was embarrassingly easy.

G told me what dates he was working the night shift so he'd be the security detail to escort the governor to his death. The others on the team knew Reyes dabbled in a bit of gambling and were led to think he was going out for a bit of debauchery in one of the underground clubs.

I insisted on one of the dates I knew G was working. Better to have an accomplice than a second body to deal with.

I knew the stars had aligned when he showed up to the meeting in the seedy motel with my very own hitman as his only bodyguard for the night.

Reyes and G entered the room, the latter pretending to do a sweep for weapons and giving me a slight smirk when he passed over the knives on my hips, ignoring them. I nodded at G to wait outside, and after Reyes confirmed his dismissal with rude and impatient words, he stepped over the threshold and pulled the door closed behind him. I had to admire how confident Governor Reyes was that his position would protect him.

Only bringing one bodyguard with him to the meeting?

Dumb move.

The Sacrifices We Make

A bit of showboating from the governor about how I should just hand over the cash so he could get on with his hectic and important life was cut off when I pulled the knives from their sheaths. His eyes flared comically large, and he started to backpedal and snivel in fear.

I had no concerns about it being a clean kill. The blonde wig and full-coverage concealer on my tattoos wouldn't point to me at all. I even wore some green contacts in the unlikely event that the shitty motel had decent cameras.

The messy and brutal kill serves as a message to others connected with The Gambit. Pushing us for more money is not a good idea, and crossing us is an even worse one.

I head into the bathroom as the last of Reyes's blood bubbles from the wound across his neck. The arc it produced as I cut across the carotid—while expected—was extremely impressive. Killing may not be new to me, but it's always unique.

I wash my hands and face, reapply the concealer, and switch out my wig and clothes for an identical set I have stashed in a bag in the bathroom. I didn't bring an extra set of boots, as they're one of a kind, but I waxed them before leaving today, so a quick wipe with a washcloth, and they're good as new.

Looking like an innocent girl with a penchant for thigh-high leather boots, courtesy of Lucas, my darling Red, I sashay back across the room, leaping over the bigger puddles of blood, and head outside.

G is lounging next to the motel door, one leg kicked up behind him, looking relaxed as fuck.

"All good?" he asks.

I nod in response, and he motions to the SUV he drove here tonight. We reach the trunk together as G pulls the keys from his pocket. He opens it, shifts a cover to the side, and pulls out three cans of accelerant.

G has a penchant for watching things light up. I should introduce him to Han.

We go back into the room and splash the fluid along the walls, the bed, and the body. On our way out, he strikes a match and tosses it back inside. It immediately extinguishes as it sails through the air.

"Fucking cheap-ass matches," he grumbles.

Yeah, it would have been cool if that had worked, but you know, physics.

He lights another, bending down to place it on the floor. It immediately catches on the accelerant and starts to snake through the room. Usually, I'd just stab and run, but the glee in G's eyes lets me know this was a good choice.

He brought the kill to me because he knows about my fondness for offing the worst of the worst. I owe him this much.

We close the door, pull the fire alarm a few yards down the hall, and go to the modest grey sedan I borrowed from my buddy Axle's shop. I toss my duffel in the back seat, and G climbs in on the passenger side.

I slide in behind the wheel and get the car started. In the rearview mirror, I see the motel guests spilling out of their respective doors with their things as the alarm blares the song of its people. At least I can rest easy tonight, knowing the other guests weren't harmed.

I start the car, and Lizzo's "Truth Hurts" plays from the speakers as it connects to my Bluetooth.

What? I like it.

G starts singing along to the catchy chorus, and it's ridiculous to see this long-haired, tattooed badass sing along. Surprisingly, he hits most of the notes.

He lowers the window on his side, letting the wintry air wash over us as we drive back to El Castillo from the sleepy seaside town.

We have about an hour before we're back, and he makes grabby motions for my phone. Once in his clutches, he sets the song to repeat the whole way home.

By the time we reach the city, we've listened to the song approximately four million times and found harmony together.

Overall, not a bad night.

I drop G off at his new house without asking for directions because I enjoy freaking people out like that. I know where all of my people live. I also spend time with them when I can because I don't want to end up like King, with people only following the rules out of fear.

I'd much rather have them play nicely because they respect me.

I drop the car back at Axle's garage for a deep clean as the moon hangs low in the sky, illuminating the streets as if it's dawn when it's only three in the morning. I message King and sweep for bugs or trackers before taking off in Black Beauty, my vintage Chevy Bel Air.

It's been a weird month.

Red took Archie's death pretty hard, trying to take the blame onto

The Sacrifices We Make

himself for Mrs. M's sadness because he introduced them. He's also been beating himself up over not finding Polly in Horvat's house, so he's attempting to take Noah's shooting injury onto himself as well, despite how many times we've told him shit happens.

The ever-gracious and hard-ass Mrs. M keeps reminding Red that without him, they wouldn't have known each other at all, and she's grateful to have spent time with Archie, no matter how short.

Noah's demeanor after the shooting has been...challenging. He's closed himself off more than usual, and not once have we talked about his request as he lay dying in my arms. I don't know how to bring it up or if it was some strange blood loss-induced rambling. So far, after his recovery, he's been surly, out of touch, and I've caught him staring off into space more often than I'd like to admit.

If the gunshot wound had been any closer to his head, I'd be worried about some kind of ricochet fucking things up, but it seems to be mood-based rather than physical issues at the moment.

The luncheon after the funeral was tense and awkward, with no one knowing what to say.

Noah was still healing from his wound and the ensuing surgery, so he was a little cranky.

Jacob and Han sat on either side of Mrs. M, who suddenly looked far older than her sixty-five years. They listened to the exploits she and Archie got up to, only cringing at the graphic stories, which were only every five or so minutes.

Red stuffed his face with all the comfort food we ordered and kept to himself.

Between the ribs, macaroni and cheese, mashed potatoes, and a mountain of rolls, we had more than enough sustenance to feed an army. He ate about three times his average amount.

Apparently, funerals make him hungry.

Red was mourning Archie in his own way as well.

Archie was one of Red's foster dad's brothers. Yeah, a bit of a tongue twister, that relationship. He was always kind to Red, teaching him how to defend himself against the other kids who picked on him.

The training wasn't all-encompassing, but it was enough to give the other kids pause before messing with young Red. After aging out of the system, they continued to keep in contact.

Archie didn't have a close relationship with most of his family these last few years because he claimed they were all dicks and couldn't be bothered. That's how Mrs. M ended up being the final authority on his resting place.

We were nearly in the same boat as her about a month ago.

Lucas was driving like a maniac to get help when Noah stopped breathing. We hauled ass to the hospital after handing off Horvat's wife to Han to stash her in lockup. We'd needed to question her, but we were in a life-or-death situation.

I was in the backseat with Noah and kept pressure on the wound to stem the bleeding.

Jacob sat in the passenger seat until the ragged cry left my throat when Noah's chest failed to rise again. Red heard the wail and swerved the car as we were careening down the road. Jacob practically vaulted over the divider to begin chest compressions as I kept breathing for Noah until we arrived. Thankfully, we were already close to the hospital when that last, heart-stopping breath left his lungs.

Red drove the SUV into the ambulance bay and shouted for help until nurses and doctors made their way to us with a gurney.

We got Noah transferred onto the bed as I rode astride him to keep my hands steady on the wound. Once we reached the operating room and the doctors attended to Noah, I was dragged out and forcefully led back into the waiting room by a nurse. As I emerged into the waiting room, Jacob and Red rose in synchronicity and rushed to my side, each grabbing a forearm in support.

They steered me to a bathroom and got me cleaned off. Jacob removed my weapons and slipped out to stash them in the spare tire cubby in the SUV before the cops inevitably came to question us. You can't just show up in an emergency room with a gunshot wound victim, covered in blood, and expect to walk out without answering some questions.

What felt like days later, but was really only a couple of hours, the cops were satisfied with our story of this situation relating to Annex Security and one of the guys' assignments. They had details on their phones of the search for Richard Blake, who was, in fact, dead, but the cops didn't need to know that specific detail.

He's been on their radar since "leaving the country," and when the guys told them they were also investigating it, we went from suspects to allies looking to close a case for them.

We said we'd visited one of the many local drug dens to look for leads because Blake's resignation hinted at drug abuse, but one of the dealers took

The Sacrifices We Make

offense and fired. We claimed the shooter had run off while Noah was bleeding, and we didn't pursue.

To explain the lack of blood at the scene, Jacob came up with the story that Noah had just emerged from the SUV, and the power of the bullet knocked him back into it. Not bad for a quick chat in the bathroom while washing blood off of our faces and hands.

I backed this story up, wearing my sweet and terrified face. I put a bit more hesitance into my words, wrung the hem of my top, and looked at the officers as if they had saved my life. Coupled with the SUV's blood-soaked interior, it wasn't a hard story to sell.

Jacob told the police and the hospital administrators that I was Noah's wife and came along for the ride since we all thought it wouldn't lead to anything.

He chose the wife angle so we could access his room and information once Noah was out of surgery. It was unlikely the cops would question that too much as they were now on the lookout for a trigger-happy drug dealer.

Noah's surgery lasted ages, and Mrs. M was kind enough to arrive with clothes and food for all of us and joined us as we camped out in the waiting room. He was kept under sedation for a few days to keep his heart rate steady and blood pressure up during the initial healing phase.

We were all sitting around the small private room while Polly, the shooter, was locked up and under camera surveillance in a safe house until we could question her. The air in the room was tense as we brooded, thinking about possible outcomes when Noah's hand flexed in mine.

I shouted for the nurse that he was waking up and breathed out the longest sigh of relief I'd ever experienced. My Captain was going to be okay.

The one good thing I can say about all of this mess is that King believes Horvat was killed in a burglary. The clean-up crew that took care of Richard Blake, the Annex board member I killed in the hotel a month prior, also handled Horvat's house. God bless Rosa and her dream team of crime scene scrubbers. I owe her a bouquet or, at the very least, a month's subscription to her favorite OnlyFans account.

Horvat's widow, Polly, our detainee, was from the East Coast and a mere eighteen years old.

Polly was sold on the auction blocks in New York last year to the asshole, who liked his girls young. Horvat kept her locked in the house but told people she was a hairdresser. Polly didn't work. Fuck, she didn't even go grocery shopping. The cameras in the house weren't just for security; they were for keeping her in line.

We locked Polly in a safe house for about a week while we ran back and forth to the hospital with things for Noah. She was happy to stay put and finally claim freedom from that asshole after living for so long under Horvat's rule.

When Noah was released, we finally had the time to question her. She didn't have much to share except that Horvat was a sick fuck, so we didn't get much on The Gambit or his plans with the other members.

We decided to bring her to the clubhouse—blindfolded, so she didn't know its location, of course—and we all quickly took to her. She was just an innocent kid in all of this.

Despite her recent trauma at the hands of Horvat, she's still got sass and snark like crazy and has a lighthearted demeanor. Jacob took point on looking out for her because his younger sister, Anna, is about that age, and he said they're pretty similar.

When Jacob disarmed the security system, she'd hidden in the linen closet. The alarm made a particular sound when Horvat's phone was in the vicinity, alerting Polly to his arrival and extending that psychological torture.

Jacob's tampering caused a different sound, prompting her to hide. When Red did his sweep, unlocking all the doors, he unwittingly gave her access to the usually locked room. She slipped in and grabbed a gun from the desk before hiding in the closet.

I truly believe she didn't intend to shoot Noah. She wanted to kill the bastard who bought her like livestock and used her in the worst of ways. When she saw the opportunity, she pounced. I can't fault her for her ambition. I would have done the same thing, but I wouldn't have missed my target.

Polly has been a sweetheart and was surprisingly helpful when Noah was still bedridden. I heard her scold him for trying to get up and move around too early.

He listened to her because, well, how could you not when a trauma survivor threatens to cry on you for not following orders? I wouldn't want to be responsible for more tears from this teenager. She's cried enough as it is.

While we've all loved helping get Polly back on her feet, part of me is glad she's getting ready to go home. Helping her makes us feel better about all of the shitty things we've done in our line of work, but it's been tough to plan and speak openly about things.

With two players down and three of my other board members forming a coalition to take out King and dismantle The Gambit, our plans are becoming more complex.

More importantly, getting Sage away from King has become goal number one on our list, and mentioning her situation could trigger Polly, so discussions on that topic have been quiet and disjointed due to interruptions.

As for the burglary, Polly acted her ass off when she called the police the day after we decided she wasn't a problem for us. She played the sobbing widow really well. The police expressed their condolences, had her write a statement at the station, and sent her on her way.

Chapter Two

Noah

AFTER BEING SHOT AND STITCHED BACK TOGETHER, WAKING UP IN the hospital was not a pleasant experience. I've been shot before, once in the calf while on a mission, but it was nothing like this.

I remember waking up multiple times before fully coming to. I was groggy, and everything was dark because I couldn't find the strength to lift my eyelids. It was a battle I wasn't winning that day, but I was able to listen.

Rogue, or Trouble, as I liked to call her, whispered words of reassurance to Lucas as they sat at my bedside and waited for me to return to the land of the living.

I heard Jacob on the phone with what must have been Han, who didn't seem to be with us at the hospital, as his voice was noticeably missing.

I hoped someone thought of calling the cleaning crew. We didn't want our involvement with Horvat getting out to the cops. I knew that'd be fun to explain away if the guys hadn't done it already.

After I'd drifted off again, a warm hand slipped into mine at some point and squeezed. I squeezed back and instantly heard Trouble calling out for the nurse that I was waking up. I didn't think I'd ever heard her raise her voice like that before. I must have been worrying her with my extended nap; it felt like I'd been asleep for a week.

"My husband is waking up, Cherise!"

Husband? What the hell happened while I was unconscious?

My eyes flew open as her words registered and swung around the room, landing first on Jacob, then Lucas. Finally, I landed on Rogue, who sat on my left with her hands wrapped around one of mine. Hers are so small compared to my giant paw clutched between them.

"Noah, are you with us?" she asked. Her eyes darted back and forth between mine, searching for clarity and comprehension.

I nodded and tried to clear my throat to speak, but she just placed her fingertips over my lips. Then, she leaned forward and whispered, "They think we're married; that's how we got into the room. You were shot as we were looking for Blake at a known crack den; the impact knocked you back into the SUV you had just exited."

Her tone told me these were the lies they had fed to the hospital and the authorities, and I had better not forget the new details.

I moved my head up and down infinitesimally as the words registered. Filling me in on the essential details until we could speak more openly was crucial as now that I was awake, I'd be questioned and had to keep the story straight.

I'd figure out that whole husband-and-wife thing as soon as possible, but it seemed self-explanatory.

The nurse chose that moment to come bustling in, and Rogue kissed my cheek as she pulled away, removing herself from the bed so I could be checked over. But she didn't step away completely. Instead, she hovered near the end with one hand on my shin, almost reluctant to lose the contact we maintained.

I was poked, prodded, and given more instructions than I knew what to do with as the doctors went over my recovery and the police followed up with questions about my shooting.

I was a lucky motherfucker. The bullet didn't do any critical or lasting damage; it just forced a lot of bleeding by nicking an artery.

I had some severe muscle shredding, but I was kept in an induced coma for three days to keep my blood pressure under control as they replenished what I'd lost and my body still while the initial healing took place.

With my "wife's" assurances that she would take care of me, I was released a few days later, and we headed back to the clubhouse.

Rogue took her duties seriously and played nursemaid for weeks while organizing a hit on the governor via text. I'm ashamed to say I got frustrated with my lack of movement and need to stay in bed most of the time.

I always knew I didn't like being sidelined, but those first few weeks

The Sacrifices We Make

were all the confirmation I needed to know that I'm prickly when I don't get my way.

Instead of lashing out at my team, I turned inward and kept to myself. Logically, I knew they were only trying to help.

I was mad at myself, mad at Rogue for putting us in that situation, and mad at Lucas, who somehow missed an entire person hiding out in the house.

I know these things happen, but fuck, I hate being caught unaware. I was paying the physical price while the others managed the logistical fallout. I tried to help, but everyone kept ushering me back to bed.

Even Polly, my shooter, scolded me a few times and threatened to tell me all about her experiences over the last year while sobbing into my healing wound. That's the one that got me to settle.

She'd been through a lot worse than me. And yet, she was dealing with it, not taking her anger out on everyone in the vicinity like the petulant child I'd somehow become.

It's been about six weeks since the shooting. Mrs. M is doing okay since Archie's passing, and now, we're just starting to get back into the swing of things. Polly went to live with her family in Delaware last week. Instead of just sticking her on a flight, Jacob went with her and helped get her settled.

He and Han organized the collection of a few of her things from the house she shared with Horvat and listed it for a quick sale. His assets, at least the legal ones, were signed over to Polly because of the common laws in California.

The sad thing is, the millions he's undoubtedly made from gun-running are in an account in the Caymans. Jacob is loosening some strings to get that handed over to her. It's the absolute least she deserves for her year with that asshole.

Jacob arrived home yesterday, and today, we're working on getting back on track. Now that I'm not on bedrest, I'm ready to retake the lead and move forward with our plans. This has been the longest month of my life. Stuck in bed, useless.

Completely and utterly useless.

If I'm not leading my team, what am I good for?

Trouble hasn't brought up the stupidity that spewed from my mouth when I asked her out as I was fucking dying in her arms. Not that I've given her any openings or been receptive to most topics of conversation since the shooting.

Who does that, anyway? Asks someone out on a fucking date when they might not be breathing in the next few minutes? Did she feel guilted into saying yes?

Somehow, the gunshot seemed to have blown apart the wall I had been hiding behind. My conversation with Mrs. M flitted through my mind as I lay in the back seat, my head on Trouble's lap, staring into her tear-stained face and watching as she looked at me with such emotion.

At that moment, all I could think about was how I had wasted my time. I had hesitated, knowing that relationships were messy. How would this even work? All five of us?

I haven't brought up "the incident"—as I've been calling it in my mind—either, because no matter how I look at the situation, I come out looking like an asshole, a coward.

Is this a midlife crisis?

I go to the balcony on the catwalk in front of my room. I lean over the edge, resting my forearms on the railing to see what the others are doing. We agreed to jump back in after Jacob got back. I feel the nerves prickling under my skin, itching to get back into work mode. It's been too long since I've been productive.

We wrapped up the Blake issue by helping the other teams "discover" that he had left the country and was now living peacefully in Montenegro. His money would set him up in the Balkans for more than one lifetime while he lived like a king.

I met with the other Alpha teams via video chat two weeks after the shooting to corroborate our findings, and by the end of that call, it was considered wrapped. Jacob laid a flawless trail, and we led the others right to it.

I see Lucas and Han in the gym. Lucas has been down since Archie died, but little jokes are starting to come through again. He introduced them, and a part of him feels bad that Mrs. M, our Mama Bear, is alone once again.

Han is holding pads out in front of him so Lucas can whale on him. Right cross, left jab, uppercut, block, spin, kick. He never falters as he continues his assault. It looks like our meeting might be happening later than I thought. I know better than to interrupt Lucas when he needs an outlet, and lately, that's been sparring.

Jacob and Trouble are sitting on the couch in the lounge area. Jacob has his arm around her shoulders, and she's nestled into his chest, sleepily raising a cup of coffee to her lips as he whispers in her ear.

When there were four of us, we usually paired off. Now, it's looking more and more like I'm on the outside, and it's a position I've placed myself in. I should have spoken up earlier and cleared the air.

I could have done it when I woke up, came home, or any of the hundreds of times she'd helped me eat or gone over details with me.

But I didn't. And now I'm kicking myself for letting those insecurities take hold. My helplessness, frustration with my situation, and not knowing if Rogue felt obligated to agree to my request created this swirling vortex in my chest. I don't know how to dig my way out of it.

Jacob tips his head back and laughs at something she says in reply. Then, while his head is turned in my direction, he sees me at the edge of the staircase and lifts his free arm to beckon me over. Trouble turns her head and catches my attention with her slight smile.

It takes me longer than I'd like to admit to going down the stairs and across the clubhouse. Yeah, I call it the clubhouse now, too. Between Trouble, Lucas, and Polly constantly referring to it like that, it just stuck. Han and Jacob started changing the name pretty early on. I was the last holdout.

I do that a lot, huh?

I drop into the armchair across from them on the couch and see Trouble tense up like she's been caught doing something wrong.

Of course, she hasn't.

She and Jacob have connected. Hell, she's connected with everyone. And how could she not? She's a ray of sunshine and perfect for us.

Rogue lifts her eyes to mine and speaks before I push the words past my lips. "Do you want some coffee, Captain?"

I clear my throat and figure it's now or never. "No, thank you. Can I speak with you for a minute?"

I cringe at my overly formal tone, but there's no way to save it now.

She nods her head, and Jacob drops a kiss on her forehead as he takes his leave, offering us space. It's considerate on his part because now, I don't have to get up again and feel that subtle twinge in my shoulder that bothers me every time I change position.

Trouble sets her feet more firmly on the floor and looks across the coffee table at me. Then, finally, she sets her mug down and braces her arms on her thighs. She looks nervous; I don't want that. I don't want her to think she's done anything wrong when she's truly been incredible.

She's been helping Lucas with his demons and regret, handling King and the fallout from Horvat's death, taking on a hit job, and making Polly feel right at home. Mrs. M thinks Rogue hung the moon because she took her ax-throwing after Archie died to distract her.

Most of all, she was there for every step of my therapy and medication schedule.

"What's going on, Noah?" she asks.

She's switched over to my real name and looks worried. I've got to fix this and get us back to equilibrium.

"Trouble," I smile as I say her nickname, "I remember what I asked in the SUV on the way to the hospital. Is your answer the same? It's okay if it isn't. I know I've been a morose dick since getting shot, and don't deserve a minute of your time. Unfortunately, my way of dealing with it was fucking stupid. I'm sorry if I made you feel like you were doing something wrong or that I wasn't interested."

She takes a deep breath, and a smile flits across her face as if she's afraid to let it stay there for too long. "My answer hasn't changed, Noah. But this last month has been hard. You shut down. You shut me out. More importantly, you shut out your team. They needed you to be who you are, and you withdrew completely. I don't understand why."

I felt this was coming and thanked small mercies for the pep talk I had in the mirror this morning.

"The hospital where I woke up was where Callie was born. It's where I learned I wasn't her father. Those memories came back, and the futility I felt back then rushed back in. I didn't want to lash out at anyone, and it was likely to happen with the headspace I was in.

"I'm sorry. I know those words don't make up for how I've been acting lately, but they're all I can offer right now, along with a promise to do better if something like that happens again," I finish lamely. It's true I can't offer more than that right now, but I'll find a way to make it up to her somehow.

She nods her head, just taking in the information. "Apology accepted, and I guess your best is all I can ask of you. But Noah, hear me and hear me well. I will not be made to feel as if I've done something wrong when I haven't ever again. Next time, talk to someone. It doesn't have to be me. Hell, it doesn't even have to be anyone on the team. Speak to a therapist or a drunk at the bar, but don't shut down again. Instead, let's find a coping method. We need you too much for you to have the luxury of doing that again."

Is it just me, or did she just pull a Mrs. M and put me in my place with a stern word and a sparkle in her eye? Those two have been spending entirely too much time together.

"Agreed. Happily." I know she's right. I can't just check out again. I have a team that depends on me and, hopefully, a girl who might actually depend on me a little, too.

"Great. So, now that that's settled, there was talk of a date. There's this Spanish tapas bar I've been dying to try." Her segue into a new topic has me feeling like I've got a bad case of vertigo.

Is that it? All forgiven? No backlash? I need some clarification. "Aren't you going to yell at me?"

"Do you want me to yell at you?" she asks deadpan, her face expressionless.

"Not particularly, but isn't that how this goes?" Thinking back to my time with Sheila, yelling was the norm.

"Not with me. You made a mistake. Admittedly, it was a long and drawn-out mistake, but you apologized, listened to me and my conditions, and agreed. You haven't given me a reason not to trust you. In fact, you got shot on a mission I was leading, and I know I apologized, but are you looking to yell at me?"

"No, what? Not at all."

"Then we're good," she says confidently. "You can take me out tomorrow night. Today, we have to go over what's been happening over the last month now that Polly's gone, and we have free rein in the clubhouse again. Who knows how long this meeting is going to last? Come on, let's get you some coffee. You know you always concentrate better with caffeine."

She's right.

Rogue

As I usher Noah into the kitchen, only wincing slightly at the grimace he makes as he stands, I take stock of the past month. Keeping all the plates spinning has been challenging, but we've been thorough and careful.

Horvat's death was officially ruled a burglary by the police just days after his death. Rosa's team did a great job on the cleanup, and with Polly's statement, everything with the police was settled quickly.

Another of the many things hovering over our heads is the partnership with Neil and Claudette. They're the two players from the Rattlesnakes we recently dealt with from a rival gang in the Pacific Northwest.

Luckily, with our machinations, King doesn't suspect foul play in Horvat's demise. After all, the police chief is in King's pocket and has no reason to lie to him or conduct a less-than-thorough investigation.

Neil's fake death on the pier in San Francisco, in front of all of those tourists I undoubtedly scarred for life, has gone over well. With Claudette's help, he was moved to a safe house and kept hidden away.

I've been in contact with King, and we've had an emergency board meeting in the meantime, but it's been smooth sailing overall. King let me see Sage last week because I kept feeding him details on Neil's boss in San Francisco, Claudette, who we've effectively renamed Anthony.

Claudette has helped keep the details coming, leading King in another direction while we regrouped at home and tossed ideas at each other about handling the chaos in our lives. It's been nice having other women around and in my corner lately.

Some tentative friendships are forming between the texts and phone calls with Claudette and hosting Polly for the past month. I have to say, it's been intimidating because I haven't had many of those in my life, but they were patient with me as I found my footing. I'm really excited to meet with Claudette in a few days. It's one of the topics we need to discuss today.

Noah peruses the mug collection in the cupboard, picking one out for the day. He ends up pulling one out that says *Have a nice day,* and on the bottom, there's a middle finger, so it will show every time he takes a sip. Cute.

I grab the coffee pot from the warmer and pour him a cup as he maintains eye contact.

To say he shocked the hell out of me this morning by bringing up the date thing would be an understatement. However, the flip-flop my heart did in my chest when he confidently broached the subject made me sure it was a good idea.

Noah's whole-hearted apology while explaining his reasoning only reinforces his position on the team to me. He is a leader through and through. He's responsible and admits when he fucks up.

The world needs more men like this.

I don't know precisely why he expected me to yell at him, but I strongly feel it has something to do with his ex. It's not something I'm going to poke and prod at because it's none of my business, but I'll just have to show him another way.

A small smile tugs his lips as I continue staring at him, lost in thought. I return it slowly and trace my bottom lip with the tip of my tongue. His eyes track the movement, and a fire grows in his warm gaze. My stare trails a path down his aquiline nose to his full lips, sweeping down his neck to his broad shoulders and across the span of his wide chest.

The Sacrifices We Make

Sex on a stick. That's the only way I can describe Noah. He's tall as hell, at least six foot four, wide like a football player, with a built body that I want to explore so very badly. His skin has a luscious tan hue, almost olive, and the sparkle in his eyes only adds to his allure.

I tear my eyes away as I hear Han, Red, and Jacob entering the kitchen.

My guys. *All* of my guys, I guess.

How did I end up living out a reverse harem novel? I mean, I'm not complaining, but damn. I have to download some new books to my Kindle; maybe I'll get some ideas for my new situation. I just added one about a woman fighting for a top spot at an acrobat school while juggling three guys to my TBR—it's time to bump it up the list.

Han reaches me first and plants a kiss on my forehead. He's freshly showered after the gym and looks longingly at the coffee pot after leaning in and whispering, "Good morning, Gorgeous. You look ravishing," in my ear, using my old fight name as my nickname. I love that he uses it, along with my real name, Ivy, when speaking with only me.

Shivers rake over my body at the contact as I remember how we came together last night. Since we almost lost Noah, it's as if every time we're together, he's more reverent, more serious. It's like he's afraid to lose me the way he almost lost his commander.

After living alone for so long, I'd never have guessed that I could form connections this deep after such a short time. It'd be easy to pull away or give in to the fear of these feelings fizzling out when things go sideways, but I wouldn't be who I am if I gave up that easily. I've got feelings for all of them, and I don't plan to let anyone go soon.

I blink up at him, his face just a few inches higher than mine, and run my hands along his shoulders and chest. "Good morning, Han," I whisper back. His smile reaches his eyes as I study his face. His Korean features lend themselves to perfect skin, and the small scar running through his right eyebrow just adds to his appeal. Besides that, his lean, athletic body makes keeping my hands off him hard.

He moves aside to fix his latte, and I notice Jacob and Red having a whispered conversation on the other side of the kitchen island. I sidle up to them and look curiously from one man to the other.

Noah remains in his position as Han joins him, both taking long drags of coffee as they watch the rest of us. Noah winks at me, and I know it's a wink of teasing encouragement. It says *You chose to be with these two; break it up so we can get started.*

I place a hand on Jacob's bicep and one on Red's. They both snap their eyes down to me as I look between them. "What's going on, guys?"

Jacob is the first to break the silence, "Nothing, nothing. Lucas wants to get some new mugs, and I've told him we have enough."

Red lets out a small laugh, and the sound reminds me of who he was before Archie's death threw him into a bit of a spiral. His dark red hair is slick with sweat, and his small dimples try to poke through his stony facade. The freckles across the bridge of his nose capture my attention as they disappear into the short beard he's been sporting these past few weeks.

He's tall like Noah but leaner, and with all the time he's been spending in the gym lately, he's getting cut as hell. We've spent a lot of time over the last month talking out his slip back into the angry kid he was when his parents died. He's been doing much better lately, but I meant what I said after our date. I don't care if he's silly or serious, so long as he's himself.

He kisses my forehead and grabs a water bottle from the fridge. Jacob takes the opportunity to scoop me up into his arms. I giggle as he spins me round and round. Then, I shriek as he starts going faster and faster until I'm almost positive my coffee is going to make a reappearance.

"Jacob! Put me down right now before I put *you* down!" I shout out.

He laughs as he slows the spinning. Both my head and stomach are grateful. He parks my ass on the kitchen island in front of him and steps between my thighs. His ice-blue eyes behind his black frame glasses sparkle with mirth as he gets as close as he can to me.

A couple of months ago, we discovered Jacob has a bit of an exhibitionist kink, while Red is a bit of a voyeur. It's made for some engaging extracurricular activities, but lately, we've kept things behind closed doors in deference to Red's issues. However, that doesn't mean Jacob doesn't steal somewhat innocent touches in front of the others. "Hi, Snuggle Bug," he greets me in his delectable British accent.

Oh, did I mention? The others were giving Jacob shit for not having a nickname for me like they did, so he's been cycling through cutesy names that I unequivocally hate until he finds one we can both live with.

I move my hands from the back of his tattooed neck and wrap them around his throat in a playful yet threatening gesture. "Find another name," I command.

"Snuggle Bug" is *not* going to be the one that sticks.

He smiles his breath-taking smile at my threat and runs his hands along my body until they settle on my waist. He shifts his position closer, making sure I feel his growing erection, and I can't help the small moan that escapes. The others are still in my peripherals, and I can just barely see Noah tip his head back and sigh in exasperation.

I release a breath of a laugh and run my hands along Jacob's chest, letting my nails scrape his nipples on my descent. He grinds into me harder, igniting every nerve ending in my body as I squirm to ease the ache building in my core, demanding satisfaction.

Dammit, Rogue! Now is not the time to fuck our British tattooed tech nerd. Later. How long is this meeting going to last anyway?

Chapter Three

Rogue

I hop down from the counter and grab Jacob's inked forearms for stability. He just plants his feet and stands his ground, so I use the opportunity to slide down the front of his body as I find my footing.

"Get your tea, and let's go," I lean to whisper into his ear.

He moves to do as I say but suddenly spins and leans down to bite the sensitive patch of skin between my neck and shoulder. My body reacts instantly, pushing my hips toward his, and I feel the flush rising up my neck as my knees go weak.

"Boys, war room. Now," I manage to command through my lust-addled brain.

Everyone hops to it, grabbing their drinks and choice of breakfast, and we make our way out of the kitchen. We cross the expansive clubhouse and march into the war room, ready for business. We take up our usual seats and prepare ourselves to plan an attack.

Everyone settles in, and I kick off the show. "King has been relatively quiet lately. His reaction to Horvat's death was expected. He checked everyone's locations via their cells, and mine pinged from San Francisco. Thanks, Biscuit." I smile so Jacob knows how grateful I am for his quick thinking, and he shoots me a dimpled grin in return.

When Noah was in surgery, Jacob took the time to adjust my phone's location. We've had it pinging from my apartment since I moved in with the guys for some extra peace of mind for when King inevitably checked up on me.

Still, after the Horvat kill, while we waited on bated breath for news of Noah's recovery, he changed the location to San Francisco, thus giving me an alibi should I need one.

"I've been feeding him information about Neil's boss, and as a reward, you all know I saw Sage last week. I gave her the note with the address to the clubhouse just in case."

Sage told me King had brought her to his home the night I killed Horvat but hadn't done anything to her. Instead, he told her he was disappointed in me and hinted at punishing her if I didn't do my job promptly, hence the tears I could hear down the phone call that set me off and ultimately resulted in one less board member for The Gambit.

Neil's boss, Claudette, is a problem we intend to settle soon without having to *actually* kill anyone, considering Claudette is pretty cool.

"You all know we voted Francesco Romano, Horvat's second, onto the board to take his place last week. He's not exactly a typical gang-banger, but he's playing by the rules.

"I'm doing recon on him, so I'll have something soon, I'm sure. As we know, no one ends up in gang management without skeletons in their closet. Until then, we let him settle in and get comfortable while I continue digging. King is already showing signs of liking him, so I'm wary." I confess my concerns, knowing they'll be received with open minds.

Romano makes me edgy. He's only been with the organization for about five years but has climbed the ladder at an impressive rate. However, he's a problem I haven't figured out yet.

King's priority is dealing with Neil's boss. According to Claudette, said boss, Neil is fine and relaxing in a safe house in Oregon. She's keeping him in lockup and out of sight until we deal with The Gambit, just in case King has spies in the northern territory.

Let's face it, he probably does.

"As far as Blake goes," Noah starts, "the other Alpha teams followed our breadcrumbs, and our trail led them to Montenegro as we'd planned. Jacob's body double worked well for security cams, and since none of the teams thought it pertinent to fly over there to verify—because he was all over the local footage in his neighborhood—the case has been closed."

Thank God.

That was my one concern. I knew the double Jacob had hired and paid handsomely looked like Blake, but I was convinced someone would check. But why would they? They had his resignation letter, the footage from the airport of the guy, and now local cameras had him settled in there, seemingly living a comfortable life.

My over-wariness makes me think that others read into things as deeply as I do.

Jacob tackles the next on our list of topics. "Polly is settled in Delaware. Her aunt and uncle seem like good people, and I made sure to encourage them to get her into therapy as soon as possible to start to heal. She made an incredible step calling them in the first place, and I don't want her to stagnate there.

"I'm working through getting Horvat's funds stashed in the Caymans, but it's taking some time. Until then, we're funding whatever her aunt and uncle can't provide for her, and I don't believe they'll take advantage of that. In any case, I've got alerts on their credit cards and the account I set up for Polly, so we'll know if there are any underhanded moves."

Bless this man. He not only connected with Polly because she reminds him of his little sister, but he also went above and beyond to make sure she'll still be taken care of when she's out of our care.

Yep, we're most definitely finishing what we started in the kitchen.

We all agreed to help finance Polly until she got back on her feet, considering her aunt and uncle weren't especially well-off. We're all making amends for things we've done in the past however we can.

"Han, how's Mrs. M these days?" Red asks, breaking his silence.

"She's okay. She's sad, understandably, but she's making peace. She told me she was glad Archie went out doing something he loved. Her!" Han visibly shudders at that comment; that is definitely the verbatim conversation they must have had recently.

A combination of guilt and grief has Red keeping his distance from Mrs. M. Red smiles at the news. Mrs. M and he always have similar quips, so I'm glad to see she's starting to make jokes and that it's okay if he decides to, as well. He tried to take a lot of Mrs. M's sadness onto his shoulders, but hearing that she's moving forward might relieve him of his self-imposed burden.

"I'm still in a funk, guys," Red admits. He lets out a sigh and continues. "Buttercup, you've been awesome in dealing with my mopey ass, but I need some action. Maybe that will pull me out of this. Even I'm getting sick of my mood swings."

Noah nods like it's a comment he expected to hear sooner or later.

"Then, let's do it. We can work on stuff from Annex until our plans form more fully, so maybe you'll feel more yourself by then. What do you think?" I love that Noah puts the vote to Red and Red alone.

"I'm in. Let's do something from Annex's server list, and we'll keep to the planning stages for now for the rest of the Annex and Gambit board members." He turns to me, "Is that okay with you, Buttercup?"

I nod my head without an ounce of hesitation. Whatever he needs, I'm in.

We spend the day going through the server and finally choose an assignment for Red. He'll be going undercover, so it takes planning and coordination. It's new to see the guys working together on an Annex assignment, and watching as they slip into their official roles is fascinating.

Evening comes and goes as we discuss the board members we're gunning for and our exit strategy for Sage. When midnight rolls around, we're all done for and starving.

The night ends with all of us huddled around the kitchen island, stuffing our faces with Noah's quesadillas. Then, finally, we trudge our asses up the stairs and into bed.

I fall onto the heavenly mattress with Jacob on one side and Han on the other, and we pass out as soon as our heads hit the pillows.

WHEN I FINALLY WAKE UP AFTER CRASHING LAST NIGHT, I'VE GOT Han wrapped around my left, Jacob snuggled into my right, and their hands linked over my hip.

I love waking up like this—surrounded by my men, who have been tentatively working on their own relationship.

They still need to have their talk. I think part of the delay is nerves, and the other part is because of everything happening around us.

It's hard to focus on getting a relationship off the ground when you're covering up a murder, hiding a teenage trauma survivor, and planning the demise of two organizations. I should know; I've been neglecting the relationship talks in favor of quickies and running takedown scenarios in my mind all day and night.

I lift my head to check the clock on the nightstand behind Jacob and see it's already two o'clock in the afternoon. Good lord, we slept for twelve hours.

All that melted cheese must have lulled us into a stupor. No regrets.

The Sacrifices We Make

I carefully free myself from the guys and watch as they relink their hands in the place I once was, and Jacob's thumb rubs a soothing pattern over Han's knuckles.

Careful to keep my sigh inaudible, I leave the room and head to the bathroom to get washed up.

I check my phone as I brush my teeth for the recommended two minutes and see I have an email from the clinic. We got ourselves tested last week and have been waiting for the results. I'm confident we'll get the all-clear, but I'm erring on the side of caution. I'm pleased to say we're all negative on every test, and Noah was tested for everything under the sun while recovering from the wound, so he's also in the clear. I also hopped on the option to keep my copper IUD *and* do the hormonal injection that lasts a few months. No babies for these super-secret spy colleagues...at least, not anytime soon.

I meet Red in the gym and share the good news. He does a little celebratory jig and bids farewell to condoms with a song he makes up on the spot. I make a mental note to fill the others in later, and we spar a few rounds before Noah pops his head in. "Hey, Trouble! Are we going on that date tonight or not?"

Red whirls to face Noah, and I use the unexpected interruption and take him down to the mat with a sweep to his legs. He's right up there with Han when it comes to his combat skills, so I use distraction tactics to beat him when I can.

I straddle his body and use my taped-up hand to cover his mouth. I lean close and whisper in his ear, "You started this with those text messages while he and I were up in San Francisco; be nice."

He nods, and I slowly remove my hand from his mouth. He grins at me and cranes his head back to see Noah at the doorway.

"Dear Leader! You finally asked again? Without having to die this time?"

Red's joke is so unexpected that Noah and I freeze as the words sink in.

"I did. Any problem with that?" Noah asks.

"No, sir," Red responds with a wink. He slaps my ass, and as I move to stand, he clamps a hand around my waist and keeps me still.

"Hey, Cap. I've already made the reservations. We're leaving at seven. Is that good for you?"

"Can't wait," he says, aiming an adorably shy smile at me. He leaves the room, and Red suddenly spins us, so he has me pinned to the mat.

"He finally asked again? When? Tell me everything," he insists with excitement in his voice.

I try to hide both my blush and my grin. But, unfortunately, I must fail miserably according to the delight in Red's eyes.

"He did. It was yesterday morning, before the war council." My laughter bounces around the gym, making Red tip his head back and join in with whoops and cheers for his team leader.

"I knew he had it in him! Fuck, I feel better. The tension between you two was killing me."

My smile only grows, and he leans down to kiss my lips passionately. His erection digs into my lycra-covered pussy, and I return the kiss with all I have. Red has been showing more glimpses of his carefree self lately, and I can't believe it took his boss asking me out to have some noticeably positive effect. Well, that and his farewell to condoms.

Red looks up and exclaims, "Buttercup! It's already five-thirty! Go get ready." Hell, I think he's more excited than Noah at this point.

He leaps up and pulls me with him. Red puts his hands on my waist and steers me up the stairs and into the shower, shoving me in before it's properly heated, and I yelp at the cold sensation on my heated skin. I pull him in with me when he tries to shut the glass door, and suddenly, we're not in such a rush.

We're both still in our workout clothes, getting drenched under the showerhead, but nothing could pull me away now.

Red steers my body until my back is pressed against the cold tiles before slowly dropping to his knees and kissing my body the whole way down. He loses the battle with the sports bra, so I save him from his frustration and remove it myself.

He playfully bites at one of my nipples as he massages the other with rough fingers. Eventually, his hands slide down my waist until they reach my shorts, and he peels them from my body with impatience.

I open my eyes to look down at this magnificent man before me through the steam slowly filling the shower cubicle. He winks and dives down, bringing me to ecstasy twice before insisting I shower off and get ready for my date.

I'M JUST HOOKING THE LAST LOOP OF MY TOP WHEN THERE'S A KNOCK on my bedroom door. I figured it'd be faster to get dressed and ready in here than in the bathroom, where any of the guys could interrupt me and tempt me into being late.

I'm already running a little behind because of the shower sex with Red.

I grab my clutch from the end of my bed and reach my door. I disengage the lock—another measure to prevent distractions in the form of tall, sexy security team members—and pull the door wide. Noah stands on the other side in a dark blue, three-piece suit, and my eyes widen as I take in his tall frame and stunning suit paired with a crisp white collared shirt, brown belt, and matching shoes. God, help me.

"Hey, Trouble," Noah says with a little smirk. Yep. He caught me checking him out. Eh, I'm not too bothered by it. We're going on a date, after all. His eyes trail down my body and take in my dress.

It's a black corset top with a fitted skirt. I paired it with black tights with seams running up the back and my skull-and-crossbones heels. I left my hair down but added some victory rolls for some drama. My lips are painted red, and my winged eyeliner is on point.

I look like Bettie Page if she were living in the twenty-first century, and I love it. It looks like Noah does, too.

I spin for him, watching his eyes follow the seams on my tights. His eyes land on my ass, and he lets out a small groan as I smirk at him over my shoulder. "Trouble. Definitely trouble," he affirms.

We laugh as I turn back around to face him, and he clears his throat. "Ready for our date?" I nod, and he pulls a bouquet of sunflowers from behind his back. "The woman at the shop insisted on roses for our date, but I know you and Lucas have the white roses thing, so I thought these could be ours."

Surprise rushes through me, and I gush because I can't help myself, "Thank you, Noah. This is really thoughtful."

I love that he went above and beyond by doing this. It's entirely unexpected and wholly appreciated. His attention to detail about Red's flower choice clues me in on how long he's been paying attention to the little things involving me.

I take the flowers gratefully, and he pulls my arm into the crook of his. He leads me downstairs and into the kitchen so I can leave the flowers somewhere.

There are no actual vases in the clubhouse, at least that I've seen, so I settle on a glass pitcher and fill it with water for the flowers. I set the bouquet in the center of the island and admire it for a moment.

"Come on, where's this tapas place?" he asks as he pulls me out of the kitchen. I got a little caught up in staring at the flowers and thinking sweet—and some dirty—thoughts about the man next to me.

He grabs my coat from the hook by the door, so I don't catch a chill. Of course, December in California isn't too cold, but if you've grown up here, even sixty degrees can sometimes feel like Siberia in the throes of winter.

Being from the East Coast, Noah is comfortable in his suit jacket and laughs at me when I burrow into my coat.

"It's on the east side of town. We'll get there in no time." We exit the clubhouse, and I notice the other guys are nowhere to be seen. "Where is everyone?"

"They went to check on Mrs. M. Don't worry, everything is fine. She just invited them for dinner. She heard about Lucas's fiascos in the kitchen while I was on bed rest and didn't want anyone getting food poisoning...again."

Mrs. M *with the assist.*

"Wait, you told her we were going out?"

He rubs a hand on the back of his neck in a sheepish move I've never seen from him before. "Yeah, Mama Bear was the one who kind of talked me into getting over my drama and asking you out. It's hard to say no to her when she tells you to get your head out of your ass." He laughs as he says the last part, and I can't help but join him.

"I'll have to thank her," I respond with sincerity. I'm happy I wasn't the only one feeling things. Noah and I had been openly flirting a little before he was shot, and I wasn't quite sure if that was him just being kind or if I was reading too much into those little glances and light touches during our game night.

Noah leads me to the truck, but it's a bit high, so he puts his hands on my waist and lifts me effortlessly up and onto the seat. I'm about to scold him for exerting himself so soon after his injury, but he holds up a hand to halt me and says, "Relax, I'm fine. I'm a gentleman, so you can't get mad."

He's right. It was chivalrous as hell, and I loved it.

He rounds the truck and settles into the driver's seat. We make our way to the restaurant as I give him directions, and we sing softly to the oldies music playing on the radio. He's got a decent voice. I wonder if I could talk him into karaoke one night.

He guides me inside the quaint Spanish restaurant, and I tell the hostess my name is Mrs. Tate and that we have a reservation.

I really enjoyed the look of shock on Noah's face at the hospital when the nurse kept calling me his wife, so I decided to extend the joke a little.

He laughs as his big hand engulfs mine, and we follow the hostess to our table.

Over small sample platters and delicious tapas washed down with a few glasses of wine for me and a small beer for Noah, we chat about anything and everything.

He tells me about his relatively normal childhood in Baltimore. He expands on the stories from his military days he had begun to tell me about during our stakeout in San Francisco two months ago. As the hours pass, we laugh, chat, eat, and drink merrily.

I share some snippets of my childhood with King, but more than that, I tell him about my parents before they let their addictions run their lives.

He holds my hand through most of the meal, and as we wind down and share a slice of chocolate torte, I realize we're the last patrons in the restaurant. I look up from his captivating stare and only see servers and cleaning staff milling around.

I look back to Noah, who follows my gaze, and he just laughs. "Looks like we lost track of time a bit. I'll grab the check, and we can head home."

I nod, and he lifts an arm to get our server's attention. The man arrives at our table in record time, the bill already in hand. No doubt he's itching to get out of here, and we've kept him longer than we should have.

Noah pays and leaves a generous tip while apologizing for monopolizing the young man's time on a Friday night.

"Sorry, man. It's our first date, and we got a little caught up in our talk there at the end." He says the "first date" part with such pride in his voice.

He's proud to have me on his arm, and I preen on the inside. On the outside, I aim a polite smile at the waiter with a dip of my head in apology.

"Yes, sir. It's no problem. You guys have a lovely night." He bids us farewell, likely bolstered by the fifty percent tip, and Noah helps me into my coat after the waiter retrieves it from the coat check. Taking my hand firmly, he traces small patterns on the back as he leads me from the restaurant.

I can't remember the last time I felt this carefree. Yeah, there's still a mountain of shit for us to wade through, but right now, at this moment, things are perfect.

As Noah's cedar scent washes over me, I sigh and tilt my head to the right so it rests on his shoulder as we make our way to the truck. He lets go of my hand and tucks his behind my lower back, resting his palm on my hip.

I'm not going to lie; Noah's got some smooth moves.

He pulls the same maneuver when we reach the truck, lifting me into the passenger seat.

I can almost feel my ovaries doing somersaults at being so easily lifted and put where he wants me. It has to be some kind of left-over caveman thing to be so effortlessly hauled around.

We drive back, laughing about what plans we could have messed up for our waiter by staying at the restaurant for so long. Noah bets he's got a hot date with his high school sweetheart, while I think he's dying to get home to join his friends online to play video games. Noah is more romantic than I gave him credit for if his first thought is young love. He tries to be all growly and stoic, but I'm slowly figuring him out.

We arrive home, and Noah insists I stay in my seat. As he did at the restaurant, he rounds the truck and opens the door for me. He lifts me into his arms, and I slide down his body at a tortuous rate as he sets me back on my feet.

I look up into his eyes, and his pupils are blown. He moves to step back, likely to give me some space as I find my footing, but I wind my arms around his waist and keep him where he stands.

Still staring into his eyes, I whisper, "Thank you for tonight."

He blinks owlishly and responds, "Thank you for saying yes. I don't know that I've ever been so scared to ask someone out."

I laugh, and he joins me as I ponder the past month. I wonder why he didn't bring it up sooner. "Does it bother you that I'm also seeing Han, Lucas, and Jacob?"

"No, Trouble, it doesn't. It took longer than I'd like to admit to become accustomed to the idea, but I don't see it as cheating the way I thought I would. With Sheila..." he pauses to ensure he hasn't offended me by bringing up his ex on our date.

He hasn't, to be clear. Sheila's part of his past helped make him who he is today. It's not my place to judge that. He continues his explanation, "It just wasn't meant to be. I couldn't give her what she needed, so she snuck around. What is it you need, Trouble? I don't want to mess this up as soon as it starts."

I mull his question over as he looks into my eyes, waiting for my answer. "I don't need much, Noah. I need trust. I need to know you've got my back, and I need you to know I've got yours.

"As for the others, I need to know it doesn't bother you, but if it ever does, you need to tell me. I need communication and understanding. I've never had a relationship like this. A relationship, period. I will mess up, and you'll need to tell me when I do."

"I can do that." His smile is damn near blinding, and I can't help but feel like we've reached an agreement to give this thing a real shot.

He moves back and takes my hand, swinging my arm gently as we walk to the front of the clubhouse. He pauses on the top step when we reach the door. I instantly stand at attention, thinking something is wrong. Someone has broken in, and the guys are in trouble.

None of that is happening, of course. Noah turns to me, and his big hands cup my jaw. His thumbs glide gently up and down my cheeks, then he tilts my head back and leans in.

The moment our lips connect, it's game over.

Stars light up behind my eyelids as they flutter closed, and Noah's lips seal to mine as he gives me a kiss that feels like years of desperation pouring into this singular moment. I feel his tongue trace my bottom lip, and I open for him without hesitation.

Noah's tongue sweeps into my mouth, and my leg pops behind me involuntarily, like in one of those movies from the fifties. I know I like to rock the looks from that era, but this was entirely unintentional, and I'd never imagined it was an actual thing that happened.

Just as I feel my heart rate pick up at the thought of moving this inside, Noah slows the kiss and reluctantly pulls himself away from me.

He drops his forehead, resting it against mine, and looks into my eyes unflinchingly. "Trouble was the best nickname I could have ever given you."

I laugh softly, and he leads me inside, walking me to my room and giving me one last kiss at the threshold.

"I want to do this right. Let me take you out again?" Noah asks imploringly.

"It's a date, Captain."

I close the door and turn towards my bed. I rarely sleep alone these days, but instead of waiting for the others to return from Mrs. M's place and having to go over the details of our date, I want to keep them all to myself just a bit longer.

I go to bed with a smile, the phantom feeling of Noah's lips on mine.

Chapter Four

Rogue

It's been three days since my date with Noah, and while he's been sweet with me, he's returned to his gruff self with the others.

Everyone knew the date was happening, thanks to Mrs. M and Lucas, but no one has pestered us about it until today. We're all sitting around the kitchen island drinking coffee and tea when Red finally cracks.

"So what the hell happened on your date? Neither of you has said anything! Is this happening or not? Are we boyfriends-in-law?" Red asks.

"Lucas!" everyone groans. I didn't even use his nickname that time, shocked into using his real name by his prying.

"Jinx!" he cries out victoriously.

Yeah, he earned that one.

"Good, now that I have your attention, will someone nod or shake their head so we know what the hell is going on with you guys?" he demands.

Noah and I both shake our heads in unison and grin at each other with giant, goofy smiles. Aww, look how in sync we are. Then, he lets the smile drop and glares at Red, who takes it in his stride and continues.

"I wish I could double-jinx you two for gestures." He follows this with some mumbling about being left out of the loop while Jacob and Han look on in apparent exasperation. Noah and I share more small smiles behind the rims of our coffee mugs, and I can't help but feel like today will be great.

I've been in regular contact with Claudette lately, and we have a meeting this afternoon to clarify our stories and start preparing for the next steps.

King called to check in the other day and knows I'm moving forward with plans to put a bullet in whoever Neil's boss is. He just doesn't know it will be fake again and that the person in question is helping us with the ruse.

We all walk away from the kitchen island as Red continues his litany of questions and concerns, but honestly, I'm not worried. I grab my bag, keeping my lips zipped, and Jacob waggles his brows at me after emerging from his room with a duffle bag full of weapons in his hand.

We decided it would be best if we all took the trip up north.

Noah is still, understandably, a little wary of trusting Claudette, but she's good people. I don't necessarily want her moving The Rattlesnakes into California to take over for The Gambit. Although, honestly, anything has to be better than leaving King at the helm of such a powerhouse gang controlling most of the West Coast.

We agreed to meet in a small town halfway between El Castillo and San Francisco. Claudette is stationed in the Bay Area, so having it between our locations works well. She's in charge of Neil's peers and the underlings in the area, so she's needed there.

We make the drive in relative silence despite being un-jinxed pretty early into the ride. The others are picking up on my pre-mission habits.

I look to my right and see Han relaxing. He looks out the window, watching the farmland and open spaces along the highway as we travel north.

Jacob is on my other side and has one headphone in as he dicks around on his phone. His right hand is resting on my thigh. When he sees me peeking at his screen, he squeezes my leg. His dimples make a brief appearance in reassurance as he tilts his phone in my direction to see the screen.

He's playing Candy Crush, not solving world hunger, despite the intent look on his face and unwavering concentration. I try to keep my eyes from rolling, but I fail miserably.

Red is sitting up front with Noah, and they have been flipping to different radio stations every time a commercial comes on. It's been an eclectic mix for the duration of the ride.

Jacob directs Noah from the backseat, and before I know it, we're pulling up in front of the most suburban house I've ever seen.

It's modestly sized, painted a drab brown, and has a large tree in the

The Sacrifices We Make

front yard shielding much of the front of the house. It's the perfect place to plan a gang's demise.

We pull into the driveway, and Noah kills the engine once parked. He turns in his seat, and Red watches the house for any sign of a threat.

"Okay, Trouble. You're running this. Claudette told you she wants to deal with you and you alone, but she didn't say anything about us being with you. Jacob, you and Han scope out the house and sweep for bugs. Lucas and I will wait here with Trouble until you say it's clear."

Orders handled, the men on either side of me offer one last thigh squeeze and a kiss to each temple on their way out of the car. They're in sync in nearly every way, and that gives me confidence that even if something is lurking in suburbia, they'll be fine.

They walk up the worn brick walkway shoulder to shoulder, each palming a gun. Jacob and Han reach the front door and disappear inside after knocking. Nerves ratchet up inside of me as I wait for the all-clear signal.

Five tense minutes later, Han exits the house alone. He makes his way to the SUV and opens the door for me.

"All good," he confirms with an odd expression. It makes me nervous, but he would raise the alarm if it were something ominous.

We make our way to the door, and Red offers to stand guard outside while the others are with me in the house. I pull him into my arms and hug him before heading in.

My hand slides soothingly over his back, and I tip my head up to whisper into his ear as I remain in his embrace. "Be careful, and if you're good, I'll let you paint me soon." He pulls his head back and looks into my eyes, searching for a lie he won't find.

"Really?" he asks excitedly.

He's hinted at wanting to do so for a few weeks, but I was a little reluctant about having him study me so minutely for such an extended period. I nod my head and give him a little wink.

"Really. Naked if you want," I assure him.

I swear, the neighbors five doors down hear his jaw hitting the floor.

"Yes, Buttercup." He salutes me and spins me in his arms. His hand lands on my ass in a playful slap and squeeze as he pushes me towards the door and the others, my laughter dancing across my lips as I go.

We cross the threshold and meet Jacob in the foyer.

"All good here. Want me with you or outside with Lucas?" he asks as he slides his bug detector into his jacket pocket.

"Here, please. Red is fine, and Claudette doesn't seem to have any reason to sabotage this," I tell him confidently.

I realize I haven't seen anyone besides my team, so I turn to Jacob and Han for confirmation. "Are there any others here?"

"No, it's just Claudette," Han tells me. His voice shows his disbelief, but the certainty in his eyes is reassuring.

"Okay. Then let's play it by ear, and if anyone is inclined to patrol, they can walk the perimeter with Red." My confidence in this meeting is well-founded, but I'll always be wary of working with others after being alone for so long.

They all agree, and Han takes my left hand while Jacob grabs my right. Noah walks ahead as we walk deeper toward the back of the unremarkable house. I don't need to be walled in by muscle, but it's not a bad place to be.

Noah rounds a corner ahead of us, following the sounds of a can being opened, and we find Claudette sprawled across a worn leather couch with her bare feet propped up on a coffee table filled with drinks.

A mishmash of margaritas, beers, sodas, and water bottles decorate the solid coffee table before our hostess. The drinks are still sealed in their cans or bottles, except for the margarita in Claudette's hand.

Good thinking. I would never take an open drink from someone in a rival gang.

"Rogue!" Claudette shouts out when she sees me behind Noah's hulking shoulders. "I'm so glad you're here. I can't wait to figure out how we're going to take down some bastards together."

Her jovial tone has me concerned.

I've just teamed up with a psychopath, haven't I?

She gets up, bounding over to me, and the hem of her royal blue wrap dress flaps around her calves. Noah half-heartedly tries to block her path to me despite knowing I can handle myself, but the little pixie fakes right and darts left under his arm.

She throws her arms around my neck unexpectedly in a warm embrace. She's a slip of a thing and stands about five feet four inches. Her wild, curly red hair is unbound and floating around her shoulders as she tilts her body back and forth during our hug, pulling me down to her height and rocking from side to side like an unrelenting tilt-a-whirl.

She pulls me from the grips of Jacob, who is visibly scowling, and Han, who has a smile. Noah is unceremoniously shoved out of the way as she drags me to the loveseat with her. O...kay, I guess we're sitting together.

The Sacrifices We Make

The guys check that I'm okay before making their way to the remaining three-seater couch to join us.

"So, this is the harem," she laughs. "How did you swing that? You said your team was coming with you, but I didn't know exactly what kind of 'team' you were. I guess I do now."

Noah coughs into the crook of his elbow as he hides his reddening face while Jacob and Han share a look, grab a beer each, deftly remove the caps, and clink the bottlenecks against each other. Claudette laughs freely, and her tiny button nose twitches with each guffaw.

I don't know what to say here. Claudette and I have been chatting back and forth since our initial phone call to arrange Neil's "death," so I don't know if I should maintain my badass work persona or act as my actual self.

My dilemma is cut short when Han responds, "We're a team, but we're also her boyfriends."

Well. I guess that answers my unasked questions as to what the hell we're doing.

"Damn, girl!" Claudette exclaims. "Look at you go. And what about the redhead outside? Is he also one of yours? I saw him through the window, and damn, I would climb him like a tree."

Okay, so my confusion is kicking my ass here. Isn't she supposed to be a higher-up in a gang? Why are we chatting about boys like two girls in high school? I never did that in high school—my homeschooling and then later enlistment in a gang kind of killed the idea of having friends.

Fuck it. I've never had a girlfriend before. Let's do this.

"Yes, he's my boyfriend, too," I confirm.

Embrace it, Rogue. Embrace it.

"That's awesome. I want a harem. Squad? Pentad? What do you guys call yourselves?" she asks in rapid-fire. She leaves no space between the questions to answer them.

"Well, this is the first time we've ever had to explain ourselves. I don't know what we're calling ourselves. I just refer to them as 'my guys' in my head," I say.

I shrug my shoulders with my admission because as much as I want to be cautious around this tiny woman, I can't help but laugh at her open curiosity and awe at our situation.

Noah is sucking down his club soda like it's a lifeline to keep him from having to contribute to this uncomfortable situation. Yet, even as he does so, his eyes remain fixed on me as the heat grows behind his stare.

Han laughs as silently as possible, but his shoulders shake with mirth at my reaction to the situation. Jacob's eyes are on mine and intensify when I refer to them as "my guys." I think he likes that one.

"Moving on," I attempt to steer us back on track. "We need to talk about what I'm going to tell King. First, I've got to kill Neil's boss, also known as *you*. He's been given all of the information we came up with together last month, but he's expecting me to make a move soon. So what have you got for me?"

"He thinks Neil's boss is some middle-management guy named Anthony, correct?" I nod my head before she continues and shocks the hell out of me. "Neil worked for me directly to gather intel on The Gambit and to test what limits he could push."

The shock must be apparent on my face as she pauses to pat a hand on my knee in reassurance.

"Aw, hell," she continues, watching me warily. "There's no easy or gentle way to say this. Ready? I sure as hell hope so. *I* am the head of The Rattlesnakes."

Claudette does little jazz hands as her declaration lands like a bomb.

Holy shit. I knew she was involved, but I didn't think the woman ran the damn thing.

"Noah, we should call Lucas in here. I don't think we'll want to repeat everything if it's this monumental," Jacob says as his eyes dart between us, likely trying to figure out if I'm in any danger sitting this close to yet *another* gang lord.

Noah nods, pulls his phone out, and calls Red to tell him to join us.

Claudette uses the awkward pause to keep chatting. "Yeah, I know it's a bit of a big reveal, but who is going to think I'm a gang leader?"

"I'll say," I admit.

It's jarring to think this woman I've been speaking with on the phone and texting is the head of a damn gang. She sends me memes every other day for crying out loud! The last one was of Miss Piggy getting spit-roasted by Kermit and Gonzo.

Will I *ever* get away from these gang leaders? Or is this where I'm meant to remain for the rest of my life? Passed from one to another? Constantly maneuvering myself away from one, only to end up working with another?

Red rounds the corner and immediately looks at my face to judge the situation. I give him a small smile to assure him that I'm okay, just a little shell-shocked if my wide eyes are any indication.

"Hi! I was just telling Rogue here that I'm the head of The Rattlesnakes," Claudette declares when Red shifts his eyes to her.

"Cool, cool."

Fucking Red.

"I figured it was best to be upfront about everything if we're going to work together on more than just avoiding my murder. My original last name was Hendrix, but I needed a change in name and location somewhere along the way. So when I moved north and took over for The Rattlesnakes, I changed it to Shuman. It holds significance and disconnects me from my family. As far as most people know, I own real estate and do property management."

She still has no idea the guys work for Annex and her sister, Mara. Or, fuck, maybe she does?

This tiny psychopath has higher connections than we thought. Still, she hasn't brought it up, so I made the executive decision to keep it under wraps until absolutely necessary.

Hopefully, my firm look at the guys will be heeded as a warning to keep our mouths shut. Noah pretends to stretch his neck up and down, letting me know he and the others will follow my lead.

Her abrupt change in name and location speaks to her desperation to get away. I have to give Claudette credit for her ingenuity.

"Okay, spill. How did this happen? And how are we going to solve the King problem?" I ask.

Han

Watching Ivy, or Rogue, as everyone else calls her, make friends is one of the most entertaining moments of the year. She's excited, uncomfortable, and unsure of how to act, yet she's doing pretty well.

I don't know why it makes me so happy she's finding new friends other than she deserves it. A little part of me is already jealous that she's splitting time between the four of us. Adding a friend would cut into that time even more.

Am I petty? Absolutely.

I know it, and judging from Jacob's raised brow as he studies my face, he also knows it.

Witnessing Ivy and Claudette hash out the details about "taking out" another of Claudette's men while secretly hiding him away is hilarious.

Claudette is offering up members of her gang that Ivy can pretend to kill like she's going through an employee roster of who pissed her off this week.

I tune back in to hear Claudette offer up yet another lackey. "Oh, or there's Toby. He's been a little shithead lately. I'd like to stash him away in a remote location far away from me. He likes to chew cinnamon gum all goddamn day, and it drives me insane."

I'm starting to think Claudette is a little insane. Poor Toby. He's eventually picked as the winner.

"How are you going to kill him?" Claudette, leader of the motherfucking Rattlesnakes, asks our hitwoman with a twinkle in her eye. Yeah, she's getting a kick out of this.

"Well, obviously, I can't do the same thing as last time, but there needs to be witnesses in case King has people watching. I can do a close-up at a club and have him lined with blood packs so I can nick one open. He'll 'bleed out' in a busy nightclub, so it's seen and reported on, and if it's in San Francisco, we can use your coroner connections again, right?" Rogue outlines the plan.

"Yes! That sounds great. Can I watch when it happens?" Claudette inquires with glee etched on her face.

Yep, insane. Judging by Ivy's bewildered look, she thinks the same.

"Yeah, but you can't be too close, or you might be photographed. The last thing we need is King connecting you to El Castillo or anyone in the area."

Rogue handled that one well. We don't want King to know we're working with Mara's sister, and since we haven't outlined that we're planning to take down Claudette's look-a-like, it's better to keep everything under wraps for the moment.

Claudette readily agrees and promises to prepare Toby for his new task.

Ivy and Claudette chat a bit longer about lighter topics, like the organizational structure of each gang, while the rest of us just watch like assholes, not called upon or needed at all. Claudette and Rogue have everything in hand, and the gang leader doesn't even have security here.

When we arrived, Jacob knocked on the door in that perfunctory way he tends to do. Claudette opened the door barefoot and relaxed as hell. She ushered us in like she was welcoming us into her private home.

I don't trust her the way Ivy seems to already. There's been a question tickling the back of my mind.

"Claudette, I'm grateful you're helping us, but why do you want to take

The Sacrifices We Make

out King?" I ask, leveling her with a stare and internally praying it's for a good reason, not just a ploy to gain more territory for her gang.

She finally breaks her conversation with our girl to look at me, and the genuine hatred I see in her eyes tells me this is serious for her.

"King is a man with too much power, and when Rogue told me about how he uses people's family as leverage, I knew I was in. It doesn't matter that he's not using mine. Don't you ever just do something because it's the right thing?" she asks. Her sincerity shines through, and my respect for her increases tenfold.

Her question makes sense, but I can't help but think that there must be something else she's got going on. She seems bound and determined to be on our side, and I don't see a reason for us to doubt her yet. She and Ivy have worked together without a hiccup so far, and her foregoing security at our meeting shows she trusts us, even if we don't yet trust her completely.

"Look, I may be pretty new at this whole gang leader thing, but that doesn't mean I'm a shit person. The last guy died, and I took control. It's not perfect, and we've had some growing pains, but things are leveling out. There are a lot of things to fix from prior management, but I'm working on it. King is a dick and needs to be dealt with. Don't think I don't have my own spies in his camp. I know he's got his eyes set on my territory. One man should not hold sole control of territory as big as that should he succeed."

Her point makes sense, and Ivy, seeing Claudette getting worked up, gently places a hand on her leg. "Hey, I get it. I don't want him expanding any more than you do. I'm glad you're with us. We'll get this figured out. And more importantly, we need to plan what we're going to do when he's removed and The Gambit is finally gone."

"So, how are we going to start chipping away at King's hold?" Claudette asks conversationally, shaking off the tension of my earlier question about her motives.

"Well, I've had some ideas," Ivy starts. "King's power on the board comes from swaying votes to his side if he doesn't have them already. Horvat is gone, but Enrique De La Cruz is another member who is staunchly loyal to King. We need to relieve King of his supporters. Undermining his moves will be easier if he doesn't have that unwavering support.

"Horvat's replacement, Romano, is still a wildcard. As for the others on the board, we're leaving them be for the moment." My girl says the last bit firmly, allowing no room for compromise.

I know Ivy doesn't want to share too much about loyalties while she's still learning to trust Claudette, so it's brilliant that she's focusing on one member at a time. Zeroing in on plans, Ivy starts breaking it down for our new ally.

"De La Cruz fought hard against the restrictions of selling to minors, and he's been bringing it up at board meetings for a while now. Hell, only a couple of months ago, I had to take out some of his dealers for disobeying the rules. What if they were following De La Cruz's rules instead? What if he were encouraging people to sell to minors and lining his own pockets? How many people do you have embedded in The Gambit?" Ivy asks.

"About fifty or so, up and down the state. They're all at different levels, and three are dealers. They don't work directly under De La Cruz, but they could mention the chain of command being involved. This is a good idea, Rogue. Rumors spread like wildfire, and suddenly, De La Cruz isn't the trusted man he once was."

The girls dissolve into giggles and whispers as they plot De La Cruz's end. The four of us watch the scene with rapt attention and try to understand the words they're sharing. I have a feeling these two will be devastating to their enemies.

After Ivy and Claudette finish their whispering, they stand up and hug each other.

A hug? Since when does Ivy hug anyone but us? *Ah, there's that misplaced jealousy again.* I have to work on that.

We stand and look on as they give each other a broad smile. Ivy looks over to us, and the grin seems genuine across her lips, reassuring me and the others in one fell swoop.

Chapter Five

Jacob

THE MORNING AFTER THE MEETING WITH CLAUDETTE, I WAKE UP A few hours before my alarm is set to ring and hit the gym.

Between Noah getting shot, Archie dying, weighing the options of whether or not Rogue can trust Claudette, and the unresolved kiss with Han, my mind is a mess of calculations and weighing the odds of someone getting fucked over or hurt.

Sure, Han and I have spent time together with Rogue, and I've woken up a few times with our hands tangled together after she slips out of bed before us, but we haven't broached the topic of what's happening with us. It never felt like the right time, with our circumstances constantly changing.

The need for some semblance of control has me taping up my hands and going a few rounds with the punching bag while death metal blares from the speakers. With every combo hit I make, I think of one of the problems, letting the endless cycle work its way through my head. It's like some fucked up form of meditation, but damn, if I don't feel better by the end of my routine.

I'm just throwing my last punch and stepping back when I hear applause coming from the corner. Han is seated on the weight bench near the door in his boxer briefs and nothing else.

I look at the clock and wince. It's only five-fifteen, and I've had music going for over an hour.

Hopefully, the others will have their doors shut and sealed off from the sound. Han wakes up early to run, so he must've seen me or heard my music on his way into the bathroom.

I grab the remote for the sound system and lower the volume. My chest is still heaving from the workout, and I smile sheepishly when I register how loud the music is. Yeah, if not for the soundproofing, the whole damn building would be awake.

My bad.

"You okay, man?" Han asks cautiously.

"Yes. No. I don't know," I admit. "There are too many things going on. Nothing is settled, and it's driving me mad. I like things orderly and structured. Not whatever *this* is," I attempt to explain as I flail my arms around to encompass the shitstorm we're in.

"Okay, so what can we solve now? Let's get something sorted out; at least that way, you won't beat a hole in my punching bag," Han offers with a chuckle and a wave of his arm at his currently dented bag.

I think it over. Can we solve King today? No. What about Sage? No. The Annex board? No. The one thing I've been trying to avoid because I'm a little bit terrified of the outcome if it all goes to shit? Yep. That's the one.

"We can talk about us. What that means for you, for Rogue, and me," I say.

Whoomp, there it is.

Han nods his head and gestures to the mat between our positions. We meet there, and both sink down to sit facing each other. I guess it's now or never.

I already feel some pressure lessening in my chest from knowing this will be discussed, for better or worse. Letting things linger like this, unsolved, isn't something I'm particularly fond of.

Han clears his throat quickly, and his chest bounces with the motion, making his tattoos dance in the gym lighting. "Look, if you'd rather not pursue this, that's your choice, and I'll respect it." He looks dejected; his face tilts toward the mat, and a frown mars his lips. That resignation makes me raise my hand and cup his face.

"Han, that's not what I'm saying at all. Look, we've been sidelined with everything, and this has been weighing on my mind. Not in the way you think," I correct his thinking when his eyes fall to the mat between us again. "I hate that we haven't explored this. I hate that it bothers Rogue that we haven't spoken yet. I hate that you think I'm not into this because I *am*."

His eyes lift with my last declaration, and his lush lips tip up in a small, unsure smile. "Yeah?" he asks gently. "You know I'm going to make you work for this. I'm in, Jake, but I think I speak for both of us when I say I don't want to lose Ivy. She's been encouraging as hell, and if she doesn't have to choose, why should we? But we have to be cautious and take this slow. I don't want everything to implode."

"You've been my best mate for years," I say, ready to voice my concerns. "What if this fails between us? We'll lose each other and Rogue; I'm terrified of that. I've fallen hard for her, Han. What if we fuck everything up between all three of us?"

"I'm not going to lie, that's a distinct possibility, and I'm sure your fucking superbrain has already calculated the odds," he laughs, and I nod my head in assent.

We've got an eighty-six percent failure projection if we start this polyamorous relationship with each other. Add in Noah and Lucas because they're not going anywhere, and that number jumps higher and higher.

"It doesn't look good, but I think Rogue set up some good rules. Communication is number one. We have to talk to each other, separately and as a group, about everything: feelings, doubts, fears—all of it. I know I'm not the best at it, and my words get stuck in my head, but I want to try," I admit on bated breath.

Han leans forward and brushes his lips against mine, our knees knocking together as we sit cross-legged on the floor. His kiss is gentle, and he sighs against my lips.

Pulling back only an inch, he whispers, "Then we figure it out together. I'll help you when you can't find the words." With each purse of his mouth as he formed the sentence, his lips brushed mine, teasing, tempting, and instilling a level of confidence in me that I didn't expect when facing the uncertainty of our relationship.

My mouth crashes into his, and he lets out a low groan when my tongue sweeps into his mouth. One of my hands rests on his jaw, directing his mouth the way I want it, as the other claps around the back of his neck, keeping him locked in our kiss. His rest on my bare shoulders, gently squeezing as we lose ourselves in the moment.

A squeal comes from the center of the clubhouse, echoing loudly in the open space now that the music is turned down. Han and I break our kiss to spin toward the sound.

Lucas is forcibly hauling Rogue away from the lounge area, his arms wrapped around her middle, as she whoops and hollers, throwing celebratory fist punches in the air as she looks at Han and me in the gym with pure glee in her eyes.

Glass fucking walls. When will I learn?

I hear Rogue shouting at Lucas in the kitchen and catch the tail end, "—hot as *fuck*, Red! How could you pull me away from that?" Her voice gets higher as she yells at Lucas, making Han and I laugh uncontrollably for a minute.

"She's a dangerous one," Han comments. "But I'm glad she was honest and has zero problems with this."

"She's one of a kind," I reply as we refocus on each other. "So, there's probably a few more things to talk about to get this off the ground, but the one I want to clarify first is my need for control." Han nods as I finish the sentence, and before I can explain that my need for control has been relaxing a bit since Rogue joined us, he jumps in.

"Oh, yes. That. I want that. Badly." *Wait, what?*

"What?" I repeat aloud because, apparently, the English language has become difficult for me.

"I. Want. That," he enunciates because he's a cheeky bastard. "I'll learn what exactly you need, and you'll learn what I want. Just like we would with any new relationship, but watching and experiencing you direct Ivy and me in bed has been so fucking hot, I can't stop thinking about it."

We go on talking for a while longer about our limits, expectations, and wants. By the time Noah comes downstairs to call us over to the war room, my cock is rigid and throbbing as I imagine all of the scenarios my mind can muster. As Noah approaches, I have to shield myself from my commander lest he put me on clean-up duty for the rest of the week.

Han

I leave Jacob at the foot of the stairs with a quick kiss as he goes up to shower, and I head into the kitchen to get some coffee.

I find Ivy sitting at the kitchen island in a flared black skirt and a knotted superhero shirt, showing off her midriff with a cup of coffee cradled between her palms.

Her mug today reads *What I really need are minions*. Lucas and his mugs. After all this time working together, I've started looking forward to the array of choices everyone settles on in the mornings. It's juvenile but an entertaining way to start the day.

I drift over to Ivy when she looks up from contemplating the contents of her cup, and a coy smile spreads across her face. "Why, hello, handsome. How was your morning?" As she asks the question, the light in her eyes has me suppressing a chuckle—like we didn't see Lucas carry her out of the lounge an hour earlier.

"How do you think it went?" I ask without shame. "That man could read me the stock market reports, and I'd still get turned on. When he turns that attention on you? Well, you get it." She laughs because she *absolutely* gets it. More than once, I've caught her practically drooling when his accent intensifies.

"Preach," she attests, raising a hand to the ceiling.

I lean in and deliver a searing kiss to her lips. She tastes like coffee, and the sweetness explodes on my tongue as I explore her mouth. She ends the kiss with a sweet peck and pulls back. "Really, though, how did it go? Can I ask that?"

"It went well, Gorgeous. We talked it out, and I'm glad I took your advice and stopped hiding my feelings. Are you sure you're okay with this?" I ask.

I know this isn't something she anticipated when she was first brought blindfolded to our clubhouse, but I think the recent developments have been positive. At least, I hope so.

We're making headway with the boards, we're all blissfully happy with Ivy, and we have vague plans to get her sister away from King. Nothing is coming together right now, but we've laid the groundwork and are prepared for when things move.

We agreed to review some of the work today before Ivy heads to her board meeting this evening when Rook Industries closes for the night. We also have to start getting Lucas ready for his Annex assignment.

"I'm glad you and Jacob have talked, and that kiss was hot as hell, not gonna lie. But the thing I'm happiest about is that you both aren't hiding things from each other. There are so many things to keep under wraps with what we do; hell, we can't even order pizza here. But we can control what we share among the group. The last thing I want is someone hiding how they're feeling. We're a team."

Her words have the intended effect and calm me like nothing else could. I feel seen, understood, and, most importantly, loved.

I move towards her, cupping her jaw with one of my hands as the other finds her thigh under the countertop. I love this girl. I think I've loved her since I was twenty-one and watched her flatten gangbangers in the ring, only to follow it up with serene touches as she wrapped my hands in the locker room after my fights.

The words come, clear as a bell in the silent kitchen, "Ivy, I love you."

Her eyes spring open, and she searches mine as the words sink in. Her lips part, and she sucks in a shaky breath. "I love you too, Han."

Thank fucking Christ.

My lips descend, and I lift her onto the counter. She wraps her legs around my hips, and we seal our new declarations with sensual touches and scorching kisses. I shove the fruit bowl out of the way and return my hands to her thighs. I lift her skirt, slide her panties to the side, and drive my fingers into her wet heat. So fucking wet, so warm, so mine. Ours.

Her head drops back as she supports herself on her elbows, draped across the counter like a goddess, as I bring her to the brink of orgasm and mercilessly push her over the edge.

I let her come down, then change the angle, putting pressure on her clit with my palm as she finds herself in the throes of a second orgasm within minutes. It's not an easy feat to accomplish, so I feel smug as hell knowing I can do that to her. I bring my lips to hers, and her kiss is ravenous.

That's how the other three find us as they come strolling into the kitchen.

Rogue

He loves me; Han fucking Shin loves me. And I can't and won't deny that I love him, too.

I know he mentioned it in a roundabout way when we discussed the past a couple of months ago, but to have him say it without a hint of hesitation in his voice gave me the bravery to do the same.

Okay, my voice may have wobbled a bit, but in my defense, I was caught unaware.

Am I nervous about the developments with him and Jacob? Maybe.

I meant it when I said that I want him to be who he is and explore his sexuality as he sees fit. But I'll admit, a tiny part of me is nervous he'll choose Jacob over me. Does Jacob prefer Han over me? Is this how the guys feel because I'm seeing all of them? We need to sit down and have a potentially uncomfortable conversation, especially if we're using the word "love" and making sweeping declarations.

The Sacrifices We Make

I don't want to make them feel jealous or nervous that I'll choose one day if Sage and I can stick around El Castillo after we get her back. I can't see myself doing that. They're all so unique and suit different sides of me. The thought of losing even one of them has my nerves prickling under my skin.

Wrapped up in the utter, soul-consuming bliss that only Han can provide this morning with his reassurances and comforting touch, I don't notice the other three approaching until there's a gruff groan.

I lift my head to see Noah standing front and center with Red and Jacob flanking him on either side. All three have glazed-over eyes and a straight-shot view of my positively drenched pussy as Han removes his fingers.

He lifts them to his mouth and licks them clean as he maintains his passionate eye contact with me, completely ignoring the others in the doorway.

"Morning, Trouble." A sly grin spreads across Noah's face as he approaches me on my left, keeping his eyes on my face. He leans in to deliver a soft kiss to my forehead in greeting and moves to the coffee machine while discreetly adjusting himself beneath his black sweatpants.

Jacob reaches us, and after sharing a kiss with Han that has me ready to combust again, he leans in and takes my mouth with his.

I taste myself on his lips, a remnant of his kiss with Han, and I groan into his mouth with pure, unadulterated lust.

"Morning, Kitten," he says against my lips. *Nope*, not that name, either. I pinch his nipple in retaliation, and he just laughs as he stalks over to the kettle.

Red is the last to join us and saunters over to me, his confidence resonating through the kitchen with each step.

Han moves to the side, and Red sidles up between my still-spread legs. He pulls my panties to the side again and bends to lick a languorous line up my center before readjusting my thong and settling my skirt back around my thighs. His tongue traces my collarbone, and he plants open-mouthed kisses along my neck.

Reaching my ear, he whispers, "Buttercup, that was hot as fuck, but next time, invite me earlier." He ends his request with a bite to my earlobe, and a whimper escapes me as my head tilts back in ecstasy.

He pulls back with a wink, and I know today will be a good day.

Chapter Six

Rogue

AFTER THE MORNING PEEP SHOW I SHAMELESSLY PUT ON FOR everyone and the team meeting we had soon after, I feel prepared and self-assured as I walk into the offices of Rook Industries.

I've got the intel Claudette and I fabricated ready to disclose to the board. Tanaka and I spoke earlier this week, and he said he's managed a lucrative deal, so he'll be able to ask for a meeting with Sage as a reward.

We ended up choosing the plan to get her out that we'd discussed months ago. After all the ideas we bounced around, this was the most straightforward with the least risk. Tanaka doesn't know who she is to me, but he knows I want to get her out, and he agreed to help me with this in return for my assistance in taking down King.

Once we've got Sage away from my bastard of an adoptive father, the last bit to work out is how to get rid of the evidence he's compiled against me.

I've got some ideas kicking around, but they still need to be fleshed out more to tell the guys. If I gave them half-formed plans with no workaround to consequences, they'd veto the ideas so swiftly that I would barely get five words out of my mouth before they turned to immovable statues with refusals on their stiff lips.

Usually, the guys are good at listening to my side of things, but these plans I keep coming up with would put me in direct danger, and I know exactly how even the mere suggestion of them would pan out.

I ride the elevator to the executive floor and smooth my face into work mode.

I know I look like a hard-ass when I'm here, but it's part of the job and necessary when working with this crowd. King can't catch on to the fact that I've been in cahoots with Tanaka and plotting his demise. There can be no over-familiarity, coded looks, or anything that could give us away. I need Tanaka to help me with Sage and King to remain squarely in the dark.

The elevator slows and announces its arrival on the designated floor. I exit and walk along the white marble hallway to the meeting room at the far end.

I wore a black, off-the-shoulder top, my favorite black ripped jeans, and the thigh-high leather boots with a silver zipper running up the back that I wore to Governor Reyes's death. The handles of the zippers are tiny daggers, and I adore them.

Red saw the boots online—along with a bunch of fabulous retro clothes—and had it all sent to the guys' PO box just before Archie died. I've only worn them for that one hit so far, but I wanted to wear something of his after Red's bold display in the kitchen this morning. You know, to make some new, non-murdery memories in these kickass boots.

I was in his room getting ready for tonight's meeting, and when I leaned forward to grab the daggers and drag them up my legs, I caught sight of him with his jaw hanging open as he trailed my thighs and settled his stare on my ass. That look led to a romp with only the boots on, my back pressed against the door, as Red slammed into me over and over again.

Now, when I look down at the boots, I don't see Governor Reyes's blood everywhere; I see Red and the fire in his eyes as he pounds into me. *Much better.*

With each passing day, Red is settling back into his usual self. I think part of it is that he's looking forward to sinking his teeth into the Annex mission. He's spending tonight and tomorrow doing recon and research, so he has a tangible goal.

We ended up putting the mission to a vote, and it was unanimous. The goal is to gain some files from Collinsworth Bank by any means necessary and forward them to the Annex bosses.

The guys were understandably adamant about avoiding any of the missions that could be a cover for some of their company's more nefarious

The Sacrifices We Make

deeds, and stealing some information seemed like the safest bet. No one to relocate, hide, or kill. What a nice change of pace.

Red has been busy pouring over the documents, and with Jacob's help, they should be able to find everything in a few weeks. Red will likely go undercover as a transfer to their branch; they're just waiting for an opening in employment to pop up.

He could end up as a teller or in management, but Jacob is ready to have him transfer in with the right qualifications, no matter the position. Honestly, any role will suffice if it gets him access to computers connected to the central server.

I see the other six members in their seats in the meeting room. Two men are on the far side of the table: De La Cruz and Horvat's replacement, Francesco Romano.

There's an empty seat for me next to the new recruit.

On the side of the table closest to me are Nina Wilson, our finance guru; Hiroto Tanaka, the CEO of Rook Industries; and Elise Batten, the high-society liaison.

King sits at the head of the table and speaks with Romano in hushed tones.

Romano looks different from our last arms dealer. He's tall with broad shoulders, has deep golden skin, and his wavy black hair is starting to grey a bit near his temples. He looks like a slightly over-forty fashion model, not someone slinging uzis on the corner for a gang.

It doesn't help that he's suave as fuck and could probably charm the habit off of a nun. He stands as I approach; my kickass boots are silent despite their killer spiked heels because Red thought ahead and got me the padded soles.

As Romano sweeps the chair out for me, I tilt my head to the other members around the room and take my seat with the slightest nod of recognition for the chivalry. He guides my chair in and resumes his seat next to me.

There's power in being the last one to a meeting and knowing the attendees waited for you to arrive before starting. Even as King narrows his eyes, I let that feeling rush over my skin.

"Now that we're all here," King begins the meeting with a petty dig at my two-minute delay, "we can discuss the agenda for the night. Romano will inform us of the progress of the trade agreement with the Vegas Crew. Rogue will tell us about her plans for those moving in on our territory in San Francisco. Tanaka has news to share about Rook Industries. Elise has the new governor under her thumb, and we'll need to be brought up to speed. Let's get to it, people. I've got plans."

I hate how he makes it sound like we've inconvenienced him when he's the one who sets the meetings in the first place. Maniacal, egotistical bastard. At least this time, he showed up. He set up a few meetings and then ghosted. Dick. I bet it's a power move.

Romano stands to say his piece about the new trade deal when King waves his hand in his direction. Lapdog.

"The Vegas Crew doubled their most recent order. They want slightly more firepower than we have now, but I'm pulling some strings to get an extra shipment. I negotiated a pushback on the delivery and a twenty percent hike in the price for the inconvenience. They readily agreed, and we'll have an extra million in the bank from the extra charge."

"Good work, Romano. You're already doing better than Horvat ever did." King sings his praises without regard for Horvat's life. It's not like there's much to lament, but still. They were allies at one point, right?

I'm curious if he's already pulled Romano under his wing. We voted him in because he was Horvat's second in command in the arms dealings and showed more promise than the others in that organization's sector. He knew the business well enough that the board didn't have to worry about training someone.

"Rogue, what have you got on Carter's boss?" King asks as he looks down the table at me. I don't feel the need to stand up to address the room, and if I did, at this point, they'd all find it odd as it's a habit I've never picked up.

"Anthony will be in San Francisco again next week, and I'll handle it. He has a couple of meetings I've found out about, but he'll be celebrating his mistress's birthday at a club. I'll hit him there to send a message to anyone else in the area with ideas of taking a slice of the pie for themselves. Thoughts?" I look around the table to observe if anyone finds fault with my plan. I see impressed looks from most of the other board members but a guarded stare from Nina. She's never been overly fond of my skills. I think I scare her.

"Good." King claps his hands together in a show of confidence. "Get it done, and make it messy. You said he isn't affiliated with any of the other gangs? Just a local who thinks he's a big fish and recruiting?"

"That's right. Anthony's from Sacramento but thought San Francisco would be easy pickings because of its divided neighborhoods," I assure him, leading him farther and farther from the truth.

"Good. I want it public and vicious enough that the news picks it up." He nods his head at Elise to share her information next. She also refuses to stand.

The aged heiress strokes the diamond necklace at her throat and commands the room with clear elocution and unwavering eye contact.

"The new governor will be touring the state and is stopping in El Castillo. He has enough skeletons in his closet that I've persuaded him to proclaim the prosperity of our lovely city and redirect any federal investigations from taking place. Not to worry, dears. I'm handling it."

King nods at Elise with begrudging respect, then invites Tanaka to share his information about Rook. "Tanaka, tell me what's been happening on the legitimate side. We see the numbers are up, and a recent article was published in one of the major business magazines. Explain."

Tanaka stands and folds his hands in front of his slightly rounded belly. He takes a deep breath, and his soothing timbre washes over us all, "Returns on investments are way up due to a startup recently acquired by a bigger tech giant. The software sale resulted in a healthy bump in our revenue, and we maintained a portion of the holdings after the transfer. Employee turnover is down, so we spend less on training and severance packages. Essentially, the business is running like a well-oiled machine, and we will all continue to be wealthy men and women in the future."

He concludes his speech without drawing attention to his own work but crediting the whole business. It was his deal that just made the company hundreds of millions of dollars. I'm thrilled he didn't turn out to be an asshole after all.

This is the kind of person I want on my team. Letting him request Sage doesn't feel as unnerving as it did before he delivered his little speech, calmly laying out the facts and taking pride in the company.

"Finally," King nods and turns to De La Cruz, "I've heard rumors of more sales to minors. De La Cruz, I will not tell you again; get your dealers in line. Send it down the line that anyone selling will be handled internally. Remind them of what happens when they break our laws."

Resisting the impulse to do a little happy dance in my seat, I thank the heavens that the rumor mill has already started. Every whisper undermines De La Cruz. If things turn out as I expect, King will lose faith in him, and De La Cruz will start looking for new allies. Could he be swayed to our side with enough pressure on all sides? Do I even want him on my side?

We discussed other business for the next hour and found that most of the house was in order. There are always a few things to rectify, but overall, it's been a quiet month.

Horvat's death was hovering over us as a problem to solve, but getting Romano installed in his place has freed us up considerably.

As the talk of promotions and who to add to my underling assassins' lists wrap up, King turns to the man on my left and asks, "Romano, what do you think of Rogue?"

"She seems...competent," he replies cautiously, and I roll my eyes. The other members have all ceased talking and are intent on watching the exchange.

A scoff escapes me. I quickly weigh my options and decide Romano can keep breathing today because he hasn't seen me in action.

Competent is an insult. I'm fucking magnificent.

King clears his throat and speaks again, "She's attractive. She's young and...competent." *Competent, my round ass.* "But she needs a firm hand; that's where you come in."

The fuck? Never again will I be faced with a firm hand, and if this man so much as tries to lift a finger to beat me into submission as King implies, I will cut off all of his appendages one agonizing inch at a time, starting with his cock.

"Explain," Romano demands with a tone of voice few are brave enough to use with King. A smidgen of unexpected respect builds for him as he asserts himself with his new boss.

Instead of answering, he shoots Romano an icy glare, warning him to watch it, and turns to me. "Thoughts on Romano?"

It's time to freak out the new guy.

"He's intelligent, doing better than Horvat, so competent applies here as well." I shoot him a wink with the last thought. "Francesco Romano is forty-three, a widower, has no children and makes approximately ten million dollars a year. He spent too much on his condo downtown in a bidding war with another prospective buyer, has a degree in business, and walks with the slightest limp on cold days because of an old football injury to his right knee."

King smirks and levels Romano with a glare.

"That, Romano, is how you answer a question. Do better," he says.

King bangs his fist on the table once, drawing all eyes to him and stopping the gawking everyone had been doing. "There is one final order of business I would like to apprise you of, not as a vote, but simply to inform you all."

The Sacrifices We Make

King straightens his cufflinks and adjusts the edges of his shirtsleeves poking out from the arms of his jacket. "Rogue and Romano are to be married. She needs someone in the fold to have by her side when she takes over. I'll hold onto this position until my last breath, but make no mistake, there *will* be a Queen after this King meets his end."

Muted gasps go around the table, and Elise has a smug smile. Tanaka looks like he's just eaten some rotten eggs, and De La Cruz is stunned speechless, as am I.

King only gives a moment's pause before continuing. "Romano has worked his way up and has the respect of his subordinates because of his tactics. Combine that with Rogue and the fear she instills in those thinking to cross us, and we will have a power couple at the organization's helm. I've given this much thought; it is the best course of action. I will not hear a discussion on this; it is happening. This is a courtesy announcement."

No one has moved since King started his "proclamation." Elise shrugs a carefree shoulder when he stops speaking, likely thinking I could kill Romano when the time comes. Yeah, I've got her all figured out now.

Tanaka and Wilson look at each other, and the former lifts a brow ever so slightly, and Wilson infinitesimally shakes her head, warning him not to say something.

They know as well as I do that there's no way out of this for me. They don't know why but understand that I follow King's orders to keep the peace.

De La Cruz looks at neither Romano nor me but at King. His anger becomes palpable in the room, and I know it's because he hoped to sit in King's chair one day.

It must have been hard coming up the ranks with King but never stepping out from behind his shadow. I think he always figured one day, his time would come. King naming me heir apparent will only cause more strain. Great.

I know, deep down, there is no way out of this for me. The threat of Sage will be hanging over my head until I get her back with me, and apparently, King thinks I'll be staying afterward. If he even sticks to his side of the original bargain, that is.

I realize how foolish I've been, clinging to a deal I negotiated when I was sixteen with the head of a criminal organization. Still, it's been what has given me the wherewithal to push through and continue living this life.

King continues to think I'm that dutiful child he brought up in this world of pain and secrecy who follows his commands without question.

Romano is sputtering his reaction and refusal to be married to a girl nearly young enough to be his daughter while the others just gawk at the new development.

De La Cruz is still glaring daggers at King, now knowing he never had a shot at the crown. Through all of King's shit, he has constantly reminded me I would end up leading The Gambit one day. Of course, now I realize it's always been said behind closed doors. De La Cruz had no clue.

King called it "continuing his legacy."

Yeah, no thanks.

It would be infinitely easier to wait to dismantle The Gambit once I led it, but how many people would die between now and then? How many loved ones will be used as leverage to blackmail people into doing King's bidding?

Nope, I can't wait around until then. The earlier, the better.

If it weren't for the lack of a dissolution plan, I'd have stabbed King through the heart with the heel of my new boots for thinking he gets to decide my future more than he already has.

With a final reminder for De La Cruz to keep his dealers in line and an internal moment of joy, knowing his end is coming soon, I leave the room and head down the hallway to the elevator.

Romano catches up with me, and I do my best to avoid looking back into the meeting room where Tanaka is asking King for some time with Sage, as per our plan.

We went over his script about fifteen times in the last two days. He'll say he heard a rumor about a dominatrix named Sage working with us and wishes to inquire about her services.

At the very least, we know she did the dom-sub scenes with Blake, so if word got out, it could be attributed to the former security director. Hopefully, with all of the money he just brought in, it'll be an easy yes from King.

Romano says nothing as the elevator doors open, and we step in together. There's nothing to say. King holds the power here, and he's right. Anyone stepping into the role of leader needs allies. The only question is, is my husband-to-be trustworthy in any sense of the word?

Chapter Seven

Rogue

As I exit the Rook Industries building after that disastrous meeting and an utterly silent elevator ride down to the lobby with my apparent fiancé, my mind spins with possibilities of gaining a new ally or enemy.

I veer left as Romano turns right upon exiting the main door, not bothering to turn around as he calls my name in a bid to discuss what just happened. I don't have the mental capacity for that at the moment.

I'm in the middle of a mindfuck of a conundrum, busy figuring out a way to tell the guys I'm ostensibly getting married, and I didn't even put up a fuss about it. I grab a cab and take it to a busy shopping mall across town.

I enter the building, pulling out my official phone to have it ping here for an hour, then at the bar and grill downstairs that operates later than the stores. I select the option to have it show me making my way to my apartment when the allotted time passes, just in case my phone is being tracked.

Thanks to Jacob's tech and a few random stops on my way to or from the clubhouse from any Gambit-themed activity, I've felt better coming and going from their place. The last thing any of us need is King finding out about them.

I stroll around the mall, eating a cinnamon-sugar pretzel as I window shop, and eventually roam to the other side of the building through one of the bigger department stores. The shops are closing soon, so I have to get moving.

It was either the mall or a bar to get lost in before switching taxis, and I wanted a pretzel.

I reach the kid's section of the department store with the mothers trying to corral their little ones and order an Uber with my burner phone. The app shows that there's already a driver outside, so I bob and weave through the tiny clothing racks and flying projectiles the hoard of five-year-olds are throwing and know that any possible tail I could have had will be stuck in that mess as I escape.

I meet the friendly driver and hop into the Prius to get to the clubhouse's neighborhood, ready to deal with the fallout of my new predicament.

Of course, I don't let the car drop me right at the gate, but we've all been using one of the local apartment buildings as our designated drop-off. Noah's right that we can't risk letting anyone know where we're located.

Polly was blindfolded on her way here, and all of the tech in the clubhouse was password-protected. Jacob made sure she couldn't uncover her location once inside.

We've gone to great lengths to ensure our security here, and I have no intention of leading anyone to our little bubble of safety.

I pay the lovely driver, and there's no need to cover the cost of bullet holes today, thanks to Elise's unsteady marksmanship. Once he takes off, I cross the street, then stick to the shadows to get to the clubhouse.

I open the stock market app on my burner phone and press the sell button to get the gate to start sliding open. I know the guys get an alert every time I use the app, as I do, so I've come to expect one of them to be waiting for me at the door. This time, it's Han; he must have been the closest.

I cross the threshold into the parking area and turn to look over my shoulder, seeing the gate start to slide shut. He must have pressed the "buy" button on the app before I could.

I turn to the entrance and see him leaning against the door frame, watching me approach. His eyes seem to be stripping me of every last scrap of fabric as I approach him.

"Hey, Gorgeous. How was your meeting?" Han asks as he pulls me into his arms and presses a heated kiss against my lips.

"It was good, but we've gotta talk. Is everyone here?" I ask.

"Yeah, let's go to the war room. You can fill us in." He wraps one arm across my shoulders and ushers me into the house. The weight of his arm helps make me feel settled, and I relish it.

How on earth am I going to tell the guys?

Han? We just exchanged our first "I love you" this morning, and now, surprise! I'm getting married! I really can't see this going over too well.

We step through the foyer, and he opens the frosted glass door for me, refusing to disconnect his arm from around my shoulders. "Guys!" he shouts into the open area of the clubhouse.

Like meerkats, they pop their heads out of various rooms, and I can't suppress the giggle that spills from my lips.

Jacob's is poking out of his office in the back. Red's head pops over the couch as he peers over at us, rubbing sleep from his eyes, and Noah's head is at an unnaturally low level as he emerges, presumably hunched over, from the kitchen.

"Captain, what the hell happened? Did you shrink?" I call out to him.

"Hey, Trouble! I spilled some lentils, and those fuckers are a bitch to pick up," he yells back.

He withdraws and walks out of the kitchen wearing a hot pink apron that says *My meat is hand-rubbed*. Red sees it and starts laughing his ass off.

"You can't laugh at it if you're the one that bought it, Lucas," Noah chides.

God, I love this place.

Jacob is doing his best not to join in, but I see his shoulders shaking and know he's losing the battle. Deciding to cut it short before our beloved leader loses his shit, I point to the war room, and Han leads me over.

We settle in our usual seats, and I ponder how best to share the news. Jacob stops beside me and gives me a lingering kiss, promising much more. *Nope. Not the time, Rogue. I have to get this out.*

Red flops into the seat across from me, the same way he did the first day we met for the first time here three months ago. The only items missing are the fun mugs, but Noah's apron more than makes up for them right now.

Noah sits at the head of the table, and all eyes turn to me. Okay, time to dish.

"Romano worked out a deal with the Vegas Crew and is looking more and more like a proficient man and not the usual gangbanger. Tanaka delivered his good news about Rook Industries, and King was pleased. He was speaking with King as I left, so he should be asking for time with Sage. Elise has the new governor under her thumb now that Reyes is gone. King wants me to deal with Neil's boss as soon as possible and liked the idea of me gutting him in a nightclub." I take a breath, knowing the easy part is over, and now, I have to work up the nerve to drop a quick bomb on them and hope for the best.

The guys all nod, knowing the plan. We reviewed this before I left so they knew what to expect from Tanaka and me, who kept me in the loop as we planned our exit for Sage. The Romano news and Elise thing are new to them, but they don't directly impact us or our plans, so they're small potatoes.

Time for the big news.

"Before the end of the meeting, King made an announcement. One involving Romano and me." Shoulders tense around the table.

We only know a little about Romano, but we're digging as hard as possible. The guys are understandably nervous about him being a new player on the board. "He appointed me his heir to The Gambit and announced my betrothal to Romano." *There, I said it.*

As the guys digest the news, I'm met with an eerie, unnatural silence. This is one of the first times they have reacted slowly to news from The Gambit side of the coin we're dealing with. I know it takes some time to process, but I expect some reactions when that's done.

Time continues to pass, and no one speaks.

"Are you guys jinxed, and I missed it somehow?" I ask, genuinely curious as to why they're so silent.

"No, Buttercup, we're just trying to give it some time to settle, and then one of us will probably ask you what you think. Right, guys?" Red looks around the table for confirmation, and I get a chorus of yeses.

Han, ever the peacekeeper, follows this with, "So, Gorgeous? How do we get you out of this? I just got you back and don't intend to lose you."

"I don't think there's anything we can do at this point," I tell him honestly.

I break eye contact with him and look around at the other guys, who all wear varying degrees of frowns on their faces. Yeah, it's not ideal, but it keeps King happy and allows me to learn more about Romano.

"I have to go through with it. King still has Sage and the evidence against me. If it were something small, I could argue it. But King made the declaration in front of the whole board. I know I've got Tanaka, Elise, and Wilson on my side, but what if I could sway another? Then we'd only have to deal with De La Cruz and King."

That reminds me of another point to bring up to the guys. "By the way, the rumors have already started. De La Cruz was called out at the meeting again for sales to minors. He's losing King's faith. Claudette works fast as fuck."

Noah clears his throat and asks perhaps the most critical question, "Trouble, how do you feel about getting married to someone you don't love?"

I look at him and let some of the anger I've been shoving down rush over me. King has no right to dictate what I do in my life. Yes, he might be my boss and adoptive father, but my personal life has always been mine to do with as I please so long as it didn't impact the business.

"I'm pissed as hell, Noah," I whisper. "I don't like it, but I know the piece of paper is not what makes a marriage. It's love, trust, and understanding. I've watched people cheat on, lie to, and steal from their spouses, all in the name of furthering their own lives and careers.

"Marriage, to me, is not the be-all and end-all, but it sure as fuck should be on my terms if I ever go that route. I gave up on the idea of a normal relationship when I had my first contract kill." My voice wavers at the end, knowing I had no choice but to go through with the first hit.

Han reaches for my hand and gives it a gentle squeeze. I look around the table and see concern etched on their brows, but no pity, thank God. I don't think I could take it at this point. Jacob rubs a hand on his neck, and Red's eyes are a swirling storm of anger.

Noah places a hand on Red's shoulder to ground him, and he dips his head. We can do nothing now but make a strategy to move forward while keeping on with our original plans and making adjustments where needed. This throws a wrench into the middle of them, but it's an impasse. This is happening, and there's nothing I can do to change it.

Jacob clears his throat, and I know an unpopular opinion is coming. "I think it's a good idea. You can keep a better eye on what's happening within the board, and you'll get a feel for Romano and his motivations. We're not finding much on him, but tying himself to you legally might give you access to him, Love Muffin." Fucking nicknames. I glare daggers at Jacob, and he just chuckles at my expense.

"NOPE!" I shout into the room, and the tension breaks when everyone chuckles. Once it dies down, I continue, "I'll keep an eye on him, maybe work my way toward gaining his trust."

Just then, a text pings on one of the burner phones in the war room. I push off the floor, letting the wheels of my chair roll me to the shelf behind me. I snag the phone and unlock the screen. Tanaka's text says he mentioned wanting to spend time with Sage, the domme, and King agreed. He'll let Tanaka know when she's available.

Talk about a productive meeting. I pass on the good news to the guys.

Red clears his throat, and everyone looks at him. "Jacob has finished the tech for the Collinsworth Bank job I'll be running, and I've done all the research I can. They recently had an upper management guy leave the company, so we'll slot me in as a transfer from another branch in a few days. What do you guys think? Could you do without me for a little while?"

My first instinct is to say no and tell Red to shove the Annex assignments up his superiors' asses because I'm petty and angry at the world right now, but I clamp down on the words threatening to spill out of my mouth. I don't have to like it, but I have to support him like he does me.

"Lucas, if you're ready, we're one hundred percent behind you. Are you sure you're good to do this on your own?" Noah asks with a bit of concern in his voice. I love how he looks out for his guys. He's a secret sweetheart and loves his team like they're his family, but he tries to hide that softer side of him.

"Yeah, Noah, I'm ready," he confirms.

"We're just a phone call away if we can help," Jacob assures him, and I swear my heart flip-flops in my chest as I watch their eyes on their teammate, propping him up with every word.

"Cool, thanks. I'll finish out here with you guys this week, then move into the apartment Annex has set up for the job. Aw, Buttercup, don't look at me like that," Red whines when he sees my face.

I didn't want him to move out, and my face clearly showed it. Damn these men, slipping past all of my defenses and encouraging me to let my guard down.

"What? I didn't do anything," I argue.

"Yeah, you did, Gorgeous," Han says. *Traitor. He's on my shitlist now.*

"Fine, I may have made a face. I don't like it, but I get it. You promise to call if you need us?" I enquire and watch his eyes light up at my question.

"You're worried about me. You like me!" I drop my head into my hands and sigh in exasperation.

"Duh, you big goofball." Red is damn near dancing in his seat.

"No, Buttercup. You *like me*, like me." *Aw fuck.* I'm not prepared to have the feelings talk today. And yeah, I *like him*, like him. With my heart rate speeding up at his declaration and my earlier thoughts, I might even be in love with him.

"Moving on." My tone leaves no room for argument, and I despise watching the little smirks on all of the boys' faces. *God, it's spreading.*

"Mara Hendrix has to be next on the Annex side," I declare. Well, that got them to focus.

The guys all look at me, and Han—my former, turned-rekindled flame and current group traitor—is apparently the most curious.

"Whatcha thinking, Gorgeous?" Han asks.

"I have to head to San Francisco in a couple of days to get things in place for 'Anthony.' Andudette will have more information on her sister than we could ever find. I'll broach the subject of getting her help on this one. She's not on good terms with her sister; maybe this is our way in."

"Devious," Jacob comments, "I really fucking like it."

We spend the rest of the night making plans and brainstorming. Some of which I can't fucking wait to put into action. Between Tanaka's progress with getting to Sage and the Mara plan firming up, I'm in a great fucking mood.

THE FOLLOWING MORNING, AS I WALK DOWN THE STAIRS TO ASSAULT the coffee machine, I see all four of my guys standing at attention. It makes me pause my descent and eye their little smirks with trepidation.

"Uh, morning, guys. What's going on?" I ask.

Jacob holds out a cup of coffee for me in a mug that says *Want to hear a joke? Decaf.* I fucking love it. I make gimme motions as I reach the last few steps of the staircase.

They all move in close, and as soon as my feet land on the ground floor, I'm surrounded. Jacob is in front of me, Han and Red are on either side, and Noah is at my back. I'm boxed in, and I've never been so happy to be in a position I can't easily escape.

Noah runs his hand behind my ear and sweeps my hair to the side, kissing my neck. A shiver works its way through me before Jacob leans in and kisses me until I forget my own name. Phantom hands take the coffee cup from me, and I instantly wind one hand around Jacob's neck to deepen the kiss as soft fingertips trail up my arm. Han quickly finds a spot to nibble under my ear as Noah's assault on the other side goes uninterrupted.

I feel hands reaching around my stomach, and with their grip on my hips, I know it's Red. They're all touching me, sharing me between them without hesitation, and my mind immediately starts envisioning scenarios where we're all tangled up together and writhing in ecstasy.

Jacob pulls back, finds Han's mouth near my ear, and kisses him deeply.

Watching that has my panties detonating before Red steals my attention with his own earth-shattering kiss.

I sigh in contentment as he eases off, and Noah, who has been in the same spot, tilts my head back to deliver a kiss in greeting that makes my damn foot pop up behind me again. *How does he do that?*

Breaking the kiss, he whispers against my lips, "We have a surprise for you today."

I open my eyes and find his light-brown ones as they capture mine. "Is it not the completely hot make-out session with my four favorite guys first thing in the morning? Because I have to tell you, this is a damn good surprise."

The others laugh around us, and Red takes over the explaining. "We're having a group date today. I'm leaving for however long this assignment takes, you've got San Francisco and a fucking marriage to deal with, and we need to have some fun before we all turn grey and end up with ulcers. Are you in?"

"I'm *so* in! What are we doing?" I ask, delight in my voice.

"That, Gorgeous, is a surprise. Come on, drink your coffee, then get dressed. Anything is fine," Han adds when he sees my mouth open to ask how I'm supposed to know what to wear if I don't know what we're doing.

There is a world of difference between my dancing and paintball shoes. When Han sees I'm about to protest the lack of criteria, he continues, "Anything, really. Although, a ball gown *may* be pushing it. Just be comfortable."

Excited by the upcoming adventure, I down my coffee in record time and sprint up the stairs as the guys sprawl out in the lounge. I ran through my choices and decided on the black jeans I wore last night, one of Red's superhero t-shirts, and some ankle boots.

I may not have my whole wardrobe here, but I've got a decent selection between the little stops at my apartment to grab a few things here and there and Red ordering things for me online. My hair gets pinned up quickly, and with a swipe of eyeliner and my deep plum lipstick, I charge down the stairs and pronounce that I'm ready.

We pile into the SUV as I ask question after question about where we're going, but Noah's stoicism seems to have transferred to everyone because no one, and I mean *no one*, cracks. Red looks like he wants to, and Han keeps looking at my face with glee. I know it's killing them not to tell me, but Jacob keeps threatening purple nurples if they even whisper a word.

We pull up outside of a strip mall, and I look around. There isn't much

The Sacrifices We Make

here, but when my eyes finally land on one sign in particular, I let out a shriek of joy that catches everyone off guard.

We pour out of the SUV, and I can't help the pep in my step as we get closer and closer to the door. Noah reaches out and pulls it open for us, and I step inside the restaurant, relishing the warm air as I remove my jacket. I am so ready for this.

"We rented out the whole place; it's all ours for the next four hours," Jacob assures me. I leap into his arms, and I'm passed from person to person as I give my effusive thanks.

A worker interrupts before I can live out some fantasies and explains the setup. He hands over unlimited play cards and explains that there are over three hundred and fifty games to play in the adult arcade, the kitchen is open, so lunch is available, and the bar is fully stocked.

This is going to be incredible.

I race off with the card in my hand, and the guys and I make our way through as many games as possible. The competitive skeeball tournament is the highlight. Noah complains that something must be wrong with his balls, and we all lose it.

As a kid, I never went to an arcade, so this is a new experience. I've always wanted to try these games, and the guys made it happen.

Jacob is unsurprisingly adept at the old-school Mrs. Pacman machine; Red dominates at air hockey and Dance, Dance, Revolution. Han is exceptionally skilled at racing games. I do only okay, but I have a blast all the same. Next time, I'll kick their asses. Noah is terrible at everything but plays along and indulges me when I drag them to machine after machine.

We gorge on burgers and chili cheese fries, down a few too many beers, and when we finish the day, we've got enough tickets between us that we get a giant teddy bear and name it Harold, after my teenaged video game buddy.

Chapter Eight

Lucas

I'M LEAVING FOR MY NEW ASSIGNMENT AT COLLINSWORTH BANK IN A couple of days, and I use the opportunity when it's just us guys to call a team meeting without our lady love.

I pulled everyone away from whatever they were working on and gathered them in the war room. Jacob and Han looked slightly confused, and Noah looked downright concerned, but I shushed everyone and motioned for them to sit down.

We're not plotting and scheming today, but what I want to discuss is serious. It feels like the right place to have the conversation: no distractions, no music playing, just the four of us.

"I know you're all wondering why I've gathered you here today," I start, and suddenly, I'm hit with the idea of doing that in an elevator full of strangers. *Now is not the time for comedic genius, Lucas. Come on.* "I want to discuss Rogue." They know I'm serious because I didn't call her Buttercup.

She's not here today because she is meeting with Tanaka, Batten, and Wilson. They've finally arranged a time that works for all of them to discuss taking down King. Our girl also wants to discuss Romano with them and see if they can share insight. She told us in no uncertain terms that we were not invited. I think it's because she wants to keep us hidden up her sleeve until the last possible moment. She's so thoughtful.

"What about her?" asks Jacob. "Is something wrong? She seemed fine this morning."

"She *is* fine," Han assures him and covers his hand with a reassuring squeeze. Fuck, those two are adorable.

Noah just watches as I run the meeting. He's not used to being excluded from the leadership role, but I'm steering this air balloon today. *Do air balloons even have captains?*

"She's fine," I echo Han, and Jacob relaxes his posture and flips his hand so he and Han can lace their fingers together. *See? Adorable.* "I think we need to have a boyfriend-in-law meeting."

Groans echo through the room, and I curse that I can't jinx groans. This would go so much more quickly if they couldn't talk.

"Define 'boyfriend-in-law meeting,'" Noah demands, ever curious.

"We should discuss what we're doing. I love that girl, but I don't want to scare her off. She's not planning on sticking around, at least not that I'm aware of, and I'm invested. I don't want to lose her. I don't want to give her up. I know it's unconventional that she's seeing all of us, but I don't find it odd. Do you guys?"

Noah clears his throat and shifts in his seat. Of all of us, I know he has the most issue with voicing his feelings, despite initiating the little make-out at the foot of the stairs the other day, so he shocks me when he pipes up. "I also really like her. I just started dating her and want to see where it goes. You're right; it doesn't bother me as much as I thought it would."

Well, slap my ass, and call me Shirley.

"I told her I love her." Damn, Han! Going in for the kill. "She said it back. I don't know what that means for the future, but I've loved her since we were younger. I don't plan on giving her up either."

"I'm in this for the long haul, too," Jacob states but casts an eye at Han after his declaration. Okay. So we're all on the same page, some further along than others, but at least we agree. Buttercup is everything I didn't know I needed, and it kills me to think of her moving on after she gets her sister back.

"We need to help her with her list more than ever. We have a vested interest other than just taking down our boards. We need her. She seems to need, or at least want us, too. We have to make it safe for her and Sage to stay once we get her back." The determination in my voice shocks even me. I'm rarely this focused and single-minded.

A chorus of agreement sounds through the room.

"Should we also talk about some ground rules now that we're all in this?" Jacob asks.

"I've got one," Han states. "No interrupting dates. We can do the group thing again because that was fun, but we'll all need to promise to respect individual time."

"Deal." My agreement is met with a firm nod and a glint in his eye, telling me he'll take me down if I renege. *Noted.*

"We keep each other in the loop if we move to the I love you stage." Jacob looks at Han as he delivers his rule proposal, and I see Han flinch a little.

I think this is the first time any of us have heard about how things have progressed with Buttercup and the "I love you" thing. With the new relationship Han and Jacob are exploring, I get why he might be feeling a little blindsided.

"Yeah, that's a good rule," Han agrees. He leans in toward Jacob, "Sorry I didn't tell you. I meant to, but I didn't know how to bring it up that we'd exchanged the words. It changes nothing with us."

Jacob nods and returns Han's soft smile.

Noah clears his throat and adds, "I'm new to this whole thing, and I know you guys have your inclinations, but I'm not one for sharing in the bedroom. The stairway was...unavoidable. What you guys do is up to you and Trouble, but I'll keep things behind closed doors if she ever decides to take things to that level with me."

Possessive bastard. But I get it. He's got his Sheila issues and thinks sharing means dividing the attention instead of doubling it. He'll figure it out one day.

Damn, I'd love to see those two go at it. I've been thinking about our Dear Leader getting topped by our girl since they went out last week.

"Okay, to recap: no interrupting solo time, keep each other informed of major milestones should they occur, make sure she and Sage are safe once we get her free, and no roping Noah into a devil's triad. Is that it?"

"For now," Han replies. "We have to be open to changing the rules as things progress, but communication will be key here, guys. I think we should also tell her we spoke. I don't know that she'll like that we met without her to discuss our relationship, but I get why you called us together, Lucas. You just don't want us to get all fucked up if she leaves. The team is sticking around; she might not."

I knew I liked Han. He gets me.

Rogue

I left the guys at the clubhouse about half an hour ago. Red made a bit of a fuss about me attending this meeting alone, but I promised to text the group chat if anything significant happened. I can only make so many concessions before I feel like I'm being managed.

I shoot a thumbs-up emoji to the chat group to indicate I'm here. I know it drives Noah crazy, but that's probably only about sixty percent of why I use emojis instead of words. The other forty percent is pure convenience.

I wait for the gate to open as I sit in Black Beauty. I've been going back and forth about what Horvat mentioned regarding King phasing Elise out, not for any reason other than she's outlived her usefulness.

He likely thinks she's just some old lady ready to retire. A cozy life in this neighborhood is not what King has in mind. No, he's probably thinking of a pine box six feet under, filled with her secrets to keep her company for eternity. However, the new governor angle should keep her alive and useful a bit longer.

The intricate wrought-iron gate slowly inches open on the hydraulics, and as I creep forward in the car, I admire the land surrounding the house. No, house isn't the right word. Mansion fits infinitely better.

The home is two stories and sprawls to either side of a large portico with a circular drive around a fountain. *Holy shit.* I knew she was loaded, but this speaks to incredible wealth.

Being who I am, I can't help but search out vantage points and notice the design of the house has turrets on either side with narrow windows, a widow's walk atop the central part of the house, and all landscaping has been kept minimal as it leads to the front doors.

Elise has herself a sniper's wet dream of a house. I know better than to assume it's just how the house was built. This has clearly been designed with defense in mind. Anyone approaching the house will be immediately seen from the grand windows, so there's little chance of anyone sneaking up on her unsuspectingly.

I expect the backyard to be designed similarly, and the curious part of me is desperate to explore every nook and cranny.

I reach the front door and find a valet waiting for me next to the grand oak doors. He steps forward as I put the car in park and comes around to open the door for me. He stands back, and I slide from the plush leather seats to find my footing on the small gravel stones lining the drive. Another person opens the door, and I look towards the door to see who else Elise has on staff today. The fewer witnesses, the better.

My anxiety is eased as Elise stands in the open doorway wearing an oversized sweater dress and black leggings. She's got bunny slippers on, and I think I'm having a stroke. I've only ever seen her dressed in her Chanel pant-suits, fancy dresses, or business-chic attire. This is entirely different than anything I'd ever have imagined.

"Rogue, darling. Come on in." Even her tone of voice is relaxed.

I'm getting the authentic Elise today as a show of good faith. She's not putting on airs or being haughty as she often is in the board meetings, and my mind struggles to reconcile this version with the woman I know.

"Good morning, Elise. Thanks for hosting." That's right, we're having our first official alliance meeting today.

Elise volunteered her house, and it's taken us ages to find a time and day that works for all of us. Our schedules have us all over the place, not to mention my work, which requires me to be back in San Francisco. I plan to head up there tomorrow after I get everything settled here and with Claudette over the phone, but my plan may change depending on how today shakes out.

She ushers me into her home, and it's everything I'd expected when I saw the outside. A large foyer with a single round table in the middle has an enormous vase of fresh flowers. Twin staircases lead to the upper floor, and doors to the right, the left, and the rear all lead to different wings. How on earth does she, and whatever number husband she's on now, not feel like they're drowning in square footage?

"I told you a slightly different time than the others because Tanaka mentioned you may have questions about the whole accidentally 'shooting at you' thing." This woman and her air quotes. I swear, they get me every time.

"Uh, yeah. What the hell, Elise?"

"Come this way, and we'll get comfortable and chat before the others arrive. I gave us an extra half-hour to go over the basics." She takes off toward the door to the right, leading the way into a sitting room that matches the splendor of the rest of the house—her little bunny slippers' ears flopping with each step. Lucas would love those.

She has a tea and coffee setup on the sidebar and offers me a drink before settling down on the loveseat across from mine. We both opt for coffee, and I take dainty sips as I wait for the conversation to start. It doesn't feel like an alliance meeting, but rather, two girls just chatting. Is this how she pulls secrets from her victims? By plying them with refreshments, and...are those snickerdoodle cookies I see on my saucer?

I'm screwed.

"So, dear. The long and short of it is that I was a woman living alone with too much time on my hands. My second husband, Oscar, was a former military man who was quite old when he passed. It was a May-December romance, you see. When he died, I went through his things and found his old sniper rifle." She takes a sip of her coffee and crosses her ankles delicately in a prim move, despite the bunny slippers, before continuing.

"Of course, I knew nothing of how to use it, but it got me thinking. I was all alone in this big old house without any self-preservation skills. What thirty-year-old woman wants to be that vulnerable, especially when limited security systems were available back then? So I took a gun course, got my license, and filled my free time at the shooting range."

I nod, seeing her point. This is a giant house with incredible acreage around it. If I were here alone, I'd be pretty scared, too, if I hadn't had the training King instilled in me.

"So, you started training?" I ask, prodding her to continue the story.

"Oh, yes. Edward, my third husband, started as my instructor. I learned everything from him, and he helped me modify the house. I wanted vantage points in case the worst happened. You can never be too careful in our line of work, you know.

"Nowadays, my security is top of the line, and I don't have much reason to keep up my training. It's why I needed the laser sight at the cemetery. I'm sorry if I scared you, dear," Elise concludes, only slightly regretful in her tone.

Scared me? *Fucking scared me?* This lady's insane.

"Elise, I think it's time to hang up the rifle. I can handle the extracurricular shootings without the laser; that way, no one sees it coming. Plus, knives are more fun. I've got this," I assure her.

That was persuasive, right? I'm a good shot but nowhere near as skilled as Han. I prefer my knives. Let's hope she doesn't think I'm rude by asking her to shelve the gun.

"I think you're right. I'll keep the shooting here on the grounds of the manor." *Manor.* Yes, that's the word for this house. Jesus, it's enormous.

Also, it's probably a bad idea to continue shooting *anywhere*, but at least it will be contained. On my way out, I'll warn the valet to spread the word to the other employees working the house and the grounds to tread carefully.

The Sacrifices We Make

"Anyway, would you like a tour, dear? The others should be here in about ten minutes, giving us enough time to see the downstairs area."

Just the downstairs?

Huge.

Fucking.

Manor.

After the ten-minute tour, five minutes of which I spent lost in the East Wing after taking the hidden bookcase door she showed me, we met Wilson and Tanaka in a different sitting room than the one Elise and I spoke in earlier. It seems like a living room, but there's no television and some uncomfortable-looking seats.

"To the dining room, people." Elise's clipped orders have Tanaka and Wilson snapping to attention and rising from their seats. We follow her through the door across the room and find ourselves in a formal dining room where the servers place soups in front of four chairs.

Elise indicates my seat beside hers and sends Tanaka and Wilson to the other side. Despite the table having seating for at least twelve, we're in the four seats directly in the middle to speak more efficiently.

Elise waves a hand, and her employees scatter through the doors, leaving us in silence. "Okay, good-ish guys, what's the plan? And are you seriously going to marry the new guy?" asks Nina. She looks from person to person surrounding her, and I can see she's nervous.

"I have a few things in the works, but as far as the Romano thing, I don't see a way out of it. King has me over a barrel on this thing. I don't want to get into specifics, but did you guys ever wonder why I haven't killed him yet? He has a few things on me that I need to get back. Then, and only then, can I gut the motherfucker." At the looks being exchanged, I know I'm not the only one with murderous intent for King in the room.

I remind them of what they've got at stake so they understand the gravity of the situation. "Wilson, he's threatened your dad in the past repeatedly, correct? Tanaka, he has issued not-so-veiled warnings about your daughters? Elise, I don't know what he has on you, but it's up to you whether or not to share. I think we all want to see him dead, but do any of your leverages hinge on being exposed or killed off when King dies like mine do?" No one nods, so I continue, "Okay, so...thoughts?" I finish as I lift my spoon filled with pumpkin soup.

Tanaka takes a deep breath and is the first to speak. "I think it is good we keep our options open regarding Romano. King has taken a liking to him, and if he can help recover whatever is holding you back from pulling the trigger, we should use it. Is there a way we can test him and see if he is mindlessly loyal to King? Some information we can let slip and see if he delivers it?"

It's not a bad idea. If the new guy wants to ingratiate himself with King, ratting on some board members would do the trick quickly.

Elise chimes in with some unexpected words, "Oh! Can it be about me? I love pissing that little fucker off, even if it'll be fabricated." *Well, damn.*

We all look at one another and nod. Now to think of some gossip that's juicy enough for Romano to pass on to King.

"In other news, we should all ensure our bases are covered. Nina, stop skimming money. If I can find it, King possibly could." Nina's face pales, and her eyes comically widen. She thought she covered her tracks.

"I...I..." she sputters. "How did you find out?"

"Does it matter? It wasn't the most direct route, but I made sure to have information on everyone on the board, and your purses were way too nice for your salary. Coupled with your mortgage and living expenses, it was easy to see you live outside your means. Without major debt to attribute it to, I dug deeper. You don't have to put it back into The Gambit but stop fucking taking it. Falsifying expense reports, even doing it well, could be detected."

She nods and keeps her eyes downcast, likely in shame of being caught —not about doing it, no. She's been stealing for years and hasn't felt remorse. I'll bet she's mentally kicking herself for making an error.

Tanaka looks at me with a bit of fear in his eyes, no doubt wondering what I found on him as I mentioned that I had information on all of them, but there wasn't anything in particular about him that I could dig up. He just got sucked further into a game he didn't know he was already playing.

I turn to Elise and see her small smile as she winks at me. Yep, she totally killed her husbands. I found the official records of her refusing an autopsy for religious reasons for each husband.

Elise is agnostic.

Chapter Nine

Rogue

After my charming visit with "team good-ish guys," I get back in the car and head to my old apartment. I mean, my apartment. Not old. I haven't permanently moved out. I'm just crashing with the guys, but the clubhouse feels more and more like home each day. Ah, who am I trying to fool? It's become home to me.

Between the game nights, helping Noah heal, and all the planning we do there, not to mention that I'm dating all four of them, it's hard not to feel the welcoming pull of a home base. I haven't felt anything akin to that since my parents were alive. Even my apartment feels barren now, even though I've lived there for years.

I pull out of the manor's grounds and turn up the radio, cruising through El Castillo with my windows cracked while the oldies station serenades me. Dream a Little Dream of Me by Doris Day wraps its notes around me, and I lose myself in the drive as I sing along. I may not have the best voice, but this song is manageable, especially when no one is listening.

After the twenty-minute trip, I pull into the underground parking structure and hear my phone ping when there's a pause between songs. I get Black Beauty into her spot and grab my purse on the bench seat beside me.

Pulling my phone out, I see it's the group text with the guys. I mean, who else would it be? It's not like I get many social texts. I see the messages started about ten minutes ago, but I must have missed the sounds over the music.

Red: Buttercup, how did it go?
Captain: Keep us updated.
Boom: Gorgeous, it's been a little while. Let us know if we have to kill anyone.
Boo Thang: Hey, Sugar Tits, like my new name on your phone? Also, send us something so I can stop barricading the door to prevent the other three from tearing the city apart to find you.

Good Lord, it's like they're all in here with me in the car. It's time to emulate Noah and give them tasks to get them off my case.

Me: Guys, I'm fine. Boo Thang, Sugar Tits is a horrible name. So is Boo Thang. I'm picking up some stuff and heading over to K's. He sent a message this morning, ordering me to go to his place. He said he has some stuff to discuss. You guys focus on getting Red ready for the assignment.

Fucking nicknames are going to be the death of me. I can't save the guys on my phone with their real names in case anyone gets ahold of it, and I definitely shouldn't use King's name for the same reason. I should have just taken the damn burner phone, but with the visit to King in a couple of hours, it seemed better not to.

I exit the car, go to the elevator, and wait for it to arrive while switching my phone to silent. I see messages on the lock screen popping up, but I stash it until I'm back inside my apartment.

The elevator takes me to the lobby, where I check in with my favorite ex-hitman. "Hi, Hugo. Has anything come for me lately?"

"Hey, Rogue. No, nothing since you stopped in last week. No one asked for you either. I'd text you if they did," he assures me.

"Thanks. How's Jim?" I ask as I look to the front door. The usual night doorman is working today, which is strange considering Jim and Hugo always work together on the same shift. Hugo's boyfriend off of work today puts my hackles up immediately.

"Oh, he's okay. Don't worry, I see your knife hand twitching. His mom is sick, so he's taking a few weeks off to help with the doctor's visits. Thanks for caring, Rogue." Hugo may be an ex-hitman, but he's a softy at heart.

I tell him to pass on my good wishes for Jim's mom and head upstairs.

The Sacrifices We Make

Stepping into my apartment is a strange experience. I was only here a week ago to pick up some weapons and a few more outfits, but the air is still and stagnant. The dust motes highlighted in the early afternoon sun have me pulling out the vacuum and tidying up the place before moving to pack a bag.

I have a couple of hours until I have to be at King's place, so the cleaning and packing only take up part of that time. My closets are nearly half-empty at this point, so I spread out the clothes a bit if anyone makes their way in here—not that they should get this far.

My security has yet to fail me, but I make a note to have Jacob look to see if there's anything else I can do, tech-wise, to shore up my defenses.

I slide the closet door in the living room and pull back the carpet to reveal the trapdoor to the apartment below mine.

Ah, Batcave, how I've missed you.

The guys have a fantastic setup, but having a hidden weapons room beneath a trap door makes me giddy.

I enter the code and the lock disengages. I turn and start my descent with as much pep in my step as I can manage while descending a ladder.

I've got an hour and forty minutes until I have to leave. I'll pack a quick bag with some more goodies from here and play some video games.

It's afternoon, so Harold Wakowski should be home from school. We can shoot shit together and curse up a storm. It's been too long since we've played Call of Duty together.

After an epic—albeit shorter than I'd prefer—gaming session with Harold, I'm back in the garage, my bags slung over my shoulder. I head to Black Beauty and drop them in the trunk before doing a quick visual sweep of my car in the garage.

You can never be too paranoid, can you?

Not seeing anything disturbed, I unlock the door and slide in. I changed into a red flared skirt, a hand-cut, off-the-shoulder T-shirt with the anarchy symbol on the front, and some black peep-toe heels. It's a bit different from my usual garb with the maimed shirt instead of a corseted top, but I love it, and that's what counts.

I make it to King's building in record time and hand off my keys to the valet. I know that sounds stupid, but my reasons are two-fold, and I do my best not to change my mind as I walk into the lobby.

The concierge nods at me, and with a lift of his phone, he confirms my appointment. The private penthouse elevator dings, allowing me access, and I enter.

The ride slows, and the doors open into King's foyer with a whoosh. The black marble tile underfoot and stark white walls bring forward a rush of memories, and I do my best to keep them at bay. I'm here for a reason and can't afford to be off my game.

The sound of my heels reverberates across the floor's hard surface with every step I take as I walk down the hall to King's office.

The hallways have iconic paintings ranging from Pollocks to Vermeers and everything in between, some copies and some originals. King likes his luxury a little too much for my taste.

I walk confidently down the hall, past the training room where he shot me, my old bedroom, and three of the guest rooms before reaching his office door. I do my best to keep the painful memories at bay, but every time I'm here, they rush back in.

His office is right next to the main bedroom, and, looking at his black bedroom door, I fight the image that comes to mind of me stabbing him as he sleeps—one day.

I knock twice and wait to be called in.

After a few moments, the handle turns, and I tamp down the look of shock attempting to flit across my face when I face Francesco Romano.

"Rogue, come in," King calls from within the office.

Romano steps to the side and extends a hand to usher me into the room. As I brush past him, I take in his classic three-piece charcoal suit and black tie. I step fully inside the space and see King behind his desk. The monitors of his security system are lit up behind him, showing different angles within the building and apartment.

Romano closes the door after I enter and joins me by the chairs opposite King's desk. I look at King but keep Romano in my peripherals. I've given no reason for King to lash out at me, but I want to keep any threats at bay.

My fiancé gracefully folds his tall body to take a seat, and after King waves a hand at me to do the same, I take the chair to the left. I know better than to simply ask King what's up, so I sit in silence until he states why he summoned me.

Romano drums the pads of his fingers on the armrests of his chair, and I cross my legs so the fabric of the red skirt drapes evenly around me as I settle in. This feels like it's going to be an awkward meeting.

"Ah, the happy couple. Romano, Rogue, are you both ready to solidify this union?" King asks. The question is not wholly unexpected, but I sit silently while waiting for Romano to answer. King raises one strong black brow and stares intently at the man on my right.

Romano's mouth is hanging open, probably hoping I've found a way to get us out of this or hanging onto the last sliver of hope that King would hear out his pleas not to have us fucking wed, but King pays him no mind and looks endlessly pleased with himself.

"The two of you will marry in nine days to cement your positions on the board. With this arrangement, I see this organization thriving. Rogue will take over for me one day, despite her reluctance to play with others. She mostly follows orders, and this one *will* be followed, daughter. You will marry. You will live together. You will keep each other in check.

"Romano, you are to be her consort. My role will be hers eventually, but you will be the one to get the underlings in line. Agreed?" His speech ends with a note of wistfulness.

Does he think he's helpful? Creating some kind of super-couple? Playing fucking matchmaker?

I let the situation wash over me as I think over the repercussions yet again, knowing there's no way I can refuse with the threat of Sage over my head. Agreeing without a fuss keeps me in King's good graces, and we can continue working around him to set things up for the fall.

I tune back in to hear Romano spouting reasons why this doesn't work for him, but I know King won't listen to a word he says. King wants him under his thumb, but because Romano doesn't have anyone he can leverage, he'll create another link—me and the power we can wield together.

Everyone wants power, and I'd wager King is betting he'll be reluctant to give it up once Romano has a taste of it.

"Fine. Christ, this is going to be a disaster." Romano turns his head toward me and has the most confused expression on his face. I'd laugh if I didn't think he'd have a stroke.

King goes to open his mouth to respond to Romano's objections but is suddenly cut off by the shrill tone of his phone. He holds a hand up to us and answers the call. "King."

He nods as he listens to the person on the other end. I have a feeling I know what this phone call is about, and I just hope King is about to confirm my suspicions.

"Good. That's all," he says before hanging up the phone and placing it face down on the desk. "Rogue, want to explain the weapons you brought to my home?"

Bingo.

Romano's head whips back to me. He's doing his best to keep his shock hidden, but I see it, and it makes me smile. I turn my head to face King more fully and give him the explanation I've been working on since I arrived at my apartment earlier.

"King, you know I'm heading to San Francisco to take care of Anthony. After this, I'm leaving to start doing some recon. He's due in town in three days, so I'd like to scope out the nightclub first."

"And you think grenades are necessary for your job?" he asks calmly.

"Only if you want me to have fun with it," I reply.

King's shoulders relax the tiniest of measures as a small smile twitches on his lips. He always had a flair for the dramatic.

I let my smile break free at the concrete knowledge that King orders his men to search my vehicle upon arrival.

The valet is undoubtedly convenient for visitors and for discovering little things about those who come here. I had a hunch he was having my car searched, but I needed to stash something worthy of an immediate phone call to confirm it firsthand.

It turns out that a bag of guns with a few grenades rolling around inside was enough of a threat. It's good to know what the threshold is.

Romano is still flustered and grumbling about things under his breath that, quite frankly, I don't care enough to hear.

"Okay," I say, "settle the arrangements, and when I'm back from San Francisco, it'll be done."

King has a pleased smirk, telling me he thinks we're right where he wants us. He knew I'd obey his command, and the allure of power calls to him in a way I don't feel.

He thinks everyone is after power or money, but he forgets that there are more important things in this world.

Or maybe he just doesn't know any better.

To be honest, I don't care about the marriage thing. I know the slip of paper isn't what makes it a marriage. It's the love, respect, and honor that hold weight. I don't have that with Romano, and I never will. It's no big deal; I'm not looking for another boyfriend.

This is just a means to an end—a way to keep King happy and looking elsewhere while the guys and I quietly move pieces into place and possibly gain another ally.

The Sacrifices We Make

I look at King, who meets my eyes as we ignore Romano's mumbles. He nods, and I return the gesture before rising from my seat and going to the door.

I'm done here, and I've got four boyfriends to tell about the new timeline. This is going to be fun.

After leaving King's apartment, I drive to my apartment instead of the clubhouse. I can easily brush it off as having forgotten something if King used any kind of tracking device. Who knows what the hell the valet could have stashed in here?

I pull into my parking spot and thoroughly search my car. It isn't until I have the hood up and my arms elbow-deep in the still-cooling engine that I find a small metal disk where it doesn't belong.

I pull it from the car and stick it on the Hyundai parked beside me. King has used trackers before, and they're a pain in the ass to find the old-fashioned way, but worth the investigation.

Someone stashed a bug detector under my passenger seat, and I have a feeling it was Jacob. It led me to the engine compartment, but it took me feeling around all the parts to get it out after the engine cooled.

I leave the bags in the car and skip stopping in the lobby to get upstairs and call the guys. I haven't even looked at my phone since I left earlier, but I want to call them somewhere I know is secure.

I enter my apartment, go to the closet trapdoor, and drop down, skipping the last four steps of the ladder entirely. I look at the names on my phone and decide to call Captain. If he's not with the others, he'll react better to the news than anyone else and agree to pass on the information to the rest of the guys.

It's not ideal in any condition, but the wedding will happen in a little over a week, no matter what the five of us have to say—well, six if I count Romano and his complaining.

The phone starts ringing, and I genuinely hope they're all together so I only have to say this once and not leave it to Noah to break the news to the others. Lucas is leaving for his mission in two days, so they're likely going over plans.

After three rings, the phone picks up, but there's no voice. It's an excellent tactic to get the caller to speak first. "Captain, it's me."

313

"Thank fuck, Trouble. We haven't heard from you in hours. Jacob is at his wit's end, trying to settle the other two."

"You sure it's just the other two he's keeping calm?" I laugh the words out. This man doesn't like to admit he gets worked up as quickly as the others, but he totally does. He's just a little better at hiding it.

"No," he sighs out in his deep voice. "When are you coming home?"

His voice over the phone is pure sin, and I realize I'm fucking dick drunk again. Noah and I have been taking things slowly, which is fine. Completely fine.

It's not fine.

"I'm not coming back to the clubhouse. I have to go to San Francisco to handle the Claudette/Anthony thing. King had someone search my car while I was at his place. I had bags packed in the back just in case, with a few heavy-hitting weapons to cause a reaction. The valet reacted, so now I know King's keeping tabs on me when I visit. My reason for the arsenal was that I was heading up to San Francisco immediately after. That's why I can't come home. I have to follow through and leave now."

The silence on the other end has me biting my lip. If Noah's unhappy with this, I can only imagine how he'll handle the following news. I decide to dive in before he can fixate too much on that. "Are the others with you by chance? Can you put me on speaker?"

"Yeah, Trouble. Hold on." Noah shouts for the others to join him while I pull the phone away from my ear and put my hand over the ringing sensation. For a generally calm and placid guy, he's got a set of lungs on him. Damn.

A few moments later, I hear some shuffling, and the guys chirp their hellos down the phone. "Hey, guys. I have some news."

"Noah wouldn't tell us anything," Red says. "What's up?"

I quickly tell them I'm headed up to San Francisco earlier than expected. Red complains and sounds frustrated with the new development, and I have second thoughts about telling them about getting married in nine days.

Still, I decided I wouldn't keep secrets from these guys, no matter how painful or irritating they may be. Everyone else in the world, sure. But them? Fuck no.

They've earned my trust. No matter how much I wish I didn't have to tell my guys, it's the right thing to do.

We will *not* break up over lack of communication, and that's precisely how this would play out in the end. They'd get mad, I'd feel justified in my actions, and the whole damn thing would come tumbling down around us.

Fuck no.

"Look, before I tell you, I need to hear you say you will do your best to react rationally. I won't ask you not to get mad because I would if the shoe were on the other foot. I'm just going to ask for some trust. Can you all agree to that?"

There's a moment of hesitation before four reluctant yeses come down the line. Blessed forces that be, Red somehow finds the courage to refrain from jinxing all of them. However, that could have stemmed any possible outbursts.

Taking a deep breath, I use my most monotonous voice and spill the details. "King has decided I will marry Romano in nine days, not in some far off, an as-of-yet undecided, possible future scenario as we thought. Nine fucking days. And I will also, apparently, be living with him upon my return from this trip. Nothing will happen with him. I am with you guys completely, but there's no way I'll get around this until I have Sage back. I don't like the idea, but it's a way to figure out future moves."

Han is the first to speak, and thank God he does. "Gorgeous, we trust you." There's a grunt on the other side of the phone, and I have a feeling someone just caught a jab in the gut for overreacting. "You do what you have to do. Do you want one or all of us up in San Francisco with you? We could leave now and follow you up there."

"No, no. Don't worry about me," I assure him.

"Red, honey?" I call out into the phone. There's some shuffling, and I'm taken off of the speakerphone.

"Yes, Buttercup?" he asks. "What can I do? Do you want me to kill Romano for you? If there's no groom, there can't be a wedding. Plus, I called dibs first."

My laugh bubbles out of me, and I let it go freely. I don't have to put a damper on my reactions with them like I do with King.

"I know you had dibs, but this is out of my control. Plus, you never asked." I shrug even though he can't see me. It's funny, but it's still true. "Your only focus is your mission. Be safe and call me if you need me. I'll be there and back as soon as I can."

"I know, I know. And I know you're going to be fine, too. I trust you. Just, please, if that douchewad even touches you, I want you to skin him alive. Can you do that for me, baby?" His voice drops to a low and dangerous tone, and fuck me, I am digging it.

Why the hell does that turn me on as much as it does? Who knew Lucas could be the possessive type? He's so free with his teammates and me. Because Romano isn't one of us, he doesn't get the same leniency. Not that the new guy would get it from me in the first place.

"I promise, Red. I'll miss you, but seriously, call if you need me. Can you pass me to Jacob?" After a quick goodbye, more shuffling ensues, and suddenly, my sexy Brit's voice comes down the line.

"Hey, Boo Thang," I tease. His laughter is a balm on the nerves I've been feeling all damned day.

"Hey, Sugar Tits," he laughs out.

"Those are not the two nicknames that stick, got it? Keep thinking, and I'll do the same. I'm gonna miss you. Keep an eye on the guys for me, will ya?"

"You got it, Love. Take care of yourself, and use the bug detector wand I stashed in your car. It's under the passenger side of the front seat. Let me know if you need anything."

I don't mention that I have already found it because it would only raise the question of why I needed it in the first place. I love that Jacob thinks of stashing detectors in our vicinity at random times. Last week, I found a small one in my purse. He even covered it with little cherry decal stickers for me.

I make a mental note to thank him properly later.

"Will do, Dream Boat. Nope. No. I take it back." God, I hate this nickname thing! Why does nothing sound right?

His laughter comes down the line. "I'll miss you, too, Sweet Cheeks."

Fuuuck. First Sugar Tits and now Sweet Cheeks...I think someone else has sex on the brain. "Pass me to Han, please?"

There was more shuffling, background chatter, and finally, some blessed silence. "Hiya, Gorgeous. I stole the phone and hid in the weapons room." I sigh, and a tremble can be heard in my breathing for the first time in a long time. I look around my own weapons room and find it funny that we both hide where the blades and guns are.

"Ivy, I hear you breathing, and it's not the steady calm I'm used to. Are you worried about us?" he asks, and his soft, caressing voice trails down the connection. "I get it. I don't like it at all, but I get it. None of us are mad at you; we want to tie King to a target for Mrs. M to throw axes at."

I laugh at the image he just planted in my head, not caring that he did that intentionally to break the tension. "You're right. It's not ideal, but it is necessary to keep Sage safe. I promise to take precautions and to be wary of him."

"I love you, Ivy. Be safe, please."

"I love you too, Han." I hear a door bang open, a shuffle over the phone, and a muffled "oof."

"Trouble? Trouble, are you still there?" Noah calls down the phone. He's breathing like he's been running.

"What's happening? Is everyone okay? Fuck, I can be there in ten."

"What? Oh, no. Nothing is wrong. Han is just chasing me because I stole the phone. Be safe, and hurry back. We'll handle things over here. Just worry about Claudette and Anthony. Or Toby. Whatever the fuck his name is. Fuck the rest."

There's a yell from the other side, the sound of the phone hitting the ground, and a muffled curse before the line goes dead. I think Han caught Noah.

Chapter Ten

Rogue

I TAKE MY TIME DRIVING UP THE COAST TO SAN FRANCISCO, TRYING to enjoy the scenery along the way and not fret too much about the upcoming jobs.

Before I left, I grabbed a new burner phone from the Batcave to redirect my mind. Reprogramming them to suit my needs and controlling what I could at the moment helped me keep my feet on the ground.

I'm sure Red will be fine. I mean, it's corporate espionage, so nothing too dangerous—hopefully, just some information grabs and downloads. Jacob will have been thorough about the tech he needs for the job, Han will have stocked him with weapons just in case, and Noah will make sure he keeps his head with his daily check-ins.

As for me, I have everything I need in the back of the car, ready to go for the assassination of Toby, aka Anthony. Although, it's technically not an assassination unless it's a political or prominent figure. In this case, it's just a hit.

I have the windows cracked and feel like the badass I am as I listen to "King" by Lilith Czar on full blast, my voice weaving in with the music. I'm not quite in "mission mode," as Han calls it since this has been in the works for a few days already, and it's not an actual dispatch.

Crossing the bridge into the city, I focus on the music and views. I decided to splurge on this trip; it's being paid for by The Gambit, after all. I won't be holed up in some off-the-grid apartment, oh no. Not this time.

I pull up to The Fairmont in Nob Hill, and the valet is quick to open my door and offer assistance to help me out. I give him a sweet smile and direct the bellboy to the trunk to collect the bags. I lean over the space and make sure everything is zipped up tight before letting him touch anything.

I strut across the opulent lobby, heading to the reception desk with my clutch tucked under my arm. My hands are primly held before me, and my red skirt swishes around my thighs. I switched the t-shirt I had on before with a black corset top when I stopped for gas about an hour earlier, and my hair is a little windblown from the trip, but my white vintage sunglasses push it away from my face.

I gather a few stares as I reach the desk, and a well-dressed receptionist stands at attention, ready to get me checked in. The bellboy is off to the side, waiting to find out what room I'm headed to. I see my bags carefully packed onto the gold-plated cart, and the one with the grenades is perched on top. Nice.

"Good afternoon, ma'am. Do you have a reservation?"

I raise a withering brow at his question, wondering how many people walk into this fancy-ass hotel without a reservation. "Yes, it's under Romano."

I phoned just before leaving El Castillo and thought it would be funny to start using my new beau's name. If King checks up on me, he'll see it and think I'm at least playing by his new rules while spending way too much cash.

"Yes, Mrs. Romano. We have you in the Presidential Suite, as per your request. I'll have the bellboy bring your bags up, and I'll show you to your room. Will your husband be joining you?"

"Not this time," I look at his nametag, "Clark." I hand over my Rook Industries expense card, and once he logs it into the system and returns it, I wave my arm for him to lead the way.

Clark the clerk takes me to the elevators next to reception, and the bellboy is already gone. He likely heard my suite number and headed up early to get my stuff in the room. I really should have insisted on keeping the bag with the grenades on my shoulder, but it wouldn't have suited the affluence of this place to be walking around with a big-ass duffel bag.

We reach the twenty-third floor, and the doors open silently. My suite is near the elevators and has a stairwell to the right. Already studying the floorplan when I was booking the room, I confirm which direction to high-

The Sacrifices We Make

tail it in case I need a quick escape. It's one of the reasons I requested this room. Well, that and the views. And the minor dent it will make in The Gambit's account.

Clark uses my keycard to enter the suite and opens the door for me. I turn left and head into the lounge area. There's a dining table and chairs, and just behind that is an oversized black couch that could easily fit me and all of my guys. The couch is aimed at a huge television mounted on the wall.

Damn, we need a couch like this. I make a note to figure out who made it so I can order one for the clubhouse.

I stroll back toward the hallway, passing Clark, who's still standing near the door, and head into the bedroom area. It's gorgeous, and the whole suite is decorated in soothing browns and velvety blacks, but the bed...oh, the bed. It's draped in beautiful, decadent, and fluffy white linens. It's a Cal-king and looks so freaking cozy. It may not have my men in it or smell like lavender like Jacob's does, but I'll sleep like a baby tonight.

The bathroom just behind the bedroom is equally luxurious and gives the finely designed ones at the clubhouse a run for their money. I wonder if Jacob used this place for inspiration.

Just before the panic sets in about missing explosives, I find my bags settled on a small stand in the closet. With a quick check, I find that nothing has been disturbed. I reach Clark, and with a crisp hundred, I thank him for his time and assure him the room is precisely what I wanted.

He leaves the keycard on the table and exits the room. As soon as the door snicks shut, I take off at a sprint and launch myself onto the giant bed.

I may have a decent stockpile of money gathered to help get Sage safe, but I never splurge on myself. I always stay somewhere exorbitant when I go on missions because the company picks up the tab, but I have never booked this gorgeous of a room.

I think it's the little—okay, big—vindictive part of me that wants to bleed the company for some cash, but fuck it. I let out an excited giggle as I wiggle on the covers and look out of the windows. The room offers a 270-degree view of the city, and I feel like a fucking queen in her castle. I love it.

I snatch up one of the burners I hid in my clutch and FaceTime Han.

He answers on the third ring, and his relief is evident when he sees me smiling. "Hey, Gorgeous! You made it okay?" he asks.

"Yes! Han, look at this place!" I can't help but squeal in delight when I flip the camera angle and show off the room I booked for my stay. "It's fucking amazing, but I already miss you guys. Is Lucas ready?"

"Yeah, Jacob is with him, and they're going over the tech he'll be using. He'll be fine. He's staying in one of the apartments nearby, so he'll be close, but we're stashing his bike at a garage down the block if he needs a quick getaway.

"Noah has gone over every inch of the plans. Everything looks good, and I've loaded him up with as many concealable weapons as I could in his pack. He'll be fine. Wanna see him?" he asks.

"I'll shoot him a text in a bit. I just wanted to show you this place and make you jealous. Just tell the guys I'm good and that I miss them." I keep the wistfulness out of my tone, but only just.

"Will do, Gorgeous. Take a bubble bath, and get some sleep. You'll need it if you're spending time with Claudette soon. That woman is...a lot." Han laughs as he reminds me of a few of the memes I've forwarded to him from her.

I laugh and send him a kiss through the phone before hanging up. I do just as he asks, filling the tub with an array of products I find lining the shelves. As I dip into the water, I let out a giant sigh. I'm delighted no one heard that. I'm a badass; I'm not supposed to sigh at bubbles, but here we are.

I get settled in with a glass of wine and a steamy book on my Kindle. As the bubbles tease my nipples, I snap a selfie with the burner phone and send it to the guys. I switch the phone to airplane mode, thinking of how frustrated they'll be when they see the message and there's nothing they can do about it. I giggle and lose myself in the characters' stories as I let the day's stress melt away.

I WAKE UP IN THE MORNING WITH THE SUN SHINING DESPITE THE likely chilly temperatures. I snuggle further into the covers and extend my legs sumptuously, enjoying each pop and stretch as I let my body unfurl into a starfish position.

I look around the gorgeous room, smiling to myself all over again. I may not love luxury all hours of the day, but occasionally, enjoying it isn't a bad thing.

Sighing happily, I reach for my phone on the nightstand. I never switched it back on after my bath. I wasn't going out last night, as Han knew, so they had no reason to worry.

I just finished my bath, fell into bed naked, and finished the smutty book I was reading. Funnily enough, I can't stop reading reverse harem books these days, and lord almighty, they're giving me ideas if all five of us ever end up in bed together. Not that it's easy to imagine Noah sharing with the others, but it's fun to try.

I power on the burner and laugh at the barrage of messages pouring in when the phone gets a signal.

Captain: Fuck, Trouble.
Red: Buttercup, I'm five seconds from ditching this mission and heading up to you.
Boo Thang: Princess, touch yourself.
Boom: I second J's suggestion. Send videos.
Captain: Third.
Red: Fourth. My cock says, "Fifth."

I laugh as more messages come in and spend time scrolling through them before doing as I'm asked. I've never done anything with a camera pointed at me, but there's a first time for everything, right? Between the security Jacob and I both put on our phones, I know it's a secure line.

I turn on the camera and aim it down the length of my body, pressing record as my hand comes into view. I watch the screen as my red-painted nails lead a trail down my stomach on their descent.

My breath starts coming in soft gasps, and I see my abdomen quiver on the screen as I finally reach my clit. I take my time, working myself up before dipping my fingers into my pussy. Thinking of the four of them watching their phones with rapt attention has me losing any last vestiges of trepidation as I pull my fingers away and see them glistening on the screen.

I drag the wetness up to my aching nub and touch myself exactly the way I like, occasionally varying the rhythm and pressure according to which of my guys I'm thinking of at that particular moment.

My hips are moving of their own accord, chasing my fingers as I swirl around my clit, and I let out a moan that I know will have Red's cock producing precum the moment he hears it. Jacob will likely be cursing about it not being his fingers playing with my body while the others watch.

Envisioning them all here, my subconscious takes over, and with my vivid imagination, it's as if they're all in the room with me. Han would be whispering sweet yet filthy words of encouragement in my ear and making me wetter and wetter as both he and Jacob descend on my taut nipples, their wicked tongues driving me mad with lust. Lucas would be impatient and drive into me as soon as my fingers pulled away. And Noah...fuck, I don't know what Noah would be doing. But I imagine him commanding my movements, encouraging me to edge until the last possible moment.

That last thought has me arching my back and finally exploding, soaking the comforter under me and trying to rein in the shaking in my thighs.

I keep the video rolling as I come down from my high, slowly dragging my fingers up my body, and flip the phone so it's now aimed at my face.

I send the camera a flirty wink as I dip my fingers into my mouth and suck them clean with a groan. I blow the boys a kiss and end the video, sending it before I can second-guess myself.

Tasting myself has almost become second nature at this point. The guys are very generous with oral, and when they kiss me after, I taste myself on their lips.

That last bit will have them wishing it was them licking me clean.

I laugh at the possibility of their incoming reactions. The video is a few minutes long, so I use the time to prepare for the day.

Sure enough, when I return to the bedroom, there are about fifty messages and a video that Lucas sent in reciprocation, all in the group chat.

Boo Thang: Bloody Christ, woman. You can be sure to expect some praise for following commands the next time I see you.

Captain: Trouble, you're in trouble. I've seen you with the guys around the clubhouse before, but that... I'm going to imagine that was just for me. Fuck, you're perfect. The way the morning sun dances on your tattoos has me hard as a fucking rock. Get back here.

Red: You know I leave for my job today. This was like sending a soldier off to war in the fucking filthiest way possible, and I fucking loved it. Fuck. I'm actually out of words. The only thing I'm thinking now is FUCK in bright, flashing pink neon lights.

Boom: You are just as gorgeous as you were when we met all those years ago. I can't wait until it's my cock you're coming around instead of your fingers, teasing you, testing your will to hang on just a bit longer. Bring your sexy ass home in one piece, or there will be hell to pay.

Red: I think you broke Captain. He just came out of his room and is staring at the wall with a blank face. Good work. Also, who knew he was such a poet over text?

The Sacrifices We Make

Captain: I'm not fucking broken, Dickhead. Get your shit, let's go.

After ordering a full breakfast, coffee, and a pot of tea, I sit in the middle of the bed with my laptop open as I review plans for the day and tomorrow's "kill." Cementing details is just intelligent planning at this point, and it's imperative nothing goes wrong in such a public place. A lot is riding on this going right.

Countless hours later, when my eyes have crossed, and I'm sure all of the bases have been covered, I meet Claudette in the lobby at four for high tea because, apparently, that's still a thing. Once more, we run through details together for Toby, aka Anthony, as we sip some Darjeeling tea and munch on petite finger sandwiches.

I hand off a vital component for Toby's upcoming demise, and Claudette promises to deliver. Despite my reluctance, she's still adamant that she be there to watch this go down in person tomorrow.

Heading into the nightclub at ten, I notice the usual crowd of drunk, young professionals looking to let off some steam before the weekend. I plan to get the lay of the land before the job. I think if someone heard the thoughts running through my head, they'd assume I'm certifiable with all of the scheming and murder plots going on up there.

There are three exit points from the club. One is the main door, which a bouncer guards at all times. The second is through the kitchens and has a security that can be disarmed, but it would require a code and more time than I'll likely have. The third is down a dark hall near the bathrooms and just has a secure padlock.

That's my backup exit plan if everything goes to shit, and I can't flee with the masses after the man gets stabbed. It's pitch-black and dingy just past the bathrooms, so I don't expect many people to make it past the restroom doors to investigate.

Taking up a seat at a high-top table surrounding the dancefloor, I watch as the sea of bodies undulates to the music. The guy at the turntables is pretty good, and he'll be here tomorrow night, too, so I expect a similar vibe. I'm nursing my beer, watching for camera angles, and fending off the fifth dude who's tried to hit on me when I feel a warm, dry hand clamp down on my shoulder.

I'm about to gut this motherfucker who dares touch me when I see the whites of douchebag number five's eyes and the fear that floods them. I grasp my beer bottle by the neck so I can use it as a weapon, and my other hand is busy rucking up my short black skirt to get to the knife strapped to my hip. Just as I bring the knife to the mystery man's throat, I hear a voice ground out, "Mine."

I know that voice. I know that timbre. It makes my pussy drip, and my will bend. I pull back the knife before I accidentally nick one of my boyfriends and look up into the icy eyes of my favorite Brit.

"'Mine' works for me. What shall I call you?" I ask playfully.

"'Yours,'" he answers simply. Jacob's delicious mouth is on mine in mere seconds, and I lose myself in his kiss as the lights swirl around us, the strobing lights playing through my closed eyelids. I break the connection because, despite the excitement I'm feeling at seeing him, I don't know what the fuck he's doing here.

"Why are you here?" I demand of him. His answer is to wrap his long, tattooed arms around me and lift me from my seat. He settles me on his lap, straddling him, as he drops us onto the stool beside mine. His hands move from my hips and land on my ass. He gives me a firm squeeze before drifting them to the front of my body. I feel them move across the tops of my thighs to slip under my skirt to find my pussy.

He's wearing a white Oxford shirt and his standard black slacks. The way the lights of the club dance across his tattooed neck and the base of his skull have me drooling all over again, just like I did the first time I met him.

"Mmm, Love. You're practically soaked. Tell me, was it from me or the attention you've had from the five morons who have hit on you tonight?" My eyes widen at his guess in the number of suitors I've had until he clarifies. "That's right. I've sat by patiently and watched five—*five*—assholes try and take what's mine. *Ours*."

Part of me wants to mess with him and tell him it was the others, but knowing he came up here for me has me answering his question honestly. "It was when you called me yours. Fuck, Jacob, why are you here? Is everyone okay?"

"Everyone's fine, other than their dicks being at full attention all goddamn day. I snuck out after we got Lucas settled in for the new job. I didn't want to wait for you to come back. And when you do finally get back, you're moving in with that douchebag, aren't you? I needed you. Now," he whispers into my ear, somehow making every word clear despite the music pumping around us.

His hand tightens on my thigh while the other finds the material of the panties and rips the part covering my dripping pussy clear in half. It's still wrapped around my waist like a useless garter belt. He takes advantage of my surprise and slips a finger into me.

"Make no mistake, Love. I will be rewarding you for the video, as promised. Though, I suppose I should also punish you for teasing us. But tonight? Tonight, I'm going to fuck you like there's no tomorrow for what you've put us through." His voice is rough, menacing in a way, and filled with lust.

I clench around his fingers as he pushes another one in, and his words register in my head. I want that; I want that desperately. I want to know what his ideas of reward and punishment are. I want to fuck him against every surface of this club. Then I want to take him back to my hotel and fuck him six ways to Sunday on the expensive furniture.

His eyes bore into mine as he rests his forehead against mine, and I watch as his lips part and his breathing speeds up. The unbridled hunger in his eyes has me on the edge, and when he grinds his palm on my clit, I lose it, tilting my head back and watching the kaleidoscope of colors wash over the ceiling as the bass from the music vibrates in my very bones.

"Dance with me," he whispers in my ear before trailing his teeth down my neck, landing at the sensitive spot just above my collarbone. I nod, and he helps me stand on shaky legs. I don't know how I'm going to dance like this, but I trust Jacob to have my back and not let me fall or look like an asshole out there.

He pulls me toward the dancefloor and then bypasses it as we head down the dark hallway toward the restrooms. People are lined up on both sides as they wait for the bathrooms, but Jacob keeps going down to the end of the hallway, where the exit lies.

He yanks my arm and spins me so my back is against the wall. His body crashes into mine as he lifts me, making my skirt hike up to my hips and securing my legs around his waist. His damn penchant for ripped panties makes an appearance again. He pulls the waistband of the black lace from my body, completely shredding it in the process, and stuffs it into the back pocket of his dark jeans.

I raise a brow at him questioningly, and he just growls out another, "Mine."

His lips drive into mine as I work my hands between us, unbuttoning his fly and undoing his zipper. Once his cock is unrestricted, I stroke him a few times, mimicking the motions of my tongue against his. Our noses bumping, teeth clashing, and his glasses gone askew; it's everything. *He is everything.*

His breathing increases as I line him up, and he finally, *finally*, pushes in.

My head snaps back and thuds against the wall behind me. Full. I'm so fucking full with this angle, and his piercings are teasing me in ways I haven't experienced before.

Jacob's hand grabs both of mine and pins them to the wall above my head. His other hand on my lower back holds me steady as he pumps into me with such urgency that I have trouble catching my breath.

His face is hard to distinguish in the dark lighting of the hallway, and it adds a flair of drama. I fucking love it.

I lean my head forward and catch his bottom lip with my teeth. I bite down and taste the slightest tinge of blood as he groans. I come as soon as the hand that was supporting my back reaches my clit. Two circles of his painstakingly teasing touches, and I'm done for.

As my muscles squeeze desperately around him, Jacob lets out an almighty roar and follows me off the cliff, biting down on my shoulder to muffle the sound.

His chest is heaving as he sucks in deep lungfuls of air and keeps me pinned against the wall. I try to move, and he just holds me tighter against him, unwilling to let me go, even for a moment.

"Love, Darling Mine, that was incredible. I didn't hurt you, did I?" he asks, his voice still carrying the post-orgasmic growl his voice always has. Darling Mine is a nickname I could absolutely live with.

"Not at all. Let's do that again." I calculate that I have enough information for tomorrow's hit and drag Jacob down the hall, past the bathrooms. The round of applause the crowd waiting in line gives us makes us laugh as we continue moving at a near run through the club.

We head out the door and back to my suite to sneak in my man, who is not Mr. Romano. I plan to make this man beg for more by the night's end.

Did I mention the exhibition thing is contagious?

Chapter Eleven

Rogue

I'M BACK IN THE NIGHTCLUB WITH JACOB STANDING AT MY SIX, playing the role of dutiful boyfriend and support, as I watch Claudette across the room with a few friends who are pretending to have a bachelorette party here, as we planned.

She said she could get eight girls together to keep more eyes on them than on the other dancers. They alternate between dancing on the crowded dance floor and staying at their table off to the side, being noisy and generally annoying with the sheer volume of their shrieks. She followed through on that promise. With the attention-grabbing volume, people either join them or send them annoyed looks.

About an hour ago, Toby arrived with two friends who are underlings employed by Claudette. He's been working his charms on a girl down the bar, and I can see him snapping his cinnamon gum from here.

No wonder it drives Claudette crazy. The man chews like a cow does on cud.

I see him get shot down again and shake my head. I don't know why he's bothering to hit on women tonight. Claudette informed him of the plan, so it's not like he can go home with any of them. Maybe he's just one of those perpetual horn dogs who forgets everything else when there's a pretty girl in sight.

Jacob is leaning against the bar beside me, keeping any wandering eyes well off of me. With his menacing stare, anyone whose eyes land on us immediately feels the unwelcome vibe and moves along.

I had a different plan involving dressing down and making myself look more homely, but this works, too. At least I got to wear Red's fun thigh-high boots, some dark wash jeans, and a black corset top.

My tattoos have been masked with a full-coverage foundation. My hair is up in a high ponytail and trails down my back, where Jacob twirls the ends in his fingers as he watches the club for signs of anyone watching us.

It's nice having him with me. I fought about it back at the hotel this morning when he announced he was coming, but I'm glad he did. I'm just used to doing this on my own and not having to worry about anyone else, but it's Jacob. He's intelligent and trained for scenarios like this. I trust he'll know what to do if shit hits the fan.

We drink our club sodas and watch as the night wears on, the patrons getting rowdier and rowdier. The time is coming; I can feel it. It's as if the seconds stand still, and things start moving slowly, allowing me extra time to account for unknowns. I slowly slip into mission mode as Jacob continues to hover close to me, giving death glares and deadly vibes to nearly everyone. His hand on my lower back tenses, telling me he knows what's coming.

I see Toby on the dance floor with a girl who looks way too drunk to be upright as he grinds into her and calls it dancing. I look up at Claudette, sitting at one of the tables on the mezzanine, and she catches my eye for just a moment and nods.

It's go time.

She lifts her phone to her ear, and I know she's alerting the fake EMTs and coroners to be ready.

I grab Jacob's hand, dragging him onto the dancefloor. Jacob slides into the dancing and indulgent boyfriend persona effortlessly, and I sway my hips to the rhythm, trying not to get turned on in the middle of a job.

It's not entirely successful.

We make our way closer to Toby as he dances in the center of the space, and Jacob returns a firm hand to my lower back, keeping me pressed against him, chest to chest, as we move to the beat.

The DJ is the same as last night, and I was right; the vibe is the same, and the beats drown out any other noise. The bodies swarmed on the dancefloor care only about the person pressed against them.

I turn my body so I'm looking at Toby's back. He's still wearing his

The Sacrifices We Make

blazer over his white shirt and navy slacks. Claudette promised he wouldn't take it off so the blood packs he has strapped to his body wouldn't be visible. It's our cover, and thankfully, his dance partner is so drunk that she hasn't noticed.

I'll make sure she gets out of here before this goes down. She's too wasted to have a level head in the upcoming chaos.

Jacob's hardening cock is grinding into my backside as he wraps my hair around his fist and tilts my head back with it. I give him a dirty, sloppy kiss as he continues to move to the music. He steps forward one step, guiding my legs with his until I'm pressed between him and Toby.

Our target feels the movement, and the corner of his lips tip up when he sees us grinding on him. He turns, ignoring the half-drunk girl who takes offense and stumbles away to her friends near the entrance. Good, she'll be able to get out quickly and with support if the girl waving a water bottle in her face is any indication.

Toby spins until he's facing and grinding into me in the front. Fuck, this is so uncomfortable, and from the vibrations I feel coming from Jacob's chest against my back, I think he's feeling the same way.

Toby is wearing the packs I passed over to Claudette yesterday at high tea disguised in a designer bag, so this should be a quick slice here and there, and they'll start to spill. I hand him the glass of club soda I managed to bring onto the dance floor with minimal spillage, with a pill dissolved in it. It'll slow his heartbeat enough to fool anyone who checks his pulse.

He tips his head back as he finishes it, wincing at the carbonation, and after a moment, I see his body start to slow with lethargy. I pull the knives from my hips and get close enough to Toby to get the job done as Jacob drapes himself over my back, shielding me from any wandering eyes.

I quickly slice the packs near his ribs and push him gently until he falls to the floor. Before he even hits the polished concrete, I'm facing Jacob, and my knives are stowed. I pretend to look over and see him on the ground. The blood is pouring from the packs and soaking the floor. I let out a scream, and Jacob cradles me like the amazing boyfriend he is.

Soon, others take up the call, and there's a mad rush for the doors while one man checks Anthony's pulse and shakes his head.

The day after dealing with Toby, Jacob and I spend the day in San Francisco doing all of the touristy shit I never get to participate in.

We ate lunch down at Fisherman's Wharf, enjoying clam chowder in sourdough bread bowls, visited Ghirardelli's chocolate factory and shop, took a boat out to Alcatraz—which I could totally escape—and walked around making goo-goo eyes at each other all day. It was our first solo date, and by the end of the day, I was surly because it was over.

He has to head back tonight, and unfortunately, I'm staying one more night. King called me this morning as Jacob and I were having slow and lazy morning sex in that awesome bed. I let the phone ring out and called him back after we'd showered.

King was as close to giddy as I'd ever heard him about the news coverage of the kill. It was announced that he was a gang leader, and the city is safer for his passing. While not condoning the violence, the police chief was thankful for the streets being cleaned up.

Claudette checked in this morning to say they got Toby out of there, and she's already a happier woman for the break from his cinnamon-gum-snapping ways. We're meeting up later.

Now that the Toby/Anthony thing has been resolved, I need to press for details about Mara. She has to be the next on our list. With Horvat recently gone, it would be too suspicious if we lost another board member so quickly. As far as Annex knows, Blake is fine, just far away.

Hopefully, the remaining members of our list will be manageable. There's King, possibly Romano, depending on where his loyalties lie, De La Cruz, Mara Hendrix, and the ever-enigmatic Patton Cross.

Fewer than before, but still a fucking mountain of a problem.

The group chat has been eerily silent as Red is using a different phone on his undercover assignment. I wish I could send him a message wishing him luck, but it's not worth the risk of blowing up his corporate phone for a few sweet words.

I asked Noah to pass on my words so he knows I'm thinking of him. Noah agreed and told me Lucas had sent a photo to show his appreciation and that he'd never be our messenger again. Lucas likes his dick pics a little too much, and you know what? I do, too.

Back in the suite, I kiss Jacob goodbye and send him on his way as I prepare to meet Claudette for drinks at a popular speakeasy downtown. I don a black dress with a tight skirt and red peep-toe heels. I wrap my curled hair up into a red bandana as the loops of the curls peek out of the top. I look damn good, so I send a photo to the boys to tease them a little. I'm not going to be living with them for a while, so this will be our new reality until we can steal some moments for ourselves.

The Sacrifices We Make

I arrive a few minutes before nine and find Claudette inside the bar. The password to enter the bar was "flibbertigibbet." How weird is that? A man in a vest and a newsboy cap opens the door when I say that ridiculous word, letting me into the basement-level bar. Cool.

Looking around at the tables shrouded in the dim lighting, I think Noah would enjoy this. He seems to have eclectic tastes but hides many preferences to avoid rocking his team's boat. But his variation in cooking gives his little secret away.

"Hey, Rogue!" Claudette pops up from the barstool and engulfs me in her hug—again—despite being half a foot shorter than me.

"Hey, C," I greet her cheerfully, pushing the guys from my mind for just a bit.

"Come, sit! Ernesto is an excellent bartender and makes a mean martini. Wow, say that five times fast." She laughs and signals for Ernesto to make two more for us as we settle onto the seats, and she attempts her tongue twister.

"So, how's our friend? Everything okay?" I ask. I texted her earlier, and she told me everything was fine, but I have to hear it from her in person. I feel responsible for the guy even though he's one of hers.

"Oh, yeah, totally fine. I got Toby carted to the safe house after three separate vehicle switches, and he's set up with Netflix and his cinnamon gum far away from me. He'll be fine."

I let out a sigh of relief I've been holding since last night. I needed to see it in her eyes that he was okay. I didn't want to kill him, and I'm not at the level of trust with Claudette that stops my brain from thinking about how she could have killed him while he was under the effects of the drug in his system.

"Oh good, okay. So what's up? Why did you want to meet?" I ask.

She eyes me curiously, then lets out a little laugh as she pats my hand resting on the bar, "Oh, honey, I just wanted to hang out."

Huh.

I'm so used to someone dying or needing to exchange information that her simple answer has me letting out my own laugh. Fair point. But I still do need some information on her sister. I'll bring that up later. There's nothing that says I can't also find some enjoyment amidst all of our schemings.

"Okay, we can totally hang out. I've never done this before, so you'll have to guide me through it. I draw the line at braiding our hair and singing Kumbaya, so be warned."

"Deal. Let's talk dick," she announces.

My drink—which *was* excellent, by the way—comes shooting out of my mouth as I try and fail to contain my laugh. The hand I used to cover my mouth is drenched in gin and vermouth. Darling Ernesto is immediately in front of me, handing me napkins to clean up the mess I've made of myself.

Claudette, meanwhile, is laughing her ass off so much I think she's going to fall right off the chair. She starts sliding to the right, and I grab her arm to keep her upright, covering it in the remnants of my drink. Whoops.

The evening passes quickly, and while we don't talk about dick, we do talk a bit about her life before she ended up with The Rattlesnakes. Her dad was an epic twat, preferring Mara to Claudette from the beginning because of her natural intelligence and aptitude for tech.

Claudette feels as though they were pitted against each other, and there was no saving the relationship. She also hinted at some wrong-doing on Mara's end, although who of us is pure these days? But her viciousness about her sister indicates she won't hate us when we remove Mara from the board.

I feel sneaky about gathering information on her sister while we're out for fun, so I dish everything. Her assistance until now hasn't come with any strings, and she's upheld her end of each bargain we've struck so far.

I tell her how we're making plays for our boards and that we don't wish to kill her sister but relocate her. We're struggling to find out how she's connected to The Gambit, and Claudette assures me she'll put some people on it and relay the information as soon as she has it.

After our talk of fucked up families is over, we enjoy our night and get to know each other. A few hours later, I return to the hotel and fall asleep with Han on the phone, whispering loving words in my ear, wishing me a good night, and telling me he's glad he's found me again.

So apparently, when King told me I'd be living with Romano, he didn't mention we would both be moving into an apartment in his building two fucking floors under his. Great.

About half an hour from El Castillo, intending to go straight to Romano's place—as I'd assumed we'd be living there—Romano texted asking where I was.

Nope. That's not going to fly. My response was less than gracious as I told him to take his controlling bullshit and shove it up his ass. Romano

The Sacrifices We Make

responded by saying he was in the new apartment and didn't know if I had a key to get in, so he was wondering if he should wait for me.

Well, fuck. I read that situation all wrong.

After figuring out where the hell I was heading and cringing when he sent the information and floor number, I apologized for my quick reaction and told him to please wait to let me in. When I arrived, I reluctantly handed over my keys to the untrustworthy valet, grabbed my suitcase and weapons bag, and told the valet to bring the rest when he had a moment.

I take the elevator up and try the door handle to our new apartment. It turns quietly, and I gently push the door inward as it swings on silent hinges. I hear Romano's voice down the hall and creep closer after setting my bags on the couch in the living room.

The apartment is fucking decadent; nowhere near as big as King's, but it looks like a miniature version of his upstairs. The front door opens into the open living space and kitchen, all housing state-of-the-art appliances and electronics, incredible modernist paintings on the walls, and furniture I'm sure costs my year's salary...and I get paid a lot for what I do.

The wall opposite the door is pure glass, offering stunning views of El Castillo and the hills beyond. To my left, a hallway disappears in an L-bend. I hear Romano down the hall, so I quietly remove my shoes and pad my way closer.

"No, she's not here yet. Yes, I'll figure it out. She's important; I know it," Romano says to whoever's on the phone, and I freeze where I stand.

Me? I'm important for what? Taking down King? Sure. But who the fuck is on the phone and knows about me? That's the part that bothers me.

"Listen, I have to go; she'll be here any minute. I'll call later." Romano continues speaking as I make my way back down the hall, replaying the confusing and yet not quite incriminating conversation in my mind.

I grab my shoes and bags, hastily crossing the room to get back outside the door before Romano emerges from the room and spots me. I toss my shit into the carpeted hallway near the elevator as gently as I can and pull the door closed softly behind me.

I stand to the side of the door as I yank my shoes back on and settle my bags nicely so they don't look like they've been heaved across the hallway. I scroll on my phone for a few minutes, passing the time, before I make stomping sounds and reach the door. I lift my fist and knock on it three times in a decidedly huffy way.

Romano swings the door open and cheerfully says, "Welcome home, honey."

I might just stab him before the wedding.

"Romano," I greet.

He stands aside to let me into the apartment, and I look around like it's the first time, and not like I've already categorized the best access points here in the living room. I drop my bags in the same spot they were in ten minutes ago as Romano takes a deep breath.

"I didn't know we'd be living here, but King insisted on having us close. He also said his heir needed nicer digs than your current apartment. I tried to talk him out of all this, but he was adamant. Are you okay?"

The glare I send him would freeze the devil's balls. I walk up to him, grip his burgundy silk tie, and yank him down until he's at eye level with me. "You think you could have changed King's mind? And here, I thought you were smarter than your predecessor. We're not in charge. He is. We do as he says because he leads the board. Unless there's a six-to-one vote, what he says goes."

With Enrique on his side, King will always have the right to do as he pleases. I don't know where Romano's loyalties lie, so I'm not banking on him backing us if we make a move. I look around the living room with its luxurious yet small couch and tiny armchair, the kitchen and island with two chrome barstools settled under one side, and peer past Romano down the hallway.

I have a bad feeling about this.

I take off, well aware I'm damn near stomping as I do. The hallway hooks to the right, and I follow the path. I see a door on the right and one on the left. Oh no. *Oh, no, no, no.*

I open the one to the right, hoping for a bedroom with an ensuite, but I'm met with an average-sized bathroom with an expertly appointed shower, toilet, and sink set up. Everything is done in white and tiled, so at least it'll be easy to keep clean, and the linens and designer soaps scream wealth.

I huff through the door and cross the hall to the last remaining door.

I swing it open and find a four-poster king-sized bed, sleek black dressers on either side and another door. The door leads to a small walk-in closet where Romano has stashed his few bags.

One bed, one couch that would barely fit the two of us seated, and no tub to make into a little place to curl up. The last option is the floor, where one of us will sleep for the foreseeable future. At least the rug in the living room looked plush.

Chapter Twelve

Lucas

Five days. It's only been five days since I started at Collinsworth Bank, and I hate it so much that if I don't start getting the intel we need soon, I swear, I'm going to start making shit up to get out of here.

I've been put in an upper-management position with a secretary who's been making flirty eyes at me since I stepped off the elevator the first day. *I am so over it, Kelsey.* Yeah, they gave me a twenty-year-old intern as a secretary who doesn't even know how to dial out of the building.

Buttercup has been living with Romano since she returned from San Francisco, and the information I've been given is limited. We didn't plan the code to cover everything, but Noah lets me know everyone is okay. The guys are handling other jobs they can do without me, and Buttercup is trying to gather intel on Romano from within their apartment now that she's back in town.

I know I'm not actually going to break any time soon. I'm a professional. I can totally handle not reaching out to the others to talk about anything other than stock market dividends and employee turnover rates. But fuck, with my girl out there, I'm damn tempted to give her a call just to touch base. Noah no longer opens my picture messages to forward to her because the last time, he said my fire crotch burned his retinas.

Mila Sin

He's jealous.

"Mr. Lewis," Kelsey calls for me as I storm out of my office. "Sir, please wait." She's tottering after me in a pair of fuck-me heels that are entirely too stripper-ish for the office.

"Yes, Kelsey?" I groan out as she catches her breath from her fifteen-foot sprint.

"Mr. Ortega wishes to see you before you leave for the day." The request surprises me as he handles the foreign markets, and my "job" is maintaining the bank's local branches. There's no overlap between our departments.

"Sure, thanks. Go home for the day. It's five, right?" She nods at my question, and with an exaggerated flick of her bottle-blonde hair, she wanders back to her desk, her hips swaying way too much. Like that would tempt me...pft, please. I prefer the type of girl who holds a knife to my cock and looks just as good in sweats as she does naked.

I cross the office floor, pass the lower-level workers in their cubicles, and go to Ortega's office. His secretary isn't at her desk, so I stride to his door, rapping my knuckles twice. "Come in," I hear his deep voice say.

I open the door and enter, ready to figure out what he wishes to see me about. I keep up my confident expression as Ortega scans me from head to toe. "Yeah, you're dressed okay. Want to join the other guys and me tonight? We have a bi-monthly tradition. Tonight is a bit different than usual, but we need bodies."

"Oh, yeah? Doing what? Poker night?" I ask, hoping for some quiet after firing two people today.

"Guys night at The White Knight. Meet me downstairs in a few hours, and we'll head out together," he confides as if it's a big secret.

"Who's going?" I ask as my curiosity piques. If there's anything to pick up from the other higher-ups, it'll likely be from guys' night at a strip club. The tech is hard at work gathering terabytes of data, but there's something to be said for gaining intel while the targets are wasted. Seems like it's time to earn my way into the inner circle.

"Most of the other middle managers, plus Mr. Ross and Mr. Hess." Okay, cool. So that's the upper management and two of the big five that run this damn place. Fuck me, this is going to be interesting.

"Sounds good; I'm in. I'll meet you out front at eight." He nods his head at my parting words, and I turn on my heel to leave.

I go back to my office and lean back in my comfy chair with my feet up on the desk. I've been here for one whole workweek, and as soon as my

The Sacrifices We Make

computer was given admin access to go through employee files, I slipped the drive into one of the ports.

I also stuck devices in a few other computers in the office, all belonging to people in higher positions than mine. Jacob has been combing through all the data he could get while I've been confidently pretending I know what I'm doing in a management role.

There isn't much to it. Just pretend to be above everything and everyone, difficult to please, and suddenly, the underlings are going above and beyond to earn the new guy's attention. It helps that I sign off on their quarterly bonuses. It makes them all the more eager.

After three hours of shooting crumpled-up balls of paper into the wastebasket, playing solitaire, and taking more BuzzFeed quizzes than any healthy person should, I ride the elevator downstairs to meet Mr. Ortega.

Jacob already vetted everyone on my floor and flagged anyone I should keep an eye on. Ortega didn't make it onto the list, but that doesn't mean I ignored him. Oh, no. I know he eats lunch at half past eleven every day and makes his intern monitor the foreign markets so he doesn't have to wake up early. He usually shoots the shit for a few hours every day with the other guys at our level but seems to get his work done relatively quickly.

I exit the building's lobby and find him waiting in the back of a black sedan with tinted windows. "Let's go, Lewis!" he shouts from the back seat. He thumps his fist on the car's interior ceiling, and his driver stands patiently by the door, waiting for me to climb in so he can close it. Here we go, I guess.

The initial silence of the drive is punctuated by Ortega's phone ringing and him chatting to whoever is on the other end. I just use my time to text Noah what's going on and that I've been roped into going to a strip club. His response is to watch my back. The White Knight is a club owned by The Gambit. Of fucking course it is. I bet Buttercup had a hand in naming it with her fondness for ridiculous names.

As the drive continues and Ortega carries on speaking to his caller, I let my mind drift. When I saw the text telling me The Gambit owned the club, it got the gears turning.

I'm on a bank intel job from Annex, which has ties with The Gambit. Here I am with the upper management, about to meet with two big dogs from the bank at a club they own. There's a connection here. I just have to figure out what it is.

We pull up outside the building, and I already have to hide my cringe; this place is a shithole. The sign depicting the name has two letters flickering, and the bouncer propped up on a stool by the door looks like he's half-asleep.

This is the kind of place The Gambit runs? Impossible.

Ortega claps me on the shoulder, "Let's get in there, Lewis. We're the last ones to arrive. I had to finish a report for Ross before showing up here, or he'd have me by the balls."

He's a dedicated worker, and I appreciate that.

We exit the car, and I wave a hand before me, indicating he should go first. The driver climbs back in and takes off, leaving us in the filthy parking lot I'm sure one could pick up hepatitis from.

Ortega walks up to the bouncer and whispers something in his ear. The big guy nods, and instead of opening the door next to us, he leads us around back to a storm grate. He lifts his wrist to his mouth, and with clear diction, not the sloth-like personality I'd assumed he had from his lazy posture out front, he says, "Bravo, open the gate. Two more for the bachelor party."

Bachelor party?

Just as I'm about to ask Ortega about it, the metal grate lifts, and out steps a man who looks like the real-life version of Johnny Bravo. Oh. My. God. I have to tell Buttercup about this when I see her. She's gonna lose her shit.

Bravo leads us down the steps and waves a metal detector over us, checking we're unarmed. It's good that I left my guns in my new fancy office. He waves us through a thick door, and as we enter, I have to stop my breath from getting caught in my throat. This room is enormous. It must be the entire footprint of the building nestled above. I thought that one above us was the strip joint, and maybe it's another one for the general public, but this room caters to the rich; that much is evident.

Chandeliers hang at evenly spaced intervals, all lit with dark lights. The walls are covered in an elegant, velvety fabric that must be a bitch to clean if someone messily blows their wad and hits the material. I do not envy the cleaning service that works for this place.

Ortega leads the way across the black tile floor and weaves between the tables until we join a big group of men sitting in a long booth. They're sipping amber liquor as a few girls make their way around, giving lap dances. Noticing a few of the guys from my office, I give them a few fist bumps, painfully aware that I may be making contact with questionable germs and fluids, and dip a respectful nod to Mr. Ross and Mr. Hess. After all, they are my "bosses," and they don't know I'm a plant in their office.

Their eyes return to the girls doing their strip show on the stages and

The Sacrifices We Make

the women giving out lap dances to the men in our group. I grab a seat and continue looking down the line of the table. My eyes pass over a few guys I don't know until they land on Francesco fucking Romano with a crown on his head.

I know it's him because Buttercup brought home a photo of the board members I drew from her descriptions after a recent board meeting. She managed to get snaps of everyone as they had their attention elsewhere.

I'm at my girlfriend's fiancé's bachelor party? The universe has a fucked up sense of humor.

White-hot rage fills my body as I look at the asshole currently living with my—*our*—girl, and I want to rip him limb from limb. I know they're getting married and that Buttercup is doing recon on him, but I'm so far out of the loop that I don't know what's happening day-to-day. I miss texting her. I miss her face. I miss her heart. And I'm fully aware I'm blaming the asshole at the end of the table.

I let the club's music wash over me as I spiral into the depths of my rage and do my best to keep it from showing on my face. How long do I have to stay here? Can I kill him? Buttercup hasn't yet, so he must not have done anything untoward. Noah would break protocol to tell me if Romano needed his face broken or his body buried.

My gaze continues to peruse the other men at our table, not resting long on any face so I can memorize who is here and how the hell we're involved in this bachelor party. My observational skills are obviously in the shitter today because I see Enrique De La Cruz right next to the man of the hour. He's speaking too quietly on the phone for me to hear him over the music from here, but I observe all the same. I quickly decide it would be rude not to introduce myself to the bachelor.

I stand up from the vinyl bench seat I'm sharing with Gerard from human resources and straighten my black suit. It's still mostly pristine if we don't mention that tiny mustard stain I got on the sleeve today at lunch. Stupid hot dog. I make sure that little fucker is hidden and stretch my legs as I walk to their side of the table.

The girls previously dancing nearby have moved on, and Romano is lazily watching the one on stage. De La Cruz is still on his phone call, looking a bit perturbed, so I give him a slight nod in greeting and turn my attention to Romano.

Fuck, he's good-looking. He's wearing a charcoal-grey suit with a deep blue vest over a crisp white shirt. He looks like he took a wrong turn off a fashion show runway and ended up in a high-class strip joint.

Buttercup said not to worry, but I don't think that will be possible now that I've seen this guy up close. Even I'm attracted to the fuck-wad. I trust her, but I'd be nervous to put anyone and this silver fox in a room together.

"Hey, man. Can I assume you're the lucky guy?" I ask as I motion to his crown.

"Yeah, hey. I'm Francesco." He extends a hand for me to shake, and manners dictate I must reciprocate no matter how much I want to grab the fork off the table next to him and jam it into his eye for stealing my girl away.

"Joshua Lewis," I reply as I shake his outstretched hand. As the bachelor goes to open his mouth, De La Cruz pops up out of his seat, firing quiet but firm directions down the line on his phone. Francesco shakes his head with a quiet laugh and points to the seat beside him, inviting me to sit down.

"Fuck, I hate this shit," he lets out as he sighs deeply.

I whip my head to face him fully and see he's exhausted. "Not your thing?"

"Absolutely not. My fiancée set this up for me," he groans.

Fucking magnificent, Buttercup.

If I know my girl at all, she's using the time he's guaranteed to be away as an opportunity to snoop for anything she can find on this guy. She's so devious; I love it.

"You must have a great fiancée for her to have set all of this up for you. How do you know the guys from my office?" I ask curiously. I want—no, *need*—to know the connection.

"I don't. The guy whose seat you just took invited them. My bride-to-be told him to take me out with friends, so here I am." He looks like he'd rather be at the dentist getting a cavity filled with fire ants than here. I also feel like Buttercup didn't tell De La Cruz to take him out; more likely, she threatened him with bodily harm if he didn't.

"Okay," I say, deciding this guy isn't so bad other than the fact that he's living with my girl, "let's make this interesting. It seems we're both stuck here for a bit. Let's make some bets." He looks at me like I've lost my ever-loving mind, and maybe I have, but I see some potential to get some answers from him.

"See Ortega down there?" I ask, and Romano nods when he catches sight of him. "He was on the phone with his mistress on our way here. He doesn't know I speak Spanish and understood every word of his little lovers' spat. I bet he passes out from too much booze by ten o'clock and misses their meeting time at midnight."

"Oh, you're on. I think he'll make it till eleven," Romano counters with a twinkle in his eye. Perfect. That means we're here until at least ten or until Ortega passes out. That should give Buttercup some extra time, as it's still early enough.

"Stakes?" he asks.

"Hmm, how about the loser buys the other a beer? I have a feeling we're going to have a lot of bets going by the end of the night, and I wouldn't want to take your retirement fund, old man. Does your girl know you're only a few years away from Social Security?" I laugh as I insult him. I find it's often the quickest way to make friends.

He punches me in the shoulder, and we continue down the line of attendees, making bets about who will come in their pants when a certain girl gets too close or who will end up barfing by the end of the night.

After an hour of shooting the shit, eating the food from the buffet, and watching the bets unfold with Romano, De La Cruz makes his way back to the table. He looks squarely at Romano and announces he has to go with a slight waver in his voice. He's sweating bullets, and judging by his look, he might even be using.

"Everything okay, man?" Romano asks.

"*Si*, yes. Those rumors are still flying around, and I'm putting them to rest." With that ominous promise, he turns on his heel and leaves the club, snapping his fingers at Johnny Bravo to open the door and let him out. I didn't even get an introduction from him. I'd be insulted if I weren't trying to fly under the radar.

Romano and I look at each other and just shrug our shoulders. Acting oblivious is hard as shit, but I know what the rumors are. Rogue has been spreading the word, with the help of Claudette, that De La Cruz's guys have been dealing to kids. King has issued a warning, and if these whispers keep up, there will be too many to deny. De La Cruz won't be a problem for us anymore because King will kill him first.

I lean back in my seat and turn down the tenth dancer of the night. To his credit, Romano does, too. "Your girl wouldn't want you getting a lap dance?" I ask. "She set this up, didn't she? I think it'd be expected."

"Nah, she wouldn't mind, but I don't want it. I'm good just sitting here and watching these assholes make fools of themselves." We look down the length of the table, and sure enough, someone comes in their pants.

Romano just drops his head and shakes it in a laugh. He raises his arm and asks the waitress to bring me a beer.

Winner, winner, chicken dinner.

We wrap up the night close to midnight, and I realize I spent the whole evening chatting with Romano, and you know what? He's actually a pretty cool dude.

I rise from my seat and bid farewell to the guys and Romano. I didn't glean much about my coworkers' connections with The Gambit, but now I've got some suspects to work with. It's time to put my nose to the grindstone and figure this out.

Monday's going to be a fun day at the office.

Noah

Lucas sends me a text way too late at night for my taste. His name on my phone confuses me until my brain catches up on the details of his name change for his current mission. My tired mind sluggishly unravels the code we're using, and I read and respond.

Lewis: Met FR. B set him up for a bachelor party. When's the wedding?
Me: Sun, 1400, parents' church.

I can't give him too many details over text, but he needs to know. There has been so much going on that I can't share. But he needed this. His mind was bouncing from mood to mood, and I think it's been good for him to have a new goal to focus on. If that keeps Annex from pushing more assignments on us, all the better.

I know Trouble sent Romano out for a bachelor party and threatened De La Cruz into taking him because she wanted a decent window to snoop. She never knows when he will be home and needs some uninterrupted time. Rogue doesn't spend much time in their shared apartment, but rather, she's taken up residence in an office at Rook Industries to coordinate the other hitmen, and they still have her on their books as Cleaning Supervisor. Cute.

We've been able to text sporadically since she moved into King's building with one of her burner phones, but she knows it isn't safe to talk freely. She found microphones in their apartment and destroyed them, but like magic, they reappeared within twenty-four hours. She's furious with King for pushing this on them, but the unfortunate nuptials tell us that he still trusts her enough to want her to succeed him when he retires...or dies. I'm cheering for the death route.

I roll over in bed and wish I had a moment to talk to my girl. I take a chance, hoping Romano is still out, and press my thumb to her contact information on my phone. It rings twice before it clicks on. "Cap?"

"Hey, Trouble. I know you can't talk safely, so I just want you to listen." She takes a deep breath and murmurs her assent.

"Lucas met Romano tonight at the strip club. I don't know how or why, but he texted me after, so I think your fiancé is still alive." Her deep chuckle whispers down the connection, and it soothes my nerves when two of my team are so far away from us.

I hear her soft breaths over the line, so I take the opportunity to speak as she listens from the other side of town. I have to reassure the girl who feels like she's slipping away from us the longer she plays this hated role on someone else's terms.

"You're our glue, Trouble. Lucas bounced back so quickly because of you. Han has you to love and care for; you know he needs to dote on someone. You're that person.

"Jacob has thrown his old scheduling, controlling ways out of the window since you showed up in our lives. He's happier for it. He's trying this thing with Han, who loves you for who you were and who you've become. And I don't know if either of them ever would have gone for this thing without your encouragement. And me? You give me hope again. So much damn hope that sometimes I'm afraid someone will come and snatch it away from me.

"I know we only had one date before you had to move out, but I'm going to date you so fucking hard when you come home. You are inspiring, you are strong, and you are exactly who all of us crave and, more importantly, want in our lives. Please don't lose yourself as you hold onto your work persona twenty-four-seven in front of Romano. Keep that sweetness for us because we love you for it."

I hear a soft sob on the other end of the line as my words make their way to her.

"Don't cry, Trouble. You're ours, and we're yours. We'll be here waiting whenever you can get away. Or we'll blow that building to smithereens to get you out if you can't get out alone. I think Han's been stockpiling since you left." The last comment has the effect I was hoping for when I hear her sniffle and a small laugh pops out.

"I just wanted to say that even though you have to marry that guy, it's not forever. It's just for now. You said he seems pretty decent and has been keeping his distance. That's good. That means you can get an annulment and marry Lucas. He was pissed his dibs were ignored."

I let out an almighty sigh and let my words continue pouring out. This emotional stuff has been buried for so long I don't know if I'm doing a shit job of it or if it's okay. God, I hope it's okay. "Trouble, Rogue, Ivy, whichever name you choose, let us know if you need anything. At all. We'll drop everything and be there in a heartbeat. Okay?"

A soft voice floats down the line as she answers gently but resolutely, "Yes, Cap."

I bid her a good night and hang up the call after she does the same. She's been away from us for too long. Her texts were getting shorter and shorter. Her personality is fading the longer she keeps up her walls in front of the man she has to marry and the surveillance in her apartment. I feel she's still in there, but a reminder to drop the mask occasionally can't hurt.

I roll into the middle of my bed, bring one of her shirts up to my nose, smell the familiar herbal and lemon scent she always wears, and fall asleep with the fabric covering half of my face and a small smile tugging at my lips.

Chapter Thirteen

Rogue

Well, it's my wedding day. I never thought this day would come. Nor did I think I'd be marrying another member of The Gambit, to whom I've barely spoken and hardly know.

Despite living together for the last week, I rarely see Romano in our shared apartment at King's place. He works weirder hours than I do and constantly travels around working on arms deals and keeping his underlings in line.

I've been spending more time than ever at Rook's offices. Instead of just texting and calling in orders from the comfort of my couch or bed, I've been living in my headquarters office. No one has said anything about it yet, but I guess that's the good thing about getting married when you're the head assassin; no one wants to be on my shitlist because I'm the bride and can gut you in your sleep.

Romano's recent boon with the Vegas Crew has not gone unnoticed by King as a stellar move. True, we earned some extra cash from that, but his burgeoning alliance and relationship with King have my attention.

With King considering taking over The Rattlesnakes' territory, he wants allies in his corner to support him if that happens, and the Vegas Crew is a good one to have backing you. They're flush with cash, so much so that Romano's inconvenience charge would be pennies to them. It's a smart move if I'm honest. He already has a good relationship with them, but Romano is helping to reinforce that.

I take one last look in the mirror, resigning myself to this stupid arrangement as the thoughts race around my head. I refuse—*refuse*—to wear white for this sham of a wedding, so I don a black, tea-length, a-line dress, an ebony veil, and a set of black pumps.

The service is taking place after the main mass of the day at Saint Ignatius Church, so hopefully, not too many people will be there. I know it will be the entire board of The Gambit, along with their seconds if they have them. I don't officially have a second, but G is the closest thing in my little squadron of murderers. Plus, I like his style when he burns shit to the ground. There's never any evidence left. The cops are still investigating the former governor's disappearance, and no one seems to have figured out he and I were in the motel he torched.

I ended up inviting Jim and Hugo to bolster my numbers. G and Hugo know each other from Hugo's days under my leadership before semi-retiring, and they were both decent enough people that a small friendship formed between all three of us. Casual and irregular, but friendship nonetheless.

Jim's mom is on the up and up after her bout with pneumonia, so they were happy to make up the majority of my guest list. I sent Jim's mom some flowers last week when she moved home, and she sent me a homemade lemon bundt cake that I unceremoniously devoured over the kitchen sink. So much for following her doctors' orders and sticking with bed rest, but damn that cake was good.

I've been sleeping in the bedroom while Romano sprawls out on the tiny couch in the living room. Half the time, I come out in the morning for coffee and find him on the floor. I bought him an air mattress when I noticed it for the second time, and he's been complaining about his back less since giving in and blowing it up. Small mercies.

I poke my veil-covered face out of the bedroom door—yes, I know I'm being dramatic with my all-black ensemble, but apparently, the bride is always right—and see the coast is clear. The bathroom door is open, and the room is unoccupied. I cross the hall to put on the dark burgundy lipstick I left in there yesterday. With a quick blot and a pop of my lips, I'm ready to go. I dump some makeup in my purse to do touch-ups as needed.

Entering the living room, I see Romano leaning against our small kitchen counter in a black tuxedo, looking every inch the model he could have been in another life.

The Sacrifices We Make

"Rogue," he falters, "you look gorgeous." His eyes sweep my body and take in the outfit I've chosen for today. He never comments on my appearance, but his sudden and unexpected comment instantly makes me wary.

"You're not getting a virgin bride, so white was out of the question." My statement jars him, as intended, and his eyes snap up to mine.

"I have no interest in your virtue, and virgins are far too inexperienced for me anyway," he scoffs. Before I can dig into that comment too much, he continues, "The car should be here in just a few minutes. Ready?" he asks resignedly. I'm glad to see neither of us is thrilled at this arrangement.

"Yep, let's do this," I begrudgingly say as I pull on my black pea coat.

He ushers me out of the apartment with a hand on my elbow and locks up behind us. We quietly ride the elevator down to the lobby, each keeping to ourselves. I'm glad he's not using the opportunity to try and mollify me in any way. We both know this has to happen, and we can do nothing to change it. This is the longest I've spent in Romano's presence since we moved in together. The silence is—weirdly—not wholly uncomfortable.

Our trip to the church continues in silence, and I take back my earlier thoughts. It's becoming uncomfortably quiet now. Romano passes the time on his phone, texting, checking emails, and basically ignoring me. I stare out the window and wonder how the hell we ended up here. We've still got about an hour until the ceremony, so I plan to cloister myself in the bridal waiting room and drink champagne. Not to celebrate but to get through today.

As we pull up to the curb, I spy a familiar blacked-out SUV across the street and know my guys are here. It gives me the boost I need to straighten my spine and put on my very best resting bitch face. I've been keeping that mask on twenty-four-seven since moving in with Romano. Hell, I know King has listening devices in the apartment; he might even have cameras, but I haven't found any. I can't let a crack show, so when Noah called me the other night and whispered such sweet words into my ear, I let my mask fall a bit.

Thankfully, I had covered myself with the blanket so the possible cameras and guaranteed microphones wouldn't pick up on my tear-stained face and wavering voice. I couldn't speak freely, but Noah was sure to make it a conversation I didn't have to participate in, even if I could. His reassurances and support rendered me speechless. Who knew that gruff and bossy man could be so sweet?

"I'll see you in an hour. Don't fuck this up, or King will ruin us both," I remind Romano just before the driver opens our door to let us out.

He nods his head and follows me out of the car. I walk with my back straight and posture perfect. I left the black veil over my face for the car ride, and thank God it was in place when I spotted the guys' SUV as my eyes flared wide for just a moment.

I take off toward the church and pull the heavy wooden door open. Stepping into the entryway, I see Father Andrews, who ushered me into the church's very own version of a vault. "Congratula—," he starts, but the word tapers off when he takes in my black dress and veil, which is more befitting of a funeral than a wedding. "The bridal chamber is down the hall and to the left."

I give him a slight tilt of my head, my mask firmly back in place, and follow his instructions, my heels click-clacking along the marble floor as usual when I'm in this building and in non-padded soled shoes. I pass through the dark hallway and make my way to the room I'll be hanging out in until the ceremony. Just as I reach the door, it cracks open, and a hand shoots out, grabbing my wrist and pulling me inside. I'm about to put the man down when I see a blur of auburn and familiar lips slam into mine.

Red.

"Hell's bells, Buttercup. I've missed you," Lucas murmurs between scorching kisses.

I try to respond, but there's no time before he's pushing me against the wall next to the door and nipping my lip with his teeth. Thank God I remembered to grab my lipstick from the bathroom.

"It'd be rude of me not to make sure you were properly fucked on your wedding day," he growls out between kisses.

I groan as he bends and runs his hands up my thighs under my dress, caressing the tops of the stockings, his fingers leaving a trail of fire as he makes his way higher. He grips under my thighs and pulls both around his waist until I'm clinging to him. While I'm off of my feet, he spins and walks me backward until my ass is parked on the desk, his mouth never leaving mine.

I love the way Lucas kisses. His whole body gets involved in the act, and I feel the flush rising up my neck from his attention. A swirling cyclone of emotions plays in my chest, and I don't know which one will come out the victor. I'm nervous about the new situation, anxious about being so far away from the guys, angry with King, and so fucking turned on I'll have to throw out my specially-made wedding-day panties any second now.

Red places his hands on either side of my face, his thumbs tipping my jaw up so I look into his eyes. "Buttercup, tell me if you want me to stop;

otherwise, we're doing this here in a church. I don't know if you're okay with that."

The warring factions in my head are quieting, and lust wins this round. He must see the decision is made as I bite my bottom lip, dragging my teeth in the flesh until it releases. His eyes track the movement, and he lets out a growl. I push back on his chest, and confusion enters his eyes until I have him pressed to the floor. I straddle his waist and work the fly on his slacks until he shimmies them and his underwear down his thighs.

I grip his stiff cock and give it a few strokes as I lean forward, and he slides my absolutely fucking ruined panties to the side. I slowly, tortuously, sink onto his cock, and the moan he lets out has me clamping a hand over his mouth to keep him quiet.

I rock back and forth, the veil still covering the top half of my face, only my deep red, smudged lips visible to Lucas. The thrill and taboo factor of doing this in a church only spur me on as I ride my boyfriend at a pace I didn't know I could set.

Lucas's eyes trail down my neck, down the dress, and finally, to where we're connected. He lets out another groan, and I press my hand harder against his mouth. He tilts his head back, plants his hands on the floor, and uses the leverage to lift his hips, topping from the bottom.

I let go of his mouth and lean back to change the angle. I shift my body, and with each roll, Red pushes his hips up, grinding into my clit and setting off sparks behind my eyelids. My head tips back, and I have to cover my mouth to stifle the scream that erupts when his free hand wraps around my body and he slips a finger into my ass. The pressure is delicious.

Within moments, my pussy clamps down on his dick, and we're both gasping and riding out our releases. God, I've missed this man. I collapse forward onto his heaving chest, peppering kisses on his neck. I'm euphoric and feeling freshly-fucked and relaxed for the first time in over a week. It's hard going from constant sex to this dry spell.

Lucas kisses the top of my head and hugs me close. "Why are you here, Red?" I ask with concern in my voice. I know we have some time before King and the others show up, but I can't help being worried that he's here and we could be caught at any moment.

"I just needed to see you. I met your fiancé at his bachelor party," he laughs as he speaks. "Did you set that up for any particular reason?"

"I wanted to search the apartment. I didn't know Romano's schedule and needed him out for a few hours, so I set it up and made sure De La Cruz was with him. How did you end up there?"

"I figured as much. That was a smart move. One of the guys from 'work' invited me. I didn't know it was a bachelor party until I arrived. Romano seems like a decent dude, you know, other than supplying weapons to other gangs and marrying my girl when I had dibs," he complains.

I laugh at that. Red's verbal stream of consciousness always gives me giggles.

"Yeah, he's been keeping his distance. That first day, he had a phone call I wasn't supposed to hear. I don't know who was on the end of the line, but he mentioned that I was important for something. I'm working on figuring it out." My confession of what's been going on has his eyes snapping open as he searches my face for something. Worry, perhaps? He won't find it. I'll handle this like I handle everything: with calculated moves and an iron stomach.

"I think playing the caution card is the right move here. Don't let anything slip, but keep your eyes and ears open. Gather what intel you can. That's all you can do right now. I know the guys are working on getting things in motion for Mara. You've got rumors spreading about De La Cruz selling to minors. Tanaka got the okay from King, and the date has been set." Lucas's summary hits the nail on the head. For now, my focus is on getting through this performance and keeping King happy.

"I'll be careful. Now, we have," I look up at the clock mounted on the wall, "twenty minutes until I have to meet King out front. Wanna go again?"

He lets out an excited whoop and spins us so my back is on the cold floor. I shriek in an entirely badass way at the freezing sensation, and we spend the next fifteen minutes rehashing some of our favorite positions. I'm left with two more orgasms and one fewer pair of panties than I had earlier.

Red and I quickly chat about what he saw at the bachelor party and his confusion about the connection. I know he'll figure it out, and we'll all rest easier when we're both back home. We use the last of our time to trade theories and ideas before I meet King at the front of the church.

We're mostly back in our clothes, and I'm fixing my lipstick when there's a knock at the door. Red dives under the desk he nearly fucked me on—with my wedding day panties clutched in his grip—as the door swings open.

King is standing on the threshold. His eyes take stock of my appearance; thankfully, everything but my panties is back in place. I'm leaning toward the mirror, fixing my lipstick, and we make eye contact through the glass.

"It's time, Rogue. Let's get you married to our ally. You know the consequences if you fuck this up?" His words have their intended shock value, and I consider whether he means I'll be dead or Sage will. "You *will* run The Gambit someday. I've been grooming you for it since you were a child, daughter. It's time for you to carry on the line."

Han

I'm sitting shotgun in the SUV with Noah in the driver's seat, and Jacob sprawled in the back. We've been here for hours already, and I don't regret sitting around while we wait outside the church as our girl marries someone else.

We arrived around twelve to be sure we would catch a glimpse of her as she entered. Noah parked across the street, hoping she would see our SUV and know that we were here to support her and if she needed us for anything. The slight tilt of her head in our direction as she exited the car at one o'clock indicates she did see us.

What surprises us is the figure slinking around the corner of the church. Lucas lifts his head as he reaches the sidewalk and sees the SUV. He waits for a break in traffic before darting across the street. He hops onto the sidewalk and rounds the car until he pulls open the back door and launches inside.

"Jacob, you British bastard, I've missed you!" Lucas squeals as he bear-hugs Jacob in the back seat. Jacob lets out an almighty oomph as he struggles to adjust his glasses, which were knocked askew in the assault.

"Lucas, get the fuck off of me!" Jacob cries.

Noah just shakes his head, knowing there's nothing he can do to stop the bromance display in the back seat. "Hi, guys! I knew I'd find you around here somewhere. Little did I know it'd be right out front."

"Hey, Lucas. Did you catch sight of our girl? She's dressed like she's going to a funeral," Noah says, and the admiration in his tone is noticeable.

"Not only did I catch sight, but I also caught these." He pulls a pair of black panties out of his pocket and holds them up. Emblazoned across the ass are three symbols. ATO. Alpha Team One. I fucking love that girl and her loyalty.

Noah spins in his seat so fast, I'm afraid the old man will break a hip. "Lucas, what the fuck did you do?"

He smirks and winks at Noah. "I helped settle her nerves. She knows we're all good and waiting in the wings if she needs us."

Jacob takes advantage of Lucas's focus on the conversation, snatches the panties out of his hand, and stuffs them in his pocket. "Mine."

Damn, I love that possessive tone he gets when it comes to our girl. My cock starts to harden, and I have to remind myself we're here with the others and not in any way able to act out the scenarios running through my head. He makes eye contact and shoots me a wink that I gleefully return. Soon.

Since we finally kissed in the gym that day, we've been talking about anything and everything—our fears, needs, desires, and limits—over and over again until it was down pat. It's a good rule when starting a relationship with a dom-sub nature, but I'm ready to move forward.

I turn to Lucas behind me in the backseat. "What's going on? How's the job?" I know he's there to pick up some details that are hopefully not too well hidden on some of the company's servers, but after Noah told us he ended up at Francesco Romano's bachelor party, I have so many questions.

"It's weird, man. Everything seems completely normal. On Friday, I was busy playing the role, and one of the other guys on my level invited me out. It's a bi-monthly thing, but he said that night would be different than their usual fare. By the way, is bi-monthly twice per month, or once every two months?" he asks randomly, and we all shrug. The answer depends on the situation.

"Anyway," he continues, "I went with him and ended up in this secret bunker strip club, and other guys from the office were sitting with Romano and De La Cruz. I don't know how they're connected yet, but I'll find out. What confuses me is that if The Gambit has ties to Collinsworth Bank, why would Annex plant an agent? Wouldn't they be working together on this?"

That's an interesting development. The only thing to do now is keep Lucas's eyes on the prize and continue pulling the information Annex needs. Of course, we have Jacob sifting through it first to build our own narrative before handing it over, but these ties and binds that cross the organizations have all of us desperate to figure out what's at play here.

I groan as I rub my hands over my face. "I don't know, man, but you need to keep getting closer to those guys. Try to connect, see who is associated with De La Cruz or Romano, and ferret out the information. The banking details are important as well, but fuck, this is getting complicated."

"Agreed," Jacob interjects. Did you put the new USB into your computer before you left on Friday?" Lucas nods his yes, so Jacob continues. "Okay, that data should be downloading if it's not already done. I haven't gotten the notification, but it should be happening soon, depending on how much information they have on that particular server. Good work."

Lucas just shrugs. He hates this job, but he's doing it well. We give him our reassurances, then talk turns to Romano.

"So you met him? The asshole marrying our girl?" I ask.

"Yeah," Lucas confirms. "Surprisingly, the asshole seems like a decent guy. We spent the night making bets about the other guys at our table. He didn't have a lap dance at all and kept his drinking in moderation. If he weren't marrying our girl, I might actually like the bastard."

All of us are a little shocked at that information, but it speaks volumes about him not getting his freak on at the strip club, knowing he isn't getting any at home from our girl. I'm curious about him, but there's no way for me to get more on him than we already have. Ivy has been thorough but hasn't been able to find anything in the flat. She sent a text on Saturday morning saying so.

Something has to shake out soon. Lucas is away, Ivy is away. Claudette has resorted to blowing up my phone since our girl is living her Gambit life, and the gang leader says she needs a texting buddy. Annex and The Gambit are connected in ways we still don't know and have me questioning everything. It's frustrating, and all the running in the world isn't helping me take my mind off it.

As we're hashing out scenarios about the phrase "carry on the line" that Lucas overheard King say in the bridal room, the doors to the church open. Romano and Ivy come out, surrounded by the other board members of The Gambit. There's no celebrating, no rice being thrown, no happy cheers. Everyone simply stands around the front of the church, saying their goodbyes, and takes off for their vehicles. Romano and Ivy are left standing with King, who claps both newlyweds on the shoulder, hugs Ivy, leans in to say a few words, and then leaves for his car.

That's it. Our girl is married to someone else.

Chapter Fourteen

Rogue

That must have been the most awkward wedding that church has ever housed.

Father Andrews was our priest, and as King walked me down the aisle, I saw only a quarter of the pews filled with board members and their seconds. This wasn't a social event but a business one. Jim and Hugo were standing in their row near the aisle, and both shot me matching winks as we passed.

I held my head up high and used the agonizingly slow march down the aisle to catalog who was on our side and who wasn't, distracting myself from the impending shackle about to be attached to my ankle in the form of a six-foot-three Italian.

King held my arm in the crook of his elbow, and after we'd walked the long march, he shook hands with Romano and placed my newly bedazzled hand in my groom's.

Before walking down here, King gave me an exquisite engagement ring "for appearances." He knows Romano didn't get me one, as he didn't need to, but King wanted to ensure I looked the part. It's a round diamond, nearly as wide as my finger, and has incredible clarity. There's going to be no hiding this thing.

As he placed my hand in Romano's, he clasped his hands around ours and gave a menacing squeeze. Message received, asshole.

Romano led me up the steps to the altar where the priest stood, a giant tome in front of him, as he cleared his throat and began the ceremony.

He blathered on about different aspects of marriage and how we were to be as man and wife. I didn't have the heart to interrupt his speech to tell him there would be no fruit from these loins and only just managed to keep from smirking at my internal tangents.

Rings were exchanged, vows spoken while I secretly crossed my fingers in the folds of my skirt, and when the time for the kiss came, I hated King with my whole being for thrusting this awful situation into my lap.

Was it cheating if there was no alternative? Could the consequences of not doing this mean punishment for my sister? I knew the guys would absolutely and resolutely tell me they understood, and they had, but my mind was trying to justify this, giving in to the slimy feeling in my veins.

Romano lifted my short black veil and searched my eyes with unease. It was the first time I'd seen him with his mask off, even if only for a moment. His hands slid around my jaw, thumbs resting under my ears, the very same way Lucas had held me only an hour before, and I had to fight the bile working its way up my throat. The cool metal of his new ring was jarring against my overheated skin, while my own felt like its own form of a collar.

Romano leaned in and kissed me gently and hesitantly. There was a moment; I saw it in his eyes before he leaned in: guilt, resignation, anger—an eddy of emotions that was shuttered from me as soon as his lids dropped.

At that moment, I knew I might end up trusting this man eventually—not with anything as valuable as my heart, but with pulling him onto my side and taking down King. His eyes betrayed how much he hated the position we were in, and the anger there told me he might be willing to take some revenge for it. Some would argue taking down King is just as important as my heart. I'm not one of those people. Not after giving it to four men I know are outside and/or still hiding in the bridal room down the hall.

Thank goodness the kiss was over as quickly as it started, and we were pronounced man and wife. The pitiful audience watching this train wreck applauded, and we led the way to the church entrance. The guests, my new husband, and I made our way out to the front steps and onto the sidewalk, everyone bidding a farewell and taking off to continue their Sundays.

I agreed to the ceremony but drew the line at a reception. King was okay with it so long as we followed all his other rules. Agreeing to the wedding so quickly earned me some points.

The Sacrifices We Make

"Rogue, Romano, I arranged a honeymoon for you to get to know each other a bit better. Take the company car; the driver knows where you're going, and there are clothes, toiletries, and everything you could need at your destination. Use this time to get to know each other. You're husband and wife now, after all." King placed a hand on either of our shoulders and gave a quick squeeze, an odd light filling his eyes. I almost want to say it was happiness, but we know that monster isn't familiar with that emotion.

King shakes Romano's hand, then turns to me. He leans in for an uncharacteristic hug, and just when I think it's all over, he hisses in my ear, "Try not to fuck anyone else while you're married to him." He pulls back and looks pointedly at my lips, which are no longer swollen from Red but must have still been when King came to get me from the bridal room. Fuck.

I nod my head at him with an austere look in my eye. King turns on his heel and walks to Walter's car idling in front of the church. How does he always find the best parking?

Romano looks at me and offers his elbow to lead me to the car waiting behind King's. We make our way over, and as Romano positions himself behind me, I look to the SUV still parked across the street and shoot a wink to the blacked-out windows and my guys inside. If they're in there, I know they're watching. The same way I would be if our roles were reversed.

ROMANO AND I HAVE BARELY SPOKEN A WORD IN THE CAR DURING THE three-hour drive. We've been through fields and over mountains and finally seem to be arriving at our destination. With King insisting we take his car, I have no doubts the driver is heavily paid to report on anything we say if the interior hasn't already been wired.

King may demand loyalty, but he doesn't trust anyone. This will be a long honeymoon of watching what we say and where. It's time to put on a good show and nip the surveillance in the bud.

The car starts to slow, and I look out across the shimmering blanket of snow on the sides of the road and the ever-thickening copse of trees until I see a small cabin. We've arrived at Mammoth Lakes Village, a charming town with log cabins set up for winter skiers and those who slip away from the cities for a weekend of frolicking in the snow, and King has put us up in a home Goldilocks would be envious of.

It's a single-story log cabin with a long driveway and no neighbors. The smoke rising from the chimney tells me it should be warm enough. It's mid-

December, and while it's not too cold near the coast, these mountain towns get freezing cold with the altitude and snowfall.

The driver parks in front of the porch steps and rounds the vehicle to let us out. Romano slides out first and reaches a hand back for me. I take it and do my damndest not to trip in my heels. I didn't know we were headed anywhere, so I obviously have no appropriate footwear. Hopefully, King wasn't lying when he said the house was stocked.

We make our way up the steps and cross the threshold into the house. It's...pleasant. There's a small kitchen to the left, an old pine table with four chairs, and linoleum tiles. To the right is a small yet comfortable lounge area with a cozy-looking leather couch, books crammed onto shelves, and no TV in sight. The hallway leading away from the two rooms must lead to the bedroom and bathroom. There can't be much more here since the house looked so tiny from the front.

After taking a look around at the cabin, I hear a car door slam and the sound of tires on the gravel. Great. We're stuck here. I turn to Romano and see him peering out of the window at the retreating tail lights. A soft curse leaves his lips, and he looks at me. We both break out into laughter at our predicament.

"Great, so we're stuck here, married, and know nothing about each other. Let's fix one of those things," I state authoritatively, knowing it is highly likely King has someone listening in.

"Fine. How are we getting out of here? I think we're about a mile from the main road." Romano's voice is resigned as he rebuttons his coat, ready to head out into the wintry air.

"You idiot. We can't fix that right now. But we can get to know each other. Let me check out the cabin while you figure out something for dinner. You didn't marry a great cook." We're stuck together, so now's as good a time as any to figure out what he's up to and lower his expectations on the wife aspect. King fucking loves him and has basically just made him a son-in-law, as well as my right hand when the time comes for me to step up in the organization. Why?

Romano shakes his head, and I pull my trusty device detector out of my purse. Jacob said never to leave home without it, and I'm glad I brought it to my wedding. King is three hours away, so even if he gets pissed about me disabling his modifications to the cabin, there's some time to prepare for his anger. What's he going to do? Send the driver back? Please. I'd have him laid out in two seconds flat.

I sweep the kitchen and living room, finding no less than three microphones, and make my way to the bedroom with them gripped in my hand. There's one in the bedroom, near the headboard, likely hoping to ensure we genuinely spend the night together as husband and wife and thus throw the whole annulment thing out of the window. Thankfully, there's nothing in the bathroom because, well, ew.

I'm about to step onto the porch when the smell of garlic wafts down the hall. Seeing as it's nearly seven o'clock, and I haven't eaten since breakfast, my stomach is firmly in favor of finishing the sweep after food.

I emerge from the hall to see Romano at the stove sautéing garlic and clams in a pan while a pot filled with linguini pasta bubbles away next to it. Oh, good God in heaven, yes. At least I know I won't starve up here.

I grab three glasses, a can of Sprite, and a bottle of white wine from the refrigerator and plop my ass on one of the spindly chairs. Romano hears my shuffling but barely pulls his eyes from the pan as the garlic browns—good man. Burned garlic ruins every dish, no matter how much you try to mask it. Once he pulls the pan from the flames, I let out a little whistle and hold up my left hand.

"Are those *bugs?*" he mouths the last word with eyebrows nearly reaching his hairline.

"Yep. Wanna drown them?" I ask.

"Hell yes."

Without further ado, I toss the tiny microphones into one of the glasses, crack open the Sprite, and pour it over the top. Hopefully, the carbonation hisses and pops in whoever's ears are monitoring us in the cabin. Petty, but I'll take my wins where I can get them.

I rise from my seat, head to the bathroom, and flush the microphones down the toilet. Buh-bye.

Returning to my seat, I flop down and sigh deeply. Romano hands over a chunk of a baguette that I take gratefully. "We're good to talk now. You know King has our apartment wired, right?"

"Yeah, I figured as much. You're sure you got all of them?" he asks.

"Sure as I can be. I have to do the porch, and I think I saw a small shed out back, but we're good in here now." My assurances make his face relax more than I've ever seen it.

"Thank God. I've been dying to rip the ones out of the apartment, but since he lives just upstairs, I know he'd either come to shoot me or have it rebugged again in a matter of hours. He did that the first time I found them on the day I moved in. The rebugging, not the shooting. I left to go get some of my stuff, and by the time I returned, four new ones were put in." He shakes his head at the situation and returns to working on dinner.

I know what he means. I did the same thing a few days after I arrived and found replacements within hours. Just as Romano drains the pasta over the sink and my mouth is full of bread, my phone rings loudly. I dig around inside my bag, shoving makeup, a gun, and sheathed knives out of the way to find it at the bottom.

Looking at the screen, I repress a grin. Romano looks over, and he just knows from the look on my face that it's King and we've successfully removed all of his devices inside the house. I can't keep the glee from my voice as I answer.

"King."

"Daughter, explain." Verbose, isn't he?

"I followed your instructions, married the man, and have safely arrived at our honeymoon. I will not let you listen if I decide to fuck him. Was there anything else, or may I return to my evening?"

I know I'm pushing my luck. I fucking know it, and I can't help myself. I've kept my shield up at all times in the apartment. I've done what was asked of me. I will not kowtow and bend to his whims more than necessary to keep Sage alive.

"Fine. It's four days, then you're back here. Hook him and keep him. He's done great work so far, and I want him to stick with us."

"Yes, King," I answer and hang up the phone.

Romano looks back at me over his shoulder as he plates our pasta, and I shrug. What else is there to do?

He carries over two plates, and the smell is divine. Linguini with clam sauce, fresh bread, a small salad, and the bottle of white wine I pulled out earlier. This might turn out to be a short vacation, after all. Too bad no one is getting laid.

"So, Romano, tell me about yourself." I hook a brow up and wait for him to dish.

He laughs as he settles in his seat and picks up his glass of wine. He takes a sip as he contemplates his answer. "You know the basics. I'm forty-three and have worked for The Gambit for nearly five years. I make decent money. What else is there to know?"

"How about how you ended up working for The Gambit in the first place? You seem to have come out of left field. It's a standard story: middle-class life, saw the chance for more cash, and hooked up with the company through mutual friends. But it doesn't tell me your motivation or why you rose through the ranks at that pace. While you were still three rungs under Horvat, I heard about the arms deals and researched your missing competition within the organization. How many other dealers did you remove? Why are you working for us?"

My questions catch him off guard, and he places his glass down. I don't think he had any idea I'd done as much research as I have. Competent, my ass. Magnificent is the word, husband dearest. "I did what I had to do to move up the ranks. I have my reasons for joining The Gambit. These are dangerous times, Rogue. No one can be trusted, despite what relationship we may hold in the eyes of the law."

I gently settle my fork on the side of my plate and look at him. "What happened to you?"

"Nothing for you to worry about. Your turn," Romano motions to me with his fork full of pasta. "Why did you go along with this marriage?"

It's not what I was expecting, but I'll play along.

"King demanded it. He holds sway, and I can't say no to a lot of the things he asks of me. Also," I cut him off before he can ask, "none of your business." I smirk at him as I lift another fork of pasta to my mouth. Despite having married a woman with zero kitchen skills, it looks like we won't starve. The man really can cook.

"Since we're stuck together for the foreseeable future, and I don't particularly love tense, awkward silences, how do you feel about a truce for the time being?" he asks. My eyes widen at his proposition, and I think it over. Friends? Aw, shit. Why does everyone want to be friends with me all of a sudden? I should give Claudette his number so she can show him how needy friends can be.

I mull it over, and without mutual leverage over each other, it just can't happen. "Groundwork needs to be laid before that can occur. There are more than just our lives on the line if we fuck this up. Don't you ever wonder how King keeps so many people loyal to him? It's either money or threats hanging over loved ones."

His hand reaches out and clasps mine across the table. "I know. I also know he has someone on you." My hand falls free from his grasp and lands on the table with a thud.

"How—" I start and cut myself off before the emotion can enter my voice. I take a sip of wine and try again. "What do you know, and more importantly, how do you know it?"

"You're not the only one who can research people, Rogue. I've been keeping tabs on the board since I joined The Gambit. It's good to know your superiors. King's been on my watch list for a lot longer than that. You think I don't know about the girl he raised and her original family?"

My jaw clenches that someone else knew about Sage and did nothing—*continues* to do nothing. Not that he could get to her in his previous roles for the organization, but hell in a motherfucking handbasket, he knows.

"Rogue, you're sure all of the tech is out of this room?" he asks me as he eyes the cobwebbed corners and cupboards. I stand from my chair and pull out the detector, doing another sweep, sure to get into the crevices and assure both of us, once again, that it is, in fact, safe to speak.

"I see you're a good person. I also kept track of your kills over the years. Never innocents, never murky sins, only the blackest of the black. You are not the monster King tried to raise, and that's why I didn't fight this marriage as hard as I could have. Yeah, I argued it a bit, but that would be expected for someone having their autonomy taken away. King is directly responsible for the death of my wife. It was seven years ago, and I've worked my ass off every day since then to get closer to him so I can fucking kill him."

Possibilities flit through my mind. Is this a trap? Has King set this up to catch me conspiring with my new husband? Is this a way to find out my loyalty? There are a million ways to play this, and with King's penchant for physical and psychological abuse well documented, I have trouble putting all of my faith into this man. So, instead, I flip the tables.

"Tell me about your wife," I prod, and he does. He tells me about her charm, character, beauty, and tragically short life. I know he's speaking from the heart when I see the way his eyes become watery. When he reaches her death, a single tear tracks its way down his cheek, and I lift my thumb to catch it. There is no charge in the air, no feeling as if my skin is prickling with electricity like when I touch one of my guys. He is just a man in pain, looking for revenge.

There's nothing more dangerous.

Long after finishing dinner and our wine, we're still sitting at the table, discussing our situation. Romano has no interest in me because his wife is still at the front of his mind daily. It's a lovely sentiment, but it must get lonely. I decide to tell him I can't make a move on King in any way, shape, or form until I retrieve the evidence he has on me.

"I need information," I tell him. Romano can't help with Sage, but he can find other information for me. "There's proof of my crimes. It's a secondary way to keep me in line, I guess you could say. He has it written in his will that it goes to the authorities if he dies. I don't know where it is or

The Sacrifices We Make

who his lawyer is regarding that information. I've already checked his usual attorneys' files, and it's nowhere to be found. I need that information, Romano. Find a way to get it, and I'll help deliver King. But we're going to have to flip a coin or something to figure out who gets to kill him because I also deserve a shot at him."

"Thank Christ." He holds out his hand, and we shake on it. "You've got yourself a deal, Rogue."

And just like that, I've got someone else on our side who I'm still determining if I can trust but who just made massive strides in the right direction.

We eat some cookies Romano finds stashed in a cupboard and discuss the other board members. I haven't told him who's on our side yet, but I'm sure from my tone that he knows De La Cruz isn't one of them.

"He left the bachelor party in a panic the other night. Any idea what's going on there?" he asks.

"I hear he's been having trouble with his dealers selling to minors. If those rumors prove to be true, King's going to murder the bastard, and I don't feel one ounce of remorse over it."

Romano nods, and I wonder if I can have some fun here.

"How was your bachelor party, by the way? Still washing stripper glitter off?"

He chokes on his cookie and glares at me across the table. "First of all, I didn't get a lap dance because that would be disrespectful to you," he sputters out. "Second, it's not my thing. Sorry, but thanks for the night out. I ended up having a pretty good time."

I quirk an eyebrow at him, indicating he should continue even though Noah told me Red hung out with Romano at the strip club. He explains, "I met some guy there who also wasn't feeling the vibe, and we ended up hanging out and laughing at the other guys the whole night. He owes me a couple of drinks we didn't get to order. I have to find a way to collect."

Oh, Lucas, you memorable bastard.

Chapter Fifteen

Jacob

I LOOK AT NOAH'S PHONE ON THE KITCHEN ISLAND AS IT LIGHTS UP with an incoming call. Usually, I'd let it ring until voicemail picked it up, but I grab for it just in case it's Rogue. Just as I push the button to answer, it rings out, but as fate would have it, a text message soon pops up.

Unknown: Cap, answer the damn phone.
Unknown: Come on, Cap. I'll withhold sexy videos if you don't call me back.
Unknown: I mean it! Okay, I don't because that one on Saturday was :fire emoji:. But come on!

I laugh at the chaos reigning on the screen while simultaneously adjusting myself at the memory of her last video, and I know it would drive him up the wall to see it all cluttered with unread messages and missed calls. This distance sucks and has resulted in a lot of videos and sexting between all of us.

I made Noah leave his phone here when he went to work out because he kept relentlessly checking it for messages from Rogue or Lucas. We haven't heard from either of them since the wedding.

After Rogue's car drove off, Lucas hopped out of the SUV and strolled down the street to his motorcycle to head back to his undercover job.

There's been nary a peep from either of them, which has everyone a little on edge.

I pick up the phone and enter Noah's passcode. He thinks he hides things so well.

"Hey, Love. Where've you been?" I ask when she answers on the first ring.

"Jacob? Hey! I'm on my honeymoon. King didn't tell us we were leaving until after the wedding and ordered us into the car. I'm up in Mammoth."

"Honeymoon?" I ask with a growl. Logically, I know nothing is happening, but I don't like the idea of her with this guy alone, up in the mountains playing house.

"Relax, big guy. I debugged the house. King doesn't have ears on us, and I check it regularly. Romano has been forthcoming with some information, and I gave him the task of figuring out how to get my evidence away from King. I like delegating. If he does it well, it'll take something off our plate."

Her reassurances only sometimes work to keep me from flying off the handle. "Fine. Lucas says he met the guy and that he thinks he's okay. Is he being good, or do we have to skin him alive and ruin his life?"

"He's being good, I promise. And yeah, I think he's a good guy. He just went out back to collect some of the wood from the shed. King stuck us in some tiny cabin out in the woods to bond or whatever. I don't think he expected us to bond over killing him," she deadpans.

I laugh at that because, well, it's hilarious and only something my girl would say. "When are you coming back, Darling Mine?" I try not to let my desperation bleed into my voice, but it's quite the herculean task. It's hard enough when she's across town and not with us here. Now that I know she's hours away, it has me feeling out of sorts.

"Tomorrow, I think. King said four days. Plus, we have a board meeting the day after that we can't miss, so I doubt he'd stick us up here for an extended amount of time."

"Sounds good." As soon as the words leave my mouth, I hear a shuffle on the other end. A groan comes through the phone, and it's distinctly male.

"Got the wood!" comes down the line, and I know our time is up.

"Great, set the fire, and I'll just finish this call with Elise." I hear her reply as the call is muted, and I start calling ridiculous nicknames down the line.

"Cupcake! Tater Tot! Angel Face!" I ramble on until I hear her laughing on the other side of the line when she unmutes it.

"Dammit, Jacob. Elise would never make me laugh like that. You're going to blow our cover."

"Fine, I just wanted to mess around a bit. I miss you."

"I miss you, too."

"Love," I start, "come back to us and be safe. I don't trust the guy, just keep your guard up and put a knife to his cock if he tries anything. Please."

"I will. I'm yours, remember. I'm not risking that."

Before I can find another way to keep her on the line, there's another bit of shuffling and a muffled voice. "Hey, I've got to go. I'll see you at the meeting, Elise. Night." Ah, she's not alone anymore.

"Sure thing, Love. Be safe."

She hangs up, and I regretfully pull the phone from my ear. I'm glad she could find some time to check in, but the roar of frustration in my brain is so loud, it's threatening to drown everything else out. I need her back here.

I clutch the phone and head toward the gym, where I see Noah on the treadmill, fire in his eyes, as Han yells encouragement. Fucking cardio.

Han is sitting on a weight bench, his legs on either side. He is wearing one of those T-shirts with ripped sleeves so the armholes gape enough to see his toned sides and a peek of his stomach. He sees me approaching the gym and winks through the glass. I hold up the phone as an explanation, and he nods.

Entering the gym, Noah sees his opportunity and hits the stop button on the machine of death. "What's up?" he asks.

I give a run-down of what Rogue told me, and as I finish, Noah nods, and Han gets this look of adoration on his face for her that only slightly reawakens the jealousy I had just tamped down.

"Anyway, she'll be back tomorrow. There's a board meeting she can't miss." I look at the other two and shrug. She left without us knowing, and while we didn't need to know her every move, this one was big.

"That's good news," Han says.

"Excellent. I'm glad she checked in and will be back soon. I hate not knowing that she even left. I just figured she was back at the apartment." Noah hates being out of the loop, so at least now he knows her whereabouts and when she'll return to El Castillo.

"I've got the data Lucas was able to patch through to us. I'll work on that for a while to see what I can figure out before we hand things over to Annex. If he's gathered enough, I'd say he'll be able to return within a few days. Thoughts?" I ask.

"Sounds good, man. Keep us updated on what you find," Noah says.

"Come on, Dear Leader. You owe me fifteen more minutes. Let's go!" Han commands in his trainer voice. Noah presses the start button with a groan and a not-so-muffled curse as the speed ramps up until he's flat-out sprinting again. Fucking cardio.

I step across the room and fix my lips to Han's for a brief kiss. With Rogue gone and Lucas on his mission, the three of us have been alternating between a state of worry, trying to dive into work, and twiddling our thumbs. It's infuriating. Training seems to be the only thing that will help Noah settle his mind, no matter how much he argues against it.

I leave the gym and settle into my office next door.

Sifting through data isn't the highlight of my job, but when I find nuggets of information that lead to development, my body vibrates with energy until we chase those leads down.

I sit at the computer for hours, looking over three of the five screens with The Clash playing in the background on repeat. I need to lose myself in work; repetition is the only way to do that.

Han comes in, delivers a plate of food Noah cooked, and leaves after planting a kiss on my temple. I can't resist the moment and lean into him while my eyes stay focused on the screen. He laughs at my concentration, and the sound settles something in my chest.

I keep going long after both Han and Noah come to say goodnight and warn me not to work too long. It's around four in the morning when I get a hit.

Fucking bingo.

Rogue

It's the third day without food, and I'm dying.

King has had me locked up in my room for a week with only a bucket for a bathroom, and when I threatened his life through the door on the fourth day, he stopped bringing me food, too.

Being fifteen and hormonal has not helped me this week.

I should have never listened in on his phone call last week. He was talking with Horvat on speakerphone, and the door was slightly cracked. I had finished my homework, cursing everything math-related in the process, when I heard his voice carrying down the hall.

He talked about guns and the fact that Horvat had fucked up a shipment along the way and was expected to pay for the loss the organization suffered.

The Sacrifices We Make

I stood outside the door for the thirty-minute phone call, and when the door suddenly swung inward and I found myself staring into King's eyes, I knew I was fucked. I was supposed to do my work, train under his regime, and follow his orders. Listening in was not one of my sanctioned activities.

King's hand shot out lightning fast as he gripped my hair near the base of my skull and swung me around toward my room. My feet scrambled on the carpet lining the hallway, and I tried to grab anything to stop the procession down the hall. He flung it open when he reached my door and threw me inside.

Well, now it's been a week, and I'm miles ahead on my schoolwork. I have learned to value a toilet in a way I never thought I would, and I would be grateful for anything to eat.

My stomach has been grumbling for days, and the hollow pit in my gut takes the last of my energy and focus. Just as I'm contemplating eating the notebook paper just to stave off some of the pain, the door is kicked inward, and King stands at the threshold.

His eyes are a menacing black as he advances toward me. He lifts his hand in a closed fist and brings it down over and over again until it's not only hunger driving me to blackout but pain, as well.

I WOKE FROM MY MEMORY/NIGHTMARE AROUND THREE IN THE morning in my new apartment with my new husband by my side.

Romano and I returned from our trip yesterday, and it's been quiet after sharing so many truths in the little cabin in Mammoth. But when you know King has the place wired, you tend not to want to make waves.

Before we left, we discussed putting on a little show for King to make him believe we were starting to get along and acclimating to the new arrangement. I don't know how much acting we have to do now that we're actually starting to get along because the jokes and little jabs are becoming easier to dish out.

I'm not going to lie; he's an attractive man. He's quite intelligent, and after talking a bit more about the loss of his wife, I see he isn't going to move on with anyone, so I know I'm safe in that regard. I don't want to be fending off advances day and night.

The one thing we disagreed on was the sleeping arrangements. I argued that King would come to expect us to be sharing a bed, or at least leaning in that direction, after the wedding. Romano put up a big fight about it until he started to actually listen to my arguments. He knows I'm right, and as uncomfortable as last night was, sharing a bed with a man I still barely know, it's for the best to keep suspicion off of us.

After tossing and turning for an hour, I dozed off again, and we both woke to his alarm at five-thirty this morning. After sharing an awkward, bleary-eyed look, we burst into laughter. There's nothing like someone seeing you at the ass-crack of dawn to level the playing field.

As evidenced this morning, he wakes up and bolts upright. I don't know if that's a daily thing, but it was funny as hell. I watched in amazement how he went from dead asleep to nearly jumping out of bed and rolled over with a grunt to catch a bit more rest.

He stubbed his toe on the nightstand, and in all the ruckus, I woke fully. He talked me into going to the gym with him this morning, and we ran in companionable silence. All it did, though, was make me miss Han.

We're in Black Beauty now, headed for the Rook building to go to the meeting King called.

Romano keeps trying to change the radio, and after slapping his hand away for the fourth time, I pull the knife from my hip and brandish it until he relents. Driver picks the music. It's a basic rule.

I pull into a parking garage around the block, and when Romano asks, I remind him of King's eyes everywhere, and I'd rather he not go through my car again.

I lock up, and we walk the three blocks to the building. Romano, ever the gentleman, guides me into and out of the elevator and opens doors for me. When he pulls my chair out this time, it feels respectful, not out of place like last time.

We're about twenty minutes early, so we sit in silence in the boardroom as the others enter. King is the last to arrive. It's funny how no one bats an eye when he's a minute late. No, that's reserved for me.

"Good, you're all here. Let's start." King calls the meeting to order, and we wait, impatiently wanting to know what's on the agenda for the day. There are no spreadsheets out with sales, no new deals to discuss that I know about. Nothing.

King makes his way to the head of the table and pulls the chair out. He spins it a few times, his hand trailing over the plush leather backrest on each rotation, and I know today will be bad. But for whom?

King addresses the room with an arrogance I've come to expect. "I don't often arrange for impromptu meetings outside of our standing one every two weeks, and should things have improved, I would have had other things to discuss. But they haven't. So I have a vote to put forward."

King doesn't often call for votes. It isn't necessary a lot of time as the only things that need board approval are a structural or personal change to the board or something that crosses between two divisions of the organization.

He looks around the table, making eye contact with us before clearing his throat. "It has come to my attention that Enrique De La Cruz has more dealers selling to minors." Before De La Cruz can even open his mouth to protest, King holds up a hand and levels him with a glare I've only ever seen directed at me when I was younger. "Now, one whisper of a rumor, I understand. There are rules to be taught and reinforced. But now, I've been hearing about it for almost three weeks from other divisions of the organization—rumors of kids OD-ing in the middle of classes or at the park. Now, I put it to you, board. Who runs the dealers?"

As one, we all answer clearly, "De La Cruz."

"And has he not been warned to follow the organization's rules that we have all agreed upon?"

Again, in unison, we ring out, "He has."

"All those in favor of removing De La Cruz from the board for his gargantuan blunder if he doesn't rein in his dealers by next week?"

Hands around the table shoot up with no hesitation whatsoever. God fucking bless Claudette and her rumor capabilities.

"—can't do this! I swear to motherfucking—" De La Cruz is making a scene, but it's hard to pay attention to the gnat fluttering around your head when there's a fucking dragon at the head of the table.

"Done. Rogue, see me after the meeting." King's words are terse and leave no room for refusal.

I nod my head. I knew this would come down to me, and I'm ready to finish this out. I didn't expect it to happen this quickly, and with the guys working on a plan for Mara while I'm here, maybe we could wrap up two board members in one week.

What is the value of this one man when it comes to the greater good? To lessen King's position and allies? I've met Enrique's second, Cian Byrne. He's smart, but he's a coward. When push comes to shove, he'll bend or step out of my way on my climb to crush King.

Regarding De La Cruz, I make no arguments about why he should be spared. He informed his dealers that I was coming. I was gutted in a bathroom because they were warned. The last dealer I was sent after also knew I was coming and hid in a shitty motel.

I'm already contemplating which hitmen I could farm this out to, but I know it'll need to be me. I don't trust the others, and I don't think I'll be able to sleep until I see this done myself.

"Any other business?" King asks. It makes sense he called a meeting just for this. As per the bylaws we all abide by, a member cannot be eliminated without a vote to avoid backlash from others. It's a good thing no one here knows that I put a few bullets in Horvat instead of a burglar. I'm sure King and De La Cruz would have had something to say about that.

When no one raises any issues, and De La Cruz is a babbling mess in his seat, we bid our farewells. I pass my keys to Romano and ask him to bring the car around. I'll be down in a few minutes, and I don't feel like having my new husband waiting around for me just outside the door.

After Romano and the others step out of the meeting room following our threatening vote, it's just me, King, and De La Cruz. King flops into his seat and sighs heavily.

"How could you lose control of your dealers, Enrique?" King sounds...disappointed? Concerned? Fuck if I know which adjective to use to describe this, but it's a level of care I don't know that I've ever heard in his voice. Not with me, not with Sage. Only when he speaks to my parents' headstones on the anniversary of their deaths—a death I'm ninety-nine percent sure he caused. Why else would he take me in other than as some twisted notion of guilt? He could have molded anyone into his tailor-made assassin and probably had an easier time of it.

"I still have control of the dealers. They're rumors, King. I've been running them for years. They listen when I tell them to pass the info down the line. No minors. I've said it since it was voted in," De La Cruz argues.

"Yes, and you've been pushing back against the vote since it was enacted, haven't you?" King asks.

"I've been arguing against it, but I haven't betrayed it. You can trust me."

King, who has been relaxed until now, sits up straight and yells across the table at his former confidant, "I can trust NO ONE! Not one person, Enrique. I don't have that luxury. I'm giving you this time to fix it, which you will do as a gesture of our longstanding friendship. There will be no mercy if you don't rectify the issue."

Until then, I'd been standing behind my chair, watching these two rehash their relationship drama. As King yells at De La Cruz, a slip of my hand causes the chair to make tiniest of squeaks, which, of course, rings out

The Sacrifices We Make

in the now silent room like a gunshot. I stare at it, adorned with the wedding ring I forgot I was wearing.

"Rogue," King orders, "you'll keep an eye on him, make sure he doesn't run. Enrique, you know we can find you wherever you go, and we'll make sure others feel the wrath of the board. Get your shit in line, or get yourself a will. Those are your choices."

King lets out a heavy sigh, and the weariness on his face is fascinating to watch. It's so out of character that I can't look away. He maintains his stare down with De La Cruz until the man mumbles something about fixing his employees and asks to take his leave.

King sends him out with more menacing words before he turns to me. "Disabling the devices at the cabin was not a good move, Rogue. What are *you* hiding?"

"Nothing," I reply with a shrug and nonchalance I do *not* feel. "It's weird knowing someone is listening in when I'm trying to get my new husband in line by whatever means necessary. I don't want your lackeys listening to me fuck him in the name of the company."

I haven't so much as touched Romano, but King doesn't know that. So long as it maintains the illusion, I'll lie about it until I'm blue in the face. The nod he sends me is one of mournful pride.

"I know you'll do what's required. Did you know I was once in love?" he asks, and the abrupt change from organization politics to his love life has my mouth opening and closing like a fish out of water. What do I say to that?

"No, I didn't. I know you've had relationships, but love was never something I'd considered." He nods his head at that, seemingly understanding my confusion.

"It was before you were born. You wouldn't have witnessed it. There are good and bad things to love, but often, the bad outweighs any small measure of joy it could bring. And one person always loves more than the other. It's an imbalance that leads to destruction. This union with Romano may not be based on *love*," he sneers at the word as if it has personally offended him, and maybe it has, "but it will be based on mutual respect. You are suited well for each other, and you will present a unified front as the leaders of this organization one day."

My chest feels a bit tight for the man who has never shown me a measure of compassion, yet here I am. Feeling my own heart squeeze, listening to his resignation. I don't know who hurt him, but I have a feeling this contributed to who he's become. I can't help but think about the guys. I can't see any of that happening with them, this desolation that surrounds his soul, tainting it until it has become darker than the blackest night. But then again, does anyone see it coming when it ends badly?

"Why the sudden talk about the future, King?" I ask, knowing he could lash out at my questioning of his motives. It's not like me to inquire about his reasons, but I need to know why he's pushing this.

Instead of icing me out, he simply looks at me and says, "I won't be around forever. A smart man preps his house for the worst-case scenario. He stays three steps ahead of the others."

With that, he rises from his seat, his shoulders slightly slumped, and I watch as he exits the doors and makes his way down the hall. I...I don't even know what to think at this point. What did he mean by that?

The ominous conversation replays in my head as I wait for the elevator to bring me down to the lobby, where I find Romano in the driver's seat of Black Beauty at the curb. He's fiddling with the radio, unaware of my approach. It gives me a moment to school my features into my usual mask, and I open the door.

"Hey, how'd it go?" he asks.

"Oh, fine. Just a bit of housekeeping," I respond quietly as my mind continues trying to figure out the puzzle. I do know that De La Cruz is on thin ice and on his way out. That seems to have been the catalyst for King opening up a bit tonight. I wonder how much feeling, emotion, and disappointment he's hiding under that mask he wears.

I'm going to process this a bit before discussing it with Romano to see if I can shake loose some answers with some good old-fashioned research.

Chapter Sixteen

Han

Ivy is acting strange. It almost feels weird to call her Ivy in my head when she's firmly wearing her Rogue mask, not letting her true self shine through at all.

She's been back from her honeymoon for nearly a week, and aside from a few texts about the De La Cruz plan going well and that Romano is keeping his hands to himself, there hasn't been much else from her. Each text was perfunctory and all business.

Noah's been her main point of contact, and even he says she has become more and more distant over the last few days. And you know that when Noah says someone is a bit standoffish, it means they're practically non-communicative.

I'm in the weapons room, stocking our stores with a fun haul, including a few extra knives I think Ivy will like when I hear Jacob shout with triumph through the ajar door of his office. I hastily, yet carefully, drop everything and make my way to the center of the clubhouse so I can see what's up.

"Bloody fucking right, I knew it!" Jacob's voice comes from his sanctuary.

I see him leaning back in his chair, his arms raised above his head in victory as his chair spins round and round, the tips of his toes guiding the movement, forcing him to spin faster and faster. He's adorable.

"Hey, what's going on?" I ask from the threshold of his office, getting dizzy just watching him go in circles at an increasing pace as he celebrates whatever conquest he's just landed.

"I cracked it. I motherfucking cracked it!" he shouts. "Ooh, they thought they could bury it, but I got it!"

Noah, who was in the kitchen making lunch, comes through the open expanse of the clubhouse to join me at the door, his head following Jacob's spinning in the chair.

"Any idea what he's talking about?" he asks me.

"Honestly, it could be anything from breaking through that Candy Crush level he's been working on to hacking into the Department of Defense servers. Your guess is as good as mine." I shrug my shoulders and know that without Jacob telling us, any speculation is a possibility.

As Jacob's spin turns to us, he plants his feet and abruptly stops his movement. "I've figured out why they wanted someone on the Collinsworth job. Noah, call Lucas home; he's done."

Noah's brows lift, an impressed expression overtaking his face. A lot of this assignment has come down to only Lucas and Jacob, and it's impressive how quickly they've gathered the intel needed. Although, I guess I shouldn't be surprised. He said he found something a few days ago, but it wasn't concrete yet. He's been working on it day and night, barely taking time away to eat or leave his office.

The original assignment was to pull records from the servers and deliver them to Mara at Annex. No one said anything about rifling through them, but of course, we go above and beyond. Alpha Team One isn't just our designation; it's an assurance that we're the best.

Noah starts to ask for an explanation, but Jacob quickly cuts him off. "I'd rather have all of us together for this. We don't need anything else about the higher-ups or how they're connected with The Gambit. I've bloody got it. There's a reason the management ended up at Romano's bachelor party."

"Fine, if you're sure. I'll go give Lucas a call and start the logistics for moving him back here." Noah pulls his phone from his pocket and taps the screen to call Lucas.

Jacob surges to his feet, and with quick and determined strides, he makes his way to me, wraps one hand around the back of my neck, and brings me in for a scorching kiss. Noah makes a groaning sound and grumbles something about needing curtains in the clubhouse as he retreats to make the call.

Jacob's tongue tangles with mine, and I bring my hands up to cup his jaw and keep us connected. His kiss is raw, exuberant, damn-near explosive.

We've been approaching this thing tentatively and slowly, but at this moment, I can't remember why. It's as if all of my good sense melted into a puddle on the floor the moment Jacob's lips crashed into mine.

His grip slides to the front of my throat and tightens as he pushes me against the wall behind me. He pulls back and whispers against my lips, "Is this okay?"

I open my eyes to see his bright blue-grey eyes searching mine, looking desperate. I nod my head, and he quirks a brow. Ah, yes. The Packet.

We've been exploring this development between us, but Jacob was unsure how to explain what he's really looking for in our relationship. So, instead of winging it, he did what he always does: research. The wealth of information available made his overly organized brain elated, so he compiled what he felt were the things we needed to discuss and agree upon.

The Packet, as it is named, outlines consent, safe words, limits, and has been reviewed by both of us point by point until we had it memorized. The Packet dictates if something is to progress, verbal consent is required.

"Yes, please." Jacob's grin comes out in full force at my words, and he keeps his hand on my throat as our lips connect again.

"Touch me," he demands. My hands raise to brush his strong shoulders, moving of their own accord, and the loss of intentional movement staggers me as my hands take on a path all their own without conscious thought.

My breath stalls in my lungs as I lose myself in the kiss, the moment, his crisp, clean scent with a hint of lavender. It instantly makes me think of his bed, of the little bottle of floral essential oil on his bedside table that he sprinkles on his pillows every morning, so the scent lulls him to sleep when he finally lays his head down after a day of data mining.

The all-consuming passion I feel as we finally give in to the inevitable has me releasing a moan Jacob echoes roughly. His hand releases my throat and comes up to cup my face with a gentleness I honestly didn't expect from him. I know he's more gentle in his intimacy with Ivy, but after discussing the logistics of his needs and my wants, I think I expected him to be dominant, rough, and in charge all of the time when it's just us.

He never explicitly said he would be that way at all times, but it's what

I had wrongly assumed. My anxiety built this up into something else: something inspiring, illicit, and both scary and pacifying all at once.

Yes, I want this the way he does, but that doesn't mean I'm not nervous I'll do something wrong or screw up somehow. Above all, I realize I've neglected the fact that he's a gentle soul, even under his need for control. I let the situation grow until it became this unrecognizable *thing* in my mind when, in fact, he's the same as he's always been. We've just added a new dynamic.

He draws back with one last swipe along my bottom lip, and my eyes flutter open, looking into his own hooded eyes shielded behind his glasses. His chest is heaving under my palms, the top two buttons of his white shirt are undone, and his hair is ruffled after my hands raked through it. The tattoos on his neck and upper chest are in stark juxtaposition to his white shirt, seemingly moving of their own volition with each ragged exhale he expels.

His thumb traces my lip as he keeps his eyes trained on mine. "Han," he commands. My eyes snap up to his instead of continuing to trace the lines of his tattoos. "Upstairs."

His words whisper across my lips, igniting a flame deep in my stomach with the promise they hold. "Please," I beg. We've kissed, we've touched, but Jacob rightfully insisted we finish going through The Packet before taking things to the next level.

Well, The Packet is done.

He spins me in his arms, pressing my chest against the wall, his hard, concealed cock pushing into my backside as he crowds me against the glass divider. He runs his fingers through my hair, suddenly tilting my head to the right as he licks a line up my neck on the exposed side. He leans in further, gripping my earlobe with his teeth, just this side of painful as his hips grind into me, and says one word. It tumbles from his clenched jaw with a growl. "Run."

He retreats, giving me enough space to turn and make my way to the entryway. I shoot through the open door, turning my head to look over my shoulder during my escape, and I see him straighten the cuffs of his starched shirt and begin to take slow, calculated steps after me.

My heart is pounding in my chest, comparing the contrast between his tender touches and this growly alpha stalking after me. Who knew a game of cat and mouse, hunter and prey, would have me adjusting my cock through my sweats as it strains beneath its confines?

I lope up the stairs and hit the top step as I hear his gruff chuckle float

The Sacrifices We Make

up the staircase. He's just placed his first foot on the step, and the look he gives me as he lifts his head and his eyes connect with mine has me taking a sharp inhale. He looks like the devil incarnate as his slacks strain against his powerful thighs and bulging cock, his bare feet tattooed all the way down to his toes, start ascending the steps. I look away and make my way to his room, internally begging for today to be the day we escalate our relationship.

I make my way into his room and have a moment to myself before he catches up to me. I spin around the space, looking for a place to hide. I want to continue this game of chase, but also desperately want to be caught. I'm just pulling the closet door closed after darting in when I hear the bedroom door close on the other side of my hiding space. A moment later, music starts pouring through Jacob's sound system. It's a heavy beat, but it's not loud enough to cover the sounds of my desperate breaths.

The closet door is yanked open, and the silhouette of Jacob fills the frame. He looks menacing, out of control, and like everything I've ever craved. He steps into the walk-in closet and takes my wrist, pulling me through the now open door and to the center of his room.

He slowly turns toward me, and I take in the man before me. His eyes are not just the normal blue-grey I've come to expect. They look almost silver in the dim lighting, and they are bright—as if he's lit up from within.

"I've got you now, Han. What shall I do with my prize?" he asks to himself. He walks a slow circle around me, and I feel his eyes trailing up and down my body as he inspects his prize.

Reaching my line of sight again, he steps toward me, his hands remaining at his sides, both curled into fists. He makes no move to touch me again now that he's caught me.

Just as I'm about to ask if this is *finally* happening, he opens his mouth. "How—" he starts, hesitating for just a second, "How could we have ignored this for so long? Pushed it under the rug? Do you feel it, too? As if there's electricity zapping under your skin? As if you'll perish if you don't succumb?" His voice ends in a whisper, almost as if he's speaking to himself again.

A shiver makes its way through my body at his tone. "I know what you mean. What is it you need right now, Jacob?" I ask boldly, hoping all of the dancing we've done around the topic and small touches are finally leading to something more. We've spent a lot of time talking and discussing how we want our relationship to work. Still, we've delayed sex to build our tenuous foundation in regards to adding the romantic element. There have been soft touches through the night, small dates when we could slip away, and kisses both gentle and reverent across the forehead, and others so soul-stealing it felt as if I'd left my body.

"You," he answers my question about his needs after a moment of thought. "I need you as you are, Han. I need your trust in this. But I also need you to remember your words if it's ever too much." He isn't unsure of himself, but I can see a hint of worry in his gaze. I think he's afraid he's going to scare me off.

"Stop is 'Red,' slow down or ease off is 'Yellow,'" I list off. We'd talked about having ridiculous safe words, but why not stick with simple? There's a reason they're the most popular. Although Ivy calling Lucas "Red" makes it a bit ridiculous and will instantly pull both of us out of the mood with laughter.

"Excellent." Jacob's praise is subtle, but his grin is impossible to look away from. "Take my cock out," he orders.

Oh, yes, *please*. I lift my hands to his button, working it through the loop and lowering his zipper achingly slowly. He may be running this show, but that doesn't mean I can't do things my way. It doesn't mean there isn't power in each of my movements as he stands above me, controlling the situation. I drop down to my knees, finding myself at eye level with the bulge hidden behind black boxer briefs.

I slide my hands up his firm, ink-blackened thighs, my fingertips reaching to touch his hard cock and bumping over each tempting piercing. I see his hardness jump at the contact behind his boxer briefs, and my own dick mimics the movement. I continue my exploration and curl my fingers around the elastic of his underwear's waistband. Peeling it down, his cock escapes its confinement and bobs in front of my face. His underwear slips over his thighs and pools at his feet like an offering to whatever god decided to put us on the same team all those years ago.

I lick my lips and dive forward as my hands push the rest of the fabric down his legs. My tongue runs a path from his base to his tip, gliding over the metal bars on his shaft until I reach the head. With a flick to the piercing at the tip, I sit back on my heels, watching the rest of the strip show.

Jacob slips one foot from the material around his ankles, and shifting his weight, uses the other leg to fling the clothes to the side. His hands deftly undo the buttons of his shirt until he's shrugging it off of his shoulders and tossing it next to his slacks.

I maintain eye contact and open my mouth wide. He takes the invitation and moves one step forward, one hand gripping his cock so hard his knuckles are pale. I place my hand over his and guide it up and down, stroking him in strong, sure strokes until I see the quiver in his abdomen start to increase.

Removing his hand, I grip the backs of his thighs and pull him forward until his cock is immediately in front of my face. I shoot him a playful wink and descend. My mouth envelops his hot, thick cock, and I work my way up and down. My lips are stretched wide to accommodate him, but the strain is of no consequence. I'm entirely too high on his taste, the feel of his muscles under my palms, and the sounds of his ragged breath above me, groans slipping free every few thrusts, every note of his pleasure still discernible over the sound of the music in the room.

Hollowing my cheeks, I work him until I feel his hips start to move of their own accord. The thrusting is still gentle, still tentative, so I relax my throat and pull him closer until I feel him bump the back of my throat.

"Oh, bloody fuck, Han," comes the growly voice above me. I relax my throat as he pushes in again and take the opportunity to swallow him down. Jacob pauses at the back of my throat, and saliva pools in my mouth. He pulls back and pushes back in, giving me enough time to breathe between each thrust as I take all of him down.

I moan around him when the taste of his precum hits my tongue on the withdrawal. He enjoys that immensely—what man doesn't?—and continues fucking my face as I encourage him with my hands gripping the backs of his thighs.

"Enough," he groans out. "Enough. I won't last much longer. Where the fuck is your gag reflex?" he asks in bewilderment.

I release him with a satisfying pop to answer his question, "Never had one," I shrug. It's not something we've ever needed to talk about.

His eyes go wide as he clears his throat before putting his index finger under my chin, and the pressure tells me he wants me to stand. I surge to my feet, my body bending to his will, my dick aching with anticipation for what's to come.

"Strip," he orders. My dick, my poor dick, gets harder than I thought possible at his command. I reach behind my neck, dragging the soft t-shirt over my head, and toss it into the pile Jacob started. His eyes never leave mine as I drag my sweats down as well. I went commando today under my black sweats, so I divest myself of the soft material and kick it to the side. I stand before Jacob naked and proud.

His eyes leave mine and trail down my body. I see the slight flare of his lids as he takes me in like it's the very first time, and not as if we'd been naked in front of each other countless times with either Ivy or the other women we'd had threesomes with over the years.

In a way, I get it. It's an entirely different circumstance, and exploring something for the first time with someone is the most natural high you can find.

Chest puffed and dick aching, I step toward Jacob. His hands finally uncurl, and he places them on the junctures between my shoulders and neck. His forehead comes to rest on mine. "On the bed," he whispers, no less commanding with his soft tone.

I retreat a few steps, his hands still on me as he follows me down. His weight on my body is euphoric. He licks his lips before he leans in for a punishing kiss that has me lifting my hips in a bid to grind with his. Jacob gives an experimental thrust against me, and his hard cock sliding next to mine elicits a groan from the back of my throat. Tongues, teeth, and breath coming together create a new soundtrack, layering over the song still playing on repeat from Jacob's speakers.

Lifting his weight and sitting back on his heels, Jacob releases me and takes my cock in his hand. His grip is firm and unrelenting, even as my hips start lifting to meet him stroke for stroke. He plants a hand on my hip, keeping my lower body from moving. I'm confident I'll have a bruise in the morning, but I'm beyond caring at this point. I want his mark on me. I want to look in the mirror tomorrow morning and be reminded of every moment that transpired.

He scoots forward on his knees, bringing his dick next to mine, and grips both in his big hand. He starts pumping our cocks together, and the sensation is indescribable.

He leans down, circling my nipple with his tongue, before biting down just as his hold on our cocks tightens to a vice that has my balls pulling up. Between his grip and the anticipation of this moment finally taking place, I know I'm close. Jacob must sense this as his grip relaxes a bit, and he leans over me, his right hand digging in the nightstand drawer.

"We're going to start off slow," he tells me. "But soon, I want you tied up, hanging from the anchors in the ceiling while I fuck your tight ass."

My mind completely empties, and tingles run up and down my spine at the image he's just planted in my mind. Good fucking God, *yes*.

"God has nothing to do with this," he assures me. Okay, my filter must be broken because I said that out loud. Jacob looks at my face and lets out

The Sacrifices We Make

that dark chuckle I love so much. He leans in, his lips next to my ear, and whispers, "Turn over."

He pulls back to give me the space to move, his hand withdraws from the drawer with a bottle of lube, and my hands clench into fists with delicious anticipation. I'm facing down, ass up, when I feel Jacob skim his hands up my thighs until they land on my ass. He lets out a groan before leaning over me, trailing kisses along my shoulder blades and down my back.

"Remember your words?" he asks me tentatively, almost as if he's afraid I'm going to change my mind now. I'm not.

"Yes. But I doubt I'll need them. Red to stop, yellow to slow down or back off." My answer pleases him if the quick slap to my ass and the soothing palm that follows is any indication.

I hear the snap of the lube bottle and feel it drip down my crack. Jacob's hand follows the line, and I feel pressure at my hole. He teases the entrance until I'm pushing back in encouragement.

"Patience," he snaps. Another smack to my ass makes me groan, and with that, he pushes one finger into me, testing the stretch. As my moans continue, he withdraws and inserts two digits, scissoring them and preparing me for what's to come.

My hips start to rock involuntarily, and I reach one hand under me to fist my own cock. The decadent pressure, my own fist tight around my dick, and the feel of Jacob's body heat behind me send bliss pulsing through my body, settling something inside me. This feels *right*. Ivy feels right, too, and I love that she's encouraged us to figure out what we want from each other without it being a detriment to any of our relationships.

Jacob adds a third finger after a few minutes, and I nearly come as the stretch becomes just this side of too much. "Fuck, Han. You're going to take my cock so good," he groans.

All I can do is pant out a succession of "Yes, yes, fuck yes," until his fingers withdraw entirely.

"Whose ass is this?" he asks me. Possessive Jacob has arrived, and I. Am. Here. For. It.

"Yours. It's yours and Ivy's." That gives him pause, but he doesn't know about the toys we'd been messing around with before she had to move in with Romano because she knew I'd been nervous about taking Jacob's cock due to the size.

He lets out a groan as his fingers sink into my hair. He pulls my head back and to the side so I can see him over my shoulder. "Has she fucked you with toys?" he asks. I nod my head, and he expels a hiss through his lush lips. "Next time, I want to see that."

With that declaration, he pushes my head back down, his hand moving to the middle of my upper back as he puts pressure there, encouraging me to sink my lower body. It traps my arm under my body as I continue stroking my cock. I hear the lube again, and the chill of the substance along my crack makes me clench for a moment.

Jacob slides his dick through the liquid a few times, coating himself. He pauses at my entrance and starts to slowly push in.

I relax my body and push back when he reaches the tight ring of muscle, allowing him entrance. He rocks his body a few times, easing his way in. As they breach my body, the piercings are a new, foreign sensation to me, but I love them all the same. He's careful as he is with everything, and the soft words of encouragement spilling from his lips continue until he's worked his way in, one tantalizing inch at a time.

Once he's seated all the way in, the tension leaves his hand, still settled on my back. "Fuuuuuck," he groans. "So fucking tight. So mine."

He pulls out a bit and pushes back in. My breath leaves my body as he pushes in again and again and again. His thrusts begin picking up pace, his hips snapping against my ass. My hand is suddenly pulled away from my cock as he reaches around me and takes it in his own grasp.

I pull my arm from under my body and use it, as well as the free one, to grip the lavender-scented pillow before me. I just know that I'll be thinking of this moment any time I smell this scent in the future. Jacob's hand commences at a punishing pace, stroking me to the same tempo of his hips driving into me from behind.

His grip tightens as he jerks me off, and his hips start stuttering in their rhythm. We're both so close to the finish line and when he guides his other hand under me to roll my balls in the palm of his hand, I lose it. My eyes scrunch shut as the shiver races through my body, and I come hard, releasing ropes of cum onto the sheet below me.

Slowing his strokes, Jacob releases me once I'm spent and grips my hips, yanking my ass onto his cock as he matches his pace to the music playing in the room. He thrusts one, two, three more times, and I feel his angle change as he arches his back and empties himself into me.

He continues pumping into me for a few moments as he comes down from his high before pulling out and toppling over to the side, taking me with him and away from the mess we've made on the sheets.

The Sacrifices We Make

I turn my body so I'm facing him, looking into his blissed-out eyes as he trails his fingertips along my cheek.

"Was that okay?" he asks me with a hint of nerves in his voice. "I've... I've never done that before."

I lean in and capture his lips with mine, leading our kiss this time. "It was perfect," I say as I pull back, relinquishing his mouth. "No need for safe words this time."

He laughs at that, knowing I'd use them if I needed them. "Wait till I pull out the ropes." His grin stretches his lips, and he looks giddy as the ideas form in his mind. I groan as my cock starts to harden again at the scenarios, and Jacob just lets out a surprisingly loud laugh as he leans in to retake my lips.

"Come on, we should get cleaned up so we can help in getting Lucas home." Jacob's reminder about what brought about his sudden elation has me experiencing a weird mixture of horniness and curiosity.

"What'd you find, anyway?" I ask, needing to know what's next on the cards for us.

Jacob tsks firmly and adds, "Really, I just want to go over this once because I know if I explain it now, you're going to run off and do something reckless. On rare occasions, you've flown off the handle regarding things affecting those of us on the team. We can't afford you blowing up buildings today."

I let out a laugh. "One time! That happened one time." Jacob shoots me a look, knowing I'm full of shit. "Okay, six times."

He leads me out of the room to clean up in the bathroom, where we dawdle a bit longer before meeting Noah in the war room. He's on the phone with someone, telling them we're done with the assignment, and we're pulling Lucas.

He nods his head a few times, and with a gruff, "Yes, ma'am," he hangs up the phone. It must've been Mara on the other end of the line. Noah knows Jacob would make any copies of data and keep it here before handing off the intel.

Thank God we're not dealing with Patton Cross on this one. That man gives me the heebie-jeebies, but he's one of our bosses, so I deal with it.

Time to get one of our missing team members home. If only we could swing by and grab Ivy on our way home, my day would be complete.

Chapter Seventeen

Romano

Despite the tentative alliance Rogue and I made during our time at the cabin in Mammoth Village for our fake-as-fuck honeymoon, she closed herself off as soon as we went to that board meeting. I don't know what I expected, but icing me out again wasn't it.

I noticed the shift after the meeting. On the way there, she had threatened me with her knife as I tried flipping to a different radio station, a ghost of a smile dancing upon her lips. Whatever she, King, and De La Cruz discussed after sending the rest of us out must have been something big. I haven't picked up anything out of the ordinary in her day-to-day since then, but it's as if every inch of our progress has vanished.

Since the abrupt change, she's been off dealing with her hitmen. I saw "G" flash on her phone yesterday, and she hasn't been back to the apartment since. I know he's one of hers, the same way I know all of Enrique De La Cruz's dealers, Elise's political and rich contacts, and Wilson's account numbers. The same way I know King's real name is Kadir.

The shrill ringtone of my phone rings from the kitchen countertop, breaking me out of my musings as I stir the vegetable soup I've been working on. I look at the number and roll my eyes. Great.

"Romano," I answer as I usually would. Who knows if King ended up replacing the bugs Rogue ripped out of the vents and furniture after the last meeting? She said King wouldn't replace them with vehemence in her tone, but I'd rather be far too safe than have him know who I'm *actually* working for.

"Who is your least favorite cousin?" Shade's deep voice on the other end of the line asks. Gotta love the security hoops we jump through.

"Damiano," I answer with ease. "Where are my guns?" I ask. My security question had to be something I could ask if someone was nearby and listening when they shouldn't have been.

"Your favorite is probably in your holster on your hip, but the rest are in storage locker number five-nine-two on the third floor."

Identities verified, I let out a breath. You never know what you'll run into in my line of work.

"Where are we on the girl?" he asks. I immediately bristle a little.

Rogue providing evidence on King has been the objective from the beginning. The marriage was a blessing in disguise, but agreeing to it too quickly wouldn't have sat right with King. I had to put up some arguments to make it more believable. That kind of inside information would be a goldmine if only I could get her to open up.

He raised her, and despite her circumstances, she seems to be able to think for herself when all he wants are mindless minions. Getting her to trust me has been an exercise in futility when she barely even spoke to me before moving in together. Even then, it wasn't great at the beginning. It was the honeymoon that had her opening up a little. Her offering me a chance to prove myself is precisely the kind of in I was looking for. When I was Horvat's second, I was never close enough to King to pick up anything of value. Aside from distancing himself from the underlings, he's notoriously well-guarded by Rogue when they're together and by his extraordinarily well-trained security team when they're not.

"Playing along, but there's been a recent setback," I answer. Once again, my mind was left on what might have happened at that meeting after I left. Rogue came out of the lobby and was quieter than usual after breaking some of the ice in the cabin. She's gone back to the way she was before the getaway, and those steps in the wrong direction only make me think this will take far longer than I had hoped.

"But there's been progress. That's good, Romano. Keep it up, and do what you need to gain her trust. Do you need anything at the moment?" Shade asks.

I think about it, and, deciding there's nothing urgent besides getting the documents Rogue needs from King before she can make a move, I get

Shade on it. Fortunately, there isn't much on the net this man can't find. I'm supposed to meet King tomorrow morning, and I'll start poking for information, but it doesn't hurt to have someone on the outside working on it as well.

"Yeah, got any ideas for an attorney? I want one who won't ask too many questions, can handle wills, and can protect my money in this marriage. Find one our mutual friend might use." Hopefully, that's enough info for him to connect the dots.

"Ah, your boss's attorney? Asking him hasn't given you results?" inquires Shade, and I hear the tapping of his keyboard over the line. He prefers the ones that click-clack every time you press a key, which drives me mad.

"Haven't tried yet. But apparently, it's a company secret. See what you can do." My tone tells him how important this could be, so with a reminder to be safe and intelligent, not to break cover, and not to get caught, Shade hangs up to get to work.

I make a few calls about the Vegas Crew trade deal. Thanks to Nina's bribes along the route, the guns are on their way, free from any local police deciding to stop our trucks. One of their guys handed over the deposit this week, and the guns were sent out. They should be arriving in the next hour or two. The money will be handed over to my second, Lee, and then it's out of my hands. I've done my job.

I spend the night reviewing my notes on the members of The Gambit that I have stored on my laptop, buried under a million spreadsheets on finance, only glancing at the door or my phone every fifteen minutes or so, wondering when Rogue is coming back. By two o'clock, I've given up hope of talking it out tonight. Repairing whatever bridge has been burned at this hour would only lead to more confusion as my eyelids threaten to close of their own accord.

I WAKE UP IN STAGES BEFORE MY ALARM CAN SOUND OFF. BEATING the clock means I don't do the "zombie thing," as Rogue calls it. The shrill alarm always has me jolting out of bed, and, having seen it a few times now, she says it looks like a corpse being reanimated.

Knowing it will be chilly outside of the blanket burrito I'm wrapped in and already dreading the meeting with King for breakfast in a couple of hours, I give in to temptation and snuggle further into the warm covers of the bed. It can't be later than five or so, which gives me another hour to snooze.

I shift on the bed but bump into something in front of me. Ah, shit.

Cracking open a bleary, overly-tired eye, I see a spill of black hair in my face and quickly figure out that I've woken up while spooning my wife. She stirs, no doubt woken by my squirming and trying to pull myself free without waking her.

She rolls over to face me and mumbles, "Captain." Huh, I wonder what that's about?

I breathe a sigh of relief that only one of us is awake for the accidental snuggling, slowly extricate myself, and only jostle her once or twice in the process. She must have come home late if she's zonked out this hard.

I grab my phone, head to the closet, pull a suit out, and enter the bathroom to get ready. She needs sleep if those dark circles I saw were any indication. She also smells faintly of smoke, almost like a campfire, and I notice it's more potent in the bathroom. I lift the laundry basket lid, and there are some clothes in there emanating the smell. I push the lid down and make a mental note to send the basket out to be cleaned today. That will stink up the apartment in no time if we keep opening the lid.

I shower, shave, brush my teeth, and dress in the small space. It's only half past five, so I mainline coffee and read the news until it's time to meet King at eight.

I take the public elevator up to his floor after pushing the button and waiting for him to give me access. He invited me to discuss my marriage and future with the organization. He didn't say much more than that, but I can't help but wonder if he and Rogue discussed it after the board meeting last week.

Whatever it is, it might give me an opening to ask about legal advice and get the name of his attorney Rogue is after.

Arriving at the penthouse, I cross the marble foyer after being frisked by his ever-present security and make my way to the grand room in the center. King is sitting at the formal dining table in the open-plan living area, dressed more casually than I've ever seen him.

He's got loose black linen pants around his legs and a plain white t-shirt covering his torso. His hair isn't styled as usual, and his bare feet are the biggest shock to my system. I don't think I've ever seen this man out of his three-piece suit and designer loafers, and it has me all out of sorts. Hell, it's why I'm always in suits. It was to make me appear more similar to him and thus curry favor with him.

The Sacrifices We Make

"Romano, come sit." He waves a hand at the chair to his right because, of fucking course, he's at the head of the table. I doubt he's chosen a different seating position since he took up the mantle as the organization's head.

I feel fucking ridiculous in my suit at this hour while he's still clearly lounging in pajamas. Although, maybe that's a tactic, a way to put me on edge in some twisted psychological ploy. Clearing my throat, I reach the table and unbutton my suit jacket as I lower myself into the chair.

As soon as I land, one server comes out with a platter of breakfast foods, and another brings a carafe of coffee. I've already had three cups while killing time this morning, but another wouldn't hurt, considering how little sleep I got last night and how wrong it felt waking up with Rogue in my arms.

King is busy making a plate of eggs, bacon, and fruit while I opt for toast and cheese and continue fueling my caffeine addiction with yet another cup.

Knowing better than to try and start a conversation with King before he's ready, I tuck into my small plate and wait. And wait, and wait. We've spent a bit of time together since I was called up to the big leagues, and every time I tried to start the conversation before he was prepared, I was reprimanded or looked at how a parent looks at their errant child when they misbehave. The asshole is only a bit older than me but lords his position over everyone, making them feel small and inconsequential in comparison.

He's just finished the last of his cantaloupe when he clears his throat, drawing my attention. "*This* is why I picked you for Rogue. You know your place in this hierarchy and can lend your support behind the scenes. So tell me, how is the marriage going?"

Biting back the retort on the tip of my tongue, I simply nod in agreement with the first part of his statement, using the moment to calm my anger. "The marriage is going well so far, I'd say. She's still a bit standoffish, but she's coming around."

"Good." He looks like he expected that answer, and part of me wants to take it back just to watch that smug expression slip from his face. "And the Vegas deal is done?"

"Yes. I got confirmation this morning. Our guys have the cash and have yet to run into any problems crossing back into our territory. I'm meeting them after this."

King muses for a second, running his fingertips along the lip of a saucer in front of him. "We need to keep an eye on them. They are amassing weapons and have been on a major recruiting spree in the last three months."

My associate up north in The Rattlesnakes' territory told me the same. They've been watching the Vegas Crew as well. But little does King know, the Crew won't be an issue much longer. "What can we do?" I ask, knowing he's putting the information out there to bait me. Horvat never mentioned anything about spying on the other gangs. I assumed it was something someone else handled for the board."

"You wouldn't have been brought up to speed on that. It wasn't for your pay grade." King waves his hand as if that's all in the past before continuing, "In any case, it's something you'll start monitoring and working on. I'll provide the backing to hire however many bodies you need to keep your sights on them. Dealing with The Rattlesnakes is enough for the moment. I want to cut the legs out from under the Vegas Crew if they step even one foot west of their territory lines. Understood?"

"Yes, sir," I respond.

"Good. As for your marriage, I'm pleased you two are putting in some effort. However, I was not too pleased that Rogue insisted on removing the bugs. That girl has always been abnormally headstrong, but if it helps her...adjust to the marriage more quickly, I'll let it slide. No more bugs are in the apartment, so I suggest you use it to ingratiate yourself to her, Romano."

Catching his drift to lock down Rogue as quickly as possible, I can't help but ask, "Why me, King? Not that I'm complaining, but Rogue is more than capable of finding her own husband. One she actually wants, no less."

King lets out a sigh as if he's dealing with a moron, and I kind of see his point. From his point of view, he must think he's allowed me to marry a beautiful girl and end up at the head of a criminal empire all in one fell swoop.

"You'll be good for her. You respect her, but more importantly, I think you understand better than most what would happen to you if you step out of line. Only instead of being a widower, like you, she'd be a widow. Understand now?"

I fix my gaze on him. The deep brown of his eyes looks almost black in the dark lighting, and I suppress the chill that tries to work its way through my body as he continues speaking. "It is unfortunate your wife got caught in the crossfire all those years ago. I would hate for the same to happen to you. Though you haven't given me any reason to blow *you* to kingdom come, have you?"

The Sacrifices We Make

Fighting every instinct I have to rip into him for bringing her up, I clamp down on my immediate reaction and shake my head. He's aware she died, and his emphasis on certain words makes it sound almost as if she were an intended target and not a bystander. I can't let that get to me right now. Amara is gone, and there are bigger things at play than my bleeding and broken heart.

I see an opening to start prodding for information and take my shot. "No, King. If you want me with Rogue, I'm with Rogue. The organization has been good to me these past few years. I'll pay my dues, but I want to align our lives. You know, further tie her to me so she doesn't get any ideas. Do you have an attorney you recommend for such things?"

I fucking hate talking about someone I respect like that, but I know the way he thinks, the way he binds people to him. I cross my fingers and hope he takes the bait.

"Hmm," he pauses as he tilts his head, considering my idea. "I think you might be onto something there. You know she fucked someone right before your wedding, right? You might want to take care of him before she gets ideas to continue that little tryst while you're married. I think wrapping your lives together from a legal standpoint might pressure her to play along. At least until you two have your own little one to raise." My involuntary shock at the last statement has not gone unnoticed.

King scoffs, "Did you think it would just be you two? Oh, no, Romano. When I said she would carry on the line, I fucking meant it. But yes, I keep a few lawyers off the books for things like this. I'll find the right one for the job. And you, you'll make sure Rogue is yours in every way that counts. As I told her, I don't need you two to be in love. I need you to back her, support her when she takes my place, and carry. On. The. Line. Oh, and we're having a meeting tonight. Let my daughter know."

I drain the last of my coffee, distractedly asking if there's anything else as the bile threatens to rise up my throat. I'm dismissed with a terse "no" and a wave of King's hand. I cross the living space and enter the elevator with a parting nod from one of King's security guys.

Instead of heading out to meet with the guys I sent to Vegas, I veer off my original course, stopping the elevator and heading to the apartment I share with Rogue. I find myself out of sorts as I exit and stomp my way down the hall. My breath is coming in gasps, and I feel the flush rising up my neck.

I tear into the apartment and find Rogue hovering over a mug of coffee that says *The Buttercup Whisperer*. I briefly wonder what that's about before shaking my head and focusing on the matter at hand.

She looks up briefly but does a double-take when she takes in my frazzled appearance. "What the fuck happened now?" she asks, voice still gravelly with sleep.

"First, there are no more bugs here, thanks to you. So, one point to you. Second, did you know King wants you to pop out some kind of heir to his fucked up kingdom? He threatened me, so that's pretty typical for a breakfast meeting, and mentioned my wife, so I'm on edge at the moment. Oh, and also, there's a meeting tonight." I think that's it.

"Yep, no bugs. I told King I didn't want to fuck you as his security team listens."

She doesn't continue with the rest of the topics—intentionally withholding information and her reaction—and I rake my hands through my hair for the millionth time since I entered the elevator, confused as fuck as to how she's so calm about this. "Anything else you want to add?"

"I'll clear my schedule for the meeting?" she says in a teasing voice that has me pacing the tiny living room as she stands, casual as fuck, in the kitchen wearing an Avengers t-shirt and some leggings.

"You honestly have nothing to say about the whole 'pop out a kid' thing?" I shout at her.

Her eyes flash a dangerous look in my direction, and she lifts the coffee mug to her lips, drinking deeply before setting it in front of her. "Be smart, asshole. Of course, King wants us to procreate. What could bring us together more? But *that's* not happening. Maybe my uterus is fucked up; maybe you're infertile. We'll figure out a way to sidestep that for the time being. King wasn't subtle when he brought it up last week."

"Is that why you shut down after the meeting?" I dare to ask. She sighs and shrugs her shoulders. "A head's up would have been nice, Rogue. He also suggested I 'take care of' whoever you slept with before our wedding. Please tell me you've stopped since we've been married for the sake of whoever it was. The last thing either of us wants is King killing someone else who matters to us."

Rogue looks off to the side with stress marring her features. Without her mask in place and the makeup she uses to shield her face from the world, I'm reminded that she's young. Way too young to be embroiled in this world and handed off to a man like me.

"It's not going to be an issue. I'm not seeing *anyone* at the moment." Her voice cracking on the word "anyone" gives me pause, but I let it go, knowing my voice is a little odd in the morning before my third cup of coffee.

"Okay. I also asked King for a lawyer to bind our lives together." As she gears up to rip into me, no doubt, I put up my hands in a gesture of surrender and continue before she can assume the worst. "Not to *actually* get us stuck together for all time, but I figure if there's someone he trusts with that, it might just be the one he has handling the information you need back."

"I—" she starts, releasing a breath, "I'm mildly impressed, Romano. Good work."

"Does that mean you'll start letting me in on your plans for King?" I ask, hoping this gains me a little favor with her.

"Not a chance. Until those are in my hand and wiped from everywhere else, you're on the outs, bud." With that disappointing statement, she saunters off, patting me twice on the shoulder condescendingly, and makes her way back to our room.

Well, at least I got a nickname this time. In the past week, Rogue's been icing me out at every turn, shooting down any attempt at conversation.

I wait until I hear the shower running and loud music pouring from the Bluetooth speakers before calling Shade.

We go through the song and dance of verifying our identities, and I dive in. "Our mutual friend wants to 'carry on the line.' He's also pulling lawyers for me. Did you get any leads on possible candidates?"

"In the twelve hours since we've spoken? Yeah, like forty-two, but I thought I'd narrow it down a bit first. Also, if what you said means what I think it means, I call godfather." Cheeky bastard.

"First, thanks. Second, fuck no," I laugh. Shade is a bit of a loon, but he's good at what he does. "Listen, there's been another meeting called tonight. I'll call you after and keep you posted, but the last meeting that was called out of the normal schedule didn't go well for one member in particular. I have a feeling tonight will be the same."

"*First*," Shade emphasizes, mimicking me, "I'd make an excellent godparent. But I catch your drift. In and out. Nothing ties you to this life once you're out." Ain't that the God's truth. "Second, keep your head down and get what you can. No one cares about the other members apart from what they have on K."

"Yeah, you're right. Anything specific to watch for this week?"

"The new governor is coming through the city in a few days. We know his route and planned stops, including visiting a certain high-society queen bee, so I'll get you the details. Otherwise, all good, man. You need anything?"

"Just that list of lawyers so I can cross-reference when I get the other list. Narrowing it down between the two will give me somewhere to start. It's the only way to get in her good graces, man."

The music volume drops and the shower turns off. "I gotta go. Keep me posted. I'll call tomorrow. Over and out."

"Over and out," he parrots back.

AFTER FINISHING OUR TASKS FOR THE DAY, ROGUE AND I PILE INTO her car and head to Rook Industries for the meeting King called. She stuffs a duffle bag in the trunk, and I'm almost afraid to ask what's inside.

When I finally couldn't take it anymore and had to know, she just shrugged and said she was prepared for anything. The mask was firmly in place, all jokes were gone, and the soft smiles she hid from the world were nowhere to be found. These days, it's like talking to someone else entirely.

She parks in the underground lot and climbs out of the car. I follow suit and meet her by the trunk, which she lifts and pulls a duffle bag from. It makes a rattling sound as she slings it over her shoulder, but maybe it's better that I don't know what she has planned. She's never brought a bag to a meeting before, at least that I've seen, so it piques my interest, but I don't bother asking when I know I won't get an answer.

She slams the trunk closed, and we make our way to the elevator in silence. The ride is equally quiet, but I use the time to slip my own mask on.

You are Francesco Romano. You are a member of the board for The Gambit. Your wife died at the hands of these assholes. You give no shits about their internal politics. You. Will. End. Them.

Repeating those thoughts for the duration of the ride, I feel a calm mask settle over my face as we reach the designated floor. Rogue steps out ahead of me, her hips sway in a fitted grey dress, and her black pumps pound out a menacing beat as she walks through the halls to the meeting room.

I follow a step behind her, keeping her within arm's reach. Maybe King was onto something with the idea I'd be backing her up. It's hard not to fall into line after this woman. She moves confidently and doesn't entertain folly when in work mode.

We're five minutes earlier than the appointed meeting time, yet we're the last to arrive. I pull the chair out for Rogue, and she leans, brushing her lips to my cheek. *Ah, we're back to acting.*

Tanaka, Batten, and Wilson are opposite us on the other side of the table, and I see more than a few eyebrows raised. Elise claps her hands together with glee, but when I look at her face, she's staring at my ass. I've batted her hands away from me more times than I can count, and despite her claiming "my mind must be slipping," I know she's full of shit.

Speaking of Elise, I've heard a rumor about her intentions of marrying the new governor and creating a political alliance against King. I have that information in my back pocket, but I refuse to give it up. I want all sides working against this asshole.

Rogue sits in the chair, and I guide it forward to get her settled. The bag is dropped on the floor next to her feet, and I take my place beside her.

King calls the meeting to order as soon as my ass hits the chair. "Board, have we given Enrique De La Cruz sufficient time to get his house in order?"

"We have." The echo of voices is ominous and something Horvat told me about the meetings. When King addresses the room about a member, we must respond. There is no sitting one out. No riding the fence.

"Enrique, have you put your dealers back in line?" King asks. His eyes roving over the bald man next to me.

"As much as I can, King. If you'll give me—" He's cut off with a bark of laughter from King.

"I will give you nothing more. You have had time. Your dealers are still doing the work we've forbidden." He turns to the rest of us. "I motion to eliminate Enrique De La Cruz from the board and, in doing so, end his life. All those in agreement?"

Chapter Eighteen

Lucas

"Banks are everything that's wrong with the world!" I shout as security guards on either side haul me from the middle of my floor at the bank. "Soul-sucking, creativity-stifling..." My words are cut off as a fist haphazardly connects with my solar plexus.

"Wanted to go out in a blaze of glory, did you?" Security Guard Number One with the sloppy punch asks. I like to imagine their names are something like Gene and Neville, but we all know that they're just walk-ons, not noticeable enough to have a designated name in the credits of this movie.

I relax my body and become a dead weight between the two guards, causing more of a headache. I've always wanted to quit a job by going out with a bang, and boy, did I.

It's just past eight o'clock in the office, and we all stayed late to connect with a conference call for one of the bank's big clients. Noah called me yesterday and said that I could come home, but I really—*really*—wanted to do this, so instead of asking for permission and telling him my intentions, I just kind of rolled with the idea and then spent too much at an arts and crafts store.

I had to come back for one last day anyway to wipe evidence of our snooping by collecting the thumb drives and SD cards Jacob gave me. So I wandered around, making excuses to go into others' offices to snag the hardware from the computers I had hijacked with Jacob's tech.

Tonight was just for me. I've got the tech in the hidden pocket in my suit jacket, and I got here ridiculously early to set this up.

When the call was knee-deep in negotiations with the client—some start-up owner with more money than he knows what to do with—and Mr. Hess was in the middle of explaining the lengths our professional team would go to to make him happy, the first chair exploded. Okay, maybe "exploded" isn't the proper term. It fell apart, and the chair's occupant, Mr. Ortega, tilted to one side as the seat part of the chair slipped away from the base. It was hilarious, and I swear, it happened in slow motion. A burst of eggplant emoji confetti and bright green glitter shot out from the chair's base, causing a mushroom cloud of sparkles in the meeting room. Other people turned to the sound and objectionable confetti boom, thus resulting in more broken chairs and eggplant bombs.

It's funny what loosening a few screws before a meeting can do. Then, of course, putting a pressurized contraption between the wheel guards and the seat portion set to detonate as soon as any weight is removed after the initial pressure. In the aftermath, I was the last one in my chair, feet propped up on the table as the client looked on in horror at the unprofessionalism and chaos through the screen.

Hess put it together pretty quickly as he dusted himself free of the offending confetti mixed with a bit of glitter—which will be a bitch to dry clean—and ended the call with the client. His face turned an intriguing shade of red, then purple, and I swear, I saw more than a few capillaries burst in the whites of his eyes.

He fired me on the spot, so here I am, being hauled out by security, having checked something off of my bucket list.

Security drags me into the elevator, each man still gripping my arm as if I'm going to run off like a new puppy, and we make our way down to the lobby. I'm shouting ridiculous things as we pass each floor, hoping whoever is still here is entertained by my nonsense. There's no point in being intentionally insane if there's no one there to witness your performance.

I run a silent check and feel the slight weight in my suit jacket on the left side, meaning the hardware is still with me, and I feel my phone buzzing in my pocket. After shouting, "If you have no interest in banking, you are not *a-loan!*" between floors three and two on our descent, I get another hit to the gut, and security promptly drags me through the lobby and out the door.

The Sacrifices We Make

I land on the concrete with barely a scratch, and I have to admit, that was super fun.

I pull my phone from my pocket and see a new text from Buttercup, but I have her saved as something boring because of this whole undercover schtick.

Cindy with the IRS: I'm coming for you with the Batmobile. Get your ass outside your apartment in 20 minutes. I've got a surprise for you.

I hope it's sex. I really, really do. This stupid assignment has taken forever, and it feels like it's been months since our rendezvous in the church.

I grab a cab and head to my rented apartment, arriving a few minutes before her appointed time. She's already there, lounging against Black Beauty in a sinful grey dress and a pair of black heels, but she's not alone. She's got her husband with her. *Ah, shit. It's probably not sex.*

"Hiya, Red. You know Romano," she says as I approach, her voice hard and unyielding. Not exactly the excited tone or breathy sighs I was hoping for, but I know she's been in her head lately. Living with someone you're not sure you can trust in an apartment monitored by a psychopath has made her walls build back up brick by brick. The man in question was looking down at his phone but snapped his head up at the introduction. When he makes eye contact with me, a huge grin spreads over his stupidly handsome face, and he extends his hand for a shake.

"Hey, man. You still owe me a few beers and an explanation of how you know Rogue."

Points to him for not calling her his wife.

"What are you guys doing here?" I ask curiously. I know this isn't a social call since she's brought along the baggage. It's also not a sex visit, so I'm doubly disappointed.

"Get in; we've got some work to do. This one," Buttercup points at Romano, "wouldn't get out of the car when we left our board meeting, so he's coming with us. Guess it's one way to know if we can trust him." She pauses for a second, looking at my dark brown-dyed hair, and lifts her hand. "Is that an eggplant in your hair?" she asks.

I hear a muffled sound, and the car gently rocks.

"Buttercup, is there someone in your trunk?" I ask curiously, my lips curling into a sinister grin. It's been ages since I've had a good tussle.

She smirks and sends me a wink; the mask she has on slips with the gesture, "Sure is. You want in?"

"Fuck, yes. Let's go. Shotgun!" I call before Romano thinks he gets any more time with my girl than he's already stealing. "We'll get beers after."

And with that decision made, we pile into the car, and my girl drives us to a mechanic's shop. The guy in the workshop, who she greets as Axle, hands over a set of keys, and once we drive into the bay, he pulls the drop-down shutters so we're sealed inside. He was good about not looking into the car to see who my girl had with her. I admire the deference others give her, and I *love* take-your-boyfriend-and-husband-to-work day.

Once the shutters are dropped, Buttercup opens her door and bangs on the trunk twice to get whoever is in there to be quiet as she makes her way to the bay doors. She locks the mechanism to the right to keep them sealed and meets Romano and me at the car's trunk.

"I'm going to need some help getting him downstairs. There's a workroom for me built into the basement section," Buttercup tells us.

I'm itching to see who's in the trunk, but I'd like to make a game out of it. I've had to be "serious Lucas" since starting the undercover job, so when Buttercup starts moving forward with the keys outstretched to unlock the trunk, I slap my hand over the lock. "Wait!" I cry out. "I wanna guess."

She rolls her eyes, but I see the smile attempting to peek through, and Romano just looks at me like I'm insane. He wants an explanation, but we can do that at a bar later.

"Well, go ahead," she prompts.

"Phew, okay. Is it King? No, there'd be more spectators. Hmm...Oh! Is it that guy who raised the price of prescription drugs so high that no one could afford them? I'd be down with that." Guesses continue to swirl in my head, and I blurt about twenty names before Romano finally lifts his hand and cuts me off.

"It seems like this could go on for a while. Shall we just move this along?" Romano asks. Killjoy. He was more fun at the strip club.

I remove my hand when Buttercup waves me away. She slips the key into the lock, and I start bouncing on my toes as she turns it. The lock clicks, and it's pushed from the inside before she can lift the metal. A bald man, namely De La Cruz, jumps out of the trunk and onto my girl. Well, that won't do.

She deflects him by snaking her forearm between them and trying to create space, but it's so unexpected that none of us can react in time. He's got a set of handcuffs clinging to one of his wrists, and as he takes my girl down, his hands wrap around her throat. He doesn't seem to have noticed the two of us next to him, but the moment Buttercup's head hits the ground, making a sound like a watermelon dropped on the floor, Romano and I are yanking him off of her with a speed I wouldn't imagine possible if I hadn't witnessed it.

Buttercup groans and lifts her hand to her head to check and pulls it away wet with blood.

Something snaps in me. Something I've kept locked down and worked hard to control. Bloodlust fills my body, and I whirl to face Enrique De La Cruz, currently being propped up by Romano with his arms yanked behind his back in a standard police hold. Someone's been watching cop shows.

I let my fists fly and jab Enrique's ribs three times, solar plexus, so we have matching bruises thanks to the security guard at the bank, and two solid punches land to his kidneys before I cross and hit his jaw so hard I hear the bone crack.

Buttercup struggles to sit up, so I bend down, confident Romano has a solid handle on Enrique, and help my girl up. She wobbles a bit, even in a sitting position, and I know she likely has a concussion. The sound of the impact makes me think her brain might be a little jumbled.

"Hey, look at me," I command, checking her pupils and having her follow my finger with her eyes. She seems a little out of it, but we have to get this show on the road. "Do you want me to finish here and have someone come get you?" I ask.

She shakes her head and immediately clutches the sides of it with her hands, regretting the move instantly. "No, fuck. Don't let me do that again. Let's get him downstairs. Mind handling the questioning, Red?" she asks me like it's a hardship. I'm going to gut this man for hurting my girl.

"Not at all. It'd be my pleasure after that move. Where are we headed?" I ask as I get her standing on her feet. She holds onto my arm and leads us down the stairs after grabbing a duffle bag from the back seat. We enter the pit where mechanics stand when changing the oil in a car; I've always wondered what's down here.

We weave our way through the toolboxes and stations they have set up—it's not as exciting as I'd imagined. To the back, there's a door with a "Management only" sign, and she flips through the keys in her hand until she holds up the one she needs.

When the door swings open, I see a dark stairway leading into pure blackness. Well, no one ever said our jobs were glamorous.

We descend the stairs after Romano and Enrique, keeping a few paces behind. Finally reaching level ground, Buttercup finds the light switch. Of course, there's only a single bulb, making this look like a seventies horror film. Enrique has to be pissing himself by this point.

The door is locked behind us, and we follow the new guy and our captive at a slower pace to make sure she stays on her feet.

Passing through a small antechamber, we face a single door. Buttercup pulls another key from the ring and unlocks it. Enrique is still breathing but struggling to stay upright despite Romano's hold.

We enter the room, and it's fucking genius.

The walls and floor are covered in a shiny-looking lacquer, and there's a drain in the middle of the floor. Handy. A single chair sits over the drain, and when Romano yanks Enrique's head up to see his destiny, the man loses his shit.

Only so many things can make the average man cry as he props his walls up with sheer determination. Extreme joy or sadness, the loss of a loved one, or facing your own mortality are surefire ways to smash those walls down. We've just broken De La Cruz by showing him his fate if the whimpered sobs escaping from his broken jaw are any indication.

Romano frisks Enrique for weapons and pulls only a single cufflink from his shirt. The other one is missing, presumably having been used to help free his hand from the cuffs. Romano frog-marches him to the chair, and I position Buttercup against the wall, giving her De La Cruz's shirt once it's been taken from its owner.

I know my girl could have gotten out from under De La Cruz. Fuck, I felt the knife against her thigh, ready to be used, but the element of surprise was on his side, and we didn't give her a chance to handle him on her own. I hope she isn't pissed at me for intervening. She would have done the same if the asshole had pounced on me with a cheap shot.

Once Enrique is settled and strapped into the chair with his handcuffs back in place, I saunter over, clapping Romano on the shoulder. "Thanks, man. I got this. Do you want to stay or go for the wetwork?"

He thinks it over for a moment and finally decides. "I'm staying. I need to know what he knows."

The two of us look over at Buttercup, who nods in assent. She's trusting him to know who I am and what I do. She's a good judge of character—after all, she's dating me—so I put my faith in her knowing what she's doing. Plus, there'll be blood on all of our hands now. Secrets build alliances.

"Before you begin," Buttercup calls, "I have some questions for Mr. De La Cruz."

The man in question raises his head to see her, "I didn't sell to minors."

His voice is sure, but the broken jaw makes it hard for him to form the words properly.

"That's not my question. If you had any patience, you'd know that," Buttercup scolds. "No, my question is quite simple. Who is King keeping from you? Who is he leveraging to keep you in line? Or did you remain loyal for so long because you're a terrible person?"

An unexpected laugh spills from the man's lips, along with a string of blood and saliva from his crimson mouth. "He has my sister. Not that it matters; she's not who she once was anyway."

"Give me her name," Buttercup demands, her voice reaching a menacing tone I've never heard from her. Even with Horvat, it was detached, calm, and composed. It is not composed now. The sister thing has to be a significant trigger for her. Hearing that someone has all but written off their family when she has so little must enrage her.

"Fuck you," he spits out. Oh, wrong answer, buddy.

I stow Jacob's hardware in the duffle bag to avoid blood transfer and drape my jacket on top. I pull a set of brass knuckles from the bag, noting that a few things in here are already a touch bloody, and I imagine they were used to subdue De La Cruz enough to get him into the trunk. Laying knives out on the floor in an arc reminiscent of a rainbow in front of De La Cruz, I hear him struggling against his binds but refuse to look over until my pretty arc is complete. I want him to see what's waiting for him if he doesn't give up answers easily.

With each blade I display, his breathing picks up. I finish organizing and turn to look at him, letting my darkness seep into my eyes. The shivers dancing up and down his spine increase tenfold.

Despite his apparent fear, his eyes keep their steely hold on Buttercup as if she's the one who ordered this when, in fact, it was his old buddy, King. By the time the bag is empty of weapons, the scent of piss has permeated the air, and De La Cruz is shaking, the handcuffs rattling ominously against the back of the metal chair.

Rogue tries asking a second time. He declines to answer again.

I let a punch fly, and Romano stands back as I work De La Cruz over with my fists and the knives. My girl peppers him with questions between attacks until he tells her what she wants to know, both about his sister and how he helped King get others as leverage to use in a bid to keep people in line. She also presses the advantage and asks how he knows Richard Blake and his ties. She's carefully pressing for information about Annex without giving away too much with Romano in the room.

She's clearly not ready to let him in on everything, but it makes for some entertaining conversation as she forms questions requiring someone in the know to decipher. Romano seems confused at the mention of Blake, but I just shake my head, encouraging him to remain silent as we work.

Eventually, when Rogue is sure she has what she's looking for, she waves at her husband to get on with it. Romano asks his own questions about an incident from some years back, but Enrique doesn't seem to have the answers he's looking for, despite the tactics I'm using, so instead, he switches his line of inquiry and digs for information on the drug trade.

I get my turn and ask him about the men at the bank and get some fascinating results. I guess he doesn't owe anyone loyalty there. With each slice, I feed into the shadows that live inside me. The ones I keep under lock and key. Since Archie died, they've been hovering in the periphery, waiting for an opportune moment to stretch their wings and consume me, even if only for a little while. I think that's why Buttercup called me to join in. She knows what lives within me. She has it, too.

It takes over four hours, but he spills what he knows, along with a lot of blood at my hands. He's drawing rattling breaths due to his broken and fractured ribs, and the shadows in me smile, knowing we're helping to end an evil man.

Romano stomps up the stairs and returns with a power washer, an extension cord, and a hose, attaching it to the plug and spigot in the room. He unloads a few rolls of tarp next to Buttercup and looks at her with pity in his eyes for her injury. She doesn't need his pity, and she needs to show him she's more alive than she appears at the moment. It won't take long before De La Cruz dies, but I'm craving that beer we talked about, and I'm ready to speed this process along while helping my girl hold on to the power in their weird marriage.

Most of the mess is contained near the drain under the chair, so clean-up shouldn't be a problem, but there's the matter of killing him outright. Buttercup must read my mind—or my impatience—and stands from her position to make her way to us. Her knife is out of its sheath, and she draws close to Enrique.

She looks at Romano, standing next to the power washer, ready to get things moving. Her gaze is stern and unrelenting as she flips the knife in her right hand up in the air carelessly, effortlessly catching it by the handle each time.

Her voice is lazy as she bids adieu to the monster before her. "I thought I'd have trouble ending you. You haven't done anything to me directly, but

I'm glad to be killing someone who gave up on their own family and helped break others in the process. How could you drag innocents into our world? Fuck you, Enrique. I hope you rot in hell."

With that, she slices the blade vertically up his stomach and ends when the ribs stop her progression. His insides become outsides, and he slumps forward as death comes for him. The blood spray isn't too bad, considering how much he lost in the past few hours, and a once-over with the power washer will get the rest of it down the drain.

Buttercup is standing there, the blood coating her right arm and her clothes a mess, and she's never looked more impressive than when she righted this wrong. I leave Romano to clean up the mess on his own as I make my way to my girl.

I tip her chin up and plant a heady kiss on her berry-painted lips. She sighs into the kiss but breaks it and peeks around my shoulder at Romano. I turn my head and see him looking at us with a mixture of confusion and sadness in his eyes.

"She's my girl, Romano. Got a problem with that?" I ask. The last thing I want to do is deal with another body tonight. Especially one that I kind of got along with last time we were in the same vicinity, but I'll do it if I have to.

"Nah, man." He turns to Rogue, "You may be my wife on paper, but we both know neither of our hearts is up for grabs. Just keep that shit on lock when we go out. You never know who's watching, and after King's threat this morning, I'm in no mood to deal with his shit."

I nod, desperate to ask what threat he's talking about, but Buttercup lets out a small laugh and completely distracts me. She remained stone-faced all night, her mask only slipping once when she found the eggplant in my hair, and I didn't know how much I needed to hear her laugh at this moment after the butchering I just finished. "This is a weird night," she mumbles. "I never thought I'd be introducing my boyfriend to my husband."

I laugh and am glad to see she's not too messed up after her head bump and lengthily interrogating De La Cruz. I'm still considering taking her to the ER, but as I run my hand up the back of her head, I see the bleeding has stopped, thank God. I know head wounds bleed a lot, but she seems okay. Her eyes are clear enough, and she's not jumbling anything around. I'm still taking these two out for a drink to ensure she stays awake longer.

We drain Enrique as much as we can, roll him in a tarp, and help Romano with the power washing after putting the body in the trunk of a minivan Buttercup snagged the keys for. He does a decent job of it but misses the tiny spatters further from the central part of the room. I don't think he's had to do a clean-up like this before. But that's okay. I'm teaching him for the next time.

We get the room back to normal and pile into the minivan. I text Rosa, one of the cleaners we keep on standby, and we drop the body and the van off at her location. I also ask Rosa to bring us some clothes to change into, and when she arrives carrying an armful of Target plastic bags, I almost laugh at the look on Romano's face.

I don't think that man has worn non-designer clothes in years if the face he just made is any indication.

We change and use the baby wipes in the bag as Rosa stands outside the van. We step out once we're all wearing something less bloody and I retrieve the hardware from the duffle bag. Rosa tries to hide her chuckle and fails miserably, climbs in, and takes off. She promises to drop the weapons bag off at a secondary location, and I text Han to meet her at an intersection and pick up the knives to clean them at the clubhouse. It's like crowd-sourcing a murder these days.

I still have some nervous energy bouncing around, so I encourage the others to head to a bar a couple of blocks away. We're in a decent neighborhood, and it's not shitty enough or rich enough for The Gambit to bother with. We'll be safer here than anywhere else, and with the way we look at the moment in our mismatched outfits and Romano's white tennis shoes, I doubt we'll even be noticed.

"I need a shower and about four hours of my kill-and-chill ritual. You guys doing okay?" she asks us, her eyes flicking between us as she ties her hair into one of those messy buns. It hides the blood surprisingly well when I lean over to check. I give her a thumbs up.

"All good," Romano says in a clipped tone that doesn't quite have me believing him.

"Yep. I owe this guy a beer," I tell her, then put on my stern voice. "No alcohol for you until your headache goes away. That was quite the bump. But maybe some juice to bring your blood sugar back up?" I offer. Buttercup just nods and follows me inside the bar.

It's one of those restaurants and bars with all of the sports memorabilia and kitschy shit all over the walls, and I love it. No one in The Gambit would be caught dead in here.

We grab one of the high-top tables and get a round of beers for Romano and me while Buttercup orders an orange juice.

Once the server drops off the drinks, we let our guards down just a

The Sacrifices We Make

smidge and look around the table at each other. Buttercup starts us off. "What do you want to know?" she asks Romano.

He lifts a finger from his beer glass and waves it between us. "How do you two know each other? I know I met you at the bachelor party, but I thought you were with the bankers, not The Gambit. And does she call you 'Red' because of your work with the knives?" The last question has me questioning his intelligence until I remember I sprayed my hair brown for work at the bank. I stifle a chuckle and decide to answer the other questions instead.

"I was with the bankers, who seemed to be tied to De La Cruz. I knew they went out a couple of times a month, and your bachelor party was the first and only time they invited me. I didn't know where we were going, nor that it was one of The Gambit's clubs. I'm looking at gathering information, and with some of the details the asshole spilled earlier, it should be a cakewalk now."

I turn to Buttercup, who just shrugs. She's leaving the rest of my involvement up to me to share. God, I love this girl. I need to find a moment to tell her without her husband hearing.

Chapter Nineteen

Rogue

After beers and orange juice with my boyfriend and my husband—weird fucking sentence—Lucas and Romano do one of those curious bro-shake things that end with them clasping hands and bumping shoulders. We chatted over our drinks about Romano's wife—the original one—and his motivations to join The Gambit. The two idiots finally let go of each other, and Lucas hauls me into his arms.

"I miss you, Buttercup. When can you come home?"

"You don't even live there right now," I argue.

"My job is finished. Did I not mention that? Tech," Lucas uses Jacob's nickname to keep *some* anonymity as he lightly side-eyes Romano, "got what he needed, and I was called back yesterday. Just had one last thing to finish up at the office." The twinkle in his eye tells me it was something I probably would have paid good money to see, but now certainly isn't the time for a lovers' chat about his shenanigans.

"That's great, Red." I look up into his smiling face and see that some of the shadows playing along the planes of his face while he was carving up De La Cruz have receded. His smile is softer again, and his eyes are more vibrant. I had a feeling he'd been going a little stir-crazy stuck in an office all damn day for weeks. Watching him unleash on that piece of scum was weirdly hot, and remembering it has my pulse jumping and my skin pebbling in eagerness.

Sidestepping the answer to his question about when I can return to the clubhouse, I pull my phone from the back pocket of the ridiculous denim mini-skirt Rosa provided. It's better than my gore-stained grey dress, I guess. "I have to let the boss know the job is done. You catching an Uber?" I ask, hoping one of the others isn't coming to pick him up because I might just be tempted to get in the car with them and never return to my shitty gang life. Unfortunately, Sage's safety and the file have me sticking with this a bit longer.

"Yeah, it'll be here in a minute."

I pull my phone out, attach a photo of my newly dead colleague to the message, and let King know the job is done.

Me: Job's done. Anything else tonight?

King: No. Check in with your crew tomorrow. I've got a list headed your way in the morning. Make sure it's handled. Local only for you.

The condescending, overbearing asswipe is just as perfunctory via text as he is in face-to-face communication. I click out of the text screen to remove the offending picture and words from my sight. Lucas is scowling next to me, and Romano is watching us with curiosity.

We didn't explain much about our personal relationship. Red just said he was a colleague and my boyfriend. Funnily enough, it was the "colleague" part that seemed to pique Romano's interest. I made it clear he wasn't associated with The Gambit four times throughout the night because the topic kept coming up.

A silver Prius pulls into the parking lot, and Lucas looks down at his phone. His face shutters when he realizes it's time for us to split up again.

He says a last goodbye to Romano, sidles up close to me, his breath wisping across the crown of my head, and leans in to kiss me one last time.

"Bye, Buttercup. I—" he's cut off as the driver of the Prius honks the horn and asks if one of us is "Lewis" through the open window. Red sighs and rests his forehead against mine while he lifts his finger to the driver, asking for a moment. "I'll see you soon, okay? You owe me a painting." His whisper sends tingles down my spine, and I clench my thighs together as the words touch something deep in my gut.

"I know. Soon, I promise."

Red gets into the car as Romano stands back a few paces, kindly giving us a moment of privacy. He steps forward and stands shoulder-to-shoulder

The Sacrifices We Make

with me. "You love him," he says with an undercurrent of disbelief running through his tone. "You love him, yet you married me because King told you to. What are you planning, Rogue?" The last part is barely audible, which gives me an excuse not to answer.

"I'm doing what needs to be done to ensure no one dies because I refuse an order." The taillights of the Prius are becoming distant specks of crimson light as they head down the street, taking my reason for smiling with it. I feel the mask sliding back into place in preparation for the next stretch of my cover. I pull our wedding rings from a pocket and hand Romano his. I slide mine on and feel the mask over my face, my personality, lock in place.

Despite the steps we've taken forward tonight, hearing King tell me his plans for me broke something in my soul. Dictating my future and mapping out my life plan without consulting me or even asking my opinion, knowing I couldn't refuse even if I wanted to because of Sage, has made me feel small. Insignificant. I never wanted this fucking life, and yet, here I am, poised to take over for him someday.

Romano checks his phone as a black town car pulls up. The driver emerges, and it's one of Romano's underlings. Well, at least he didn't see Red. Although, brushing him off as someone we met at the bar would be an easy sell.

Knowing that I need to set up a meeting with the other hitmen, I send a mass text to the group chat. In the message, I arrange a meeting for tomorrow and inform them of a time and place. Those not on an assignment will meet with me, and I'll pass out the new contract kills. Whoopie.

I'M THIS FREAKING CLOSE TO BANGING MY HEAD ON THE TABLE AND shooting my men myself. We've been at this for two hours, and if I have to hear one more time about how Cassius gets the best assignments, I'm going to stab the others in a bid to stem the arguing.

Cassius, the man in question, lifts a brow, and his dark skin glimmers under the fluorescent lighting. We're currently holed up on one of the floors being renovated in the Rook Industries building to hold our meeting. All six hitmen who weren't out on assignment are here, and a few more are dialed in via video chat.

Cassius is a colossal motherfucker. Six and a half feet of muscle, wider than an NFL offensive lineman, and obvious as hell in a crowd. That said, he manages to stick to the shadows better than anyone on my team. He can sneak up on even the most cautious targets and have them broken and bleeding out in mere minutes. He doesn't have many scruples when it comes to his job, just a thirst for violence, so he gets the ones I don't want to hear details about.

"What else have you got for us, Boss?" asks G. My "second" is sitting to my right, fiddling with the laptop we have the absent members of my crew synced up to. I've doled out half of the list King sent over this morning. I won't be taking any on because only one of the names is my type of victim, but he's six hours away, so he's not entirely local.

"Javier and Cain, I want you two on the hotel owner in Los Angeles. Jonathan Voorhees can't be running girls from the port to the Nevada border to hand over to the Vegas Crew. He's got deep ties to The Gambit, and going around us isn't part of our agreement." This was the assignment I'd have loved to participate in, but with King's orders that I only take on local jobs, I had to dish it out to someone else.

Javier looks at his partner Cain, and they nod their heads. They've been working together on jobs for a year or so now. I noticed their easy camaraderie when training them, and they continue to suit each other well. Cain is the brains, Javier the brawn. Together, they're deadly and work in unison seamlessly.

"Yes, Boss. Do you have anything particular in mind for him?" Cain asks.

"Make it hurt." Thinking of that man being degraded and torn into pieces brings a sinister smile to my face. I wish I could be part of this one. "I want him broken and begging for forgiveness behind a strip of duct tape before you end him. Make him feel like he's undoubtedly made the girls feel."

Cain's chin-length blond hair bounces as he nods eagerly. His tanned hands are twisting in front of him, and I know he's already thinking of how to make it fun. Javier is average-looking and doesn't draw attention when they're out on a hit. He gets lost in a crowd because he always wears his baseball hat with nondescript clothing. He was made to blend in and get the job done.

Fabio, or Alex, as his birth certificate says, our plant in the entertainment industry, chimes in from the video screen, "I'll be done here in a couple of days, and Toronto is cold as fuck. What's next on my roster? Please tell me it's somewhere tropical."

As he begs for warmer climes, he shakes out his honey-colored hair—the asset that gained him his nickname as it looks exactly like that romance cover icon from the eighties and nineties with those same signature locks. "Fabio, I've got you on the docket to handle one in Sacramento, so you'll hit that one on your way home. It's not the tropics, but it's better than the wild north. Any objections?"

"No, Boss. Lizzy was harder to track down than I thought, and I've been freezing my balls off up here for almost a week. Happy to be headed back to California in a couple of days." Fabio is a lady killer. Literally. He was sent after Lizzy Perdue for going to the police about The Gambit after her husband—a prominent Hollywood producer—failed to make payments and got himself killed. By the sound of it, she'll be taken care of tomorrow.

Most of the hitmen in my crew have a problem with killing the few women who find their way onto a list, even if they've done the same thing as one of the male targets we have. Either women are way smarter at covering their tracks than their male counterparts, or they go against The Gambit less often. Honestly, I think it's the former.

I send Fabio to get it done when a woman eventually makes it onto our radar. He gets close to them, lures them in with his body and attention, then ends them in a way that looks like an overdose in their own homes. Crafty one, that man. He's got crazy mommy issues, but it works for the job.

"Fine. You all know why I give you certain assignments, do you not?" I ask. The muted chorus of nods and "Yes, Boss" goes around the room.

"With how things are headed, we might be getting a bigger piece of the pie. I like this team. I think you're all good at what you do, but don't get cocky. Do your job, and do it well. Send messages when needed. Report back to me when you're all done. Those of you on a job, be safe, and please be smart. I don't want to have to train a new bunch of recruits any time soon. Don't make me."

My threat looms over the room, and I dismiss the crew with a wavd. My six guys file out, and the remaining three on the video chat are brusquely cut off when G slaps the laptop lid closed.

"I don't know how you fucking do it, Boss," G states.

"Do what?" I ask, exasperation seeping into my tone. I hate these meetings. The face I have to wear, the tone I have to take...all of it just reminds me of how deeply entrenched in this life I am, and while I fucking hate it, it's like a part of my soul calls to this in some way. Giving orders and ending assholes is easy for me. It's not the sum of my parts, but it *is* a part of me. Call it conditioning from the years under King's reign.

"We only all get together, what? Like once every two months, maybe three? Yet we're all on the same page and kept busy between meetings. You manage to take into account our personal time off and keep even the argumentative fuckers in line. I want to be you when I grow up."

I laugh at that. "G, you're five years older than me."

"Doesn't matter. You run a tight ship, and you've experienced more than the fuckers you manage could ever dream up in their worst nightmares. You wanna...I don't know...Go get a cup of coffee or something?" G's voice trembles during his question, making my suspicions rise.

"You know I'm married, right, G? You were at the wedding," I respond when his question sounds more like a date than a simple cup of coffee. I waggle my ring finger at him, nearly blinding him with the rock. I wear this stupid thing to all meetings and functions, but it has to come off for kills.

"Yeah, and you looked hot as fuck in your black dress and funeral/wedding veil, and it doesn't seem like you're enjoying being married. But something *is* different with you." His eyes rove over my body, looking for imperceptible changes before I sock him in the gut and slam his head down on the table. It lands as a groan of pain escapes his lips.

"Look, I know we just finished some work together this week and spent some time in each other's company, but I am not someone you want to get involved with. I'll go for a drink because I'm exhausted after this meeting and need the caffeine, but don't get any ideas, G. We've worked together for years. If it didn't happen back then, it's not happening now." My stern voice is back, mask firmly in place, and G's head nods as best he can as his cheek is smashed into the table in front of us.

"Yes, Boss."

With that, I release the pressure on the back of his neck and let him up. I circle my finger in the air in a lets-wrap-it-up gesture and start heading toward the elevator. G is quick to grab the laptop and cord and follows me out of the office space.

"Hey," he starts, "you think anyone suspects us for the fire?"

"I sure as hell hope not, G. Why? You getting sloppy in your old age and leaving evidence behind?" I ask, a teasing lilt in my tone. He's only a few years older than me, but I like teasing him about it.

"No, I just haven't seen De La Cruz since he left the storehouse and we torched the place," he confesses with a worried glance from the corner of his eye.

"And you won't. He's been voted out." The elevator arrives, and G is still standing in the same spot he was in moments ago as I step into the box.

"No shit?" he asks, eyes wide and jaw slack.

"No shit."

The Sacrifices We Make

I'M READY TO DITCH G AFTER COFFEE AND SANDWICHES—HE ORDERED me one because he said I was acting hangry and stabbier than usual—and take an Uber back to the apartment when a dark SUV pulls up onto the curb in front of the cafe.

G already has his hand under his jacket, likely pulling the Glock from under his arm before I can tell him to cool it. I know that SUV.

"G—" I start but am ceremoniously cut off as Red creeps up behind him, wraps a strong forearm around the front of G's neck, and gets him into a chokehold. A balaclava-covered Han plucks the gun from my companion's holster while Red applies enough pressure to make him pass out in less than ten seconds. He's carefully lowered to the ground, and the guys come to stand on either side of me, grabbing my arms tightly but not painfully.

"Hey!" I shout at them. I need him to be okay, and leaving him on the sidewalk doesn't seem like the smartest thing. I know he'll be up soon because chokeholds don't make you pass out for too long, but still. He's my employee!

The SUV was enough of a distraction to allow someone to sneak up behind the guy who would take over for me if I were killed. I have to increase his training.

"Trouble, put up a bit of a fight for the nice bystanders, and let's go," Noah commands from the driver's seat. They all have matching masks and look like some weird alt-rock boyband. I giggle internally but then start shouting for help.

G begins to stir and opens his eyes just in time to see me tossed into the car and taken away.

I look at the men on either side of me, Jacob and Han, then up at Noah in the driver's seat and Lucas fiddling with the radio from the passenger seat. "What the fuck? Want to explain why I was just 'abducted?'" I ask.

Oh, I got to use Elise's air quotes.

"We figured out that you couldn't get away from the apartment too easily, but if one of your men saw you kidnapped, you had a good excuse for being out for a while. Plus, when we finally get Sage back, King will have someone else to blame," Jacob explains as if it's the most logical thing in the world. And you know what, it kind of is. It's fucking brilliant. King will have me chasing down leads on the mysterious threesome that kidnapped me because, let's face it, I'd totally escape a kidnapper or three. Jacob stayed in the car so G won't know there's a fourth.

"Give me your phone, Love." Jacob sticks his hand out, palm up.

I hand it over warily and watch as he pulls out the sim card and switches it with another. "This will show your phone as moving south instead of north if King or your buddy back there tracks it. We're headed to the clubhouse," he explains.

"Why?"

"Gorgeous, first, because we miss you. Second, Jacob finished pulling and sifting through the information from the bank. He wants us all to go over it together and won't tell us shit until you're there." Han says the last bit with a little ire in his tone. He's obviously been bugging Jacob about it, and the man hasn't caved.

The guys on either side of me are careful not to get too close. Either they see I'm feeling a bit unlike myself, or they've noticed my walls have built back up, despite the small crack Red put in them yesterday. I see Jacob eyeing my wedding ring with a flash of disgust on his face before he schools his features and turns toward the window.

It's nearly eight in the evening by the time we arrive at the clubhouse, and the guys are not going to like the mood I'm in after sitting silently beside them in the car for most of the trip. They're all still wearing their masks and not speaking.

I miss the crap out of them, but I find myself shutting down that part of my personality more and more as the days slip by, and I'm stuck living with Romano and under the watchful eyes of King's minions dotted all over our building and the office.

I'm angry at the whole situation, and finally, taking certain things into my own hands has me enraged with myself for not doing anything earlier. Between the minor moves I'm making on my own and my lack of a plan to see the guys, I know I've been coasting and letting the situation dictate my actions, not my wants.

I'm struggling to let my walls come down, even though I know I can trust my guys. My tone of voice is cold, my mind walled off. I don't know what will pull me out of it, but knowing I'm in that place, mentally, is enough reassurance for me that soon, I'll be able to.

Too many things have happened lately. There's the whole getting married thing, the implication that King wants me to pop out a kid, not trusting Romano, and G and I secretly burning down the storehouse that had the cache of drugs De La Cruz was selling. Oh yeah, I added a *very* important name to the list without King knowing and doled it out to Javier and Cain, letting them think he was trafficking girls instead of drugs. I'm slowly cutting King off at the knees, with him being none the wiser.

My pieces on the board are moving into place, and I'll be poised to take King down soon without repercussions. I just have to get Sage by my side and the evidence in my hands. I know it's the same as six months ago, just before I met the guys, except that pawns have been removed and I've been working hard on my position.

I couldn't have done this without the guys' help, encouragement, and planning, and it makes me feel inadequate at the moment. The important thing is that King is losing allies left, right, and center, and his grip on his throne wanes with each strategic move I make.

We approach the gate, and Jacob opens the trusty app on his phone. The gate pulls away from the latch, and Noah parks the SUV in the lot. We all pile out one by one, and I'm the last to slide out, not feeling particularly happy after being abducted and feeling a flush rise on my chest about having choices taken away from me, even if it was well-intentioned.

Han unlocks the clubhouse door and stands in the center of the open doorway, looking every inch the avenging angel as I slowly make my way across the concrete. The air is crisp this evening. It's fortifying and smells like new beginnings. He pulls his ski mask off and stuffs it into his back pocket. The others do the same as we make our way forward.

Han's face is hard to see with the backlighting from the clubhouse, but as I draw close, he steps from the door, and his features become clear when bathed in the moonlight. He's ecstatic I'm here and seems to be wearing a megawatt smile. How can he be? I've been gone for weeks, I'm married to someone else, and when I dealt with De La Cruz last night, I called Lucas instead of him, and I just stewed in silence the whole way here.

Regardless of my internal turmoil, Han steps forward and sweeps me into his arms. He plants a kiss on me that, were I in any other headspace, would have my knees weak and my pulse racing. I lazily return the kiss and pull back too soon for his liking.

"Gorgeous, are you okay?" he asks.

"Yeah, fine." I offer a small smile, and his shoulders lower from their tense position. The others also let out tiny breaths of relief from behind me. "Let's get going. I want to know what Jacob found."

Han says nothing about my clipped tone, just casts a worried glance over my face and guides me into the clubhouse.

I make it three steps past the entryway and am immediately engulfed in a bear hug by a streaking blur from behind. "Hi again, Red," I choke out, trying not to inhale and crack a rib in his embrace. He drops a messy kiss on my cheek, nibbling his way to my mouth before I'm snatched away into Jacob's inked arms.

"You saw her yesterday, dickhead. It's my turn." His arms wind around me gently, and he tips my head back with a finger under my chin. "You're here," he breathes. "You're home." His lips descend, and I give him a chaste kiss in front of the others. I try pulling away, but his grip on my chin tightens until I'm opening for him, losing myself in the kiss, but my mind is screaming that this isn't what any of them signed up for.

He releases me as a shadow falls over us. I open my eyes and see Noah looming behind Jacob. "Hi, Trouble."

"Hi, Cap."

"God, I've missed you." Remembering his love letter whispered over the phone in that same hushed tone has me pulling my walls back up before I drop into a puddle on the floor. He opens his arms as Jacob releases me, Han and Lucas standing opposite us, and I make my way into Noah's hold.

His warm hands settle on my hips after drawing me close, and the heat from his fingertips seeps into my chilled skin as he finds the gap between my top and my jeans. He doesn't move to kiss me. Instead, he dips his head until we're nose to nose and searches my eyes with his own honey-brown orbs. "Are you okay?" he asks, his breath soft against my lips.

I nod, our noses bumping before a smile graces his lips. I pull back, and he releases me, sensing I'm not in the frame of mind to exchange small talk. "To the war room?" I ask.

"Yeah, Buttercup. Jacob's been in there all day setting up and won't let us see what's going on," Red gripes.

Confused about how he's hidden things from them when the walls are made of glass, I look to the war room and see he's hung sheets along the walls to block out the others. I can tell he's taken linens from everyone's stashes because there are his own giant sheets, one set of Lucas's Superman sheets, Han's usual plaid pattern, and a deep grey that I can only assume belongs to Noah.

I look at Jacob confused, but he only lifts a shoulder and says, "I only want to run through this once, and I know if they saw any of it, they'd interrupt with questions."

"Fair enough," I say.

"Gorgeous, let's head in. Lucas, can you grab drinks? I have a feeling this'll take a while," Han directs.

"I'll help," Noah offers. Lucas nods gratefully, and after a quick consensus, we all decide beers sound good.

Han takes my hand on one side, Jacob on the other, and they lead me to the blocked-off room. Jacob opens the door with a flourish and ushers us in ahead of him. As soon as my foot crosses the divide, I look around with awe. Jacob has either gone completely insane, or this whole room has become an arts and crafts project.

There are photos all over the walls, the whiteboard is filled top to bottom with information and acronyms I can't decipher, and there are yards and yards of red yarn connecting photos and companies together. My breath catches as I find a photo of my parents on the wall. I follow the string connecting them to Patton Cross, the board member from Annex we've had the least luck with, and King.

My breath catches, and my knees threaten to buckle without even knowing the information at hand, but I know it can't be good. Jacob catches me under the elbow and guides me to a chair. He pushes me in and drops a kiss to the crown of my head. "It's bad, Love, but we're here," he assures me. How can they be here with and for me? Look at this shitstorm I've brought into their lives by agreeing to work with them.

I take a steadying breath, following the strings around the room, but it's giving me whiplash as I trail from one side to the other and decide to wait until Jacob explains it to all of us. There's no sense in reacting until I have all of the information.

Han drops into the seat beside me as Lucas and Noah return from the kitchen with beers for everyone. This is going to be a long night, isn't it?

"Okay, Jacob," Noah starts after he takes his seat at the head of the table, "what have you got for us?"

Lucas is perched on the edge of his seat, following the strings around until Jacob claps his hands and gets him to refocus. "Okay, so the bank has information and accounts for all of the members of The Gambit. More importantly, it's been funneling information to a contact within the Annex. I think I've got it, but it'll require more digging on the Annex servers. I didn't have time for that, though I have a program mining for information in a certain government branch. I want to float my theory past you while the software does its job."

Jesus, he's breaking into government servers? What the hell is going on? The way his eyes are lit up, it's evident he believes he's onto something, but without proof, I'm going to withhold excitement until it's concrete.

"Okay, bear with me here. The bank seems to use investments and loans to launder money for The Gambit. Rogue, you'll need to confirm with Nina Wilson." His gaze sweeps over me until I nod in agreement. "So, here's what I'm thinking. De La Cruz and Horvat, er...Well, I guess now it's Romano, collected the drug and weapons payments and ran it through The White Knight strip joint and other clubs down the coast, all of which do their books with Collinsworth Bank. The dividends from the investments and stock market gains are deposited into Rook Industries, which then pays all of you, correct?"

I nod, as my pay comes from the Rook Industries payroll.

"On the plus side, I've found a way to get Horvat's money out, and it is currently being transferred to Polly because of California law." Jacob's statement has me repressing a grin, knowing that Polly is getting the least of what's owed to her and the bank assholes are losing that nice chunk of change.

Jacob continues. "Okay, off to a good start with my theory. So the question was then, why are we gathering information for Annex? I tracked the shit out of their emails, transactions, and financials for the upper management. And one person was suspiciously missing, considering the bank is also where Annex does their banking. Mara.

"Patton Cross even has his personal accounts there. Well, at least three of them. So did Richard Blake. Why does Mara have nothing?" he asks rhetorically.

Before any of us can attempt to theorize, Jacob continues, "I think she's working with the feds. The information gathering and assignment came from her, and she's the only one who doesn't have ties to the bank from our two organizations. Why would she be gathering information if it doesn't pertain to her? You could argue it's about the company, but it's too fishy that she's not involved with the bank when everyone else is. The only answer I could come up with is that she's gathering it for someone else. But who? That's the big question.

"Remember the person she meets at that random coffee shop on Saturdays when she has 'massage' in her calendar? What if that's her contact? Her handler?

"I'm combing database after database, trying to match a few of the photos we took of him during our stakeouts with employee records, but I'm not coming up with anything yet. It's the only narrative that makes sense," Jacob mumbles at the end as if he isn't quite sure it's accurate but is determined to make it so.

"Okay, so why are my parents on the wall?" I ask. I'm both excited and

The Sacrifices We Make

terrified to hear the reasoning. Will these be the answers I've been subtly digging for since I got the original police files from the box at St. Ignatius church? Or will it just turn me in more circles until I don't know which way is up and I give up hope completely? Please be the former.

"I was able to pull some old records from your parents' schools, including teachers' notes. I found King's real name. Your mom was mentioned as always in the company of Kadir, another student in her class. They seemed to have been best friends or were even dating at some point. Anyway, her English teacher mentioned a poem your mom wrote and attributed the muse to Kadir. I got hold of an old photo someone posted of their class for one of the reunions, and lo and behold, the boy labeled as Kadir Acar had his arm around your mom's shoulders, and it's King, looking at her with more than friendship." A shudder wracks my body at the thought of that monster being sweet with my mother, and I cringe as I wonder what the fuck she was thinking. Although not all monsters are born, are they? Some are made. I would know.

"Okay, so they knew each other. I know that. King has mentioned it in the past," I reply. That facial expression King is wearing in the photo Jacob is pointing out on the wall is new, but that kind of look can stem from childhood friendship.

"But did you know they lived together? They got an apartment on the west side of town. They lived there for a few years after they finished high school," Jacob informs me.

"What? No way. That doesn't make sense. She was with my dad then." I look around the table at the others, hoping for someone to back me up on this, despite knowing they don't know enough about my parents' history to have any clue if that's true. I'm grasping at straws here because I was born when my mom was twenty-one. She would have been living with King when I was conceived. That would mean...

"She was, Rogue." Jacob takes a deep breath before continuing, "She was living with King, or Kadir, as he was known then, while he worked his way up the ranks with your dad. She left the apartment about six months before you were born—according to the lease agreement, she terminated the lease with the building's management and moved in with your dad. They got married within a month of moving in together. Your dad, Joseph, was, by all appearances, your biological father. It would require a DNA test, but I think your mom left King for your dad."

"King said he loved someone before I was born. It was my mom?" I ask in disbelief. From what King said, I always knew they were close growing up, but *love*? Thinking back to our conversation after the last board meeting, when he confessed his love for a woman and said that it had ended badly, it must have been my mother. Did Mom create the monster who raised me? Or was that The Gambit?

"It looks to be that way, Buttercup." Red looks at the photo of my parents and follows the red yarn to the photo of Patton Cross, the last male member of the Annex board. "What does Cross have to do with all of this?" he asks.

"That's where I'm drawing a blank," Jacob says to Red, then turns his head to me, "but he's named as your godfather."

Noah slams his beer on the table, the rush of liquid bubbling as it escapes the top, soaking his hand and the table in the process.

"That's not possible," I choke out. I've never met the man. Who the fuck were my parents that I have an infamous killer no one can find evidence on as a godfather, and the man who raised me is the head of the most prominent criminal organization on the West Coast? My life is a clusterfuck of epic proportions, and who knows if I'd have ever found out if it weren't for the men in this room, the men who didn't sign up for any of this. Yeah, we agreed to work together on the boards, but the emotions—the feelings—were never part of the agreement. They must loathe me right now; the woman embroiled in this chaos and forged in its flames.

Seconds slip by as I process everything Jacob has uncovered. The secrets, the lies, the subterfuge by everyone involved...it's just too much. What the fuck does Patton Cross have to do with anything? Is King actually my father? A shiver rakes down my spine at that thought. It isn't ideal, but knowing it's possible doesn't change our relationship. It doesn't make anything he's done okay. If anything, it makes it worse. And my mother. What the hell did she do? My head is confused, and my heart is in pieces at the bottom of my ribcage. Just when I thought I had started unraveling this mess, more is revealed. Although, maybe it's more like separating the individual threads that make up a knot. That knot is the perfect metaphor for where and who I come from. Seconds turn into minutes as silence reigns supreme in the room as the guys wait for me to say something, *anything*.

I keep my eyes downcast, though I know they're all staring at me. I can't face them when it comes to this. I should get out of here before I bring more down on us. Apparently, They've got one boss working with the feds if Jacob is correct, and the other is...God, he's nothing to me, but there's a connection, and I need to find out what it is and what it means. I can do that on my own. There's no need to involve the guys more than they already are.

I scoot my chair back, putting my hands on the table to prepare to stand from the chair. My ass lifts a few inches when Noah's voice rings out in the suddenly stifling room. "Don't you fucking think about it, Trouble. Sit down."

He may be a leader, but he isn't my leader. I work alone. I don't know what I was thinking in teaming up with these guys. "You don't need this," I say, my voice small and nearly unrecognizable to my own ears.

"No, we don't," he confirms. "We don't need you. We want you. There's a big difference there, or have you been away from all of us for too long?"

Han groans and drops his head into his waiting palms, burying the heels of his hands against his eyes. "Noah's right and wrong, Ivy. Don't listen to his angry tone, but listen to the words. We don't really *need* anyone, but you fit us. We *want* you because you're you, not because of who you come from. We'll figure this out." His head snaps over to Noah, "Don't be a dick about it. She's ours, and you're making it seem like a bad thing. Be helpful or shut up."

Noah grunts at Han's words as Lucas and Jacob follow the conversation like a tennis match, bouncing from one team member to another. I'd laugh if it were under any other circumstance.

"Do you all want out?" Noah asks the room.

"No," rings out from all of us. I surprise myself with how quickly my answer comes because I am too selfish to give these men up despite the complications.

Chapter Twenty

Rogue

"Jinx!" shouts Noah.

We all shut our mouths and send glares in his direction. Yeah, he won that one fair and square, conniving bastard, but the tension in the room is killing me.

Red shifts in his chair, obviously wanting to speak his mind but unable to do so. I don't know the full consequences of violating a Jinx, but I've seen a few punches thrown for close calls. Violent bunch, I tell ya.

Han and Jacob thread their hands together and lean back in their chairs, watching the scene unfold. I keep my ass in my chair as directed, and Noah rises and stalks around the table to position himself between me and the table.

"Now that's enough." His voice is stern, and he's taking charge of the team, the room, hell, the fucking clubhouse. "Why are you picking a fight, Trouble?" he asks me, knowing full well I'm jinxed and can't respond. "Is it because you miss us? Is it because you're feeling insecure being forced away from us?"

The mother fucker is right. I'm mad, frustrated, horny as fuck, and livid all at once that I've been away for so long. I miss them. They're my oxygen, and I've been suffocating while playing a role I despise. I've kept my mask up twenty-four-seven around Romano and in the apartment for fear of being betrayed. I'm just so tired of being stuck in my own head.

I look up at Noah, who keeps his eyes on mine, searching for the truth I've kept sheltered behind the sky-high walls I've built up since the last time I was around the guys. Since King issued my marriage decree. Since my future was decided—*again*—without my consent.

I let the wall slip a bit, and tears start to well in my eyes. Noah's hand reaches under my chin and tilts my head up, not letting me drop my gaze to the floor or hide the emotion raging in my eyes. I wish I could speak right now. I don't know what I would say, but looking into each other's eyes is a soul-shattering experience, and there's nothing to distract me from it.

Noah's thumbs wipe the tears away as they trail down my cheeks, and he leans in to kiss my forehead with such tenderness that I didn't even know he was capable of. Red slides out of his chair and stands to my left as Han and Jacob come around the table. They pull my chair away from the table while I'm still sitting in it. They kneel in front of me like knights before a queen. I'm still stuck in this chair, but feel surrounded and comforted. I'm exactly where I need to be. *Want* to be.

Han's hand strokes my hair behind my ear, and he leans in to nuzzle his nose in my neck. He trails his tongue up to my ear and gently bites down on my earlobe, eliciting a shiver radiating from the very center of me. Jacob's hand is resting on my thigh, tracing a small swirling pattern, and Red, dear Red, is watching it all and adjusting his cock in his sweats. I'd say he was being crass, but the emotion in his eyes tells me it's not just because of his voyeuristic tendencies.

"Guys, get to Tech's room," Noah says, using Jacob's rarely-used team nickname to avoid breaking the jinx. "I think our girl needs some time with us. She needs to remember who she is and what she means to us despite the doubts running through her mind." My ears perk up at that, and my spine snaps to attention.

I look between the guys, and they nod, leaving Noah and me in the war room alone. Did he mean all of them? I instinctively move to rub my thighs together to ease the ache building in my pussy, but Noah steps forward, blocking my attempt at relieving the pressure between my thighs. His arousal is evident in my line of sight, and I lick my lips in anticipation.

Sex doesn't fix everything, as we all know. But it does bring a level of intimacy that I've been missing since last seeing all of them. Noah knows this, and he's found an exciting way to remind us all—mostly me—of our shared bond. His fingers wrap around my wedding band and pull it from my finger. It lands on the table and rolls across the sleek tabletop like a penny.

My issues with the information brought to light are quickly waning with the promise of adoration I see in Noah's eyes. He leans close and whispers, "I see those questions brewing, Trouble. I don't know how this will go yet, but I want to find out. I think you need us to show you we're in. And trust me, we're *all* in. The question is: are you?" I nod vigorously in response to his question. I want all of them. I want nothing more than all of my guys around me, filling me, tasting me, loving me. "Then let's go."

He runs his hands down my sides and under my thighs. In one swift movement, he has my legs wrapped around his waist, and my arms come up and anchor around the back of his neck. He peppers hot kisses along my jaw as he strides out of the war room, and my head tilts back in ecstasy. I'm confident I'm leaving a wet spot on the front of his pants, but I couldn't care less at the moment.

He carries me up the stairs quickly. When we enter Jacob's room, I see the dimmed lights and a roaring fire playing on the projector, lighting the room in a warm orange glow.

Noah sets me on my feet and spins me around. Han and Jacob lie on the bed, a space between them for me, and Lucas is standing at the foot of the bed, just waiting. Noah encourages me to step forward, and it looks like he'll be directing this show because the rest of us are jinxed.

"Get on the bed, Trouble." My knees quake at his command, and I take unsteady steps forward. Sure, I've had Jacob and Han together. Red has watched us in the past and joined in soon after. But I've never had all of them in the same time frame, in the same space. And I've never had Noah at all, aside from sweet kisses and fleeting touches. I want to see what makes our commander growl in that unique way that lights my panties on fire. I want to watch Red lose his shit as I get pounded by one of the others.

Dropping into Jacob's green velvet chair, Noah spreads his knees wide and settles in. Like a king atop his throne, he dictates our moves and relishes in the control he can exhibit here. I look at Jacob as he nods at Noah, relinquishing his steadfast control to his team leader more quickly than I'd anticipated.

Noah doesn't seem like the type to join in on group activities; he's a leader through and through. I don't see him stripping down and joining us all on the bed, but this seems to be a compromise for him. He's involved, but not directly. He barely hesitates as he waves a hand for me to join the others on the bed, and his praising growl is music to my ears as I move to follow his command.

I place my knee on the bed and bend forward to get up. Red takes the opportunity to run his hand down my back and over the curve of my ass as I crawl, adding extra sway to my hips for Red and Noah to relish, to join Jacob and Han. The former grabs my face and pulls me in for a delicious kiss that has my toes curling in my boots. Han strokes up and down my arm closest to him, and his sensual touches, coupled with Jacob's hard, punishing kiss, have me rethinking religion because this right here is as close to heaven as I've ever experienced.

"Take her clothes off," comes Noah's command from the far side of the room.

At once, the guys stop what they're doing, and with teasing touches, I'm quickly divested of my top, and Red works my boots off my feet. Jacob shifts so he can yank my jeans down my legs as Han situates himself behind me and unclasps my bra, dragging the straps tortuously down my arms. The scrape of the material along the goosebumps they've provoked has me shivering.

Jacob leans forward from between my legs, his fingertips trailing the waistband of my panties, slipping a single finger under the elastic as if he has all the time in the world while I gasp for breath at the attention. He peels them from my body, and I use the moment to look at my other two boyfriends. Red stands at the edge of the bed; his right hand is on the back of his neck as his left rubs his cock through his jeans.

Noah has his legs spread but leans forward with his elbows resting on his knees, watching the show we're putting on for him. "Hold her legs open, and let Tech have a taste."

Han immediately hooks my legs with his, pulling them apart and exposing my glistening pussy to the others. His hands come around my body to tweak my nipples as I maintain eye contact with Noah. He's still leaning forward, and as he watches Han maneuver me the way he wants, his head tilts up, and confidence enters his stare. He always liked being in charge. Who knew it would translate this well to group activities in the bedroom?

"Now, Tech," Noah coaxes.

Jacob scoots up the bed and takes my chin with his thumb and index finger, tilting my face so I'm looking directly at him instead of the man directing us from across the room. His gaze is fierce as it catches mine, and looking away is no longer an option when I see the lust and—dare I say it—love shining in his blue-grey eyes.

Red groans at the sight, and I do my best not to look at him next. Jacob wants my attention right now, and fuck, it's impossible not to look at him. His face, bare of glasses, leans in toward mine, and he gives me a brutal kiss, trailing down and leaving scorching, open-mouthed kisses and licks along my neck, collarbones, and breasts. His tongue blazes a path down my stomach, quickly dipping into my navel as he descends.

Finally, after a torturous few seconds, he reaches my clit. I let out a mewling cry as he swirls his tongue around that throbbing bundle of nerves, tightening my grip on Han's thighs, my nails digging into the firm muscles. As Jacob dips his tongue into my aching pussy, I'm sure I leave blood-stained marks with my nails on my captor's legs.

Jacob maintains eye contact with me as he devours me, his tongue setting a punishing rhythm, thrumming against my clit, until he looks to Han, who is teasing my peaked nipples in time with the tonguing I'm receiving from Jacob. The heat in Jacob's gaze as he flicks between the two of us as quickly as his tongue flicks against me has me detonating.

My head is thrown back onto Han's shoulder as his arm bands around my middle, keeping me in position and not letting me curl forward as my stomach muscles contract. The pressure is exhilarating, and the constraint across my abdomen has me begging for more. Without words, of course, because I'm still jinxed, and I'm not risking anyone stopping what we're doing because of some silly childhood game we take way too seriously.

I crack my eyes back open when I feel Jacob nip the juncture of my thigh. He lifts himself on his forearms and quickly kisses my lips before diving to my left and doing the same with Han. I watch, enraptured, as Jacob's tongue peeks out, sliding into Han's mouth, and the man groans at the taste of me still on Jacob's lips. It takes everything I have not to join in on their moment until a hand settles behind my head and pulls me closer.

The three of us are locked in a triple kiss, and even with my eyes closed, I know precisely whose tongue belongs to whom as we fit together. My hand reaches out for Jacob as Han's body is behind mine, his erection digging into my ass, and the angle makes it difficult to reach as he continues to pin my legs down, his arm still across my stomach.

"Our girl here seems to like being held in position. Isn't that right, Trouble?" Noah says. Jacob pulls back from the kiss, and I chase his mouth as he withdraws. I nod as I try to catch my breath. My eyelids flutter as I open them to look over Jacob's heaving shoulders to catch Noah's gaze.

Han continues trailing kisses along my neck, his hand never having left my breast as he kneads it deliciously. Noah looks at Jacob and nods. I don't know what that means, but I'm eager to learn. "Red, keep our girl busy," Noah instructs.

The man in question looks at me, quirking an eyebrow at Noah's use of my nickname, and I shrug. Everyone needs a nickname in this game, and it looks like he's borrowing. Red reaches behind himself, pulling his shirt over his head in the way only guys seem to be able to do by gripping the back of the collar and drops the material to the floor.

His hands playfully undo the button fly on his jeans, and I wiggle in Han's lap with every button set free. He lets out a breathy laugh and leans to his left, opening the bedside table drawer. I'm distracted by his rummaging around, but I keep my eyes on Lucas as he shucks his pants, kicking them off to the side as he makes his way to me.

"Feed her your cock, Red." *Fuuuuck me*, Noah's got some secret dirty talk buried under that proper etiquette he loves to use.

Red hops onto the bed in one lithe movement, never losing eye contact. He walks across the fluffy duvet, his abs contracting as he balances on the cloud-like mattress. When he's right in front of me, he puts a hand on my head, and my mouth drops open in encouragement.

He's always had a bit of a dominating vibe, and they all do, aside from Han, but I've never had him handle me this way, with such surety in his movements and grip. I dart my tongue out, tasting him, and his flavor explodes on my tongue. I groan and wrap my lips around him. I grip his thighs, using the leverage to pull myself into a kneeling position, away from Han, who helps push me up in the tight space between them with a firm hand on my ass.

I lick and suck and stroke until Red is groaning along with me, thrusting with abandon into my throat. I choke as he pushes in and holds for a moment, his hand still wrapped up in my hair, and as he retreats, I suck in a breath, ready for more. Han pulls my elbows to the middle of my back, and my breasts push forward with the movement, making Noah groan from his chair. I feel soft material wrap around my arms just above my elbows and realize I'm being restrained.

"Break the Jinx for your safeword, or if you want us to stop, okay, Trouble?" Noah asks, and I nod vigorously, making eye contact so he knows I hear him and am fully on board with what's happening. I can't help whimpering at the sensations as the material binds tighter and tighter on my upper arms behind me.

The Sacrifices We Make

"How's it coming, Tech?" Noah asks. Red's cock pops out of my mouth, and I look to where Jacob is standing on the bed, silk ropes hanging from the anchors in the ceiling I wondered about all those months ago. *Of course.*

Jacob holds up a finger, indicating just another moment, and Red uses the timing to continue thrusting into my mouth. His groans are becoming more and more breathy as he gets closer and closer to the edge.

I feel a hand under my chin and pop off Red to look at who's got hold of my face. Jacob is grinning down at me and lifts a brow. I nod my head. I am absolutely, positively, one hundred percent okay with everything happening here. I just wish Noah was with us on the bed, but I think that's something we'll need to work up to if he ever wants to join us. This is an excellent middle ground with him directing us.

"Mech, lay down on your back. Tech, over his face. Trouble, on top. Red, behind our girl." Noah has assigned us our positions, and my pussy clenches as I envision it in my mind. Han drops to the bed, his pants and shirt stripped off and thrown to the side, and with a lingering lick of Red's cock, I turn and straddle my first love. He pulls me down for a quick kiss, his tongue plunging into my mouth, greedily taking sips of my pleasure for himself. Then he positions me so I'm parallel to his body, levitating over him with a bit of space separating our torsos as his sturdy arms keep me balanced above him as my arms are still restrained behind my back.

I feel the movement behind me, and Red spears two fingers into my dripping cunt, pulling the wetness up to my asshole. He works a finger in, and I groan at the sensation as Han's hips shift rhythmically, his cock bumping my clit with each pass, causing a delicious shiver to rake over my body. My hips chase his as I crave and silently demand *more.*

Jacob starts passing the rope over and around my torso, framing my breasts and either side of my pussy and ass. I'm trussed up, breathlessly awaiting whatever magic is about to happen. Noah commands Jacob to lift, and with a slight tug, I'm weightlessly hovering over Han, my hips still connected with his, but my upper body is suspended. Jacob did the ropes well. There's not too much pressure anywhere, and when Red pushes his fingers in my ass, I sway forward along Han's length.

The moan that escapes me is obscene.

"Ready, Trouble?" Noah asks from his goddamned chair. I'm going to burn that thing, so next time, there's nowhere for him to sit, looking relaxed as all hell while I balance on the edge of insanity.

I look at him over my shoulder, unable to beckon him closer with my finger because of the restraints, and I refuse to break my silence for fear of this stopping altogether. He must see the desperate look in my eye because he shakes his head. He does, however, lift his hips and slide his sweats down his thick thighs and grip his cock with a firm hand. I see a bead of precum glistening on the tip and lick my lips. I want them all so badly; it feels like I'll break if I'm denied. "Guys, our girl is looking fucking hungry. Give her what she needs."

Han and Red lift my hips in tandem, and I'm lowered onto Han's cock. He starts pumping from under me, and the feeling is divine. I sway with each pass, but Red grabs my hips and steadies me. I feel the lube drip down my ass, and Red slides his cock along my crack, coating himself in the slick substance. He notches the head against my hole and works his way in, one tortuous pass at a time as I try to push back into him. Han groans under me at the sensation, and I echo it. There is nothing like being filled like this. At least, that's what I thought until Jacob moves in front of me.

His tattooed thighs move to either side of Han's head as he lifts my chin. He leans down, tucking my hair behind my ear, and I look down at Han, who has started pumping into me harder and harder, eliciting groans from Red behind me as their cocks stroke that thin wall between channels. Han's tongue is out and tracing Jacob's cock as it stands proudly above his face. Oh, fuck. *Oh, fuck, fuck, fuck.* That is hot as sin, and I can't look away. I clench around both Han and Red as they continue fucking me like they can't stop.

I raise my eyes to Jacob's cock and focus on the head. He pushes into my mouth as Han's hand wraps around his length, helping to keep it steady for me in my bound position. Han lifts his head and sucks one of Jacob's balls into his mouth while reaching between us to rub tortuous circles over my clit. I come with a loud moan, and Jacob growls so loudly, I'm thankful, once again, we're in a secure location.

Red's thrusts are getting more and more erratic as I feel his gaze burning into the three of us, no doubt a result of the combination of my earlier work, the feel of my tight ass squeezing him to oblivion, and the show we're putting on for him now. With a few more pumps, he pulls out of me, and I feel jets of his cum landing on my ass. His hand comes up and rubs it into my skin, marking me in a way I didn't think I'd find so fucking sexy—so claimed.

Jacob and Han continue their frontal assault, and I hollow my cheeks so that every time Han pumps into me, I move forward onto Jacob's cock, causing him to groan. Within minutes, we're all shattering. Jacob is the first to recover and removes my restraints with deft fingers and only a few lingering touches to the sore spots.

"Trouble, you okay over there?" Noah asks. I lift my head from Han's chest and make eye contact with the silent watcher in the chair. I nod my head as a sleepy smile overtakes my face. "Good," Noah drawls.

Red, Han, and Jacob share a look, quirked eyebrows on each of them, and they nod, obviously communicating something I'm not privy to with their nonchalant shrugs and easy silent conversation. They each kiss my lips and clear out of the room. Cleaning up and rest sounds good, but I've got one surprisingly dirty yet shy Captain to enjoy.

"Rogue," Noah says from his godforsaken chair, releasing me from my silence. "You sure you're okay?" he asks.

"Yes," I breathe as I try to regain my senses. I'm flopped on the bed, the pink marks from the ropes decorating my skin. Nothing hurts, but the reminders will keep me on edge until they fade. "But I need more, Noah. Please."

He looks at my face, gauging my seriousness, and in a swift movement, he stands from the chair. He drops his sweats completely and pulls his shirt over his head. I've never seen him naked, and Christ, what a tragedy. This Adonis is all mine, and it's time I claim him completely.

He saunters toward the bed, his thighs flexing with each step, and I lick my lips in eagerness. His eyes take in my body, and I lift up to rest back on my elbows, tipping my legs open so he can enjoy the view of the devastation his orders contributed to.

He plants a knee on the bed and moves over me with surety and grace. He doesn't do anything in half-measures, and I love him for it. The need to tell him rises up in my body, and I can't slow the words as they spill from my lips. "I love you, Noah Tate."

His eyes drop to my lips as he watches my truth outflow into the world. His brow furrows as if he doesn't believe me, but I'll never let him doubt my feelings. Not when he goes to great lengths to show me that he loves me as well. Between the phone call a few weeks ago and the sensual reassurance I've just received at the command of this man, I know he cares for me and will battle his own insecurities to give me what I need, and it's something I plan to reciprocate at every turn. I drop onto my back, using my hands to grip his cheeks and direct his face to look at mine.

I drop all of the walls I've ever hidden behind, and he must see the truth in my eyes as I repeat myself, "No. You don't get to doubt me. I've never given you a reason to. I. Love. You." I enunciate each word clearly so there is no room for error. "You are kind, strong, infallible," with each adjective, I deliver a kiss to his lips, the last one has me biting his lip and dragging him down with me, and his weight settles over me.

"Now, you've had your fun with me and the others. It's our turn," I tell Noah as I pull back to issue my own orders.

"Trouble, I love you, too." My breath catches in my throat. I never thought he'd return the words so quickly. I expected to wait on tenterhooks with his past and mistrust after what his ex, Sheila, put him through. But there's no wavering in his voice. No uncertainty. Just the stark fact that this is not one-sided in any sense and that we're all feeling this connection I never want to lose.

I propel upward, and Noah grabs my hands, lifting them above my head as his mouth descends and keeps me pinned to the bed, taking everything from me yet leaving me with so much more.

My back arches, searching for more contact, and he obliges with his hips shifting against mine. His cock nudges at my entrance, and I'm so wet, he slips along my slit until I see stars. He withdraws, leaving one hand holding my wrists higher up on the bed as the other grasps his own cock. He gives it a few pumps, and within moments, he's guiding himself into me, sliding into my ravenous pussy one delicious inch at a time.

Growing impatient, Noah plants his hand next to my head and thrusts the rest of his length into me, and I choke on air. So new, so perfect. How can I feel this way after being fucked six ways to Sunday by my other guys? None are better than another, but they're all so different; each experience fills a fractured part of my soul. I'm starting to understand monogamy doesn't work for people with souls as fractured as mine. Different pieces require different things that no one person can provide.

The groan Noah expels is hedonistic as he withdraws and slams back into me. Oh, fuck. He repeats his movements, dipping his head down to tease my nipple with his tongue, then withdraws and blows cool air over it, watching it in fascination as it peaks and pebbles. He pays the same attention to the other as his hips continue to snap against mine, driving me higher and higher up the bed and into nirvana.

My groans, moans, and chanting his name have reached a crescendo as he continues his movement, my body writhing under his. He suddenly pulls all the way out, and I groan at the loss of fulfillment. He hauls me up and flips me over as effortlessly as he flips fucking pancakes in the morning.

His hands hook around my hips, and he pulls my ass into the air. He impales me on his cock, picking up the rhythm he had earlier. His hands

The Sacrifices We Make

are leaving bruising marks on my hips as he anchors me in one spot. I grip the comforter below me, my hands flexing in the soft material, likely tearing it open with the force of my grip. I lower my torso so my breasts are pushed against the material to keep them from hitting me in the chin with the force of his thrusts. Yeah, big tits can cause self-harm. Watch out, ladies. Men, be aware.

Noah's grunts and rumbles are picking up the pace, and his rhythm is losing its finesse. He's getting close, and I'm honestly shocked he's lasted this long after watching the show the four of us put on earlier.

He dips one hand down and starts playing with my clit, and I fucking lose it. I come violently, screaming into the duvet as my pussy clamps around his cock, milking him for all he's worth.

He stills as he pushes into me a final time, his cum pouring into me and making me feel entirely satisfied as his fingers keep up their rhythm on my clit, drawing out my pleasure.

Withdrawing his cock, Noah must notice some of his seed spill out of me because there's a swipe along my slit and his fingers push their way into my cunt one final time. "So fucking sexy, Trouble. Look at my cum spilling out of you." I groan and arch my back at his words, letting him see all of me and soaking in his praise.

He helps to turn me over and drops down next to me on the bed. I'm exhausted and need to clean up, but in a few minutes, when I regain some feeling in my legs again.

Noah leans close, "I love you, Trouble. And we're doing that again."

I laugh and nod my agreement before it occurs to me that he could mean the group or solo session. I like to think we're leaving all options open. He may not join us on the bed, but I think we'll all be in agreement that he can direct us again. Remembering the look in his eyes as we followed his orders has me almost raring to go all over again.

Chapter Twenty-One

Jacob

When I wake up in bed, it feels too warm, and my legs are trapped. I fruitlessly try to move them to get more comfortable, but a hand snakes around my middle. I grin, knowing it's Han and relishing the feel of his body wrapped around mine. It might be a bit warm, but it's cozy, too.

"Well, aren't you two a vision?" comes a soft voice from the foot of my bed.

I lift a hand, indicating the intruder can bugger off during my snuggle time, but something seems off about the voice.

I crack open an eye to see Han standing at the end of my bed with a cup of coffee in his hands as his loose pajama bottoms hang perilously low on his hips. I groan and close my eyes once more at the sight.

I'm afraid to find out who's behind me until I remember what happened last night. I seriously hope it's Rogue snuggled behind me.

"'Fraid not, Cuddle Muffin." *Aw, fuck.* I must've mumbled that last thought out loud. Rogue's fingers pry one of my eyelids open until I'm looking at her with a watery eye because she's held it open for too long, and the dim lighting is way too much for me at the moment. She's in front of me, grinning like a fool.

"Who?" I ask in a timid whisper.

"It's Red. He likes being the big spoon," she laughs as she pushes away from me and snuggles into a different set of arms. And there's Noah.

After we gave those two some alone time last night, we went back into my room to clean up, change the bedding, and put away the toys so I could sleep in a cum-free bed. They came in following their showers, and after being unjinxed and talking late into the night, we all nodded off one by one in the early hours, having turned the evening into a big group sleepover.

I see Noah's hand trail up and down Rogue's bare stomach as she lies on her side facing me. He moves closer to her naked tits with each pass, and I watch as he grazes her hard nipples. She lets out a breathy moan, arching her back in a languid stretch until her ass is pushing back into him. Plucking at the peaks, he plays them until she's squirming in front of me. I'm about to trail my tongue down her stomach to find her hot pussy, but suddenly, there's a hard cock against my ass.

"Rogue, Darling Mine, you have to stop," I beg. "Lucas is getting way too excited."

"Jacob?" comes Lucas's sleepy voice behind me, his lips pressed against my shoulder. I feel his mouth pull into a smile, and he nips at the decorated skin just above my collarbone.

"Yep."

"Well," Lucas pauses, "we could let this be weird or let it go. Or we could continue last night's escapades."

Noah's voice comes from the other side of Rogue as his head pops up over her shoulder, "Morning, Trouble. I was having the best dream."

"I'll bet, big guy. We should stop. I have to get going," she says regretfully.

"No," Noah whines like a petulant toddler, pulling her snugly against him. I honestly didn't think he had it in him to let her see his playful side so early. He messes around with us sometimes and gets some pranks over on Lucas, but he's let Rogue into our circle quickly, and it's nice to see that relaxed smile on his face.

"I have to, you know that. Jacob has some digging to do on Mara, and I have to make sure my work went according to plan. Plus, I have to come up with some insane story about how I escaped three kidnappers. Any ideas on that one, guys?"

"What work?" asks Han, still standing at the foot of the bed. He ignores the kidnapper question because Rogue will surely think of something that plays to our advantage.

"Oh, uh..." she trails off. She's never hesitated like that before. I know there are certain things she can't tell us, but this one has her looking a little ashamed.

"Rogue," I intone. "Share, please."

"Fine. It's not that bad, but we didn't talk about it beforehand, not that we could, what with the whole being married and living elsewhere and listening devices in my apartment," Rogue rambles on, and with each word, I get increasingly anxious.

"I kind of burned down one of De La Cruz's warehouses that stores drugs the other night. G was with me, you remember him? I took him with me for the governor's hit. Anyway, we did that earlier this week, and I kind of set up some other hitmen to take down one of the guys funneling drugs in for the organization. Oh, and G's assignment last night was to hit a few more warehouses. I thought it'd be fun to blow up our drug trade."

No one moves. I don't think anyone is breathing at this point. You could hear a mouse fart in the silence.

"I'm..." Noah starts, propping himself up on his elbow, his face hovering over Rogue's. "I'm sorry? Did you just say you detonated a drug cache, organized a hit on their smuggler, and arranged for more blows to The Gambit's empire?"

"Uhh, yeah. Pretty sure that's what she said." Thank God Lucas didn't make an old joke about Noah's hearing. Now is not the time.

"Yep," she says succinctly.

"Why didn't you call us?" Han asks from the end of the bed; his voice is a bit softer than usual. He might be feeling a little left out about blowing shit up, but he knows this is her deal.

"If anyone had seen you, it would have been reported to the higher-ups, or God forbid, King. There would be a manhunt for you across the state. I couldn't risk it. G and I could always play it off as an assignment or checking in on the worker bees if we were seen before getting the job done," she explains.

I'm not happy she put herself at risk, but as always, I remind myself that my girl knows what she's doing. Despite how badly I want to kneel before her as her knight in shining armor, she's not some helpless damsel in distress.

"That makes sense, Trouble. But next time, can you keep us in the loop?" Noah asks.

"Yes, sir." Her retort, no doubt meant to be quippy and sarcastic, has Noah groaning and pushing his hips against her, moving her closer to me.

"As interesting as *that* new development is, we should probably make a plan," Han drawls from his spot at the end of the bed, noting the effect the "sir" had on Noah.

Rogue rolls towards me, taking Han's space, and presses a kiss to my lips. Morning breath is real, people. I do my best but end up pulling a face that has her smacking my shoulder and clipping Lucas on the chin because he still hasn't moved his face from the crook of my neck.

Damn, I love cuddles. I don't even care who they're from.

It's been two weeks since the sleepover to end all sleepovers, and the files we gathered from the bank have been handed over to the Annex management team. I've had eyes on Mara since my suspicions that she's working for a government agency cropped up. After more digging, I'm confident I know who she's been meeting with instead of going to her massage appointments.

It's her handler. It has to be.

So that's what brings me to this seaside cafe at ten in the morning on this overcast day. We've been trailing her but decided only one of us should approach her to fish for information. I insisted on going as she knows me through the tech training and recruited me from CalTech University.

The dark-haired man is gathering his things and getting ready to leave. I see the opportunity and leave the truck to reach the front door. I spy Mara through the windows, gathering her phone and an envelope to deposit in her purse and pulling out money to pay her bill.

The man stands from his chair and reaches out to take her arm as I walk through the door. "Ms. Hendrix!" I shout across the bustling little cafe.

The man's shoulders tense. His back is to me, so he doesn't know who's calling out to her, but it's always bad news for a clandestine meeting if someone is recognized. Mara pats his hand and leans close to him. She whispers something in his ear as I weave through the tables, and he takes off through the cafe toward the kitchens; bathroom or quick exit?

It doesn't matter, really. I'm not here to see him.

"Hi, Ms. Hendrix, fancy meeting you here. What are the chances? Can I buy you a refill?" I ask.

"Mr. Waters, I was—"

"Nonsense, it's no trouble at all," I insist. I use the flustered moment to wave down a server, order a cup of English Breakfast tea, and gesture for

Mara to place her order as I collapse into the now vacant seat. She orders a chai latte and raises a brow at me.

I grin in response, loving that I've boxed her into staying. Despite the face she puts on at work as a hard-ass, Mara was raised by her father to have manners and to put business first. As her employee, she grants me the audience without much fuss.

"What can I do for you?" she asks.

"Oh, nothing much. I just have a few work questions, if you don't mind. I was planning to schedule something with your assistant next week, but seeing as we're both here, it should only take a moment," I implore, concern lacing my tone.

"Well, I suppose I have enough time for one more drink, so let's get to it. What's on your mind?" Mara prompts.

"Why don't you have an account at Collinsworth Bank?" I ask candidly.

Her eyebrows shoot up, and her face becomes more like her work mask. "You were only supposed to deliver the files, Mr. Waters, not dig through them."

"Ah, well, too late. My question is, why does everyone but you have an account there? Why did we gather that intel in the first place? Is it for leverage on The Gambit or taking down the company your father helped build?" My questioning ends, and there's a lull in the din of the cafe. I watch as Mara tries and fails to fight the twitch in her fingertips as my inquiry sinks in.

"This is a dangerous game you're playing, Mr. Waters."

"I'm well aware, and we want in," I tell her simply.

"There is no room for you in this. At least, not in the way you're thinking." She repositions her legs, perhaps finding comfort in her fidgeting, and wrings her hands together on the tabletop.

The waitress comes to drop off our drinks, and I pay immediately. Who knows when I'll have to take off, and I'd rather not be waiting around for the bill or, God forbid, rush off without paying unintentionally. I waited tables in college. That was the worst.

I prepare my tea how I like it and lift my eyes to Mara's green ones. She really does look like Claudette if she was put through old-school librarian training and got lost in a closet full of shoulder pads. I mean, seriously, when did those make a comeback? Mum will be so pleased.

"Look, Mara. May I call you Mara? I insist you call me Jacob. There's more going on than I think you're aware of. If this is for the greater good, consider ATO part of your team. We'd like to help. How can we do that?" I ask, desperate to get some kind of information about what's going on. With the new influx of intel, it seems we spent the first half of the mission with blinders on.

"I can't tell you anything. But keep doing the assignments I post on the server and get the results to me. I'll keep the work coming, and it'll help if you guys don't mind doing the boring shit no one else wants to do." Color me surprised; Mara cursed!

"We're in. But," I lean in close, bent over the table and in her face, "if you fuck us over on this, we will come for you. And we won't be alone."

Her eyes search mine to see the gravity of the threat I've just laid down, and instead of any fear slipping in, she nods her head. "I can't tell you much of anything, but the assignments are the key. There's information to be found, and we need to be the ones to find it. I don't like the direction the company has taken in the last few years any more than you guys do." She lifts a hand to stop me as I open my mouth to ask more questions, "Yes, I know what you've been doing to remove people safely, and thank fucking God, but there was nothing I could do to step in. I've helped where possible, but I don't have much wiggle room."

"Cross?" I ask. Knowing the only person left with the power to steer the company is the man we know so little about.

Mara just nods and looks around the shop. "Look, I really do have to go, but keep doing things. Look for the phrase 'nail them to the wall' in the assignments. Those will be from me."

We shake hands over our teas, and there's finally a shift in our favor with the board. Rogue has her team of "Good-ish Guys," as she calls them, and it looks like we may have just found ours.

I've run over everything with the guys twice over the last week since meeting with Mara, and sure enough, when I opened the Annex server and filtered through the assignments, there were a few in there that had the code phrase in the body of the assignment text. We immediately snagged those assignments. The bank job had the term as well. I wonder which other agents she has on her side if the code has been going back at least a month.

And is it Patton Cross we're against? Or King? Or both? I need more information, but breaking into government servers takes time. And even

The Sacrifices We Make

then, not everything is recorded electronically until a job is done to prevent this very type of hacking.

The four of us are sitting in the war room, and it's not the same without Rogue. She's been able to slip over here once in the three weeks since our sleepover, but it's not enough. Lucas is constantly moping and painting anything and everything. One wall of the clubhouse has become his canvas. White roses, yellow sunflowers, sugar skulls, cartoon-style cherries, and Rogue's many tattoos are painted on the wall.

The monitor beeps and indicates there's someone at the front gate. I flip on my monitor and see Mrs. M in the Shaggin' Wagon, waiting to be let in. Knowing that she'll start honking soon and drawing unwanted attention if she isn't admitted immediately, I key in the code on the laptop, and the gate starts rolling open to let her in.

Lucas and Han hop out of their seats to help her because she always brings food, while Noah and I follow more leisurely. "You okay?" he asks.

"Yeah, mostly just glad I was right. Doesn't bring our girl home, though, does it?"

"Not yet. Hopefully soon," Noah replies shortly.

Mrs. M and the others enter with boxes and catering trays full of food. The boxes are left on the coffee table, and the food is carried into the kitchen.

"Happy Valentine's Eve eve, boys!" singsongs Mrs. M.

Ah yes, February twelfth—Mrs. M's unofficial holiday. Thankfully, we prepared early this year and bought and wrapped our gifts for her in August. The first time we celebrated with her, we learned that she expects —nay, *demands*—Valentine's gifts.

"Happy Valentine's Eve eve, Mrs. M," I say and kiss her cheek. She pats my shoulders and tells me I need to hit the weights more. God, I love this woman. I make my excuses and run to fetch the presents stored in one of the spare rooms.

I grab the boxes and notice there are five instead of four. I'm curious who's being a suck-up and got Mama Bear two gifts instead of the one we agreed on. I'm mulling over who to reprimand when I smell the faintest hint of lemon and lavender coming from the small box on the top of the pile and know that our girl really is *our* girl if she's buying gifts for Mrs. M.

I carefully make my way back to the others and move to settle the gifts on the kitchen island. Everyone is chatting and being generally merry when Mrs. M sees the stack of gifts and screams. I jostle the precarious pile and manage to only just hang onto them as she bounces up and down on her stool, making gimmie hands to get at the goodies. "Patience, Mrs. M!" I scold. *Honestly.*

"Fine," she pouts, following it quickly with a smirk. "Can a few of you grab the pile on the coffee table? Gifts first, food later."

Coming in with a tower of boxes each, I look at Mrs. M, who shrugs. There are the presents with her usual Spongebob Squarepants wrapping paper—she bought it in bulk two years ago, and it's been with us for every birthday and holiday since—but there are white-wrapped boxes mixed in, breaking up the wall of cartoon sponges.

Tearing into her pile of presents, she unearths a new pair of her favorite clogs from Han, a juicer from Noah, a lockpicking kit from Lucas, and the cross-stitched pillows from me with dirty phrases on them. She lifts the small present last and, with renewed vigor, rips into the fucker. She pulls out a USB and asks me for a laptop which I happily provide. We gather around and watch as a single file shows in the folder. It's a video, so we press play and wait.

Rogue's face fills the screen, and she starts speaking. "Happy Valentine's Eve eve to you, Mrs. M, and my guys. I have a feeling you're all watching this together. I'm sorry I can't be with you all, but you know King has been poking around and asking Romano where I've been running off to. Not to mention the whole kidnapping thing. He's still got me on lockdown, and I can't risk him finding out about you. I put this together knowing I won't be there with you guys to celebrate, despite Noah texting me repeatedly and Han agreeing to add my box to the day's stash."

We all look at Noah, who shrugs and says, "I miss her." I swear we all sigh, and I just know he wants to jinx us again.

Rogue's voice continues from the screen, "I'm sure you all just gave Noah some shit. Are you done? Can I continue?" She laughs softly. "Mrs. M, my gift to you this Valentine's Eve eve is one-on-one lessons with me on how to use your new knife. I bought you one, and I'll deliver it at our first lesson when I'm sure you won't stab anyone in the eye. There is a photo of it in the box where you found the USB drive." Mrs. M thinks that keeping the knife away from her is bullshit but admires the photo all the same when Rogue cuts off her upcoming tirade. "The rest of you, my guys, Mrs. M has gifts for you from me. I have plans to check in with Han in a few days when I'll give him this video on a flash drive, but I know I can't trust you not to peek if I hand over the boxes, Red."

"Hey!" he protests loudly at the screen.

She continues after a slight pause, perfectly timed with Lucas's

The Sacrifices We Make

outburst. "You know I'm right. Mrs. M, if you wouldn't mind, could you give Red his gift? Jacob, turn on the kettle, please. Pause me until he opens it." I lean over and hit the spacebar, still in awe of how well our girl knows us, and do as she asks. Mrs. M hands Lucas a medium-sized box that fits in his hands easily as I fill the electric kettle with water and set it to start. He weighs the box, shakes it, sniffs it, and still doesn't have a clue.

Ripping off the paper, he opens a plain cardboard box to find a matte-black mug nestled in an abundance of pink fluff. "Uhh, not as cool as my other mugs, but I love it all the same. Is it supposed to be black like our ops?" The kettle reaches its boiling point and flicks off. He sets the mug on the counter and pulls out the pink material, which turns out to be a pair of bunny slippers. He hugs them to his chest as I press play on the video.

"The slippers might be a little goofy, but I saw them on Elise at our meeting and knew I had to get you a pair." Lucas smiles and immediately bends down to slip them on his feet. Rogue continues speaking on the video, "Okay, Red, fill your mug with the water from the kettle and pause me till it's done." I press pause again and wonder if Rogue ever thought she'd end up with the kid from the AV club as one of her boyfriends.

Lucas walks across the kitchen tile in his slippers, mug in hand, and pauses at the kettle. He pours the water and taps his foot, bunny ears flopping with each tap.

His back is to us, and he lets out a choked sound. "I take it back. This is the best mug I've ever owned." He spins around and shows off the once-black mug. It's now white, having changed with the hot liquid inside, and says *I love you with all my boobs. I'd say heart, but my boobs are bigger.* I resume the video.

"I wanted to say this to you the last time I saw you, but it wasn't the right moment. I finally realized there is no 'right moment.' There is only right now. I hope you love it. I love you, Lucas." Her voice is calm and steady, and nothing but pure love shines in her eyes.

"Mrs. M, if you would do the honors? Noah is next," Rogue directs. Lucas puts his hands to his cheeks and tries to hide his blush and overwhelmed reaction as Noah is handed a large box. He manages to resist the urge to rattle it to guess what's inside. "Okay, you got it, Captain? I'm assuming so. Open it quickly because asking you to pause me repeatedly cramps my style." We all laugh at that before she continues.

"Captain, rip the damned paper. Make a mess." He does as she asks, and it amazes me that she knows what we will do in advance. He was looking for the seam to unwrap it carefully, but clearly, she's pushing him out of his comfort zone, and it's a joy to witness. The paper gets shredded off as he looks at a black box. He unlatches the small silver clasps and gapes at what's inside.

"This is for our next date. I'd like to plan this one if you don't mind. I want to go paintballing with you. It's up to you if you want to invite the others, but I want us to do something fun and reckless. I know you always hold it together for everyone, so my gift to you is letting go a bit. Let's make a mess, get down and dirty, and fuck shit up just for the hell of it. Okay, big guy? I love you, and I'll see you soon." Noah lets out a little grunt, but a grin overtakes his face.

Mrs. M pats his arm and smugly says, "Told ya so."

It dawns on me that she's said I love you to everyone but me at this point. Lucas and I were holding down the nonverbal love fort after she said it to Noah a few weeks ago, but with the mug and her declaration, I'm the odd man out.

"Jacob's next, Mrs. M." She leans over and hands me a wrapped flat packet, about the size and feel of a padded envelope. I tear into it, careful not to tear the contents. "This is for you *and* me, you and Han, or even just for you. It is yours to do with what you please, but I really want to test it out with you." I pause the video as I look at the furniture blueprints in front of me.

She designed me a new gamer chair.

More than that, she designed me a gamer *sex* chair. The armrests have built-in restraints, and there's a hook behind the headrest to attach cuffs or rope. The whole thing lays back flat but is weighted on the base to accommodate the extra movement and weight. She's even had the headrest stitched with "Tech," and fuuuuuck me; it has massage features for certain areas.

Han peeks over my shoulder and sputters out a cough. "Yep! She gets first dibs on that thing, but I definitely want a turn." Lucas pops up over my other shoulder and cocks a brow as he tilts his head to see all of the features. "Woah," he says. "I may even want a turn on that thing."

Mrs. M shushes us and hits play. "It's being delivered to G's house for me when it's ready, and I'll get it to you. It takes a while to customize something like that, but I hope you love it. I also hope you know that I love you, Jacob. I'm sorry I'm not there to say it to your face, but I will be." She wipes at her cheek, and the tear on her fingertips breaks my heart. We have to get her back here. Pronto.

"Last but certainly not least, my darling Han." The man in question beams at the endearment as Mrs. M puts a box in his waiting hands. He unwraps it and pulls the top of a shoebox open, looking inside as his mouth hangs open. "These are highly illegal and extremely dangerous. Please be very careful. I'm giving you this in hopes that you'll be my partner in crime for my next job, where I might require some of your expertise." I peer into the box and find explosives. Han's face is lit from within, and he's nearly bouncing on his toes.

"I know you guys said you just wanted me to tell you next time, but I think you'd all feel better if I had someone with me. Han will be that person if the job is incendiary-related. Boom, Handsome, Han, you were the first man to show me kindness since my parents died. You were my first in so many things, and I love you for who you were then and who you are now."

Rogue has made eye contact with the camera since she started speaking, but now, it is intense, unflinching, raw, and emotional. "This was way harder to do than I expected. I love you. All of you. And it kills me that I'm here and not there. Soon. I'll be back soon."

Chapter Twenty-Two

Rogue

IT'S TODAY. IT'S FINALLY FUCKING TODAY.

I've been living with Romano for way too long. King has been eerily quiet, only insisting I don't venture out for fear of another abduction, and I miss my guys.

After Valentine's Eve eve, I received messages and calls from the guys expressing their thanks and declarations of love from Noah and Han. Jacob and Red said they wanted to wait and say it to my face. And if everything goes according to plan, that day is today.

I texted Noah earlier this morning to tell him that Tanaka contacted me, and his appointment with Sage has been arranged for Thursday—the least sexy night of the week, in my opinion.

Arranging Tanaka's "date" with Sage took longer than expected because she was booked solid. I don't know whether to be proud or disgusted. I know it's not her choice, so the revulsion is firmly aimed at King and the people running the escort business.

I haven't seen her in a while, and I hope she's hanging in there. It won't be much longer now before we can get her out.

According to Noah's text, I have my meet-up with the guys today. He handled the logistics, promising we wouldn't be caught where we're headed. A storm of butterflies takes flight in my stomach at the thought of finally getting to see them, touch them, and breathe them in again.

Addiction? Quite possibly.

After texting King that I had to meet with one of the hitmen and help on a job, I climbed into a taxi. It was the only excuse he would accept for leaving the building. He insisted I take a guard with me, but after ushering them into the apartment and giving them a drugged water bottle, I slipped out of the building and into a taxi waiting for me outside. I changed cabs at the bus station and gave the new driver the address Noah had sent me. After a fifteen-minute ride, we approach a huge building I've never seen. "Skate Express" is written in giant neon lights on the side, and I see a line of people waiting for the doors to open.

Seriously? A roller skating rink? I heard these died out in the late nineties.

I exit the car and make my way to the line, joining the queue of overly excited children and worn-out parents, only gathering a few looks at my lack of offspring in tow at what is very clearly a children's venue.

I feel a movement behind me a second before a hand wraps around my waist. I know it's one of my men because who else would approach a woman giving off my stay-away-from-me vibes?

"Buttercup, you look divine," Red says as he leans in close, his breath whispering over my ear. His hand stays on the sliver of skin between my t-shirt and skin-tight jeans, and my walls drop just an inch or two.

I turn in his embrace and take in the faces I've been missing for weeks. Red's eyes are bright and cheerful, telling me he's as excited to see me as I am to see him. He softly kisses my lips, whispers, "I love you," and turns me to see the others hovering in the wings.

Han opens his arms, and I'm gently passed into them. He engulfs me in a warm embrace, whispering his greetings and love into my ear as the barricade I hide my true self behind slips down a little more.

Jacob approaches from behind, the heat of his body warming me as he wraps his arms around me, his palms against my belly. He tugs me back a bit and rests his chin on my head. He kisses the top of my head and leans down to catch my earlobe with his teeth. He lets out a small growl as his hips push into my rear, and with the slightest breath, I hear, "I love you, Darling Mine." My eyes slip closed as I revel in his words and touch. A smile plays along my lips, and I know that I'll be back to my true self with one more hug.

I open my eyes and see Noah staring at me with hunger in his eyes,

The Sacrifices We Make

watching the others get their contact first. Always the selfless leader, our Noah. I step away from Jacob, and he easily releases his hold.

I quickly stride the remaining two steps as Noah opens his arms. He lifts and spins me like Han did that first day in the clubhouse. I giggle, and his lips crash into mine.

Remembering where we are and the children present, I break the kiss before we forget our surroundings and smile against my Captain's lips.

"Hi, Trouble. I've missed you."

And there go the last of my defenses.

"Hi, Captain. Did you really pick a roller rink for our meeting?" I jokingly ask.

"Would anyone follow you to this place? And if so, there are so many kids and parents around that they'd lose track of you in no time. I booked us a party room. It's someone's birthday today, and she never told us."

I think for a second and realize, yup. It's my birthday. It's not like I've celebrated it since my parents died, so it's easy just to ignore it.

"I thought this could be fun," Noah says. "Jacob knew the date from his research, but when you texted about a meeting, we decided to make it a whole thing."

The line moves forward as the doors open, and people are admitted into the rink.

"I love it," I assure him.

Paying the entry fee and getting our rental skates, we enter a vast room with arcade games lining the walls and an enormous skating rink in the center. I opt for classic roller skates, and the guys all choose rollerblades.

"Do you Want to talk shop first or skate first? We're doing both, but the order is up to you, Gorgeous," Han states.

"Skate first, please," I say as I bounce on my toes, and my smile stretches across my face in a ridiculous display. This is kind of awesome.

We lace up—or, in their case, buckle up—our skates and hit the rink with the kids. No one is exceptionally skilled besides Noah, so we make fools of ourselves and laugh as we do laps around the rink. Noah attributes his ease to his years playing hockey as a teenager, and it shows. Jacob clings to the wall to avoid wiping out and only just manages to keep his feet under him.

After twenty minutes of going around and around the rink, we make our way to the party room Noah booked and find chocolate cake, soda, pizza, and hot dogs. Ah, the joy of kid's party food.

Grabbing plates and dishing up the goods, we settle in. "Okay," Noah starts, "what's the plan?"

"Well, Tanaka's meeting with Sage is happening. He has the day and time but not the location. I checked, and it seems they frequent only two or three hotels in El Castillo for the higher-paying clientele, which Tanaka is. The fee he's paying would make some small countries weep. His reward for the tech sale is the opportunity for the date. He still has to cover the charge."

"Okay, so let's make a plan of attack for each. We'll need a location near the entrance to watch when Tanaka enters. He's still good with the scheme, yes?" Jacob asks.

"Yeah," I answer. "Tanaka and I had lunch again a few days ago with the other Good-ish Guys, and everything is settled. He knows what to do and insists on doing it. Most of it was his idea, honestly. The timing is down pat, and it'll require me to take out a few of Sage's security guys, who will be stationed out in the hall. King briefed him on the security details and requirements for an evening with my sister."

"*Us*, Trouble." I look at Noah with a confused face. He just sighs. "You said, 'It'll require *me* to take out a few security guys,' and you should have said *us*," he clarifies.

"Fair point," I concede. Having a team like this to back me on something so personal is still so odd.

Red holds up a hand and exaggeratedly finishes chewing his pizza, obviously wanting to say something but having enough manners to not speak with his mouth full. Finally done, he takes a drink of his soda and licks his lips. "That's damn good pizza. But I call dibs on being with Buttercup in the hotel. You know we can't all go in there."

"Deal," says Jacob. "But a couple of us will be in the hotel itself while one keeps the car running."

We spend the next two hours alternating between stuffing our faces and making plans. Noah said we couldn't go skate again until we had a strategy. It took a while, but I'm happy with the results.

The night is cut short when Romano calls, asking why there's a burly guard passed out on our couch and telling me King asked where I was, so I say my goodbyes and cab it back to my building to deal with the mess I left at the apartment and wait for retribution day.

The Sacrifices We Make

It's Thursday. The day I finally take something back from King. He's strong-armed me into marrying a man I don't love, told me I need to have a child with the old ball and chain, and brutalized my body in the name of training. He also possibly killed my parents—but seems to have been in love with my mother—and had my sister stashed away since infancy. E-fucking-nough.

I may not be able to kill the bastard today, but I can sure as shit make his life harder when he loses leverage over me. I mean, sure, he still has the evidence, but I can only deal with one problem at a time. Getting Sage out has been job one since I started training. Killing King and getting away with it, job two.

I crack open my eyes and look to my right. Romano is wide awake, staring at my face across the no-man's-land center of our bed.

"Are you sure about this?" he asks me for what must be the hundredth time in the past two days.

My answer is always the same. "No, but it's the best shot I've got."

He sighs at my answer, knowing full well that someone could get hurt today. I can't let him in on all of the plans, but I did ask him to keep King occupied tonight, so he knows something big is going down. With De La Cruz gone, the drug trade abruptly cut off and in shambles, and Horvat murdered, King knows someone is coming for him, but he isn't sure who.

I've basically been on lockdown after my "abduction" and subsequent release. I fed King a story about how three men in ski masks took me, and after being bound and gagged, I was to deliver a message to him. I told him they had threatened him and The Gambit, claiming they would be the ones running the city in no time. King scoffed at the idea but still warned me to stay home.

I've been doing all of my work online, and the hitmen have all accomplished the tasks I've set for them, thus cutting off the drug supply train at the moment. King and De La Cruz's number two are currently working on a new avenue.

King doesn't know I slipped his guard the other night to meet with the guys. I came home to find him still passed out on the couch with Romano sitting in one of the armchairs, shooting glances at the man to check if he was still breathing. When the man came to, I threatened him with my very favorite knife, then offered him a spot on my team with the possibility to work his way up if he kept his mouth shut. He started the next day.

After tonight, King will likely put me on the kidnappers' trail and believe it's their fault he loses Sage. It'll take some well-timed hints, but I know he'll be looking for their next hit. Sage's kidnapping will fit that narrative perfectly. My guys are geniuses.

I look at Romano's face, and I swear he's aged at least ten years in the few short months we've been married. I always knew being married to me would be taxing. He opens his mouth, closes it again, furrows his brow, and finally spits out the words he's been mulling over. "Just be careful. You may be my wife only in name, but I'd care if you got killed, Rogue."

That right there is how I know he's a good man stuck in some dreadful circumstances.

———

I MEET THE GUYS AT THE DESIGNATED SPOT AFTER TANAKA WAS GIVEN the location, knowing we're risking being seen together but having decided it was worth it. G and Fabio were put on "Rogue Watch," as they call babysitting duty, and I told them to take the night off because I was staying in anyway.

I may have lied. I've never given either of them a reason to doubt me, and as their boss, my word is law.

The guys and I had options picked out for each of the possible local hotels, so it'd be easy to coordinate on the day of Sage's extraction. It was just a matter of knowing which one we'd need to be at.

I meet them at the Indian restaurant around the corner from the hotel, and we grab a table near the window to watch and wait. If only we had known the location further in advance, we could have installed Red or one of the other guys as a hotel worker to make access a little easier. As it is, we've only known about the location for the last hour. It was impossible to get eyes on the inside. Still, we did have a moment to get a small plan formulated based on the original but with contingencies for this particular scenario.

It took a few dozen phone calls, some careful maneuvering on all sides, but our plan is settled. As we sit around munching on appetizers and drinking tea, I look at the guys who have been there for me when I'd given up hope on humanity.

Between King, the hitmen, and the jobs I do, I'm not surrounded by much good in my life. I try to hang onto it when I find it, but sometimes it's more difficult than trying to breathe underwater.

Noah and Red sit on either side of me, the latter's arm around my shoulder, his lips tracing small patterns on my neck; the former has his

The Sacrifices We Make

hand on my thigh, inching higher and higher, testing my resolve. Jacob and Han sit opposite us in the booth, their hands laced together, these little looks passing between them that show the love and devotion they have for each other. As if they sense me looking, their eyes meet mine, and I see that same love and devotion aimed at me.

I have never in my life been more content. More loved. More cherished.

We sit in silence as I watch the clock tick down. Tanaka should be arriving any moment, and Noah has the best position to see through the window to the hotel entrance. This whole plan hinges on him showing up. Every second that passes, my nerves creep to dangerous levels until I'm in my deadly calm mission mode. Han notices immediately, of course, and reaches across the table to take my hand and runs his thumb soothingly over my knuckles. The same way I've seen Jacob do to him when he's not resting well.

It takes another few minutes, but Noah nods his head. He's seen Tanaka arrive.

It's showtime.

Jacob settles the bill with the waiter up at the front as the rest of us gather the coats and hats. We want to be as covered as possible for the security cameras, and winter has provided us with the perfect excuse for layering up.

We exit the restaurant, Han and Jacob veering to the left after calling a goodbye as Red, Noah, and I head in the other direction. We have plans set about where we'll be in the hotel, and it didn't matter which hotel he chose, as they're all laid out similarly, it's just a matter of a few feet to the left or right.

Noah takes up his post near the entrance and slips Red and me each an earpiece. We're headed inside to have a drink in the lobby with Han and Jacob, who should be showing up in about ten minutes.

Red threads his arm through mine, steering me through the revolving door and into the lobby. This is it. I can't fucking believe after all this time, if everything goes to plan, Sage will be free.

We settle at the bar, and my date for the evening orders me a gin and tonic and gets a bourbon for himself. I've never known him to drink the stuff, but I guess when you're undercover, you make different choices. It must be usual for him when he's working a job.

After the bartender sets the drinks and coasters in front of us—lingering a little too long on my cleavage, now free from my coat—I feel the air charge with electricity and a warm body behind me. My hair is brushed to the side, and Jacob plants a soft kiss on my exposed shoulder.

"Mine," he whispers in my ear. Every time he lays his claim, I feel like jumping his bones.

Coincidence? I think not.

He drops onto the stool next to me as Han takes up his other side. We sit and chat about nothing to keep curious eyes off of us. We pretend we all work for an asshole boss in an accounting firm, and every time one of the guys says what a hardass their boss is, Noah grumbles at us through the earpieces. It's fun, and I can't remember the last time I had fun on a mission. It must have been the governor job with G.

We pass the time, and when I feel the burner phone vibrate in my pocket, I check the message. Everything is ready to go, and Red and I need to move. *Now*.

I settle my hand on Red's and nod toward the elevators. Jacob makes a big show about waving us off paying, saying he and Han will handle the bill. We stand, drape our coats on, and make our way across the expansive lobby. Han and Jacob will split up, one staying in the bar for coverage and one making their way to the service entrance around the back of the hotel.

We ride the elevator up in silence. Red's hand in mine, his eyes on me as we pass floor after floor. Tanaka texted that he told Sage what was going on and that she knows what to do.

As we reach the twenty-third floor, the doors open, and there's shouting coming from down the hall. I sprint out ahead of Red, him hot on my heels, as I barrel my way through the cracked door and into the hotel suite Tanaka told me they were in.

Around me is pure bedlam. Tanaka is on the floor, a gash in his head seeping blood into the expensive carpet; Sage is being held by one of the escort company's security guards while the other is on the phone. The dickhead on the phone sees me first, and I don't give him a moment to prepare. I charge him like a motherfucking linebacker as my hand reaches back to pull the knife from my hip and ram him with my shoulder.

I hear Red come barging in after me, and he stops short, likely assessing the situation. I land on top of my target, wrestling him to the ground. I use my arms and legs like a vise around his own to subdue him. Thank God Han made us do so much grappling training when I lived there. Must remember to thank him if I survive this.

Within moments, I have the man stomach-down as I pin his arms with my legs while sitting on top of his body and yank his head up. I drag my knife across his throat, so he bleeds into the carpet instead of letting the blood hit the walls, leaving a bit less of a conspicuous mess to clean up.

When I feel the fight leave the man's body, I snatch up the phone he lost in our altercation and examine the screen. There's no name, only a number, and the phone is still connected. I lift it to my ear, expecting to hear someone asking what's going on but instead, there's nothing. I'm not speaking first, asshole. Nice try.

I click to end the call and look at Red, trying to carefully maneuver the last thug, who still has Sage gripped tightly in his arms, into a vulnerable position. When her wide, fearful eyes meet mine, I shake my head. She can't get out of this on her own, and fighting her captor won't help; Red and I will have to handle it. She lets out a resigned and fearful sob, making her petite chest rise and fall in short bursts. She's going to have a panic attack before we get her out of here.

Her movements spur Red into action, who feints left and attacks right, getting a slice across the man's arm as he raises it to defend his face. Red doesn't pull his firearm, knowing as well as I do that as soon as the guard sees that, he'll kill my sister, knowing he has no escape. Sage is still perilously close and stuck in the middle of a knife fight. I come at the man from the other side, and he whirls to fend me off, giving Red an opening. He sinks a blade into the man's side and yanks it back out.

As soon as the blade is in, he slackens his grip on Sage. I use the opportunity to pull her from his arms and push her behind my body. I feel her turn to the door and tighten my grip on her wrist. "Stay here; there could be more coming. We'll finish this, then we're out of here."

She gulps, her blue eyes wide with fear, and nods her head.

Red presses his advantage and advances on the man while I block Sage with my body. I have to check on Tanaka as he lies there on the floor, groaning in pain as he comes to, but Red and thug number two are getting closer and closer to his prone body.

As I'm watching the two men trading punches and Red landing hits with his knife, never letting up enough for the man to draw his own weapon, nor having the opportunity to pull his own gun from his coat pocket, I see Tanaka reach for the man's ankle. The guard throws a wild and unexpected punch at Red that speaks to expert training, forcing him to retreat just long enough for the man to lift his leg away from Tanaka, pull the gun out of the ankle holster, and fire one shot into Tanaka's chest and one in his head.

Sage's security guard's choice to end Tanaka ends up costing him his life.

I've never seen Red move the way he does when he leaps through the air to close the gap before the man can swing the gun in Red's direction. I shove Sage behind the couch in case the man fires, and it's a good thing because the gun goes off again, the bullet's trajectory only a few feet to my left.

Red's knife descends and embeds itself into the man's eye. It pushes through, and he uses the momentum to drive it in and shifts it, shredding whatever finds its way in the blade's path.

Being held up partly by his body's shock and partly by the death grip Red has on the knife, the man begins to sag. Red pulls the knife from the man's gaping eye socket, grabs the gun from his slackening grip, and fires twice in the chest and once in the head.

Thank God there's a small silencer on the gun, but we should still get out of here before anyone decides to investigate. It's not altogether silent, no matter what Hollywood would have us believe, and I don't want to take any chances with Sage's life now that she could finally be free. We just have to get the fuck out of here.

I go to pull her from behind the couch, but she leaps in the other direction toward Tanaka, frantically checking him for a pulse despite knowing she won't find one.

"He saved me. He told me you were coming for me tonight and that I had to hit him on the head convincingly and leave with the guards, and you'd get me away in the hallway. I hit him, but I must have hit him too hard or something. I was scared, so I just closed my eyes and swung the lamp like a baseball bat." She sucks in a deep and shaky breath.

"He spun, and his foot got caught on the leg of the table, and he crashed into it. The security guards heard it and came in. The customers aren't allowed to mark me, so they were probably going to step in. When they saw me with the lamp in my hand and him bleeding all over the place, they grabbed me, and that's when you showed up. He shouldn't have died, Ivy. He shouldn't..." Her words trail off into a mumble as she keeps repeating the last sentence over and over.

There's nothing I can do for Tanaka now, so I wipe the tears trying to escape and start making a plan. I make a mental note to have the guys tell Rosa to make it look like a mugging gone wrong. At least that way, his family will have his body back to bury it as they wish. He was a good and decent man who worked to support his family, despite the caustic nature of the organization he became entangled with. He did not deserve this ending.

I hold a thin and frail Sage in my arms, hoping she doesn't faint before we get to the vehicle, but the chances of that are slim. The tremors wracking her body make it hard to keep a grip on her as I try and fail to get her up on her feet. She obviously hasn't been exposed to these kinds of things like I have, so I have to remember to take it slow and be calm.

Red helps me to get her up and moving; all the while, she's still mumbling about how she's responsible, and we make our way out of the room as I refute every piece of blame she tries to place on her own shoulders. This one is on me. I switch on the comms, let the guys know we're on our way, and tell them what we need from Rosa.

I really have to send her more gifts for cleaning up my shit. If she does this one well, and Tanaka is removed with dignity, I'm buying her a goddamn house.

Sage is shaking the entire ride in the elevator, and Red's black coat is covered in blood, but it shouldn't be too noticeable on the cameras. We exit on the parking level, and Noah is there with the SUV ready to go.

"Han and Jacob?" I ask.

"In the truck on the way to the clubhouse. Are we still keeping Sage there?" Noah asks.

"Yeah, it's the safest place for now. Did someone call Rosa? Does she know how to handle Tanaka?" I ask. Noah nods and puts a reassuring hand on my knee from the front seat after Sage and I climb into the back. Red takes shotgun and sends a sympathetic glance over his shoulder at us. He knows how much I liked Tanaka and how little he deserved that finale. He's no doubt watching that I don't put my walls back up to deal with this.

We set off into the night at a fast clip and head in the direction of home. Noah resists the urge to ask about what happened until we're all together, and right now, I'm extraordinarily thankful for that.

I only want to go over this once. But more importantly, I want to give my sister a hug and celebrate the fact that we got her away despite the bitter consequences.

Chapter Twenty-Three

Noah

Three days into having Sage living with us, I finally see her poke her head out of the guestroom. We put her in the one beside Rogue's, but our girl hasn't slept in there in months. I still think of it as her room, in any case. Hell, even when she was living with us full time, she was in one of the other's rooms more often than her own.

Rogue had to go to Tanaka's funeral today with the rest of the board and her stupid husband. She's been trying to get here to be with her sister, but with De La Cruz's second, Cian Byrne, having stepped into his boss's old role, the drug storage places having been blown to smithereens, and the loss of Tanaka, there's been a lot of emergency meetings called.

Rogue says King hasn't mentioned Sage being gone yet, and he likely won't for the time being. If King thinks someone's taken her, he'll guard the fact that he no longer has as much control over Rogue as he once did.

Sage has stayed in the guest room, as is her right, and we deliver food and supplies she may need as she sequesters herself away, coming to grips with finally being out of her old life. I would say she was free, but she's stuck here until we can either safely move her or remove the threats looming over her life and Rogue's. Lucas has started chatting with her through the slightly ajar door after delivering her meals and seems to be making some progress.

The woman in question peers into the central area of the clubhouse from her doorway and cracks it open a bit wider. I watch from my peripheral vision as she tilts her head back, assuming a more confident pose, and pulls the door open all the way. She takes a few tentative steps out, takes two back toward her room as if she's changed her mind, then spins and starts walking along the catwalk toward the stairway.

Rogue introduced us to her the night we got her back from the escort service, but the girl was so shaken, I'd be shocked if she remembered any of our names. Trouble told Sage that we were her boyfriends and that she'd be staying with us. We would never touch her, harm her, or presume to dictate what she does. When our girl made those promises on our behalf, looking each of us in the eye as they were delivered, we simply nodded, offering our names to her in greeting.

Sage starts making her way down the steps to the lower level, and I see her pause as she finds me on the couch in the lounge. It's only for a second, but it's enough to tell me she's still feeling unsteady. I relax my posture, trying to rid myself of that solemn facade I wear so often.

She reaches the ground floor, and I lift a hand to invite her over. She hesitates but then squares her shoulders and makes her way to the couch opposite the armchair I'm currently occupying.

I wait until she's settled before trying to start a conversation. With how little we've seen of her, we haven't had a chance to speak. Trouble has been able to get here once since the night we brought Sage here. After visiting with her sister, tears were evident on her face, and a weary resignation had taken up residence in her eyes. She only told us Sage was dealing with it and that we should give her a little time.

We went over everything the other night in the war room after Trouble got her situated in the guest room. She told us what Sage said had happened, and it's clear the situation got out of control, ending with Tanaka's death. After the debrief, she had to head back to keep suspicion off of her.

"Hey, Sage. I'm Noah, one of Rogue's boyfriends." She nods her head and keeps her eyes on mine. Despite her initial hesitancy when coming out of her room, she's slipped into a calm yet confident mask.

"I remember," she says. "Plus Ivy has told me all about you guys. You're the boss, but she likes you, even when you get growly. Her words, not mine."

I let out a little laugh at the description, and it trips me up a little when she uses her sister's real name. Between "Rogue," "Ivy," and the myriad of

The Sacrifices We Make

nicknames floating around, it gets a tad confusing, but you only have to hear the affection in each of our voices to know who we're talking about.

"Okay, that's good. Your sister was telling us a bit about what happened," I say and immediately regret my words as her shoulders inch up toward her ears and the tension grows. I internally curse myself for bringing it up and needing to know everything all at once. I decide to press later; for now, simple assurances will do. "None of it was your fault, Sage. That rests squarely on our shoulders for the plan and the man who pulled the trigger. If we take it one step further, it's King's fault for putting you in that position." She looks at me with tears in her eyes. "None, Sage. *None* of it is on you."

Tears slip, unbidden, from her eyes and trail down her cheeks. She's still basically a child, and after living stashed away, God knows where, and with God knows whom, she's understandably uncomfortable. "I know. I feel so terrible for that man, Tanaka, and his family. Has Ivy said if she's coming back today?" she asks.

"Yeah, she should be back in a few hours," I assure her.

"Okay. I'd like to get to know you guys. Her, too, I guess? We've only seen each other briefly over the years. I don't know much about her." It hits me how hard our girl has been working to free her sister when she doesn't know anything about her other than the situation she ended up in.

"We can do that. Can I get you something to eat? Drink?" I ask, wanting to make her feel more at ease. I mean, we are dating her sister. All of us are in love with her. Plus, if she ever gets second thoughts about us, it would be good to have her sister backing us. But, more importantly, Sage just seems like a genuinely nice, lost young woman.

"Water would be good. Maybe some food, if it's not too much trouble?"

"You got it. Anything in particular you want? I can whip something up for us. It's nearly dinner time anyway. The guys will be hungry soon, and I'm craving something home-cooked. Want to help me?" I ask hopefully. Anyone has to be better than Lucas at helping in the kitchen, and it might be a way for us to get to know each other while keeping our hands busy instead of just staring at one another across the coffee table.

"Yeah, that sounds great," she responds quickly.

We make our way to the kitchen, and I put her to work chopping vegetables while I prepare the broiler and grill attachment for the stove. We're having Korean-style pork belly because the meat was on sale this morning, and Han has been complaining that my Ethiopian cooking adventures have gone on long enough.

I'm focused on the meat sizzling on the indoor grill as Sage puts the side dishes into little bowls. I chose this meal, hoping the sharing aspect of food would extend to the conversation. I hear Han and Jacob make their way into the kitchen, whispering furiously over something, but they suddenly stop talking altogether, having seen our guest has opted to join us.

"Hey, Sage!" says Han cheerfully.

"Hello," Jacob echoes.

She lifts the knife in a little wave, giving herself a break from cutting the kimchi into bite-sized pieces. "You know, you look a lot like your sister when you do that," Lucas says from the doorway.

We all let out a little chuckle and marvel at the similarities. Sage and Rogue don't look too similar, but I know Rogue dyes her hair black, and while Sage's pale skin is unmarked, Rogue is covered neck to toes in tattoos on one side. However, it's the little smirk and blade-wielding that show the familial resemblance. "You're actually right, Lucas."

She pauses, looking at the knife in her hand, and cracks a small smile. Being compared to her sister is obviously a good thing in her eyes instead of the usual sibling rivalries we all hear about.

"Okay, boys, stop comparing. You," Sage says as she either regains her confidence or pulls on the domme mask she wore for work and points the knife at Jacob, "grab the dishes. And you two," she points between Lucas and Han, "start moving stuff over. Someone figure out when my sister is going to be here."

With that, everyone springs into action as I pull my phone out, turning my face to hide the smile threatening to break free. The last thing I want to do is make Sage feel self-conscious about taking control. After all, she'll be in control of the rest of her life. It's time she learns how to do it.

Me: Hey, ETA?
Trouble: 10 minutes. Food?
Me: Covered.
Trouble: ::thumbs up emoji::

Fucking emojis. If you can't beat 'em, join 'em.

Me: ::kissy face emoji::
Trouble: ::shocked emoji::

I look around and see everyone following Sage's orders, so I start piling the meat into the serving dish, cover it, and make my way over. I drop it off in the center and go back to the fridge for drinks after getting everyone's preference.

Han lifts the lid of the dish behind me and groans in pleasure. His mom makes the best Korean barbeque, but I know mine is a close second. She just won't tell me the secret to her ssamjang sauce.

All of our phones make a short chime, telling us Rogue is here. Lucas hops up out of his chair and races for the front door, shoving a hand in Jacob's face and pushing him back into his chair to be the one to welcome our girl home.

Sometimes it's eerily similar to living in a frat house, but the laugh that pours from Sage is totally worth it. She doesn't seem like she's had many opportunities to smile, so I'm glad we're providing some entertainment.

A few minutes later, Lucas leads Trouble into the kitchen, and she looks spent.

"How'd it go?" I ask, taking in her all-black ensemble and red-rimmed eyes.

She looks at Sage, likely knowing the guilt she's carrying. Sage just nods at her sister, indicating it's okay to go over it with us.

"It was okay. Heartbreaking, devastating, but okay. Only a few from the board attended, but most of the Rook Industries employees were there, along with his family, of course. Nothing but kindness from everyone. I..." She pauses. "I know we can't tell the family what happened, but I want to make sure his girls don't lose their spots at their schools because of funding.

"Jacob, could you set up some kind of life insurance payment to be sent to them from me? But, obviously, don't include anything about me?" she asks shyly.

"Yeah, Love. I can do that. We'll work it out this week and get them whatever you want," he assures her.

Trouble grabs a stool, plopping down on it as if her bones are too heavy for her to carry anymore. I step up behind her, resting my hands on her shoulders, squeezing gently. She doesn't have to carry anything alone anymore. That's what we're here for.

"I feel guilty. I know we contributed to the outcome with our plan. I also know we weren't the ones to pull the trigger or start this mess, but I still feel it. I got Sage out, everything I've wanted for years, and he lost his life." Her voice fades to a whisper as she finishes voicing her thoughts.

Han takes the stool next to her and clasps her hands in his own. "I know, baby. I know." Han's hands keep hers from withdrawing as he looks deeply into her eyes. "How do we help you?"

Rogue

"That'll be two thousand dollars, Sagey-poo!" Red shouts across the kitchen island.

Yep. Sagey-poo. That's happening.

The man who decided to call me Buttercup at our first meeting can't think of anything better than Sagey-poo. I'm slightly disappointed.

"No!" my sister shouts at him. I look at the board, and yeah, she landed on his fancy-ass Boardwalk Avenue property with the hotel he painstakingly built and mortgaged all of his other properties to fund.

"'Fraid so. Gimmie!" Red is well into his sixth beer at this point, and the rest of us aren't far behind.

When Han asked me how they could help, I said the only thing I could think of. Family dinner and game night, like my parents used to do with me. Sage was still far too young for games and more interested in her pacifier at that age, but if I can make some memories with her, I'm damn well going to do it.

"God, you're awful," she tells Red. "Are you sure you want to date all four of these guys?" she asks me after casting a judging eye over my boyfriends.

When she asked me about the guys on her first night here, I didn't know how to explain our relationship or what degree of exposure to healthy relationships she had seen over the years. I just told her they were all my boyfriends. She said, "Cool," and that was that.

She didn't ask for too many details the way I would have, but I guess when you grow up in the line of work she's in, things like this don't come across as weird.

Sage lines up some Monopoly money in her hand and starts sliding the other across the top, making it rain. Red immediately gets up and starts performing some impressive stripper moves to earn his keep, making the rest of us snort in laughter.

"That's it. I've mortgaged everything I have to pay that one," she points to Red. "I think I'm done for the night."

"Probably a good idea," Noah says. He's nearly out of cash, too. Who knew Red was the real estate mogul of the group?

As we pack up the game pieces, I ask Sage, "Can I stay with you tonight? There are a few things I want to talk about before I have to get back to my apartment. Someone is covering for me tonight, but I won't be able to come back again for a little while."

The Sacrifices We Make

"Sure, but I snore, so if you stay the night, be warned."

"You snored when you were a baby, too," I laugh.

Her face turns serious for a moment, "I'd really like to know about our parents and our old life if you don't mind revisiting that."

"That's part of what I want to talk about. We'll go over all of it, but tonight, you need to know what the circumstances are. I have a job out of town tomorrow, so I'd rather get you up to speed now."

"Sounds good," she says as she nods.

We say our goodnights, and Sage gives a wave while telling Han he has a workout buddy in the morning. I make my way around and give each of the guys a small kiss. I know Sage knows we're all together, but she doesn't need to see it.

We make our way upstairs and into the bathroom to get cleaned up for bed. Teeth brushed, faces bare and washed, we pad along the catwalk to the guest room.

I call out a last goodnight to the guys as they make their way into the bathroom on either side of the clubhouse. Stepping into Sage's room, I see it's a replica of my guestroom here. Simple furnishings, a small bag of clothes I bought for her stashed in a corner, a bed, and an empty dresser. If she's staying here, I'll need to get her some more things to make it feel like home while we work on removing King.

Sage crosses the room, reaches into the duffle, and pulls out two sleep shirts I bought for her. She tosses one to me and says, "I always sleep nude, but I figure that'd be weird if we're sharing a bed." I laugh because, of course, she does. I do, too.

I strip down and toss the shirt over my head. It hangs to mid-thigh and is super soft. Excellent choice. Sage is nearly naked, but when she turns to grab the shirt from the bed, I see raised and shiny skin on her back in an odd pattern.

"Sage, what happened to your back?" I ask because it looks familiar. Really familiar.

"Oh," she says, trying to shield the mark from my sight. "It's my rune. King says you have one, too."

I lift my shirt to show her the algiz on my abdomen; the one King carved into me as Horvat held me down. It's one of many lining my stomach, but it stands out as the most prominent. She moves closer, tracing it with her fingertips as goosebumps break out over my skin. I place my hand on her shoulder and turn her body. On her lower back, there's a replica of my abdominal scar.

"Is this the only one?" I ask, my tone deadly calm as an inferno of rage engulfs both my vision and soul.

"Yeah," she trails off as she takes in the others on my stomach, each earning a small touch from her slim fingers.

"I'm going to fucking kill him," I growl out, promising my sister this with every measure of intention I possess.

My declaration causes her to gasp, and before I can calm her, my phone dings from the bedside table with an incoming text.

I open the message and find it's from Romano.

Hubs: Vegas Crew is gone. Wiped out. Happy three-month anniversary.

The End...for now.

Back Matter

Afterword

Daaaang. Okay, I know a lot happened in this book. Noah was all like, "I'm alive!" and you were probably all like, "I'm going to fucking kill Mila!" But then you realized we needed that grumpy grump and loved me for letting him live. Right? It was a close call, y'all. Anyway! Then we found out Claudette is a little psychopath, Jacob and Han worked it out (yeah, buddy!), Rogue had to go and marry Romano, we don't know if we can trust that dude, we got Sage back, but lost the lovely Tanaka in the process. And, last but not least, The Vegas Crew has been wiped out! Onward!

Volume Three

Content Warning

Content warning:
This book has explicit moments, from murder (described graphically) to sex (also described graphically) that some readers may find objectionable. There is also long-term illness and brief mentions of past childhood trauma. Please proceed with caution, and if this isn't for you, turn back now.

Prologue

Rogue

HUBS: VEGAS CREW IS GONE. WIPED OUT. HAPPY THREE-MONTH ANNIVERSARY.

My phone falls from my hand and lands with a dull thud.

The Vegas Crew is gone? What does that mean? And why does it sound like Romano—my husband, but only in name—had something to do with it?

For the love of God. We *just* got Sage back. King, thankfully, hasn't mentioned her absence yet. We buried Tanaka earlier today. And now this?! *Fucking hell.*

I look across the guest room at Sage as she wrings her hands in front of her body. Why does she look so nervous? Oh yeah, because I just told her I would kill the only parental-type figure she's had in her life.

Well, maybe that's not true. I know little about Sage's upbringing, but now *really* isn't the time to get into it.

"Sage," I start, my voice calm, "I have to go. We'll talk about our parents and King when I get back. For now, listen to the guys. They'll keep you safe and hidden. When all of this is over, I'm giving you the life you want. The life you deserve. Okay?"

She nods her head. "I promise to listen. I know you're all keeping me hidden, and I don't want to go back there." A visible shiver wracks her body, and I know I will eventually need her to give me some information about her previous residence. I'm taking G with me, and we'll burn that shithole to the ground.

I pull on my pants and strip off the oversized shirt I had planned to sleep in tonight, trading it for the outfit I had on earlier. I scoop my phone off the floor, and with a quick kiss to Sage's cheek, I fly out of the room and down the stairs, where I find my guys all lazing around the lounge area in various states of slumber.

"Hey! Look alive!" I shout at them.

Instantly, they pop up and clear the grit from their eyes, zeroing in on me and the possible new threat I've just delivered to their doorstep.

I drop my phone on the coffee table, screen displaying the message, and wait for the reactions.

"Have you really been married for three months already?" Lucas asks.

Not quite what I was looking for.

"Not the bloody point, Lucas," Jacob reprimands as he sits back in the armchair. "Alright, Love. How does this change our plan?"

"I don't fucking know, but I have to get back to my apartment. I mean, the apartment I share with Romano. Fuck, I need just one place to live; this is getting confusing and annoying to explain." I know I'm rambling, but my mind is going a thousand miles a minute, and I'm just trying to find some equilibrium.

"Good plan, Trouble. Keep us informed. Do you want one of us nearby?" Noah puts his fingertips to his chin as he thinks it through.

"I'm good. But I've got to go. King will be ready to tear the building down and everyone in it." I quickly kiss each of my guys and sail out the door. Cruising through the streets of El Castillo in the early hours is always an eerie experience, but when you don't know what's waiting at your destination, it adds a whole new level of unease.

I pull into the parking garage, skipping the valet at this late hour, and ride the elevator up to our apartment. Entering the living room, I scan the small yet opulent space and find it empty.

I stomp down the hallway and find Romano starfished on the bed. I take off one of my boots and decide I am not above violence.

Launching the boot, a sick sense of satisfaction flows through me as it hits him squarely in the stomach, and he lets out an almighty "Oomph."

He bolts upright and has a gun drawn and leveled at my face. I quirk a brow, and he lowers it, flicking the safety back on. Hmm... question for later. I've never actually seen him with a firearm, despite leading the weapons division of The Gambit.

"Rogue, did you... did you just throw a fucking shoe at me?" he asks incredulously.

"First, technically, it was a boot," I say with a huff. "Second, what the fuck was with your message?"

"I thought you'd want to know," he explains ineptly as he puts the gun on his nightstand and wipes a hand down his face.

"And the whole anniversary thing?" I inquire.

"It really is our three-month wedding anniversary. The two thoughts were unconnected, but I now see the confusion. I heard about the takedown from a friend and thought you'd want to know before King did." His explanation does nothing to quell the nerves I've felt since he sent that goddamn text. He makes minimal eye contact, and I know he isn't telling me everything.

It's fair, I guess, as I certainly don't tell him everything. I make a mental note to do some more digging on Husband Dearest.

"King doesn't know yet? How is that possible? How did you find out?" I ask in rapid-fire, hoping to trip him up with the inquiry.

"I have people in Las Vegas. One of them called when they didn't hear from their guy on the inside. He investigated and found out the feds took them down. The whole damn organization, just gone."

"Holy shit." My words escape in a whisper.

If The Vegas Crew—an institution that has stood stock-still since before the days of Sinatra—can go under, then I'm sure The Gambit is next on their list. After all, they're among our greatest allies—or rather, *were* our allies. We kept them happy, and they did the same for us. They were a powerhouse gang with more money than they knew what to do with, able to pay off politicians and law enforcement with ease. I once heard a rumor that they even had the Vice President on the payroll.

"Yeah, I expected you to come back after getting that text. I know you were busy tonight, but with news like this... King's going to be out for blood soon. I'd rather him not be suspicious of you. It would make my life very complicated," he says with a yawn.

"How considerate," I deadpan.

"Come on, let's sleep before he breaks down our door in the morning when he hears the news." He turns down the blankets on my side in a blatant invitation to climb in. I walk into the closet and change into an oversized t-shirt and shorts. Emerging and flopping down into bed, I decide I can deal with this shit after I've had coffee in the morning because he's right. There will be hell to pay, chaos to manage, and people to investigate.

Tomorrow is going to be a long-ass day.

Chapter One

Rogue

I lace up my old shit-kicker boots and tuck my knife into the hidden sleeve.

One more douchebag to go this week. I tilt my head from side to side and crack my neck, swinging my arms in wide arcs to limber up before slipping into mission mode.

Romano pokes his face into the bedroom and gives me a curious look. He raises his dark brow, and the front of his hair flops over his eyes. "Are you ready?"

"Yes, dear," I say sarcastically to my 'husband.' My confidence slides into place as I grab a few more knives, strapping them to my hips, and drape my leather jacket over the ensemble. I'd set off a *lot* of metal detectors in this getup.

It's been a month since The Vegas Crew was arrested on charges ranging from grand larceny and racketeering to the occasional murder and bribery of political figures. We've been lying low, keeping our noses to the ground, and trying to fly under the radar. Fuck, the last thing I need is to get sent to federal prison so soon after getting Sage free.

I shake off the thoughts of impending doom and cross the bedroom to seize my go-bag on the dresser. Romano ushers me into our living room.

He's clad in black pants, a dark V-neck t-shirt, and a pair of polished Italian boots—quality leather, no doubt.

Grabbing the guns from the coffee table and sliding them into our shoulder holsters, we both turn to the door as Romano pulls a bomber jacket over his murder-and-torture outfit.

"Let's go kill a pimp," we say in unison. I resist the urge to call "jinx!" He doesn't know the game, and it pains me being so separated from my men. This shit needs to be done and over with so I can go back to the clubhouse to see them and Sage.

My brow lifts at our declaration, thinking it's rather blunt of him. He's picking up traits from me because of our extended cohabitation. We've been married for over four months at this point, and with spring in full bloom, the days feel extraordinarily long and wearisome.

As for my—*our*—job today, it's not quite Gambit sanctioned, but things need to be handled.

I tapped G and Fabio for assistance on this one because they're loyal to *me*, not The Gambit. Romano, despite my initial worry, wants to help. Over the last few months, he has proven himself somewhat trustworthy, and I'm using this as another test. He won't know where the girls are moving to, but he is sticking near me so I can watch him.

We arrive in the parking garage. I slide into the driver's seat of Black Beauty, and after a quick stop at a parking lot for a clandestine meeting, we head out of the city. The further from El Castillo we get, the more Romano's knee bounces.

"Are you nervous? You weren't shaking when we took care of De La Cruz." I ponder over what could freak him out about this job. Although, maybe this is the standard response to a planned murder, and I never got the memo.

"No, it's not that. It's the simple fact that I had my dossier on Enrique. I knew what he did before you drove us out to that workshop. I don't know this guy, and that makes me edgy. Hell, I didn't even know you had plans to go off and kill someone until twenty minutes before we left."

I laugh. "So you're nervous because you're under-prepared for a job you didn't know about and, most importantly, were not invited to, and somehow that earns me a tense partner? Great."

He scoffs in my direction and mutters, "I am not *tense*."

Sure.

I turn up the radio, and we cruise closer to San Jose, closer to a man who has earned his death.

We pass by the swanky start-up companies, the expensive homes, and tree-lined streets—all promising bright futures here in Silicon Valley—until we reach the address on my burner's GPS. We don't need King knowing we took a trip out to visit Sage's pimp, so we left our usual phones at home. Thank God burners have evolved with the times and we're not stuck using the gray bricks from the nineties without navigational abilities.

I've got the local base covered with two body doubles I sent to dinner downtown in a crowded restaurant on the west side of El Castillo. It's why we stopped in a public garage for that meeting, and Ashley and Tim, our doubles, emerged from the property for their lovely meal with clones of our phones tucked in their pockets as we drove away in the rental car I parked there last night.

Maneuvering onto the quiet street, I watch the neighborhood carefully. It looks the same as it did on Google Maps last week and the same as when I snuck out here two nights ago.

Ron Mitchell is the pimp that runs the ring handling Sage and the other top girls. I've got a death so sweet planned out for him, and while I didn't need the extra backup, I'm glad to have it.

My guys know I'm working this job with two of my own associates. They weren't pleased to be left out, but they're figuring out the Mara Hendrix shit and her work with the feds. The good news is they accept my job and never try to change me or what I do. They understand I don't see it as an optimal career path, but I can handle myself.

I never planned to come here and dole out punishment; I only ever wanted to free Sage. But after hearing about their conditions, not to mention the guards who abused their power, I had no choice. Those women are sisters, daughters, aunts, and important people to someone out there. I'd been selfish, only thinking of my family.

Thanks to my sister mapping it out for me, I know the layout of the building. I've learned she enjoys and is rather talented at drawing, so her sketches are detailed and as proportional as she could guarantee. I pulled the blueprints from city hall, and the general outline was on point, but according to Sage, they've changed the interior.

There are a few standard-looking storefronts on the bottom floor with what look like apartments above, but inside, the walls have been taken down, making the four buildings into one.

Two large eight-seater vans pull up behind me and switch off their lights. I push open my door and approach the first.

"Hey, G," I greet. He runs a hand through his short brown hair and gives me a wink. His blue eyes are sparkling with glee and he rubs a tattooed hand over his stubbled jaw. G is handsome; I'm not going to lie. Even though he and I would never work, he's going to make someone else really happy someday.

"You ready to do this, Boss?" he inquires.

I didn't exactly tell him everything, but he knows it's a pickup of girls who we're moving to safety. I had to brief them so they'd know to be calm and gentle to the women who have endured far worse than anyone should. Fabio drives the van behind him; the two vehicles should be enough to transport everyone.

"You're ushering out at least ten girls and getting them to this location." I hand him a slip of paper, and he unfolds it, letting out a long breath as he realizes a six-hour return trip is in his future.

"Okay, sounds good. I've got a new playlist loaded; this is going to be fun. I named it the G-Spot." This man and his love for pop music is always a treat, but his naming abilities could use some work.

"Let me check on Fabio, and we'll head in." I make my way to the other vehicle with the second slip of paper in my grip. If they get separated, I'd sooner they each have the address than rely on spotty cell service along the road.

As I approach the van, I spy Fabio examining the tips of his hair for split ends. Good Lord, how did I end up with these guys on my team? I roll my eyes, and I hear G chuckle behind me.

"Fab, focus, man!" I whisper-shout at him. He keeps his head tilted, but lifts his eyes to mine.

"Hey, Boss. You look good," he declares as he glimpses the guns nestled in the shoulder holsters under my jacket.

"*Focus*. Here's the address." I turn my body to include G in the conversation. "I'm leading us in. You're each grabbing as many as you can fit in the van, and leaving immediately. I'm staying behind to wrap up some loose ends. Understood?"

"Got it, Boss. Do you need any clean-up or help with the body?" Fabio asks with unbridled glee in his eyes. He's been itching for a kill, and part of me wants to agree.

"This one is mine."

He nods his understanding and hops out of the car.

Romano joins us, and we stand there, hidden from the windows of the building by the vans, as I locate our access point. I sign a few tactical hand signals I taught the guys years ago, and they nod. Surprisingly, so does Romano.

I hand everyone a ski mask, inspired by my guys and their "kidnapping" a couple of months ago, and they pull them over their faces. We approach on silent feet, and no guns ring out, proving Sage's memory of rotations was correct. I drilled her on them until I was sure she was certain.

The first door we encounter is to the bail bonds' place. "Safe Word Bail Bonds" is a ruse for the brothel they run in-house, so I reach out and turn the handle, feeling the satisfaction of it turning without a hitch. I pull the door wide as Fabio and G enter with guns drawn. Five shots go off, and I hear the dull thud of at least two bodies hitting the floor. A startled gasp rings out in the silence, but I see G lift a finger to his lips.

Fabio whispers, "We're here to help, lovely. Do you want to live?" The woman nods frantically as I step into the dingy space. She eyes me with trepidation.

"Good. Where is everyone else? And can you keep your shit together long enough to help us get them out?" I ask.

She struggles to lift an arm, and I realize the bastards have her strapped to the chair. Her breasts spill out of her bralette, and bruises decorate her hips, visible through the peach lace of her matching panties. I pull a knife from my hip but wait until she confirms she'll cooperate. Otherwise, I'll duct tape her mouth shut and leave her here. I don't need any surprises.

Wiggling my knife in the air, I pin her with a hard stare until she agrees. "Yes, of course, I'll help you, idiot. There are twelve girls upstairs, one is out on a job, and one disappeared a month ago. They said she was on an extended assignment, but I think they killed her." Well, she started with sass, but by the end, her tone is melancholic.

"What's the name of the missing girl?" I ask, having a hunch.

"Sage."

"I got her. She's safe. Now, let's get the rest of you out of here." She eyes me again with skepticism in her gaze. "Long blonde hair, scar on her back that looks like the letter Y with a line through the middle, and really fucking good at drawing? I promise you, she's secure."

Tears well in her eyes, and her gumption comes back. "Let's do this then, girl. Ron went out, but I can help with the rest."

As I cut through her bindings, the guys stash the bodies in a closet off to the side.

G wipes his hands on his jeans and stands next to our little helper. "What's your name?" he asks.

"Trinity." She lets out a deep breath. "It's Elenor, actually, but they made me use Trinity. Sage was the only one who got to keep her name for some reason. God, it feels good to use my real name."

I wonder how long she's been living here and forced to assume a new identity. Sage's life was hard, but at least King didn't give her a new name, too. She got to hang on to a little piece of her old life, whereas I had to give up everything aside from our intermittent visits. Consoling Elenor, I place a comforting hand on her shoulder and turn her body toward mine.

"Elenor, I'm glad to meet you, but I won't be telling you my name just in case, you know? These are my colleagues. We're here to get you guys out. How many men are still here? When will Ron be back?" I fire off in rapid succession. Elenor seems no-nonsense, so I'm hoping she'll answer as quickly.

"The girls are upstairs. There were two guards down here, and Mr. George, one of our regulars, is upstairs. There are four guards to watch the girls up there. Ron has an office in the storefront next door." She points at the doorway opposite the closet the guys stashed the bodies in.

"He went out about two hours ago; he's usually out for at least four. The stairway over there leads to the girls and guards. They play music at all hours, so they won't hear you coming." I groan at the mention of a patron. A new factor that shouldn't matter if we can sneak up on him.

Sage gave me similar specifics. There were always at least two guards on the bottom floor, while the rest were upstairs on their nights off. They liked to visit with the girls who weren't working that night.

Elenor shows us to the door hiding the staircase, and I hear the music thrumming through the walls. "Okay, Elenor, the girls know you as Trinity, right?" She nods in confirmation. "You stay here. I'll send them to you and my coworker here." I put a hand on Romano's shoulder. "You guys will bring them to the vans across the street." Romano squares his shoulders and agrees quickly.

"These two," I gesture at G and Fabio, "are going to help me upstairs, then drive you up north. I've set up a safehouse based on what Sage has told you would need. I know it might be difficult for the girls to trust us, but I promise, it's safe. Listen to them and the woman who meets you at the house. She's going to keep you hidden until you all decide what to do next."

Elenor nods as Romano moves next to her. He casts an assessing glance over our helper, likely wondering the same as I am. Will she be stupid or helpful? His eyes connect with mine, and I see his determination to help.

His being here has changed my plans, but an extra set of hands can't hurt. I'm getting the girls out and gutting the men responsible.

I take the lead as G and Fabio follow me up the stairs. The heavy beats of the rap music grows louder until our footsteps are muffled, and we reach the top.

I open the door a crack to peer out. Doors line either side, stretching down the hall. Sage told me they reserve the first few rooms for clients, while the ones toward the rear are for the guards and girls.

Seeing that the coast is clear, I swing the door open and spin to the first door on the right. G takes the one on the left. Fabio is on hallway-watch duty as he brings up the rear.

I find the space empty aside from a bed and a few strategically placed mirrors. G's room across the hall is identical.

We make our way down the hallway, checking six rooms before finding one housing a young woman with dark brown hair and a split lip. She draws in a shuddering breath as she sees my ski mask, and I hold up a finger to halt her impending scream. "We're here to get you out. Go downstairs and find Trinity. She and my friend are waiting. Go!"

The girl scrambles off of the bed, hitting the floor to pry up a loose floorboard. She lifts out a plastic grocery bag that has a few items in it. That right there tells me these girls haven't lost hope.

Her big doe eyes find my own, and she whispers, "Thank you," before darting into the hall with the bag clutched in her hand and down the staircase.

One.

It continues that way until we reach the room next door. A burly man has his dick buried in a teenager, lost to the rhythm of his thrusts as I come up behind him. I yank him away from the woman before running a knife along his throat.

Thankfully, the girl is facing away from us, so she doesn't see the carnage. At the loss of his body against hers, she sags forward onto the mattress, likely thinking she's done for the night.

"Hey," I whisper, and her head whips around to find me covered in blood and still holding the knife, with the client at my feet. "We're getting everyone out. Grab whatever you can't leave behind and meet Trinity downstairs. Go."

Unlike the first girl, she takes nothing, just springs up, grabs a t-shirt, and rushes out. These girls have been through enough shit that she doesn't bat an eyelid at a dead client on her floor. And yet, she trusts a woman in a ski mask who promises help. Desperation drifts in the air, and in their shoes, I'd choose a woman taking down disgusting pigs over staying put any day.

On and on it goes until the last guard is dead. G, Fabio, and I make quick work of the upstairs level, bearing in mind the numbers Elenor told us. When I'm sure they match up, we descend the stairs to find Romano and Trinity in the main room.

"Is that everyone?" I ask Elenor.

"Yeah, that's it, aside from Brittany. She's the one out on a job with her two guards," she answers.

"Okay. Boys, get them to the address. There's a woman there with red hair who will help get them settled and keep them hidden until we can get them to their families. Her name is Claudette, and she's a friend. Be nice."

I look at Elenor to give the bad news. "Listen, it might be some time until I can deliver you home, but I promise you will be safe and looked after until then. Listen to what she says, stay hidden, and please don't let the girls do anything stupid."

She nods her agreement, and I send G and Fabio to the vans to take them into Claudette's territory. She's waiting for them at the safe house and promised a place for them until we can ship them home.

———

THE DOOR SWINGS OPEN, AND AN IRATE-LOOKING MAN ENTERS. HE'S dressed in a three-piece suit, entirely too debonair for this part of town. He stops the moment he crosses the threshold and sees me in his plush leather chair behind the desk. My feet are up on the polished wood with my ankles crossed atop his closed laptop.

"Well, hello, Ron." A sinister smile overtakes my face—now free from that stupid ski mask—and I watch the confusion flit across his gaze. He's been out for the last hour while we cleared the girls and I set up shop in his office.

Sage told me all about Ron and how he preferred to be dominated inside the bedroom and make her life hell outside of it. It's half the reason I decided to come back and free the others. After growing up with King, the least I can do is help someone else get out from under an asshole's thumb.

Sage mentioned she was his favorite, the one he called downstairs when he wanted a "scene." He must miss his favorite girl by now, and I have plans to use that in my favor.

"I am a gift for you, Pet. Sit."

He hesitates, and Romano moves from his position beside the exit, yanking him into the room. The door closes behind him and he forcibly shoves Ron into the chair opposite the desk.

Ron isn't a big man. Romano must have at least four inches and fifty pounds on him. Struggling against the hold on his shoulders, the man finally realizes there's nowhere to go and stops squirming. I see the bulge in his pants grow and know he's into this. Ugh, men.

"That's better," I coo. "You've been a very bad boy, haven't you?"

His eyes widen a fraction before he tries to hide it behind an impassive mask. Too late. I saw fear mixed with desire flash in his eyes. I can work with that.

He looks to the left above the desk, where he had a camera positioned to monitor the office. Too bad I disabled it when I did my bug sweep after getting the girls out. Not only did I find some fancy cameras hooked up to a closed-loop server, but there was also a nice cache of weapons in the false bottom of his desk drawer. I may just keep one or two when I'm done, to add to my collection.

Ron may be the scum of the earth, but he's got good taste in weaponry. Dropping my feet to the floor, I rise from the chair to make my way over to him. I kneel in front of him, running my palms up his thighs. My fingertips trail across his chest before I run them along his arms until his hands are in mine.

He peeks up at Romano, who smiles encouragingly. I filled him in on the likely scenarios while we waited for Ron to return.

Placing Ron's palms on the armrests, I cross my hands before my belly, reaching for the hem of my top, as if to remove it. Instead of the shirt, I pull away with two blades and impale them into the backs of his hands, effectively pinning him in place.

As he's yowling in pain, Romano tightens his grip on the man's shoulders, and I return to the seat behind the desk. This could take a while, and I want to be comfortable.

"A little birdy told me you like girls with my bone structure. Is that right, Ron?" His cries of agony are mere whimpers now, the adrenaline pumping through his body as it mutes the pain. That's okay, I'll make it hurt again soon.

He looks up at me, searching my face. I see the flare of recognition when he studies my face. "Sage..." he whispers. His lids close heavily as he sighs, having made the connection. He knows his fate is sealed.

Mila Sin

I remove my jacket from the top of the desk, revealing the lineup of small daggers I made. With a flick of my wrist, one goes sailing across the room and embeds itself in Ron's shoulder, inches from Romano's fingers.

"One," I count. "I have ten of your little knives here. How many girls have you threatened with them? How many have you made bleed?" I ponder aloud, not expecting an answer, and am proven correct when he grunts and keeps his mouth shut.

Sighing, I pick up the second dagger in the line. I let it fly, and it lands inches below his rib cage, sinking into the soft flesh of his abdomen. "Two. Where is the girl out on assignment? When is she due back?"

Again, he stays silent.

I work through the ten daggers, pinning him in vulnerable but non-lethal spots as Romano's hands stay clamped on the man's shoulders. My questions have all gone unanswered so far, but I'm in no rush tonight. No, I will relish this.

I round the desk, keeping my pace slow and measured. I want him to understand I have no problem drawing this out and making it painful and prolonged.

"Please," comes his whispered voice as I stand over him and watch as his blood drips from the chair and creates a puddle on the floor. The scent of urine permeates the air as I approach and my lips tip up in delight.

"Tell me. Tell me everything, and I will end this," I tempt Ron with my soft tone.

He shakes his head in refusal, and I sigh in satisfaction. Popping my knuckles, I prepare for the warfare I intend to rage across his broken and bloodied body. For Sage, I will bloody my hands, cover myself in unforgivable sins, and revel in it, knowing justice has been partially served. There's still the matter of King, but that's for another day.

I pull the knife from his right lung, listening to his wheezing breath with joy dancing along my spine. I tilt his head back by the short hair at the crown of his head and jam the blade into his eye.

His wail of agony bounces around the room, taking root in my soul and calling to the monster within me. The monster who trained for this; the one who dances in the blood of her enemies and smiles with glee as she does so.

Since we started, I haven't looked Romano in the eye, knowing his opinion of me will be tainted after tonight. But I simply don't have the mental capacity to care right now.

"Kill me. Just fucking kill me already," Ron begs. The knife is still embedded in his eye socket as the other one wheels around wildly.

"Nope," I say, popping the P on the end and watching tears fill his remaining eye.

His death is inevitable. He knows it. I know it.

The blade comes free of its sheath at my hip, and I study his hand, still pinned under a dagger on the armrest of the chair. Romano pulls a length of rope from the small cabinet next to the desk and ties it on Ron's upper arm.

Time to start sawing.

An eternity later, the man is in pieces, having died along the way. I drew it out as long as I could in vengeance for my sister and the pain he caused her, both emotionally and physically. He may not have been the one to inflict *all* the damage, but he certainly didn't help. No, he farmed her out to disgusting men and women who take out their rage, pain, and desires on others.

The last thing I did before lighting that building up was take his severed hand and unlock his phone using his fingerprint. I got the details for the last girl, Brittany, and I know someone who would want to help kill some assholes.

Romano didn't interrupt once or try to stop me from doing what I needed to do. He helped spread out the pieces of Ron around the room, hour after hour, and I respect him for that.

As Romano and I return to our apartment after stopping off at a safehouse to shower and change, my phone pings with a message.

G: All settled, heading home.

Me: Great work, thank you.

G: So who's the redhead?

Me: She's none of your business, G. Keep your cool, man.

G: Can you put in a good word for me?

Me: I'll think about it. Night.

Good. One less thing to worry about. The escorts are staying with Claudette until I can kill King. I mean, it's not like we can bring them home and thrust them back into everyday life. There are only so many ways to keep someone hidden, and if King finds out that they've miraculously returned to their families, what's stopping him from just retaking them as leverage again?

No, we have to keep everything under wraps for a while longer.

I show Romano the message and watch as his face relaxes before my eyes.

This was definitely a new adventure for my husband and me. We exit the car and ride up to the apartment in silence. We follow the carpeted hall to our door and trudge to the bedroom, battle weary and bone tired.

It's been a long fucking day, and I need some sleep. Dismemberment is hard fucking work and takes forever. Silence engulfs the small space between us, and there's a furrow between Romano's brows. I don't think he's ever seen someone taken apart before. Ah, well, first time for everything. His hands were remarkably steady on the bone saw.

I opt to take an additional shower as Romano sets up the coffee machine for the morning. After a quick, but thorough, wash, I crawl into bed. I don't stir as I hear Romano moving around the bedroom. I'm too tired.

He collapses into bed as the gray light of dawn slips through the curtains. Brittany is still out there, and I've got a plan brewing.

Today, I'm seeing my sister and sending her the fuck out of town. When King gets wind of this, he's going to go on a rampage. Between this and the recent news of The Vegas Crew wipeout, I don't want anyone caught in the crossfire.

I wake four hours later, my body still too hyped up on adrenaline to sleep deeply, and I look to my right. Romano is lightly snoring. It's weird, but after these past couple of months, I've become used to the rhythm of his breaths as I slumber.

Kill and Chill didn't happen last night because of the exhaustion, so I plan for a slow morning, thinking through everything and making new plans while *Vikings* plays in the background on our fancy television.

Romano joins me in the kitchen a few hours later, his hair rumpled and his pajama pants clinging to his hips. He's thinned out since we got married. Stress?

"Morning," he rumbles.

"Morning, dear," I joke, continuing the routine we've had in place now for a few weeks.

"Everything quiet?"

I simply nod my head and drink my orange juice as I scroll through my phone, checking the group chat with the guys. My morning was slow and calm, dressing myself and spending time reading was the perfect way to unwind after last night.

"Do the girls need anything?" he asks quietly.

I tilt my head and look at him. "Yeah, clothes, essentials. The safehouse had some stuff, but I want to grab some more. Those girls deserve to be spoiled after everything. Want to go shopping?"

He nods, and we hit the mall, quickly grabbing as many things as we can from the department store and stuffing my car to the brim.

Chapter Two

Han

I stretch my legs out, lazily waking up after a night of recon with the guys. Jacob and I crashed after showering away the remnants of our last job. Perching in a sniper's nest while watching our mark took hours. That roof was dirty, grungy, and disgusting.

I don't know why I'm awake. It feels too early.

My hips shift, and my dream carries into my waking hours as warm, wet heat envelops my cock. A moan escapes my lips as I feel pressure at the base, and my eyes fly open.

I look down my body and find Jacob lying on his stomach between my legs, the tip of my dick in his mouth. *Oh, fuck.* My head drops back to the pillow, and I lazily bring my hands to his silky hair, enjoying the buzz cut on the sides, and running my fingers through the length on top.

After months—*years*—of both of us cycling between want, need, lust, and love, we finally got our shit together. These days, we spend more time in each other's company than ever before, adjusting to our new relationship and learning what makes the other tick outside our friendship and team dynamic.

Jacob promptly moved most of my day-to-day stuff into his room after our kiss in the gym. When I looked around with a raised brow and noticed we were cohabitating, he merely shrugged, grasped my neck, and kissed the hell out of me.

It was hard to argue with that.

He squeezes my dick as my fingers run through his messy hair, and his hum reverberates in my bones. My breath catches, and he realizes I'm fully awake now, not just dream-caressing him—which he says I do often. My hand palms his cheek as he releases me.

"Morning, Love," he rasps out, and for a moment, I'm confused because that's what he sometimes calls Ivy. "Han, lie back and let me suck your cock. Then, I want to try something."

Jacob has the uncanny ability to make anyone do his bidding with that sexy-as-fuck accent, but add in the sleepy rasp, and I'm a fucking goner. His promise of what's coming has me reclining against the pillow and rocking against the hand planted on my hip.

According to our *many* conversations about what we both want in bed, Jacob is open to experimentation. I think today is a research day and I'm damn near giddy.

His tongue lashes at my pulsing veins as he draws me farther into his mouth. He fondles my balls for a moment before slipping his fingers to the sensitive skin behind my balls, pressing as he hollows his cheeks. The curses and groans of pleasure flowing from my mouth encourage him to continue.

I know this is new to him, but he's doing a marvelous job of it. I've been with other men before, but he hasn't. But Jacob approached this like he does everything; with thorough research and enthusiasm. He pops off my dick for a second to coat his finger in saliva before returning to the task at hand. His finger slips between my cheeks, and he swallows me down as much as he can manage with a slight gag as his finger presses at my entrance, and I drop my calves over his shoulders to give him more space as my hands fist the pillow behind my head.

"Jacob, yes, more. Please." My words fall on deaf ears as he slows further, dragging out my pleasure and taking his sweet time.

It takes only a few minutes before I'm on the edge, and Jacob pulls away from me completely, letting my legs drop down to the bed and placing his hands on my thighs, quivering with impending release under his grip. He moves into a kneeling position and drags his bottom lip through his teeth.

"You edging me?" I ask with a curl to my lips. I sit up, leaning forward to give his cock one long, lingering lick from base to tip, before tackling him to the bed.

"What is it you wanted to try?" I ask as he cleans his hand with the wipes from the drawer. "I need to come. Jacob. Please."

"I want you to fuck me." His voice is hushed, quiet in the dawn of morning, and vulnerable. So fucking vulnerable I want to wrap him up and give him whatever he wants.

"Are you sure?" I ask.

He nods his head. "Definitely. I want to experience everything with you. I followed your example and played with some toys." A grin sneaks over my face at that, imagining Jacob working his body over with a dildo, readying himself for me.

I lean in, kissing him roughly, the way he likes. "I love you, Jacob."

He grins and quips back, "You're just saying that because you want my arse." His accent and words always become decidedly more British when he's turned on.

"Not a chance. I'd be equally in love without it. I love your mind." Kiss. "I love your generosity." Kiss. "I love how you take care of us." Kiss. "And I love how open you are." Kiss. "Get over it, Jacob Waters. I love you."

His eyes shine under the dim lights. Sometimes, I miss the natural light from the sun, but our security is more important, so the windows lead nowhere but are backlit to give us a feeling of the outside world without leaving us vulnerable. "How we ignored this for so long baffles me." His voice is one of awe. "I love you too, Han."

Smiling against his lips, I feel his cock stir against my thigh. I move my hand to reach for him, but his fingers snake out and grasp my wrist, halting my progression. A lazy grin overtakes his face, and it has my breath stalling in my lungs.

"Come here." His voice is still a rasp through the air, and his beautifully adorned skin looks darker as the shadows play across his tattoos. I do as he commands and drape myself across his body as he pulls me closer. He snuggles in, pressing a desperate kiss to my lips. "Be patient with me?"

Jacob hasn't shied away from touching me during sex, and this morning was far from the first time he's had my dick in his mouth. But he mentioned that he's tentative about bottoming, despite wanting to try it. I've told him countless times that it's impossible to mess it up if it's us, but he's still unsure of himself.

It's strange to see this man, who commands both Ivy and me in bed, have doubts—not in us, but in his ability to please me. My heart swells at his determination to try, and I love him for it.

I kiss his lips, his cheeks, his neck. Slithering down his body, his cock slides between my lips, and it's hard as a fucking rock. Pumping it a few strokes and running my thumb over the piercings as I bump along each one, I work my hand between his cheeks. He spreads his legs further apart, knees bent as his heels rest on the bed. I use my mouth and run it down his sac, sucking one of his balls into my mouth before humming, causing his hips to rear off the mattress.

I give the other the same treatment and gather saliva before moving down. I lick his taint, using my fingers to press after I move lower still. Jacob gasps at the sensation and grabs his knees, pulling them toward his head and opening beautifully for me. I want him further down the bed, so I hook his thighs with my arms and pull, scooting him right to the edge of the bed. Kneeling on the floor, I lean in and lick at his hole until he's fisting his own cock and groaning in delight.

Working my digit past the tight ring, his hips move in time with my gentle thrusts. I keep my slow pace, and he begs for more.

"Han, get the lube. Then get your dick in my ass. I need to feel you."

I grab the lube from the sex toy bin under the bedframe and apply it generously. The first touch of the cool liquid has him clenching. I stifle a chuckle and know that from now on, he'll warm it for me first rather than just squirting it on my ass.

I work one finger in, noting his tension and going slow. The first time is rarely a walk in the park, so I pay careful attention to the cues. His grunts of discomfort slowly start to change as I take my time.

"You're doing wonderfully, Jacob. That's it." My encouragement falls from my lips easily as I continue pumping.

Slowly, he relaxes enough for me to add a second digit. He grunts at the intrusion, and my eyes fly up to his. They're wide and glassy, but he nods his head, telling me to keep going.

When his breathing becomes shallow and choppy, mixing pain and pleasure into one, I scissor my fingers, taking care that he's well-prepared and comfortable.

His heels slip once or twice as he moves his body with the rhythm of my pace. I notice he's ready, and I remove my hand. He groans at the loss of contact, but I need the moment to slather my cock in lube. I clamp my hands on his knees, pushing them apart and line up my cock. He takes a deep, steadying breath, and his eyes are fixed on mine, eager and timid, all at once.

"Relax and let me in. It's going to stretch, and you'll love it. Just. Let. Me. In." I punctuate each word with a small press forward. His teeth clench in anticipation; this dominant man giving up control for a bit is not only physically taxing, but mentally as well.

He nods his head and I feel him do as I ask. The surrounding squeeze is indescribable. His muscles tense as I slide out, then back in. I start a slow, steady pace to help him acclimate to the sensation.

I watch as his face grows slack, the sensation new for him, and he fights to keep composure. Not on my watch. Before long, his breath is punching out of him with each snap of my hips against his ass, and he's grinding back into me with urgency as he works his dick in his fist.

I smack his hand away and palm his cock. I pump him hard and match my pace. This man is everything. So calm, so patient, so fucking *good* that I can't see straight. My love for him and Ivy both settles deep in my heart. I know there's no comparison because they're different people. Love isn't finite. Why can't someone love two people equally?

Jacob clenches around me, and I shout my release, pouring myself into him, as ropes of cum decorate his chest from his own orgasm.

Hours later, I'm in the kitchen having a cup of coffee. My mug today reads: *If your eyes hurt after drinking coffee, you have to take the spoon out of the cup.* Sage is sitting on a barstool, staring at me across the marble island with a raised brow.

"Can I ask you something?" she asks.

"Yeah, sure. What's up?"

"So I know you're all with Ivy." She pauses, and I nod in confirmation. "But, how does all of that work?"

Well, I don't think she's talking about the sex. This isn't a conversation I planned to have today, but it's happening. My thoughts from earlier come crashing into my head, and I realize I've found the perfect way to explain our dynamic to Sage. "It means we're her boyfriends and are all head-over-heels for her. Your sister doesn't tell us who we can and can't love. She knows we can love multiple people. Which is why she's encouraged Jacob and me."

She nods her head as she processes the information, her knees coming up to her chest as she folds in on herself. It's a pose I've seen her do countless times over the last month. If anyone larger than her tried it, there wouldn't be space on the stool for both their ass and heels. Noah keeps overfeeding us, but she's consistent in her small portions.

I forget Sage is only eighteen sometimes. She's intelligent, determined, and has effortlessly slid into life here at the clubhouse... mostly because she keeps to herself, aside from mealtimes.

No matter what we plan, whether it's dinners, lounging around, or trying to chat, after thirty minutes, Sage retreats to her room. I get it. She's had a rough life. An ache settles in my chest, thinking about how she's under lock and key here, instead of living her life. She should graduate high school this year, and yet, I don't know if she's ever been to school.

I doubt it. She's smart, certainly. But formally educated?

"I just..." She trails off, unsure of how to continue. She tucks a strand of her long blonde hair behind her ear and clears her throat. "I just want to know that you guys are good for her. She's sacrificed too much for me. I realize that. She kept King's attention on her and did horrible things to see me, not to mention save me from that place. She deserves the world, and instead, she has a sister whose baggage has baggage."

I'm getting the *what-are-your-intentions* talk, aren't I?

"Sage, let me put your mind at ease." I place my cup on the counter and lean forward so even if she tries to hide behind her sheet of blonde hair, my candidness will be clear. "I am in love with your sister. Noah, Jacob, and Lucas are, too. We each got there at different times, and Jacob and I have our own thing, but it takes nothing away from what we share with her individually. Most of us may have only known her less than a year, but she fits us, Sage. Ivy is the strongest, most compassionate, and, yes, the deadliest woman we've ever known, but you know what else? She is absolutely perfect for us—*each* of us. It sounds cheesy as hell in my head, but I'm going to say it anyway. She completes us in a way none of us were expecting or looking for. When you find something that makes you feel like you're on top of the world, something that builds you up and makes you a better person, do you fuck it up? Hell no."

Finding my stride, I continue, "She is our person. She may not live here with us right now, is legally married to someone else, and has baggage—as we all do—but any one of us would do anything to see her happy. Even if that means letting her go, should she choose to leave at some point. There comes a time in your life when you'll find someone who makes you feel that way. Embrace it, and put their happiness above your own because they'll do the same for you. You'll find your way together. And we're nowhere near the end of our road yet with the things the five of us still need to do before we can ride off into that sunset, but fuck if we're not doing everything within our power to make it happen."

She looks me in the eye, not wavering for a second as she studies my face. "Fine, I approve."

"Didn't know I needed your approval, but it's good to have it," the voice behind me says.

I spin with a great, big smile. There's my girl.

I stride up to her and grasp her hips with my hands. She sighs as I lay a firm kiss on her lips and giggles at her sister's deviousness.

"You sneaky devil," I tell Sage as she bursts out laughing. She's always freer when Ivy is around, presumably because they've had a relationship all her life, albeit an irregular and guarded one.

"I had to know. Plus, this way, she knows, too." Sage hops off the stool and comes around the island to hug her sister. "Hey, what's up? I didn't know you were stopping by today."

"I have some news," Ivy says to both of us. My brows lift, silently asking if she wants us all together, and she nods her head.

We leave the kitchen and find the other three hovering just outside the kitchen area. As we walk to the war room, they each pat me on the back or thump me on the shoulder. Yup, they all heard my speech too, and we're in this for the long haul.

Ivy sits us down and wrings her hands together. "So, I took out Ron Mitchell last night."

Sage lets out a heavy sigh and leans back in her chair. "You did?" she asks. "And the others?"

"The guards are gone, at least the ones who were there. We moved the girls to a safe house until we can send them home. One was out on assignment, but I have a plan to get her."

Lucas raises his hand as if he's in elementary school. Ivy indulges him, "Yes, Red?"

"Uh, who's Ron Mitchell?"

Sage fills in the gaps with a tremble in her voice. "He ran the escort business. At least, my division of it. I told Ivy about it when she came to visit a couple of weeks ago. She said she'd handle it; I just wasn't expecting it to happen so soon." She turns to look at her sister after answering Lucas. "You're sure he's gone?"

"One hundred percent. I know you spoke with other escorts from other... establishments like this one up and down the coast, but consider this one dismembered." I think she meant to say *dismantled*. "We'll keep digging for information on the others."

Noah breaks in without raising his hand like a doofus. "Do you need any cleanup, or is it handled?"

Ever the pragmatist.

"It's done. After the job, I set the place on fire." Her assurances don't mollify Jacob or me as I spy the tension in his clasped hands.

"G was with you?" Jacob asks without missing a beat.

"G, Fabio, and Romano." She winces a bit when she says the last name. "I didn't intend to take Romano, but he proved to be useful and passed a test he didn't know he was taking. G wasn't there for the fire, but I did it in his honor." Jacob just nods his head. He knows better than most what Ivy can do after doing all of that research on her kills over the past few years. She may have caught a blade to the gut the day she met us, but we've never doubted her ability to do her job; I think we all just wish we were with her.

"Alright, Gorgeous," I say, "what's next?" Instead of dwelling on what could have possibly gone wrong, moving on is usually the right move.

"Sage's relocation." The woman in question snaps her head up in alarm.

Ivy explains, "Look, I'd love to keep you here, but the other girls were asking for you. Do you want to go with them or stay here? I think it would be safer for you there with what we're planning."

Clearing her throat, Sage looks around the table at all of us. "I'd like to go there. Thanks, you guys, for babysitting me, but I should help with the girls. There's a lot that we all have to deal with, but maybe it's better to do that together?" she wonders aloud. "Where are they?"

"Up north with a friend. Han, do you have anything going on today? I can't disappear for that long with the chaos happening within The Gambit. Would you drive Sage?" Ivy asks me. That right there tells me how much she trusts me. I know she's left her sister with us this month, but transporting her and trusting me to deliver her safely is the biggest "I love you" she could have ever presented.

"Sure thing," I answer. There's nothing I wouldn't do for this woman. Things have been up in the air since the feds took down The Vegas Crew. King has become more paranoid than ever, and it's been tough for Ivy to get here. It doesn't change my feelings, though. Anything she asks is hers.

"Okay, great. I'll get you the address. I brought over a bunch of stuff Romano and I picked up at the mall for the girls. Extra clothes, toiletries, stuff like that. Are you okay delivering all of that, too?" she asks. I'm glad she has kept up her King evasion and the extra coverage with Romano in tow would help. Usually, it's the mall, the grocery store, or the sports center when there's a game. But either way, she always makes a stop to make sure she isn't followed here.

"Sagey Poo," Lucas starts, and Sage rolls her eyes at the nickname. "Why don't you get your stuff packed and make a list of anything you might need?"

"Yeah. Will do," she whispers. She lifts her head, making eye contact with Ivy as she stands from her seat. "Thank you. For Ron. He was an evil man."

I see Ivy blink furiously, trying to combat the tears called forth on her sister's behalf. She hides it by nodding her head resolutely. "Anytime."

Sage leaves the war room and makes her way upstairs to pack.

I don't like the fact that none of us were with Ivy to take down Ron. There are only so many times she can blow up a warehouse drug cache or murder a guy without me before I get twitchy. Also, I still have the explosives she gave me for Valentine's Eve eve that I'd like to use. I'd also *really* like to know how she got her hands on that level of explosives. That shit's incredible.

"Oh, Buttercup." Lucas sighs. "I love you." He has stars in his eyes as he stares at her. He sees our expressions of confusion. "Before you ask why I decided now was a good time to mention it, just look at her! She took down a pimp last night. She handled her shit, and she looks out for everyone. Plus, that dress is perfect."

She chuckles at him and smooths her hand over the dusty-pink dress. Noah stands and goes to her side. He puts a finger under her chin and lifts her face. "I don't want to lose you, not now that we've finally started this relationship. I hate that we weren't with you, but please be careful." His deep and rough voice is brimming with emotion as he echoes my thoughts. "We're here when you need us. Always." He dips down and delivers a searing kiss to her lips that has her sighing when he relents.

Go, Dear Leader, go! So much for keeping everything behind closed doors.

A small voice sounds from the door. "I'm ready."

Sage is standing there with a duffle bag packed and ready for our drive up north.

We stand as one, each giving Ivy a kiss on her head as we exit the room, aside from Noah, who hangs back.

Jacob brushes his lips with mine and tells me to be careful after helping to move the bags from Ivy's rental car to the SUV. She wasn't kidding. She bought a ton of stuff. I'm sure the girls will appreciate the gesture.

THE DRIVE UP NORTH IS CALM AND UNEVENTFUL. SAGE AND I FLIP through the radio stations and stop at a gas station for some road food. She learns that honey-mustard pretzels are the best, and Diet Mt. Dew is disgusting. It's weird to think of all the things she's learning that the rest of us take for granted.

We pull up to a modest house out in the suburbs, and I text Claudette that we're outside.

She meets us in the driveway and helps carry things in for the others. She drops them in the living room and it's eerily quiet. "Where is everyone?" I ask.

"They're hiding out. Strange car, strange man. What do you expect?"

Fair enough. Claudette introduces herself to Sage, not offering a hand or touching her, and I know she's in good company with the tiny psycho. Any sexual assault survivor needs to be treated with care. And physical touch is far, *far* on the back burner.

Claudette explains where her room is, and Sage takes off after promising she has her phone with her, sending me a wave as she goes.

"They'll be safe here?" I ask.

"I have snipers in the trees and I wired the house with alarms to hell and back. I worked something out with the local high school to get them enrolled online if needed. And when this is all over, they'll be free to continue their education at my expense or move on, if they want. Fuck, they can live here forever if that's what they need."

I see the alarm nodes on the windows and doors, knowing they chirp every time they open. Jacob showed me tech like this when we were outfitting our clubhouse. The girls are safe, and the snipers in the yard give me extra confidence.

"Okay. Well, there's stuff for everyone in the bags there. Please take care of them, Claudette."

"It's my honor to do so. Don't worry."

She puts a hand on her hip and glances around the house before speaking. "Hey, who were those two that dropped the girls off last night?"

"G and Fabio. They seem to be good guys. Why? Thinking of recruiting them?" I ask with a laugh.

"Sure... 'recruiting.' Let's use that word. They seem fun." She strokes her index finger on her chin as she muses aloud.

"Oh, no. No way, Claudette." Christ, this woman. She's taken to texting me at all hours when Ivy isn't around. Maybe giving her G or Fabio's number would free up some time for me. Unfortunately, I don't have their contact information. Dammit.

"I'll pass along your interest, but don't hold your breath, Claudette. And for the love of God, no more Kermit memes. Please."

She laughs and waves my plea away like it's not serious. It is.

I leave, knowing Sage has one of our burner phones to call us if needed, and slide back into the SUV. There's a text waiting for me from Ivy.

Gorgeous: Found the last girl after going through Ron's phone. She's at The DuMonde Hotel in San Francisco for the week. Room 418. Happy hunting.

I look at the GPS and see I'm a mere forty-five minutes from the destination. Happy hunting, indeed.

Rocking up to the cheap hotel, I leave the car parked in front of the lobby doors, and take the keys with me. I'll be long gone before the tow truck makes it here. The receptionist yells at me as I go marching through the lobby and run up the stairs, pushing through the door marked for the fourth floor. Two goons are sitting on a bench next to the door I need.

I walk by as if I'm headed for my room before turning around and shooting the oaf closest to me in the head. His colleague stands and tries to take the gun from his hip, but I'm faster. One bullet embeds in his shoulder to slow him down and one in his skull.

There's no silencer, so the shots ring out in the hallway loudly enough for the idiot who paid for the girl to open his door. That's much easier than searching the corpses for the key. I shove him backward and he falls onto the bed. I give him the same treatment as the second goon, but instead of the shoulder, I get him a little further south.

The girl scrambles off the bed, clinging to the wall. I speak quickly because we have little time. "My girl got the rest of the escorts away from Ron. They're in a safe house an hour away. They're waiting for you. Here," I say as I dig my phone out of my pocket. Sage answers the video call on the first ring and her face fills the screen.

"Han, what's up?"

"Sage?" the girl croaks.

"Brittany, hey! Are you okay?"

"This guy just shot my client in the dick. I'm good. But what's going on?"

I break up the chit-chat. "Sage, is Brittany safe to come with me? We have to get out of here before the cops show up."

"Brit, go with him. He's the best, and he'll bring you here. Go!"

Brittany nods and follows me from the room. I give her my t-shirt and scoop her into my arms. I haul ass across the lobby and get her settled in the front seat of the SUV.

Thank God this place has no cameras, or maybe shit like this wouldn't happen if they did. At least I won't have to change the license plates and get Jacob to deal with the footage.

The receptionist standing by my truck is no longer yelling when she sees the obviously traumatized young woman in the front seat.

"Go," she breathes. "I saw nothing."

Chapter Three

Noah

THIS LAST WEEK HAS BEEN PURE CHAOS. AFTER HAN GOT SAGE UP north safely and settled with the girls, he returned, and we dove into work mode. We'd already done one assignment for Annex Security, our shady-as-shit employer, last week. It was a simple info grab, and Jacob could do it remotely after Lucas pickpocketed a keycard from an assistant.

Today, however, we're scouring the server for a new assignment.

Jacob pulled up the list of jobs and noticed a few of them—currently in progress by other teams—had the phrase "Nail them to the wall" within the description. That seemingly flippant line is the glaring beacon Mara told him to look out for.

He's checking the backlog to see which units consistently take those assignments. Maybe we can determine if others are involved in her machinations.

So far, only Beta Team Two has popped up repeatedly on those assignments. Among the eight groups Annex has on hand, they are the ones working on those the most. They're a newer unit, hence their beta status, but they've been doing extraordinarily well for such new recruits. We have little information on them, but I think it's safe to say they're plants. They haven't fucked up once, and we're operating under the theory that they're federal agents working with Mara, as that's what Jacob swears Mara is.

Yep, somehow, we've ended up working for a security company moving within the underground criminal world while also being managed by the feds. What a clusterfuck.

The data Jacob collected was from a shipping company located down in Long Beach. It didn't require a trip, thankfully, as it's a few hours away, and I'd hate to leave Trouble up here all alone. I have faith in her, but it still makes me uneasy. What if she needs us?

We're all sitting around, going through the server on our respective laptops. Lucas is more fidgety than usual and keeps patting his stomach. It's not his usual hungry rub across his middle, but some kind of weird patting and petting. After twenty minutes of catching his movements from my peripherals as we're neck-deep in the server and flagging potential jobs, I can't take it anymore.

"Lucas, what the fuck are you doing?" I ask with a sigh.

"What? Me? Nothing." His eyes wheel around the room, avoiding my stare, so I know he's lying. He's excellent on missions and at undercover work because he loses himself in the role, but there isn't much he can hide from us. He'll tell us when he's ready, and I decide to let it go.

We've chosen a kill order to handle this quarter. Not that we'll kill the team, considering their only offense seems to be setting up a rival security firm. But that's reason enough to get them on the server. We're going over logistics and how to remove Nicolas and his team from his stronghold in Bakersfield. The debate over whether we stash him somewhere for a few weeks, *then* move him or get him to another country immediately is in full force when Lucas giggles. A fucking giggle.

"Alright, Lucas, out with it. What the hell is happening? There's no way you just giggled at the Motel Starlight." I sigh. His glee at the random subject has me confused, and his wiggling in his seat is distracting in the worst way.

"Nothing, seriously, man, I'm fine," he says before patting his stomach in that weird way again and failing to suppress another giggle. He clears his throat, then shouts and jolts out of his chair like his ass is on fire.

He leaps away and drops to the floor on his hands and knees.

What. The. Fuck?

I tilt and look under the table at what he's inspecting when a brown and white tuft ambles into his hands. He swoops it up and cradles it to his chest. He slips the creature under his shirt, and when he finds his seat again, and I rise from my position, he meets my eyes and must see the questions lingering in them.

"Oh, uh... I guess this is as good a time as any." He lifts his shirt, and in his lap is a hedgehog. A rodent. A little beast of a thing that blinks into the harsh lights as Lucas runs a delicate finger along its back, making cooing noises.

Jacob eyes the prickly little bastard, shrugs, and returns to work. Han looks at me and must see the incredulity on my face. He jumps in to ask the pertinent questions.

"What? Why? And how?" His tone informs Lucas that he can't get out of answering.

"This, gentlemen, is a hedgehog. I'm calling him Sir Lancelot. Get it?" We each roll our eyes. "I found him in our parking lot. They're not from around here. Not to mention illegal in California, so I think someone had him as a pet and lost him. I can't exactly put up signs with my phone number because animal control would just come and take him. What if they put him down? I'm keeping him. He's cute, huh?"

We meet Lucas's monologue with silence. At the lack of affirmation and coos over the "cuteness" of this thing, he lets out a groan. "Whatever. He's freaking adorable, and I'm not giving him up. Buttercup is gonna love his name."

The little beastie, who was snuggling into Lucas's hand, pops its head out and looks at me when I start speaking. It's unnerving. "Fine, but he's your responsibility, and keep him out of danger zones. I'm talking about the weapons rooms, the servers, anywhere there's tech he can chew through. Oh, and the kitchen. We don't need to pick up a disease eating something he's climbed all over. Just your room, you hear me?"

The creature stares at me through my speech, and I'm nearly confident I see a tear forming in the corner of his beady little eye. It's not that I'm afraid of animals. I just don't like the ones that carry God-knows-what on their skin, in their saliva, and yes, in their shit. No way is that thing getting near me. It takes a tentative step forward, away from Lucas, and toward me. I roll my chair away from the table, desperate to regain that space.

Lucas laughs for a moment and snatches him up. "Fine, I'll put Sir Lancelot back in my room, but he will need to go out now and then. I wonder if they make harnesses and leashes for hedgehogs. We could go for walks."

Jacob pipes up at the absurdity, "They're illegal, you fool. You *just* said that. You can't just take him for a walk in public."

"I mean around the parking area. Geez," Lucas grumbles as he leaves the war room. "And no one tells Buttercup! I want it to be a surprise!" Yay, something else to add to our never-ending list.

Who do we know in Animal Control?

With a plan forming for the group in Bakersfield, I leave for my team leader meeting. I'm curious about how Mara's going to play this. There is only so much she can hide that Jacob won't be able to dig up. Between her allegiances being called into question, and the clandestine meetings, it's painting a pretty vivid picture.

My plan today includes checking out the other unit leaders and grabbing a moment with Mara after the meeting. I have some questions.

The other leaders and I are waiting in the Annex Security lobby on the upper management level. Taking advantage of the few free minutes I have, I text Trouble.

Me: Hey, Trouble. Got plans later?
Trouble: No... wanna make some?

I fail to hide my grin as I stare at the screen, knowing all the while I must look like an idiot, but I don't care. I'm too in love with this woman to mask it.

Me: Yeah, can you meet me at 698 Baker St. Around 7?
Trouble: Sure! Do I need to bring anything...weapons wise?
Me: Just yourself. I got the rest.
Me: ::kissy face emoji::
Trouble: ::heart emoji::

Ah fuck, there I go, using the emojis again. I refuse—*refuse*—to let anyone know those damned things are growing on me.

A message from Han pops up in our team group chat. He's trying to locate Lucas because Sir Lancelot is curled up on the couch in the lounge, alone. I'm sure this is only the first of many successful escapes; I just hope the thing doesn't chew through all the wiring.

The receptionist looks up from her computer at us, crowding her pristine lobby, and raises her voice to be heard over the chatter. "Ms. Hendrix will see you now."

As one, we stand and make our way to the conference room. The only time we use her office is when it's our evaluation time, and even then, it's a toss-up whether it's with her, Cross, or the former combat specialist, Blake.

We find our seats in the conference room and in strides Mara Hendrix, closely followed by Patton Cross. She's dressed in her usual bland pantsuit, her hair in a bun, and glasses perched on her nose. She's nothing if not consistent. Cross is wearing his usual three-piece suit, fancy as shit loafers, and has a white pocket square peeking out from his breast pocket. If not for the hard glint in his eye and hair greased to the side the way most gangsters in El Castillo arrange their hair, he would look as if he could run a Fortune 500 company. Thinking it over, I'm sure if all business ventures this company had were legal, they'd make it onto that list.

They find their seats at the head of the table, and the one usually reserved for Blake remains empty. Saying a silent, thankful prayer that they've moved on from his disappearance, I let out an imperceptible sigh. It's only a matter of time before they fill his spot. It's been months since he "resigned," and I know they've been meeting with prospective candidates. The only question is who they'll settle on. Someone from within the company, or will they bring in fresh meat?

The meeting is the usual monthly hoopla with bonuses given out for completing assignments, recognition, and reprimands, and all the while, I wish I were anywhere but here. How did I end up working for a company that has no scruples about killing off the competition? Fuck my life. I'm getting too old for this shit.

Technically, we could all retire at this point. We've got enough saved and invested to do so without needing to pinch our pennies. Righting our own wrongs and helping people escape the reach of Annex had become our reasons to continue. Now we've got Rogue. And my new motivation is removing the asshole who's dictated her entire life.

Some might say it's fucking stupid to throw everything you have into a woman. Into making her happy and treating her the way she deserves to be treated—spoiled, even—but that's what I want. It must be the way I'm wired, because I once thought Sheila was that person for me. Boy, was I wrong. It's why I've been so careful in starting this relationship with Rogue and the men I consider my brothers. If for one moment, I thought they didn't have her best interests at heart; I don't know what I'd do. She deserves the best. I only hope we can be the ones to give that to her.

The meeting wraps up after a quick forty-five minutes, and Cross dismisses us. As Mara stands, I rise from my chair and wait until she and Cross have left the room. The guys and I shake hands, and I pay special attention to the leader of Beta Team Two. He's a couple of years younger than me, dressed in black tactical pants, and has a hard glint in his eyes. He looks me up and down in an assessing manner and introduces himself.

"I'm Nick Grand; you're Noah Tate, right?" he asks as he shakes my hand. He's met me before, but I feel something in my palm and know this is a ruse.

"Yeah, that's me. Nice to meet you. I saw you at the last few meetings, but you know how these things can go." I call the last meetings to attention because while I'm confident I've vaguely met him in the past, his designation and the slips of info Mara has given us just made him a lot more interesting.

"Too right. Last time, DTT was up in arms about no bonus for their corporate espionage. I don't know why they'd expect one. Management found them out. Man, what a disaster." He references Delta Team Two's latest fuck-up.

"Idiots," I agree. There's a reason they're the last team on the totem pole. I'm nearly certain they'll be replaced before long. Among the eight teams, they really are the worst. I like my spot up top. So long as the new guy here doesn't come for it, we'll be a-okay.

He gives my hand a final shake and releases it. I feel the slip of paper he transferred over in my palm and hold it securely with my thumb. I tuck my hand into my pocket, depositing the note, and continue with a few pleasantries.

When the room has cleared out, I stroll to Mara's office.

She's sitting in her plush white chair behind her desk, and her fingers are massaging her temples. "Ms. Hendrix," I greet from the open doorway.

She straightens up immediately. "Oh, Mr. Tate, come in."

I do as she asks, closing the door behind me. "Our team has been going through the server for new assignments, but we think there's a delay. The assignments posted are always from days before. I think there's some kind of lag in the system."

My complaint is a complete ruse, of course, but it gives me the coverage I need. "I'm going to write my private email here. If something comes up, could you let us know? Until the lag is fixed, this will have to do." I snag a pen and a sheet of paper from her desk. In tiny writing in the corner, I write out, "Can we talk in here?"

Turning the paper toward her, I watch as she hastily shakes her head. "I can't believe you're having problems with that." She sighs, answering both the question on the page and the entirely fake issue I've brought to her. "Can you rewrite that, Mr. Tate? That's incredibly illegible."

I roll my eyes and turn the paper again, jotting down meeting details. This was a possibility, so Plan B is now in full effect.

"I'll work with IT to get that settled. Take the assignments on the list that you have access to, and I'll have my assistant keep you updated on the other ones."

"Sounds like a plan, Ms. Hendrix. I'll be in touch."

I remove myself from her office, knowing there's nothing else we could plausibly discuss without arousing suspicion from whoever is watching her. I'd be nervous about us leaving it at that, but at least now I know the office has bugs. Hell, the entire building probably does. The only question is: Is it the feds or Cross? She suggested he was behind a lot of the moves when Jacob cornered her in that coffee shop.

AT SEVEN ON THE DOT, MY PHONE LETS OUT A CHIRP. TROUBLE.

Trouble: I'm here. But where is here?

I carefully refold the note that Nick Grand gave me and stuff it in my pocket. I have to discuss it with both the team and my girl, but right now, I have a date.

Rushing out the door and down the stairs, I find her standing on the sidewalk in a full black skirt, black heels, and a white corset top. She knows I love those damn things. She pinned her hair up, the loops and swirls of her curls and waves gently nestled in a bandana tied off at a jaunty angle on the top of her head. *Fuuuck me.*

I swing the door to the building open, and she turns toward the noise. A smile overtakes her face, and all the worry from the day melts from my shoulders.

She bounds up to me and throws her arms around my neck. "Hiya, Cap."

Her kiss is sweet, deliberate, and rocks me to my core. How could I have ever thought Sheila was the one for me? I've never felt this way about someone else, and while I loved Sheila before she ripped my heart out, this all-consuming passion and bliss is something I want to keep and treasure for the rest of my days.

I reluctantly break the kiss, boop her on the nose in greeting—because apparently, I've lost all sense of myself—and lead her inside. We climb the stairs of the building, and I wipe my nervous hands on my slacks. I swing the door inward, and Trouble just looks at me from the corner of her eye with suspicion before entering my second 'home.'

She steps into the living room, and twirls around the open space, taking in every square inch. "What is this place? Noah, did you get us a sex pad?" she jokes.

"What? No! This is my apartment." Her jaw drops open a little, and she looks around more earnestly this time. I can tell she's looking for little pieces of me here, and she finds them sprinkled around. There isn't much because the clubhouse is home, but the photos of my army days interest her.

Her eyes widen when they finally come back to mine. "Is this where you disappear to sometimes?" she asks shyly.

"Yeah. I mean, we have to maintain residences outside of the clubhouse to throw off suspicion, but I haven't been around much lately. I thought maybe we could have a date here." Am I an asshole for killing two birds with one stone? Kind of. Will she understand that? Definitely.

"Well, I like it. It suits you." She wanders over toward the kitchen and opens the oven door. "Good Lord in heaven, Noah. What have you done?"

What? What happened to my meal? Did I burn it? Impossible.

I rush to the oven and yank the door all the way open. Everything looks fine.

"This looks incredible!" she exclaims.

With an audible sigh of relief, I close the glass door and spin her toward me. I place my hands on her cheeks and tilt her face to mine. Looking into her eyes, I say, "Don't scare me like that. Do you know how long it takes to prepare a roasted rack of lamb?"

She shakes her head at my question.

"Hours, Trouble. And while I appreciate the excitement, let's avoid the mild heart attack next time, please."

"Yes, Sir," she answers with a coy smile.

And there goes my dick. It rose to half-mast the moment I saw her downstairs, reached uncomfortable levels with her kiss, and now, I'm lucky if there's any blood left in my brain at all.

I plant a gentle kiss on her lips and direct her to the island. She hops up on a stool while I step into my pantry, discreetly adjust my throbbing dick, and grab something random to pretend to have needed. She looks at me inquisitively as I walk back into the kitchen clutching a jar of... pickled peppers. Yeah, I probably should have paid attention to what I was grabbing, but I'm committed now.

"Want one?" I ask.

"With dinner? Isn't that a cherry-glazed rack of lamb? Do pickled peppers go with that?"

"Not particularly, but I had a quick craving. Maybe you're right. Let's stick with the bread."

Smooth, Noah. Real fucking smooth.

Dinner goes well, with not a pickled pepper in sight. We chat the way we did at the tapas restaurant on our first date, only this time, there's no server impatiently hovering, waiting for us to leave. We devoured the lamb, demolished the potatoes, and picked around the salad because it was basically a filler.

I left soft music playing in the background, oldies because I know they're Trouble's favorite, and when she sways in her seat because of the melody or possibly the wine, I can't resist. I stand and extend my hand to her. "Can't Help Falling in Love" by Elvis Presley plays on the stereo system and never have I heard more fitting lyrics.

"Care to dance?" I ask.

She gently places her hand in mine, and a thrill runs through my body. I guide her up from the table. Elvis croons from the speakers, and I use my phone to increase the volume. We sway back and forth, a sense of deep contentment settling in my chest as we softly sing along and lose ourselves in the music.

AFTER DANCING FOR A FEW SONGS, ROGUE'S HAND TOYS WITH THE hair at the nape of my neck—the brush of her fingers slow and intimate. Goosebumps trail down my back at her touch, and my arms tighten around her. She rests her head on my shoulder as we glide around my living room, and I press a soft kiss to her crown. Her movements slowly turn more seductive, and my half-mast boner from earlier comes back with a vengeance. Okay, to be honest, it hasn't gone down all night, but it's suddenly drawing more attention as her hips sway so close to mine.

She tilts her face toward mine, and her gaze drifts from my chest to my heated stare before finally settling on my lips. Her tongue snakes out, and my eyes follow the movement, incapable of doing anything but. She sucks her lush lip into her mouth and bites down, her teeth raking over the supple flesh.

She rises on her toes and presses her lips to mine in a soft, chaste kiss that leaves me wanting more. My hand reaches the back of her neck, keeping her close as I push forward, continuing the kiss.

My tongue sweeps into her mouth, and I groan at the taste of the dessert wine mixing with her own flavor. Her hands wind around my neck, and her fingers thread through my short hair.

The scrape of her nails sends goosebumps trailing down my arms, and I feel my cock stiffen further. She takes control of the kiss, making me growl and give up control for just a moment. It occurs to me that this will be our first time; just us.

Last time, the guys carefully made their way from the room to give us our moment alone together. They know I'm not really one for public displays, and that's precisely what it would have felt like if I'd joined them. I immensely enjoyed directing them, but I have no plans of participating physically. At least, not yet. Although, I have a feeling if this woman crooked her finger in my direction, I would join them in a heartbeat. Knowing Rogue, I doubt she would push me to do something I'm not ready for. Or willing to do. It's just not who she is.

My hands grip her hips harder, and I lift her from the ground. Her legs wind around my waist as her kiss deepens. The heat of her core against my body has me groaning at the contact.

She pulls back. "Noah?"

"Hmm?" I answer with my eyes still closed, nipping at her lips because I can't fucking help myself.

"This place got a bedroom?" she asks huskily, causing my cock to throb with want.

I spin and stride down the hall. She lets out a giggle at my furious pace, and holds on for dear life as I turn a corner at a break-neck speed.

I enter my room and toss Rogue onto my bed. She lands on her back with a tiny bounce, her hair spilling from the up-do and her tits from her corset. How in God's name did I get so lucky?

She stretches her arms above her head, and I brace myself over her on my forearms. I let my hips drop, pressing into her center through her skirt. My lips trail a path from behind her ear, down her neck, landing at the swell of her breasts. She wiggles under me, looking for friction, and grinding her clit against the bulge in my slacks. She gasps quickly and begins fumbling with the clasps along the front of her top.

"Leave it." My voice stops her hands, and she settles them on my hips, pulling me closer.

"Yes, Sir." Her statement is a breathy whisper, but there's a playfulness to it. I don't need the "Sir" part, but I do like how she lets me lead. I know she's a powerful woman, capable of handling her life, both sex and regular, but I want to direct her. Need to.

A groan escapes my throat, and I slide down her body, unzipping the skirt at her waist. She lifts her hips and allows me to divest her of the garment. Her panties are black lace, and the garter belt straps run under the waistband to connect to her thigh-high stockings. Isn't it supposed to go the other way?

Dragging my eyes away from all that lace, I ask, "Did you put these on in the wrong order?"

She merely replies, "This way, we can keep the hose but lose the panties."

If my mind continued functioning after those words, I wouldn't have noticed it. It's as if she's short-circuited all electrical impulses in my body.

I didn't know this was a fetish for me, but here we are. Learning new things every day.

I grasp the waistband of her thong and drag it down, avoiding the clips attached to the lace-topped stockings—I don't want to accidentally remove those in the process—and slip them over the heels she's still wearing. She looks incredible.

Half-angel in her white corset, half-demon in the black lace framing her pussy. The colors are a mimicry of the tattoos covering half of her gorgeous body. I glide my hands up her silky calves. This woman was made for me, for each of us really, and I hope like hell I don't fuck this up.

I follow my hands with kisses along her tattooed thigh, and as she arches her back, she runs her fingers through my hair and directs my head straight to her clit.

"Please, Noah."

Her words are my undoing. I descend and start with slow strokes to her clit; long, languorous licks that have her tightening her hold on my head. I switch the tempo, going faster, little flicks of my tongue driving her mad. Her thighs clamp over my ears as I increase the pace yet again. I pry one away from me and use the gap to add a finger to her soaked core. I slip one into the first knuckle, and at the sensation, she groans and pushes further toward me.

Keeping the pace on her clit with my tongue, my finger pumps in and out. When it's coated in her arousal, I add a second.

"Faster!" Rogue urges me.

Her thighs rest on my shoulders, and the heels of her shoes are digging into my back. The fervor in her tone has me complying. My shoulder twinges a bit as I drive my tongue in and out of her at an increased pace, unable to get enough of her. I hear her breath quicken, her thighs shake near my ears, and I pull away.

"What the fuck?" she asks, her tone threatening.

"You're going to come on my cock, Trouble. Repeatedly." She lifts a brow, and there's passion and fire in her gaze. Her chest heaves with the unfulfilled release. The near-edge is only going to make it better when she sinks down on my length.

I stand from the bed and beckon her to the foot of the bed with a curl of my finger.

"Undress me."

Her hands fly to the buttons on my shirt, deftly undoing them with quick flicks and a frustrated growl at the last button before popping it off and sending it skittering under the bedside table. She shoves the shirt over my shoulders, and I work on taking it off while she undoes my slacks, pushing them down my thighs. I shuck off my clothes and look down at this woman before me, kneeling on my bed. Her hands rake a trail down my chest, making my skin tingle and my cock jump. Catching the edge of my boxer briefs, she torturously slides them down my legs, bending her head to catch the head of my cock in her mouth. Oh fuck, if we start that, I'll never last.

I grasp her upper arms and fall to the bed, pulling her on top of me in a spin-like move. She settles her thighs on either side of my hips and grinds down on me. Her wet pussy sliding over my length. So wet, so fucking warm.

"Ride me, Trouble. Make yourself come on my cock."

She needs no more encouragement than that. She lifts, tensing her thighs. Balancing with one hand pressed to my chest, and using the other to line my dick up with her entrance.

She sinks down inch by decadent inch, and I watch as I disappear inside of her. Satisfaction blooms deeply in my chest at the sight and the feel of her surrounding me. This incredible woman who would burn the world down for those she loves has chosen me. *Us.* When I bottom out, I can't stop the groan that escapes my lips. I look up at her, this goddess, this queen, and my breath stalls in my lungs.

Slowly, she moves. Her hips start a rhythm, and my hands come up to help guide her body as she uses me in the best way possible.

Up.

Down.

Grind.

Rogue's breaths come in short bursts, and her hands on my chest curl, her nails digging into my skin. The pain is exquisite. I'm confident I'll have crescent-shaped scabs on my chest in the morning, and I don't fucking care.

Her pace increases, and her head bows back. She removes her hands from my torso and props them on my thighs behind her. Her movements are becoming less fluid, more rabid as she controls our motions. I try to keep myself still. I want her directing this, but my hips pump up and down of their own volition.

Rogue brings one hand to where we're joined and massages her clit. A few swirls later, she's coming so hard, it feels like her pussy catches my cock in a vise, and I never want it to let me go.

She collapses forward, still grinding her clit at the base of my dick, and I act without thinking, flipping us until she's under me, reminiscent of the first time we made love.

I stuff a pillow under her hips and sit back on my knees. The backs of her thighs are pressed against my chest, her ankles up above my head, when one shoe goes flying off. Fuck it.

I withdraw and power into her. My cock slowly slides out of her before punching back in. The rhythm keeps her on edge, and she whimpers at each loss of contact.

In.

Out.

Grind.

Unable to stop myself when I feel her pussy fluttering around me, I lose all control. I find a tempo she likes and drive it home. With a pinch of her clit between my thumb and index finger, she flies off the handle once more.

As her pussy tightens around me, I follow her over the precipice and release deep inside of her with a groan I'm sure my neighbors won't appreciate.

Her eyes are still closed after her climax, and her tongue darts out to swipe at her lips. My mouth is dry as fuck as well, so I ease out of her, reveling in the sound she makes at the loss of my heat, and grab a few water bottles from the kitchen.

When I return, she's still in the same spot, eyes closed but smiling.

I run the cold bottle up her body, and she hisses at the touch when it meets bare skin.

"Trouble," I softly call as I nip at her ear. Her eyes flutter open. Her pupils are dilated, and she tilts her head in my direction. "I love you."

"I love you too, Noah."

"Good, now drink. We're doing that again."

"Yes, Sir." Her laugh comes out at her own words, and she swipes the water bottle from my hand.

After fully undressing her and carefully hanging her clothes in the closet, we meet at the bed. It takes three more rounds before we're both sated and ready to drift off.

It isn't until seven the following day that her phone dings on the nightstand, and she pouts that she has to go.

Chapter Four

Rogue

Last night and this morning were perfect—or they would have been if my phone hadn't chirped. Thankfully, I left my official phone at the apartment and used the clone without GPS that Jacob made for me.

The elevator arrives on my floor, and I walk into my apartment. I text King back once I'm inside and in the kitchen. I don't want a text arriving while I'm out, then having him watch me walk back into the building with my GPS pinging from this address. The lengths I employ to keep my ass covered are getting ridiculous.

King: Breakfast meeting in my apartment. Just you. 9:00.
Me: Okay.

Simple enough directive: leave the husband at home. Speaking of Husband Dearest, where is he?

My feet quietly pad down the hall to the bedroom. I crack open the door and see him starfished on the bed again. Seems he likes his space when I'm not here. After spending the week preceding our wedding sleeping on the couch, his body is probably reclaiming every inch it can.

In the closet, I grab some leggings and a Henley shirt, and tiptoe back to the bathroom. Smelling like sex when I show up at King's place isn't ideal. Or maybe it is. He's been on me about the pregnancy thing, so he might just think it's Romano.

My clothes are simple loungewear, and my hair is mussed from last night. I'm going with the whole just-got-fucked look to throw suspicion off. The coffee pot emits the most glorious aroma, and I follow my nose toward the kitchen. I round the corner and bump straight into Romano, sloshing his coffee all down his front.

"Shit! Sorry," I apologize as I rush to the kitchen to grab a towel.

I return to find Romano just standing there, staring down at the mess of coffee, not having moved for fear of spreading the liquid gold along the hall.

"Totally fine. Where are you off to? Another 'adventure'?" he asks with a grin.

"No, nothing so fun today, unfortunately. I have to go meet with King." Well, that killed the fun banter. Romano's eyes shutter and he straightens his shoulders.

"Do you need me with you?" he asks.

Despite being thrown into this situation headfirst, I've got to hand it to the guy. He's remarkably calm and has adapted to our new arrangement really quickly. I doubt when he signed on for running guns under Horvat all those years ago, he imagined he'd end up in this position—poised to co-lead the motherfucking gang.

"No, orders were for me only. You know how King can be. Speaking of, what's going on with The Vegas Crew? Are we expanding east?" I ask. We certainly *cannot* take on more territory. It'll only make toppling this entire organization even more difficult.

"No news yet. I met with King yesterday, covered for you as you asked, but there was no talk of plans. He only griped about how they could be reckless enough to get caught."

I figured as much, but it's good to have that confirmed. It's only been two months, and Vegas's assets are still frozen, with too many law enforcement agencies on high alert. Moving in immediately would trigger every red flag imaginable.

I get the worst of the spill off the floor, and Romano goes to clean up. I've got to get moving, or I'm going to be late. We all know how that would go.

Dashing to the door, I exit and press the button on the elevator while stuffing my tiny wallet and keys into my bra. Waiting for permission to ascend to King's floor, the seconds tick by as nothing happens. After I've pulled my phone out and have my thumb hovering over King's name on the screen, the elevator starts its journey. Weird. It never takes that long when

I'm expected. His security team is usually manning the monitors at all times from their offices throughout the building.

The elevator arrives, and the doors slide open to reveal the usual pristine living space King calls home. The scent of breakfast food trails through the apartment, so I head to the kitchen.

King stands, leaning against the counter in a pair of black linen loose pants, a white t-shirt, and bare feet. His chef is at the stove, dutifully flipping omelets and settling fruit on a platter. King takes a sip of his tea with his pinky in the air as he meticulously watches the chef arrange the slices of mango on the edges of the dish. *Pompous ass.*

King catches sight of me in the doorway and nods his head slightly. I nod back, a bit confused at the scene I'm witnessing. I don't think I've ever seen King this informal before with his staff. Sure, he has on his designer pajama pants as he always does in the mornings, but he looks almost relaxed. There's no scowl marring his face, no threats of death in his eyes. It's throwing me off.

Clearing my throat, I greet him with my usual terse, "King."

He lifts his head and tilts it to the side curiously as he sips his tea. "Ah, Rogue, yes. Take a seat."

King follows me and sits at the head of the table while I take the chair to his right. The chef comes out, laden down with food dishes, and after a few trips, excuses himself and leaves the apartment. The sound of the door closing echoes around the space, and I'm left wondering what's going on as my heart beats irregularly in my chest, waiting for whatever bomb he's going to drop.

There's no security, a chef quick to leave, and King in his pajamas. Romano told me he was casual about their breakfast meeting soon after our marriage, but hearing it and seeing it are two different things.

"Eat. We have a lot to discuss." My childhood conditioning kicks in, and I instantly grab an omelet from the serving tray and pile fruit on the side of my plate, avoiding the grapes because *ew*. King does the same, opting for bread and jam as his side dish and tops up his own coffee before pouring one for me.

I lift my fork full of fluffy eggs and wait him out. He'll start the conversation when he's good and ready. Until then, the only thing I can do is eat in relative peace and hope whatever he tells me doesn't sicken me enough to bring it all back up. King digs in, and after ten minutes, he breaks his silence.

"Are you pregnant yet?" His words register, and I choke on my eggs.

"It's been three months. I told you to give him a reason to stay loyal. Whether it's because we attach him to you or the offspring."

Hackles up, I clear my throat and calmly deliver the speech I've had in my back pocket for this exact moment. "I went off birth control after your orders. I have my ovulation chart and have been persistent in trying. It could take more time; most women who are trying to get pregnant conceive within a year. If nothing occurs between now and then, I've already looked into IVF. But I'm young, we're both healthy, and there's no reason to think it won't take in the next month or two." I see his eyebrows rise at the IVF mention, but I have an argument ready to head that off. "IVF is a good route, but could potentially interfere with work. I figured you'd want all hands on deck after what happened with The Vegas Crew."

According to research, IVF hormonal treatment is manageable, but only because women are badass and our bodies endure a lot for reproduction. But we do it with a smile on our faces and iron in our veins. He nods his head at the last part of my speech, so I'm hoping he drops the topic.

"Fine. Keep at it. I want things settled by the year's end."

Sure, sure. Except that I have an IUD I've grown quite attached to, motherfucker.

Considering the conversation on my womb rental closed, King rips off a piece of bread and points it at me. "I'm glad you brought up Vegas. I want that territory under our umbrella. The Rattlesnakes will push back on that, along with the other organizations in Southern California and possibly the Midwest leaders on the other side of Vegas's territory. The area would be an excellent addition. It's time we got the heads together and ironed out a new treaty. I've got something planned for the summer."

That surprises me. King rarely plans things out himself. He hires a myriad of people to do it for him. Curiosity gets the better of me. "What are you proposing?"

When I question him, anger flashes in his eyes, and reflexes have me shrinking back a bit. It's not enough to be noticeable to most people, but King sees it, smirking at the power he still has over me. I square my shoulders and wait for his response.

"We're having a party, darling daughter. It'll allow us to host some prominent figures and remind them of our reach. We will also mingle with the other organizations, ending with a signed and sealed treaty. Invitations to submit treaty negotiations are ready, and I'm making the announcement at the next board meeting."

I honestly didn't expect a detailed answer like that. Ideas flit across my mind as I soak in the information. Claudette will be in attendance; that's one on my side already. Getting the Southern California assholes to negotiate will be hell, but anything is possible when the Vegas territory is up for grabs.

"Can I help organize it?" flies out of my mouth before I've thoroughly thought things through. I have a plan forming in my mind, and I don't want to miss the opportunity. Even if it ends up sucking, I can skip it and arrange the standard party stuff. King eyes me with a cocked brow and skepticism in his gaze. I get it. I've never volunteered for anything aside from taking out an asshole.

"You have enough on your plate. Have an heir in your belly, then we'll talk. Elise is heading this one up." My ears perk up at that. If there's anyone I can convince to let me in on the details early, it's that sniper-wielding, bunny-slipper-wearing, high-society whacko.

"Yes, King," I agree, knowing I can bug Elise for details. I wonder if I'll need to blackmail her.

After finishing our breakfast in silence, I think we're done with conversation when King ruins that hope for me. What's one more dream dashed, after all?

"Marie, it isn't safe out there. Stay here." His hand reaches across the small space between us, and he grips my hand with enough force to have me stifling a small gasp at the unexpected contact. He never touches me anymore. Before, it was to hurt, to punish.

Marie? What the fuck?

"Uh, King, Marie was my mother."

"What? No, your mother was Maria. Vain woman, naming you after herself. I'm glad she's out of our lives." His emphasis on the name tells me he's confident that he's right, and it has me questioning myself for a moment before I conjure up the image of my mother's headstone, which clearly says "Marie." And my name has nothing to do with hers.

"What's happening, King?" I ask, unsure what the fuck is going on. My shoulders hike up to my ears with uncertainty.

He responds, but his voice is too low to hear it. The mumbles continue for a few seconds as I lean in closer to hear. His hand lashes out to grip my arm, and he squeezes with incredible strength. As I'm busy training my eyes on the vise around my forearm, bracing for a hit how I used to, I miss his face transforming. When I look up again, his eyes have rolled back, and he's tense, his back arched dramatically in his chair, seizing.

Ah, shit.

I rip my arm out of his grasp, and as soon as his arm is free, he tilts to the side, smacking his head on the table's edge on his way down. I turn him on his side, as he instructed me when I was a kid. It's been at least fifteen years since he taught me, but he drilled it into my brain.

He had a seizure once when I was living with him, but we never spoke of it again. The single time I brought it up, he beat me horribly. I learned my lesson to never ever breathe a word of it to anyone.

The unfortunate part of this whole situation is that I can't let him die, despite wanting him to seize or bleed out until there's no bringing him back. I know the repercussions would be catastrophic for me. My teeth grind as the thoughts come, unbidden, weighing the options before me.

Yes, I might have Sage back, but I don't have the evidence he's collected against me since I started in this line of work. Keeping one hand firmly on King's shoulder and tilting him to the side, I use the other to grab my phone from my back pocket.

What a day to not have security around.

I quickly unlock the phone and dial our resident doctor. He lives a floor below King, acting as his private physician for years. Dr. Shaw is an unassuming man with a bald head and no sense of humor. He answers on the first ring, his tone clinical and sure.

Shaw assures me he'll be up in a minute and that he can bypass the elevator security with his own electronic card. I stay on the phone with him and listen as he instructs me on what to do. His voice is calm as he walks me through the steps. I try to keep my composure and hope that the man before me doesn't die during the call. That'd be just my luck.

The elevator doors open seconds later, and Dr. Shaw rushes over to us with a medical bag at his side, dropping it next to me as he checks King over, avoiding the blood pooling under his head.

"How long was he seizing before you called?" he asks.

"Ten seconds, maybe less. He's had one before, but it was years ago. I was just a child. What do we do now?" I ask, my tone damn near frantic as my hands shake, looking for something to do.

"If it were just the seizure, I'd say ride it out until it stops. But with the head wound, we need to get to a hospital. Saint Gregory's has one of his doctors always on call. Get an ambulance here. He'll hate knowing he rode in one, but I can't patch this up and get the scans as quickly as they can. He pays handsomely for priority and discretion."

I do as Dr. Shaw instructs and grab my phone off the floor. I dial 911, then the lobby number, so they can admit the EMTs when they arrive.

The wait isn't long because everyone knows this building caters to the elite, thus lighting a fire under the ass of any emergency responders in the vicinity. The wailing sirens can be heard from outside of the building far more quickly than I would have thought possible, and yet, the moments drag on, each lasting an eternity. Time ceases to have meaning as my pulse pounds in my ears and my nerves are shot to shit.

After a few agonizing moments of questioning my choice to even ring the good Dr. Shaw, instead of letting him finally die, two EMTs enter the penthouse, making their way over to us. They keep him steady, preventing him from moving from his position on his side.

The minutes seem endless as he convulses on the floor. I've never known one to go this long. After another thirty seconds, the shakes ease, and I help the EMTs load him onto the gurney.

We rush downstairs and get King loaded into the ambulance. They ask if I'm family, and it's easy to say I'm his daughter in this situation; I need information. Dr. Shaw hops into the back with me after giving the EMTs a stern glare, just begging them to argue.

The ride to the hospital is agonizing, grueling even. Seeing the man before me lying supine on the gurney, tubes attached, and electrical nodes taped to his chest, I can't help but wonder if this will finally be his end. My nerves and elation at the prospect war with each other in my mind, only adding to my anxiety and jittery limbs.

He's dashed into the back once we arrive, and I set up shop in the waiting room, filling out documentation with what little information I know. Fuck, I don't even know his last name and I doubt he'd want his first name out in the world. Filling out that portion with just "King" seems to do the trick, as the nurse doesn't even bother to check the rest of the form. Dr. Shaw disappeared with King when they wheeled him in and told me to sit in the waiting room and we'd know more soon.

Apparently, King has connections absolutely everywhere.

The double doors proclaiming "no access" taunt me. I want to know if this is the end and I'll have to slip into hiding when that motherfucking documentation gets out. It may be a heartless way of thinking, but I need my ass covered if this goes sideways.

I take a seat in the orange plastic chair and begin my watch. I quickly thumb out a message to my guys, letting them know what's going on, followed by a text to Romano, who abandons everything and joins me at the hospital.

Romano comes rushing into the waiting room through the double doors. It's still early enough in the day that traffic shouldn't have been bad. And yet, he still took thirty minutes. He plops into the seat next to me and searches my face to see if I'm okay. The concern in his eyes is comforting. He clasps my hands with his own.

Even though I know this could be the end, and a big part of me hopes it is, it still saddens me to think that the only person I currently have as a parental figure is lying in the back, possibly dying. It makes no sense. Sweat beads my forehead as we begin our wait.

This man, this person, this father who was supposed to take care of my sister and me, ended up hurting me worse than most would dare to imagine. Romano brings his palm to my face and redirects my eyes from the floor to his own.

"Rogue," he calls to get my attention. "King is going to be fine. I pulled some strings. A surgeon here owes us a favor. I called him from the back of the Uber when you told me which hospital."

It's easy to see why this man moved up the ranks so quickly if this is what he can get done from the back of a cab. "He's had a grand mal seizure and likely has a concussion with the bump and gash on his head. They don't know how he'll recover, but it was still early when the surgeon and I spoke. I'm sure we'll know something soon. He's not in surgery, they were just stitching his head when the surgeon checked in on the prognosis. He seems to be okay, and they've stabilized him. Now, we wait. They won't let any family back until they examine him. After some tests and blood work, I'm sure they'll let you see him."

"Thank you, Romano," I tell him. My voice shakes, and I don't know what to make of it.

Words can't express what it means to me, knowing that there's someone else in my corner within the organization. Yes, I have my wonderful guys, but they've been sequestered to a small corner in my life. I want them front and center at all times, but no way can that happen anytime soon, and it fucking kills me.

Taking the information Romano has given me, I reach out to the group chat. They filled the chat with message after message, but I refuse to read them. I know it will be platitudes and things that I can't hear right now. The texts will be in favor of him dying or fear if he lives. Either way, I'm of two minds, and I can't bear to work through the scenarios; both are equally beneficial and equally horrible.

A few more minutes pass before the nurse comes around the desk. She makes her way over to us and asks, "Family of King?"

Romano stands as I nod my head. He helps me to my feet with a gentle hand and wraps his arm around me. "Yes, this is his daughter, and I'm his son-in-law. How's he doing?"

The nurse clears her throat and says, "There's bleeding in his brain. The seizure and the impact to his head caused some trauma. However, the doctor doesn't see why he won't eventually recover, but the physician has some things to go over with you if you have a moment?" Of fucking course, we have a moment. We're here waiting for news, not rushing from one thing to the next.

I nod my assent at her stupid question. She leads us through those taunting double doors, down yet another stark, white hallway, and to the door of an office, two floors up. The name on the door says Dr. Hansen, Neurology. She knocks timidly before opening the door to the office and gives a nod to the man as she backs out of the room.

Dr. Hansen stands and extends his hand toward us. Romano shakes it firmly, pumping it up and down twice as he introduces us. "I'm Francesco Romano, and this is my wife, Rogue," he tells the doctor. I'm grateful he never actually uses my legal name. But I'm still pissed he knows it.

"Where is Dr. Shaw?" I ask.

"He's with King, monitoring things, as directed. Nice to meet you both. I wish it were under better circumstances. I'm Dr. Hansen, and I've been King's primary physician in this hospital for the past few years."

Years? I know he's had at least one seizure, but to have a specialist on hand reeks of more information than I'm privy to.

The doctor before me seems like a relatively average person, not someone in the gang's employ. His brown hair has salt-and-pepper hues woven through most of it. He has a neatly trimmed beard, the usual white coat, and a pair of glasses perched atop his nose that lends him an air of gravitas.

"I'm sorry, Dr. Hansen. Did you say years?" I ask, the disbelief apparent in my tone.

I find I get more answers when people are unsuspecting about what I do and what I'm capable of. My sugary sweet demeanor has been incredibly valuable over the years. He nods his head, waving his hand to the seats before his desk.

"I'm afraid so. Normally, it's hospital policy to go over the results with the patient in question. However, King is in an induced coma at the moment. The trauma to his brain was quite severe. We're monitoring the size of the bleed to see if it stops before the pressure gets too high. If it stays relatively low, the body will reabsorb it. If it continues bleeding, we'll need to drain it. We know nothing at this stage, but we should know if his end-of-life plans have changed."

I bring a shaky hand to my lips to cover the gasp threatening to escape. King can't fucking die. He can't. There are too many things up in the air right now. All of this will have been for nothing if he dies now and I get sent to prison.

Romano clasps my hand with his and squeezes. He knows exactly what I'm thinking. The evidence is somewhere. King is lying in a bed, vulnerable, giving us the perfect time to start an invasive search for the documentation.

The doctor clears his throat and thinks carefully before saying what's on his mind. "With King's condition, you know we can't avoid it. If you can help me find Ivy Montgomery, that would be helpful. I have paperwork here that she signed, giving her power of attorney and appointing herself as King's end-of-life caregiver."

I squeeze Romano's hand so tightly, I'm positive he's losing all circulation. "I'm Ivy Montgomery. Rogue is the nickname King gave me as a kid." I pull my ID from the small wallet I had stuffed in my bra before breakfast. The paperwork has my signature on it, but I definitely didn't know about this. I'll bet King just forged it and paid off his lawyer to notarize and file it. Good God, that man and his manipulations are going to be the death of me.

Dr. Hansen examines it, then hands it back, a comforting look on his face.

I clear my throat. "I'm out of sorts and seem to be missing some information. What condition?" I ask.

"His early onset Alzheimer's," Dr. Hansen says, in a befuddled tone. "Jesus." He shakes his head. "He didn't tell you, did he? With the paperwork signed, it seemed as if at least someone knew."

Thoughts race through my head. Early onset Alzheimer's? When the fuck did that happen? And why was there a seizure? The doctor sees the confusion in my gaze and sighs deeply. Romano sits silently beside me, tracing circles on my back for who knows how long at this point. I didn't even notice him start while I've been ensnared in my own head, going over outcomes.

I look at Romano's face and see the men having a silent conversation with raised eyebrows and furtive looks in my direction. I straighten my spine and will myself to hold it together. From happy dancing or crumbling to the floor, I'm not sure.

"Dr. Hansen, can you please explain what's going on? Why did he have a seizure? Is it related? I don't know nearly enough, it seems. I appear to have legal responsibilities, and yet, I know nothing of his condition. Do I have the right to know? To even ask?"

"Yes, Rogue, uh, Ivy. You do because he selected you to dictate his end-of-life care. Seizures are par for the course, especially with his form of Alzheimer's. He hasn't had one in nearly a month now, but this has been the biggest, by far."

Holy fuck. How's this even happening? What went from a breakfast meeting has turned into planning the end of my adoptive father's life.

No matter how much I hate the man, I'm not sure I'm equipped to deal with this at the moment, but it seems I have to. Romano turns his attention to the doctor and takes over. "When was he diagnosed?"

The doctor refers to the chart and says, "Almost fifteen years ago." Right around the time I moved in, soon after my parents died. I level my gaze at the doctor and ask the question I'm dreading. "Will he make it?"

Part of me hopes he does, and part of me hopes he doesn't. But I need to know so I can prepare, not only for myself but for Sage. If we have to run, I'd rather know sooner than later.

Dr. Hansen wobbles his head left and right, making an unsure gesture. "At this stage, we need to wait and see. We don't know what the long-term effects are. We don't know if he will even wake up from the medically induced coma once we stop giving him the medication. I know it's frustrating to hear, and I know it's not something we can prepare for. But we need this documentation, just in case." He slides the paperwork over to me. I see King has filled out a few things, recognizing his sharp handwriting. He has indicated to leave him on life support as long as possible.

Half of me wants to scratch that option out and fill out the page for a DNR—do not resuscitate—as the directive.

Although, if he is legally alive yet vegetative, it gives me time to find that motherfucking evidence, so it doesn't end up in the wrong hands when his life finally ends.

Chapter Five

Rogue

IT'S BEEN THREE DAYS SINCE THEY ADMITTED KING TO THE HOSPITAL. Romano and I have been running back and forth, attempting to be in two places at once. The board would have met last night, as per the usual schedule, but obviously that couldn't happen. We couldn't tell them he was in the hospital, but we did our best to make excuses, saying that King was otherwise occupied.

Cian Byrne—De La Cruz's replacement—while being easy to push around when I direct my withering stare at him, is chomping at the bit to take more on. He's ambitious, but way too green to take anything more on than cleaning up De La Cruz's mess. Well, supposed mess.

At least with Claudette reining in her plants in our drug trade and putting an end to the rumors, he thinks he's doing a bang-up job. The only issue is the product. Since I had my hitmen take out one of the supply lines down south, he's been trying to make new connections. The caches G and I blew up left him severely short of product. Unfortunately, everything south of the border is funneled into the Southern California gangs. The new guy has his hands full with that, but he's making inroads in dealing with the Irish mob up in Chicago.

After the doctors evaluated King and tested for everything under the sun, they told us to wait and see when he wakes up. They're pulling him out of the medically induced coma as his brain bleeding has slowed and didn't require surgery or draining. Now that the worst of it seems to have passed, the doctors are hopeful he'll wake up on his own soon. It can take anywhere from a few hours to a few days.

Romano has been by my side the entire time. After the first day of endlessly waiting in King's room, or near the nurses' station, we went back to the apartment to regroup. Dr. Shaw is at the hospital, so he told us to take some time. We gathered a bag of clothes for each of us, planning to spend the foreseeable future at Saint Gregory's.

I let the guys know what was going on, but I haven't been able to see them since all of this happened. They've been working on a new assignment from Annex, planning things out so they don't have to kill anyone this time.

Trading text messages back and forth while sitting in the cushioned chair in King's room has been my only reprieve. My mind is a tempest of emotion, guilt, joy, resentment, and despair. As much as I want King to die, I want it to be by my hand. I want it to be done in a way that will ascertain I'm safe at the end. But sometimes, my mind likes to whisper things like, *He's the only family you have, other than Sage. Haven't you lost enough already?*

It's been about two hours since the last nurse came by to check King's vitals. Dr. Shaw is in constant communication with both me and the hospital staff, stopping by every few hours to check in now that Romano and I have set up residence in King's room. He's nice enough, and only doing his job, but I still irrationally hate him for helping me save King.

Everything seems to be going well, but King isn't responding to sensations below his waist. I want to dick punch him just to test the theory. They're not sure if it's a permanent situation or something he'll recover from in time. *Again, wait and see.* Fuck, I'm tired of that phrase.

I've been wracking my brain trying to conjure examples and instances when Alzheimer's could have been fueling his actions. Honestly, with the way King swings from emotion to emotion one day to the next. It could have been at any point, really.

Ten minutes later, as I'm playing Candy Crush on my phone and trying to beat Jacob's high score on a particularly awful level, I see a flicker of movement from my peripheral. I look at King and see nothing has changed. I chalk it up to a flicker of light, even as I continue my stare-off with his relaxed body. A few minutes later, I see the slightest twitch of his fingers. His eyelashes flutter as he slowly comes to.

I don't immediately call for the nurse the way I did with Noah when he started waking up from his coma. God, there are too many of those going around for my sanity. I simply sit and wait, wanting to see what's going to happen next.

Despite the dim lighting in the room, his eyes squint before slamming back closed as he groans.

King's voice rasps as he tries to speak. I stand from my chair and make my way closer to his bed. His eyes open again, moving in my direction, and he finally sees my face. "Marie," he scratches out.

Again with this Marie stuff. I guess now, knowing that he has Alzheimer's, it's understandable. My mom looked the way I do. She had dark hair like I've dyed mine, but she wasn't covered in tattoos. Our faces have the same nose and green eyes, but my facial structure is similar to my father's, along with my naturally blonde hair.

After Jacob dropped the bomb that King and my mom were living together during the red-yarn catastrophe that took over the war room, the shock finally wore off, and I studied the pictures he found of my parents. I looked nothing like King, so I decided that was that. There was no way he could be my actual father.

I grab the water cup with the straw that the nurse left from the bedside table and position it near his mouth so he can drink. If he still thinks I'm my mother, maybe this is the time to get some answers. He takes a few sips, and I pull the cup away before he can have more. He looks up at me curiously. I reply to his silent bid for more with, "If you have too much, you'll get sick."

I give him another moment, just one or two, to get his bearings and help adjust the bed, so he's sitting more upright instead of lying down.

He looks longingly at the water cup. Once again, I put the straw to his lips for another drink. After a few more sips, he looks around, confusion coloring his voice. "Marie, what happened?"

It's now or never. If King has slipped into the past, I can get the answers I've been searching for since I was a child and lost everything. I carefully respond, infusing emotion into my voice and doing my best to sound sweet like I remember my mother doing. "You had a seizure. You're in the hospital, you're okay, but they have to keep you for observation a few days longer."

"Did the doctor say why I had this seizure?" he rasps out, clearing his throat to push the words out after not speaking for days. A flicker of fear enters his eyes, and I get the feeling this is the same emotion he must have had the first time it happened. To be so young and relatively healthy, getting sidelined by seizures must have been terrifying. Before I let myself feel too sorry for him, I press on.

"No, they didn't. Not yet, at least. I'm sure the doctors want to speak with you about that. Can you tell me the last thing you remember?" I ask, threading my voice with concern. Shit, I should have been an actress.

"Yeah, you had just come home, and we were planning what to have for dinner. You wanted Chinese, and I wanted Thai; we can never decide. Did it happen in the apartment or at the restaurant?" he asks. "Did anyone see?"

Deciding to be as truthful as possible, so I don't cause any excess confusion, I answer as best I can, "It happened at the apartment, and we were alone. I got you on your side, and the paramedics were there within minutes. You stopped seizing after five minutes, but because it went on so long, they insisted you stay here for observation, which was the smart thing to do," I chastise him when he opens his mouth to object.

"Can you describe the last week for me? What do you remember?" I ask. If I can figure out what year or time he's thinking of, maybe I'll have a better shot at getting something out of him.

Sitting in that god-forsaken chair, waiting for King to wake up, I had a lot of time to do some research on early onset Alzheimer's and grand mal seizures. The most common side effect for both is memory loss. Who knows how much recollection he actually has at present?

"Oh, Sweet Marie." The words are sweet until the heart rate monitor starts beeping more rapidly. His features contort until his face is flushed red and his jaw ticks with anger. Fists clench at his sides as he studies my face. "I remember last week; I remember everything. How could you fucking do that to us?" King screams as he gains whatever memory his condition and collapse have triggered.

"Do what?" I ask, startled by his outburst and taking in the quick rise and fall of his chest.

King closes his eyes, and a grimace of misery washes over his face. He takes a deep breath and says, "After all the years that I've been there for you, stood up for you. Fuck, even when we were kids, I defended you from the bullies, the mean girls who called you names in elementary school. And this is how I'm repaid? Me? Kadir, the one who has stood by your side, because your parents were royal assholes and pushed you out, who has watched with pride as you've become the woman you are?" He pauses for a moment to catch his breath and clear his throat. I let his angry words crash over me, knowing nothing will interrupt him now.

"I know you fucked up. Joseph is a smooth talker; I never should have introduced you two." His voice is pained, defeated even. "I know he offered you things I can't—security, a safe home, hell, vacations now and then. But you always told me none of that mattered to you. But for you to go behind my back and leave me for him." His tone drops to regret and remorse, finally whispering, "It's what I deserve, anyway."

I think back to when Jacob was going through my family history in the war room and his red web of connections. He noted that King and my mother were living together, yet she was also with my father.

King speaks to her—well, me, I guess—as if she's a lover, but his words don't indicate that they were anything closer than friends. Was his love unrequited? King sighs when I don't answer.

"Marie, I know you're pregnant. The signs are all there. Please don't leave me for him. Please don't. I will raise that baby as if it's my own. You can't trust Joe. I saw something a month ago that proves he's not who he says he is. I know you're planning to leave. After all, that baby is his, but don't you see, my Sweet Marie, we could be so much more. He never even has to know about the baby. It will be ours to raise, ours to love."

I hang my head as I imagine my mother would in this situation. I wonder if this is how their conversation actually went all those years ago. The pure anguish on his face shows he did, in fact, love my mother. I wonder if it would have been possible for him to raise me as his own with her by his side.

But that's not the reality we live in.

Something changed along the way. From the period his mind is in now to when he adopted me, eight years passed. Has he been this way since my mother left? Or did it develop over time along with Alzheimer's? And how many of my childhood experiences resulted from his condition? Is this just who he is?

Part of me wants to blame my mother for my upbringing, for making this man into the monster he's become—the thing that goes bump in the night—the man who holds power so tightly, as if letting it go, even an inch, would cause the world to crumble around him.

Romano walks into the room, and King whips his gaze over to him. A flash of recognition passes over his face. The seconds tick by as he regains lucidity.

"Romano," he announces before looking back over at me. "Rogue, what's happening? Where am I?" It looks like our trip into the past is over.

"King, you're in the hospital. You had a seizure during our breakfast meeting a few days ago. The doctor informed us about what's been going on. I'm listed as your power of attorney, so he was legally obligated to tell me so we could handle the what-ifs. Hansen and Shaw should be here soon enough. I'll call for the nurse now that you're awake."

He nods his head in his usual lofty demeanor, obviously thinking all of this is beneath him. He knows we now know about his condition, and he doesn't look too pressed to discuss it. I push the button beside King's bed to alert the nurse that King is awake and grab my phone to call Dr. Shaw. I turn before quickly wiping a stray tear away.

Romano

All manner of medical personnel checked King upon his waking. We were told about his seizure and long-term effects, especially coupled with head trauma. It seems as if the damage was not overly extensive, but he is still having trouble feeling things below the waist, ruling out walking at the moment. They insisted on keeping him a few extra days, but with the way things have deteriorated over the past few months, they're not optimistic about his prognosis.

It's been two days since King woke up, and all of us are going a little stir-crazy.

When I walked into the room, Rogue had silent tears tracking down her face, but King acted as if everything was normal. When I pulled her aside later—as King discussed his condition with Dr. Hansen—she told me he had slipped into a non-lucid state upon awakening and thought that she was her mother. That would have been a tough pill to swallow for anyone, even more so for Rogue, knowing that he had loved her mother and possibly killed her.

I sent Rogue home today and told her I would sit with King. He's been lucid the entire time. Mostly, just handling business from his phone as per usual. Part of me wonders if that's his preferred method because it's easier to be distant and walk away from a call or text when confusion strikes rather than a room full of people.

He alternates between flipping through random channels on the television in the room's corner and growling at messages coming through. The last part is entirely understandable, as some people in The Gambit require that hands-on approach, which can be exceptionally frustrating.

I handle my business from the visitor's chair near the window. Part of me wants to look him in the eye and sink a knife into his gut as he lies there, helpless. The other part of me knows I need Rogue for the big picture. And to have her on my side, that fucking evidence needs to land in our hands. There's a good likelihood I could make it all go away, but if it leaks to the press, there's not much I'll be able to do.

In either case, I need to do this her way. It's frustrating as fuck, but manageable. I look at King as he stares down at his phone, typing out messages.

I see his eyelids getting heavier and heavier. It's late in the evening, and despite not physically doing anything, the mental exhaustion of being in the hospital is enough to take anyone down at an early hour. Boredom always wins.

He sets his phone down on the bedside table, adjusts the blankets around his waist, and leans back into the nest of pillows behind him. "Are you going to stare at me all night?" he asks.

I laugh. "King, you know if I left, Rogue would have my balls, and I rather like them attached to my body. Thank you very much. You're stuck with me." He lets out a chuckle at that.

"How are you getting along with my daughter?"

I answer him honestly, grateful to not have to lie this time. "Really well, actually. Our sense of teamwork has finally fallen into place," I say, thinking about our work with Ron Mitchell, that disgusting pimp who we painstakingly hacked to tiny pieces with a weird sense of camaraderie. King just nods his head and lays back on the pillow, his blinking becoming slower and slower.

His eyelids finally droop and don't open again. I continue working on my phone, directing arms dealers, running routes, and checking in with the people who need to continue the day-to-day work. At nine o'clock, the nurse comes in with a plastic bag filled with King's personal items. She peeks over at the bed and sees he's asleep. She gestures to the closet and walks on silent footsteps. Before opening the door and setting his things inside, she pats me on the shoulder and whispers, "You're a good son-in-law."

Yeah, if only she knew.

Surmising that King is out for the night, I stand from my chair after the nurse leaves and pull the closet door open. I lift the plastic bag, and inside, I can see a small billfold and a handkerchief.

The little leather holder has a few plastic and paper cards, but nothing that sticks out to me as irregular. As I rifle through, I realize one of them is the electronic key for the penthouse elevator.

Shit, yes!

I stuff the cardholder into my jeans pocket, snag my cell phone from the table next to my chair, and waltz out of the room. An apartment needs investigating, and I know just the guy to disable the cameras in the building while en route.

I quickly text Rogue to see if she's at home and call Shade while waiting for her reply. We go through the usual song and dance of verifying our identities, and I tell him what I need.

"Oh, man. Do you know how long that's gonna take me?" he gripes.

"Well, you'd better work fast because I'm going to be there in about fifteen minutes." Despite it being nearly ten at night, there's traffic on the roads of El Castillo.

"Fifteen minutes! Are you insane?"

"Maybe," I answer. "But this is the break we need, so I know you'll get it done." I'm nearly certain he can hear the glee in my voice. It's been far too long since I got to do something fun.

I hear him clicking away on his keyboard over the line and know he's getting the job done. I ask him what he's doing, and he only shushes me. Apparently, he needs silence when he's working. Who knew? I keep the phone to my ear as I draw closer and closer to our apartment building. Listening to Shade curse and threatening to find a new job, leaving me to find a new handler, makes me chuckle in the back of the car.

Two blocks from the building, I finally hear him say into the phone, "It's done."

I thank him and hang up, confirming the payment and tip to the driver before exiting the car a few buildings down from ours. I call Rogue to get her involved. If anyone can help me with the next bit, it's her.

"Miss me already, honey?" she asks when the line connects.

"Of course, but I need you to occupy King's security for about an hour."

The silence stretches for so long that I pull the phone from against my ear to check if I dropped the call. I see it's okay, so I press it between my ear and shoulder and call her name into the mouthpiece.

"What are you up to, Romano?" she asks quietly.

"The nurse dropped off King's wallet, which I assume was in his pocket when he went down. In his little cardholder was the electronic key to his apartment. I'm getting that evidence for you, or at least finding out where to get it. I'm sick of sitting on my ass and waiting for something to happen, waiting for the research to shake out. This time, I'm going after it, and I will bring it to you."

Her breath catches as I deliver the end of my impassioned speech, and she whispers, "Thank you, Romano. I'm on it. Where are you?"

"Downstairs."

"All right, grab a cup of coffee around the corner. Give me ten minutes, and I'll have everything ready to go. The camera feeds?" Rogue asks curtly.

"Handled," I tell her.

"You're going to have to tell me how you did that one day," she says with a laugh before hanging up.

Walking toward the closest intersection, I enter the coffee shop and waste time sipping my drink and comparing prices on mugs until it's time to go. Sneaking into the parking garage, I hop into the elevator and wave the electronic card in front of the reader. The doors close as the light turns green, and the car rises.

Shade only handled the cameras, not the overall electronics, so I didn't want the doormen to see me arrive in case anyone figures out someone's been in King's apartment. I didn't want them saying, *"Oh, yeah, Romano came home right around then."* It's better to be far too cautious than stupid. I spend the ride to the top contemplating if this whole thing will bite me in the ass. Eh, still worth it.

The elevator dings as the doors slide open to reveal King's foyer. I poke my head out and take a quick look around, thankfully seeing no one.

Feeling a level of confidence I definitely shouldn't, I enter the apartment. The tiled floors are gleaming, and the dining table is clear, meaning someone has been in here since King collapsed. He probably has a regular service to take care of it, and knowing what I do about King, I doubt a few broken dishes and an overturned chair would be a cause for alarm from his regular staff.

Everything looks tidy and in its place, the same way it has every time I've come to this apartment. Pretending to be on King's side, and working for him exclusively, has been an exercise in self-control. Having met in his office more than once, I follow the familiar path as I walk on light feet down the hallway to the solid door.

The entire time, I'm praying that Rogue has sufficiently sidelined his security. Knowing her, and who she handles for The Gambit, I have no doubt.

Okay, a little doubt.

Moving as quickly as I can around the desk, I pull drawers open and rifle through them, looking for any pertinent information—purchasing orders, stock options, a few business magazines... junk. King's giant ass desk that he lords over us from behind is completely and utterly full of junk.

I reach the bottom handles and find both of them locked. This fucking desk has seven drawers, and yet only two are locked? My spine tingles, telling me I've found something important.

Searching for the key proves fruitless. I rummage through the pencil holder atop the desk and find a few paper clips that will have to work as a lock-pick set. I wish I'd grabbed my set from downstairs first.

Working with the makeshift tools, I do my best to keep it clean, but the scratches on the lock face blend in with others already present. Finally, the flimsy lock gives and I'm able to pull it open.

After I have the first drawer open, I do the same with the second. This one proves a bit harder to break into, but not impossible. I end up cutting myself during the process and have to pop my thumb into my mouth before the drops of blood land on the carpet. I can't leave DNA evidence behind.

When the lock finally disengages and the drawer opens, I do my best to resist giving myself a pat on the back in the middle of an empty office. Lord knows Shade is probably watching the cameras and having a good laugh at my expense. I quickly decide what the most important things are. I pull out all the paperwork I can find. King, knowing he has Alzheimer's, likely prepared for a worst-case scenario during a lucid period.

After twenty minutes of shuffling through an endless stack of paperwork, I find a small slip of paper toward the front of the drawer. It's wedged between the base and the front of the cabinet.

I pull it out and turn it around. It has six carefully printed digits. From my research, I know it's Rogue's birthday. I also know that six digits are often necessary for a safe, especially an electronic one.

Could it be that easy? I rush to the kitchen, knowing that there's likely a stray plastic bag stashed somewhere. I strike gold when I find one in a lower cabinet. Sweeping all the paperwork into the bag to take it with me, I drop it by the couch to take on my way out. I can go through it later. King won't be released for another day or two, so it gives me tonight to go through everything. Who needs sleep?

My last task is to find the safe itself. I search the office top to bottom, coming up empty even after pulling the paintings from the wall, like this is a damn movie.

I tear out of the room, making my way to the bedrooms. I find nothing in King's room, having moved absolutely everything I could find before meticulously putting it back into place.

The clock is ticking, so I continue down the hall, finding Rogue's room, or at least, what I think is her old room. The space is entirely bare, aside from a pine twin bed and a small dresser. There is no personality here, nothing to show a child once filled this space. My heart aches for her knowing what she's gone through. I can only imagine the sheer terror of living with King for so long.

I find a third door, which I assume to be a bathroom. But after attempting to open it and only meeting resistance, I know there's more to it than that. I recall seeing a bundle of keys in one of King's drawers and rush back to his room, hoping one of them would fit this lock.

There are a handful of keys on the ring, and I make my way through. Finally, the sixth one fits. Knowing I'm up against the clock has me fumbling and dropping them to the floor after withdrawing from the mechanism. I turn the handle, and the door swings inward. I step inside, expecting to find anything other than the sight that greets me.

King has painted every wall of this torture box in a lacquer similar to that of the workroom in the mechanic shop Rogue, Lucas, and I used to kill De La Cruz. I now see where she gained her inspiration for that particular workshop. The room has an assortment of weapons stashed on stainless steel tables and hanging from the wall. An anchor is in the ceiling with a tenterhook dangling from it, obviously used to string up the victims he handles himself instead of passing over to Rogue.

King has a veritable arsenal two doors down from his own bedroom. If that doesn't tell me someone's paranoid, I don't know what would. Thinking of Rogue growing up here, probably having seen this room or experienced the terrors I'm sure it's held, has my stomach flip-flopping and bile creeping up my throat. I take a turn around the room, examining each corner until, finally, I notice an oddity.

There's a stainless steel surgical table pushed against one corner of the room, but it's not quite flush with the wall, as if someone has moved it. It has a second level close to the base for supplies, but for now, it only holds metal bins for organ removal. At least, that's what they look like on medical television shows.

I make my way over and take the handle of the cart, pulling it away from its intended position. As it rolls away, I see an imperfection in the wall. I grab a knife from the wall, not having time to waste, and work it open. Inside is a keypad. I type in Rogue's birthdate, and a hydraulic whir sounds above me.

Chapter Six

Lucas

"No, Sir Lancelot! Let go!" I whisper-shout at my hedgehog, hoping he'll release the wires he's got in his jaws of death. If he proves Noah right, I'll never hear the end of it. Alas, my reprimand falls on tiny deaf ears.

I scoop up my miniature friend and make my way out of the living area of the clubhouse. Noah's going to fucking kill us.

Last week, we did some recon in Bakersfield for the upcoming job, so we've been away, and Sir Lancelot has to re-mark his territory. Do hedgehogs do that? Eh, it's the reason I choose to believe. All four—well, five—of us were in the car when we got a message from Buttercup, telling us that King had suffered a seizure during their breakfast meeting.

She's kept us up to date via text, but it's not nearly enough.

After gathering intel, we made our way back north to El Castillo. We got home just in time for King's discharge from the hospital.

Buttercup has been feeling the strain, but today is for resolving it. We cleared our schedules and made a plan to get together.

On cue, my phone chimes from the coffee table, announcing that the rolling gate is opening. Showtime, little dude. It's unseasonably warm to be wearing a hoodie, but it's my method of concealment today.

I gingerly stuff Sir Lancelot into the front pocket and sprint to the entrance, disengaging the lock and sliding the reinforced door open. There she is.

"Honey, I'm home," she says with a laugh.

Careful not to squish my new friend, I draw her into a hug at my side and plant a kiss on her forehead. "God, I've missed you."

"You, too, Red. What's new?"

"Well, I'm glad you asked!" My enthusiasm seems to be contagious as her smile stretches wider to match mine.

Pulling away, I grab her hands in mine and walk backward, leading her into the center of the clubhouse. "Stand right there and close your eyes," I whisper conspiratorially.

"Guys!" I shout after looking to the upper level and seeing Han and Noah's bedroom doors ajar. They'll hear me, and someone will grab Jacob on their way down.

Buttercup jumps about a foot into the air, and I realize my mistake at having her close her eyes before shouting two inches from her face.

"Lucas McCreary! What in the ever-loving fuck was that? I should *never* trust you when you tell me to close my eyes. You and your stupid adorable grin and magic cock have lulled me into a false sense of security." Her griping continues a moment longer before she lets loose a big exhale.

"Sorry, sorry," I tell her.

Her eyes slide shut once again, but she cracks one open. "Are you gonna yell again?" she asks.

"Just one more time." My smirk makes her roll her one open eye. I echo my earlier shout, but this time she's prepared.

I look up to see Han leave his room and open Jacob's door. Loud music escapes from the previously sealed room for a moment before it switches off and Han leads Jacob out by the hand. Noah glances over the railing, a big grin splitting his face in two. All three of them rush down the staircases to reach us in the center.

Buttercup, who dutifully keeps her eyes closed, is greeted with kisses from everyone and a playful ass pinch from Jacob. She whirls around and whacks him in the chest in retribution as the other two lean out of the way to avoid any ricochet. Everyone moves closer, surrounding our girl as she stands patiently.

"Was that the surprise?" she asks with her eyes still squeezed shut.

"Hold out your hands," I instruct.

"Is it your dick?" she asks with suspicion.

"No, just... Please?" I beg. She sighs with her compliance.

Han and Jacob each rest a hand on her shoulder and Noah's hands skirt around her waist, resting on her hips.

Sir Lancelot is going bonkers in my pocket. I stick my hand in and quickly run my finger down his back soothingly to calm him down. Noah's going to give me shit for having him out in the open, but he'll forgive me when he sees the look on our girl's face.

I carefully stick my other hand into the pocket and nudge Sir Lancelot into my waiting palm. Withdrawing him from the compartment, Noah sighs. I give Sir Lancelot a small kiss on the nose and warn him to be good under my breath, extending him toward Buttercup.

He lands in her upturned hands, and she lets out a small shriek. Her eyes fly open when she feels his little feet kneading her palms with his tiny claws.

"Red, why is there a hedgehog in my hands?" she asks. I can't tell if she loves him or hates him yet, and it's got me on pins and needles. Is this how parents feel when they introduce their kids to people? What if she doesn't like him?

"He's our new team pet!" I tell her excitedly.

"Oh my gosh, he's so cute!" she gushes, and her voice goes up high at the end, doing a little excited scream to punctuate her statement.

My eyes flick from her face to Noah's, and I see his eyes roll. It's nice being proven right now and then.

"Can we keep him?" she asks, her voice breathless in wonderment.

"Absolutely!"

Noah lets go of her waist and withdraws his hands slowly. "This is a bad idea."

"Why?" Buttercup turns to face him.

"Do you know how much care that thing needs?" the big grump asks.

"We have to take him with us everywhere. He came with us on that job last week, and it was an educational experience, let me tell you. He needs a certain environment, certain food, and I just don't know if we have the time for it right now." Noah's explanation makes sense, but that doesn't mean I have to like it.

Jacob extends a finger and carefully pats Sir Lancelot on the top of his head. "What are we going to do, Noah? It's not like we can just let him go. He would get run over by a car or something."

"Yeah," Han adds in agreement. "Plus, they're illegal in California. We can't just give him to a pet shop or a shelter; they'll put him down."

Buttercup looks up at Noah, blinking furiously, and appears to be holding back tears. He takes one look at her wide eyes and trembling lip and throws his hands up in exasperation. "Fine."

Buttercup lifts her hands and rubs her nose against Sir Lancelot's, resulting in a happy squeak from our little charmer. She lifts the hedgehog toward Noah's face. "Say 'thank you'," she tells the pipsqueak.

"Wait, what's his name?" she asks me.

"Sir Lancelot." I grin as her eyes sparkle with mirth, connecting the name with the quills on his back.

"It's perfect," she affirms with a nod of her head.

In her excitement, she pushes Sir Lancelot closer to Noah's face. He drops into a duck and roll, lets out a tiny shout, and scrambles away. Is he... scared? I knew he wasn't a fan, and he never got close to our new pet, but *this* is an interesting reaction. Oh, this is going to be good.

Noah pops back up to his feet, clears his throat, and pretends the last three seconds didn't happen. "Lucas, why don't you go put him away in your room." His tone is all business, but there's an underlying waver to it that isn't usually there.

Buttercup brings Sir Lancelot closer to her chest, nuzzling him, and asks, "Does he have to go? Isn't there some kind of container we can put him in while we eat? I just met him."

Knowing how in love our Dear Leader is, there's absolutely zero chance he'll deny her request. I scamper off to find a small container.

Another chime sounds, alerting us that the rolling gate is opening again. Jacob pulls his phone from his pocket and grins when he says, "Mrs. M is here."

"Oh, thank God, it's been ages since I've seen her," says Buttercup.

Han and Noah go to the front door to help Mrs. M with whatever food she's brought today. We had a tentative plan for lunch, and weren't sure if she would show because no one confirmed anything with all the stuff going on lately. But I should know better by now; Mrs. M never misses a lunch date.

The guys come in carrying catering trays full of food, and our Mama Bear follows behind, chastising them for not calling more often. With all the changes we've had in recent months, it's nice to see some things have stayed the same. While I'm grateful for most, including Buttercup, sometimes I think our lives are too complicated and miss the simplicity we once operated under.

Mrs. M finds our girl standing with Sir Lancelot in her grasp, and the two women coo and aww over our recent addition. Eventually, we all settle around the kitchen island, sharing a meal and good conversation. We rehash what's been happening in the last few weeks and keep the conversation light, avoiding topics of death and dismemberment.

We're in the middle of cake and coffee when Mrs. M clears her throat pointedly. "I have some news," she says. All of us put our forks down and stare at her. She rarely prefaces an announcement like this... she just says it. "I've met someone," she declares.

My mouth drops open.

She was clearly nervous about bringing this up, and part of it is probably because she knows how close I was to Archie. She grasps my hand over the island and looks deep into my eyes. "Lucas, honey, you know Archie will live on in my heart, but I'm an old woman, with not a lot of time left. I'd like to spend it on a beach in the Caribbean with a handsome man between my thighs."

Cue retching. That was way more information than needed.

No one says anything. They're all waiting for me to respond. I lean forward, kiss her cheek, and tell her, "I'm happy for you. If he's a good man, we will support you in anything. And if he isn't, well, you know how to take care of yourself." I shoot a wink at her so she knows I'm cool.

Sometimes it's hard to reconcile the fact that this little lady ended up killing her first husband. It was well-deserved, granted, but she doesn't give off the same killer vibes that the rest of us do sometimes.

Buttercup cheers from her stool and does a wiggle in her seat, carefully holding onto Sir Lancelot. She hasn't put him down through the entirety of her meal, and Noah keeps casting side-eyed glances at our little friend.

"Red is right. If he ever does anything to you, you let us know, and we'll drop everything to handle it for you if you don't want to do it yourself."

Mrs. M releases a sigh, letting me know just how nervous she was to bring this up. I never wanted her to hide parts of her life or who she was dating. She should share any big news in her life without fear. A flush of guilt rises on my cheeks because the secrecy was in deference to my feelings.

Noah clears his throat, and I graciously pretend I don't see the sadness seeping into his gaze. "When do you leave?" he asks. Among all of us, he's closest to Mrs. M, and we all know he sneaks over there when he needs a verbal ass kicking.

Mrs. M sighs and says, "In six weeks. My gentleman friend, Richard, or Dick, if you prefer, doesn't know it yet, but that's our plan." Buttercup lets out a laugh, and the rest of us join in. It's exactly like Mrs. M to plan a move to a new country with a partner and not tell them about it in advance.

We all raise our cups of coffee and clink them together over the countertop, saluting both Mrs. M and her love of Dick.

Mama Bear leaves after a few hours, and the rest of us look around, wondering what we will do without Mrs. M around to keep us in line.

We're sitting in the lounge when Buttercup suddenly sits upright. "Oh my God, I forgot to tell you guys! I have my own surprise today."

"Yes, Darling Mine. What is it?" Jacob asks.

"Do you remember that couch at the hotel in San Francisco?" she asks him. I'm still jealous he got to go visit after she sent that hot as fuck video our way.

"Oh yeah. That thing was comfortable and great for..." he trails off.

She ahems, fighting a blush on her cheeks, so I know *precisely* what that couch was good for. "Well, I ordered one, and it should be here in about a week."

"Here, as in the clubhouse?" Noah asks.

"Well, yeah. I didn't order a sex couch for *my* apartment." Jacob falls back into the armchair, laughing. "I just meant," Buttercup continues with a glare directed toward Jacob, "I'd like to sit with all of you and not be so spaced out every time we want to hang out." She waves the arm not holding Sir Lancelot, indicating the space between all of us in our current lounge set up.

Han leans over and presses a kiss on her forehead. "That was a great idea. Jacob came home and said how big it was." A small laugh escapes because that's who I am, and every innuendo is fair game.

The back of Buttercup's hand lands on my chest in a playful slap. I lean over, careful not to squish our hedgehog baby, and press a kiss to her lips in thanks.

"So, what do you guys want to do?" she asks. "I don't have to leave for another hour."

"I have an idea," says Noah. "Jacob, help me out here." They both stand and go to the staircase, whispering between themselves. Curiosity gets the better of me, and the scenarios in my mind are fantastic.

A few minutes later, a mattress comes sailing down over the catwalk railing from the upper floor. A second one soon joins it, and I figure out pretty quickly what they want to do.

Han and I stand up, move the mattresses together and flop down on top of them, leaving a space between us for our girl.

"Cuddle sesh!" I call out. Noah and Jacob laugh the entire way down the staircase. When they rejoin us, we pile onto the makeshift snuggle pad and spend the next hour just chatting, touching, and loving our girl. As much as I miss having my girl to myself, or sharing her between my team and me, sometimes it's these little things I miss the most.

Rogue

I reluctantly left the clubhouse after spending a fantastic afternoon with the guys. Sometimes I really hate the back and forth. At least with Sage in the safe house up north, I don't have to worry so much. She sends daily updates about life and her school work, so my mind is more at peace.

I'm in the back of an Uber, heading back to my apartment, knowing what's waiting for me and dreading the coming evening.

After Romano's snooping in King's apartment, he came back, and we rifled through paper after paper, finding information on The Gambit, on King's past, and even a bit about my mother. There's a lot to go through and piece together, but I don't know which direction to take without the complete picture.

The one good thing is that Romano found the evidence I needed to get back—the hard copies—King had it stashed in his bottom desk drawer. There isn't as much as King always insinuated there was. The only issue is we need the will to amend the release of the documentation when he dies. Or we need their copies of the evidence. There's no way King only has one set.

Romano discovered three lawyers listed on the papers and is checking them all out to see which one King might have been more likely to use. He says he's using his contacts to investigate each and the waiting is infuriating.

We brought King home a couple of days ago, and he's still bedridden. His memory fluctuates between past and present, but more than that, he is still having difficulties with his lower extremities. The doctors say it could be temporary, so they advised therapies that Dr. Shaw is currently setting up.

After a relaxing afternoon, I finally make it back to my apartment. Romano is currently upstairs with King, sitting with him and taking care of his needs. He offered to take the afternoon when I said there were a few things for me to take care of. He's actually been really great with King when he slips into the past.

I needed a slight reprieve from King constantly mistaking me for my mother. I can't keep having the same conversations about how she/I don't love him the way he thinks he deserves. Part of me is happy to know that my mom didn't fall for what King was selling. I couldn't take it if she had. Despite his evident love for her, the conversations keep circling back to the unrequited aspect.

I take a shower and dress in comfortable clothes, knowing I'm spending the night upstairs at King's apartment. It's not ideal, and it's not somewhere I enjoy being, but he needs to stay alive. Gathering a few things, I shove them into a tote bag to take with me for my next stay at Chez King. Ugh.

After being given access to the penthouse, I emerge into the foyer to see King lying on his hospital-issued bed and Romano propped up on the couch. They're laughing and joking, and the crinkles around King's eyes look unnatural to me. I don't suppose he's laughed much in the last two decades.

His guffaw is loud and infectious, and coming from anyone else, it'd be easy to join in. Who knew hiding under that monster was someone who still liked to joke and have fun?

How much of his personality that I've known over the past fifteen years is a product of his disease and his deterioration? Is it a defense mechanism? It'd be easy to understand if his brain has created these walls and these paranoid personality traits to keep itself safe.

"Francesco, you're a funny guy. You should definitely join our organization." Ah, so we're non-lucid again. He gives the spiel to join the organization every time he re-meets Romano.

"You know what, Kadir? That sounds like a good idea." Playing along has become our go-to because explaining things sometimes turns violent. "We'll talk about that next week when we hang out again. Hi," Romano says when he sees me.

"Marie?" King asks, whipping around and craning his neck to see me.

"Hi, Kadir. I just finished work."

"Welcome home," he says with a smile.

It's interesting when his brain blends one era with the next. He seems to know that this is his apartment. But the dead woman he seems to have loved once upon a time is somehow occupying the same space. It's both heartbreaking and makes me feel like some form of justice is being served.

"Marie, this is Francesco, my new friend," King introduces us.

"Hi, Francesco. Nice to meet you." I extend my hand, and we shake as if this is the first time we've met and not that we are actually husband and wife, forced into this position by the asshole between us.

"You, too. Kadir was just telling me all about you. Only good things, I promise," he says with a wink.

I'm sure.

Yesterday, he yelled at me/my mother again for leaving. It's getting harder to stomach all the things he says. Thankfully, today is a better day.

Romano excuses himself, citing a busy day tomorrow, and I walk him to the door, whispering furiously the entire way to sum up the day in the least amount of time possible.

"What's been happening? Anything new?" I ask.

"No, nothing. He was lucid until about an hour ago, and since then, we've just been shooting the shit."

Letting out a groan of frustration, I swear under my breath. I didn't know King was even sick, let alone slipping in and out of lucidity over the years. Shaw assured me it wasn't as bad before the seizure, but it wasn't great either.

Romano puts a hand on my shoulder in reassurance as we quickly whisper about the turn King has taken for the worse. "Remember what Shaw said. The seizure may have damaged a bit of his brain, and they don't expect him to last long. We need to be patient. I've got three leads on lawyers, and I'm close."

"Okay. Keep going, please. I'm staying here tonight to make sure he's okay." It's not like I can let him die now. Dr. Shaw visits twice daily, and King flipped out when his security team captain arrived to get new orders. I told him and his guys to work at the Rook Industries building for the foreseeable future, leaving a few men behind for building security here. There's no point in them waiting around for King. He's clearly not leaving soon.

Romano says goodbye and rides the elevator down to keep working on the files. I cross the apartment and sit down opposite King, and a flash of recognition crosses his eyes. "Rogue," he says, clearly surprised. "How long have you been here?"

"Oh, a few minutes. Romano just left and was here while I had a meeting with the other hitmen."

"Okay, good. Keep the wheels turning. I don't want anyone catching wind of this."

"Will do, King." My response comes out as it usually would before I knew he was sick. Old habits, huh?

We sit in silence, both of us scrolling on our phones. This is how most evenings go. Each keeping to ourselves, not having much to talk about while we whittle away the hours, waiting for the other to crack. My resolve finally shatters under the weight of the last few weeks. I need to know what the fuck is happening and what this asshole's plan is.

"If I'm supposed to take over this organization, King, give it to me straight. Why did you never tell me about this?"

He sighs as he puts his phone down. "I couldn't tell you about this," he says. I don't bother asking him why; my raised brow does it for me. "You were supposed to be my child," he says. "You may not actually be mine, but you should have been. Someone had to raise you after Marie died, and if you'd known about my illness, you might have said something to someone. Then where would you have ended up?"

"How could you do what you've done to me? How could you take in an innocent child, raise her in bloodshed and violence? And then turn around and claim to have loved her mother?" My voice is quiet, yet menacing in its tone. My hands are balled into fists at my sides. Tension radiates through my body. There's no good excuse for what he's done.

His face is flushed as he stares back at me, teeth grinding at my audacity to question him after all these years. "You may not be mine by blood, mine by rights, mine by genetics, but make no mistake, Rogue. You. Are. Mine. That backbone of steel that you have? *I* forged that. That sharp mind and quick wit? *I* fostered that. You were a shaking, scared, timid child that the world would have chewed up and spit out when you arrived. The first person to raise a hand to you would have broken you beyond repair. And now? Now, you have a name that this city, no, this *state*, fears. You are a woman to be reckoned with and have an organization at your back to command. You are a Queen, primed for the throne." His voice is strong, proud even, but as he continues, it lowers.

I loathe to admit he's partially correct. Who wouldn't be a scared child after their parents were ripped from their lives at such a young age? It's also true that my name, my title, is feared among those depraved men and women unlucky enough to get onto our radar. But I did that. Twisting my new role to my advantage when every other option had been stolen from me was my choice. Ridding the world of those people was my pleasure. He doesn't get to take credit for that.

"I'm not saying I made the right choices," he continues, "nor am I saying I did a great job of parenting. I'm saying I've made you into a woman fit to rule. I feel myself slipping more and more every day, Rogue. We know I'm going to die soon. But I'd rather do it knowing you're ready. It's why I made you marry Romano. You need someone at your side. You can't go through it alone the way I have. If something happens to you, the way it has to me, you need someone to have your back. To support you when all you want to do is lay down and die."

King keeps his gaze locked on the wall beside the television. His avoidance of eye contact is startling. He's not a man to back down, but it sounds like that's what's happening. I remind myself of who this man is—this monster who used manipulation to turn me into one, too.

Tears prick the corner of my eyes with his confession. He doesn't get to wreck so many lives, then just give up. No. I refuse to let that tiny sympathetic corner of my brain get any louder than it already is. "You were a horrible father," I tell him. "Hearing your intentions does not justify your actions. Children should not be shot for doing the wrong thing. A child should not be stabbed, beaten, bloodied, or starved for not learning quick enough. A parent should nurture them."

"And what about Sage?" I ask, gripping my thighs so tightly my nails dig through the material of my leggings. "What did she do to deserve the treatment she received? She was a child, separated from everyone she knew. What toddler deserves that?"

"She went to a woman I paid handsomely to raise her. You think she would have done well here with you? You should be grateful she was raised away from me if you hated it so much. She doesn't have the stomach for violence like you do, Rogue. She grew into a woman men covet, and that can be used in a different way. She was given a choice at sixteen, the same way you were. Join or move on." His hands fist in the sheets at his sides.

"She learned early what it took to work as an escort. Her caretaker prepared her for the life. Trained her to be what we needed. When the choice came to fall in line, to become the domme the local escort service was missing, or leave you and everything she knew behind, what do you think she chose?"

His eyes slice across the room, and I refrain from screaming in vain at his cavalier attitude. "You may be sisters but you couldn't be more different, aside from the small tether of family you cling to and the scars we all bare at our most vulnerable."

King's hands ruffle the blankets at his sides. He pushes them down and tugs up the soft t-shirt covering his torso.

It's in the exact spot mine is; his own Algiz rune scar. "My father raised me this way. It made me into a formidable man. A man that is not easily overtaken. I used what I knew to make you unbreakable, Rogue. Sage doesn't have the same backbone that we have." It's as if he thinks that justifies his actions. Abuse repeating the cycle of abuse breaks the whole damned world.

"That doesn't make it right," I tell him. "If anything, it makes you a coward for not deviating from the system that raised you. The human body and mind can only take so much before it breaks."

Proving my point, his eyes gloss over, and he loses what lucidity he had. Whether it is his brain shielding him or his own guilt that flipped the switch, I'm glad right now that this conversation can't continue. I don't have it in me tonight. As his memories come back to the surface, taking over his lucidity, I let the tears fall. The need to hold it in has passed as he slips away.

"Marie?" He looks at me curiously. "Why are you crying? What can I do?"

Wiping my cheeks with the back of my hands, I assure him I'm fine. I tell him it's time for bed and unlock his bed's wheels. I push him toward his room and know I won't sleep tonight, rehashing every word we shared.

Chapter Seven

Rogue

THE FOLLOWING MONTH CONTINUES IN MUCH THE SAME VEIN. KING slips in and out of lucidity with more rapid changes than ever before. King is never on his own as Romano and I are constantly monitoring him. This, of course, leaves time for nothing else.

It means seeing less of the guys, so we're back to secretive video calls and secret texts when no one is looking.

After numerous calls with his doctors, nurses, and every specialist on this side of the US, I came to learn that his symptoms are indicative of the final stages of Alzheimer's. When King noticed a change, he went to see Dr. Hansen after Dr. Shaw reached his limitations.

The good doctor informed me he told King his time was almost up. His symptoms would continue to worsen despite the medication he's on. The seizures have also become more frequent in recent months. They're a side effect of early-onset Alzheimer's, but none have been as bad as the one that landed him in the hospital last month. He's had two since being moved home, and I called Dr. Shaw immediately. He did examinations after the events, but because it's par for the course and there was no head injury like last time, there was no hospital visit.

The timeline is making some sense to me. Nearly six months ago, to the day, King announced I would marry Romano. Just three months after meeting my guys, King dropped this bomb in my lap, and now, we're just two weeks away from our six-month anniversary. Jesus, time flies.

In his own sick and twisted way, it seems he's been setting me up for when he finally became incapacitated and couldn't lead the organization any longer.

Pondering King's machinations makes my head spin. I've been running the timeline backward, trying to figure out when all of this could have started or at least started getting worse. Having the doctor's clarification helped me make sense of everything.

Over the past month, we've had hundreds of conversations with me acting as my mother to ease his transition into his non-lucid states. We've had just as many talks regarding the future of The Gambit when he's present. His vision for my role as the organization's leader won't come to fruition, but it's good to know what *not* to do.

Every so often, I catch him watching the skyline from his panoramic windows as he lies in bed and his face changes to one of despondency. If we're talking about the future, what's the point when his damned evidence clause can snatch it away as soon as he dies? I know he's hiding something about that but haven't been able to suss it out yet.

If it's not me or Romano here, King loses his shit more than usual, so we've taken up health care instead of other, more qualified candidates. Teleconferencing Dr. Hansen and Dr. Shaw is now a near-daily thing.

I waffle back and forth with my feelings, slowly making peace with the fact that my last "parent" will soon pass on, internally raging about his diagnosis, and wanting to scream at him before driving my knife into his gut. The emotions cycle constantly, and it exhausts me.

I hate being here all the time, but I'm using it to my advantage. Finding out things about my mother, despite the skewed view King has of her, makes me feel closer to her than I have since she died.

With staying here, my morbid curiosity can't help but explore the apartment I once begrudgingly called home. It only took one look into my old bedroom for the memories to come rushing back. Food deprivation, beatings, you name it. I quickly shut the door, and haven't looked back.

The weapons room, my torture chamber, mocks me with every pass. Each time I go past it, my feet pause, and my heart rate quickens. I never manage to lift my hand to try the knob. The crushing memories eat away at me day in and day out. But what are my alternatives? My only option is to deal with this shit, learn about the past, and hear unwanted details of my future.

When King is of sound mind, he reviews the details of The Gambit, informing me of facets I didn't know about before. He discusses the connections between board members and politicians and what strings to pull when the time comes. King is a veritable encyclopedia of leverage.

He's brought up Sage once or twice, raging at the fact that Ron Mitchell's place burned to the ground, and they haven't found any of the girls. He blames the group that "abducted" me for stealing Sage out from under his nose and killing his most lucrative pimp.

King tries to send me out every few days to go find the masked men, but I use that time to go to my apartment and have Romano sit with King for a bit. My reports back to him always claim I'm getting closer, but no luck so far. Little does he know those men are *my* men.

I'm currently sitting on King's couch as he reclines in the hospital-issued bed at my side. Of course, he complains about it to no end in his lucid state, saying the sheets are too scratchy, the pillows too uncomfortable. So after an online shopping spree during the first week, because the complaining was driving me insane, I finally kitted his bed out with something more acceptable to him.

We spend the days in the living room with daytime soaps and various game shows on the TV to keep him calm. *The Price Is Right* is the show that keeps him level the longest. According to the internet, it's one that everyone watched when they were home sick from school. I wonder if that's what King did when he was an elementary student.

Of course, I wouldn't know because my schooling was done at home, and there were no sick days. God bless the internet and its infinite wisdom.

King always reverts to a time when my mother was living with him. He speaks to me/her with affection in his tone. It's hard for me to hear, but he's also given me more information about her than I've had since she was alive.

I learned my mom was a cheerleader in high school and that King was on the soccer team. They were best friends and shared everything. He ended up giving up soccer and all extracurricular activities to work full-time for The Gambit. He says he wanted to save money for his future, the future he planned to build with my mom. Hearing him talk about the little house he would buy for them on the coast is enough to make me realize this man has lived in his own fantasy world his entire life.

His dreams are big—well, *were* big. And if things had gone his way, perhaps my mom would still be here. Maybe he wouldn't have killed her? But that's not the way it went. King's reality jumps are rarely after the point of my mom moving out and starting her life with my dad.

I don't know whether it's his brain's way of shielding him from the pain he felt or if his mind just won't—or can't—process that. Perhaps it's because my mom wasn't in his life for those years, and my looks don't trigger those memories.

Romano and I have had many conversations about introducing him to the new era; reliving the same few years must be exhausting. I know it is for me.

The one time Romano brought up my father's name, Joseph, King went into a fit so violent that we had to strap his arms to his bed rails. Since the seizure, he still hasn't regained feeling below his waist and obviously can't walk, but his arms work just fine. The lamp on the table next to him met a grisly death as he launched it across the room at the mere mention of my father's name. We learned quickly to avoid all topics revolving around my dad.

A few nights ago, I was chatting with Han over the phone, and he mentioned the idea of bringing up Patton Cross. If anyone knows about the criminal underworld back then, it's King. If he's stuck in those memories, then it will be as fresh now as it was back then.

As the big wheel spins on the game show, King sighs. "Marie," he gently calls out, rolling his head on his pillow to look in my direction.

"Yes, Kadir? What is it?"

"Do you remember when we went to that retro car hop restaurant? The one where they bring the food out on roller skates?" he asks.

I grab the remote for the television and mute it so we can talk. "No, remind me." It's a sad truth, but sometimes I have to play dumb, so he'll explain what the hell he's talking about. If I try to tell him it happened twenty-something years ago, he gets upset and the entire day is down the toilet. This is my small way of breathing life back into my mother's memory, and if I'm stuck doing this, it's better to get something out of it, so I play along.

"You remember! It was about six months ago, right after we finished our graduation ceremony from high school. We took my car and went cruising through town just for kicks. Neither of our parents could make it to the ceremony, and we wanted to celebrate, but the party down at the beach sounded awful. So, instead, we made our own."

"Oh, that's right," I say, encouraging him to continue his memory.

"I still can't believe you spilled your milkshake all over the floor of my car. It took me three hours to clean that up. That was a good night," he says. "I should have kissed you then," he confesses, almost to himself. Ducking my head, I pretend to blush while fighting down the gagging noise attempting to break free.

"Hey, Kadir, I have a question."

"What is it, Sweet Marie?" he asks.

"I recently heard about a man named Patton Cross."

King lifts his head sharply and stares in my direction. "What did you hear?" His tone is sharp, almost carrying its own warning that I should be careful what comes out next.

"I heard he was a dangerous man and that we should stay away from him." I figure that's safe enough.

"He's unstable. Extremely so." King affirms.

"What does he do?" I prod.

"He is one of the worst in this city. They've been trying to pin that spate of murders on him. But there's not enough evidence. There's *never* enough evidence. He's highly trained, highly skilled, and highly lethal. Promise me, if you hear any mention of him, you duck your head, pretend you heard nothing, and get the fuck away." King's voice is nearly panicked now, and I've yet to hear this type of fear from him. What the fuck?

"I promise. You sound like you know him." A gentle prod here, a tiny poke there... the more information I can get, the better. He is on our list, after all.

"I've met him, and he's not a man you ever want to know. He was with The Gambit for a few years and trained as one of their hitmen. But his methods were too grotesque for their leaders. He has a violence in him that can't be contained. The bosses were talking about putting him down, but no one can seem to find him. And when they do, he's always prepared. Fuck, he's taken out six of our guys already."

"Do we know what he's after?" I ask.

"Everything."

A FEW HOURS LATER, ROMANO COMES UPSTAIRS WITH LUNCH AFTER I give the elevator the approval to reach the penthouse floor. He waltzes in with bags of Indian food and a sandwich for King.

No matter what we want for lunch, King goes in the opposite direction. It's frustrating as fuck and requires two stops every time someone picks up food.

Romano looks over to me, and I nod, telling him that it's King we're dealing with in the present, not his past self.

"King, how are you feeling today?" Romano asks.

"Fucking frustrated," he says as he reaches for the sandwich. Romano hands it over and puts the rest of the food on the coffee table. We've set up the room for absolutely everything. King would never admit to needing help, so we've slowly just started doing everything in his living room, making sure one of us is with him constantly.

"Glad you're here, Romano. I need to talk to both of you about something."

Romano settles onto the couch next to me, placing his hand on my thigh in an affectionate gesture we agreed was okay, especially in King's presence, to confirm our relationship.

"How are things going with you two?" he asks.

"Excellent, King. You made a suitable match. We get along well and agree on nearly everything." Romano's answer is straightforward and well-rehearsed.

King nods his head as if he knew he was right all along and digs into his sandwich. I slowly shred the naan bread in front of me and resist talking about our lives with the man who already dictates so much of them.

"Rogue, it's time." King's voice is firm, and my head snaps up.

"Time for what?"

"Time for you to take over officially." My hands pause their shredding of the bread.

"Officially take over? That can't happen until you're gone. I'm running things from here when you drift away and delaying the board meetings, so the others don't find out about your condition."

"I can't lead from a hospital bed, Daughter. I feel myself slipping in and out more and more often; the seizures are coming almost weekly at this point. The next one is going to take me out. I can feel it." His voice is firm, with no hesitancy, no delay. He's clearly thought this through.

"And the evidence?" I ask. "You dying negates all the work you did in grooming me for this role. Why bother if it's going to send me to prison anyway?"

"It's with my lawyer," he confirms. "There are copies here in the apartment locked up in my safe, the details of which you'll receive when I'm dead. But the ones that you need to remove are with my attorney. No one wants to die shitting themselves, shaking on the floor, and biting their own tongue. I don't want to die thinking it's another time period rather than now. You need to give me a gun to end this. The will states that if Alzheimer's kills me, you're free and clear, but I need this done with. A gunshot will trigger the clause to release the evidence since it won't be a result of the illness."

My eyes lock on to his, and I see Romano relax against the back of the couch, giving us a clear line of sight to each other. This man, this asshole, who has run my life, is now asking me to give him the easy way out.

A plan takes shape in my mind, but it's not the way I always dreamed it would be. No, now it's like shooting a lame animal to end its suffering. Nowhere to go, no way to run, and in no way a fair fight.

"Get your lawyer here. Remove the clause about releasing the evidence. Have him give back whatever he has, and you have yourself a deal."

"Done," he says.

The silence that followed King's declaration was deafening. It's been half an hour, and he's been himself. Stuck in the present, stuck in a bed, and stuck with a diagnosis he doesn't want. Romano cleaned up and cleared out all the mess from our lunches. He cracked the windows to remove the smell of the Indian food and the tuna sandwich King insisted on. The early June air breezes gently through the apartment and clears my head, along with the smell of the food.

King picked up his phone and contacted the mysterious lawyer Romano had yet to find. The man dropped everything and rushed to King's apartment as soon as the call connected.

When the tablet chimed on the coffee table, Romano leaned forward and checked the screen. In the elevator was a portly man who looked no different from any other middle-aged white male lawyer I'd ever seen. Romano flips the screen so King can see, and upon recognizing the man, he nods his head. Hopefully, we get through this without him slipping into the past. This happens *today*.

Thirty-five seconds later, the elevator doors whoosh open, and the man steps into the foyer. He clenches the handle of a briefcase in one hand, and his tan suit looks far too expensive for what anyone should spend on clothing.

He sees us in the living room and makes his way over.

"King," he greets.

"Jonathan, come in."

Jonathan makes his way toward King's bed and rests his empty hand on the bed rail closest to him. "So, it's finally caught up with you, has it?"

"Unfortunately, yes. I was sure a stray bullet would take me out sooner, if not my daughter." King is extraordinarily indifferent when talking about his own life. And yet, when he talks about taking his own life, it's the most sincere I've ever heard him.

"Right. Well," Jonathan says, "I have the paperwork here. We can amend the will. I've only heard you mentioned as Rogue, but I take it you're Ivy Montgomery?"

"That's me."

"And you are?" he asks Romano.

"Her husband and signing as 'John Doe', or whatever clever name we can come up with. King seems to have developed an aversion to his entire security team, so it's just the three of us. Well, four, including you now. Welcome to the club." King is not amused at that.

The morning of our breakfast meeting, King had apparently slipped into his non-lucid state and sent everyone packing aside from the chef. When we returned with King after the hospital, he did the same. I didn't argue with him and confirmed that they could go; they'd been reassigned within a day. It was an opportunity for me to gather intel without others in the vicinity. King wouldn't even take on the nurses that the hospital recommended. And let me tell you, emptying King's catheter and bedpan are not experiences I wish to relive. Thankfully, Dr. Shaw walked us through it and he gave us strict orders not to let King up. With his mobility issues, he would need a helmet and a walker, not to mention more people keeping him steady.

"Right. Okay, let's get this going then." Jonathan opens up his briefcase and pulls out a stack of paperwork. "This is your will. If you'd like to make an amendment, we can do that instead of starting from scratch. I need you to initial, here, here, here and sign here." He points to the little stickers he must have put on the papers during his ride over here. "It's simple to remove a clause, and I can backdate it as needed."

King grabs the pen from Jonathan's hand and swishes his initials and signature where needed. "I want this backdated at least three months. I want it filed and ready within the hour."

Jonathan nods his head with respect and puts the paperwork in front of Romano to sign as a random named witness, backdating the signatures by a few months. It takes some mental math, but we get there in the end.

The lawyer then hands over a few flash drives from his briefcase. "I have not plugged these into a computer since you gave them to me. We have downloaded none of it, as per your instructions. You can verify that with anyone who works in tech."

"Good. You've done decent work, Jonathan." King, ever stingy with his compliments. Jonathan dips his head once again and stands up straight.

"I can't honestly say it's been a pleasure, King, but thank you for your business. Who do I send the bill to?" he asks.

"The usual. My death won't affect that, but I'd send the bill fast, just in case."

"Very good." Jonathan picks up the paperwork he needs, and I assume he'll have it notarized illegally, but he has an hour to get things under control.

"Call us when it's done." King's tone leaves no room for argument, and Jonathan leaves as quickly as he arrived. Romano and I just look at each other. All of that work to get King's paperwork and evidence, and, in the end, the man called the lawyer himself.

My lips twitch as I try to keep a smile—and my laugh—contained at the irony of the situation. Romano does the same, his eyes sparkling. Eventually, I can't hold it anymore, and I throw my head back with laughter, collapsing onto the couch. Romano follows suit, and King's eyes ping between us.

"I made a good match," he says.

"I think I should do it in the room. Rogue, what do you think? Easier clean-up and body removal. My funeral instructions are in the will, which Jonathan will go over with you when it's done."

A small part of me feels guilty about my plan, knowing he can't fight back. It's a part that I try to squash, but it rears its ugly head. And I realize I am not the monster King tried to raise. I am my own woman, with my own mind, convictions, and ethics. For so long, I have wanted to drive my knife into his heart and watch the light seep from his eyes. But I know I'm not the only one who imagined this scenario.

I look at the man to my left—my husband, my confidant in some ways. He's earned this kill just as much as I have, but instead of being the one living with physical scars, he lives in emotional turmoil, still pining for a woman who has been dead for years because of King and his organization.

Romano meets my gaze with a question in his own. I nod my head, letting him know we will do this together.

One last kill as husband and wife.

The call comes through that the paperwork has been filed and the will uploaded and backdated within the system.

Noting which company he worked for, I texted out a request to Jacob to monitor the situation from his computers. I wish we had known which law firm was handling the will in advance, then we could have avoided all of this. At least now, with the name Devonshire and Young, we know which servers to break into.

I text Jacob that they filed the paperwork and send him on his way to investigate. King says nothing as I thumb out texts on my phone, informing the guys of what's going on. It doesn't take long, and within fifteen minutes, Jacob has the confirmation I need, having been double and triple-checked. Someone backdated it within the firm's system and the notary's records. He says we're good to go.

I peek up from my phone to find both King and Romano watching me intently. This man has earned his vengeance. It's time to deliver it.

It takes no time at all to wheel King to his torture chamber. For all of my reluctance to enter this room over the past month, I find it surprisingly easy now. A way to put my own nightmares to rest.

King's lack of mobility is a bit of a hindrance. We get his bed to the mouth of the hallway, and Romano strides down the hall and enters King's room. He comes back with a set of keys and swiftly unlocks the door to the concrete chamber, getting the key right on the first try. Looks as if I couldn't have gotten into the room even if I was brave enough to try.

King chuckles under his breath and says, "Of course you looked around. Find anything interesting?"

Romano looks at King, simply shrugs, and looks heavenward.

Romano props the door open and comes back to help me move King. Once inside the room, we get him laid out on the surgical table shoved in the corner. Romano wheels it straight to the center of the room and over the drain.

His only view is the chains hanging from the ceiling, unless he tilts his head in our direction. It's a good thing he doesn't. I've kept my face expressionless, but Romano has a sadistic twist to his lips, marring his face. There's a darkness in Romano that he tries to hide. He unleashed it a bit with De La Cruz, but I have a feeling I'm about to see an entirely new side of him today.

"Anything you want to say beforehand?" I ask as I close the door, twisting the key in the lock with a final click.

I turn to face my adoptive father.

The last thing I want to do is say my last words to him when he is not aware of everything he has done to me, so I intend to speed this along.

"You with us, King? I'm not about to hand you a gun if you've stepped into the past again. You might end up shooting me in your anger at my mother."

"I'm with you, Rogue." He looks offended that I'd ever think he could hurt my mother, but he doesn't know I've found the original reports from my parents' deaths. I plan to get to the bottom of that now.

"Your method of parenting was shit. Your treatment of my sister, deplorable. The way you hoard and keep people as leverage to keep your underlings in line is disgusting. You hurt innocents. You hurt people who don't deserve it. You *kill* people who don't deserve it. You may have trained me to be a queen. But The Gambit is going in a new direction," I assure him.

"But most importantly, I am ecstatic that no other child will lose their parents to you and your fucked up empire." My words drip venom and I see him flinch.

"There's something you should know, Rogue," he says. "Your talk of vengeance should encompass more than just me. If you want to avenge your parents, you're going to need to take out Patton Cross." My fists clench at my sides.

"What does he have to do with my parents?"

"He swayed your father from The Gambit and had him working as a double agent. When your parents tried to pull out of the gang life altogether, Cross paid your house a little visit. The way he killed your parents... well, that was Cross's signature style. You'll find out about him soon enough." The roar of blood in my ears is deafening as a sinister smile takes over King's face. He's not going to make things easy on me. When has he ever? Knowing my parents had their throat slit while my sister was sleeping down the hall is not something I enjoy thinking about.

Part of me had assumed it was King since I received the official reports from Saint Ignatius Church. I thought it was in retribution for my mother leaving him. Perhaps jealousy, even. If he couldn't have her, why should my dad? But hearing it's likely the last person on our list fills me with glee.

After King, my target will shift, and I'll have an empire at my back to get justice.

I nod my head, showing King I've processed the information, and stroll over to the wall to choose a weapon. His eyes follow me as I stroll past the guns, the easier option, and stop in front of the wall of knives.

"There's something you should know," I say conversationally to the man on the table. "I've been putting things in place to kill you for the last nine months. Do you know who took Sage? I did. Who killed Ron

Mitchell? I did. The things you do and the people you associate with are your downfall. Ruling with fear and an iron fist earns you no mercy, King."

I look at Romano and see his gaze fixed on King, lying on the table, and his eyes are alight with anger. "Now, while I would love to kill you, I'm afraid I'll have to pass the task on to my husband, who, by the way, I've never slept with, do not love, and am divorcing as soon as you're gone. No way am I letting you kill yourself. Someone else deserves that honor."

Romano lets out a laugh that's damn near maniacal. "But, darling, we get along so well," he jokes.

King's eyes whip over to Romano at my confession and his sarcastic retort. His tone of voice is acerbic and would scare even the most hardened criminal.

"And what is it you have against me?" he asks. "Your wife had her own secrets. She may have died, but I've given you a new one. I've given you more money than you know what to do with. I've given you power, influence, and anything else your heart desires."

"What my heart truly desires, King... is yours. Carved from your chest and ripped from your body. You and your organization stole the one person who mattered to me."

I step up next to Romano and hand him the knife. As strong and fearless as I know I can be, I can't do this. I can't be the one to kill him, not after the last month. Maybe I wouldn't have been able to do it at all.

In a roundabout way, I got my closure and a direction to take for my vengeance. It's time for Romano to find his. I lean back against the door, getting comfortable for what is sure to be a very long few hours.

Romano does not rush. He takes his dear, sweet time despite the screams ripped from King's throat. He is methodical and uses a precision I'm envious of. I also see he learned a few things from when I dismembered Ron. As King's end nears, he's staring into my eyes as tears of pain fill his.

I do not blink.

I do not hide my joy.

I watch the man who raised me and tore me down as he takes his last breaths.

Romano has split his chest open. The skin carefully peeled away, and his rib cage cut away. The bone saw lies on a table, just out of King's reach. His only salvation, inches from his fingertips. He fought with his upper body strength at first, but Romano found some restraints and affixed his arms to his sides.

I watch as Romano digs his hand into King's heaving chest and squeezes his heart. King gasps in pain as the air leaves his lungs and his heart constricts.

Romano lifts his other hand with the knife and carves a circle around the organ powering our mutual enemy. The light fades from King's eyes, and his blank stare is still fixed on my face.

Romano rips his fist out, pulling King's heart with it, and drops it on the floor next to his feet. His booted foot comes down in a vicious stomp, crushing the heart beneath its treads.

Chapter Eight

Jacob

It's been three hours of waiting to hear what's happened with King. Rogue texted me at seven to check if they backdated the will in the system and filed it correctly.

She said little via text, but she announced that King was dying tonight. Making sure things were going according to plan was the *only* reason I wasn't banging down her door and handing her the knife.

Lucas sits beside me on the oversized couch that Rogue ordered for us. It arrived two weeks ago and has quickly been named the best couch in the world by all of us. Lucas's leg has been bouncing up and down for hours. He's alternated between a state of pacing and sitting while staring blankly at the walls of the clubhouse.

I get it. I really do. Knowing that the woman you love is out there, handling shit that shouldn't even be on her plate, is an exercise in self-control we all despise.

Han is in the weapons room, meticulously cleaning and organizing everything despite having already done it a few days ago. I hear Noah in the gym on the treadmill. You can always tell when he's worried because he voluntarily does cardio. The whir of the treadmill stops, and moments later, I hear the pounding of the punching bag.

We've all texted the group chat multiple times and received no answer, which has us at our wits' end. I'm on my phone, and for once, I'm not playing Candy Crush as I wait for something—anything. No, instead, I'm reading the will repeatedly. But I also know these things take time. I look at the clock, and my self-imposed time limit is almost up before I storm her building to find her.

I did some digging while I was in the law firm's database. She only asked me to check if they filed everything correctly, but it was an opportunity to see what was actually in King's will and not just the clause that kept her from reclaiming her life all these years. King is an extraordinarily wealthy man, understandably. It makes sense, being the leader of a criminal empire. But the thing I found most interesting was that his will was updated about six months ago. Within it was a clause that if the Alzheimer's or seizures caused his death, the evidence would be squashed. A smart provisional plan, and one I doubt he shared with Rogue.

How awful must it have been to be responsible for the life of a man you hate without knowing that he included that provision for natural causes? More than once, I'd seen her fret when no one was watching. Or, rather, when she thought no one was watching.

I'm always watching her. I can't seem to help it.

There's more in the will than she knows. Guaranteed.

Another half an hour passes when my phone finally chirps that the gate is rolling open.

I clicked to the video surveillance to double-check, and sure enough, Rogue is striding across our parking lot, headed straight for the door. Lucas looks over at me curiously, but I don't spare him a moment.

I launch myself over the coffee table, my determined strides taking me straight to the glass doors leading to the foyer. I haul them open and cross to the reinforced door, unlocking it and sliding it open.

Standing there, looking as if the entire world is falling down around her, is Rogue.

She looks as if she's been through a war. Her hair is a mess, swept up in a bun atop her head as tendrils float around her face, there's blood on her shoes, and her casual outfit is wholly disheveled. My heart stutters at the sight of her.

Her green eyes are brighter than usual, tears clinging to her lower lashes. She blinks up at me owlishly, almost as if she's unsure why she's here.

I grab her hands and haul her into my arms. She lets out an almighty sob and relaxes into my embrace. Her hands instinctively wind around my waist, but I feel her knees buckle. I crouch down, sweep my hand under her legs, and carry her like a husband carrying his bride over the threshold and into the main clubhouse. Lucas is on his feet, instantly rushing toward us. He quickly assesses Rogue, making sure she's uninjured, and guides us to the couch. Lucas lopes off when I tilt my head toward the front door I abandoned to get her inside.

He returns a moment later and stands warily off to the side before stopping next to me, his eyes roving over Rogue once more.

Rogue's sobs have not stopped. In fact, she's crying harder now. I turn my body and collapse back onto the couch. Lucas takes up one side as Han and Noah make their way to us. We surround her on the couch while she buries her face in my chest. Part of me wonders why she is grieving for a man who made her life hell. Another part understands this was her last parental figure in any sense of the word, even if he was an awful one.

I trace my hand along the side of her face, pushing her unruly hair behind her ear. With her constant care of King, seeing her has become more and more infrequent. She didn't know about the natural causes clause of the will, so she was there constantly, making sure he didn't die.

Romano obviously offered her reprieves, but she was too afraid to leave King's side, even taking up residence in his living room. When asked if he had other rooms, she simply mentioned her old bedroom and that she wouldn't be setting foot in there.

Lucas runs his fingertips up and down her arm, comforting her in the only way he can at the moment. Noah and Han are exchanging glances, having a conversation between themselves without words. Noah eventually takes a seat to my left, pulls Rogue's shoes off, and settles her feet onto his lap, gently massaging them. Han kneels before me, caging Rogue in and helping to surround her with the men who love her.

It takes another thirty minutes for her to calm down enough to take more normal breaths. No one rushes her. No one presses for information. We just give her time to gather herself. She clears her throat as if she is about to speak, and another wail pops out. My heart breaks as I hold her close and offer her comfort any way I can. She nestles against my chest but extends her right hand to Han. He clasps it as if she is his lifeline, and if he lets go, she will cease to exist.

Lucas murmurs words into her ear from behind, letting her know she is loved, she is cared for, and that whatever happened was necessary. We don't even know what happened, but it doesn't matter; we will support her in anything.

She slowly lifts her head and looks around. My hands are busy holding her tightly against me, so Han wipes his thumbs under her eyes and clears the wetness from her cheeks.

"Hiya, Gorgeous," he coos.

Her breath is shaky. "Hi, handsome," she breathes.

Rogue suddenly looks at Noah as if he squeezed her feet to let her know that he's with her as well. "What do you need, Trouble?"

"I need to talk it out. And, yet, I need to bury it at the same time and never mention it again." Her exhale is deep and wary. "It's so stupid. I shouldn't be grieving. Why does it feel like a part of me has died with him?"

"Because a part of you has. The part that King had control over. It's gone now. It's okay to be a little all over the place," Noah assures her. Rogue steadies her breathing and finally turns to look at everyone, swiveling her head back and forth, making eye contact with each of her men.

"Buttercup," Lucas draws her attention. "We're here for whatever you need to do. Anything. Simply name it."

Seeing that she's ready to talk, I pull her closer to me, squeezing her tight. "Do you want to tell us now or later? What's better for you?" I ask.

"Now," she says, "while it's fresh in my mind. I don't want to forget details and leave them out."

She launches into the explanation, telling us how King wanted to end his own life. My mind connects that to the fact that they would have given her evidence to the authorities because a gun isn't a natural cause. In the end, King did right by her, not allowing her to take the fall for his death since he had planned to do it by his own hand.

Rogue tells us how she agreed to his demands, only insisting they amend the will, about how her mind churned with methods of doing it, how to end the man who had taken so much from her. She tells us of the indecision she faced. That despite being a killer, she would have had trouble ending King.

Romano was with her the entire time, through King asking for aid in killing himself, through the will amendment, and through the end. Despite inadvertently stealing her from us, he was there for her at a time we couldn't be. And for that, we owe him everything.

We knew he had his own vendetta against King, so it seems to have been a simple choice for Rogue to allow him to deliver the killing blow when she couldn't. They agreed to his terms and wheeled him to the room that Rogue vaguely mentioned in the past. This was the room he trained her in, punished her in, and has given her nightmares since she was a child.

She explains to us how she modeled her kill room at the mechanic's shop after this one. Lacquer on the walls for easy washing, a drain in the center for blood. The only difference being that King's room had an arsenal setup.

She sniffles mid-speech. "I couldn't resist it in the end. I told him about how I've been working against him for months. It was as if a cartoon villain took over my body, delivering a monologue listing the deeds I'd done to undermine him. I wanted him to know it was me. That the girl he broke in so many ways could rise and take back what he stole. I explained how I took Sage and killed Ron. I said so many awful things, but I needed him to hear them before he never heard anything again."

King told her about her father's involvement with Cross and that he was the one to end her parents when they wanted out of gang life. She's convinced he told her the truth and said she had never seen him more sincere. It lines up with Cross being named as her godfather. It lines up with the past that man has covered up over the years—the murders, the brutality. And it lines up with the last member on our whiteboard.

As Rogue recounts King's last seconds at the hands of Romano, she tells us about the moment his eyes locked with hers and didn't waver until his end. She says there was regret in his eyes, perhaps even a bit of pride and respect.

When she reaches the part where Romano shoved his hand into King's chest and gripped his heart, her tears come again. By the time King's heart hits the floor and Romano stomps on it with his boot, tears are tracking down her face.

I instantly decide to check out that bastard, Romano, once again. That cold, clinical vengeance she described doesn't come from nowhere. We let her speak until her voice turns hoarse, only offering soft touches of reassurance and the space to get it all out. Once she's spent, she slumps into my arms, defeated. Each of us keeps a hand on her as Rogue stares off into space, letting the conversation ebb and flow around her.

The guys and I speak softly, comparing impressions, theories about Patton Cross, and theories about Romano. I rhythmically trace my hand up and down Rogue's neck, feeling her pulse point and making sure she's actually here, finally free of King.

What does this mean for The Gambit? Does Rogue pick up the mantle? Or does she let it collapse around her?

Noah's hands inch higher and higher up her legs with each pass. I think we're all in the middle of assuring ourselves that she is here.

That she is okay.

That she is ours.

Rogue's hands don't miss the opportunity to reach out to us either, finding comfort in our arms.

I think back to the first month or two she was with us. She often steeled herself before allowing even a brush of our fingertips, and I know part of that was because when King would touch her, it was with a malicious hand that we simply don't possess—not toward her.

Her hands wrap around my neck and pull my face close to hers. I rest my forehead against her own and softly whisper, "Darling Mine, how can we help?"

"I need to not think for a moment," she confesses.

I stare deep into her eyes, lean in, and take her lips. It's a gentle whisper of contact between us. I feel Han's hand on my knee, encouraging me to tend to our girl. It may not be the healthiest choice, but it's what she wants. Who am I to deny our girl? I feel Lucas's hand trailing up and down her back in reassurance. With every downward stroke, his hand bumps my arm as I have it banded around her back.

Rogue squeezes her thighs together, and I hear Noah exhale to my left.

We talked about the night we all came together, how Noah directed us. He's not sure if he'll ever be ready to join us all on the bed, but right now, I don't think he cares.

See, that's the thing about Noah. He has his preferences but will bend for those he loves. Hence the reason he tried to make it work with Sheila for so long. It wasn't until she drove the final nail in the coffin of their relationship that he finally pulled away.

Since then, he's been guarded. Until Rogue. I've never seen him let someone in the way he did Rogue once he finally got over his fear and went for it.

Rogue deepens our kiss until her tongue duels with mine, the challenge clear. Gentle isn't exactly what she's going for right now. She wants to feel loved, honored, and not like a monster for inwardly breathing a sigh of relief at her adoptive father's death. She wants to feel alive.

Her fingers toy with the hair at the nape of my neck. She gently follows the outline of the tattoo at the base of my skull. It thrills me that she knows the shape without having to see it. She watches me as much as I watch her.

I break the kiss and put my forehead against hers again as I feel a shift in her legs. Noah palms both of her knees and gently pushes them apart. "Are you sure?" he asks.

She nods her head against mine, and when I give her a look, she answers appropriately, "Yes."

We've talked about blanket consent. Rogue assured us she's always willing when she's with us, and if she isn't, she'll just say so. But in this case, with all of us, words feel like the right thing and not just a nod.

Rogue's leggings leave little to the imagination, but they're in the way. Despite how much I love seeing her in them, they've gotta go. She unwinds her arms from around my neck and tosses them straight up into the air. Lucas's hands come from behind, grab the hem of her shirt, and drag it up and over her body until she's free. He deftly unhooks her bra and slides it down, baring her chest to us.

She pushes her hands against my thighs and lifts her body. Han and Noah, working in tandem, remove the leggings by each holding one side of the waistband and dragging them down her legs.

Doing my part for the group, I grab her lace panties and pull, shredding them as I often do. I can't even explain why it turns me on the way it does. Han asked me once, and the only way I could describe it was to equate it as the last thing standing in my way before reaching what's mine. She rolls her eyes at my antics and lets out a soft laugh.

Lightening her mood brings a smile to my face. What she doesn't know is I've stocked a drawer upstairs with plenty of replacements.

Naked in all her glory, she lies draped across me like an offering from a god who is far too kind to us.

Noah puts his hands back on her knees, pushes them apart, and slowly trails his fingertips up her thighs.

I look up and see everyone's gaze trained on the path Noah is blazing with his rough hands. Han's hand travels to her clit as he kneels next to Rogue, and I watch him on the opposite side of our girl, my eyes drawn to his movement as if he's magnetic. He traces slow, torturous circles around her swollen nub.

Lucas's hands wrap around her body and worship her breasts as her nipples stand at attention. His palms cover her breasts, and his rough, calloused hands drag over her pebbled buds as her back arches, seeking more.

"Please," she says when Noah's fingers reach her pussy.

Finding her wet, he drags it up to her clit, giving Han some lubrication to continue his torture.

I take her mouth with mine in a fierce kiss, stealing the breath from her lungs. Our duel for dominance continues where it left off earlier. I feel her body bump against mine when Noah drives his fingers into her.

Unrelenting.

Unmerciful.

She gasps against my lips, and I swallow the sound. I pull back, looking at what my teammates are doing to her. Noah's fingers are slick to the knuckle, driving in and out of her heat. Han circles her clit faster and faster, and her hips buck in time with their ministrations. Lucas pinches her nipples in tandem, causing her to throw her head back against his shoulder as she reaches her climax.

Lucas mumbles in her ear, too low for me to make out the words, but it has her gasping and grinding her hips hard against the rest of us. She lets her scream out as the orgasm washes over her, making me thankful we have no neighbors and a soundproofed building.

"More," she moans. "More, I need more. Please."

This girl should never beg unless it's for my cock, seconds before slipping inside her. I want her to have what she wants without needing to ask, and I want to be the one to deliver it.

Shifting until my body slides out from under her, I place her carefully against the back of the couch. "You remember what this couch does?"

"Oh, yes," she confirms. Her pupils are blown as she recalls what we did to the couch in that San Francisco hotel room.

"Everybody up," she says as she claps her hands together in a stunning display of self-control.

Everyone does as she asks, and I get Han to help me move the coffee table out of the way. Rogue fiddles with something on the side of the couch after removing the pillows and tossing them to the side. Within seconds, the couch has unfolded, the backrest is tucked under, and everything expands, turning it into a massive surface we can use.

That's right. It's not just a couch; it's an orgy bed that nearly rivals the size of mine upstairs.

Lucas strips out of his clothes in the blink of an eye, and Noah follows suit. Han and I look at each other, and the heat between us is enough to start a blaze in the room. He moves closer, clasping my face with his palms, and lowers my face those couple of inches for a scorching kiss.

Having collapsed onto the giant bed, Rogue's jaw drops, and a moan escapes her, telling me this is turning her on as much as it is me. Han slowly drags his fingers from my face, down my chest, to the hem of my shirt. He unbuttons from the bottom, slowly making his way upward.

I reach for his shirt and drag it up his body, only breaking the kiss for a moment so the material can pass between us.

Han pushes the shirt over my shoulders, and with each torturous pass of his fingertips against my chest, Rogue's breathing increases. We fumble for one another's belt buckles, quickly undoing them and the zippers of our trousers. We push them over the other's hips until they drop to the floor.

Our cocks strain toward each other, and Han steps into my space fully and grinds his hips against mine. He palms my arse and pulls me closer. The heat of his dick has me biting his lip and breaking the skin with my teeth.

I feel hands on my hips, fingertips digging into the waistband of my boxer briefs. They pull slightly, and I look down to see Lucas with a grin on his face and his hands sliding my underwear down my legs.

Rogue is doing the same with Han's boxers, albeit her hands are more sensual on Han than Lucas's were on my body.

Noah stands to the side, his chest heaving as he takes in the sight before him.

I share a quick kiss with Han before focusing on our girl. She sits back on her heels in the middle of the bed. Neatly. Obediently. As if she is the perfect submissive. But that's the thing. I don't need her to submit. I love who she is. This strong, fierce woman doesn't have a genuinely submissive bone in her body.

I love the challenge. Adore it even.

Noah takes a step forward tentatively. Rogue reaches a hand out to him, palm upward, and crooks a finger in his direction. He's powerless to stop himself as he moves in front of her.

He stops just before reaching the couch, staring down at this creature before us. Rogue fists Noah's dick with one hand, pumps it twice, and lowers her open lips all the way to the root of his cock. Impressive.

Pulling back, she uses saliva to work him over with her hands until his hips subconsciously press forward at every downstroke.

She grips him hard at his base and lowers her mouth until she's taking him in at a feverish pace. Noah's hands reach down and grasp the sides of her head, his fingers weaving through her messy hair. He starts off gentle, but I know as well as any of them that when our girl has your dick anywhere near her body, there's no stopping our natural reflexes.

Noah's hips drive toward her, and I see Rogue swallow around him. He pushes, keeping himself lodged in her throat, and she welcomes it.

I stand behind Han, my hips gently grinding against his arse as we watch the show before us. I reach around Han's hip, taking his cock in my hand and grip as I stroke him, matching Rogue's rhythm.

Noah pulls his hips back and tells Rogue, "Enough."

He reaches under her arms, pulls her to a kneeling position, and swoops down, pulling her legs out from under her, so she falls backward onto the couch.

Despite the three of us just standing around watching, it doesn't feel as if they've left us out. It feels as if this is how it was always supposed to be. Lucas stands next to Han and me, his eyes riveted on the scene before him. Noah steps forward, and his knee bends as he climbs onto the bed/couch. He throws a look over his shoulder and sees the three of us standing off to the side.

Noah first looks at Lucas, who nods vigorously, telling him to get the fuck on with it. He twists a bit more and looks at Han and me. I've crouched down slightly, so my chin is resting on his shoulder, my hands still working his length and cupping his balls.

We both nod at the same time. What our girl wants, she gets. He turns back around, and from our vantage point, I can see the look in their eyes. They're connected. In a way that only two people deeply in love can be. I know it because it's the same look I share with both Rogue and Han. There's no shying away. No hiding who you are. Just pure love and respect flowing between them.

Rogue curls her torso and grasps Noah's shoulders, bringing him down on top of her. She whispers in his ear, and a grin overtakes his face. He nibbles on her neck before his mouth slowly trails down her body, stopping at each breast to pay it the attention it deserves.

He drags the tip of his tongue down her torso until finally reaching her clit. His face is hidden by her thighs as she clamps them around his head, keeping him in place. Noah's hands brace on either side of her hips, and her body rocks in rhythm to his tongue as he claims her body with his mouth. Rogue throws her head back and uses one hand to undo the hairband keeping it out of her face. It fans around her head as she twists and turns in ecstasy.

She tilts her head in our direction, and she opens her eyes, watching my hand moving slowly over Han's length. She grabs Noah by the back of his head, fingers white-knuckling it as she rides his face. Noah pulls back with a smirk, and Rogue pulls him up toward her.

"Fuck me," she groans. Noah, never wanting to deny Rogue, lines himself up and thrusts into her, her tits bouncing with the power of his movements.

"You like them watching us?" he asks. His tone is deep, his voice betraying how much it's affecting him.

"Yes. God, yes."

"Lucas," he calls, "hold her steady."

Lucas snaps to attention, his hand finally disconnecting from his cock as he makes his way around the couch and grabs her arms, pulling them above her head.

He leans forward, kissing her upside down as Noah grunts his approval. The kiss is sloppy, all-consuming, and makes Han release a groan as he thrusts into my hand.

Noah's powerful back muscles ripple as he holds his weight off of her. He flexes with each push forward, and seeing our girl come undone, even if it's not by me, is an aphrodisiac all on its own. I see the strain in Rogue's arms as she tries to pull them from Lucas to touch Noah.

She's wiggling beneath him, her hips driving up to meet him thrust for thrust.

Noah's hand lifts from the couch, and he circles her throat with it. He holds her steady as Lucas continues kissing her, keeping her pinned in place as he reaches closer and closer to his undoing. Lucas groans at the display before him. Watching like this, seeing things happen to our girl as we stand helplessly to the side, gives me an appreciation for his voyeuristic tendencies. It's hot as fuck.

"You want to come?" Noah teases Rogue in that deep voice of his.

"Yes, Noah. Yes!"

He leans back, his knees still braced on the edge of the couch, as he picks up her hips and positions her precisely the way he wants her. Lucas's hands toy with her breasts, pinching and caressing. Her arms are still where Lucas held them, but now they grip the lip of the couch behind her, keeping her steady.

Noah's hips snap forward, again and again, pushing them both toward their climaxes. And finally, his thumb circles her clit, and he follows her into oblivion. They're both gasping for air, and Noah tumbles down on top of her, kissing her sweetly, gently even.

He rolls to the side, removing his weight from her, and Lucas lets go.

Rogue lifts her head and looks at Han and me. The mischief in her eyes sparkles. Han, ensnared in her gaze, takes a step forward, pulling me with him.

"Buttercup," Lucas says. "Are you ready for round two?"

A smile lights up her face, and she agrees readily. Perfect.

Now, I may have let Noah run the first round we were all together. But now it's my turn. The wicked glint in my eye must be noticeable because Rogue quickly delivers a kiss to Noah before rolling to a section of the couch with more space.

"Lie back, let your head hang off the back," I tell her firmly. She complies, dropping her head, and it falls at an unnatural angle off the side of the couch. She opens her mouth directly in front of Lucas, showing her intention. I whisper in Han's ear as the others are distracted. "Do you want both of us?" I ask.

He turns his head to look me in the eye. "Are you sure? We've never...in front of..." He takes a deep breath. "You're ready?"

"Yes," I say confidently. "And you?"

"Absolutely."

He steps forward, pulling me with him as Rogue separates her knees, letting her thighs fall to the sides and giving us an unobstructed view of her positively dripping pussy. Han and I groan in unison when we catch sight of it.

I give Han a deep kiss and nudge him toward her. He lowers himself on top of Rogue, teasing her body with his fingertips and his gentle touch. Her chest is heaving, and her breath comes in short pants as Lucas steps in front of her face, her eyes trained on his cock.

"Open up, Buttercup," Lucas says, a teasing tone in his voice and his dick hard and ready in his grip.

She quickly rolls her head to look at Noah, who's simply watching us. He shoots her a smile of reassurance as Han moves his body between her thighs, lining himself up and driving in at the same time that Lucas pushes into her throat.

Han and Lucas both exhale as Noah intakes a breath through his teeth. The sound is a symphony to my ears.

Han coats himself in her slick center and rocks his hips, grinding on her clit each time. I trail my fingertips down his back before reaching over to the coffee table, pulling open the drawer. Inside, I find knives, a gun, handcuffs, and a bottle of lube. You know, the usual.

When the couch arrived, and it took all four of us to get it set up in the lounge, I stocked the drawer just in case. The knives and gun were already inside.

I pull the lube from the drawer, kicking it shut with my foot, and pour a generous amount into the palm of my hand. Slicking it up and down my dick, I rub the rest against Han's ass after warming it, making sure we're both prepared.

Noah catches the bottle when I throw it his way. Talk about an assist.

Han groans at the contact. My finger teases his hole, and each time he withdraws from Rogue, he opens himself to me, and I slip the first digit in, reaching the knuckle. After I'm sure he's ready, I add a second. I stretch him, and Han sucks in a breath, holding it as he continues his movements. Lucas has his eyes trained on us as he continues his thrusts into her mouth, holding himself in her throat and withdrawing after an extended time.

I gently touch Han's shoulder blade, pushing him down toward Rogue's body, which he kisses and laves with abandon.

He pauses for a moment so I can line myself up. I withdraw my fingers, wrap my hand around my cock, and push past the tight ring of muscle. Han tenses for a moment, then lets me in.

I see over his shoulder as Rogue drops Lucas's cock from her mouth and cranes her neck upward to see what we're doing.

"Fuck, yes. Red, are you seeing this?" she asks in excitement. He murmurs his agreement as he fists his cock and continues stroking himself so she can watch the show Han and I are putting on for her.

Han kisses the fuck out of her, then tilts her head back.

Lucas directs his cock back into her mouth and comes undone in a few thrusts, his abs flexing as he empties inside her throat. She swallows everything he gives, and he drops to the floor, creating a makeshift pillow with his forearms as they watch Han and me before them.

Han kisses Rogue, uncaring of Lucas's cum as his tongue sweeps into her mouth.

I hold myself steady inside Han to give them a few moments. When they break the kiss, Rogue groans out, "Move, for the love of God, somebody move!"

Well, she asked, and we all know I'm not one to deny our girl. I pull myself back and snap my hips forward into Han, which drives him deeper into Rogue. They let out twin moans, and Noah's breathing increases to my left.

"Oh my God," Han groans.

I pull back and press forward yet again, moving them both up the couch, and Lucas uses his arms to keep them steady. Noah clasps Rogue's hand, squeezing hard. The combination of all of us coming together, Han's ass clenching around my cock, and the sounds my girl is making are my undoing. I still myself, and Han takes over, his hips colliding forward into Rogue and back onto my cock have him gasping for air as he works himself between us.

His thrusts forward and back come quicker and quicker as the seconds tick by, and it's not long before he rips my orgasm from me, coating his ass as I pull out and paint his cheeks. Han, able to get more movement without me at his back, lifts his hips, circles Rogue's clit, and bites down on her nipple. She screams a release that reaches the rafters as she comes. Han is quick to follow, his neck bent as he buries his face against her neck.

Chapter Nine

Rogue

The only thing worse than realizing it was three in the afternoon when I woke up was having to leave the warmth of the bed and my guys to send a text message to each of The Gambit's board members and Dr. Shaw.

My phone is tucked into the clutch that I gratefully remembered to take with me after last night's events. I remember not feeling steady enough to drive, so I ordered an Uber and practically barked at the poor man to drive faster.

The small bag made it into the clubhouse, and I found it in the foyer just inside the rolling front door, where I had apparently dropped it upon entering.

Calling a meeting for that evening via text, I got the usual posturing about busy schedules from a few members, particularly the new guy. But after threatening life and limb, they quickly changed their tunes.

They may not know what's going on, other than King has been absent for a bit, but all of that was about to change.

Taking over this organization was never my intention. Fuck, my only concern used to be getting Sage out and making a break for it. How stupid I had been as a naïve sixteen-year-old making deals with the head of an empire. I was never going to get out, but I let myself cling to the belief like a lifeline. I guess when you're tossed so few of those, you hang on to the one you find with dear life.

Doubling over, the weight of the empire settles on my shoulders, crushing me under its heavy expectations. I have to lead this, foster relationships, and cultivate prosperity and cohesion between its leaders, all so I can tear it down.

I don't have long before the guys wake up, so when the feelings come, I let them in. My heartbeat pounds as my breathing becomes short and choppy. This is far bigger than anything else I've taken on. There are so many lives at risk and in my hands.

As the implications and their heavy consequences start running out, I focus on my breathing. There was no other way. There was never any other route.

I'm taking these metaphorical lemons life handed me, and I'm about to squeeze them in some motherfucking eyes.

I type out a quick message to Sage. First, to check that she's okay. She affirms she is after just a few seconds, then I ask if she's free to talk.

My phone chimes with an incoming video call far more quickly than expected, so I race across the clubhouse on silent feet to not wake the guys. I reach Jacob's office and pull the glass door shut behind me. It's not soundproof, but it's quiet enough.

Sparing a glance through the glass walls, I spy the guys sprawled across the expanded couch and watch as they fill my empty spot with each other, snuggling in. God, they're cute.

"Hey, Sage. Are you okay?"

. . .

"Yeah, I'm fine. Just getting a little stir crazy. At least with escorting I could get out of the house." She laughs at the look of horror on my face and says, "Too soon?"

"Just a touch." I force a laugh. I don't know if I'll ever feel comfortable with those jokes.

"Sorry, sorry. Honestly, nothing beats the safety we're all feeling."

"I get that," I tell her. "I have some news. Are you sitting?"

"No, but I can be." She moves through the safe house, giving me a glimpse of where she's living before she enters a dark room. She flips on the light and closes the door, settling herself on the bed and propping the phone on a pillow. "Okay, hit me," she says.

"So, you remember how about a month ago I told you King was sick?"

"Yeah," she says cautiously.

"Well, last night, he passed away." Rip the Band-Aid off. Neither of us owed him anything, and while he hid the worst of his personality from her, she had seen enough to know he was truly awful, despite having put her in some form of foster care after our parents were killed.

Her eyes are wide, her mouth slightly open as she processes the information. We've been talking about it nearly every day via text or over the phone when she checks in. We all knew the end was possible, especially with the diagnosis of early onset Alzheimer's and the subsequent seizures that go with it. But I think nothing will prepare you adequately for the sudden news that someone has passed. I don't plan to tell her exactly how it happened or who did the killing, but the vital information is now out there.

"Wow. Okay, so what does that mean for you? For us?"

"It means I'm taking over The Gambit for the time being."

Her intake of breath is sharp, a knife to my chest. I never want her to look at me the way she did King. The good thing is, I don't plan to keep this role for very long. I tell her I'm making some changes. I'm planning on bringing the whole damn thing down so she and I can find some peace. After all, who deserves it more than the people the organization took everything from?

"Isn't there anyone else who can do it?" she asks, a mix of worry and indignation in her tone. I wobble my head back and forth, considering the options. I don't want to brush her off without even considering the option, but this has to be done any way I look at it.

"No. At least, no one I trust deep enough to get things done right. But that means you have to stay put. I can't handle this if I'm worried about you the whole time." My tone is pleading; I know it. But honestly, I don't think I can take another curveball at this stage.

She lets out a deep breath, resigning herself to another few months of hiding. "Anything you need, Ivy. Please, please, please, be careful. Let your guys help you. You know they want to."

. . .

"I plan to do exactly that," I tell her with a smirk as plans flit back and forth across my mind. "All of this will have been for nothing if you wander out and get snatched up again. I know I sound like a broken record, but just stay safe, and I'll keep you updated."

"What about you?" she asks, a scoff on her lips. "When will you have given enough? When will you be free?"

Probably never, I resist saying. But I keep my mouth shut. Everything I am doing is so she can live freely. If I get to do the same, all the more reason to throw everything I have at this. But she is my priority.

Ignoring her questions, I give her reassurance the only way I can. "I have plans for my future that don't include The Gambit or being a pawn in somebody else's game. I can't tell you much right now. Because honestly, I'm still working through the options, but I'm putting myself in a position to fix this. It won't bring our parents back. It won't make up for the time that we've lost. But, hopefully, it'll stop someone else from going through what we have."

Picking up the big sister tendencies that I never got to exercise as a teen, I stare into the phone at her wide eyes and beautiful blonde hair. "Keep doing all of your schoolwork, and I'll keep checking in. If all of this shakes out, we can start looking at colleges in the fall for you. The one good thing about being a top dog is that no one can tell me what to do now. The alternative is you are a weakness for me, and I need to keep you hidden. So, nose in the books, ass in the house. Deal?"

"Deal. Oh, by the way, Claudette stopped by yesterday and told me to have you call her. She said she hasn't heard from you in a few days and is threatening to drive down to El Castillo to kick your ass."

. . .

"Jesus, it's only been three days! I talk to her more than I talk to my guys, and it's still not enough."

Sage shrugs her shoulders. "She's needy. What can I say?" Her laughter floats down the line, and after a few goodbyes and promises to keep safe, we hang up the phone, and I make my way to the center of the clubhouse.

One guy is missing from the snuggle fest, and I follow my nose to the kitchen, where I sniff out fresh coffee. My phone dings in my hand, and I check the screen. Noting that Cian Byrne is the last to confirm for tonight's meeting, I vow to make his life a little more complicated. I sigh, knowing that the meeting is at eight o'clock tonight at Rook Industries. As much as I want to change the location because every time I walk in the door, I'm reminded of Hiroto Tanaka, it's central to everyone, and the last-minute call will be heeded.

I find Noah in the kitchen, in his boxers and an apron slung around his neck, as he makes pancakes over the stove. His hips and thoroughly biteable ass shake back and forth as he mixes the batter while the radio in the corner plays "Now Is The Start" by A Fine Frenzy. It's peppy and upbeat, and I make a mental note to add it to G's public playlist on that streaming website.

Despite being a terrible dancer when it comes to pop music, his hip shake is something I stop in my tracks to admire. I quietly make my way behind him, wrap my hands around his middle, and press my face to his back. I deliver a kiss to a shoulder blade, and he tilts his head back so he can see me.

"Morning, Trouble. Or, 'afternoon,' I should say."

. . .

"Hey, Cap. How are you today?" He knows I'm asking about more than just his general welfare; I'm touching on the group thing we did last night.

"Good. Great, actually. I'm glad you came to us last night."

I sigh. "Me, too. More than you know."

He spins in my arms, pulling me into his warm embrace, and kisses my nose. "I love you," he says, and tears threaten to spill from my eyes as I revel in the words and the feeling.

"I love you, too. I'm so, so grateful that you guys found me last year." He pulls me in tighter and gives me one of his great bear hugs. He doesn't mention the tears, doesn't wipe them away, just lets me feel what I need to until the scent of burning pancakes reaches my nose, and he spins around.

"Ah, shit!" he exclaims. I laugh and make my way over to the coffee machine as he swats me on the ass with the spatula.

Sweet nectar of the gods. Is there anything better first thing in the morning? Well, maybe an orgasm. Speaking of which, the other three make their way into the kitchen, finding me near the machine sipping my coffee out of a cup that says *Sorry in advance for doing a ton of stupid shit.*

What? It seemed fitting.

Good mornings and I love yous are exchanged, check-ins about what the guys are doing today are mentioned, and I clear my throat, knowing I need to broach the subject sooner rather than later. "So... I called a board meeting for The Gambit tonight."

In unison, they swivel from what they were doing to stare at me.

"Today?" Han asks.

"It has to be today. I can't leave it for later, and I need to make some plans. All of which I promise to include you in," I assure them as I see the following questions forming on their lips. "There are too many things up in the air and not enough known about what's going to happen next. Loyalties need to be affirmed and everyone has to be on board. I want to use this advantage to assess Cross and work from inside to take The Gambit down. I don't know how it's going to happen, but if Mara is involved with the feds, I need a contact."

Noah straightens at the mention of his boss. "I organized a meeting with her for next week. Whether she shows is another matter entirely, but I extended the invite."

"That would be great. Mara's the only one I know involved who isn't loyal to The Gambit someway or another. There are so many agents in The Gambit's pockets that I would be unsure who is approachable from our roster. They get enough bribe money from us that I bet one would attempt to take me out in hopes my replacement would keep paying them."

"We're on it, Love." Jacob's assurance is everything I need to hear at that moment.

. . .

The hours pass peacefully. We sit in a circle on the clubhouse floor and toss a foam ball back and forth as we chat out ideas and make plans with Sir Lancelot running between us in a pen on the floor. All too soon, my time is up.

At five o'clock on the dot, I gather my things, and Han helps me into the passenger seat of the truck to bring me home. Taking the Uber, while smart, didn't leave me with a car at the clubhouse. The good thing is, I don't have to hide my movements as much at the moment. As the new leader, my comings and goings are my own. At least, until people find out they have a Queen instead of a King. A weight lifts from my shoulders as I let the window down, and the early summer air drifts across my skin. I'll be back to the sneaky comings and goings soon enough because of my new title, but for now, I bask in my relative freedom.

Romano and I are tense for the entire drive to the Rook Industries building. It's a short one, but the silence stretches before us like an unending highway.

Last night, after Romano crushed King's heart beneath his boot, he let out a heavy sigh of relief and hung his head. The man ultimately responsible for his wife's death was finally dead. Revenge exacted, we rolled up the body in a tarp and got to work disposing of it and the evidence.

I had Rosa, my new go-to cleaner since the guys introduced us, come to King's apartment to take him away. It's nothing the building attendants hadn't seen before. And now that he was gone, who was going to report us? And to whom? They'll all be answering to me now.

This evening, after Han dropped me off, I met with Dr. Shaw. I explained a version of what happened and that King wanted to end his own life. He said it's not uncommon and something a lot of terminal patients opt to do. He signed the death certificate, took it to be filed and legalized, and I paid him handsomely for his time and attention to King. I encouraged him to take an extended vacation, and he pondered Morocco for a bit before settling on The Canary Islands.

Easing my foot onto the brake, I pull the car into the alley next to the building. King's eyes may not be on me anymore, but the valets here don't know that yet.

The tension doesn't feel like it usually does when I approach the building. No, this time, my skin is thrumming with anticipation. I park the car and slide out. Romano meets me on the sidewalk and we approach the revolving doors. He extends an elbow in invitation, and I slide my hand through the gap he leaves for me.

I see myself in the shiny exterior of the building. My sky-high white pumps and the form-fitting white dress I'm wearing scream elegance and sophistication. The tattoos peeking out on my right side from the neck of the garment to my fingertips, and from the hem at my calf to my shoes, scream individuality.

Half dark, half light.

King's sentiment about my split personality flits across my mind before I lock that shit down and straighten my shoulders. I tuck a runaway curl back into my updo and fiddle with one of my emerald earrings. One moment of weakness before the mask slips back on.

I look the part because tonight, I become Queen.

I glance up at Romano as he looks down at me. There's some wrinkling at the corners of his eyes as he fights a grin, and he nods his head at me in a show of respect and admiration. "Ready?" he asks.

"Let's do this."

The guards at the front door are silent. Taking in my outfit, the confidence in my pose, I see them all incline their heads. They know what's happening tonight. I informed their boss—who works for me—that I'd be taking the throne. He was eager to meet my request for their presence in case anything got out of hand with the power changeover.

We make our way through the lobby and into the elevator. Romano pushes the button for the thirty-fifth floor, and we rise.

The elevator doors open when we arrive, and I step into the stark white hallway. Surrounding the elevator doors are six security team members. More importantly, my team members. I've always assigned the best of the best to King, and now they're here to do my bidding.

Romano waves a hand in front of me, ushering me ahead of him. Security flanks me on either side as I traverse the hallway to the conference room. Through the glass doors, I see everyone is seated. All are accounted for except for one addition, whom I've instructed to arrive fifteen minutes after the meeting begins.

One of the security members rushes ahead to pull the door open for me. At my entrance, heads swivel in my direction, and I see a smile overtake Elise's face. As one, they all stand as I step into the room.

Romano follows me in, and the security guards take up their positions outside the door, lining the hallway. They're my insurance policy if I can't get to my knife quickly enough to deal with a threat. It's always good to have a show of firepower when taking over an empire.

. . .

I make my way to the head of the table, and Romano pulls the chair out for me. I stare down at King's old seat, and a thrill of power runs up my spine—sadness, as well—but power more than anything else.

"Thank you for joining me today," I say clearly, my voice unwavering. "Everyone, have a seat."

Romano pushes the chair in behind me, and I settle in. He takes the seat to my right and nods to everyone as he undoes his suit jacket and sits back comfortably.

"We're here today for two reasons," I explain. My tone is even, calm, and collected. I take my time, measuring out my words and not rushing or succumbing to emotion. For however long I run this shit show, I don't plan to run it with fear, the way King did.

"Item one is that King is no longer with us." Raised brows circle the table, and I watch expressions ranging from relief to suspicion.

Nira Bhatt, brought up as Tanaka's replacement on the board, raises a delicate hand. I nod for her to speak. "May we ask what happened?" Her all-business tone is firm, but I see the way her hand shakes when she looks at me. It seems as if someone told her about my old job.

"He had a degenerative illness that he did not disclose to the rest of the board, nor myself until it was too late." Skirting the actual death circumstances makes me feel as if I'm a liar. I am in so many ways, but I'm choosing to protect Romano and myself. Regardless of my intentions, the guilt gnaws at my stomach.

. . .

Elise taps her nails on the table. "Is that why we haven't seen him lately, and he canceled the meetings for the last month?"

"Yes," I confirm. "King was resting at home, essentially in hospice care. Romano and I watched over him until the end. He died last night, thus resulting in the emergency meeting today.

"Now that you know, we can move on to the second order of business. As you all know, King appointed me to be the next leader of The Gambit. Are there any objections?" I ask, trying to keep the menace from creeping into my eyes as I internally dare someone to speak up.

Nina, Elise, Romano, and Nira all relax back into their chairs, obviously having no issue. Cian Byrne, however, does not feel the same. "What makes you fit to lead?" he asks, thinking that suddenly having a seat at the adult table doesn't mean I won't hold him down and rip his tongue from his throat.

I hold up my fist, ticking off finger after finger as I explain myself. "Let me help you understand, Byrne. King named me as his heir apparent a little over six months ago in front of these very board members. I was raised in this organization. I know how it runs. I plan to make changes and have had them on the back burner for years. Who here can say the same? You're new, and I get that, but this is not the time to pull out the measuring stick. I guarantee my dick is bigger than yours."

Elise chuckles as Cian's mouth gapes at my words. He slinks back against his chair; the fight leaving his body at my declaration. I always knew De La Cruz's replacement had ambition, but with enough pushback, he'll retreat down from anything. It's part of the reason I didn't mind killing his boss in the first place, knowing I'd be able to bend this man.

. . .

Romano stands and clears his throat. Here goes the vote. "All those in favor of Ivy Montgomery, aka Rogue, taking over as leader of The Gambit say 'aye.'"

"Aye," comes clearly from each member's mouth, the loudest from Romano.

"I accept. Right, the first order of actual business: spread the word to your people that there's been a change. Things will continue as usual for the time being until I decide otherwise. I will bring big things before the board, as per the bylaws. Mind your people and your divisions, and I have a feeling we'll all get along just fine."

Murmurs of agreement go up around the table, and I watch as the members become more relaxed. They won't be micromanaged, but I need to know what we're dealing with. "I'll be meeting with each of you individually over the next month. I want to know everything about your division so I can better lead this organization."

I see the security guards shifting outside the glass doors. "Last, I have another announcement to make." The door swings open, and in walks G. He's dressed in his usual dark jeans and t-shirt combo, his boots scuffing the pristine floor.

He spies a chair at the end of the table and makes his way over to it. "This is my second, Giacomo, more commonly known as G, and I propose him for my spot as leader of the hitmen for The Gambit. I expect him to carry on my legacy in the same manner."

G's eyes flare wide, and I know he wasn't expecting this today. "Shush, you, or I'll offer the job to Fabio." His mouth snaps shut, and he sits silently while we decide his fate.

. . .

"All those in favor?" I ask.

Another chorus of agreement goes up around the room, and my agenda is settled for the night.

"We're done for tonight. Contact Romano or me in case of an emergency, otherwise, keep doing what you're doing, but Cian, if I hear of even one minor getting their hands on our drugs, I'm gutting you, got it? Do better than De La Cruz."

"Yes, Queen."

It takes my mind a moment to catch up with what just happened. I am no longer Rogue. Now, I'm the Queen of The Gambit. *Oh, fuck, that's weird.*

As is the tradition for a new leader, when the meeting comes to a close, everyone approaches me individually. Nira is the first, and I tell her exactly what I intend. "I want everything shifted to legitimate business. Your division and your section should be thriving. I know Tanaka left big shoes to fill." My throat catches for just a second, and I continue speaking, hoping she doesn't notice. "But I have full faith in you. I checked your records and was impressed. I hope you continue the corporation the same way he would have." She shakes my hand and agrees, both of us surreptitiously wiping the welling tears from the corners of our eyes as we remember Tanaka.

Next to approach is Nina. There's a slight tremor in her voice when she greets me personally. "The stealing won't pick up again, will it?" Her head shakes vigorously. "Don't forget I can find it, even if you try to cover your tracks. I will not threaten your father to solidify your loyalty. He is safe from The Gambit and from me. Continue doing your job, and if everything is in order at the end of a six-month trial period, we'll talk about a raise." Her eyes are wide with suspicion at my generosity, but she grabs my hand and shakes it with glee.

"Yes, Queen. I won't let you down." Ugh, weird.

Taking the moniker "Queen," is part and parcel of the leadership role. Non-negotiable. It's odd considering I've been called Rogue since I moved in with King. Just when I thought we settled the nicknames, I get a whole new one.

Cian steps up to me, and I feel Romano's hand on my lower back as he stands at my side, offering me the unspoken support King spoke of so highly. Respectfully, albeit begrudgingly, Cian murmurs, "Queen."

"Cian, I have plans. Just clean house, and follow directives, and I promise you will be fine. Do your job and don't be an asshole." He nods his head at me wearily. "Whether or not you can trust me? It's a feeling I would also experience if the shoe were on the other foot. I am not here to make your life harder," I assure him. He steps away after bidding me a good evening.

G bounds up to me, stopping short when he looks up at Romano's face. "Rogue. I mean, Queen. Yeah, that's going to take some getting used to."

"Fuck's sake, G. At least try to be a professional." I laugh to take the sting out of my words and hit him with a quick eye roll. He fights a smile, but pretends to take this seriously. "I'm really glad you're here. I need your eyes on the other members if I'm not around them. What do you say?"

"Consider it done." After our fun day cleaning Ron Mitchell's escort operation, I know his loyalty to me is unfailing. After all, the girls are still safe up north, and he knows exactly where they are. He didn't know there were snipers stationed in the trees at Claudette's expense, but it's a test of his loyalty that he and Fabio both passed with flying colors.

He leans in uncharacteristically and presses a kiss to my cheek, whispering in my ear as he draws back, "Give 'em hell, Queen." I repress a smile at his words and his tune as he whistles Bohemian Rhapsody on his way out the door.

Elise is the last to approach. "I always knew you were going to be Queen," she says.

I laugh at that. "You didn't think to warn me?"

"Don't be a shithead, girl. You were made for this role." I scoff, but she interrupts me. "Think about it. Who else could have this many people on their side right out of the gate? Who else could put that little Cian asshole in his place so quickly?"

I realize she's absolutely right. If they had brought in anyone else as the leader, we'd be up to our necks in problems already, and it's only been twenty-four hours.

"Queen, I want out," she admits. "I'm old, I'm tired, and I want some peace. I know the bylaws say death or tribute is the only way out, and since I plan to enjoy retirement, I've got a tribute you might enjoy."

I suddenly realize why she waited to go last. The only two to witness her vulnerability are Romano and me. "Yes, I'll agree to the terms, no matter the tribute. But I need two months from you, Elise. I need to learn your business, how to run it, and how to make it function. Can you give me that?" I ask.

"Two months to learn what took me decades to perfect? Yeah, sure." She shrugs, and I laugh at her flippant manner regarding her life's work.

"I also need you to help me with the party King assigned to you."

"Oh, dear, I've almost got it settled. It's going to be perfect."

"There are going to be some changes," I tell her. "And I want to help implement them."

Chapter Ten

Rogue

The sunshine and cool air are refreshing as I leave El Castillo far behind and follow my phone's GPS, making my way up the coast to visit Sage.

I follow the usual maneuvers to avoid possible tails, despite finally being out from under King's thumb and now arguably the most powerful woman in the state. Only having had the meeting with the board yesterday, who knows how quickly word has spread? King may not be following me anymore, but taking up the leadership role brings its own threats.

I stopped by Axle's shop this morning and swapped out Black Beauty for a midnight-blue 1968 Chevrolet Camaro. My original plan was to take one of the stupid minivans or sedans we keep on hand for sly jobs. You know, the ones where you don't want anyone to notice you? Yeah, I bypassed that sand-colored, soccer-mom car and went straight for this gorgeous girl.

There's a car show happening in Monterey Bay this weekend, so it will just look like another car enthusiast on their way to the festival. Oh, how the attendants would swoon over my Black Beauty. Maybe next year.

The windows are down, it's bright and early in the morning, and I've got my body double, Ashley, at the apartment. She and I met at the mechanic's shop, and she took Black Beauty back to the apartment building, stopping for donuts along the way as a viable excuse for being out first thing in the morning.

I did something uncharacteristic today—I trusted Romano.

After what we went through, I can to a certain extent. Last night, I told him I would check in on the girls, and he only asked what I needed him to do. That was easy. Hang out with the doppelganger at the apartment or go out together, and if anyone is keeping tabs on me, they'll see me on my doting husband's arm.

Ashley and I really look similar, and her fake tattoos, custom ordered to match mine, are a perfect decoy. Our faces are slightly different, but we're indistinguishable in the right outfit and some big-ass sunglasses.

I take the coastal highway up north, enjoying the scenery. The early morning surfers out on the waves dot the horizon, and I let some peace wash over me for a few minutes.

It's not long before I'm pulling up outside the safe house after circling downtown a few times and taking back roads to reach the outskirts and hills of Sacramento.

This may still be Gambit territory, but Claudette has bought an inordinate amount of property south of her border. I'd be pissed if she wasn't helping me along the way.

Wooded areas surrounded the sprawling ranch house on three sides, and I see the glint of a gun amongst the trees. If I hadn't been looking for it, it would have gone unnoticed. Putting my hands out the window, I show I'm unarmed—at least as far as they know—and open the door from the outer handle.

Opening the door from the outside of the car, I lift out of the low bucket seat. Keeping my hands up and slowly putting them behind my head, I fully turn in a circle, my heels sticking a bit in the mud, but manage to not fall on my face.

Upon facing the left side of the house, I hear a whistle, too perfect to be a bird call, and know I'm in the clear now that I've been identified as someone permitted to approach the house. I'm glad Claudette has the security measures set up the way I asked. The former escorts are used to guards at this point, but I wanted the place watched at all hours because it would be fucking tragic if someone swooped in and grabbed the girls as soon they got out.

I pull my phone from the dashboard, holding it up quickly to show the snipers that I didn't grab a weapon, and quickly text my group chat with the guys that I'm here safe. There's also a text from Romano that makes me laugh.

Romano: This girl is way too cheerful too early in the morning.

Me: She may be a body double, but no one could replicate my surly morning demeanor when your alarm rings.

Romano: I'd take your grumbling over her incessant talking any day, Queen.

Me: Fuck, don't call me that. I'll be back in a few hours.

Romano: Be careful, Wifey.

Me: That's worse, Romano. Way worse. Wanna get divorced?

Romano: Next week?

Me: Sounds good.

I know it'll take longer than a week, no matter how many palms we grease, but we'll get things started. It's as if our marriage is pulling at my skin. Yet another lie I'm living while telling my own guys that I love them. I know it doesn't bother them, but it bothers me, and that's enough to light a fire under my ass.

I slip the phone into the back pocket of my favorite black ripped jeans and tug the hem of my leather jacket down. What is it about getting out of low cars that fucks with your entire outfit?

I move around the trunk and call out, "I brought stuff, so I'm getting it out of the trunk. It's clothes and a few essentials, so if you need to come and check it, now is the time."

A man moves from the shadows of the tree line, and I look up at the big motherfucker.

"Queen," he greets.

Great. Word already made it up here.

"Hey, I've got outfits for the girls, new things, so they're not constantly recycling."

He motions for me to open the trunk, and after sifting through the bags stuffed in the back, he offers me a hand in bringing them up to the house.

He places them on the doorstep and takes a few steps back. When I look at him curiously, he blushes. "Claudette threatened to cut off our balls if we get anywhere close to the girls, and I plan on having kids someday."

I can't help it. A laugh slips out of my lips at the guard's words and cautious retreat to the treeline. Well done, Claudette, you tiny psychopath.

I ring the bell, and ninety seconds later, I hear six locks come undone and a security system beep from the other side of the door. I appreciate the level of security the girls have here, and I really hope they don't feel as trapped as they were before.

The door swings open, and before I fully register who's on the other side, I'm engulfed in a hug as blonde hair swings into my face.

"Hey, Sage," I rasp out. She caught me unaware, and there's no more breath in my lungs.

"Ivy! You're here!" Her squeal is loud enough to wake the house, and I quickly shush her, hoping for a bit of quiet so we can talk without too many interruptions at first. I'd like to officially meet the girls, but not yet. I need to be with my sister right now.

"I told you I'd come as soon as I could. Hey, help me with this, please. I brought goodies. We can dole them out later, but first, I want to talk." She hears the tone of my voice and pulls back from our embrace. Her eyebrow cocks, and she's looking at me with unease. It's nothing terrible, but I'd rather she be attentive and not focused on anything else.

We move the goods into the house and bring them into the living room. Everyone else must still be asleep. It is only eight o'clock, and in this quiet area, it must be easier to sleep later, away from the bustle of city noises.

She settles on the loveseat, and I drop next to her, letting out a sigh. Breathing has suddenly become more manageable now that I'm with her in person and she's safe. The security outside has a lot to do with that, and I make a mental note to throw some cash at Claudette to give them a bonus.

"So, what's going on?" Sage asks.

"It happened. I'm the leader of The Gambit now, and I've taken control. The guys and I are working to bring it down. I'm going to need your help with something." She eyes me warily, as if she doesn't think she'll be of any use. "The girls here, do they have places to go back to?" I ask.

"Some, yes. Some, I'm not sure. A lot of them have been quiet about where they're from since they showed up. I don't think anyone is missing them at home." Her eyes are mournful, and she sniffles once before straightening her shoulders. "What can I do?"

"I need information from them. Whether taken or sold, I need to know where to track down their people. If their families sold them, you can tell them I'll handle their relatives involved, if they wish."

She nods her head. "Yeah, I can do that. Hey," she interjects, changing the subject, "I got an A on my English paper!"

"That one about themes in early twentieth-century literature?" I ask excitedly.

"That's the one! I'm waiting to hear about my math exam, but it felt good when I finished." Her head ducks down, and she blushes.

"Hey, even if it's not perfect, that's totally fine. I'm proud of you for picking school back up. I think it's the right thing to do," I assure her.

She smiles, and I see the joy in her eyes at the praise. I want her to have a normal life, a college education, boyfriends or girlfriends—one at a time or multiple, whatever, it's not like I'm going to limit her on that—and whatever life she wants to build for herself.

When Han told me that Claudette was working with the local district to allow the girls to finish high school, I nearly wept. Claudette got her and a few others set up with online schooling to finish and get their GEDs. Sage is bright, and the woman who looked after her before she started working as an escort made sure she knew what she needed to. According to Claudette, Sage mentioned that the abrupt stop to her education bothered her, and every phone call we've had since she moved here has included little snippets of her excitement and love of learning new things. I don't think we realize how thirsty our minds are for knowledge until it's denied.

After a basic run-down of what happened last night, Sage and I sit back to talk about the safe house. The girls are all settled in; they've worked out a chore chart and schedule for cooking and cleaning. I included two smartphones in the haul I sent up here with Han and Sage. Both are untraceable to anyone other than us. We linked the phones to the computers at the clubhouse in case of any nefarious deeds. It's how I communicate with Sage and how the others can stay up to date on outside news.

They banded together, and after living through what they have, none of them have been stupid enough to risk contacting anyone. Jacob set up their phones to alert him if anyone attempted anything, but mostly, they've been just checking the news, watching TikTok videos, and catching up on what's been happening in the world since they joined the escort service.

I asked Claudette to teach the girls how to use the phones. Sage isn't the only one working on her education; a few of the others opted in as well. They have nightly study sessions together and are keeping each other accountable. It's like some twisted version of a survivor's sorority, and I'm grateful that Sage has people in her corner.

About an hour later, the house comes to life as the other girls in the house wake up and make their way to the kitchen and living room for coffee and conversation. I'm introduced to a few of them as Rogue or Ivy after warning Sage to keep my new role to herself. We sit around, sipping coffee and tea while munching on pastries from the pantry. There is a woeful lack of snarky mugs, which I need Lucas's help with for my next visit.

About an hour later, Claudette shows up and waltzes into the house like she owns the place. I mean, I guess she does, but still.

"Claudette!" half of the girls shriek in welcome. They pop up from around the couch and crowd her with hugs, the new clothing hanging over their shoulders as we distributed everything I brought.

Elenor has a hat, set jauntily atop her head, and the difference between how she acted when I got everyone out and now is like night and day. When I went to the kitchen to grab another cup of tea, she followed me in and told me that one girl, Brittany, was still having a hard time. Her physical injuries from the fucking guard I sliced open were long healed, but her emotional health was still suffering.

Claudette joins us in the living room, plopping down on the floor between Elenor and another girl named Mimi, settling in comfortably. She's dressed in cut-off shorts and an olive green tank top. Her red hair tied up in a bun on top of her head, instantly giving her four more inches with the mane's volume.

"Girls, did you know we're in the presence of royalty?" she asks cheekily.

They all whip their heads in my direction, and my face heats at the attention. It was easier to take as they joined us one by one, emerging from their rooms. But now, I feel like I'm on the spot.

"Nonsense. Just a woman with a vendetta," I assure them.

"Your secrets are safe with us," Elenor says. "You got us out. We owe you everything."

The girls surrounding us nod. "You owe me nothing. I'm just glad you're all okay."

Claudette makes a zip motion across her lips while the girls are all focused on me, and I give her the stink eye for outing me. I look at the girls, who all have genuine looks on their faces. Trusting anyone is going to take time, but all I see are eager faces. "Seriously, Ivy," Sage says. "If you need anything, we're here."

"That's good to know, but I'd really rather keep you all safe up here until I settle things. Even then, if you don't want to go home, I'll help you get set up in a new place. I just need your patience."

"We can do that," says Rachel, one of the quieter girls. "They're right. We owe you everything. If you need us to stay put in a safe space while you work on whatever you're doing, I think we can manage."

A chorus of agreement sounds out around the room, and I see pride sparkling in Sage's eyes. A tear comes to my own at the look in her gaze. I will do her proud in this and return these girls home if they were taken from their families or get vengeance for those who can't do it themselves.

Noah

Trouble has been Queen for a week, and after her appointment to the role, I reached out to Mara immediately to make sure she showed up at the meeting. I powered through the lobby of the Annex Security executive floor, blowing past the receptionists, and stomped down the hall to her office. I threw down a file folder, yelling the entire time about putting my team at risk on the last job because there was new intel they didn't update us about.

The upper right corner of the folder had my demand to meet scribbled faintly on the corner. I pointed it out with my gaze and watched Mara's eyes widen fractionally when she noticed it.

According to Rogue, Mara is the only person she knows of at the moment working with the feds and not in The Gambit's pockets. It's logical to use Mara as an option. If she approached someone on the payroll, they might try to cut her out and replace her for their own gain. The last thing we need is another enemy gunning for her.

Days later, Rogue and I sit back in the VIP box at the stadium, watching our local ice hockey team, The El Castillo Grizzlies, warm up before the game against the Arizona team.

Rogue is weirdly enthusiastic, listing stats and marveling at the speed the players exhibit on the ice. Who knew she was a fan?

"Oh, and look! There's Volkov! He was the lead scorer in our league last year. Weave, Volkov! Weave!" she shouts at the glass as if he can hear her through it.

He's only warming up. This might have been a bad idea for a meeting location if the warm-ups alone get her this distracted. Rogue is dancing around in her seat to the pregame music and snacking on a plate of nachos we grabbed earlier.

Mara's ticket is down at will call, and only an idiot wouldn't figure out that's where she's supposed to go. The teams emerge from the hallway for their introductions. My girl is standing, pressed against the glass, as her eyes flick from the ice to the jumbotron to see their stats. She reads them quietly to herself and shakes her head in disgust when the announcer introduces the other team. An El Castillo girl through and through.

As the ref drops the puck for the face-off, the door to the VIP suite swings open. Mara quickly closes the door behind her and looks around the room, letting out a sigh of relief.

"This spy shit is for the birds." My jaw drops at her tone. I've never heard her sound or look so casual. She's wearing jeans, an oversized hockey jersey, and a beanie in The Grizzlies' colors despite the heat outside. She's fully dressed as an overzealous fan, and I bite back a grin. I look at Rogue, who's in the same exact outfit.

The two women look each other up and down, and a grin overtakes Rogue's face. "Really?" she asks incredulously. "You have an O'Connor jersey?"

"What? He's..." She blushes. "Talented." I'm entirely sure she didn't mean talented. Ugh, this is going to take a while with two hockey fans, isn't it?

"Mara Hendrix, meet Ivy Montgomery." It's weird calling her that, but she insisted on using her real name for this meeting, so they started with honesty. Plus, roping in the FBI means she'll need her name clear on any legal paperwork.

Mara steps forward and extends a hand. "Hi, Ivy. Nice to meet you." My girl mimics the sentiment and gestures to the seat next to her, facing the glass.

"Keep your eyes on the game; we're just two superfans and our friend there"—she tilts her head in my direction as I keep my post at the door—"spent too much money to impress us."

Mara chuckles at that and nods in agreement.

"I'm working on taking down The Gambit from the inside."

Mara does the exact opposite of Rogue's instructions and turns to stare at Rogue. "What? How?" she asks, finally picking her jaw up off the floor.

"That's not the important part, Mara. I'm willing to work with the feds on this one, but I want to walk out of there and live my life afterward. There's access to enough testimony and witnesses to bury the entire organization. I'll help them get the worst of the worst, but my next appeal is to you." Mara waits. Her grip on her knees is nearly white-knuckle now. "Patton Cross," Rogue says.

"Woah. Look, I'm certain there will be some interest in taking down The Gambit. The person I'm working with would be a good fit for that, but Patton? You don't know what you're up against."

"Believe me, I most certainly do." I hear the severe tone in Rogue's voice and do my best not to leave my post to comfort her. Mara doesn't need to know how close we are. "I know he's responsible for all of those murders about twenty years ago. You can shed some light on how he ended up working for Annex. He's systematically taking out anyone who poses a threat to him and starting his own criminal organization to replace The Gambit. I will not take mine down only to hand the state over to that asshole."

"Well," Mara huffs, impressed. "You undoubtedly know what you're talking about. I'll reach out to my contact. Do you have a number he can reach you at?"

Rogue, prepared for everything, leans forward and pulls a slip of paper from her back pocket. "Burn that after you memorize it and pass it to your person. I expect an ironclad deal out of this, Mara. Tell your contact I've done my homework, and if he shows up with something less than ideal, I'll turn the organization in his direction."

Is it normal that my dick gets hard at her threat? Fuck, she's magnificent. I subtly shift my weight from foot to foot.

Rogue suddenly jumps up and cheers as the stadium erupts in cheers at the goal The Grizzlies just scored. Mara follows suit, cheering for the home team.

I see her slip the folded paper into her own pocket, and the two sit down again.

"How did Cross get involved with Annex? Break it down for me?" Rogue asks. "He was a plague on the streets, then suddenly he disappears for a few months and shows up in your firm."

"The former board swayed him to the company. He was vicious, and we were dealing with threats on clients by other gangs. Specifically, The Rattlesnakes up north and a New York chapter of the Bratva. We needed someone who could get in and out, clear the threats.

"They brought Cross on because of his efficiency. My father, one of the board members then, was against it, but they outvoted him. And now, he's got too much power for us to do anything. It's why when I noticed what was happening, I reached out to an old contact with the FBI. He brought me on board and we've been collecting evidence but so much of it is circumstantial. Cross is building his own empire. The last thing any of us need is that asshole leading an army. He'd paint the entire West Coast red."

A shudder runs through my body at the imagery.

"I won't give him the chance," Rogue assures Mara. "What about the rest of your family? Are they involved in this?"

Mara shakes her head. "I haven't seen my sister in nearly ten years. I don't even know where she is. My father passed away, and after that, my mother moved to Cape Cod. It's just me here, trying to single-handedly save my father's legacy and this company before Cross burns it all to the ground."

"Pass my number along to your contact soon, Mara. I am not a patient woman, and I've already got plans in motion," Rogue warns.

"I will. Shade will be in contact soon."

Mara leaves soon after the promise of a phone call, and Rogue and I settle in to watch the game. It's a thrilling match, made all the better by watching my girl scream at players like she can impact the game from here.

When the final buzzer sounds, Rogue is dancing in her seat, our team having beaten Arizona by two goals. I gather her to my chest and kiss her deeply, wanting a bit of her passion for my own.

I open the door to the suite to lead her out. I've got her for the rest of the afternoon, and I plan on spoiling her rotten. Rogue's hand is in mine and I'm nearly power walking down the long hallway, using my size to gently nudge people out of my way. Time is of the essence, people!

"Noah?" I hear from my right. Turning, I come face-to-face with Sheila.

Christ, it's been nearly a year since I've seen her. Her blonde hair is tied up in a messy bun, and she's wearing a sweatshirt. I look around, expecting to see her husband or Callie, their daughter, but she's alone.

"Hey, Sheila."

Rogue crashes into my back after I stop short and looks curiously at the woman trying to get closer to us. Her hand rests on my back, lending me support if needed. She knows all about Sheila, of course, but she remains quiet beside me. My rock.

"It's good to see you, Noah." Sheila tucks her hands into her pockets, looking me up and down before noticing Rogue beside me. "Hi," she says, sticking her hand out. "I'm Noah's ex. Nice to meet you..."

"Rogue," she fills in the blank.

"Wait, I know that voice. You're the one who yelled at me on the phone a few months back." She delivers her words with a laugh. "You were right. I was clinging to something that never would have worked in the long run. Thank you."

"You're welcome," Rogue says, visibly relaxing as her shoulders pull back and a smile lights her face.

I don't know what's happening here, but it's odd. "How are you? How's Callie?" I ask.

"Oh, I'm fine. Callie is doing well. Healthy, happy. William got a job in Michigan, so we're moving in a month. Things have actually been going well since Rogue here yelled at me to get my shit together. She was right. I was horrible. I've been working on it and have finally reached a good place."

I look down, and my girl is smiling. I'll never forget when she stole my phone while we were on a recon mission in San Francisco and yelled at my ex. No one has ever done something like that for me before.

I look back at the woman I once shared a life with. "That's really great, Sheila. I'm glad to hear it."

But she's not looking at me; she's looking at Rogue. "You seem good for him. I read energies, and yours match."

Ah yes, the energies thing. I put little stock in it, but my girl is beaming up at me. "Well, I certainly keep him on his toes. I mean, some days, it must be exhausting." Her words are for Sheila, but her eyes are locked on mine.

"You two seem great together. I have to run; I see my friend over there." She lifts a hand and waves at a brunette farther down the corridor before turning back to me. "Noah, it was really great seeing you. And I'm truly sorry for how I handled things after we split. Calling seemed like the wrong move after everything, but I'm grateful for the opportunity to tell you now. Rogue, I hope you don't think less of me after our chat last time. Or at the very least, I hope you can forgive me."

We both assure her all is good, and she takes off to catch up with her friend. Rogue stands on her tiptoes and kisses me gently.

"How do you feel?" she asks, knowing the damage Sheila inflicted all those years ago.

"Surprisingly okay, actually. I'm glad Sheila's doing well, and I wish her all the best," I tell her confidently. The words ring true, and a weight lifts from my shoulders. They're fine. Callie is okay and in what seems like a now-stable home.

Following the flow of the lingering crowd from the stadium, we emerge into the warm evening air, and I kiss my girl with everything I've got.

Chapter Eleven

Rogue

After my blissful—and slightly dramatic—afternoon with Noah yesterday, the high came crashing down just in time for King's funeral.

Instead of doing a speedy one, we opted to postpone it to plan a goodbye that would make King—or rather, his *will*—proud.

He was annoyingly specific about what he wanted for his final send-off. He was cremated, as per his wishes, thus keeping King's end a secret. I just had Rosa keep him on ice until I called Jonathan, King's lawyer handling the will, about the funeral details.

So, he was tucked in a freezer for a bit, then brought to a crematorium Rosa had on standby. The whole funeral was ridiculously over the top and entirely King's style. I had the lovely job of calling everyone to let them know the details. And while a few laughed on the other end, more than a hundred opted to come to the burial.

We stood outside in the sweltering mid-June heat at Saint Ignatius Church. *Why is it always this fucking church?*

His grave is next to my mother's, where the path once laid. They dug that up at King's behest to have him beside her. Because he was cremated, he doesn't even need a full plot, but his will dictated his ashes be put into a full-sized casket. Wasteful. I don't know who he bribed to make this arrangement happen regarding the footpath being rerouted, but my money is on Father Andrews. I don't trust the bastard. He knew about the vault downstairs, he married me to Romano, and now here we are... watching as he reads the eulogy from the well-worn tome before him.

Either I'm just paranoid about everything, or there aren't enough priests at this church.

The graveyard is full of people. Many of whom work for The Gambit. Others are openly gawking at me in my black lace Dior dress as the organization's new head. Fuck, I'd be doing the same—checking out the newbie. You can pick up so much by someone's body language, which is why I'm standing stock still, my arm threaded through Romano's and my oversized sunglasses covering half of my face.

They see a silent, proud woman, holding her own as others take in their first free breath in years. Me? I know my constraints have only tightened since taking this role. I have to act the part in public, so here I am. Acting my ass off.

I've shed many tears over King's death since it happened. Was I ready for him to die? Absolutely. Do I still feel guilt? Definitely. I know I probably will for a while, but the fact that he was ready to end his own life eases some of that. Whether I did it myself, when he was sick or healthy, I don't think I'd ever have been able to do it without a weight settling over my heart afterward. It's just not who I am.

The sermon goes on, and I toss the first handful of dirt over the coffin, along with a red rose that I brought for the occasion. It's a flower I knew none of my guys would ever give me, so I'd rather that flower than another. The last thing I want is Han or Jacob giving me a flower that reminds me of King.

I gather Romano's arm up once again, and we stand toward the back so others can follow our lead. The procession begins, and after each person adds some earth to the coffin, which only contains his urn, they turn to me. I've shaken hands with nearly everyone in attendance and kept my post by the old oak tree until every single person has paid their respects to King and welcomed me as the new leader.

Romano, to his credit, stands by my side, accepting condolences and congratulations. I think I block most of the afternoon out because when I truly focus on my surroundings again, we're at the hotel bar across the street where I'm sitting between Romano and Elise. They're both slinging back shots of whiskey like it's the last bottle in existence and there's a prize at the bottom.

"Rise and shine, honey cakes!"

What the ever-loving fuck is that? I bolt upright in a room that is definitely not mine, and my head pounds with regret at the sudden motion.

"What the what?!" I shout back at the intruder. I slip my hand under the pillow and pull a knife out. Good to see I haven't lost my self-preservation instincts.

I hear a groan next to me and look down. Looking up won't happen until my eyes adjust to the light. Romano is holding a gun steady at our intruder, obviously having hidden one within reach before going to sleep as well. His eyes are half-open, but he clicked the safety off and has it pointed toward the human-shaped blur in front of us.

"Put that away, boy, or I'll take it from you and beat you with it." The voice is recognizable, and I place a hand on Romano's steady arms until he drops them.

"Morning, Elise," I grumble.

"Elise? What the fuck happened last night?" Romano asks.

I smack him on the back of the head and mouth, *Language.*

I'm proven right when Elise steps closer to the bed, dressed in dark brown leggings and an oversized, but incredibly soft-looking, long sleeve t-shirt, and pinches his thigh. Elegance in violence. I can get behind that.

"Watch your mouth, or I'll pinch higher." She turns and opens the curtains, effectively blinding us both. "You two can't handle your whiskey. You crashed here after the bar. I couldn't let our new boss die of alcohol poisoning. Now get up; breakfast is in fifteen minutes."

With that, she turns on her bunny-slippered heel and leaves the room. Romano and I take a moment to process the words she spoke, and I flop back down onto the pillow, keeping the knife out of range.

"Fuuuck, my head," he groans.

"Ditto."

"We should get up," he insists.

"But it's comfy. What are these? Like thousand thread count sheets? You go, I'll die here." I spread my arms and legs, making snow angel motions on the luxury linens.

"Stop being melodramatic, Rogue. Think of the coffee Elise must serve in this place. It might be worth it. Plus, you said you were going to plan the party with her today. There's no getting out of it now since you're already here." His smug tone is enough for me to draw my last vestiges of strength, and I flip over the blanket, following it until I'm straddling my husband, knife to his throat.

"Melodramatic?" I ask, my tone icy.

"Just a smidge, Wifey. You going to kill me? It'll be a hell of a lot of paperwork and cover-up if you do," he taunts.

I think about it for a moment, and his eyes widen. I laugh, and he finally exhales. "You're right. Let's go. Caffeine first, then I need to help plan the party of the century."

"I can stay for the planning if you want some help. Plus, there are a few things we should talk about. But we don't exactly have time before breakfast." Romano's statement makes me squint at him with ire. People can discuss anything if they'd just stop tip-toeing over topics and get to the point. I had this same rant in the car the other day, so he knows what I'm thinking. He sighs before dropping his hand over his face, blocking out his nose and eyes. "I have someone who wants you to call them."

"Well, that's not ominous or anything," I deadpan.

"Just. Hold on." He flips me back onto my side of the bed and rummages around on the floor next to the bed, pulling up his pants and sifting through the pockets until he finds his phone. I watch him dial a number I'm unfamiliar with, and he rolls his eyes as he says, "Damiano." Then a moment later, "Where are my guns?" He could be speaking with one of his underlings and wants me to put them in line with my scary voice. But why do this when we're both nursing a massive hangover?

"I have someone here who you should speak with," he says before handing the phone over to me.

I put it up to my ear as I stare down at the man next to me. I wait. No way in hell am I speaking first.

"Rogue? Or should I call you Queen now, Your Majesty?" comes a raspy, deep voice on the other end.

"Who is this?" I counter.

Romano just sighs next to me. "Rogue, meet Shade. Shade, Rogue." His voice is loud enough to carry over the phone. Shade? Aw, hell. That's who Mara mentioned at the hockey game, isn't it?

The implications that Romano and Shade know each other smack me in the face. I turn to him, not an ounce of kindness in my face when I cover the bottom of the phone and whisper-shout, "You work with the feds?!"

Romano lifts his hand, and his fingers are a hairsbreadth apart. "Little bit." He has the excellent sense to look sheepish at the big reveal. "I needed you to reach out first."

"You know I can hear you both, right?" Shade says through the phone. I groan.

"So, you're the contact with the feds. What department?" I ask.

"Little of this, little of that. Call it a task force set up to take on The Gambit with a few from all the major acronyms." Well, shit. CIA, FBI, NSA, ATF, DEA, good God, the list goes on and on with possibilities.

"I assume Mara Hendrix reached out? You really should make sure she doesn't name-drop you to anyone else," I chastise.

"But, Rogue, darling, I had to get your attention somehow. No, really, only those two call me Shade. It's safe enough." His laugh is soft, although he sounds like he smokes a pack a day.

"Alright, we've met, and Romano and I have breakfast in five minutes. Let's get down to brass tacks. I want an ironclad deal that I'm out of this if I hand over everything. *And* I want Romano in on the plan, whatever it is. He may be a sneaky son of a bitch, but he's blood in at this point." Romano's eyes widen at my statement, and I realize he may not have given all the details of King's death to his colleagues, so I amend my statement. "Husband and all of that, you know."

Smooth, Rogue.

"I ran it up the flagpole when Ms. Hendrix said you'd reached out. We're willing to cut a deal for your help, leaving you untouched, but that's it. We will prosecute everyone else within The Gambit *if* your evidence is good enough. I cannot cut a deal for other Gambit members to remain free."

"Deal. Have it to my office in the next day or two, and we can get this show on the road. Oh, one other thing." I pause for effect because it's fun. Him taking the possibility of G and Fabio off the table for immunity puts a wrench in things, but I think I can swing it just fine. "Do you also want Patton Cross?"

Romano's eyes, which finally shrunk down to their normal size after my almost-slip about killing King, fly open at my question. "The fuck?" he mouths silently.

"I want immunity for myself and four others—not involved in The Gambit, to be clear—and we'll give you a nice present at the end." My negotiation skills are on point today, and my back straightens with pride at my own steady voice.

"I don't see why not, so long as they're not Gambit members. The paperwork will arrive in twenty-four hours. I'll need names for the others," Shade murmurs down the line as the keyboard clicking continues.

"No. No names. I don't want *anyone* to know who they are until they finish their roles. Do you know how many people in your organization now answer to me and would love nothing more than to replace me when they catch wind I'm trying to bring this shit down? Who knows how many Patton has on his payroll? I'm not taking that risk. The powers that be can know my full name. Very few would connect that girl to who I am now."

"That's going to be a harder sell," he says regretfully.

"I know, but I have a feeling if you can get Mara involved and keep Romano alive, you're the guy to work on this. Can you do it?" My patience is running thin, and I really want to get moving on plans, not to mention breakfast.

He clicks away on his keyboard through the conversation. "What are you doing? Typing this out?" I ask incredulously.

"No, I'm running the risk assessment of adding another element to this. Hold on." Time ticks away as he works his numbers. He and Jacob would probably get along well.

"Yeah, okay. I'll keep the names out of it. I'll get you immunity for your four accomplices, but I expect Cross at the end of this, or the deal is off. Many people are going to bite the bullet with this, my bosses likely included, if your information is up to date. Bringing in Cross and toppling The Gambit would create a power vacuum in the state. We'll work on what to do next on my end. Have Romano give you my number, and you call if you need anything." His voice drops an octave. "Oh, and Rogue, trust Romano. He's a good guy."

"Yeah," I admit. "I'm starting to see that." I look at Romano and see his eyes shining with authenticity. Despite only having heard my side of the conversation, he seems glad of the way it's going.

"Later, Shade!" I merrily sing-song then hang up.

"Well?" Romano asks.

"Well, we've got a breakfast to eat and a party to plan. Let's get to it." I clap my hands together and race off for the bathroom.

"I'm sorry, you want to do what?!" Elise shrieks over her croissant.

"I want to change the party to a masquerade. I want the heads of the western US gangs in attendance, and the guest list to include anyone and everyone high on the food chain, whether it be politics or law enforcement.

Oh, and I want them to know it's non-negotiable." I take a sip of my coffee and a bite of my snickerdoodle.

God, these are good.

"You... The entire party... It was *planned!*" Elise argues.

"Look, Elise. You want out? This is my condition. I can handle it myself, but I know what you'd say. You'd say you could have done a better job of it. And I don't want to hear those words in two months. Nor do I think you want to say them." I level my gaze at her and see Romano take a bite of his pastry and lean back in his chair, refusing to get involved.

Life isn't that kind, though. "Romano! Pay attention. Talk your wife out of this," Elise reprimands him.

"Not a chance. She wears the pants. Err, well, today it's a dress. But you know what I mean. This is happening. You might as well get on board now."

I look down, noting I need a change of clothes for the rest of the day. I'm still in my funeral dress. Gross. It may be Dior, but after the funeral and the bar? Blech.

I nod my head gratefully at Romano and am rewarded with a danish-filled toothy smile. Also gross.

"I am more than willing to help, Elise. You just tell me what to do." My assurances do not look well received.

"It's fine. It's fine." She throws her hands up in the air. "Can I keep the venue?"

I look at Romano. He nods his head after checking his phone discreetly under the table.

"Yes, that hotel is fine. But block out both ballrooms. I want nothing else happening in the hotel then. In fact, buy out all the rooms. We'll pay to move people to another place. I want the hotel empty aside from our party. Attendees can have rooms in the hotel, but no civilians." She rolls her eyes at me, muttering about how I'm going to create a deficit my first few days as Queen.

"That's fine. I'll help bankroll it if needed." She eyes me skeptically, but what she doesn't know is that I saved money from every one of those hits I did, on top of my salary from Rook Industries. I live simply, my only indulgence being my car and my vintage wardrobe. I saved up everything else for Sage and me. Even after paying Tanaka's family handsomely in a poor attempt to assuage my guilt, I've got more than I know what to do with. I know the guys would look after Sage if anything were to happen to me.

"No, the coffers should be fine. I'll speak with Nina and get it squared." She side-eyes Romano as if she's hesitant to say the next bit in front of him.

"He's fine. Speak freely, please, Elise. When have you ever held back?" She chuckles at my words and sips her tea.

"You're right. My tithe." Oh, that's right. According to The Gambit's bylaws, she has to tithe or die to get out. Most people don't get to choose.

"The work you're doing is more than enough, Elise. When it's over, just go. In fact, I insist." I'd rather she not get caught up by the feds if given a choice. She's a hardass, but she'd never miss this party. I'll think of a way to detain her before the night's festivities.

"No offense, dear, but if you die, I don't want the next sap coming after me because you thought a party was sufficient." Her brow lifts, and she looks at Romano as if he'll be the next sap in question.

"That won't happen, Elise." Romano's voice is calm but firm.

"I'm not taking that chance. Listen, kids, I've got more money than half the people in this state combined. I don't mind letting a bit of it go. It's not like I can take it with me. I want to travel before I'm six feet under, and the only traveling I can do is through walls to scare the shit out of people." I stifle a laugh at her imagery.

"Okay...so what do you propose?" I ask.

"My house."

Time stops. "Which house?" I ask as I squint my eyes. I know she's got quite a few, and to dangle this carrot in front of me is just cruel if she means the log cabin she's got up in Canada when she knows I hate snow.

"This house." Her pinky finger is up in the air as she sips, and I desperately want to grab it and bend it back to threaten her if she's messing with me.

"You want The Gambit to have your house?" I ask to clarify.

"Not The Gambit, dear. You. I know those bylaws forward and backward. The tithe needs to be made to the ruling individual, not the organization. My first husband helped draft those when the times were changing, and we didn't barter in stocks and bonds like the earlier board members."

I can't help myself. I look around the opulent dining room, the antique furniture, and try to imagine myself living here. It's too big for just one person, but maybe if this all blows over, we can all live together? There's enough space for me and the guys. We'd need to update a few things, but holy hell in a handbasket. This could be *incredible*.

"You've got yourself a deal, Elise."

Romano chooses that moment to lean forward and cut in, "I want you to know, Elise, I would never come after you if I end up in Rogue's position one day."

"Her name is 'Queen' now, Romano. Might as well get used to it. I don't think The Gambit has or ever will see another woman quite like her leading the way. Even King's mentor, Jaqueline, while fierce, was crushed under the boot of the men surrounding her. This"—she nods at me—"is a woman to bring this organization to its knees as she keeps it in line."

I'm instantly reminded of King's explanation for his shitty parenting, molding me into a woman to lead The Gambit, and as much as it pains me to admit it, they're both right. I can do this. It may be messy, but I'm going to end this.

Chapter Twelve

Han

"I wish we could have stayed at the fancy-ass Hilton across town," Lucas gripes.

"Yeah, well, we're supposed to stay under the radar. You know this is how these things go." Noah's reassurance falls on deaf ears as Lucas lifts the bedspread and examines the sheets, looking for mysterious stains, most likely.

"Look, Lucas, I know you're twitchy being away from Rogue right now, but it's only for a few days. She told us to go ahead. We left Jacob behind just in case she needs backup, but it sounds like she's getting things figured out." I keep my voice calm as I lay it out for him the way Jacob did via text when I expressed my same concerns.

"I know, I know. I just don't like it." His little tirade continues as we examine our little suite at this three-star hotel. It's got two bedrooms and a pull-out couch, so we'll all be able to spread out comfortably. The kitchenette is dated but relatively clean. He puts Sir Lancelot's little travel cage on top of the Formica table and leans down. "Hey, little guy. I'll get your hamster ball from my bag, and you can explore. I don't want you finding a hole in the wall and disappearing on me," he says in a sing-song voice as if he's talking to a baby instead of a pet that doesn't understand him.

He's cute, I'll give him that, but Noah was right. Watching out for an animal while on a mission is going to be an interesting experience. Lucas refused to leave him with Jacob, stating, I kid you not, "He needs his mama." Sir Lancelot has gotten bolder as the weeks have passed. He often ventures out of Lucas's room, and I always find him up on the kitchen counters. Good thing Noah hasn't seen that yet; he'd flip his lid.

I send a text to Jacob, letting him know we're settled into the hotel.

Me: Hey, we're here and checked in.

Jacob: Good, good. Check the fridge. There should be something in there for you guys. If not, I get to call the lovely front desk asshole again to fix it.

I walk over to the fridge, curious as hell what he planned for us, and inside I find a selection of beers, three sushi plates from a chain restaurant, a container of fried bananas in a vanilla sauce, and when I pull the freezer open, there's deep-fried ice cream. Dammit, he's awesome.

Me: You mean this feast you've had delivered for us?

I snap a picture and send it.

Jacob: Yep, that's the one. Enjoy guys. I've got Noah's leftovers, so I figured you guys could use some good food, too.

Me: You're the best.

Jacob: Love you, Han.

Me: Love you, too.

I try to quell my pitter-pattering heart as I pull the sushi trays from the fridge and settle them on the tiny kitchen table.

"What's this?" Lucas asks as I go back for the beers.

"Jacob is taking care of us, even from up north."

Lucas looks at me and raises a brow. "You've got a little something," he trails off as he wipes a thumb on my cheek. "Oops, my mistake, it's just some extra *looove* seeping from your pores," he teases.

I duck my head and fight the heat rising to my cheeks. "My pores are perfect. You're just jealous."

Noah walks around the table and smacks Lucas's head. "Leave him alone."

Lucas rubs the now-sore spot behind his ear. "Fine. It's cute, that's all. I didn't mean anything by it. And yeah, I really am jealous." He palms his own cheek in sympathy.

"I know, Lucas. I know," I assure him as he examines my face to see if he offended me with his teasing. "All good, I promise."

We dig into the food, appreciating that Jacob got each of us our favorites, and make purely sexual sounds when met with the fried bananas and ice cream.

God damn, that man is incredible.

I can't sleep. I roll to the side and check out the alarm clock on the bedside table. It's two-fifteen in the morning, and my mind does not want to be rested for tomorrow's job, it seems. I pull my phone off the charger and open my texts.

Me: I can't sleep.
Jacob: Neither can I.

Taking a chance, I text our girl.

Me: Hey, what are the chances of you being awake right now?
Ivy: 100%. This place has shitty curtains, and the full moon is too bright. I'm halfway tempted to tie socks around my head to block it out.
Me: Take pictures if you do. Or…
Ivy: Or?
Me: Are you alone?
Ivy: Yes.

I quickly exit the messages and pull up the video chat app on my phone. I click Jacob's name and find him lying in bed, his hair deliciously rumpled and a tired look on his face. "Why are you still up?" I ask him.

"Couldn't sleep. I got off the computer an hour ago, I promise. What about you?"

"Not sure, but I have an idea to help us all get to bed." His eyebrow hitches at my words, and he catches my meaning.

"Wait, all?" he asks, obviously confused about what's going on and thinks I mean one of the other guys in the hotel with me.

"Ivy. She's up, too." He nods his head in agreement, and I click to add her to our group call.

"Hello, boys," she says. I look at our girl, her hair fanned out around her. The absolute picture of sin. Her eyes are hooded, and I see her bare shoulder moving on the side of the frame.

"What are you doing, Ivy?" I ask, dropping my voice an octave or two. Just the sight of these two on my screen has me ready to go. I wish they were here.

"Who, me?"

"Yes, you." Jacob's tone leaves no doubt who's in charge. I may have started the call, but he's the one directing us.

Ivy lifts her fingers to her lips, and they glisten in the moonlight. Holy fuck.

Jacob's breathing comes harder as we watch her curl her tongue around her first two fingers before sliding them down her chin to her throat. The camera follows their progression, turning upside down. I spin my phone so I can watch it right side up, and Jacob's face suddenly flips on the screen, and I know he's doing the same thing. Great minds.

Her fingers inch their way down her body, stopping to pluck at a nipple on their way down.

"Fuck," Jacob expels harshly. "Darling Mine, don't tempt me. I will drive to your place right the fuck now."

"But you don't know where I am."

The statement catches me off guard for a moment because, honestly, how many places could she be? But she's safe, and that's what matters.

"I'll figure it out," he assures her before directing his attention to me. "Han, are you naked?"

I quickly shuck my boxers and kick the comforter to the floor. "Yes," I breathe as I try to keep my composure, watching the slide of Ivy's fingers along her tattooed line of division as they disappear below her mound.

"Oh, fuck." Jacob's voice is pure sin as he watches the scene unfold with me.

"Darling Mine, where are you?" he asks.

"I'm not telling you that. But I can tell you I'm wet, I'm horny, and I want you both so badly." Her words end in a moan, and I see her fingers pump in and out of her.

"Do you have any toys with you?" I ask.

"Maybe." There's a rustling sound as her hand withdraws and disappears from the screen. She tilts the screen so we can see her flushed face. Her cheeks are red, her eyes hooded impossibly low. She flips the camera angle, and she's in a space I've never seen before. Is this where she and Romano live? No, it doesn't look like the rooms I've seen on video chat in her and Romano's place and King's penthouse. The sheets are pure white, and the comforter pools around the side of her body. There, lying on top of the bedding, is an array of toys. Butt plugs, lube, dildos, clit suckers. Fuck, this girl has an arsenal. My curiosity about her location takes a back seat when I see the display of toys next to her.

"Holy shit," Jacob and I breathe at the same time. Thankfully, no one jinxes anyone, and Jacob clears his throat.

"On your hands and knees," Jacob orders. Ivy sets up her camera against what I assume to be the headboard and has the camera facing her. I see her face and the top of her ass as it's propped up, her knees under her. "Good girl," Jacob coos. "I want you to put in the plug, then wait for instruction." Ivy grabs the pink plug, coats it with lube, and works it into her tight hole.

Jacob lets out a sigh at the sight of her following his commands, and I bite back the groan inching its way up my throat. "Han," he barks. I know he's losing his cool, but if there was ever a reason, this is it. "Put the phone on a table or something. I want to see you, too." Ivy's moan is sinful as I prop the phone on the bedside table sideways so my body fits into the frame. "Well done," Jacob praises.

His phone follows suit, and as Ivy stares into the camera, Jacob and I have our heads tilted to the side to watch the show we're all co-starring in.

"Rogue, use the purple one," Jacob says. "Han, no touching until I say. That cock is mine." A shudder wracks its way through my body at his possessive words, and my hips involuntarily thrust upward at his orders. Fuck, I want his hands on me, and I want my dick in Ivy so fucking bad. A whisper of sound escapes my lips, and Jacob gives me a wink. He knows how torturous this will be, but I have faith he'll get me there in the end.

Ivy grabs the selected toy and slides her hand under her body. I know now why Jacob wanted the camera focused on her face. When she positions it, a look of serenity crosses her face, and her eyes slam shut as she pushes the dildo inside. God, is there anything better than watching our girl come? If there is, I haven't found it yet. "Slowly, Darling Mine. Whose cock are you imagining in your pussy? Whose is in your ass?" Jacob's voice is serene, but there's an undercurrent of tension running through it. He's as affected as I am; the only difference is that he's touching himself to the sight of Ivy while my hands lie uselessly at my sides. My ass clenches with each stroke of his cock and movement of Ivy's arm as she works the dildo. I've never been jealous of a piece of purple silicone before, but I guess there's a first time for everything.

"God," Ivy groans at the dirty talk coming from Jacob. "Han is in my pussy, pulling out far enough to alternate between driving into me and bumping my clit with every other thrust." Our girl's eyes screw shut as she tells us what she's imagining in her mind while we wait with bated breath.

"Jacob, you're in my ass, your fucking piercings teasing me. Fuck, I want it. I want it so badly."

Jacob's growl sounds over the line, and I watch as his hand moves faster along his length until his hips are shifting up with each downstroke. He trains his eyes on the phone, and I curl my hands into the surrounding bedspread, fighting the urge to touch my cock as this plays out. Between Jacob's words and Ivy's imagination, I'm having a hard time restraining myself. Jacob must see it over the phone. "Rogue, open your eyes. Look at our man. He's shaking with need, and he's not allowed to touch himself. Do you think you can make him come with just your words?"

Ivy's eyes crack open as her arm continues working the toy. "Oh, yes," she breathes. A wicked smile overtakes her face. "Han, does that feel good?" she asks. "Every time you pound into my pussy and Jacob pushes into my ass, you feel his cock through my walls. His piercings tease you as much as they do me. Just when you think it couldn't get any better, you feel his hand leave my hip and find your balls. He cups them firmly, tugging a bit, just the way you like it. You're on the brink, Han. You just need a little push." Her words pick up speed as her hand does the same, moving the toy in and out of her. Jacob groans, and his fist works his cock faster and faster. His breathing comes in pants now as he listens, enraptured by her scene.

"My pussy starts fluttering around you. You know I'm close. Picking up the pace, you wedge your hand between us so your thumb can circle my clit. You plant your heels into the mattress for better leverage, and that's when Jacob's hand drifts lower, leaving your balls and venturing to your ass." My ass clenches in phantom anticipation as my heels dig into the mattress, mimicking the positioning she describes. I spread my knees, the night air washing over my heated skin. My fists are curled, white-knuckling the surrounding sheets. My hips drive up. Up into an Ivy that isn't here, but her words make me wish it so.

"Just then, when you think you can't take anymore, Jacob slips his fingers inside me, stretching me as you impale me on your cock. I clamp down around you as Jacob drives his hard, pierced, monster cock into my ass, stroking your dick with his. My mouth drops to your nipple and bites." Ivy screams her release, and Jacob's groan echoes the sentiment. I keep my hands fisted at my sides as my hips drive up into nothing, my ass clenched, imagining Jacob's cock against mine with our girl between us. With nothing more than the cool breeze of the air conditioner in my room, I come on a roar at their words, their pleasure. Spilling across my abdomen, I gasp for air. Fuck, I've never experienced anything like that. It's as if losing touch opened my mind to imagine the scenario Ivy described.

I roll my head to the side and see the same contented smile shared on all three of our faces across the screen.

Ivy grabs the phone and flops into the bed after removing the toys. "I love you both," she says with a sleepy yawn. "Think you'll be able to sleep now?"

"Oh, yes, Darling Mine. And we're definitely doing that when you're both home where you belong."

We nod our agreement, and after our whispered words of goodnight, I pull a towel around me from the closet and leave my room to use the bathroom just off the living room.

I crack the door open, hopeful I haven't woken up Noah, who opted to take the couch so Lucas could have the other room for him and Sir Lancelot. So imagine my surprise when I find Noah awake and at the kitchen table, peering into Sir Lancelot's travel cage. He must have swooped it from Lucas's room.

"Listen, you," he says to the hamster. "We're going to need to make this work. Trouble likes you, so you're sticking around. Let's make a deal. You don't poop on everything, and we'll call a truce." Sir Lancelot squeaks at Noah's voice and does a circle in his cage. "You're not so bad. But let's maintain some distance for the time being, huh?"

Noah presses a fingertip to the cage, and I swear the hedgehog does the same, giving him a high-five prison-style.

I leave my room when Noah leans back in his chair and stops talking to the animal as if he's going to respond. I wave him off when he asks if everything is okay and smother the smile threatening to break out across my face. If our girl knew the lengths Noah would go to just to see her smile, she'd fall in love with him all over again.

For a security team, these guys were woefully underprepared for an ambush. We finally made it to the Bakersfield job. After nearly a month and a half of surveillance, recon missions, and invading their tech, we could finally make a move.

Muffled sounds escape their leader through the gag. "Look, Nicolas, we're not here to kill you, but we needed it to look like we were just in case anyone was watching," Lucas explains. More grumbles. "Would you stop talking for a second? It's rude to interrupt."

Noah rolls his eyes, the only part of him visible beneath the ski mask. "Someone hired us to take you out. It's up to you if that happens. Or you can go hide out for a few months in another country. Your call." The men settle as they look up at our leader.

We've got them trussed up and gagged, sitting in a local bar that won't open until this afternoon. Not too many drinkers at eight in the morning, and this is definitely not the place to have brunch and mimosas. The floors are dirty, the wood paneling on the walls needs updating, and the only light emanates from the neon beer brand signs hanging at uneven intervals. A dive bar is too tame a name.

"Listen," I butt in because if no one explains it quickly enough, we'll all be here for hours. "We're here to get you out. Someone is gunning for you, and I doubt you want to be involved. So, what we're going to do is get you packed up, make it look like you've 'disappeared,' and when all of this blows over, you can come back." One guy speaks behind his gag again, making no sense. "You cannot bring your families; you can't contact them either. For all intents and purposes, you need to look like you're dead. We've got someone else handling the news reports, but it will be safest for your loved ones if they grieve you and appear to think you're dead. I know it's not ideal, but would you rather our bosses send us after them?"

They shake their heads when I finish my explanation. Noah moves forward and releases the gag in Nicolas's mouth. "Who sent you? I swear to God, I'll come back from wherever you send us and end the motherfucker." Well, he's pleasant.

"Does the name Patton Cross ring any bells?" Lucas asks. No tact, that man, I swear.

The team and Nicolas all widen their eyes, and jaws drop open at the name. "Look, we're not working for him exactly, but his orders came to us. We're offering a way out. Take it," Noah insists.

"Yep, we'll do that. Fuck, Annex is after us?" Nicolas asks.

"Not sure if it's something you've done in particular, but he seems to eliminate security teams left and right to establish his own foothold. We're not exactly sure of the endgame, but the information they gave us on you is that you're threatening one of Annex's clients." Confusion flits across Nicolas's face. "Yeah, I thought so. Anyway, only the five of you were on the list, so we'll ship you guys off and get word to you when it's safe to come back."

"Yeah, we understand that." Of course, they do. They're in security as well. They know that even a phone call to a girlfriend or wife could change their attitude, so they no longer look like they're grieving their loved one. Cross seems to have eyes all over the state and connections we can't possibly uncover all at once, so everyone has to play their part.

"Good," Lucas cheers as he claps his hands together. "We've got you booked on a private plane headed to Costa Rica in a few hours. You'll be staying with a friend of ours there, so we'll let you know when you can come home. We've got to wait until a certain pilot lands, but as soon as he's on terra firma, we'll drop you off. Anyone want a beer while we wait?"

The men nod, and we untie the gags to make proper introductions. Well, kind of proper. We're using fake names while keeping our masks on, just in case. If they're found by one of Cross's contacts at some point, he'll be able to see who did the mission on the servers, and we'd be fucked either way, but at least it's a small measure of comfort we can cling to.

The men all look around the seedy bar, and as we have a few hours to kill, I hop over the bar top to get us all beers. We're waiting here until the last possible moment to get them to the airfield, so why not?

Nicolas is forthcoming with every scrap of information on Cross he's heard over the past decade. Most of it is rumors we've all heard before about the sandman that used to haunt the streets of El Castillo, but some of it is new. Apparently, the big massacre in Southern California is rumored to be Cross's work. Well, his and whoever his second was back then. Nowadays, we haven't got a clue who that could be or if he even has a right-hand man. He must, right? Is it the same person from back then?

We talk theories, and as time slips by, we get things put back to rights before the owner of this place comes in to open for tonight's crowd. I slip out the back of the bar and get the rental SUV as close to the door as possible, and everyone piles in. We get the men onto the private plane with forged passports Jacob cooked up and send them on their way with a promise to contact their host when it's safe.

The three of us look at each other, still clad in our ski masks, and burst out laughing. "Well, I have to say, that might have been the smoothest extraction we've ever done." My phone rings in my pocket, and I pull it out to see it's Jacob on the line. "Hey, what's up?"

"Uh... I think you guys need to get home. Like now." There's confusion in his tone, and it has me turning the wheel and hauling ass out of the private parking lot.

"What's happening?" I ask.

"Someone's trying to get into the clubhouse. And by someone, I mean approximately fifty armed men."

Chapter Thirteen

Rogue

I'M IN THE MIDDLE OF SHADOWING BYRNE WHEN MY PHONE RINGS. I hold up my hand to stop his explanation of the drug pipeline he's been using and pull my phone from my bra. Not the most dignified move, I know, but why fix what isn't broken?

I see it's Jacob calling, so I rise from my seat in Byrne's office and step into the hall as I answer.

"What's up?" I ask, my voice playful because, after last night, I want more.

"I need a pickup." Jacob's voice is quiet as he whispers down the line. He's not panicking, but he's certainly not thinking about sexy times, either.

"Fuck, okay. Where and when?" I ask, slipping into work mode.

"As soon as possible, Love. The alleyway behind the bakery is a block over. The one that sells the croissants Noah can't quite figure out the recipe for."

"I know it. I'll be there as soon as possible. It might be about twenty minutes. Are you safe?" I ask.

"For the moment, yes. I'll hide behind the dumpster there if I get there before you do." With that, he hangs up the phone, and I leave without a word to Byrne.

I parked Black Beauty under the streetlight in the parking lot when I arrived, so it's easy to find her as I come barreling out of the building and into the open area. I slide into the car, my hands damn near fumbling with the keys as I put them in the ignition. Getting the car started, I peel out of the lot, desperate to get to Jacob. I don't know what the fuck is going on, but they've never called me for a pickup before. I know the others are away on a job, and he stayed behind to handle the tech side and be here for me if I needed him. Not that anyone would admit to that, but they're all a little wary of leaving me behind. I appreciate it, but now, it's unnecessary. I've got my team that I've trained at my back.

If only the guys could see the meeting I had with the other hitmen and security team, they'd know I was okay. The respect in their eyes proves I was right. I do not need to lead with fear or leverage the way King did.

I fly through the streets of El Castillo, barely stopping at red lights and barreling through stop signs on my way to Jacob. Every scenario under the sun runs through my head at what could be happening. Damn him for not giving me a heads-up.

I reach the mouth of the alley and carefully maneuver my boat of a car through the narrow passageway. The last thing I need if this is an attack is to make too much noise or leave paint chips somewhere. Fucking evidence.

I roll to a stop, my foot gently easing onto the brake just behind where I assume the bakery is. It's hard to tell from the backside, and the names printed on the doors back here are so faded, I'd be surprised if anyone could read them even in broad daylight.

I turn off my headlights and wait. I palm a gun in one hand and a knife in the other. Jacob would never lead me into a trap, willingly or otherwise, so it's more for backup if he needs me.

In the moonlight, I see something move ahead of me. I refocus my eyes, seeing nothing until it happens again. The utility hole cover slowly lifts until there's an inch between it and the ground. I lean out the window of my car, one shoulder resting on the dirty brick wall next to me to steady myself in an unnatural position as I watch it slide onto the asphalt.

I keep my gun trained on the target because while it could be Jacob, it's hard to see the tattoos clearly despite the moonlight.

Hands come up from the depths, anchoring on either side of the hole, and muscular arms and shoulders follow when Jacob hoists himself out. He swings his hips and ends up sitting with his legs dangling in the opening. He looks up and makes eye contact with me. "Hey, Love. We should get out of here." He reaches back down into the hole, grabs a duffel, and quickly stands to hide the evidence of his escape. Cover back in place, he strides to the car while I check both ends of the alley, ensuring we're alone.

There's an alcove just on the right where Jacob waits, and I pull the car forward. There's no way to open the doors here, but when I pull up to his position, he grips the roof of the car and swings his legs in. He slides through the open window and lands on the seat with an "Oomph." He leans over, drops a kiss on my cheek, and places a palm on my thigh as I hit the gas.

"What's going on?" I ask, my voice betraying none of the nerves I currently feel racing through my body. I swing the steering wheel to the right to make our way back to my side of town.

"The clubhouse is being breached as we speak. I've got surveillance up and running, so we can watch live if you find somewhere to pull over."

I am desperate to see what's happening, so I swerve the car into an empty parking lot, grabbing a section far away from the lamps. I kill the engine and turn expectantly.

Jacob fishes a tablet out of the duffle bag, and after entering four passwords, from what I can tell, the screen comes to life. I see sixteen different camera angles, and when he slides the screen to the right, another sixteen feeds appear. Damn. I knew he had the place wired, but I think I underestimated exactly how many cameras were in place.

"Are these always running?" I ask.

He quickly looks in my direction, then does a double-take when he registers my flushed cheeks. "Oh, Darling Mine. I have our last encounter on tape if that's what you're asking. But now really isn't the time."

Yep, I'm going to need to watch that.

"But normally, the outside ones are always on, and there's one focused on the main floor of the clubhouse at all times. Before I left, I flipped the switch to get them all recording. Want to have some fun?" he asks.

He turns the tablet in my direction and clicks on one image. A man in full tactical gear is tearing a hole in the wall of the clubhouse exterior. He and a few others with him are hacking at it with crowbars, creating and widening a hole big enough for someone to slip through.

Once it's suitable, the leader of this little group makes hand signals to follow him, stick close, and take the structure's occupants in alive. Well, that's a blessing. At least they're not there to kill anyone. Just drag them off to who knows where.

I see one side of Jacob's lips curl up as he fiddles with something on the screen. Once the men are all inside the building, my Brit turns to me. "Will you do the honors?" he asks. There's a myriad of buttons on the right side of the screen, and he points to the red one. I take a deep breath and press.

He switches the camera angle, and I see the corrugated metal exterior of the clubhouse to the left of the men on the screen and what looks like solid concrete on the right. They're boxed in. There are yellow lights along the floor, creating the backlighting of all the windows in the clubhouse. I watch as the men creep closer to what I calculate to be the war room when a cloud appears above the men, slowly descending. The first guy coughs, covering his mouth as best he can with his forearm. It's tough to do in the small space between the two walls, and his semi-automatic weapon gets in the way when he lifts his arms.

The first guy drops to the ground, and his voice calls out over the speakers on the tablet. "Gas! Gas! Back up!" Their leader speaks into a comm device on his wrist about it being a trap. The others are slow to listen to his command, and I watch as, one by one, they all drop to the floor, unmoving. The leader hangs on longer than the others, having reached a lower altitude more quickly, but it's only a few seconds more until he's out.

"One team handled," Jacob chirps merrily.

The next screen shows a group converging on the opposite side of the building, where the kitchen is roughly located. It doesn't take long for them to break into the outer wall, but having heard the other man's "gas" comment, they don't bother trying to follow the walls. Instead, they take a battering ram to the kitchen window over the sink. It's back-lit with a stronger light, so I'm able to watch as a battering ram invades the space Noah loves so very much. My blood pressure rises with the assault on our living space, but Jacob just squeezes my leg reassuringly. "Wait for it."

Once everyone is inside the room, Jacob points out the green button to me. I press it with glee, knowing something awful is about to happen to these men violating the clubhouse. It may not be my *home* exactly, but it's one of them, and I'm glad to see the structure's defenses in action.

A heavy metal grate comes down, blocking the exit from the kitchen, and another drops over where the window now stands, empty of its glass. The metal barriers box in the men, and I watch as their foreheads light up with laser dots. Nice. Jacob quickly switches screens, and I see a multitude of angles from the kitchen, each trained on one man in the space. My Brit presses a white button, and I see the men's eyes all jerk up to the ceiling. "Who are you?" Jacob says in a menacing tone.

The men look around as if they'll see where the disembodied voice is coming from. "Lower the weapons," one man bravely says.

"Who sent you?" Jacob asks. I watch as one man's pants turn dark with a urine stain and know he's the one that's going to crack.

He proves me correct when he answers, "Someone hired us. We don't know who. That's the complete business model."

The man next to him socks him in the gut, telling me he was truthful. Mercenaries? *Come on.*

"Get out," Jacob booms over the speakers. He presses a button for the grate over the window to lift, and there's a mad scramble to leave the kitchen. "Don't forget your men on the other side. Remove them, or I'll remove them for you."

We watch as the men reach the second wave of soldiers in the parking area and instruct them to get the men from the other side. Within ten minutes, their team has moved out, and the clubhouse is empty again.

"Who the fuck sent mercenaries?" I ask, my tone shrill and far too squeaky for my liking. "Should we have kept one to interrogate? No. That'd only make them come at you harder." I just hope it wasn't a dumb move.

"I don't know, but we'll find out," Jacob answers my first question and ignores the verbal vomit that followed. His words don't assure me as much as they should. Well, fuck. I can't bring him back to the clubhouse, and I haven't really told them that Elise gave me her manor yet. After declaring it her tithe, she snapped her fingers, and her attendants brought all of her bags down the stairs, and they left in a flurry. She left behind the furniture, food in the fridges and pantry, and linens. I've been living there for two days, but I didn't expect houseguests so soon. I wanted to do the updates before surprising them. Well, no time like the present.

A thought occurs to me. "Wait, how did you connect to the sewer to get out by the bakery?" I ask.

"Oh, we have a few escape routes built in, just in case. That one is the most convenient for a pickup. The others lead to apartments around the neighborhood."

Genius.

I lean forward and kiss Jacob squarely on the mouth before starting up the car again. "Let's go home."

"Uh, Darling Mine? Where are we?" Jacob asks as he looks at the wrought-iron gates at the end of the long drive. The forest surrounding the land hides the house, and the only person to see us onto the property is the security guard I installed at the gate.

"Home." My reply is met with raised brows, and I watch as he pulls a gun from his hip when my "guard" approaches the car.

"Rogue, where the hell have you been? I've been fielding calls from Byrne all damn night when you just up and left him." Fabio's voice gets higher as he approaches the car.

I quirk a brow and watch as Jacob slowly holsters his gun at the man's tone. He mouths, "Who the bloody hell is that?" I know he's confused because it's when his Britishisms come out to play.

"Fabio," I reprimand with my tone. "Is that any way to talk to your boss? In fact, your boss's boss, now?"

"If that man weren't making goo-goo eyes at you the whole time, I'd have a different way of speaking, but he is positively smitten!" Fabio leans down to peer into my window and wiggles his fingers at Jacob, who just looks perplexed as fuck at the whole situation.

"Enough, Fab. I've got another car coming in hot, probably about," I look at Jacob for an estimate, and he holds up a finger, "One hour. Three men, black SUV."

"And a hedgehog," Jacob grumbles out as if he's embarrassed.

"That's right. And a hedgehog. They're to be permitted in. No talking to them, please." I have a feeling Fabio and Red would get along famously, and I'd rather they start their bromance after we all get out of this alive.

"You got it, Boss." He walks back over to the guardhouse, and the gates swing open. There's no one else I'd have guarding my front door than G or Fabio, but G's been busy since taking over my role.

King's former guards, now mine, are stationed around the property's perimeter at their captain's insistence. He and I had a long chat yesterday about the fortifications Elise had put into place, and while her security is top of the line, sometimes there's nothing better than a man with a gun walking the fence.

I roll through the entryway of the gate and watch in the rear-view mirror as it swings shut behind me, Fabio sticking his arm out of the guardhouse with a thumbs up. *Doofus*.

The driveway is long and newly graveled, so as we slide between the trees on the road, Jacob cranes his head this way and that to get the lay of the land. It isn't until we pass the last bend on the path that the house comes into view. "What the fuck..." Jacob drawls out as he takes in the sight before him.

"Welcome home, honey," I tease. As much as I wanted this to be a surprise, maybe it's better to get their opinion in advance. I mean, if they want to live with me, eventually. I think that's where we're headed. Forever.

I pull up to the rounded driveway and circle around the fountain until I'm parked just past the front door, leaving a space under the awning for the SUV that's due to arrive later. Jacob's mouth opens and closes like a fish as he looks around until he finally whips around in his seat and gives me a stern look. "Keeping secrets again, are we, Love?"

The heat in his eyes lights my panties on fire, well, metaphorically, and I squirm in my seat under his fiery gaze. His eyes drop to my legs as they rub together, trying to ease the ache.

"Just a few. But they're all good ones, I promise." He looks at me like he doesn't believe the words escaping my lips, hauls me across the bench seat, and kisses me like he's going off to war.

"You bought a house?" he asks incredulously. "You're staying?"

"I hope to. I want to." Trailing my fingertips down his neck, I rest my hand over his heart. "I love you, Jacob. And the others. I don't know how any of this is going to go in the next few months, but I want this to be our home when it's all over if-" I snap my mouth shut before I say the last words of that sentence. *If I survive.*

Clearing my throat, I continue, "I didn't buy it. The house was the tithe from Elise for her to leave The Gambit. She told me the other day, we signed the papers, and she and her employees packed it up and left. I've been here two days, and I'm still exploring, but it's big enough for us, and with a few modifications and a remodel, it could be somewhere we'd enjoy."

"I'm sure it will be. And Rogue, we will get through this. Together. All of us. If you think we're letting you get away after we've just found you and you're finally so close to being free, you've gone mad, woman." He laughs. "You're stuck with us. And the damned hedgehog."

A snort escapes my lips, and Jacob pulls back, looks me in the face, and throws his head back in laughter at my undignified sounds.

"Come on, you've got to show me around your..." He looks at the house. "What do you even call this thing? An estate?"

"A manor." I waggle my brows, feeling fancy as fuck with my new digs.

"Well, milady. Let's go." He opens the door and reaches back for me, taking my hand in a Victorian manner, and guides me up the steps to the front door. I put the pad of my thumb on the handle, and the beep admits us inside. Gotta love the no-key thing. I swing the door open and watch Jacob's face as he takes in the foyer. There's a circular table in the center of the space with white lilies on top, a solarium to the back, and the wings of the house branch out on either side. Two staircases are leading to the upper level, one on each side of the foyer, and they curve up to meet the landing on the next level. His eyes wheel around, staring at the paintings on the walls and the ornate banisters running up the stairs. His fingertips trail along the brocade wallpaper as he inches further into the house.

"Rogue. What. The. Fuck?" His head finally turns back in my direction, and a blush rises on his cheeks when he sees me beaming at him.

"Come on, let's do the tour." I pull out my phone and quickly text the guys my new address and tell them not to talk to the man at the gate under any circumstances. Just sit there, looking straight ahead, and wait for the pretty iron to swing inward.

Han's response is confused, to say the least, but he knows I got Jacob out, and we all have a lot to talk about. Between what went down tonight and the whole Rogue-has-a-manor thing, it's going to be a long night.

I show Jacob the bottom floor of the East Wing before my phone chirps. I pull it from my bra and see Fabio has admitted the guys. They speed off in the SUV, kicking up the new gravel, and I lead Jacob back to the front of the house so we can welcome them in and fend off the tirade of questions I'm sure is about to rain down on us.

Noah parks the car right behind Black Beauty, and three doors open simultaneously. Han launches himself up the steps and throws himself into Jacob's arms. "What the fuck happened?" he gasps out as Jacob's arms band around him tightly, assuring him all is fine.

"We had a few visitors. Rogue picked me up, and we got to use some traps I hooked up. I'm fine, she's fine, and you guys are okay. I'd say it was a successful night."

To stop Jacob's deadpan retelling of it all, Han grabs the back of Jacob's neck and plants a kiss on his lips.

Bye, panties. Fuck, that's hot.

"Uh..." Lucas says. "Where are we?" He jostles Sir Lancelot's carrying cage, and he lets out a little squeak at the motion.

Jacob looks at me and starts laughing. "Time to explain it all over again."

"Uh, this is my new home. Well, *our* new home, if you want. Wanna come in?" A few months ago, I would have nearly stuttered these words out. But seeing Jacob's reaction to the idea gives me the confidence to offer the house to all of us. It's relatively fast, but if I can marry someone I don't love with only two weeks' notice, why can't I plan a future with the men I've come to love over the past nine months?

I'm met with three wide-eyed stares before Noah climbs the steps to the entryway and scoops me into his arms, carrying me over the threshold like a bride as the others follow us in. "I love it. And I love you."

Chapter Fourteen

Lucas

I STRETCH MY LEGS OUT ON THE SOFT BED, AND MEMORIES OF LAST night come crashing into my mind.

The combination of seeing off the other team to Costa Rica, the panicked phone call from Jacob, the breakneck drive back to El Castillo, and the confusing address Buttercup sent us made us all crash last night. When Han got the text with an address, we realized she must have taken Jacob to a safe house to spend the night. It's not like they could go back to her place, which she may or may not still be sharing with Romano. We had barely spoken the past few days with the funeral arrangements and mission we were handling.

When we got the notice not to interact with the gate guard, we figured he would let us in. The man with the long hair stared at the car for so long, assessing who was inside, before finally letting us through after seeing Lancelot. We drove up this curved driveway like a bat out of hell because things seemed sketchy, but we stopped dead when Buttercup opened the door to this huge fucking house like she owned the place. Turns out she does.

We had the briefest of tours before getting into a small debate about who got to sleep where. All of us wanted time with Buttercup, and after the whispers turned to whisper shouts, she finally drew the line and made us have a rock-paper-scissors tournament to settle the debate. We thought about pulling a bunch of mattresses to a central location, but we were all so tired and crashing from the adrenaline that we could barely lift our eyelids at that point.

I crack open an eye to see the expansive room and feel a brush of warm air on my neck. Yeah, Han's going to be pissed. I won the last round with my throw of paper.

Tightening my arm along Buttercup's back, I hug her close before rolling her so she's flat on her back, and I withdraw my arm carefully. There's room for three in here, so I can maneuver where I want to go. I slide the soft comforter down and gently kiss my girl on her neck. She lets out a breathy sigh, still sleeping, but I plan to wake her up in the best way. It still seems super early, so I want to taste my girl, get her off, and then let her catch some extra rest.

I trail my lips down her neck, across her collarbone, and lave one of her nipples with my tongue. I make sure there's not an inch of skin unworshipped before moving to the other. Featherlight touches of my fingertips trail down her sides, over her ribs, before finding the swell of her hips. I drag the tip of my tongue down her body, and my hands hold her hips in place.

She squirms for just a second, a moan leaving her mouth as mine reaches her bare pussy. I love that she sleeps naked. Last night, she entered the room, promptly shed all of her clothes, and threw them into a pile on a chair. She brushed her teeth, came out of the bathroom, and flopped onto the bed, not moving. Poor thing is absolutely exhausted running a criminal empire.

I gently lick her, and her breathing comes faster. I work my way from her clit to her opening, not once alternating my tempo, just indulging. As I slide my tongue into her wet heat, I feel fingertips brush through my hair and anchor my face to her. "Lucas," she says assuredly. I peek up and see her head is still back on the pillow, and she's in that blissful place between dreams and reality.

Using my tongue, I drive her higher and higher, feeling her thighs clamp over my ears while my nose brushes her clit. Her back bows up, and then she curls forward as the orgasm grips her fully. My mouth continues its assault, wringing every drop of pleasure out of her. Her pupils are blown when her gaze connects with mine, and a sleepy smile overtakes her face.

She flops back down onto the pillows, and I can't help but tease her with a few more licks.

"Good morning, Buttercup," I say, mouth still muffled as she's yet to release her grip on my hair.

"Mmm... morning, Red." She yawns wide, completely undignified, and releases my hair from her clutches.

Sitting back on my heels, I look at this gorgeous girl in front of me, wondering how I—*we*—ever got so lucky. I lean down, trailing kisses from her inner thighs to her knees, picking up a leg and reaching her ankle. I blow a raspberry on the bottom of her foot, and she draws it back, out of my grasp.

"We have to get up! We haven't eaten in a while. Well, you haven't." I wink. She sighs. "You got a kitchen around here?"

Her eyes narrow at my questions. "Uh, yeah. It's downstairs." She fights off another yawn. "I'll show you."

"Nah, Buttercup, you rest. I'll find it." Hovering over her, I kiss her lips sweetly before leaving the bed and using the facilities. I take care of business, brush my teeth, wash up, and exit the bathroom. Halfway through getting dressed, I look over and find her softly snoring. Yep. Exhausted.

I snag Sir Lancelot's travel case, first ensuring he's actually inside—the little dude seems to escape at the most inopportune times—and softly close the door behind me when I enter the hall.

I look up and down the ornate hallway, confused about which direction I should actually take. Eh, it doesn't matter. There's always time for an adventure. But not too much time. Adrenaline makes me hungry.

Taking a stab at a direction, we walk one way, finding a dead end, then turn around and go the opposite way. I'm not even sure which room I came out of at this point. After passing what feels like twelve doors, I find the staircase. It's the double one that leads to the foyer. Okay, I remember that room from last night. I look in both directions, seeing no one coming down either hall that meets in the middle here, and pull Sir Lancelot's case closer, looping the strap around my neck. I quickly touch the banister to the curved stairs and find it smooth as silk. Fuck, I've always wanted to do this.

Turning to the side, I do a little hop and rest my ass on the smooth wood. I tilt my body forward a bit and scoot my ass until gravity takes over, and I'm flying down the railing. "Woo hoo!" I shout into the spacious room. The end is coming up quickly, and there's an ornament at the base. I keep an arm tucked around Sir Lancelot's cage and use my legs to pop my ass off the slide. I stumble a step, catching myself on the fancy wallpaper-lined side of the stairs, and throw my hands in the air like an Olympic gymnast. That was fun.

After three more mandatory slides down the banister, I finally stop when Sir Lancelot squeaks. It's totally his food squeak, not his nauseated squeak. Don't ask how I know that. Time for grub.

I pass through the living room, a second living room, a dining room, a library, and finally, give up, turning around and walking in the other direction. I need a map.

The smell of breakfast food reaches my nose, and I follow it. It's never let me down before.

It seems to come from a part of the wall in the dining room. I press it in different spots until, finally, there's a slight click. The door bounces outward an inch, and I use my fingertips to pry it open. I step into a pristine white-tiled and light wood room; it's like an IKEA showroom kitchen. Jesus, fuck.

Noah is standing before the stove whistling merrily, and I softly close the door behind me with a nearly inaudible click. I lean against the wall and watch the happiness radiating off of our Dear Leader for approximately ten seconds before he spins around with a plate, and the whole thing goes flying as he sees me. *Whoops.* I leap into action, snagging the dish out of the air before we break Buttercup's new things.

"Tsk tsk, Noah. What will Buttercup say when she hears I snuck up on you?" I ask.

"Where did you even come from?" he asks, looking around the room. There's a doorway to his right that he definitely would have seen me enter. Shrugging my shoulders, I decide to keep that little kernel of information for another time. I wonder if there are more hidden doors. Popping out and scaring Noah might just become my new favorite hobby in this house.

"Oh, here and there." I wave my hand nonchalantly. He narrows his eyes at me, eerily similar to how Buttercup did just before in the bedroom. "Whatcha making? I'm hungry," I say, rubbing my stomach and hoping to derail his line of thought.

"Frittatas, and there's also bread in the oven. If you remember, I don't sleep well in unknown places, so I just figured I'd get breakfast going. By the way, did you get turned around on your way down here?" he asks.

"Oh, definitely. I've seen at least three offices, ten bedrooms, and three living rooms, and I'm pretty sure there's a wine cellar over that way," I wave my arm in the possible direction.

"This place is massive, but it's so confusing. I hope we can talk about some renovations and restructuring of the layout," he muses. A soft smile crosses his face. "Can you believe she wants us to live with her?" He shakes his head at the thought.

"What's that look for?" I ask.

"I just... I never thought I'd find someone like her. She's fucking perfect."

Laughing at the marvel in his tone, I nod and quickly agree. You know what a new house needs? New mugs. Looks like I'll be trolling Etsy for insane drinkware today.

"Oh, hey, I saw a rosemary bush outside when we got here last night. Can you grab me a sprig?" he asks.

"Sure, if I can find my way out of here." I deposit Sir Lancelot on a countertop far away from Noah and walk through the obvious door to the room. Just as I'm crossing the threshold, my eyes snag on a map the kitchen staff must have used. Smart. I snap a picture with my phone and follow the instructions to get outside. I step out into the early morning air and take a deep breath. A lush green lawn surrounds the place and provides some safety in spotting any imminent threats. Nice. I stick a flowerpot against the open door so I don't get locked out and find the bushes Noah mentioned.

I grab a few sprigs because he always ends up needing more than he asks for and head back in.

Jacob and Han join us a few minutes later, looking refreshed and happy. They link their hands between them, their eyes alight with mischief. They were also apart recently, so it's good they got some time together, too. I know we're all jonesing for time with our girl, but maybe when we're not all wrung out on an adrenaline crash.

Noah is in the middle of adding the rosemary to the baking dish. Han and Jacob are mixing their morning beverages of choice, and I've got a carton of orange juice at my lips while standing in front of the open fridge when two men enter the kitchen, guns drawn.

Immediately, Han has his weapon out and trained on the two idiots dumb enough to pull firepower in our presence. Noah slides the bacon off of the cast-iron pan and hefts it with his oven-mitt-covered hand, and I slide a jug of milk from the shelf in the fridge and have it gripped by the neck, ready to throw as a distraction.

"Who the fuck are you?" one guy demands to know, and I take a moment to realize it's G, the man we knocked out when we "abducted" Buttercup for some time together a few months ago, and Fabio, the guard from the gate last night.

"Woah, lower the weapons." Noah is calm and puts down his skillet in a show of good faith. The pink oven mitts are a big plus in this situation when he raises them up near his ears. I stifle a snort at the image. "You let us in last night. Rogue invited us."

"Who opened the back door without disarming the security code?" G asks.

I let go of the milk bottle and lift my hand in the air. "That was me. The big guy over there"—I nod my head at Noah—"needed rosemary for seasoning. I went out to grab some from the bush out there."

"And you're sure no one followed you in?" Fabio asks, his weapon still level with Jacob's chest. Meaning Han still has his weapon on the long-haired man.

"I had eyes on the door at all times. No one came in. I locked it again when I came back," I assure them.

"Why are there no cameras on that door? This whole place is wired; I spotted a ton of them this morning from my window."

"Ah, we think Elise used that door for her lover to sneak in and out. Apparently, he's the dad of one of her staff." Fabio smirks with the explanation.

A voice comes from the entryway. "Weapons down, all of you."

"Morning, Trouble!" Noah calls from the stove as he puts the bacon back in the pan.

Everyone reluctantly does as she says, Han being the last because the pretty boy over there had his gun trained on one of his lovers. I get it.

"Sit down. Let's do the introductions." Buttercup comes to kiss me quickly, and I hold her to my side. What if these assholes are judgmental? We don't judge each other, but they might. I don't want to see one ounce of hurt on her face if they're dickweeds.

"G, Fabio. This is Lucas. That's Noah at the stove. Han and Jacob, who, if you shot, I'd have one of you digging the grave for the other. Guys, this is G and Fabio. Fabio is the one with the hair, obvs. Oh, and that's Sir Lancelot," she says, waving a hand at the hedgehog cage.

There's a murmur of hellos, and everyone takes a seat at the vast island countertop. Noah continues his work on breakfast, and G shuffles over to the coffee machine, grabbing two cups and preparing them for himself and Fabio. After dropping them off at their spots, he looks at Rogue. "Anything for you, Boss?" That's so weird. But I do like the respect in his tone.

"That's okay. I'll grab it." Buttercup swoops out of my lap and grabs Han and Jacob's mugs they'd abandoned in the kerfuffle, peers inside, and dumps the contents down the drain. She makes everyone their beverage of choice, not needing a word of confirmation about what each of us wants. After dropping off mug after mug, I see Noah slide a little closer to her. She turns, grabs his face, and plants a kiss on his lips as she stands on her tippy toes. She drops back down on her heels and looks at G and Fabio, daring them to say a word. I look over and see their eyebrows in their hairlines, and they both bring their mugs to their lips, excusing themselves from speaking.

Buttercup lets out a satisfied little huff and helps Noah dish out the meals. Han grips her hip, pulls her in close, and kisses her on her way back around the island. She melts in his arms the way I've only seen her do with him before he passes her to Jacob, who playfully nips her lip with his teeth.

"G and Fabio are Team Rogue, aren't you, boys?" she tosses out casually.

Chapter Fifteen

Rogue

Elise drains the last of her teacup, her pinky staunchly in the air as she peers across the table at the California Governor opposite us.

High tea at this fancy-ass hotel is not what I had in mind when it came to learning the ropes of her division, but, unfortunately, it's how business is done.

"Run that by me again, Gerard." She doesn't phrase it as a question or an invitation. Oh, no. That's a direct order if I've ever heard one.

I longingly look at the finger sandwiches on the three-tiered plate before me as my stomach growls. Lesson number one: don't take food in anyone's presence unless you trust them. Although, that's debatable, too. Hell, even my drink is untouched, and we've been here twenty minutes. Elise has some brass ones for indulging.

"Government agencies are circling. With the changeover, it's expected, but I'm getting pressure from all sides to set up meetings with the new head of The Gambit." He looks at me. "Ma'am." His nod is deferential, but it still makes me uneasy.

"Who?" I ask, loquacious as all get-out.

"Police chiefs from up and down the coast, the commissioner, the district attorney, and a few ADAs, a couple FBI and NSA heads stationed on this side. It's a long list, Queen."

I sigh. I knew this was coming, and I've put it off as long as possible.

"What does this information cost me, Gerard?" I ask calmly.

"Nothing, Queen. Just doing my part as the go-between. But I'd recommend setting things up sooner rather than later. The NSA guys are notoriously self-important, and the longer they wait, the bigger the problem they may be for you."

I consider his words. Nothing comes for free. I turn my gaze to Elise, who has her hands primly folded in front of her as she fiddles with her delicate wristwatch. A tiny shake of her head tells me he's still after something. "Come now, Gerard. Don't be shy. You've just brought me more information than I had five minutes ago. What'll it be?"

He clears his throat after taking a sip of his tea, and it rattles when he places it back on the saucer. "I, uh..." *Good God, we're going to be here all day. Spit it out, man.* "I want to quit."

Well, that's a surprise. "Quit?" asks Elise, clearly as shocked as I am.

"Yes. This is too much for me. I never wanted to get involved, but with Reyes dying, I had to step in. I want to finish my term, in one piece if possible, and get the fuck out." His eyes shift around the room, and I follow his gaze to glance at his security team stationed throughout the room. There's also one undercover two tables away, but he's too obvious with the way his head keeps tilting in our direction.

"You have yourself a deal." He sighs in relief at my words, and I get a startled look from Elise.

"It'll take time to bring the next one to heel," she warns.

"I'm aware. Tell me, Elise, what did you have on Gerard here to keep him so loyal?"

"He was having an affair with Reyes' chief of staff, Ethan. Oh, and he touts the party line that homosexuality is a sin. Politics is a messy business when it's filled with liars."

"That would sink your career and a lot of possible future avenues for you. No one wants to hire a hypocrite," I muse aloud.

Gerard is sweating bullets under his two-thousand-dollar suit. I don't blame him. "That's why I want out. I need to figure things out without the spotlight. I want out of politics. This is a disaster."

"I stand by my deal. You're out at the end of your term. What is that? About six months from now? So close. But you're going to do more for me, okay, Gerard? I know it's hard being in a role you hate. It's almost over," I coax.

"Anything. Name it."

Elise lifts a brow at me, and a smile breaks out across my face. I have my very own messenger to bring the underlings to me rather than the other way around. "I need you to deliver some invitations. According to your schedule, you're traveling the state to beat your chest about how infrastructure spending isn't necessary at the moment—which it absolutely is, you idiot. So on your trip, you're going to find these people"—I hand him a typed list of names—"and deliver these invitations personally. And I expect to see you there as well." I hand him the signed and sealed envelopes, along with a separate one with his name on it.

"What is this?" he asks.

"Why, it's a coronation, my dear." Elise's voice drips in condescension. "You know we wouldn't just hand over power without a party."

Gerard says how he's busy and can't make it, but Elise cuts him off with a ruthless slice of her hand through the air. "Nonsense. You'll be there." Her blue eyes are steely, and even I know not to challenge her when she's got that bloodlust in her gaze. Gerard nods his head subtly, and Elise reaches across the table to pat his cheek twice like he's a child. "Good boy."

With that, she turns her attention back to the tea before her.

Efficient. I like it.

Gerard is trembling slightly in his seat when I lean closer and whisper, "You're almost out, Gerard. Keep the endgame in mind."

We sit silently for another ten minutes before Elise and I stand, say our goodbyes—with varying degrees of threats laced within our sweet words—and make our way to the hotel's lobby. She stops me a few feet from the door. "You're cut out for this, you know?" Her words don't carry the reassurance she thinks they do. Hell, her only goal before was to get rid of King. She's done that. There were talks of dismantling The Gambit, but I'm pretty sure that was all Tanaka. Elise is not a good person, despite what I want to believe. She's just happy the threat has changed, and I—mostly—like her.

"I know." My voice is resigned, and she does the same cheek pat to me she did to Gerard in the dining room.

"You'll do okay. Next week, we meet with Senator Clarence; don't forget."

"How could I?" I laugh. The amount of reach this organization has is insane. I always knew we were at the top of the food chain, but fuck, it's still mind-blowing.

She turns on her heel and pushes her way through the revolving doors. Her driver is there to take her to her penthouse apartment in the building next to King's. Well, I guess it's mine now. Jacob went through the will, and King left everything to his successor. I signed the paperwork last week, and my bank account is obscene now. I'm not wasting it; I'm just sticking it in various offshore accounts linked to my name and Sage's should the worst happen in all of this.

I'd rather set her up with blood money than no money.

I leave the hotel, my black dress and high heels vivid in the large pane windows as I walk by. The role may be new, but I'm not changing who I am to fit it. I'll just have to break the damn preconceptions and swing my rockabilly ass until the job description fits who I am. Not the other way around.

I PULL UP TO THE GATE FOR MY DRIVEWAY AND NEED TO STOP SHORT when there's a small, red Mazda Miata parked in front, and the gate is still shut. I don't know who the fuck's car this is, but the door is hanging open, and the guardhouse's door is closed. If Fabio had to kill someone, I really hope he did it off of the property.

I put Black Beauty in park and push my door open. Walking up the drive, I listen carefully, but there's nothing around me except the chirp of birds in the late afternoon. I eye the tree line and see nothing, knowing every moment I'm not within my compound is a risk. *Fucking Fabio!*

I reach the guardhouse door and pull it open quickly while palming the knife I pulled from my glovebox.

Fucking Fabio is right.

He's sitting in his chair. His head is tossed back and jeans around his knees as a tiny redhead bounces on his cock as she fists his hair.

"Claudette!"

She bounces a few more times, her green dress hiked around her hips as Fabio grips her waist, then finally turns her head to look at me. A blush riding her cheeks almost as hard as she's riding Fab.

"Hey, Rogue." She lifts a hand and waves merrily, still bouncing away.

Fabio, on the other hand, has more sense. His head snaps up, and his blue eyes are hooded but panicked. "Fuck, Sweet Pea, we have to stop."

Claudette is still doing her thing, ignoring his words. "I'll uh... give you a few moments." I turn, but before shutting the door, I shout, "But Fabio, you're in charge of cleanup for the next month for this stunt."

I hear his not-so-happy groan, and I laugh—he hates dealing with bodies. It really is the best punishment for him. Five minutes later, Claudette comes loping out of the guardhouse with a big smile on her face.

"Have fun?" I ask from the hood of my car, where I've been leaning, waiting for them to finish.

"Meh, so-so. I prefer the older ones who want me to call them Daddy. I've got issues. What can I say?" she adds after she sees my raised brows at the Daddy comment. She laughs wickedly. "Jesus, your face. It was a joke. Kind of. Come on, let's go! I've got presents."

Her squeal is just this side of painful on the eardrums, but I roll my eyes and hop back into my car. Fabio opens the door to the guardhouse, waving us through as the gate opens. He blows Claudette a kiss, and I hear her laughter from here. Ten bucks says she never goes near that man again. So much for a "lady killer." Claudette would eat him for breakfast.

We park under the portico and make our way inside. The guys should be around here somewhere. Last I heard, Lucas was dedicating eighty percent of his time to figuring out the house's layout, Jacob was working on the security systems, Han had taken over renovation planning, and Noah was working on moving their stuff from the clubhouse to here as discreetly as possible.

The couch I bought for the clubhouse confirms it. It's now the prominent piece of furniture in the main living room. There are also boxes upon boxes on one side of the room, and I see a new camera installed in the room's corner, facing the orgy bed. I mean "couch." Cheeky Brit.

I find the intercom on the wall that Jacob got *somewhat* working again and press the button. A horrible screech echoes back at me. Fuck, he needs to fix that soon. "Guys, Claudette and I are in the living room with the black couch."

Weird fucking sentence, but necessary as we've found four living rooms so far.

The static crackles on the intercom before I hear Lucas. "Jacob, the comms are doing that shrieky thing again. We'll be there in a minute, Buttercup."

Claudette flops onto the couch, and I do my best to hide my wince as she sits in the exact spot I'm pretty sure I left a puddle during our five-way in the clubhouse. Let's call it payback for me having to witness her fucking Fabio.

"Thanks for coming, Claudette. You're early. Any chance that was intentional?" I look at the antique clock on the wall and feel like a pretentious asshole when I remember how much that thing costs, according to Google.

She laughs and shrugs her shoulders. "*That* was a happy coincidence. I didn't know he was working at your guardhouse. Anyway, the traffic was decent. I usually allow an extra hour for it, but the freeway was perfectly empty this afternoon." Hmm, somehow, I doubt that. Eh, she's here. Might as well get down to it.

"What's happening with you and Fab?" Prying isn't usually in my nature, but when one of them guards the entrance to my home, I'm damn well going to make it my business, no matter how much I trust him.

"Oh, we met when he and the tattooed one dropped off the girls. Nice guys. Pretty, too." She looks around the room, avoiding eye contact. Hmm...

I remind Claudette I know how they met because I'm the one that sent them there, and she nods distractedly, no doubt imagining the two of them. Internal drooling happens to the best of us. I get it, girl.

The guys all come trailing in from both sides of the room, as there are multiple entryways. One leads back to the foyer and the other to the rest of that wing. See? Maps needed.

"Hey, Han!" shouts Claudette when she sees him. "Did you get the meme I sent yesterday? You didn't respond." Claudette sounds a little put out at his lack of reply.

"Yep. I could have sworn I sent back an emoji. Sorry, it's been crazy around here. Totally my fault." He's such a nice guy.

Claudette shrugs it off and leaps to her feet to give him a hug. I know they were texting when I wasn't free to do so, but I didn't know they were friendly. A slight tinge of jealousy clouds my thoughts for a moment, but I shake it off. I know he loves Jacob and me. He wouldn't do that to us.

The tiny psychopath's hug is quick before she moves along and squeezes Jacob around the middle, high-fives Lucas in some intricate handshake they make up on the fly, and she extends a hand to Noah. "You don't seem like much of a hugger," she says as she looks up at his face. All of them tower over her, but with Noah's bulk, he seems gigantic next to her. He takes her hand, lifts it to his lips, and kisses her knuckles. I swear I see her swoon from here.

"That's enough of that," I say.

Noah looks down at me on the couch and studies my face. "Are you... Trouble, are you jealous?" he asks incredulously.

"What? No! We just have a lot to talk about." My defense is weak, even to my own ears, and Lucas chuckles beside me. I whack him with the back of my hand, aiming for his chest, but the height makes it difficult. He doubles over at the impact. Whoops, I think I got him in the solar plexus. My bad.

We drop the backrest of the couch to make it a flat surface, and everyone joins me on the couch. Noah puts an arm around my back, his palm pressed into my lower spine to keep me steady as I'm seated on the edge without a backrest. "Okay, let's talk territory. I'm getting the official requests from the surrounding gangs about The Vegas Crew's now open area. What do The Rattlesnakes want?"

Claudette is busy looking at my guys with way too much appreciation in her gaze. I snap my fingers in front of her face when she stares a little too long at Jacob. "Hey! I was watching that!" she complains. One look at my face tells her I'm not messing around here. "Fine, we want nothing. The territory is too far out of the way for me to manage effectively, and *some* people are still having trouble adjusting to me in the leadership role. I just don't want The Gambit taking it. You guys are too big. Give it to one of the Midwest gangs. You can do that, right?"

I shake my head. "It's not mine to give, but we're going to mediate it. I have no interest, and neither do you. You and I can help be the sane voices." I realize the irony as I say the words. Claudette isn't exactly sane in the broadest sense of the term, but with no vested interest in claiming the territory, she and I are the best to mediate.

She giggles and rolls backward a bit. Han shoots out a hand and catches her before she topples off the edge of the couch. "This is going to be so much fun. Those guys who brush us off as inept or underqualified now get their futures decided by us. There's some karmic justice, bitches!"

"Christ," Lucas says. "Has anyone been a particularly annoying asshole? You can probably fuck them over in the deal."

Claudette's eyes light up like Christmas. "Oh yes, the guys from SoCal think we belong in the kitchen, barefoot and pregnant. I'd love to help take some of their territory away."

"We'll see about that," I say, again being the voice of reason.

"Okay, so no Vegas territory. That's good. The other thing is, we're having a party. More of a coronation, really."

"Ooh! A party!" She claps her hands together in front of her like a grandma, all palms.

"Yes, yes. A party." When she looks at me, I know she wants more enthusiasm. "Weeee," I deadpan, and she dramatically rolls her eyes at me over my lack of enthusiasm.

She huffs, and Jacob takes her attention with a careful touch on her arm. "Look, we need Sage and the girls to attend the party." Claudette is already shaking her head before Jacob has finished speaking.

"Not a chance, Johnny English. They're finally safe and coming around. This could set them back." My respect for Claudette doubles in an instant. That she's putting their interests first is how I know I made a good call befriending her all those months ago.

"I know," I tell her, and she refocuses on me. "We don't need all of them, but a couple would be helpful. I haven't asked Sage yet because you see her more than I do, despite talking to her every day. You know better if she's in a stable mental place that she can do this. No harm would come to them. I will be there the whole time and lop the hand or dick off of any man who dares touch them. The appendage would be their choice."

She considers for a moment. "I think Sage would be okay. And possibly Elenor. I'll see if any of them would be willing, but so help me, Rogue, if they come back more damaged, it'll be your hand I take."

"Deal." I stick my hand out to shake on it, and she takes it gleefully.

"Well, now that's settled, who's hungry?" Noah asks.

Everyone's hands shoot into the air, and Noah looks at me curiously. "I thought you went for high tea?"

"I did, but I didn't want to end up poisoned somehow, so I refrained from partaking." Lucas looks at me as if I've committed the greatest sin against humanity he can think of, and I laugh at the look on his face.

"Smart," Han jokes.

We all scramble off of the couch, and Noah leads the way to the kitchen. We only get lost once along the way, but it's better than earlier in the week.

Noah instructs everyone to take a few things, and when we're all laden down with food that smells good enough to shove my face into—utensils be damned—we go to find the dining room.

We drop off our goods, and Lucas moves to the side to grab plates and cutlery from the sideboard for everyone. I see him discreetly pull Sir Lancelot from his hoodie pocket and settle him in a small basket on the side with a bit of food he pulls from his jeans pocket. I resist the urge to roll my eyes but make sure no one else—particularly Noah—saw him.

Plates set, we all pull out a chair and sit down, three to a side. I hate sitting at the head of the table, but for negotiations with Romano, it felt necessary. Speaking of, we're finally meeting with the lawyers tomorrow to dissolve this sham of a marriage.

Noah dishes out the roast he cooked, and we all dig in with the enthusiasm of people who haven't eaten in days. But in reality, I know it's likely only been a few hours for Lucas.

My phone vibrates in my skirt pocket, and as much as I'd love to leave it for another time and not be rude at the dinner table, I discreetly slide it out and wake the screen.

I do my best not to choke on my drink, but it's a close call. There, on my screen, is the message I've been waiting for.

Queen,

We're due for a meeting soon. Your predecessor didn't like to share his toys. I have a feeling you and I will get along better.

Tomorrow, 10 am, Annex executive offices.

Cross

I carefully take the napkin from my lap, place it on the table, and look up to find Noah's face across from mine. He's having a conversation with Lucas about the dietary needs of hedgehogs when he finally looks over at me. He must see the look in my eyes because he complains about forgetting the dessert in the kitchen.

"Trouble, can you help?" he asks as naturally as he would at any other moment. Damn, he's an excellent actor. He really got into the wrong line of work all those years ago.

"Sure."

We walk down the hall and make it to the kitchen, listening to the raucous laughter we left behind as Claudette tells a story about one of her underlings.

Noah spins me once we enter the kitchen and kisses my lips hard as my back slams against the fridge. His tongue teases the seam of my lips, and I open for him on a groan. Reluctantly, he pulls away. "What happened?" he asks, his breath feathering across my lips as he searches my eyes.

"Cross reached out. He demanded to meet me tomorrow."

Noah considers for a moment. "Put him off. We're not ready yet. Make up something. *Anything.* Move it to next week. Or even the week after. Please."

It's the "please" that has me taking his request seriously. He's not one to beg, and I know he's afraid for me, but regardless, this has to happen at some point. Later would be better. But drawing it out is only going to fuck with my nerves.

"Fine. How do I answer that?" I ask honestly. "He sounds like he's expecting a yes."

Noah leans in, nipping my earlobe with his teeth. "You are the queen, are you not?" His breath sends shivers racing down my spine. "You're certainly ours. Use that power, Trouble."

I moan as his hands tighten on my waist, and his tongue dips into the hollow near my neck.

"Fine. Fine. Yeah, I can do that," I tell him as much as myself. Noah withdraws, and I thumb out a reply.

Cross,
I'm confident we can work together. I'm unavailable at the moment. Transitions, you understand. I will meet you in the first week of July.
Looking forward to making your acquaintance,
Queen

It takes seconds for his reply to come in.

Queen,
Fine. July 3. We'll arrange a time and place the day before.
Looking forward to working with you.
Cross

I show Noah the reply, and his lip instantly curls in disgust. "Yeah, I'll just bet. The Gambit kicked him out all those years ago, and he wants his own empire. He's going to put you on the back foot with this and make it appear like you need him. You don't, but bringing him on in some capacity could work with what we talked about the other day."

He's right. The plan we cooked up alongside Romano hinges on a few things. And now, with the meeting set for two weeks away, it gives us time to collaborate. Having Cross closer could be one key to making it work. I consider it for a moment before realizing the noise of the others has died down in the other room.

"We should get back," Noah says reluctantly and grabs the chocolate cake from the countertop, handing me a tub of vanilla ice cream to go with it.

We make our way back to the dining room to find Lucas and Claudette locked in an arm-wrestling pose, grunting and groaning, trying to push the other to defeat. Claudette holds on for longer than I would have guessed before Lucas slams her hand down on the table. "Ha! Tied! One-one!"

I can't help the chuckle that escapes my lips, and Han hops up to take the ice cream from me before I drop it as my body doubles over in laughter. Tied!

Han pulls me onto his lap when we reach his seat, and I snuggle in for dessert and teasing touches.

It isn't long before Claudette notices the shift in the room's atmosphere and makes her excuses.

"Keep in touch, okay?" she says to both me and Han.

"Yes, Claudette," we answer in unison.

Jacob follows her to the door to walk her out and send her on her way. Two seconds after he returns, I thumb out a text to Fabio.

Me: Please don't bone my guests in the guardhouse. This is a classy joint, Fab.

Fabio: I tried not to, Boss. I really did. She's persuasive.

Me: Next time, lock the door.

Fabio: And leave her unsatisfied... Boss, you know that's not how I operate.

Me: Then change your ways.

Fabio: Did she happen to leave her number for me?

Me: Nope.

Fabio: ::crying emoji::

I can't help the laugh that bubbles out of me.

Chapter Sixteen

Rogue

IT'S HAPPENING. OH, GOOD GOD, I NEVER THOUGHT THIS DAY WOULD arrive.

I stand in front of Judge Ramirez, gleefully signing the paperwork, a sweet smile stuck on my face.

It took some digging, but Shade found us a judge who would grant us a divorce within a week of asking. There was no division of assets as we agreed to leave the possessions with which we entered the marriage. No kids. No property shared. Ramirez looks over the documentation before him, likely seeing my sudden influx of cash, stocks, and property, and glances at Romano's face. My soon-to-be ex-husband just smiles back. Ramirez lets out a little huff of obvious exasperation, wondering why someone would give this up, and continues his perusal of our documentation.

"And you've tried to mediate and have done everything within your power to make the marriage work?" he asks us.

"Yes, Your Honor," I say sweetly. "Better for us to part now and remain friends. No animosity. We're simply not suited for each other."

He nods his head, and with a flourish, he signs the paperwork.

A weight I hadn't noticed lifts from my shoulders. "Well, that's it. We'll get this filed, and they'll mail you the final paperwork. Congratulations to you both."

Romano stands, re-buttoning his charcoal gray suit jacket, and sticks his hand out. "Thank you, Your Honor."

I stand and bob my head in thanks. He's not on my payroll, nor does he know who I am. That helps. The few people I've seen over the past few weeks have treated me with more than their usual respect and/or fear. One woman even had a bit of a visceral reaction, nearly shrinking into the potted plant next to her at Rook Industries. I made a mental note to check over her work for the company. No one hides like that unless they've done something wrong.

Romano leans in close to the judge to say a few words as I gather my handbag from the ottoman next to me, making sure my identification and copies of the documents are secure inside. He places a hand on my lower back and guides me from the room.

We reach the main floor and lobby of the courthouse before I pull my phone from my bag. There's a text in the group chat.

Cap: It's time to party, Trouble. Bring the ex home with you. We owe him a beer.

That's it.

The chat has been suspiciously quiet since I left, but I think they gave me space to get this done without dwelling on my "marriage" being one of King's last wishes. The guilt gets better daily, but like anything, there are good days and bad. Hell, a week ago, I locked myself in the gym toward the back of the house and beat the hell out of the punching bag just to find a release for the anger that gripped my heart. Han broke down the door and brought me back to my room for a bubble bath and an epic snuggle session. It comes in waves, I tell ya.

I tilt the phone screen to Romano, who's checking his own phone, and he nods his head. "Yeah, let's go. I have some other news as well, and it'd be better if everyone heard it at once."

What now?

The drive to the house is quick in Romano's G-Wagon, and I can't help but wonder if it's government-issued. When I ask him, he scoffs.

"Yeah, like I'd want them tracking me everywhere. Give me some credit, Rogue." *Well, then.*

We reach the gate, and my alternate gate guard lets us in after I send him a hand signal.

I hop out of the car as soon as we're in front of the double doors. I press my finger on the scanner, and the door opens. The alarm beeps, so I press in the code as Romano steps through. I close and lock the front door and hear nothing. Romano lets out a laugh as he stands before the table in the center of the foyer. I cross the tile, my heels loud in the space, and I draw up short when I see what's on the table.

A note and two Nerf guns.

Buttercup and Bachelor-
Game on.
-ATO

Kicking out one foot, then the other, I fling my heels across the room, and they clatter against the door to the solarium. I grab a Nerf gun and find more clips of darts behind the note. I stuff them into the top of my dress and prepare for war. Romano follows suit, quickly ditching his jacket and rolling up his shirtsleeves.

He signals for me to go right and him left. I nod and take off through the open door to the living room. Searching, I see nothing amiss in the room, but I stick close to the wall so no one can sneak up on me. I move through the room, making my way to an office, a guest room, a stairway to the wine cellar, and finally reach the end of the wing.

A dart whizzes by my shoulder, and I twist out of the way just in time to avoid the little orange foam dart of death. The prize for winning is unknown, but that doesn't stop my need to claim victory.

I take off running through the earlier rooms, stopping at the door to the wine cellar, and slip inside. Leaving it cracked, I keep my gun at the ready. There are racks of the stuff down below, but up here, it's just a small landing space and a steep set of steps behind me.

I wait patiently for only a few moments, and my heart races when Noah comes stalking through the hall. His footsteps are careful and sure, the Nerf gun raised in his hand as if it's an actual weapon. He has his head slightly tilted, listening for movement. I keep my breathing steady, watching my target through the gap in the door. I notch the gun barrel between the wall and the door frame and pull the trigger, timing the shot with his steady pace.

These damn guns are slower than real ones and make an awful "thwump" noise when they fire. Noah must hear the shot because he stops short, and the dart sails just in front of his nose. Yeah, I aimed for his head.

His head swivels to my position, and I yank the gun back, duck down, and race down the stairs. I hear his thundering steps behind me. I launch through the room, hiding behind a shelving unit.

If I can circle around, I can get him before he finds me. I look for a clear path, but I've spent little time in this room. Sure, I know where the entrances and exits are, but I don't know the intricacies of the shelving units. Unlike Noah, who's always in here grabbing wine to go with dinners. Unfair advantage. If it were Lucas who was after me, at least we'd be on even footing.

I can't hear Noah behind me, but I know he's there by the eerie feeling on the back of my neck. I snake my way through the shelves and get to the stairway. If I can keep sight of that, he'll have to pass by, eventually.

I silently reach behind me and undo the hook at the top of my dress's zipper. This thing is restrictive, and it's making me slow. I hiked the skirt up as I moved through the house, but it was still not enough. I plan to ditch this, and I'll grab a pair of yoga pants and a tank top when I get upstairs.

Romano has shared an apartment with me for months. I don't care if he sees me in my underwear if we cross paths. Plus, he's on the other side of the house.

An idea so beautiful in its simplicity occurs to me. I gently place the Nerf gun on the floor and let my hair down, sticking the pins on the rack next to me. It tumbles down my back, and I shake it out as if I have an audience, and hopefully, I do.

I reach behind my neck, moving the zipper to the middle of my back before I have to change my arms' position to grasp it again. It trails a few inches down my back, slowly revealing more skin before I feel a hot, huge hand on my own. A nose nudges my neck, and the scent of cedar and sandalwood surrounds me. Noah carefully takes the zipper in his hand and drags it the rest of the way down my back, stopping a few inches past my thong's waistband.

My head drops back to his shoulder as his hands push under the material coming around to my breasts. The small space amplifies his groan, and as he plucks at my nipples, I grind my ass back into his hard cock behind me. His lips skate over my shoulder, and his hips push forward with each rough pass of his calloused fingers over my tits.

Focus, Rogue. Focus!

I spin in his arms, noting his flushed cheeks and glazed-over eyes. A sly smile hooks one side of my mouth up as I slide the dress from my shoulders and push it over my hips.

Noah's gun is behind him, leaning against the wall next to us, a few feet from mine. Letting the dress pool at my feet, I drop to my knees and trail my fingers down the bulge of his jeans. I unbuckle his belt with unhurried hands, pop the button, and undo the zipper before pulling his jeans and boxers down to his knees. Raking my fingernails up his thighs, his head drops back with the sensation. I make my move while he's not looking.

I grab my gun and fire a dart at his stomach. It harmlessly bounces off his hard abs, and he looks down at me. The passion in his eyes has me suppressing a grin. I don't think he—or his cock-would like it very much if I laughed right now.

"You're out," I whisper. "But you should still get a prize. Can I lure you onto my team?"

He nods his head, and the incredulity at my actions dissipates immediately. The clatter of the gun on the tile is loud, but Noah's groan is louder when I draw him into my mouth. His hand fists in my hair, holding me in place as he rocks forward. I hollow my cheeks and encourage him with my nails digging into the backs of his thighs. Aware we're on the clock, and one of our opponents could discover us at any moment, I hasten my movements on his cock and drag my nails on his thighs again. He moans my name as his speed picks up, jamming his fist into his own mouth to muffle his sounds of pleasure.

His breathing is coming quicker now. His eyes snap open, and he maintains eye contact as he powers down my throat. He keeps his hand firm but gentle in my hair. I arch my back so his visual is his hand fisted in my hair and my lace-covered ass. I pull back. "Quickly, Noah. We have to win." He laughs and picks up his pace.

I cup his balls, and when I swallow, I press just behind them, and Noah explodes. He looks down at me with awe as I pop off his cock and lick my lips, using my thumb to catch the excess. His breathing is ragged, and his thighs are shaking under my hands.

I hop up to my feet and grab my gun. The ammo clips are a bit more challenging to keep on me now, but they have little hooks, so I clip them along the waistband of my panties. I look up to see Noah staring at me, his mouth agape and his eyes devouring every inch of me. "Fuck. You can lead me to hell looking like that, Trouble. You're every wet dream I've ever had."

I give him a wink and pump the Nerf gun before leading us up the stairs and out of the wing. We reach the foyer, and shots rain down on us from the landing above. Noah pulls me behind him and returns fire quickly.

"What the fuck, Noah!?" I hear Han shout. "You switched teams?"

"She got me. I'm hers now."

A mumbled curse reaches my ears from Han's position. He tries popping his head around the corner, and Noah fires off two more shots. "Let's go," he encourages me. We take the stairs two at a time, and at the top, he takes the left wing, and I take the right, similar to how Romano and I split up. I bet there's one of them on each level in each wing. It's how I'd spread us out if given the leadership role. I stalk the hallway toward my bedroom. What are the chances Han went into any other room than that one? Hedging my bets, I power through the hall and open the door to my room. Nothing is out of place, but as soon as I step through the door, I'm pressed against the wall, Han's delicious body at my back.

"Hiya, Gorgeous."

"Wow, Han, is that a Nerf gun, or are you just happy to see me?" I ask.

"Both." His laugh is infectious, but the gun at the center of my back is hard to mistake. "But I think I know how you swayed Noah to your side. I won't fall for it."

With that, he fires the gun, but no dart connects. *A misfire! Are you freaking kidding me?!*

Taking advantage of his confusion, I spin in his arms and use my foot to push us off the wall. Lucky, sure, but who am I to say no to an advantage during a game of cat and mouse?

I pushed us hard enough that we landed on the bed. Han's gun stays in his hand because of his years of experience, but I stretch our hands above his head, giving him no reprieve as I grind down on him.

"Nope. Not falling for it, Gorgeous." Han grits his teeth as I move my hips, and I see his resolve cracking. I lean down and kiss the hell out of him, releasing his hands and bringing my gun to his chest. I fire once, and the orange dart rolls off of his chest after making contact.

"That's okay. You're mine now, as well. Want to go find Jacob and see if we can get him on our side, too?" I ask.

He shakes his head in defeat but flips us on the bed. "Fine. Stupid gun. I should grab a new one."

After tossing on some clothes, we leave the room. We make a quick but stealthy stop in Lucas's room—because who else would have a Nerf gun arsenal—to pick up a new piece for Han. It was a close call. Lucas had rigged some sort of Nerf bomb, and we narrowly avoided the shower of darts when Han flung the door open.

I reload the clip because a full clip is always better than a half-spent one. It's just thoughtful planning. We find Noah and Jacob locked in a standoff in the home theater. They're on either side of the seating, trading shots back and forth. I take aim when Jacob pops up, and I hit him in the dick. Oops.

He looks down incredulously, and Noah, who didn't see the exchange, pops up and hits him right over his heart. How did he do that? These things don't have the trajectory of a standard bullet. Hence the dick shot.

"Yeah, yeah, I'm out," he groans. I try to hide my laugh, but Jacob's glare tells me he sees it anyway. He makes his way over to me, throws one of his inked arms over my shoulder, and the four of us make our way down to the bottom floor where I left Romano. We veer off to that side of the house, and when we enter the library, Romano is there, fucking with the bookshelves.

"What's going on?" I ask. He whirls with the Nerf gun drawn, but when he sees it's all of us together, no guns at the ready, he drops it. That's when I hear it.

There's a thumping and banging behind the bookshelf. I double over laughing, and when I finally recover, everyone is staring.

"Lucas found the hidden passageway," I gasp out between laughs. "And he can't get out."

I hear the guys chuckle behind me, then Lucas. "Buttercup! Is that you? How the hell do I get out of here? This wasn't on the map!"

I lose it all over again, and this time, the guys join in a bit more enthusiastically. I reach Romano and gently nudge him out of the way. "Do you surrender?" I ask Lucas through the bookshelf.

"What the hell? Buttercup, there could be rats in here! Get me out!"

I hear Noah behind me, "So hedgehogs are okay, but rats are where he draws the line? Unbelievable."

Pressing my toes to the tiny lever at the base of the bookshelf and pulling on *The Lion, The Witch, and The Wardrobe* by C. S. Lewis, there's a soft hiss, and the bookshelf swings forward. Lucas comes diving out of the space behind the wall and lands on the carpet with a dull thud before rolling onto his back. I lift my Nerf gun and peg him on the knee. He didn't agree to my terms earlier, and I needed to ensure victory. Speaking of, just in case Romano and I aren't actually on the same team, I whirl and get him quickly on his foot. I smile broadly at his scowl.

Romano extends a hand down and helps Lucas to his feet. Lucas surprises all of us when he throws his arms around Romano. I hear him whisper, "Thank you for talking me through that and not leaving."

Their bromance makes me weirdly happy. Romano, on the other hand, seems mildly uncomfortable. He pats Lucas on the back twice, then gestures for me to lead the way. We traipse down the hallway and end up in the second lounge area. One of the ones without an orgy couch. I wonder if I should get one for every room? A discussion for later.

Noah opens the mini-fridge in the sidebar and pulls out beers for everyone. "So, how did it go?" he asks.

Romano clears his throat and gives them the news they were waiting for. "We're divorced. It's being processed, and with the pressure the bureau is placing on the judge, it should be legal in a matter of days."

Lucas, Han, and Jacob all whoop, and we clink our beers together in celebration. Noah, being the mature man he is, extends his hand to Romano. "Thank you for getting it done so quickly. I know you have your own reasons, but our girl being legally tied to someone else didn't sit right."

"Our? Our girl? Like... all of you?" He looks between all of us, and I realize he knows about Lucas but not the rest. *Well, fuck.*

"Got a problem with that, Romano?" I ask.

"Fuck no. I'm glad you have all of them watching out for you. I, uh... have some experience in the poly lifestyle. You'll get no judgment from me. When it works, it works." He sees my mind trying to process the information, and he laughs. "Rogue, I've been around for a while. You know a bit of my past, but not all of it."

I nod my head, putting that topic on the back burner for another time, and the guys all pat him on the back quickly. Being the stand-up guy he is, Noah was just trying to thank him and unknowingly let out some vital information. Romano has proven himself trustworthy so far. I'm monitoring him anyway, but I don't want this getting back to his handler, Shade, or their bosses.

"This stays between us. Please," I beg, clasping my hands together in front of me, showing him how serious I am about this.

"Agreed." His agreement comes easily. "I lost my wife. I don't want to put anyone's loved ones in jeopardy. They'll remain your four accomplices, unnamed and unspoken of by me. You have my word."

Noah studies Romano for a second before nodding his head. He believes him. Han's hand on my thigh releases a bit, knowing no judgment or outing is heading our way.

"Anyway, I wanted to talk to you guys about something." Romano piques everyone's interest with that statement.

Lucas makes a circular motion with his hand, urging Romano to spit it out. The man in question just laughs.

"Look, while King was in the hospital, I got into his apartment."

"I remember. I helped distract security for a bit while you snooped," I confirm.

"I found his safe," Romano says.

"What the fuck? Where?! I searched most of that place for that thing the entire month we were there. Why didn't you say anything?" I ask with fire in my tone. Any chance I had, I scoured that apartment. There was nothing in the blueprints, nothing around the office, his bedroom, unless... it must have been in either my room or the torture room. The two places I couldn't bring myself to spend any measure of time in. After my fruitless search, I was halfway convinced he used one of the safe deposit boxes at Saint Ignatius Church.

"It was in the concrete room; there was a section of the wall with a small keypad. The code is your birthday." His eyes have a bit of sympathy in them. He knows about the conversations King and I had. More often than not, during that last month, King's talks of my mom and the pregnancy were him trying to convince me/my mom to raise the baby with him.

"King died twenty-five days ago, Romano. Why not bring this to me sooner?" I ask.

"With the transition? Don't you think you've had enough going on?" I'm about to shred him from head to toe about withholding because I was "busy," when he follows it up with some sound reasoning. "I also wanted to verify what I found instead of sending you on a wild goose chase."

"And what did you find?" Jacob asks.

Romano's thumbnail scrapes at the beer's label, gently picking at it as he gathers his thoughts. "Evidence. Lots of it. There is your work, of course. It's where I got the paperwork from. I wasn't entirely honest about where I got it the night I delivered it to you. It was important for you to know I had it without revealing all of this." Understandable. I don't like it, but I get it. "There's evidence against your father and Patton Cross as well. It's why when you offered Cross to Shade and the higher-ups, you surprised me. What do you have on him so far?"

Scoffing, I reply with a firm tone, "I'm not answering that. I want everything you got from King's hidey-hole, and I want to work through it because I'm supposed to meet the psychopath in a week and a half. I need to walk into that meeting armed to the teeth with secrets and weapons. Sometimes, the darkest secrets cut deeper than a knife."

"I agree," Romano nods as he answers. "You need to know everything. But, Rogue, it's not pretty. Your father... there are things he did that you won't enjoy hearing."

"I'm an assassin, Romano. I may not like it, but I've got a stronger stomach than most."

Jacob's hand on my lower back gives me a bit of strength to face what's coming. Romano clears his throat. "I digitized everything. It's on a secure cloud that only Shade and I have access to. I can download it for you immediately. Just give me a computer."

Jacob stands immediately, ready to dive in, and leads Romano to the office he set up.

"Buttercup, you okay?" Lucas asks gently.

"Yes. No. Fuck. I can never answer that question."

Han presses a kiss on my temple. "That's okay. You don't have to. We'll get this sorted out. And you're absolutely right. You need to know everything. And we're here for when it tries to break you." I lean into his touch.

"I love you," I mumble against his neck as he hugs me.

"I love you too, Ivy."

Lucas runs a hand along my thigh, grounding me in the moment. I look at the guys surrounding me, and I know no matter what the evidence is against Cross and my father, Joseph, it happened. Knowing about it won't change the fact that they've done evil things or that the man whose DNA I carry was also a possible murderer.

I think about my last visit to their graves before King's funeral. I stood there, wondering if this was what he would have wanted for me. As it turns out, maybe it was.

Chapter Seventeen

Rogue

THE ONLY THING WORSE THAN DOING A BODY DUMP IS DOING A BODY dump in the middle of a date when the guy has no idea. Han looks across the table at me, takes my hand in his, and squeezes gently. "So you've been busy this week," he comments.

"Yeah, I was taking care of a few of Cian Byrne's underlings."

"Oh, what have they been up to?" he asks as he sips his cappuccino the server just delivered.

"The usual. You would think after taking care of those six dealers that De La Cruz couldn't rein in, they would be smarter. But I guess they thought the rules would change with the change in regime."

"Did Cian give you the list of dealers to have G handle?" Han asks as he enjoys his coffee.

"Not exactly. I noticed it when I was shadowing our new board member last week. There was a discrepancy between sales and the product he had on hand. With it being so far from tax return time, we usually have a dip in the market after everyone spends their return checks. It didn't line up with previous years. Plus, Claudette's guys are watching for me as well."

"Well, I'm glad that you're taking care of it. We have another assignment for Mara coming up next week, but it's one we can do from home. Jacob's got the server rooms nearly settled, and the rest is just find and retrieve. At least it's not a bank this time, and Lucas doesn't have to go undercover. He was jumping for joy when he heard he didn't need to do the whole corporate schtick again."

I chuckle to myself, imagining Lucas's happy dance. Settling into the house has been easier than we expected. The guys got what they needed from the clubhouse using the secret passages leading to the various apartments around the neighborhood. Then, we had a moving crew get the things they couldn't drag out with them. It's funny, finding a moving company willing to do the work at three in the morning was not that difficult. It only took an extra five thousand dollars to get it done. With King's money burning a hole in my pocket, it was easy to throw the cash at them rather than have it sitting in my bank account. I don't want the money. Nor do I want the business. I just want to move on and be who I am, not this name whispered like a threat to anyone stupid enough to cross a criminal empire.

One thing at a time. I hope my end game lands me safely where I want to be, but I've got my bases covered, just in case.

"That's great news," I tell Han. "I'm glad it's one where you're sticking close to home. Noah has a meeting with Nick Grand coming up. He's the leader of Beta Team Two. We think he's a plant. Perhaps the entire team is. But he slipped Noah a piece of paper with his contact information, and they're setting something up for next week."

Han looks like he's doing complex mathematical equations in his brain and I can't say I blame him. "As much as it pains me to say this, I think we need to line up all the players on the board," I say and drop my head forward.

"Yeah, I think you're right. How the fuck are we going to manage a giant team meeting like this without raising suspicions?" Han's question immediately has me thinking of venues and planning how to do this without anyone catching wind of it.

I shrug and ask if he has any ideas. The only thing I can think of is a massive Zoom meeting, but if even *one* person isn't in a secure location and on a secure line, we're all fucked.

"I don't know, Gorgeous, but we'll figure it out. You have Alpha Team One at your command." Han's waggled brows make me laugh. He releases my hands so we can start on our dessert.

We're currently floating on a yacht in the middle of the bay. It felt easy to leave my problems on the dock at the harbor. Now, as we discuss them, it's like they're all breathing down my neck again. Fuck. We need a vacation. Maybe we can go visit Mrs. M and her Dick on their Caribbean adventure? But we will definitely rent a place far, *far* away from where she and her beau are undoubtedly knocking boots.

Why are we out floating around at sea? Well, Han asked me on a date, and so we had to make do with the plans I already had. Let's just hope he doesn't get too upset with what's about to happen. Carving my spoon into my chocolate cake, I watch as the molten chocolate spills out.

God, this place has good food.

Han is working on his fruit sorbet, and I keep sneaking glances between bites of my chocolate cake. He asks the server for another spoon, and we end up sharing desserts. *Goodness, we're cute.*

We finish our coffees after finishing dessert and talk about this and that. It's rare to find time alone together, living in the house with all of us essentially on lockdown. You would think a manor would offer more opportunities for sneaking away together, but we all end up in the sex couch living room or the kitchen more often than not. We all just seem to gravitate toward each other.

I keep slipping out to handle Gambit business, and the guys are working on getting the place up to scratch for their own work.

We take a walk along the deck of the boat after proclaiming we couldn't possibly have another bite. We reach the railing at the bow, and next to me is a bench with a picture of life jackets on it. There's a smudge of blood on the corner of the lid, barely noticeable in the moonlight. Rosa's getting sloppy.

While Han is admiring the lights reflecting on the water from the city, I gently lift one of the bench tops. They're about six feet long and three feet wide, not exactly big enough for the bodies I brought on board, but it works. I pull a pair of gloves from my bra and slip them over my hands. Time to get to work.

"Oh, do you see that there?" Han asks as he points across the water. "We once infiltrated that building." He goes on about the memory as I heave the torso of the first dealer over the railing and push.

The splash gets Han's attention, and he looks over at me. Leaning to the side to see around my voluminous skirt, he notices the bench stuffed with bodies and the cinder blocks next to them that I'm tying around their limbs to help them sink.

"Ivy, what the fuck?"

My eyes plead innocence, while my bloody gloves display my culpability.

"Are you tossing bodies into the water?" he asks, his tone one of disbelief. "This was supposed to be a romantic date!"

I shuffle on my feet for just a moment as I hide my hands behind my back, fluttering my eyelashes in innocence. "It can be two things!"

He pinches the bridge of his nose and exhales deeply, counting to three a few times before removing his hand from his face.

"It can be both," I state again. "But I'm kind of on a time crunch before they start to smell." My excuse falls on deaf ears.

"Why didn't Rosa handle this?" he asks.

"She has another job tonight. I told her to stick them on the boat and I'd deal with it."

After three more repetitions of his counting, he blows out an exhale, and simply says, "All right. Do you have another set of gloves?"

I thrust my chest out to him. Tilting with my chin, I point him toward my left breast. "I stuffed a pair in there for you too, just in case."

"I have to buy you a purse or a backpack or something," he says. "You can't keep stuffing things in your bra."

"Why not?" I pout. "Purses are easy to leave behind. I'll consider the backpack. Maybe."

He laughs while mumbling to himself about insane women, and reaches into the top of my bra to grab the gloves. He snaps them on, lifts the second bench's lid, and the two of us get to work, tying the weights and heaving body after body over the top of the railing. Once the sixth one hits the water, we peel off our gloves and Han shoves them into his pocket to toss later. We can't just throw them in with the bodies; the fish don't deserve that.

"Well, Gorgeous, I have to say, this has been the most interesting date I've ever been on."

"You know what, I have to agree. At least you know with me it'll never be boring." He hooks an arm over my shoulder and pulls me in for a kiss.

"That's true."

I blow out a deep breath and look at the cityscape before me. The meeting with Cross is in three days, and after going through the information Romano brought to us and my own digging, I feel as prepared as possible to get this over with.

Han and I spend another hour on the boat, watching the waves, the lights across the bay, and sharing a bottle of champagne. Despite the intermission, the date is incredible.

We eventually make our way home, but instead of going straight in, we lie out on the grass in the yard, hands linked, and look up at the stars. I don't think it's just me who wishes for everything to go well when a shooting star passes over us.

I SMOOTH MY HANDS DOWN THE SKIRT OF MY TIGHT, BLACK, KNEE-length dress and steady myself on my dangerously high black heels after exiting the car.

I didn't want to attend this meeting without a weapon, so Han made it happen with barely a word. Knowing the security of the building, we determined that the guards would demand we hand over any weapons at reception. They'd then send us through metal detectors and pat us down, so we got creative in our concealment.

G and Fabio are with me on this excursion because I didn't want to show up without security and it's not like I could have brought one of my guys. Romano is recognizable in our circles, and I didn't want this to be a boys' club meeting. So, I made do. I trust these two implicitly.

They flank me on either side as I push through the double doors. The lobby is pristine, and there is a bank of security guards and desk attendants before the elevator, just as the guys said.

The guards tell G and Fabio to hand over their weapons before we pass through the metal detectors and enter the elevator to reach the executive floor. They put on a show of not being pleased with abandoning their hardware at the desk, displaying their disgruntled nature to the men locking up their weapons.

But it's exactly as we planned. If they are packing, the chances of me doing the same are low in the eyes of most guards. After they're patted down to make sure there are no weapons, I receive the same treatment, although, a bit more gently.

A man waves us through to the elevators, the doors waiting for us to enter. We step inside, and I hand over a few of the ceramic knives that I have hidden between my thighs. The guys move in close, blocking any camera angles, and slip the sheathed blades into their waistbands to have at the ready if needed.

With my skin tight dress, it doesn't look like I could hide anything. But by sticking them to my inner thighs, I've smuggled in my own arsenal. Sure, they patted down the outside of my body. But my skirt trapped my legs tightly together. And it's not like they were going to ask me to hike it up in the middle of the lobby.

The mirrored doors slide open, and we're met with yet another pristine lobby. I wonder if they designed this with Rook Industries in mind. After all, Patton once worked for The Gambit. It wouldn't surprise me if he brought some of that over to his new enterprise. The receptionist stands as soon as I exit the elevator, still flanked by my friends/guards.

"I'm here for my ten o'clock with Mr. Cross," I tell her succinctly. I keep my arms folded across my chest and look down at my watch as if I have somewhere else to be. In reality, I've cleared my schedule for the week just in case I need to bury a body and do the cover up.

"Right this way, Ms. Queen," she says, the picture of professionalism. "He's expecting you."

"I should hope so. He called the meeting," I deadpan, mask firmly in place, ready to take on whatever this is.

We trail after the receptionist to the biggest corner office in the place. Frosted glass walls frame each office, and Cross's is no different. She gently raps on the door twice, and we hear Cross beckon us inside.

She pushes the door open, holding it as the three of us enter. There he sits. My godfather.

He's dressed in an all-black suit, his polished, shiny shoes are visible under the desk. A sun-tanned hand rubs across his stubbled jaw and his short, dark hair is swept to the side. But the thing that stops me in my tracks are the ice-blue eyes staring back at me from an expressionless face. The eyes, though, convey everything.

He stands slowly, as if deciding whether to show me the respect I deserve in my position. "Queen," he greets.

"Cross," I reply in the same tone. The receptionist asks if we'd like anything to drink, and of course, we all say no. I'm not giving them a chance to poison me. They're going to have to work for it if it's my death Cross is after.

"Please, have a seat." Cross waves a hand at the chair across from his desk. I approach it and gently lower myself. There's still a sheathed knife strapped to my inner thigh, so I have to ease myself down or risk giving away the fact I'm not unarmed. G and Fabio take up the spots behind me on either side.

"Gentlemen, I'm sure that we're fine," Cross says, trying to dismiss my men. "You may wait outside."

"Oh, no." I shake my head in refusal. "These two stay. See it from my side. Taking over an empire such as The Gambit requires me to have security with me at all times. Please meet G, my replacement as lead assassin, and his second, Fabio." Both men incline their heads and nod with respect, playing the roles I've issued them.

We discussed this meeting at length over the past week. Between cleaning up the dealers and getting these two up to snuff on what's required as a personal security team, my week was disgustingly full.

"I understand, Queen. Although, there are some things that should probably remain between the two heads of organizations, don't you think?" Cross asks.

I tilt my head from side to side, pretending to consider his point of view. "That may be, Cross, but I don't know you. Can I trust you? Should I?" I muse aloud as I tap my index finger on my chin.

"I'm sure we could change that," he suggests.

"In time," I assure him. "Now, what is it you want from me? I've had countless meetings such as this over the past month with other figureheads. It becomes quite draining, so let's get to it."

I don't want him thinking I've been looking forward to or dreading this meeting for the last two weeks. Making him feel unimportant, unworthy of my time, and one of many is a tactic I've used to get that little extra oomph out of people in the past. Here's hoping it works again.

He chuckles as he settles in his seat. "I have to say, you're not what I was expecting."

Waving my hand in a circular motion, I encourage him to continue his thoughts aloud. "I don't know whether that's a compliment or an insult," I playfully tell him. He seems the type to play with his food before he murders it.

"I like it," he affirms. "It's definitely a compliment. King and I were not on the best of terms during his tenure. I'd like to start a partnership with you."

"A partnership with The Gambit? What can a security firm offer us that I can't hire directly and indoctrinate myself?" I ask, genuinely curious about what resources he's willing to throw around.

"I can offer you already trained men. Men you don't have to spend your time breaking in. I can also offer you contacts to a group of ready-to-attack mercenaries." He looks at G and Fabio behind me. "No offense, gentlemen. But you know as well as I do, that your training takes time."

He refocuses on me. "I can offer you trained technology experts at the top of their fields, teams ready for tactical use, and the biggie: insight into multiple government agencies who are looking to take you down."

"And what would you like in return?" I ask boldly. "Come now, Cross. We both know nothing is free in this life. Don't be coy."

"I want to lead with you."

"I'm sure my husband would have something to say about that," I gently chastise him. "Well, ex-husband now, I guess. Make no mistake, he is still my right hand. I just didn't like the whole shackled-to-one-person-for-all-eternity bit."

Cross lets out a laugh. "No one will be around forever. I'll wait for my turn. We can trade stakes in each other's companies. I'm open to negotiations."

"Once you prove your loyalty," I counter quickly. "I am not a stupid woman, Cross. I know the value my organization has, and I will not sell a piece for less than it is worth."

I see his fingers grip his desk so hard the knuckles turn white with the pressure. What did he think was going to happen? That I'd walk in and he'd impress me with his company and smooth talking? *Please.*

"Why didn't you and King work together?" I ask, point-blank.

"He holds grudges. Well, he *held* grudges." A smile curls upon his lips as he thinks of my former father figure. "I was once with The Gambit, but we didn't quite see eye to eye on what was necessary to achieve their goals. I will admit, King did a good job of getting the state in line. But there are still some corners outside of your reach. Los Angeles, for example, San Diego? Those are key cities if you want to expand into Mexico. The opportunities are there, Queen. It's up to you to take them. And I'm willing to help you along the way."

"Again, what is it you want in exchange?" I speak slowly, enunciating each word, because I'm still waiting for the full answer.

"I want off my leash," he says. "Your time as an assassin is responsible for more than a few of my men's deaths. King, despite his shortcomings, kept a few things hidden from me, including your identity and location." I release some of the tension in my fists and send up a silent prayer of thank you to whoever is watching over me for that small mercy. I don't like this man's attention on me at all, let alone the possibility of being on the receiving end of his anger.

He continues, "I will help you expand in exchange for half of the territory. With your numbers and my knowledge, we could run the entire coast. Once Los Angeles and San Diego are in your grasp, we could expand north into The Rattlesnakes territory. They had a change in leadership recently and are ripe for the picking. Not to mention The Vegas Crew's area. You know the feds took them down, right?"

"That's even more reason to be cautious," I remind Cross.

"No one knows anything about you. Not even I, Queen," the man before me confesses. "I only know you were a former hit woman. No one knows your name or where you came from. Believe me, I've been looking. If you were to disappear into the wind, who could find you? The time to strike is now, while you're relatively anonymous. I won't be the only one sniffing your trail, and the feds have a lot of resources. Why not build up your loyal following now?"

I consider his proposal. Slowly reeling him in under the guise of giving him what he wants is a good way for me to keep him under my thumb. Relaxing back into the chair, I pretend to think things over.

I can't seem too eager, so I make a show of tilting my head up to G, who nods. I turn to Fabio, and he mimics the motion exactly as we practiced. They know I need him on our side, so their support will offer him the idea that two more of my men approve of him, in case he ever betrays me. Not that he'll get the chance. Any move he makes against me will have these two putting him in a pine box faster than Cross can blink.

"All right, Cross. Give me two days to consider and weigh the options, but I like your terms. That territory is too big for just one person to rule. I'm not so egocentric as to deny that."

His smile is sinister as it breaks out over his face. I resist the urge to shudder.

With that, I stand, smoothing my dress over my hips. His eyes follow the movement and I tamp down the urge to shudder yet again. This man gives me the heebie-jeebies. Keeping the disgust from showing on my face is taking far more control than I wish to admit.

I extend my hand to him, and instead of shaking it, he raises it to his lips to kiss my knuckles. I fight the urge to vomit at the contact.

"Good day. I'll contact you in two days with my answer," I tell him, trying not to wipe my hand on my dress and then burn the damn thing.

"It's been a pleasure, Queen. I look forward to your acceptance."

I spin on my heel. Fabio opens the door, and they follow me out of the office. They fall in line as we make our way through the hallway, my heels clicking with each step on the pristine tile.

An office door is open across the space, and I almost do a double-take when I spy Mara Hendricks behind her desk. She looks so much like

Claudette, it's ridiculous. If not for their entirely different wardrobe style choices, one would easily mistake them for twins. Granted, one is more sane than the other. I keep my pace as G and Fabio watch ahead of us, thankfully not seeing Claudette's sister in the vicinity. Based on both of their recent texts about her, I wouldn't be surprised if they suddenly detoured to go hit on her.

We enter the elevator and make our way downstairs. We stop at the lobby desk, and the boys grab the weapons we left behind. Gently patting his guns, G lets out a relieved sigh as we exit the building and coos that he's never leaving them again. Ridiculous.

"So?" Fabio asks.

"I have to make a deal with the devil. Are you guys good with this? He may approach you to take me out." I must show my concern on my face because G makes a sympathetic noise and bear-hugs me.

"Queen, we gotchu, girl. I'll shove a knife so far up his ass, it'll tickle his uvula if he makes a move on you." *Big softy.*

It doesn't take me two days to contact Cross.

Within six hours, I've sent confirmation and orders on the first things we need done after having a nice long chat with Romano and the enigmatic Shade.

Chapter Eighteen

Jacob

"No, you can't be by the south entrance, that's where Han and Fabio are going to be stationed." Noah's exasperation at the logistics of the party next week is spreading to the rest of us.

"Fine. Then I'll stay by the east wall then, opposite you," Lucas tells him.

"That works, Red," Rogue reassures him.

We've been circling locations for the better part of two weeks, and with the big party looming in ten days, we're all a little tense.

Romano swivels on his stool as he looks over the blueprints of the hotel spread across the kitchen island. His eyes track the space and the set-up Elise, Rogue, and the party planners put together. "What if..." he muses aloud. "What if I put Shade over there?" He points to the security space just to the side of the ballroom. "We have enough bodies, but I have a feeling you, Jacob"—he nods at me—"will want to stay where you can see what's going on. Shade's not overly fond of fieldwork, but he could be close by instead of at the main office on the computer."

I mull over the idea. Do I want to be nearby in case things go sideways? Absolutely. Do I trust this Shade guy? Eh, kind of. But anything is better than being stuffed in the security closet and out of reach in case something happens.

"That works. He and I should meet up this week to go over everything in advance." I know the others want our group together for this, so I don't mind the switch.

Romano lifts his phone and presses the screen. "Damiano." A moment passes and a small smile breaks out on Romano's face as he asks about guns. I know that smile. It's the one you get when you talk to your teammate. "Hey, we have an alternate plan. You'll be at the hotel with us."

I hear a muffled voice coming from the phone and laugh at the curses falling from Shade's side. "Yes, yes. I know. But we need you closer just in case, so Accomplice Three can be in the room as extra backup." I still laugh that despite Romano knowing our names, he kept his word and only refers to us as Accomplices One through Four. Shade certainly knows our names by now if his skills are up to snuff, but I have a feeling Rogue may hang the whole King-killing over Romano's head to keep him quiet.

More grumbles from the other side.

"I know you like your office and the van, but that won't cut it this time. You and Accomplice Three will meet this week to go over everything. He's being very generous in sharing his tech with us, and you'll play nice. Okay?"

"Fine." The word comes clearly across the line, and I can't help but laugh at the tone. Yeah, I get it. I'd rather be in my office, surrounded by screens and assurances than in the thick of it. He'll be fine, if not just a touch uncomfortable.

Romano hangs up the phone and writes Shade's number on a corner of the blueprints before ripping it off and handing it to me. I nod gratefully and start making plans in my head about how the handoff of data will go. I created a few things over the past month as we prepared for the party and handing it over to the feds seems like a bad way to go, but fuck it. I'm happy to sell the tech if it's for the right price.

Han clears his throat. "Well, Romano. I think that's it. We've got positions, weapons, federal back up, the timing, hell, even the food picked out. The invitations have all gone out, and attendees have all responded with agreements within the time frame. Let's think it over and meet in a few days to go over it again. But now, we've got other work to do."

He sighs. "Yeah, I have to meet with a few people today. Fuck, I hate the planning stage." We all laugh at that and make consoling sounds in agreement.

Of the plans we've concocted over the last month, this one is one of the most straightforward, and after running the numbers, it's the most likely to succeed.

Lucas walks Romano out and arms the security panel. The monitor in the kitchen shows Romano leaving and Fabio at the gate sending up a one-finger salute at his retreating G-Wagon. I hate to say it, but over the past few weeks, G and Fabio have grown on me. I also think it's hilarious that Fabio keeps asking Rogue when the redhead is coming back. Seems like Claudette made quite the impression on our long-haired friend.

Han leans toward Rogue and places his hands on her shoulders, gently kneading away the tension in them. She drops her head back and groans at the sensation.

We've all been extraordinarily tense lately. The planning, the deception, the excuses that all four of us came down with something and are currently bed-ridden is keeping us from needing to work for Annex. Mara, of course, backed up our story after Noah convinced her it was in the best interest of taking down Cross.

Finding out he was the one who sent mercenaries to our clubhouse was a shock. Apparently, one of Nicolas's team members contacted his wife somehow. She didn't keep it quiet enough, and whoever Cross has in Bakersfield noticed. It means he knows we're not killing off competitors as directed. Mara played dumb to the whole thing, and threw us under the bus, as we instructed her to. It turns out money can buy mercs, but it can't guarantee they're good ones.

The four of us have been in lockdown since the event, and while we're avoiding jobs like the plague, it means only Rogue is going out to get things squared as needed. Between running the empire and handling our moody asses, she's been working herself to the bone. Which is why I set up a little surprise for her today.

The workers finished the room a couple of days ago; it was just a matter of stocking it with all the online purchases I recently made.

Noah, Lucas, and Han are in on the surprise, laughing at my sneaky tendencies to get this done. Fuck, it took me nearly two weeks, and I did it all under the cover of night, or when Rogue was out working. I didn't want to ruin the surprise. I paid Fabio a few thousand dollars to keep his mouth shut, but he still insists on checking each package that arrives to ensure I mean no harm to his boss. After the fifth box, he started blushing every time he handed one over after storing it in the guardhouse until Rogue left or went to bed.

Rogue melts into Han's touch, and Lucas slides in front of her, wedging himself between her spread thighs.

He leans down and kisses her lazily, as if they have all the time in the world, when in reality, we may only have ten days, depending on how all this goes down.

Noah rolls up the blueprints on the island as I watch Lucas, Rogue, and Han. The latter turns and winks at me, mouthing, "Later."

He knows I'm excited to show Rogue my surprise, but he's right; she needs to rest now.

"Darling Mine, what else do you have to do today?" I ask the half-asleep goddess.

"What time is it?" she asks, cracking open one eye and pulling her face away from Lucas's.

"Just after three."

"Ugh, I'm supposed to call Elise to go over final party details. It's all done, but she wants to run through it again." Her groan at the idea echoes around the kitchen.

"Fuck that," Lucas says. "I'll call her and tell her you're sick. I can pretend to be your doctor."

"No, no. It's fine. I can call her myself." She extricates herself from the sandwich and brings her phone up to her ear. "Elise, I've got awful cramps. Let's reschedule for tomorrow or the day after. Yeah? Okay, I'll see you in a couple of days then. Thanks. No, I'm okay. I'll see you soon."

The four of us look at each other across the island. That's it? Rogue takes in our expressions and just laughs. "Every woman knows the pain of truly awful cramps. We offer sympathy in those times, and copious amounts of ice cream."

"Do you need ice cream?" Lucas asks tentatively.

Rogue just shakes her head, kisses him quickly on the lips, and excuses herself. I take her arm in mine and escort her to her room. We really need to tear down a few walls in this place. The rooms are a decent size, but everything is so sectioned off. Rogue showed us some ideas for the renovation, and Han has completely taken over. I've seen some of the work he has planned for when all of this is over, and it's going to be glorious.

"Come on, Darling Mine. To bed," I murmur as I lead her up the stairs.

She doesn't even strip out of her clothes before flopping onto the mattress face first. I prop myself up against the headboard, and she snuggles into the crook of my arm, sighing heavily when she finds a position she likes. Pulling my phone out of my pocket with my free hand, I start up Candy Crush. I'm going to be here for a while, I think.

A SOFT HAND GENTLY CURLS AROUND MY MIDDLE, AND I SLOWLY blink my eyes open as I smile.

"Hey," Rogue says from my side.

"Hey," I reply, my grin carving deeper into my cheeks. "Did you sleep enough?" I ask.

My eyes need a moment to adjust to the dim light filtering in through the still open curtains. Dusk then.

"Yeah, I needed that. Thank you." Her voice has a tinge of worry to it, and I know just the way to make that disappear. I lean closer and she tilts her face up to me. Pressing my lips gently to hers, I luxuriate in the sigh that escapes her lips. Her hand roams dangerously low toward my trousers, and I halt its progression with a clamp on her wrist.

"Give me a moment," I beg softly. I pull my phone out and quickly text the guys in our group chat.

Me: Everyone up?
Noah: Yes, in the library.
Lucas: Walking Sir Lancelot around the backyard.
Han: Gathering supplies in the shed out back.
Me: Good, meet in the library in 5 minutes. Lucas, secure Lancelot. We're going to be there awhile.

The texts of confirmation come pouring in, and I hear doors opening and shutting through the house. Despite being such a big place with a lot of upgrades, Elise never soundproofed. It makes sense, I guess, if she was the one running the place. It's not as if her employees were going to complain.

I slide my phone back into my pocket and cup Rogue's cheeks. Staring into her green eyes, I whisper, "I have a surprise for you."

Excitement shines back at me, and she moves her hand south again. "No, Darling Mine. Not here. Get up, get undressed, and follow me."

She scrambles off of the bed and sheds her clothes almost faster than I can track. She stands proudly, naked, and gives me a gorgeous view of the tattoos running along her skin.

"Good girl," I say in a deep tone, watching as a small shudder overtakes her body. I noticed the same thing happened the first time I said it, so I've been using it for the past few months. Praise kink? Maybe.

I take a giant step forward and throw her over my shoulder, caveman style. Her ass next to my face screams for attention, so I bring a palm down on it quickly and she squeals. The skin pinks so beautifully. I stride to the door and make my way downstairs. The entire time, Rogue has her hands meandering over my ass. I spank her once more, and her arousal thickens the surrounding air. Fuck, this was a bad idea. How am I supposed to show any measure of restraint like this? Her hands still and I turn my head, biting her ass cheek next to me, and she groans low and long. Oh yeah, that's how. I'd restrain myself forever if I got to keep hearing those noises spill from her lips.

I march through the open library door and find Noah, Lucas, and Han huddled together. As one, their heads snap up and wicked smiles play upon their lips.

"What are we doing in the library, Jacob? Not the books! We can't defile the books!" Her laughter escapes, but when I set her down, and she takes in the other three, it cuts off abruptly. Noah's eyes are tracing her body, Lucas is doing the same, while Han's gaze pings between the two of us.

"I've been working on something for us, Darling Mine." She looks back at me, questions swimming in her eyes.

"Oh? And what's that?"

"Lucas, if you will?" I ask. He was skeptical when I told him what I wanted to do after exploring the hidden passageway he got trapped in. Apparently, he hadn't moved away from the door when he found himself locked inside for fear of rodents, but I certainly explored every nook and cranny of the network of tunnels and found some *interesting* spaces.

Lucas presses the lever, pulls on a different book than last time, and grins wide when the shelf swings forward. This time, the book is the Kama Sutra. One guess as to who advocated for that change.

"Follow me, Buttercup," Lucas says, stepping into the dark hallway.

Rogue looks at me, confirming it's okay, and I give her a nod in encouragement. Noah walks beside her, and Han takes my hand as we follow suit.

I outfitted the rough stone-hewn hallways with LED lighting that emits a soft glow, so as Lucas leads us down the passage to the right, we don't trip over each other. He pauses before a door and looks over Rogue's head at me. I pull a key from my pocket and insert it into the big wooden door. Turning it, I hear the tumblers move, and the door swings open on slightly rusted hinges. That's next on my list.

I step through and Noah puts his hands over Rogue's eyes, leading her blindly into the room.

I quickly adjust the lighting so it's softer and have a quick look around to ensure everything is in its place.

Nods from the guys tell me they're all prepared and on board with what's going down tonight. Noah removes his hands from Rogue's eyes, and she blinks as she takes in the room, and I look at it from her perspective to further appreciate the wonder on her face.

The walls are the same stone as the hallway, but I've hung fairy lights along the corners where it meets the ceiling to give off a yellowish glow. Electric candles flicker on every available surface, and an enormous bed sits against the back wall. Rogue takes a few steps forward and reaches for one of the cupboards I brought in. She cracks open the door, and I know exactly what she'll find without having to look. An array of toys, floggers, and paddles.

The next cabinet holds ropes, chains, cuffs, silks, and spreader bars. The next has recording equipment, in case she wants to film us again. On and on it goes. She reaches the Saint Andrew's cross and looks hesitant, but I shake my head when she eyes me questioningly. Han requested that one.

"Turns out Elise had a few rooms hidden down the passageway. This one seemed the best fit for an extracurricular...area." My words softly echo in the cavernous space, and my dick rises, thinking of hearing Rogue's shouts and moans reverberating around me in here. "Everything in here is brand new, don't worry, we're not playing with Elise's personal collection." I think we all unintentionally shudder at the same time. Shame I can't jinx that. Thinking of everyone jinxed and under my command like we were under Noah's direction has me hardening quickly.

That'll happen one day.

"When did you do all of this?" she asks me.

"Over the last few weeks. Fabio knows far too much about our sex life, if you ask me. But he insisted on checking each package that came through. He's completely loyal to you. Also, he blushes when he sees anal beads. Just a heads up." Rogue shakes her head and laughs.

"Can we test some of it out? Now?" Her chest is moving rapidly as she sucks in air with excitement. Her breasts move in time with her breathing, and the sway of her hips as she circles the room has us all entranced.

I look at Han, and he nods his head. He's in. Lucas is always up for fun, but I get his approval, anyway. Noah, the one least likely to join in the group activities, nods as well. *Interesting.*

"Yes, Darling Mine, we can play." A small grin overtakes her face, and she looks at Han next to her. I'll be honest, I've thought about all of us together a lot since the last time. It's been playing on repeat in my mind. And while Noah will probably sit out, just having his eyes on us is enough to fuel my need to put on a show.

Lucas may be the only self-proclaimed voyeur of the group, but after our escapades while jinxed, I know Noah loves it as well.

I lean in and fiercely take Rogue's lips with mine. Lucas, having undone his pants, fists his cock and leisurely pumps it as he watches us. Releasing Rogue, I push her gently toward Lucas. Han approaches me, cupping my face with his palms, and leans in. His kiss has my eyes closing as the passion erupts between us. I gently nip his lush lower lip and crack my eyes open to see Lucas holding Rogue as his tongue duels with hers.

I refocus on the man in front of me, running my fingers through his silky black hair and deepening our kiss. The four of us move in time with each other.

Han drags his shirt up over his head and slides his sweats down his legs until they pool at his feet. He lets out a groan and shifts his hips closer to mine. The feel of his hot cock against me is always my undoing.

Rogue hops up and Lucas catches her, wrapping her legs around him as he moves closer to the giant bed. I guide Han backward until the back of his thighs find the mattress. I use two fingers and poke his chest until he collapses back, his legs dangling over the side of the bed.

Lucas drops Rogue, and she bounces on the bed next to Han. Both breathless with anticipation, they stare up at the men before them.

Han turns his head and grasps Rogue's chin with firm fingers. He tilts her head toward him and delivers a searing kiss.

Fuck, they're so beautiful together.

Lucas is quickly divesting himself of his clothes, and I follow suit. My wrinkled shirt quickly falls by the wayside, along with my slacks. I kick them out of the way and lean over Han, pulling his attention away from our girl.

"Lucas, Jacob," Rogue demands. "Fuck us."

Never one to deny our girl, Lucas lunges forward onto the bed between her thighs, and his thumb circles her clit as his mouth latches over a nipple. Han groans at the sight, turning his face to me.

With my eyes, I beg him to watch as I trail my lips down his torso. I grip his thighs, moving them to the sides so I have an unobstructed view of everything. Finding his cock hard and ready, I lean down, licking along the length of him. I drag my tongue slowly up to the tip of his cock, and his back arches at the sensation. I see his hand reach out, and he takes Rogue's in his.

Lucas eyes me from the side and releases her nipple with a pop. He skates his tongue down her body until he finds her clit. With a nod of my head, we both dive in. The unfamiliar feel of a cock on my tongue has taken a bit of getting used to, but fuck if it isn't powerful. Han throws his head back, and he's murmuring a chain of curses, comprising a litany of *Oh, fuck* and *Yes, please.*

Rogue lifts her head from the mattress to see, and it must make her wetter, because Lucas lets out his own groan at her taste. He is unrelenting in his strokes and licks.

With one hand, I hold Han steady and feel the head of his cock bump the back of my throat. I do my best not to gag at the sensation, but I'm still learning how to do this. I bring my other hand up his thigh and roll his balls in my hand before skirting a finger under him and playing with his tight hole.

Han's hand has reached across Rogue and is playing with one of her nipples as Lucas continues his assault on her clit. Not wanting Han to finish too soon, I slow my strokes, keeping him on the edge.

I think of the show we're putting on for Noah and resist the urge to check how he's handling this as he sits off to the side. Rogue, however, has no hesitation in pulling him into this.

"Noah," she calls. "I need you." Rogue arches her back on the bed next to Han, and her breathing comes in quick gasps.

Noah quickly obliges, removing his clothes, and stepping forward and standing at the head of the bed. "What do you need, Trouble?" he asks.

"I need your cock, pleeease." She draws out the plea as Lucas groans between her thighs.

Noah grabs under her arms and hauls her higher on the bed. Lucas moves with them, barely breaking away from her in the movement. She tilts her head back and pulls him closer, guiding his cock down her throat. The angle gives him a straight shot, and he cradles her face as he slides into her mouth.

Lucas breaks away and looks at me, a glint in his eye. I nod my head and let Han's cock free from my lips.

The two of us move toward the cabinets and select our toys and necessary lube for the evening. We make our way back to the bed, lubing the toys as needed during our return.

I kneel on the bed between Han's legs, and his eyes are fixed on Rogue's mouth wrapped around Noah's cock. At the dip in the mattress, he looks down at me. Pupils blown and his hand on his cock, stroking to Rogue's rhythm.

"You want her lips around your cock, Love?" I ask. Han nods his head. "Greedy man," I chastise playfully. Noah growls at my suggestion and continues driving down her throat.

I lean down, taking a nipple into my mouth as I slide a slick finger around his tight asshole. With each pass of my tongue over his peaked bud, he relaxes into my touch.

I hear Rogue's moans around Noah's cock, and I know Lucas is doing the same.

Determining my man is ready for me after carefully stretching him with my fingers, I scoot closer, kneeling just before him, and notch the head of my cock at his entrance. I rock back and forth a few times until my head slips past that tight ring and finds its way home. Han's face tenses then relaxes as I enter him, and he tries to grind his hips to get me moving.

Not so fast.

With my dick in place, I wrap Han's legs around my thighs, locking him in place and reach beside me. Picking up the modified fleshlight I found online, I hold his hard cock in my hand and slide it over the tip. Han's moan echoes around the room, and Rogue watches us with rapt attention. Once he's sheathed inside the fleshlight, I hit the switch and the vibrations cause Han's back to arch dramatically from the bed as if his soul is trying to leave his body. The silicone bumps and ridges inside are designed to tease his frenulum and seem to do their job. I'm glad I opted for the heated model if the look on his face is anything to go by.

I pump his cock in the device a few times, and his strangled moans continue to spill from his lips. Testing my movement, I snap my hips forward and slam into his ass.

I follow the line of Noah's body to Rogue, who has her own nipples pinched in a vise grip as Lucas works between her legs. He chose a vibrating dildo that attaches to the underside of his cock at the base, giving him two phalluses to maneuver, one for either hole. Every time he pushes into her, she'll be completely filled. Lucas lubes the purple dildo after preparing Rogue, and slowly eases into her. After a few minutes of gentle thrusts, she's writhing on the bed, moaning around Noah's cock for more. Lucas powers into her, his pace unfaltering.

Today didn't seem like the day for the paddles and pain play, but toys are always welcome in our bed.

Lucas and I move, our hips snapping together in synchronicity, and I watch as both Rogue and Han come undone. They link hands across the small space between them on the bed and ride out their orgasms together.

I follow Han over the cliff when I feel his body clench around me. Emptying myself into him, I remove the toy and kiss my way up his chest to his lips. His free hand rakes through my hair, anchoring me to him as we watch the others.

Rogue groans when Lucas shifts, his bodyweight hitting a new angle. Rogue's eyes snap open and connect with Han's as Noah continues thrusting forward. As she groans, Noah comes with a roar, shooting his cum down her throat. He steps back, looking down at her with such love in his eyes. You'd have to be blind to miss it.

He leans forward, kissing her gently before taking her breasts in his hands. Biting along the outsides before spiraling in toward her nipples. It's too much for her to take, and with another scream, she comes again. Lucas follows soon after.

All three simultaneously turn their heads toward Han and I. Rogue leisurely moves a hand in our direction and swipes her finger through a pool of Han's cum on his abs and brings it to her mouth, groaning, as it hits her tongue.

The five of us collapse on the bed in different states of undoing. We're all desperate for touches and reassurances as the party draws nearer. Knowing this is undoubtedly our most dangerous mission ever has us all nervous and needy.

It's hard to describe the feelings tumbling through my mind, but we're treating every time as if it's our last.

Chapter Nineteen

Rogue

I draw up the zipper on the deep burgundy dress and smooth my hands down my stomach. These damn butterflies are driving me insane.

"You look amazing, Buttercup," Lucas groans as he lounges on my bed.

He's in jeans and a Rogue X-Men shirt, which he proudly displayed earlier with a smug smile, before following me in here to keep me company while I prepared for tonight.

Who knew hosting a party for the prominent gang leaders of our region and influential politicians, police commissioners, and federal agents would wreak such havoc on my stomach?

"Thanks, Red," I mumble my reply as I tuck in a few loose strands of hair. I braided it into a crown atop my head, further emphasizing my new role. There are going to be more than a few people looking to undermine me tonight, so I'm going in dressed to the nines, with a stony demeanor to match.

Lucas is on his stomach, his chin propped up in his palms as he watches me in the floor-length mirror. His eyes skate down the dress, paying careful attention to the curve of my exposed back, and settling on my ass. I turn around and snare his attention with my eyes. "Help me with my shoes?" I ask sweetly.

Bending over in a half corset is tough on the best day. Today, it feels like if I exert myself too much, I'll stop breathing altogether. Lucas slides off the bed and reaches for my black pumps with the ankle strap. He kneels before me, running a hand under the fabric that falls to my toes and guides his hand up my calf. I point my toes and he slips the shoe on, placing it on his thigh to do up the strap.

Repeating the motion with the second shoe, I now stand four inches taller than before and am nose-to-nose when Lucas rises. Careful not to mess up my makeup, he leans in and delivers a sweet kiss.

"You've got this, Buttercup." His reassurance is so very welcome, and I crush my chest to him in a hug.

"Thanks, Red."

"We'll be there right on time. Exactly where we're supposed to be. You just wow them and do what you need to. One of us will always be watching you. Okay?"

"Okay." I shake out my hands to remove the last of the tremors, but before I can slip into mission mode, Lucas speaks again.

"When we get through this, expect a proposal." With that parting line, he spins and tucks my arm into his. I can't wrap my mind around that possibility in the face of tonight, so instead, I lean in and kiss his cheek.

"I love you, Lucas," I murmur against his auburn stubble.

He turns to look me in the eye once more. "That had better not be your goodbye, Buttercup."

I duck my head and mumble out a noncommittal response. It could very well be the end.

We descend the stairs, arm in arm, as Lucas leads me to the kitchen. I hear the grandfather clock in the living room chime out five times. Well, at least our schedule is on track, which means Noah and Han should be back any minute.

No sooner does the thought cross my mind when I hear the chirp of the alarm and Noah's gruff voice in the foyer. They join us in the kitchen, and I look from one to the other in rapid succession.

"Is everything set?" I ask.

"Yep, good to go," Han assures me. Noah's nod in affirmation calms some of the unease.

Han pulls a bouquet from behind his back, and I note the dramatic blooms. The black dahlias are robust and nestled among greenery that only makes their petals appear more dramatic. The burgundy on the petals is a near perfect match for my dress.

He leans forward, kissing me gently on the cheek as I admire the flowers. "Thank you, Han. They're gorgeous."

"You're Gorgeous," he jokes. "I saw your dress in the wardrobe last week and thought you might need an extra accessory." He pulls a smaller bloom from the bouquet and tucks it behind my ear, sliding the shorter stem into my tucked-up hair. "There. Perfect."

Tears gather on my lower lash line, and Han is quick to wipe them away. "Shh, it's okay," he assures me as he gathers me close. Noah moves against my back and drops a kiss on my crown.

I laugh out a small huff as I refocus. Right. Now is not the time for that. I clear my throat, gently wipe away the tears and check my reflection in the microwave door. All good. No raccoon eyes today.

Jacob comes rushing into the kitchen and lets out a sigh when he sees me. "Sorry, sorry! I was just checking things one more time. I thought I'd missed you."

"You almost did. G's picking her up in three minutes," Noah says as he checks his watch.

"Fuck, sorry, Darling Mine." Jacob strides over to me, takes the bouquet out of my hands and hands it to Lucas. "I love you. You're going to be fine. You know what to do?" he asks as he gently bends to look me in the eye.

"Yes. And I love you, too. Speaking of," I say more loudly to catch their attention. "Can I say a couple of things and you all pretend you're jinxed so I can get through it? I seem to have mere minutes, and this is important."

They all nod their heads and focus on me.

"I love you all. My life would have been awful if I hadn't met you. I certainly wouldn't have Sage back, and I wouldn't know this feeling—this ache—deep in my chest. I would do anything for any of you. You took my life and flipped it upside down."

I take a deep breath to steady myself. "This may not go the way we want it to. We all know that, no matter how many times you assure me that it'll be fine. We know better than to assume an easy ride. So, if anything happens to me, please promise you'll look after Sage."

Lucas looks devastated, but nods his head when I make eye contact with him. There's a tear tracking down his cheek, but he lets it go along its path, maintaining his focus on me. Noah is silent in his resignation, but nods just the same.

"Han, Jacob, promise me you won't give up on each other. Your happiness means more to me than I can tell you. Now that you've finally admitted it to each other and embraced it, don't shut it out if I'm not there to encourage you, okay?" They both nod, lacing their fingers together.

"Finally, someone please make sure Claudette holds it together. I know she's a psychopath, but she's *my* psychopath." Thinking of Claudette coming in and raining down her brand of crazy on Cross has me certain she'll follow me to an early grave if this goes sideways.

No, this has to end today.

"Where the hell is G?" I ask aloud, getting antsy at the upcoming plans.

"Here, Boss. Just giving you a minute," he says as he peeks his head into the kitchen from the hallway. Dammit, he heard everything. Eh, could have been worse.

The guys line up, each giving me a big hug and a passionate kiss as I'm passed down the line to leave the kitchen. G waits patiently at the threshold, and when Noah finally lets go, I slide my arm in his and he escorts me to the front door; the guys trailing behind us.

G opens the limo door, and I slide into the back. "See you in a few hours," I call out to them. They shout out their encouragement, and G closes the door before hopping into the driver's seat. We roll down the gravel drive and no matter how confident I am in our plan, I can't help but swivel in my seat as we leave, watching them grow smaller in the distance.

Fucking hell, this had better not go sideways.

G AND I DRIVE DIRECTLY TO THE HOTEL. I NEED TO GO OVER everything before the party starts, and I want to make sure everything is absolutely perfect.

I step out of the limo as G opens the door for me.

The doorman at the Harold Heights Hotel is quick to grab the handle of the lobby doors and ushers me in with a wave of his arm. The hem of my dress floats around my spiked shoes as I sway into the building. There are no other guests here, Elise having rearranged their reservations, but the workers are current hotel employees, soon to be replaced by the agents Romano and Shade are bringing in.

I reach the front desk, and the receptionist there shakily points me in the correct direction after assuring me everything is as I requested. The obscene amount of money we just dropped on this soirée nearly always elicits this reaction from those who don't have it. Creating a vacuum of fear because this much money should be illegal to spend on a party.

The hotel owner is waiting for me in the lounge, and as I approach, I extend my hand.

"Mr. Wells, thank you so much for accommodating our requests."

"Queen, I would never deny you, and you humble me with your generosity." Oh, yeah. I gave an extra sum to divide between the staff we are putting out for the night and ensure they set everything up accordingly.

"Everything is ready?" I ask as I look around the space. It's glaringly empty of other patrons, precisely as requested.

"Yes. We moved everyone's bookings to our sister hotel or others in the area. A few for your party have rooms requested, but I expect them in the next hour. We stated that there was no check-in until half-past six this evening."

Excellent.

"And your people know what to do?"

"Yes, we had a meeting a few hours ago to ensure it. Their replacements are already here, preparing in the staff lounge."

"And you made sure your insurance was up to date?" I ask. It was my one caveat to having the party here. The owner is a bit of a cheapskate and had the cheapest insurance policy possible. I don't want him holding a grudge if things don't go as planned.

"Yes. I upped the plan as soon as you and Mrs. Batten contacted me a few months ago and swapped mine for the best policy money can buy. I'll switch it back if everything goes smoothly." His money-hungry ways make me laugh. This man is worth nearly as much as me, and it seems stupid to not properly insure your biggest earner. But alas, it's his livelihood, not mine.

"Shall we? You requested the adjacent ballroom for a pre-party meeting, and it's almost time." He extends his arm, and I rest gentle fingertips on his forearm.

"Yes, let's."

He leads me to the elevator, going up one floor before veering to the right. The ballroom to the left has people moving in and out quickly. All are carrying flowers, decorations, and extra seats.

This is about to be a party no one in El Castillo will ever forget, and more importantly, some semblance of balance should return to the area after Shade and the feds take in the worst offenders on the West Coast.

He leads me to the room, and I find G already there waiting for me. He nods his head as I enter the space, assuring me it is clear of bugs and any possible interference.

Mr. Wells brings me a bottle of water and a glass, leaving me and G to wait for our guests.

"Ready, Boss?" he asks.

He looks self-assured and confident, but I see the small tap his toes are doing against the red carpet of the room and realize he's looking for reassurance as much as I am.

"I think so. I've covered every base. It's time to get this done."

Moments pass in silence as we wait. The first to find us is Elise. She joins me at the table, tutting over the lack of decor in the second space. We argued over it for more time than necessary. This is just a meeting room. No reason to dress it up if it's only going to be used sparingly. Nina and Nira join us soon after, and once the women sit in the seats across from me, I dive in.

"Look, this is more than a party tonight. I need you four to leave early tonight," I say as I nod at G to include him in the conversation.

"Leave early? Girl, you must be daft. The work that went into this—" Elise argues before I cut her off with a stern tone.

"Is inconsequential if you spend the rest of your life behind bars, Elise."

"Behind bars? Honey, we own so many people; it's obscene. No one would dare lock us away."

Nina and Nira don't move. They just watch our verbal volley with interest. "Can you explain, please?" Nira asks. She was a suitable replacement for Tanaka. Her calm and firm tone is made to lead companies.

"I can't. Not without jeopardizing everything. I need you three to leave after the negotiations. Immediately after. G, you're out at nine o'clock."

Nina and Nira nod at the request, and Elise eyes me with suspicion. "Darlings, give us a moment." She waves off our fellow board members with a dismissive hand and observes G. "Are you okay with this plan?" Elise asks our lead hitman. "She's your priority, after all. You're willing to leave her?"

G squares his shoulders before answering. "I am. If it's what she needs, it's what I'll do. I'm not fully versed in the plan, but I'll do what she asks."

"Hmm." She doesn't seem convinced.

"Look, Elise, you wanted out? This is your shot. Take your shit and run. In fact, I've got a friend in the Caribbean you might get along with. She'll take you in as things settle down. I assume your finances are liquid?" I ask.

"Of course, dear. Everything is owned by different names and companies. I can cash out if needed," she says, as if I'm stupid for thinking otherwise.

"Good. Do it. Hide out for a day or two. I can get you new documents if you don't already have them; come back but not to El Castillo. And not for a few months at least."

She eyes me as if I've just told her to abandon her firstborn in the woods.

"Fine. I've got spare documents, so don't you worry about that. And you'll be okay in all of this?" A modicum of concern enters her tone.

"It needs to be done."

"That's not an answer, dear."

"It's the best one I've got."

G helps Elise to the door after our talk and returns to join me.

"She's in the next room chastising the staff for placing the flowers a few inches too close together." I laugh at that. Fuck, I needed some reprieve.

"G, I need you to follow Elise, Nira, and Nina. Make sure they get out. You're okay to come back eventually, but not today. *Promise* me you and Fabio will get out."

He tosses an arm over my shoulders. "Sure thing, Boss. You know we want to live to see tomorrow." He laughs, but his joke hits a little too close to home.

Noah

The ballroom is an alluring sight to anyone not currently freaking the fuck out. I glance at the men and women on either side of me, each tasked with keeping their clients safe from harm in this snake pit. Everyone in attendance is masked, but their identities are easy to suss out with their attire and haughty voices. I note none of the guards along the walls are enjoying the party the way the guests in the center of the ballroom are.

The gauzy midnight blue material strung from the chandeliers to the outer corners of the ceiling creates an almost midnight feel with the fairy lights tucked within the material. The walls are dark blue, and the silver candles on every available surface give off a soft glow throughout the room.

Dark floral centerpieces are at each table, and most people mill about the room, chatting with other attendees and posing for pictures as the flashes of the cameras reflect off of their opulent masks.

I observe as Rogue mingles amongst the crowd, Romano always at her side. Their masks are two halves of the same coin. Rogue's is a delicately made silver piece that covers her eyes and cheeks, each loop and swirl of the metal unique and detailed, but together they form a swan in the middle of her brows. The diamond teardrop running along her nose gives her a regal air that denotes her new status. Romano's mask is solid, but the same detail is etched onto the brow piece, and the edges match the diamond at the center of Rogue's mask.

Romano may not be her husband anymore, but these people don't know that. They see she shows him respect, and as the leader of The Gambit, that means something, so they all do the same.

They're currently chatting with Governor Gerard, and he looks close to wetting himself in fear. Romano keeps his hand on my girl's lower back, and it grates on my nerves every time I catch sight of it. Irrational, I know. But still.

Rogue turns slightly in my direction, and even though a mask covers half of her face, I know the look she's likely pulling right now. A cross between a shoot-me-now grimace and a sly smile. It's her usual face when she's working.

Her silver mask highlights her deep green eyes, and as I trail my gaze down her face, I know she must catch sight of me because one side of her lips tips up in a secret smile. I echo it and turn my attention elsewhere, hoping my simple green mask hides the lust blooming on my face.

I've clocked at least ten heads of state or federal organizations since this party started nearly an hour ago. The press thinks it's a shareholder meeting for Rook Industries, and in a way, it kind of is.

We let it slip to the press that it was happening, and with attention on the event and the star-studded list of investors, we simply had to allow the press in for a portion of the evening.

The gang leaders agreed because they are also here to foster those connections with the politicians and less-than-reputable investors.

The reason for this was two-fold. One, it allowed fewer people to be carrying weapons under the guise of keeping up appearances. And two, it gave Jacob a chance to show off his tech while forcing everyone to play nicely. At least for the first hour.

Claudette showed up right on time with two of her men as her guests and the permitted two security members, all wearing some variation of black masks with gold detailing. I recognize the two men on either side of her as Neil Carter and Toby, the two men Rogue "killed" on King's orders. Bold statement bringing them here, but then again, only King, De La Cruz, and Horvat would have recognized them and they're all dead.

They walked into the room and immediately made their way to the mayor of San Francisco. Claudette's red hair floats around her in a wavy mess that conjures the image of an Irish faerie. Her green dress is airy and light, and the two men in tuxedos befitting the event flank her on either side.

Among the crowd of politicians, influential figures, and gang lords, are the paparazzi, Sage, and two of the other former escorts, Elenor and Mimi, all floating between the army of wait staff currently delivering appetizers to each of the tables. The eerie sea of masks in the dim lighting brings a sense of foreboding that has chills raking down my spine. The masquerade theme sums these people up perfectly. Showing one face to the world as they move in the shadows, unseen and making backdoor deals amongst each other.

"Paps out in fifteen," Shade's voice crackles in my ear, breaking up the monotony of the surrounding din.

Thank God.

As if on cue, Elise raises a microphone to her mouth and alerts the crowd to the evening's events.

"Good evening, everyone, and thank you for being here at the Rook Industries shareholder's meeting. Dinner is about to be served, and our lovely photographers have a little over ten minutes before you're booted. Sorry, boys. Next time, invest, and you'll get an invitation." The crowd and photographers laugh at her teasing.

"Please, eat, drink, and mingle with your tablemates. We'll kick off the speeches while you're eating so as not to bore you to death." Huh, who knew she could be funny?

The photographers quickly make their way around the tables and snap photos of the attendees and their meals before Elise very clearly *ahems* into the microphone, and they make their way out.

Security is ready downstairs to ensure they leave the property and don't accost the guests for information on their way out of the venue.

Conversation flows freely amongst the guests at the tables. I watch as a man in a red half-face mask chats with a woman in an elaborate blue butterfly mask about insider trading. She tells him that the shares in a popular Silicon Valley company are heading for quadruple digits, and the man immediately calls his broker to buy up all the shares he can. He rewards her with information on immigration loopholes that are less loophole-like and more illegalities.

We're positioned around the room, observing, and I resist the urge to look across the room for one of my teammates. I know we positioned Lucas directly across from me on the opposite side of the room, and Han and

Jacob are on either side of the main entrance, propping up the back wall. From here, we have a good vantage of everyone and everything.

Deals, bets, and transactions are going down at every table, better suited for a back-alley handoff than a swanky gala. That they do it so openly shows that they think the new leader of The Gambit, our girl, would never set them up because she has done enough to get tossed in jail with them.

Once the wait staff leaves and the guests dig into their dinners, Elise retakes the microphone. "Thank you all for dealing with that. We're not sure how the press got wind of the event, but I assure you, we will find out who told them and fix the leak." A murmur of praise goes around at the old lady's promise of violence.

"Ladies, gentlemen, and the rest of you, I give you: Queen."

A polite smattering of applause and a small dash of fear make their way through the room. Her former job ensured she'd at least have their respect through the transition.

She floats across the dancefloor, and the spotlight follows her every move. Her red dress and black mask make her look like the Queen of Hearts in a fucked up version of Alice in Wonderland. The braided crown atop her head is a perfect symbol of the power she wields. And the black dahlia tucked behind her ear reminds us we're with her. Entirely.

"Let's get to it, shall we? I'm sure we'd all like to have this wrapped quickly." The crowd laughs, and Rogue shrugs. "I am my father's daughter, after all. He wasn't a very patient man. I seem to have learned that from him."

Whether she means King or Joseph, I don't know. But it seems as if both lacked patience from our research.

"If you are here for treaty negotiations, we will meet in the next room immediately. If you are here to 'shmooze' said leaders, please enjoy yourselves. I don't expect this to take very long."

The crowd claps at her declaration, ready to move on to shady deals with who it involves. When we divide The Vegas Crew's old territory amongst the players, the people in those regions will need to know who to meet with.

Rogue places the microphone on a nearby table and makes a beeline for the exit. Romano stands from their table and follows her to usher a leader and their second into the adjacent room.

Claudette and one of her men stand, following her out, leaving the other at the table to continue discussing things with the mayor.

Two men stand up from a nearby table. One wears an emerald mask, and the other, a mask so white it reflects what little light shines in the room. They must be the Southern California contingency. Their territories aren't labeled like the other gangs, but they control Los Angeles and New Mexico, Baja California, and Northern Mexico. They are more of a coalition than anything else.

Finally, a well-dressed woman in a silver slinky dress and a man in a suit with a bolero stand up and make their way across the room. The man must be Vic, the rancher from Texas, and Christie, the homemaker from Chicago. Together, they run the Midwest, ruling the area stretching between their two locations with an iron fist. The population of their turf is smaller, considering the farmland between, but they produce drugs en masse for the other organizations.

The crowd watches the eight of them leave, and whispered conversation breaks out among the remaining group. Elise waves a hand at the band to play some music, and in my ear, I hear Shade's voice. "Photos gone."

Did I mention Jacob's tech? Upon arrival, the press needed to submit to an inspection of devices for safety purposes. Hotel security switched out SD cards with ones that wiped data as soon as they stepped outside of the perimeter Han and I set up earlier. And that handy little trick to email images directly? Unfortunately, those little SD cards set up emails as usual, but never sent the files anywhere.

Let's just say the NSA has some reverse-engineering ideas and wants to talk to the creator, aka Jacob, when this is all over.

Deleting the images wasn't entirely necessary, but we have backup copies on the server that Shade is guarding—and working next to—in his little cubicle nearby. The photos arrived in real-time to our secure server, giving us some backup evidence as needed. We just didn't want any accidental images of Rogue out there after this is all over.

The earpiece crackles in my ear once more as the doors to the ballroom close. I lift my eyes and meet Lucas's concerned gaze across the way.

Rogue's voice comes through softly. "Watch them. Keep your eyes on Cross. I've got this."

Lucas hisses, "Yes, Queen." But it sounds more like *Yaaaas, Queen!* Despite everything, I fight a chuckle.

Chapter Twenty

Rogue

Pulling the double doors shut behind me, I slip the key from my pocket and lock the other gang leaders and myself into the smaller ballroom.

Tradition says we're not permitted to leave until we have agreed upon everything; it prevents loose ends. I plan to expedite things as much as possible because this doesn't fucking matter in the end.

Claudette and Toby, Angelo and Miguel, Vic and Christie, Romano and I. A small but extraordinarily deadly group. This should be fun.

The only things in the room are a medium-sized circular table, chairs, rolled-up maps of the territory stretching from the Midwest's land to mine here on the coast, and a collection of notepads and pens. There's a printer in the corner and a single smartphone on the table. It's not as if we need more to get this done.

"Let's get this done, ladies and gentlemen. I expect this to move swiftly. Neither The Rattlesnakes nor The Gambit have an interest in the territory. Our own are too demanding to add to it now, so the two of us will mediate. Any objections?" I ask as I remove my mask. The others follow suit until the collection is on the table.

Angelo and Miguel shake their heads, and Vic and Christie look suspicious but eventually agree as well. I mean, they knew this was coming. I was clear in my communications. They're just being difficult, and I don't have the patience for that today.

"Angelo, Miguel, what is your proposal?" I ask, pinning Miguel with a look, silently telling him to speak for the two as Angelo can be a bit of a hothead.

"We want everything stretching from Southern Vegas through into Texas, effectively redrawing current lines. This will ease our travels between Mexico and the States, giving us control of the border. We will give free passage for the inconvenience, and the Midwest group can have everything north of the Vegas Strip, stretching from The Rattlesnakes' territory to The Great Lakes, giving them control of the Canadian border."

Vic's eyebrows shoot up. "You want the most lucrative of the Vegas territory *and* my home? Sorry, Miguel. That's a hard pass, brother. You must be high."

Claudette clears her throat, calling attention to her instead of the maps I've started sprawling out across the table. Redrawing territory lines might take a while, so I hope she's got an idea. "You could negotiate a treaty for passage, but Vic is right." Her head tilts in deference to the man seated across from her. "While the area north of the strip is quite lucrative with Reno and Tahoe, it doesn't come close to the value Vegas itself offers. Try again, Miguel."

Angelo studies Claudette, his eyes roaming her face as if he's seeing her for the first time. "Stop staring," she snaps. "It's rude."

He doesn't look adequately chastised at all when he replies, "And what would you suggest, honey?"

"Split Las Vegas entirely and agree to work together. Everything North can go to the Midwest, everything South, to you boys. Simple," she says slowly, as if they're kindergarteners having trouble grasping color mixing lessons.

"And my home?" Vic says.

"Split Texas," I offer with a shrug. "West for SoCal, East for you. Your home is located east of the division line. You keep a portion of the border, and it still gives you the Gulf."

Negotiations continue for nearly thirty minutes, each side arguing why they need certain areas for either the drug or skin trade, all eager to fill their coffers with minimal work. Claudette and I exchange looks as they blather on and on about their businesses, but my ears perk up when talks shift to the human trafficking ring.

I'd always known it happened in the back of my mind, but hearing it discussed so casually has me gritting my teeth and Romano slipping a hand to my thigh under the table and squeezing in warning. He's right. It's not my fight today.

Angelo goes on about how they use one of the detainment camps near the border east of San Diego as a hunting ground for fresh product—aka bodies—and it has me seeing red. Vic laughs that they do something similar and lists the awe-inspiring number of people on their payroll. From border patrol to detainment center employees and overseers, the list goes on and on. They bond over the people they have in common working for them, and my stomach turns.

Claudette and Toby sit silently by, waiting until the topic changes. She has a calm look on her face, but I've known her long enough to see that simmer of rage in her eyes.

Finally, after far too much posturing for my taste, we reach an agreement on the territory. A variation of our ideas, splitting Texas and Vegas and creating an alliance in that area.

Each side tosses out names the other will need to contact now that the lines are shifting. Senators, a few governors, investors, and fuck, even the sitting vice president gets a mention.

We agree on similar terms of the last treaty, permitting all to form an alliance against those who overstep. It's cut and dry, not needing too many adjustments, only names and new territory agreements.

Shaking hands across the table, we seal the deal, and I quickly scan the document with the phone we had on the table. I let the program put it into typeface and send it to the printer in the corner. We all bend our heads, signing our lines as the leaders, and the secondary people in the room sign as witnesses. Scanning the document once more, I fire off emailed copies to everyone, and we all gather up our documents.

Honestly, it's not like this would hold up in court, but it's the pomp and circumstance of the whole thing. Committing yourself, signing your name, acting as if this is a legitimate business when instead it's warfare dressed up as civility.

Ready to celebrate the victory, the other leaders and I put our masks back on our faces and leave our small ballroom. We each hand off the documentation to our respective security teams stationed just inside the doors, and I look around the grand ballroom. Guests are drinking and dancing, allowing themselves the debauchery they always have to shove down and hide at other events.

I see Elenor, one of the former escorts cozying up with the DA for the state, his hand possessively on her hip as they take a twirl around the dance floor. Sage is chatting with a group of men who own a string of gambling houses in my territory, but pay us very well to stay in business. Mimi is being held a little too close for my liking by Cross near the bar. Each wears a scarlet-red mask to draw attention to themselves. A party like this without a few working girls would have been a tip-off.

Cutting through various groups, I make my way toward Cross under the guise of telling him all is going according to plan.

As I approach, he maneuvers Mimi away, his eyes roving over my body with a greedy look in his eye.

"Queen," he greets, lifting my hand to his lips and sliding a kiss over the knuckles. Only his lips are visible beneath his matte black mask, matching his way-too-expensive suit. Armani, if I'm not mistaken.

"Cross."

"Is everything settled?" he asks before taking a sip of the amber liquid in his glass.

"Yes. SoCal is spreading through Arizona, New Mexico, and focusing on the border through the middle of Texas. In a matter of weeks, they'll be distracted and pulled thin. Between the work we did last month and the new arrangement, it'll be easy pickings." He meets my assurances with a sick look of glee in his eyes.

"What's next?" he asks. "Should I just kill them and get it over with? I'd like that territory."

That's the problem with men like Cross: it's never enough. He'll always be reaching for more, and the thought of having that massive territory and that amount of influence is addictive.

"It's possible, but we'll have to move swiftly. The ink has just dried. No one accounted for another player to move in." *No one but me.*

He lifts his head, looking across the room, and after nodding, his second approaches. "Queen, I never introduced you to Dario. He's been my partner in this for years. Fuck, what's it been?"

"Twenty-five years," Dario answers with a smug grin. "It's been fun, but King stepped on our toes a bit too much. Remember the old days?"

I shudder to think what the old days looked like, especially with the rumors I'd heard about Cross. Finding the opportunity to sift for information, I take the plunge.

"Was it always just you two?" I ask, sliding closer to Cross to better hear his answer over the noise of the ballroom.

"No, we have a loyal band of associates, some of which have lasted longer than others," Dario says smugly, looking at me and my closeness to his boss.

"What constitutes a death order for you?" I ask, turning my gaze up to Cross. "I don't want to cross any lines I'm not supposed to."

He seems pleased at my question, the deference I offer, and the respect in my tone.

"Well," Dario starts, drawing my attention back to him, "don't double-cross, don't work for both sides, and we're in this until the end."

I look at him and see the interest in his gaze. "Oh, I can't imagine anyone wanting to be rid of you two." I giggle slightly, and it pains my personality to do any form of sucking up to these two.

"A few over the years tried to step out of the life."

"There's really no choice for me, being Queen and all," I intone. "What happened to the ones who tried?" I ask, letting my tone take on a breathy quality, as if the thought of killing turns me on. I feel like I'm channeling Claudette with the crazy pouring out of my mouth.

"I usually handle them," Dario says. "But if they've pissed off Cross enough, he'll pay them a personal visit."

I hang on to every word he says before turning to Cross. I lightly run a hand down his chest, and he traps it over his sternum. "And what do you do on these 'visits'?" I let my eyes drop to half-open, my breathing picking up. To me, it feels like I'm just struggling to breathe, but Cross's eyes drift to my lips. "Is it terribly bloody?"

"Yes, Queen, it is. There is no escaping this life."

"King told me about how you killed his first love"—I lean in close to whisper in Cross's ear, fighting the roil in my stomach and the bile threatening to spill—"just before his heart was taken from his chest. Was that your favorite? Getting one over on King? Imagining the pain in his life after taking the only thing he ever cared about?" I ask as I close my teeth around his earlobe, biting harder.

His breath hisses through his thin lips. I lean back, trailing my tongue across my lip and keeping my body close. His eyes follow the motions with laser precision.

"Joe and Marie. He worked for me for years. His thirst for blood was as deep and depraved as my own. Yours as well, I venture. He wanted out, knowing it wasn't possible. He started making moves to uproot his family and get the hell out of dodge. But I caught wind of the very first money transfer. After watching him slowly start putting things into place, I struck, slicing his throat and his wife's. That she was King's old girlfriend or whatever was the icing on the cake. Their kids ended up with the wife's sister. Does that scare you, little girl?" he asks, his voice is pure dominance. I send up a silent, albeit begrudging, "thank you," to King for masking our locations all these years.

"Scare me? No. You know who I was before. I've dipped my hands in more blood than I can remember. There are some that stick with you." I sigh deeply, shoving down my rage at my parents' murderer clasping my hand, and close my eyes briefly to center myself.

I needed the confirmation, but that doesn't make it any easier to hear it.

"Queen!" I hear Elise calling from nearby.

"Oh, excuse me, gentlemen. I need to work the room. Is there anyone I should sway to our side as I go?" I ask Cross, then turn my head to Dario to include him in the discussion.

"Maybe the mayor from Calabasas. It'd be good to build a foothold in politics there." I nod my head at Dario's request, dragging my hand down Patton's chest as I go.

I hear a growl in my ear through the earpiece before Jacob's voice comes through. "Mine."

"Not now, you great British oaf. Rogue, keep it going. We've got a lot to use, but more can't hurt," Shade's rasp echoes in my ear.

Romano takes my arm as I pass by, escorting me to Elise, where she's moving people out of the way to find me. Reaching her vicinity, she clasps my forearms tightly. "I'm not feeling well. I'm going up to my room to lie down. Where's your man? He can escort me," she says. It takes me a moment to realize she's talking about G.

I look over the heads of a few guests, my heels giving me the height I need, and spot him chatting with the mayor of San Francisco. I lift my arm, and he disengages, heading right for me.

"Elise needs an escort upstairs. She's not feeling well," I tell him as he approaches me. He nods and presses something on his phone to summon Fabio. "In fact, Nina and Nira were also looking a little sloppy with the drinks. Can you two bring them up?" I ask.

"Sure thing, Boss. Have fun." I watch as he collects the women on his way from the room, Fabio swinging Nira into his arms and carrying her from the room as if she'll stumble if she walks on her own. They leave the ballroom, and I let out a small sigh of relief.

I spy Cian Byrne chatting with Sage, and my hackles rise at the sight before me. His hand is placed possessively on her hip, and she's leaning slightly away from him, uncomfortable with his touch. Before I can shove my way over there, Romano approaches them and pulls Cian into a conversation, and Sage slips out of his grasp. She finds the other escorts, and with a nod, I send them on their way. They've done more than enough for the night, and Sage knows where to take the others.

I see Claudette's security guy, the one who met me at the safe house, take her hand in his and walk through the open door and out of sight. Good.

After a few minutes, he returns and nods to Claudette, who's chatting up a district attorney.

Looking at the clock on the wall, I see the time is dwindling down. Everyone here is on the list Shade and I compiled; from the gang lords to the influential people in the room. A whole lot of people are going to be unhappy in the morning.

Romano stops near the back of the room, conversing with one of the security guards stationed along the wall.

He wanders over to where Han is standing, and I see them exchange quick words before he moves on.

The server before him offers him a flute of champagne, and Romano takes it with his left hand, quickly thanking the man before making his way toward me.

His right hand lifts, and the gun he'd been hiding is pointed at my chest. Romano fires off two shots. The wind knocks out of me at the impact, and my body goes flying backward, crashing into a table.

The red liquid around me bubbles as it escapes, and it's hard to breathe. My vision dims with the force of the impact, and it gets darker as Romano stands over me.

"Good riddance, Queen."

Chapter Twenty-One

Han, Lucas, Noah, Jacob
Fuck.

Chapter Twenty-Two

Lucas

The sound of silence has never been so deafening. As I watch Buttercup go barreling backward into the table behind her like an anime character made flesh, my heart stutters in my chest.

Blood pools around her and her silver mask is knocked askew. Romano stands over her, his words clear in the quiet, loud enough to be heard around the ballroom. "Good riddance, Queen."

My eyes connect with Noah, and he fixes his gaze on Rogue as her breathing slows and a bellow of rage steals my attention. I look at Cross near the bar, and the lower half of his face, the only part visible under his masquerade mask, contorts in rage.

Other guests stare at Romano in shock while the security teams move forward to find their bosses in case Romano turns the gun on any of them. The seconds passing feel like eons as I stare down at my girl, supine on the flattened table. The dress bunches around her calves, shoes still hanging on by the ankle straps I did up this afternoon for her. Her arms splayed to the sides as if she's an offering for the gods that let this shit happen.

I draw my gun and level it at Romano's head along with everyone else in the room who's still carrying a weapon. Seeing her blood surround her on the collapsed table has my darkness swirling inside of me.

"Relax," I hear in my ear. "It had to happen." Shade's voice, while usually calm, has an eerie quality right now. Noah's eyes whip up to mine, and he stares at me curiously. "Move to the next stage. Trust me."

I inch toward the side exit next to me, ready to bar anyone from exiting.

Noah does the same across the hall, and I look to my right to see Han and Jacob at the back wall, both moving as if on auto-pilot.

Other members of the security teams are swarming their charges and moving them toward the exits.

Angelo takes Romano in an armbar while Miguel hisses in his face. "What the fuck was that?"

"She can't lead. I'll be taking over. Thank you, Romano," Claudette says as she steps over Buttercup's body and reaches the man our girl trusted.

She plants a kiss on Romano's lips and pulls the gun from his waistband, firing two shots into his chest. He stumbles back before sinking to his knees. Angelo lets him go as he collapses to the floor.

The silence is heavy in the room after the gunshots. The non-gang members are standing slack jawed at the display. More than one probably recalculating how to gain favor and influence from the new person at the top of the food chain.

The changes in territory and interests have just dramatically shifted again, and I see a fair few of the politicians eyeing Claudette with interest. Since taking up her post as the leader of The Rattlesnakes, she's kept her operation up north, except for her small foray into San Francisco, but they don't know that. Suddenly, she's poised to take over the state of California.

Not wanting to witness more carnage, the teams move into formation around their employers. Claudette swings the gun wildly. "Weapons down, all of you." When one man tries to pull his gun, she fires a shot into his kneecap with eerie precision.

"I said drop them!" she roars.

With everyone focused on the bodies before them, avoiding the crazed gleam in Claudette's eye, she steps forward, snagging Governor Gerard by the neck. She pulls him in front of her, keeping the stage to her back.

She wraps one hand around his throat, and the other has the barrel of the gun pressed to his temple. The man is sweating bullets, his eyes swinging around the room, looking for help that will not come. Not when she's holding the most influential man in the state. Without him turning a blind eye, so many of the deals the men and women in this room make wouldn't happen.

The look in her eyes must convince them, and I watch as every guard puts down at least one weapon, me included. "Kick them to the center," she coos. "Good boys."

Her two security guards gather them into a pile out of the attendees' reaches.

The remaining four gang leaders are still weaponless after their territory meeting, and security knows it's unlikely this will escalate if they do as she says. The few politicians near me gape at their hired muscle for following her orders, but they know there's a better chance of surviving if we do as she says.

Once there's a pile of guns at her feet, she stands on her tiptoes to see over the crowd. I watch as she finds a clear line of sight to Han and Jacob and says, "If you'd be so kind, darlings."

Han and Jacob open the doors, and the servers who had been serving everyone all night come filing in, dressed head to toe in Kevlar and sporting automatic weapons. Everyone's hands shoot up, and as some make their way toward me at the side exit, I pull the door open behind me, and uniformed officers spill into the room. I look across the ballroom and find that Noah has done the same with his door. Feds surround the attendees on all sides and are handcuffing and leading them away. We watch as Claudette takes off running during the commotion.

She slips past me at the door as an officer wraps handcuffs around my wrists, and she hauls ass down the hallway. Two officers give chase, cutting her off at the staircase, forcing her to go up instead of down to safety.

I'm downstairs, rubbing my wrists, when the two officers who were chasing Claudette come marching out of the building. "We lost her. But she has to be in there somewhere. We're watching all the exit points, so we'll see when she makes a move."

The other one turns and says, "The fire alarm is blaring in there like a siren. It seems like a genuine alarm, so we've cleared out."

Noah nudges my shoulder, letting out a little wink. The four of us haven't spoken since we arrived downstairs, and Shade told them to let us go.

Han and Jacob take up positions on either side of us, and we stand in a line, looking up at the grandeur of the hotel.

Han looks down, checking his watch, and I hear him quietly say, "Five, four, three, two..."

The surrounding officers watch in horror as the sonic blast of the explosion rocks the center of the hotel. My shoulders jump up before the sound even registers. The building shudders and there's a ripple of movement under our feet before the center of the building sinks into a hole.

It crumbles from the inside out, and watching the floors topple down like dominoes has the entire police force gathered silently, watching the devastation unfold.

We all stand a healthy distance away, watching until the last of it lies in a heap, covering half a city block. The dust plume is still hovering, but the concrete and glass have settled after a seemingly unending ten minutes.

"Who was still inside?" one captain shouts once the building is lying in ruins before us.

"Still unaccounted for are Nina Wilson, Nira Bhatt, Elise Batten, and two of The Gambit's hitmen. The bodies of Ivy Montgomery and Francesco Romano were inside. The coroner still hasn't arrived, so we were told to leave the bodies."

"Fuck!" the captain grouses as the building finally stops shifting and lays in rubble before us. Huge slabs of concrete are the only thing left intact as shards of glass decorate the asphalt of the road.

Rogue

One month earlier

Romano and I sit at my desk in the corner office at Rook Industries. After the day I've had sending Cross all over Southern California to pave the way for his expansion, I need a drink. Shade was clear in directives regarding who to send him after, promising me they would be able to gather evidence to use when the time came. Guess what? Trusting people doesn't get easier.

Looking at Romano across from me, I see he's exhausted, too. Living a double life is sucky. "I need you to kill me," I tell him.

He looks at me in disbelief because, yeah, that's not a sentence I ever thought I'd say.

"If anyone gets out of the charges or out on bail, they need to think I'm dead, so they don't come after me," I clarify.

"And when they come after me for killing their Queen?" he asks.

"Oh, darling, that's where I come in," Claudette says from the speakerphone. She's been surprisingly quiet the entire time, and I'd bet my ass she muted herself for the element of surprise.

"Who are you?" Romano asks.

"Claudette. Nice to meet you, hubby. Or wait, are you guys still married? You sound hot. Rogue, can I steal him?" she asks. Romano's brows hit his hairline, and I slap a palm over my mouth to keep the laughter from bubbling out. That'd be a disaster.

"We're still married, unfortunately. Finding a judge to bribe takes time," I answer.

"Shitsticks," she says. "Anyway. I'll get rid of you as well, so you'll be free and clear. Then, we dismantle The Gambit brick by brick."

Romano looks at me, his head tilted. "You're sure about this? You'd have to change your identity. Alternative name, fresh look, possibly new place to live if the other two aren't convincing enough."

"I'm sure. Just make sure everyone else is safe. Shade had some ideas for that." Shade and I have been chatting recently. I floated a few ideas past him, and he agreed this was the way to go.

Romano pulls his phone from his pocket and dials Shade. They do the usual song and dance about identities, but then he switches it to speakerphone. "Hello, Queen, to what do I owe the pleasure?"

"Oh, fuck me. Who is *that*?" Claudette asks, her tone low and sultry. "Are you married to that one, too?"

"Not now, Claudette. I'll introduce you later," I reprimand her. "Shade, how do you guarantee to keep my accomplices safe?" I ask, knowing the answer but enjoying the big reveal as Romano's face is set in a scowl. He and the guys have been getting along really well lately, and I know he'd be pretty broken up about it if something happened to them.

"Why, I hired them last week. They work for me now, and they won't be hauled in."

Claudette chokes on the other side of the line. "Oh my fucking God!"

"Can it, lady. Or I'll come find you and punch you in the tit." She laughs at my threat but keeps her mouth shut.

"And when they're out of the building, Rogue? What happens then?" Romano asks.

"Then, I go home and start my life over. I live the way I want to, with a new identity, and none of this follows me, deal?"

"Deal," the other three say.

Present day

I pace across the tile in the house's foyer and wait for my guys to get home. Fuck, waiting around is the worst! I'm beginning to see their side of things when they ask to come with me on missions. I gotta be better about letting that happen because this is torture.

The security system beeps, and I pull up the surveillance on the tablet clutched in my grip to watch as the guys' SUV comes tearing down the gravel driveway. It skids to a stop under the portico as I fling open the front door.

Jacob jumps from the passenger seat and climbs the steps to me, wrapping me in a hug and planting kisses all over my face. "Jesus fuck, Love. I never want to see that happen again!" Han slides around and holds me between him and Jacob, trailing kisses on my neck. He pulls away and puts a hand to the base of my spine.

"You're still bleeding." His voice holds a bit of reprimand, but I laugh. I'm not. I closed it with some superglue, but I didn't want to take a shower and miss their arrival. The most I did was tear the dress and Kevlar corset off and throw on my favorite sweats I found in the laundry room. I don't care if they're dirty. They do the job.

"I didn't expect the impact to send me that far back onto the table. Stupid fucking crystal everywhere. I'm fine. The Kevlar and blood packs did their job. Just a couple of bruises, that's all. Oh, and I'm burning that dress and corset as soon as I can," I grumble.

"Does Kevlar burn?" Lucas asks from next to me. "Hi, Buttercup. Good to see ya." I land a playful punch to his gut at his carefree tone, and he wraps me in his arms. I note the tremor under his skin and know he is more affected than he's letting on. "There was too much blood. I knew you had the packs under the dress, but when I saw the blood under your head, I almost shot Romano myself."

"I'm fine. I promise." He scrutinizes my face to check if I'm telling the truth, and sees that I am. Being away from them was the hardest part, but now that they're here, I feel like I can breathe again for the first time since the bullets hit my chest and knocked the wind out of me.

He drops a kiss on my cheek and runs a hand over my hair, trailing it down to the very ends before rubbing a lock through his fingers as if checking I'm really here and okay.

Noah is the last to reach us, circling the car. "Is everyone else safe?" he asks. He steps up to my other side and I've found myself in a cage of my boyfriends, and it's a damn good place to be. I know the usual phrase is a sandwich, but surrounded like this by all four, it's like a warm and toasty boyfriend baguette with me nestled within.

"Yep. Romano and I met Claudette on the roof. We took the zipline down after Sage and the girls, and got them into Elenor's car down the block. They're here in the guest rooms in the west wing. G texted that Elise used the zipline as an excuse to pinch his ass, but they're fine. She took off to the private airstrip, and Nina headed north, likely into Claudette's territory. Nira went straight to the coast and had a boat ferry her out to international waters before planning on taking a helicopter to Vancouver."

I sigh after the recount of the escapees, and Noah's hand is steady on my back. A reassurance I didn't know I needed, but wholly appreciate.

"And Cross?" I ask.

"Detained. The work you had the bastard doing over the past month, evidence compiled, and confession to your parents' murders you caught on tape tonight are enough to put him away for life. You're free and clear, Trouble," Noah assures me.

"Thank God," I breathe.

The five of us move through the house, ending up at the oversized black couch. Noah and Jacob quickly pull the levers and rearrange the cushions to create a space we can all crash in. The guys and I all undress to our underthings just in case Sage, Elenor, or Mimi wander into the room. We don't want to give them more trauma.

Han brings the first-aid kit in and fusses over the cut on my skull, cleaning up the blood and marveling at my superglue job. He says I might need to cut some hair to free it from the binding, but who the hell cares? He frowns at the bruises decorating my ribs from the bullets' impact, but there's nothing to do for those. Thankfully, I don't need to bind them as nothing broke. I just need to be patient. *Oh, joy.*

Once I'm tended to, he drops the medkit box, hauls me into his arms, and collapses with me down onto the couch. Sleep overtakes me immediately, and I drift off, curled between my guys. A little sore, but a whole lot alive.

Chapter Twenty-Three

Han

Soft whispers make their way to my ears, and I slowly come to, breaking that dream-like state to find the source of the quiet sounds.

Craning my neck, I spy Sage and one of her friends at the entrance to the living room, peeking their heads in. Mimi, my tired brain reminds me of her name. Jacob stirs next to me and tightens his hand on my hip as he groans at my movement.

I gently peel his hand from my side and sit upright. His face is relaxed, his glasses a foot away from his head, on the edge of the orgy-couch. No one bothered to get ready for bed last night. We all needed to crash and did so in various states of undress on the oversized fold-out couch in deference to our guests.

Sage pokes her head back in and stifles a gasp when she sees me giving her a pointed stare. She mimes lifting a fork to her mouth and presses her hands together in a plea. I slide off of the bed, moving Jacob's hand to Rogue's so he has someone to hold on to in my absence.

I grab a pair of pants from the floor, not mine by the size of them, and head toward the entryway, gripping the waistband and keeping them from falling around my ankles. My feet shuffle on the warm floor as I cross the threshold and find Sage and Mimi standing in the foyer wearing sweatpants and baggy t-shirts.

"Hey, Han. Sorry to wake you. Good morning. We need food, please, and we can't find the kitchen." Sage looks contrite for the wake-up call, but I get it. It took us forever to figure out the layout of the house. We all have the maps memorized now, but the paper copy is in the hidden kitchen.

"Morning. Yeah, come on." I walk off, trying to clear the sleep from my eyes, and the girls trail after me.

Elenor is coming down the stairs and quickly rushes to catch up with us. I lead them through the halls until I find the familiar doorway. Fuck, I'm glad we're renovating. This place is too confusing.

Mimi sighs in relief when she sees the big coffee maker and rushes over to it, pulling the jar of ground coffee from the counter and beginning the prep work. Sage opens the fridge, pulling out cheeses, a carton of eggs, milk, juice, and breakfast foods as Elenor sits at the counter and drops her head to her folded arms.

"Are you guys okay in here for a bit? Do you need anything else?" I ask, hopeful they're good, and I can go back to bed. "Here's a map to the place. You guys can use it but it doesn't leave the house, deal?"

"Deal," says Elenor. The word is muffled against her arms as she curls up against the counter.

"We're set. We'll find everything we need. Go back to sleep. Thank you, Han." Sage throws a smile so similar to Ivy's that I do a quick double-take. It's almost eerie. They don't look alike, what with my girl's dyed black hair, fuller frame, and copious tattoos, but now and then, the likeness smacks me in the face.

"Okay, cool. Can you guys give us a day? We'll start working on getting everyone settled where they want now that this is all over, but can that be tomorrow?" I want to spend the day snuggling my girl and making sure we're all okay after watching her get shot and crash into that table last night. I'm not ready to have her out of my sight for long, and even this trip to the kitchen is making me anxious.

"Yeah, totally. Just lock the door to wherever you guys are, and we'll keep out if we wander around. You're redoing this place, right?" Sage asks, studying the copy of the map we have taped to the fridge.

"Definitely. The work starts next week. And thank you." My voice is still thick with sleep, and I rush back through the halls, the laughter of the girls trailing after me until I find a bathroom and wash up.

Opening the door to the living room, I find the other four precisely as I left them. Ivy is in the middle of the couch, Jacob holding her hand between them, Noah spooning her from behind, and Lucas wrapped around Jacob's back.

It's fucking cute how they snuggle up, but I know it's a comfort thing, not a sexual one. Lucas mashes his face into Jacob's neck, and my cheeky Brit huffs out a laugh, letting me know he's awake and enjoying his cuddles.

I shuck my clothes after closing the door behind me and kneel on the couch between Ivy and Jacob. He cracks an eye open, seeing my naked body, and with the hand trapped under his side, he lifts his hand and crooks a finger in my direction. I crawl between him and our girl, my dick half hard as I look over them.

"You just going to sit there?" Ivy asks, her playful tone deep with sleep.

Jacob and I both laugh at the comment. I slowly run a palm up her tattooed thigh, finding the lace of her panties on her hip. I lean down, nipping the soft skin, and run my tongue up the valley of her side before it swells at her chest.

Fuck, she's perfect for me. For us.

She shivers at the contact, and Noah's hips press against her ass when he feels her stirring.

"How's your head?" I ask.

"Haven't had any complaints yet," she jokes. At my concerned face, she clarifies, "Fine, no headache, and I think the glue held overnight." I shake my head at her use of household items for patching up wounds.

"Can I check it?" I ask.

"I looked last night a few times. It seems fine," Noah grumbles from behind Ivy.

Still, I need to check. I gently nudge her hip until she's face down on the couch, and I crawl up her body, sitting just behind her ass, so my semi-hard dick rests between her cheeks. I bend forward to move her hair out of the way. The glue is still holding the cut together. It's only as long as my pinky, but head wounds bleed like crazy, so it looked a lot worse last night before I cleaned it up with a few alcohol pads.

Ivy, feeling me stroke her hair back into place, uses the opportunity to grind her ass back against me. She stills suddenly. "Are the girls okay?" Her tone is slightly panicked, and she raises her torso, propping up on her elbows.

"They're fine, Gorgeous. I just showed them where the kitchen is, and they agreed to give us today to recuperate." She sighs at my words, flopping back down and stretching her arms in front of her.

Lucas lets out a tiny snore behind Jacob, and he just laughs.

Ivy subtly moves under me as I run my fingertips down her back, undoing her bra. Her breath catches, and her eyes slide shut. Noah leans forward, taking her lips with his in a passionate kiss. Jacob's hand roams down her side, and she shivers at his touch.

Noah

Trouble's hips grind against the couch, looking for any form of relief, and I deepen my kiss against her lips.

I feel her moving against Han and lift my head to watch him slide her panties down her thighs. She spreads her legs slightly. I see her arousal between her legs, shining in the morning light as it pours through the bay windows. *Fuck.*

Jacob continues his delicate touches along her side as Han wedges his shoulders between her thighs and nips at the soft skin on either side. I dive down, taking her lips with mine—morning breath be damned—and her breathing comes faster as Han moves closer to where she wants him.

I tease, nip, and suck the lush flesh of her lips, giving her just enough to split her focus between the two of us. She mewls into my mouth as I muffle the sounds Han elicits from her.

This beautiful creature. This amazing woman who helped topple an empire is actually ours. I make a silent vow to keep her out of harm's way if I can, or stand at her back if she finds herself in the thick of it again. There's nothing I wouldn't do for her.

Trouble takes advantage of my slow, languorous kisses, and moves her mouth to my jaw, my neck, before settling her chest over my torso, licking, biting, and sucking every inch of flesh she can reach.

I prop my head up to see Han give a long lick from clit to taint in one slow sweep. She tenses for a moment before relaxing into it as he spears his tongue into her tight pussy. I groan as she fists a handful of my hair and has her other hand wrapped around Jacob's cock.

"Now, now, Darling Mine," Jacob chastises, pulling her fingers free of his length. "Touch yourself while Han works you over with his tongue. I want to hear you scream."

Ivy's breath catches, and she slides her hand under her to follow his command, and Han dives back in, messily licking and fucking her with his tongue.

My hand reaches for her ass, and I knead one firm, full globe. The grip I use is punishing as I wrestle with the thoughts flitting through my mind. Watching her sacrifice herself like that, willing to trust Romano to put the bullets in her Kevlar corset and not her head, was something we argued about for weeks.

But she was right. It's the only way she could walk away from this. The others needed to see her "die" in case they get out on bail or evade the charges altogether. They're going to blame the hostess of the party the cops arrested them at. She says she'll do a makeover, do what she needs to in order to disguise herself, but it still makes me edgy. Everyone they arrested at the party is currently in lockup, and it's not as if she associated with many others in the organization aside from her legion of hitmen who she claims all respect her enough to shut the fuck up.

Her arm muscles bunch and her body shifts as the circles on her clit go faster. Han matches her pace with his tongue before pulling back and shoving two fingers into her pussy, and she detonates. Her back arches as her hips lift, drawing out her pleasure with slow strokes on her bundle of nerves as Han's fingers keep up their relentless pace.

"Good girl," Jacob coos, and she whimpers at the words. "You're ready for more, aren't you?"

She nods her head, face pressed to the couch. I'm staring at her face as she gasps when Han pushes in a third finger. "Oh, fuuuck," she moans at the friction.

"Han, push her to the cusp and keep her there." Jacob's words wash over us and Han nods his head, eager to do as he's told.

He stretches her, and I see his thumb move upward. I follow his lead, spreading her ass so he can press against her tight hole. Her hips are bucking, matching the pace.

Han suddenly withdraws as Trouble's legs start quivering with her impending orgasm, leaving her a sweaty, panting mess. Jacob grabs Han's wrist and brings his fingers to his mouth. Ivy turns her head in time to see Jacob's tongue curling around his index finger, licking off her juices.

Lucas, having woken amidst the screaming, groans at the sight. "Buttercup, I want to fuck you, then yell at you for getting hurt, then fuck you all over again."

"No objections. Somebody had better make me come *now*."

I grab her and pull her over my body. I lift her hips and on shaky knees, and she sinks down on my cock in one smooth motion. Her head goes flying backward as she grinds down on me, and a silent scream escapes her lips.

From the corner of my eye, I see Lucas stand up and move behind

Rogue. He palms his cock in his hand. "Holy shit, Buttercup. Ride him. Please."

She widens her knees a bit more, and with her palms on my chest, nails digging into my pecs, she moves. A fantasy come to life; that's our girl. Not only is she the most badass woman any of us have ever known, but she's also the kindest. The most loving. And ours.

She uses her muscles to lift, then slides down my cock, slowly ramping up the speed with each motion. My hands are steady on her hips, and I plant my feet on the couch behind her and start taking over the movement. I push up hard, driving my cock in and out of her while keeping her in place. I see Rogue's eyes roll back into her head.

Her pussy flutters around me before I pull her down for a wet, messy kiss, distracting her for a second because I'm about to do something new.

I lift one hand from her hip and curl my finger in Lucas's direction. Am I ready for a full on group thing? It's something I've struggled with since this all started. I want to make my girl happy. It doesn't make me uncomfortable in any sense. These are all people I'd happily lay down my life for. I think the idea that it's wrong or different has stopped me.

Thinking about the time I directed everyone, or we used the couch in the clubhouse, the hidden sex room in the passageway... none of it felt wrong. It was exciting, exhilarating even. It was us working together as a team, all five of us, to reach new heights and give each other love and pleasure.

Lucas looks at Jacob and Han, who each shrug a shoulder. Lucas glances back and I give him a firm glare as Rogue presses her face against my neck, her teeth digging into the skin there. When have they ever denied an order from their Dear Leader?

"Do you want more, Love?" Jacob asks as his tone deepens and his cock stands at attention. Han runs his hand along his own length and works Jacob's boxers off while he watches the three in front of us.

"So much more. I want all of you, everywhere. Alone or together. I want this forever." Her voice is high, frustrated with the denial of her orgasms.

I gently slow my thrusts, shifting to lower my legs, and the movement makes Rogue jerk in response. Lucas runs a fingertip down her crack, slipping past her asshole, and I feel pressure against my cock as he slips his index finger inside with me. Rogue moans as he stretches her, and I tense for a moment, but just as quickly, Lucas removes the digit, trailing her wetness up to her ass, and presses in.

The unfamiliar feeling of Lucas's finger pressing against Rogue's inner wall and adding pressure to my dick causes me to groan and shift my hips. The experience is new to me, and forces Rogue to squeeze my dick with her muscles. It allows Lucas to slip into her ass deeper. As Lucas moves, each press forward alternating with my gentle thrusts, Jacob wraps himself around Han's back, the two of them watching us with rapt attention.

My God, this is better than I expected. I don't plan on sharing every time, but this could get addicting. This feeling, this pressure, the look on my girl's face as we work together to bring her to the brink.

Jacob

"What do you think of both of us fucking our girl?" I ask Han as we watch Lucas prepare Rogue.

"Well, I had planned on it," he says as my hand circles his cock. My motions are smooth and sure as I tease him with touches.

Lucas lines up his cock once Rogue is ready and demanding more. He prepped her well, using his fingers and the slick he gathered from between her thighs, so he's able to thrust into her ass with one motion, and she screams as her orgasm finally washes over her. Noah's grunt at the pressure is nearly just as loud, and he fists her hair, bringing her down to his lips for a bruising kiss.

When she recovers enough from the initial sensation, Noah and Lucas move in tandem. One sliding out as the other slides in. The symphony of flesh is addicting, and my hand moves faster on Han's cock.

"Did you like having Lucas's finger and Noah in your tight pussy at the same time? Do you think your cunt could take two cocks?" I ask Rogue.

"So good. So fucking good," she chants as her back arches between our two teammates.

I lean close, biting Han's earlobe and whispering, "*That* is what I meant when I said '*both*' of us. I want us together in her hot, wet pussy." He shudders at my words and I watch as goosebumps break out along his body.

Noah and Lucas make Rogue come again, and Lucas pulls out of her, painting his cum on her lower back. Noah lets go when she does, spilling himself inside of her. Our girl collapses forward, resting her head on Noah's chest as Lucas drags a finger through the mess on her back, marking her with a giant "L." He grabs a shirt from the floor and gently runs it over her back before flopping down next to Noah.

Lucas holds up a hand for a high five, and Noah pushes him so hard he rolls off the couch with an oomph.

Rogue lifts her hips, letting Noah's dick slide free, and they both moan at the sensation. She kisses him and pulls away, gently whispering, "I love you."

He mimics her sentiment and helps her shift off of him. She climbs across the empty space on the couch, reaching for Han, and pushes him backward. I move out of the way, guiding them down with a firm hand.

I lean over, kissing Han with ferocity before turning my head and doing the same to Rogue. "Fuck him, Darling. Fuck him, and I'll fuck both of you." My words are an order, a command, a plea, all rolled into one. I want them both so badly it aches.

She works her way down Han's length, and when she's fully seated, he spreads his legs, calves hanging off the couch and feet planted on the floor. She grinds down on Han's dick, Noah's cum easing the friction between them.

Her gasp catches in her throat as Han experimentally shifts upward, plunging in and out of her. I reach between them from behind, and circle the base of Han's dick, giving it a firm squeeze before working two of my fingers into Rogue's dripping cunt.

My fingers pump in time with Han's thrusts, testing and stretching as I go. I gently put pressure on her walls, widening her until I slip in another finger, and another.

I glance back and see Noah watching us, his concern clear on his face. It's a lot for anyone to handle, but our girl is loving it. Crying out in pleasure and demanding "More, more, more."

He's reclined on the bed, watching. Lucas shifts his body to get an unobstructed view, slowly rising to his knees as he stares without blinking.

The fit is so tight it's hard for Han to move much, but Rogue takes over, rocking her hips and driving both of us in.

She's mumbling incoherently, and sweat beads on her brow as we work in tandem to bring her to orgasm. She cries out as Han's fingers find her clit and press hard. He doesn't have to move; the pressure alone sets her off.

We let her ride the wave, and as her breathing evens out, I notch my cock at her entrance. Gently pushing on her back, I encourage her to lie flat along Han's fevered body, exposing herself to me behind her.

"You're going to take our cocks, Darling. And you're going to fucking love it."

"Green, green, green," she chants, giving me the go word, proving that while she's in the throes of this, she wants to continue even as her arms shake on either side of Han's head and her thighs are doing the same near my hips.

I double check on Lucas and Noah, wanting to make sure they've heard her enthusiastic agreement. The last thing I want is someone pulling me away. Our girl was made to test limits, to tempt us into anything and everything we can offer her. So long as we do it safely, with consent, and enough preparation, anything is possible.

I quickly slide my dick in the space between where their bodies connect. I glide it along Han's cock, coating myself in the juices smeared on and pooled around him.

Han's eyes snap open at the feel of my piercings bumping along his cock as I enter her. Rogue's mouth drops open, her eyes closed in pure bliss, and she hisses out, "Yesss."

Finally, fully seated, I give a tentative thrust. "You okay, Loves?" I ask.

Han voices his "Yes," but Rogue is less filtered. "Yes, fuck, Jacob. Move. Move. Move! Fuck us. Please!"

I move my hips, and Han does the same. We alternate pulling out and pushing in. I keep my hands on her waist, and Han holds her shoulders steady, careful to not touch her bruised ribs from last night. My grip on her will surely leave matching dark marks within a few hours, but for all the control I exhibit, I can't bring myself to loosen my grip.

It's as if the events of last night are on repeat in my mind, and despite finding her home and safe when we returned home, part of me never wants to let go. She shouldn't have been in that position in the first place.

The slide of my dick is methodical, measured, and it's driving both of them crazy.

Rogue's chanting gets more and more obscene as she praises deities I've never even heard of. I feel the first flutters of yet another orgasm from her, and Han pulls her mouth down to his. Sinking one hand between them, I find a hard, pebbled nipple aching for touch. Rolling the peaked bud between my fingers, I pinch roughly as I deliver a smack to her arse.

The scream she emits reverberates around the room, and I move my hand from her ass to find Han's sac, giving it a gentle tug. He follows Rogue over the cliff, and once both of my lovers have reached their bliss, I find my own and collapse over both of them.

I lean forward, kissing Han gently. "That was... wow."

Rogue seems to have blacked out for a second because her eyes fly open, and she sighs, wiggling between the two of us.

"Rest, Darling. I'll grab some wet cloths to clean up." My still-hard cock withdraws from our girl, and I make eye contact with her.

"I love you," I whisper between kisses.

"I love you, too."

"And I'll spank you if you ever do anything like that again," I grunt. She meets my threat with a laugh.

"Is that a promise? I hope it never comes to me being fake shot again, but I will volunteer if it leads to more spanking." She chuckles again and rolls to the side. Noah and Lucas are sitting on the opposite end of the couch, looking at Noah's phone.

"What's going on?" Rogue asks with a yawn.

"We have to go to work tomorrow. Apparently, there are a lot of details we need to debrief on, and almost losing our girl doesn't constitute a week off. I don't know if we're going to like working with Shade." Lucas sounds bitter as he says the words.

"It's fine. And you didn't 'almost lose' me. I just got a little banged up on the way down. I need to arrange some things, anyway. But today, let's just relax. The rest of the world can wait."

And we do. We spend the day laughing, cuddling, and deciding what to do next while sneaking furtive glances at our girl, making sure she really is okay. After all, now that we don't have anyone gunning for us, we can do anything.

Chapter Twenty-Four

Noah

"Morning, Cap!"

It's six in the morning, and I didn't expect to find anyone in the kitchen so early. It's our first day at the office, and I wanted to get the coffee started and breakfast going, so we begin on a good note today. There's going to be a lot to go over, and an empty stomach helps no one.

"What are you doing up, Trouble? In fact, didn't I just leave you in bed?" I ask.

"Yep, I snuck in here while you were in the shower. Now sit. I'm making breakfast."

Before following orders, I walk toward her, take her face in my hands, and peck her sweetly on the lips. "Morning."

She sighs at the contact and leans into me as I pull away, chasing my lips. She pouts so fucking cutely. I give in and claim one more kiss.

I wrap my arms around her and pull her close. She's dressed in one of my t-shirts and nothing else as far as I can tell. I'm tempted to sit her ass on the counter and do a full exploration, but something dings, and she pulls away.

"Sit." Her orders have me snapping a quick salute and finding a barstool at the island.

"What are you making?" I ask, looking curiously at the ingredients she has before her.

"Omelets. I'm terrible at a lot of things, but eggs are hard to mess up." Not true, but if it keeps that smile on her face, I'll choke down the runniest eggs ever made.

She opens the oven door, pulling out two wire racks with toast, and with careful fingers, she stacks them and drops them in front of me. "Butter these for me, will you?"

"Aye, aye, ma'am." As I work on that, she turns to the counter and whisks the eggs. Her ass moves side to side with the quick movements, and I end up buttering half of my fingers instead of the toast. This is going to be torture.

I drop the knife and bread, hop off the stool and kneel behind her. I run my nose up her thigh, and she tenses for a second. "Whatcha doing, Cap?"

"Having breakfast. Keep cooking. We're on a time crunch." A shiver wracks her body, and I trail my nose up her thighs. She gasps when I find her clit with the tip of my tongue, and widens her legs, allowing me better access. "Are you sore?" I ask before diving in.

"Yes," she breathes. Her hand reaches back to my head, and she runs her fingers through my hair, keeping me firmly in place. "But not nearly sore enough to tell you to stop."

I slide over her bare pussy, and she drops the whisk. "Nuh-uh, keep cooking," I tell her. My voice muffled as I spear my tongue into her channel.

The whisking starts again when she removes her hand from my head. The motion moves her sinfully over my mouth. My hands on her thighs are firm, slightly bruising, but she leans into the pressure.

I swirl, nip at her folds, and bury my face in the sweet, sweet heaven that is my girl. How did I ever think anything less than this was love?

In minutes, she's crying out, her legs buckling as her orgasm washes over her. I keep my hands on her legs, propping her up. I pull back and notice the whisk on the floor. Bad girl.

I grab it and toss it into the sink, scoring a three-pointer. I rise from my crouch and pin her against the counter, hips digging into the hard edge.

"I love you. Ivy, Rogue, Trouble, Maven of Mayhem. Whatever you want your new name to be, I'll love that, too," I whisper my honeyed words next to her ear, and she leans into my warmth.

"I love you, too. Noah, Captain, Dear Leader." Her grin tugs her cheeks up, and I deliver a quick kiss, smearing her juices along her lips. She groans at the taste of herself. A glint of mischief enters her eyes, but the others will be up soon, and there's simply not enough time. Is remote work an option?

I step away, grabbing a towel from the cabinet and wet it at the sink to clean up my face and my girl before washing the whisk and handing it back.

The whole time, she watches me, her green eyes sparkling in delight.

"Morning!" Lucas calls from the doorway, and Sir Lancelot squeaks from the floor. His little white harness and leash firmly attached. "I have to take the gremlin out for a walk." He stops speaking abruptly. "What—Oh, what did I miss?"

"Nothing, nothing!" Rogue shoos him out of the kitchen with flapping hands. "Take care of Lancelot, and breakfast will be ready in fifteen minutes."

"Yes, ma'am!" Lucas rushes off because not much can get between him and food, but his little buddy is the exception. I hope Lancelot is ready to run instead of walk this morning.

I have to admit, the little monster grew on me. I ordered a box of mini-balloons for the damn creature. He likes them so much, but his quills pop them, and he gets sad. So I ordered a thousand of them. They should be here tomorrow.

Toast buttered and omelets on the stove, I help Rogue get them plated and add in toppings for the guys. After all the time we've known each other, we've rarely had mornings together in peace, and learning how to be a polycule will take some time. Yeah, I Googled polyamory.

I'm excited to see where this goes. Waking up nestled in blankets and each other, sharing in our morning routines, and learning preferences the way a normal couple... or pentad, would.

Han and Jacob walk into the kitchen hand in hand, and I can't help the smile that takes over my face. They've been blissfully happy since Rogue stepped into our lives, but they also feel more settled now. I've seen the little looks over the years, determined to keep my nose out of it, but I'm so glad they finally went for it.

"Morning," they say in unison, and before Rogue can jinx them, I interject.

"Take a seat, guys. I'll grab drinks."

Rogue looks at me as if I've betrayed her, and I run my tongue along my lip, distracting her with memories of our earlier adventures. She plates the last omelet just as Lucas walks in with Sir Lancelot leading the way, his little nose in the air.

Everyone grabs a seat, food and drinks piled high, and we dig in. The toast was mostly buttered, and we forgot salt in the eggs as Rogue whisked them, but they're fine. No one complains, and everyone compliments the chef with high praise and subtle touches.

After breakfast, we get our shit together and say goodbye to Rogue in the foyer. She balances on her tiptoes as she kisses each of us, wishing us a good first day at work.

We're dressed in suits, I'm holding two bags containing additional evidence to hand over to Shade this morning, and Jacob is holding a cooler with the lunches Trouble packed for us.

When she saw us all lined up after breakfast, our sharp suits each unique and well fitted, she nearly dragged us all back to the oversized couch. Yeah, we clean up well.

"Buttercup, remember, he needs food every two hours. There's a box in my room with a bunch of snacks for him. He can have eggs, too. You should walk him around lunchtime and in the afternoon. Or, you know what? Maybe I should just bring him. They won't even notice him."

"No!" we all shout. Everyone side eyes everyone else, just waiting for someone to call jinx on our first day at work. I laugh because that would be highly unprofessional and also, exceptionally funny.

"Go, Red. I got him. Don't worry. I have some stuff to do today, but none of it will interfere with his schedule. I promise. I'll tell him his Mama loves him." She laughs because Lucas calling himself the hedgehog's "Mama" will never not be funny.

"Fine." He sighs.

Jacob opens the door, and we all file out, shouting back I love yous and general mushy shit. I love it.

The drive takes an hour, and upon arrival at the enormous glass building, we're scanned, put through metal detectors, patted down, and generally inconvenienced. I guess when you work for federal agencies, they take that stuff seriously.

Shade told us which office to go to in his message yesterday. When I give the number to the guard escorting us, he raises a brow. He enters the elevator, waves his electronic card in front of the reader, and pushes the button for us.

We ride up in silence, each of us committing every access point and detail to memory during our ascent. The doors slide open, and we're met with a dark gray hallway, an open area with computer stations all to one side, a big screen in front of them taking over the entire wall, and a slew of offices on the right. The "pit," as I've decided to call it, easily occupies two floors to accommodate the enormous screen on the wall, and the offices appear to be on both levels at the back, a railing separating the top floor from the pit.

I look at Jacob, and his eyes are bugging out at the sight. There's so much tech down there; I'm certain it's fulfilling a different kind of fantasy for him.

The guard stops before a plain black door, the numbers 842 shining silver on the dark space. Our escort raps his knuckles lightly before a voice calls out. He opens the door, admitting our entrance, and closes it behind us as soon as we're inside. Sealing us in with the man we only know as "Shade."

A solid wood desk is cluttered with papers, a laptop hanging off one side, precariously balanced, and four cell phones in a pile. The walls are all a dark color, the bookshelves matching the paint and the lights are a soft LED glow, giving the whole space a modern, yet intimate feel.

The man behind the desk can't be much older than me. He's got dark hair, a five o'clock shadow at half-past eight in the morning, and a black t-shirt on. A leather jacket hangs off the back of his chair, and I have to admit, this is not the look I was expecting for our contact.

"Morning, gentlemen. Jesus, who died? You all look like you came from a funeral." The man's appearance may be unfamiliar, but that voice was in our ear just the other night.

"Shade," I reply. Jacob has his body half-turned to look out at the pit while Lucas and Han take two of the four seats in front of the desk. "What resulted from the setup?"

We've been covertly on the payroll for a little over a month now, but this is the first time we're meeting face-to-face. It's amazing what you can do with technology these days. They ran our background checks, sent over the paperwork, hired us, and gave us our orders without ever having to step into their offices. Now that the job is done, I'm itching to find out what happened.

Jacob refocuses on the meeting, and the two of us drop into the remaining chairs.

"We've apprehended the leaders of the Southern California gangs, the Midwest group, and more politicians, investors, and people in power than expected. Fuck, we even got my boss's boss because this was my operation. Strictly a need-to-know basis meant I could bring in who I wanted until it was done. The audio from the centerpieces picked up more than enough to indict nearly a hundred people, and the mics you guys and the escorts were wearing got the rest.

"As for Cross, the jobs Queen had him doing to 'prove himself' were set up by us obviously, so we have surveillance. It could be construed as entrapment, but he and his associate, Dario, gave more than enough detail to Queen about her parents' murders to put them behind bars without bail. And you'll find, we can delay a trial as long as necessary."

I sigh in relief. "What else?"

"We ascertained the locations of four other escort services where the girls were there unwillingly, busted up a human trafficking ring in Los Angeles, and raided more than a dozen meth dens across the Midwest. People are rolling over, sharing information, hoping to cut a deal. Lower offenders, we'll offer a reduced sentence if it benefits the whole, but most we won't. And we'll offer nothing to anyone who has personal ties with you four or your girl. The Vice President is trying to use his connections to get out, but nearly twenty people gave up information on him, so he's sitting pretty in one of our cells."

Shade takes a breath.

"Now the bad news. Claudette is still missing, and the ambulances that had her guests in them never showed up at the hospital. When they were escorted downstairs, they were bruised and bloody. The police officers said they were fighting each other. New laws won't let us bring them in without medical attention first, so they were loaded into the nearest ambulances and sent off with police escorts. The ambulances arrived at the hospital, but the men were nowhere to be found. There was only the Senator's guard with the gunshot to the knee."

Shade shakes his head in disbelief. "I don't know how they did it, but fuck, that was some good magic. We're also missing five members from The Gambit. Elise Batten, Nina Wilson, Nira Bhatt, and two hitmen we only know as G and Fabio." Not news to us, but definitely to Shade. "Any ideas, gentlemen?"

"They were in the building, weren't they?" Han asks.

"Yes, and unfortunately, the charges for the explosives seem to have originated from the floor below the ballroom. It's unlikely we'll recover bodies. Romano met up with us later, informing us that Queen was home safe, and expects our promises to be kept. They will be." He laughs. "You tell her I have a job for her if she wants to play for the good guys this time."

Lucas laughs. "I doubt it, man. She told you 'no' a month ago. I doubt her answer has changed, but you can try."

Jacob stares intently at Shade. "What are we supposed to call you? I assume 'Shade' was a cover name for this job. Do you want that to continue? We tend to be nickname people anyway."

Shade laughs. "Right. My name is Ambrose Reese. Most people call me Reese."

"Good to know," I say. "And Romano? He's back to work?"

Reese sighs. "Not exactly. He's taking a well-deserved vacation after nearly six years undercover. He grabbed his motorcycle from my garage and said he'd be back in a month after we did his debrief yesterday. His phones have been switched off, and he said he needed to deal with his shit before coming back." A look of genuine concern crosses his face briefly, but it's gone as quickly as it appeared.

"Anyway, what are we working on now?" I ask, redirecting us to why we're here.

"What do you guys know about terrorist cells?"

Rogue

After the guys left for work, I roused Sage and the girls to give me a hand.

Call it bonding or necessary work, but this is equal parts fun and torture.

"Hold still, Ivy!" Sage scolds me. "Brad Mondo says I have to do it this way, or your hair will turn into ramen noodles and never be pretty again."

Elenor rolls her eyes. "Can you tell she found YouTube while we were at the safe house?"

The smell of bleach is ridiculously overpowering in the bathroom, and with all four of us in here, it's hot as hell, too. Coupled with the soreness I'm feeling *everywhere* after our adventures yesterday, it's wholly uncomfortable. It doesn't stop the shiver from raking down my spine at the thought of doing it again, though.

Mimi insisted on painting my nails, and Elenor, having watched far too many YouTube videos, has a tattoo gun working on the previously ink-free left side of my stomach. I watch her work, noting that she took her free lessons seriously. She had to pass a test for the first one and now I have the guys' initials tattooed on my inner thigh. A-plus work.

I feel like it's some unconventional version of a salon, but I'll take it because I hate the original ones. Who wants to make small talk when the person cutting your hair should pay attention to the task at hand? Plus, it's not like I could ever share anything about my work or personal life. Maybe it'll be different now. I should try again.

Four hours later, my hair is now a platinum blonde with silver tones, and it reaches a few inches past my ears instead of my ass when it's straight. I feel forty pounds lighter, and when I twist my head from side to side, the hair kisses my shoulders.

I look like an entirely new person. Which is the whole point. My stomach is wrapped and bandaged, the cling film preventing any dye from dropping onto the work. It was time to cover up that Algiz rune King gave Sage and me. Instead, we both got two cages with two birds escaping.

Before wandering through the house, I walk Sir Lancelot and feed him his snacks—which are disgusting bugs, for the record. Sage and the girls are packing up, getting ready to return to the safe house with the others. They want to stay there until we move everyone to make sure the transitions go well. My plan is to work on it now that I can fly under the radar again as an ordinary citizen.

I find Han's renovation plans, make a few adjustments, and call the contractor, offering him an insane bonus if he can get the job done within a month. He readily agrees, even when I tell him there will be no bonus if he delivers even a day late, and two outside contractors will inspect it to evaluate the work before payment.

Money really can move mountains, it seems. King left me enough to live thirty lifetimes lavishly, but really, I just want to make this one count.

My guys arrive home at five-thirty on the dot from their first day at work, and they find me in the library with my Kindle in my hand.

I adore the library and the feel of a paperback in my hands, but apparently, shipping smutty books takes time, and there's a new one that dropped yesterday that continues the acrobat story I read a few months ago. After this one, I plan on diving into the satire reverse harem I keep seeing mentioned on the Facebook groups. Do I have a fake account just to be part of the book community there? You bet your ass I do. Give me the recs. All of them.

Jacob pauses in the doorway, and my eyes flick up to meet his.

"Holy shit," he breathes.

Han, Lucas, and Noah crane their necks around my Brit to see what caught his attention. I'm wearing a black satin robe. My hair is shiny and polished as it hangs straight, and my makeup is natural and subtle. My lilac nails are a change for me, but they complement my silvery hair beautifully.

All four of them are comical as they stand there, their mouths open and eyes wide.

"Welcome home, honeys. How was your day?" I joke.

Noah is the first to recover from the shock because isn't that just the way. "It was good. We confirmed everything with Shade. Your immunity kicked in. You just have to give a statement, but you provided more than enough evidence. They will leave you out of it, although Shade wants you to join us."

I give it a thought, as I have ever since his offer came in a few weeks ago. "Do they offer contract work? I don't think I could deal with going into an office every day or doing the undercover thing. But I'd happily help you guys out when needed. I planned on doing that anyway, but maybe it'd make planning easier," I ponder aloud.

"Oh, about that," Jacob starts. "We negotiated partial remote work. We don't have to go in every day, but will work the way we did with Annex. Mostly from home or on the job, with check-ins now and then. I may go more because their set up is incredible. Love, there were easily two hundred computers, and a whole wall dedicated to a shared screen."

My smile stretches wide. "Really?" I ask. "That's incredible. I'm also glad you guys won't be doing the nine-to-five grind. Wait, what happens with Annex now?" I look at Lucas, who slowly runs his eyes along my face. He's no doubt noting the difference the hair makes. I really do look *so* different aside from my tattoos and general physicality. But the hair makes my face look more open, younger even. The light makeup is contoured to highlight my cheekbones and subtly change my face shape.

He meets my eyes and fills me in. "They're letting Mara keep control. Because she worked with them from early on, subverting Cross's orders and helping to bring in some of the evidence, they cleared her of any wrongdoing she may not have been aware of. She also brought on Nick Grand's team to work from within Annex as Beta Team Two. By the way, it was his team leading the charge from the entrance Jacob and Han opened at the back of the ballroom. We saw him at lunch and got to chatting. Not a bad dude. Anyway, it wasn't until a year ago that Mara noticed something wasn't right, but acted correctly in bringing the information to the feds. We're just lucky she scoured the reports to figure out who she couldn't approach. As for Collinsworth Bank, where I was stationed in December, it turns out Cross was in the middle of turning the execs in his direction to keep tabs on The Gambit members' finances. He was looking for weak spots everywhere while King was still running things."

Mila Sin

Shit. That man had a serious obsession with working for or against The Gambit. I wonder if it's because they kicked him out all those years ago. Like going to your high school reunion to show off your banging new bod to an old flame, or at least, that's how the movies depict it.

"That's good news. And he's secured? Not getting out on bail or anything?" I don't let fear enter my voice, but I need to know what kind of blowback I should expect.

"Nope. They've got more than enough to keep him in prison for a very long time," Han confirms. "Along with most of the attendees at the party."

I smile, knowing I've done a good thing, taken back my life, and helped to put some horrible people away.

"Claudette, G, and Fabio are up in The Rattlesnakes territory. Nina and Nira are long gone, and Elise landed in the Caribbean. Mrs. M texted me to say the 'snooty eagle' had landed. Call me crazy, but I'm pretty sure those two are going to get along famously." The guys laugh, and I see Lucas crane his neck to find Sir Lancelot.

"Oh, Noah," I draw his attention. "A box of mini balloons arrived. I thought they were condoms at first, but the pictures of tiny hedgehogs printed on the balloons made me think otherwise. What's that about?" I ask sweetly, knowing the answer.

"Shit," he mumbles, his cheeks turning an adorably ruddy red. "They, uh… They're for Sir Lancelot. He likes to play with them."

Lucas looks at Noah with wide eyes and envelops him in a bear hug. He wisely says nothing, even as Noah pushes him off, but I'm almost sure I see his eyes well with emotion.

"One more thing," I say as I stand from the chaise, leaving my Kindle off to the side. "I can't go by Rogue anymore. If it's okay with you guys, I'd like to keep the ridiculous and adorable nicknames, but I'd like to try being Ivy again." My throat struggles to let the words pass. All the guys have soft expressions on their faces, and I know I've made the right choice.

The house is in my personal name, and the only people who know my real name are men who signed off on my immunity paperwork, in this house, or in Mrs. M's beach hut.

They nod as one, and Jacob opens his arms to me.

I rush into their embrace as they surround me.

Never in a million years did I think I would find the kind of love, affection, respect, and adoration that I've found with these four. Our time together has been chaotic, to say the least, but I wouldn't trade it for anything.

The only question now is: What's next?

The End

Epilogue 1

Lucas

Two Months Later

Buttercup leads me through the house to the closed off portion of the west wing. Since the renovations finished a month ago, we've had more furniture deliveries than I can count, and the Amazon guy is practically family.

I trail after her, watching her blonde bob shine in the updated lighting of the hallway.

We did a big walk through when the construction crews finished the job, but as soon as we and the two additional contractors signed off on it, Buttercup paid the bonus and sealed this section off.

I honestly hadn't even thought of it since then. Our rooms are in the east wing and the common spaces are downstairs. With work for Shade taking up a lot of our time and Buttercup helping get some of the former escorts back to their families, or handling the ones that sold them, the past two months have slipped by.

The good news is, the people that were arrested at the party are all awaiting trial from within jail. No bail was granted as everyone involved has the means to flee to a non-extradition country, but the evidence collected guarantees they won't ever be leaving. I think the minimal

Epilogue 1

sentencing I heard going around was somewhere around the fifty-year mark. No possibility for early release or parole.

Sage is still up at Claudette's house, but will be moving in with us in a few weeks once the last of the girls are relocated or set up where they want to be. Claudette made good on her promise to house the girls if they wanted to stay and even signed the house over to Brittany, the girl Han grabbed from that shitty hotel, and Elenor. They didn't want to go home, and wanted to continue their education there. Claudette, of course, pays for anything they need and even keeps a few of the guards on hand for security.

The doors along the hall are fewer now than they were before. We expanded most of the rooms, restructured where possible, and gutted the place. During the reno, we all camped out in the same room to stay out of the way, and Ivy was pleased as hell that they did everything on time.

She takes me to the last door on the second floor and, with a flourish, opens it, ushering me inside.

I step into the bright white space, the morning light filling the room with its golden glow. There, in the center, is an easel holding a large canvas, a chaise lounge, and more art supplies than I've ever seen.

I spin around the room, looking at each detail, taking in everything and nothing at the same time because it's overloading my brain. "Is this an art studio?" I ask. My voice cracking at the wonder of it all.

"Yeah, I wanted you to have a space to create. Is it okay? I did a bunch of research and got everything they said was essential and then some. If you don't like it, I can—"

I cut off her insecurity with a fierce kiss. This woman. *This. Woman.*

"I love it, Buttercup. Don't worry about that. Oh my God, is that a pottery wheel over there?" I ask as I spy the bench behind her. "I've always wanted to try that!"

"Well, you could do that today. Or..." She pulls the tie on her white robe, and the sides part to reveal a very naked, very sexy Buttercup. "I did promise you could paint me one day."

Oh, yes. Oh, yes, yes, yes.

She laughs, and I look up to realize I'd been staring at her for just a beat too long.

"Come on. On the chaise? I want to paint you like one of those French girls!" I shout, misquoting Titanic. Snatching her hand in mine, I practically drag her across the space. Pulling the robe from her shoulders, I kiss each delicious inch as it's revealed. Just when she leans into it, my fingers

Epilogue 1

pluck at her nipples, teasing her until she's panting. Then I gently guide her onto the chaise. She reaches for me, but I swat her hands away.

"No, Buttercup. I want you hot and bothered and aching for me as I sit there, re-memorizing every curve of your body, every nuance of your skin and tattoos."

She sticks her lower lip out in a pout, and I kiss it away. "Would it help if I was naked too?" I ask.

She nods her head enthusiastically. I step away, pulling my t-shirt over my head and dropping my sweats on my way to the easel. It's a big, primed canvas, and I can't wait to fill the blank void with an image of my girl.

Grabbing a palette and a roller cart full of oil paints, I position them so they're behind me and I have an unobstructed view of the goddess before me. I see a Bluetooth speaker on the side and sync up my phone to play classical music in the background.

I start with the curve of her waist, that dip between her ribs and hips that slopes gently, enticing the eye to follow its path. Her legs are crossed at the calves, but they move to ease the ache building between her thighs, tensing and releasing. The line is so simple on the canvas, but the curve is sinful.

I focus on her torso, the arm that drapes up over the top of the chaise. When I paint, I can't focus on the whole subject when I start, so I miss the look in her eyes until I finally reach her face. Her eyes are roving over my body as the brush moves, trailing down my arm and back again, running down my body until I feel the prickle of awareness run along my skin anywhere her eyes touch.

I focus, despite my cock's insistence that we abandon this to join our girl. Adding splashes of color here and there, I keep it as lifelike as I can, focusing on the tiny details that make up Buttercup.

Painfully hard, literally, I ignore anything and everything, desperate to get this done. No, a painting doesn't need to be done in one sitting, but it's hard to stop once I've started. The sun has moved across the sky, and the lighting creates new shadows across Buttercup's body. I glance up and see the studio lighting she had fitted and curse myself for not flipping on the switches when we started.

The door behind me opens, and I hear a disgruntled groan. Unwilling to break concentration, I ignore it and hope whoever it is will go away.

No such luck.

"Uh, what's going on, guys?" Jacob asks.

"He's painting me," Buttercup replies.

Epilogue 1

"But why is he naked?"

"Because it's fun and he enjoys torturing me." She laughs before quickly straightening out her face. I may have told her to keep still a few dozen times already.

The air shifts as Jacob moves closer to me, examining the canvas before me. "Wow, Lucas, that's incredible."

I mumble my response as I work on her tattoo of the two birds escaping their cages. Mixing the soft lines of her body with the sharp tattoos is coming along better than I expected.

This might be my greatest work yet.

"Anyway, dinner is ready if you guys are hungry. Noah sent me to find you. We haven't seen you guys since breakfast. I fed and walked Sir Lancelot, too." Jacob leaves after giving us a heads up, and I properly look at Buttercup.

"Is it already dinner time?" I ask.

"Must be, but we can continue if you want. I've never seen you so focused," she says, keeping her body still. We've been at this for what? Eight hours? Holy shit. Well, the good thing is, I'm almost done.

"Can we go another thirty minutes or so?" I ask.

"For you, Red? Anything."

I smile to myself. There's a detail I'll add to the painting, so minuscule, I doubt she'll notice unless it's pointed out. But I'll know it's there.

Epilogue 2

Rogue

Seven Months Later

March in Antigua is hot. Good Lord, is it hot.

The breeze from the sea helps, but the humidity is making my thighs chafe like nobody's business. Noah and I walk along the path from the beach to our rented cabana, and his hand grips mine. Despite the wetness on our palms from the island air, we keep them clasped the whole way.

We decided to visit Mrs. M and her Dick for our eighteen-month-iversary, as Red calls it. Yep. Exactly eighteen months ago, he slid into my backseat, and I almost gutted him in a parking garage. Imagine how different life would be if I hadn't listened to my instincts in asking questions first.

The white sand of the beach reflects the warm sun, and the breeze picks up my dress. I untangle my hand from Noah's, keeping the damn material from betraying me and showing off the goods to the nice people sunbathing around us. Noah laughs as I gather the material in one hand, a curse upon my lips, as I slip my hand back into his.

Vacation looks good on the guys. I spy them lounging around the wooden platform on bright white cushions under the gauzy canopy. We've been here a month, and everyone is sporting a deep tan and relaxed faces.

Epilogue 2

Captain hasn't bothered with a shirt since we arrived, and I can't say I'm mad about it. He grills every evening, and we spend the days on the beach and the evenings eating, drinking, and spending time together.

Red has the most bizarre collection of swim trunks I've ever seen and likes to surprise us every day with a new print. Today, it's flamingos smoking joints. We went snorkeling yesterday, and he's been dragging me around to all the adrenaline adventures the island offers.

Han has two looks while on vacation. Board shorts in black or white linen pants. Both make me drool. He's been my luxury companion on the trip so far. We've done massages, facials, and he took me to a local fight night to relive the glory days of our misspent youth.

And Jacob? Jacob switched off his phone when the plane landed and hasn't looked at a screen since we arrived. Well, except for one. My Kindle. He's been reading some of my smutty books for "inspiration." Let me tell you, some of those books have been damn inspirational.

All of this to say; it's been paradise.

We go home in eight days because the longest I could bear to be away from Sage was six weeks. She's staying with Claudette while we're away, and I get daily updates. Her schooling recently finished, and she passed all of her classes, even touting a healthy GPA along the way. She's talking about going to college in the fall. I'm on board now that we've broken shit from the inside, but I know a part of me will always fret. She's also looking after Sir Lancelot while we're here. Lucas calls her his stand-in mama.

She's worried too, if her college choices are any sign. All of them are within four hours from us, and with the money King left for me, I'm planning to buy a helicopter to get to her quickly if she moves anywhere outside of El Castillo. Pilots aren't too expensive to keep on retainer if needed. I'll build them a guesthouse on the property. I think it will bring us both peace of mind.

We reach the cabana, and I see Jacob biting his lip as he reads one of my books and there's a slight flush on his cheeks. Yep, he must be at a sexy scene. I laugh and flop down on the large white cushion in the center.

"Do you guys really want to go back to work?" I pout. "We can stay here. Drink mimosas with our breakfasts, grill fish in the evenings, and fuck all day in between..." I trail off suggestively.

All four of them whip their gazes to me, and a feral hunger skates across their faces.

"Now, now, Trouble. You know Sage wants to go to school. We can't be

Epilogue 2

here if you want to stay close to her," Noah says, echoing my thoughts from earlier.

"Fine. But we can come back, right?" I ask.

"Definitely." Han leans over and kisses me indulgently. My hands skate along his strong arms, pulling him down with me.

"Insatiable, the lot of you!" a voice cackles from nearby, drawing attention to us. Dammit. Mrs. M's enormous white sun hat enters the cabana before the rest of her. "There are children present, Ivy! At least show them the proper way to do it!" I shove myself to a sitting position, making Han roll away in the process as he laughs.

"Hi, Mrs. M," I greet, properly chastised and embarrassed. The flush on my cheeks has nothing to do with the sun or the feel of Han's lips against mine. Nope. It's all being caught by Mama Bear and her beau, Dick.

The two of them join us, and Jacob fishes some water bottles out of the cooler in the corner for our guests. We've spent time with them almost daily, catching up and learning about their life on the island. Dick, while not overly chatty, is a kind and calm man. He's perfect for balancing out the enigma that is Mrs. M.

We all sit, talking and enjoying the sunset together, already lamenting that our time is almost up but making promises to come visit again soon.

Just as the last sliver of sun dips below the horizon, Lucas hops to his feet. "Mrs. M, Dick, we have plans to get ready for. But we'll see you guys tomorrow, okay?" Lucas rushes out, hastily packing up stuff from the day.

"Oh, yes. Okay, dears. Be good! Have fun!" Then she leans in, giving me a big hug and whispering, "I'm so glad they found you." As she pulls back, there's a tear trailing down her cheek. She wipes it away before the others see, and I'm left puzzling over that as she and Dick walk up to the beach houses.

Jacob helps me load up my stuff, and we follow the same path Mrs. M and Dick did. There are only five houses along the shore here, all spaced out and available for renters. However, we booked everything, putting Mrs. M on one end of the beach and us on the other. No one needs to be that close when vacation sex is on the table. Or the couch. Or the floor.

The guys usher me into the master bedroom, telling me to get ready for a night out as they hang out in the living room. I wash, leaving my hair wet and working some product through it because straightening it in this humidity is a recipe for disappointment if I want it to last longer than five minutes, and put on a white linen dress I found at a shop yesterday.

I strap sandals to my feet, my tanned skin vibrant against the all-white

Epilogue 2

ensemble. Braiding back the front of my hair so it's half out of the way, I dab on some berry lip stain and mascara.

The noises from the living room have died down, and it isn't until I'm grabbing my teal clutch that the absence of noise begins to bother me. I slip off my sandals and pull a knife from the bedside table, palming the grip with a steady hand. I turn the handle, watching the door crack just a bit before my foot pulls it the rest of the way.

The coast is clear, which is both good and terrifying. Where the hell are they?

The terracotta tiles are cool under my feet as I make my way to the living room. Nothing. Nothing and no one.

I spin in place, checking the exits and looking for signs of a struggle. My eyes land on the big kitchen table and there, in the center, I see a bouquet of flowers that make little sense when grouped, but for me, they mean everything.

Pristine white roses from Lucas, bright yellow sunflowers from Noah, rich black dahlias from Han, and full light blue hydrangeas from Jacob.

A smile lights my face as I step closer. There's a note tucked just under the base.

Follow the lights.
-Your guys

I look around the small house, wondering what they mean, when I see an LED flower near the front door. My feet rush closer, completely ignoring the fact that I have no shoes on so I can figure out their game.

Opening the door, I see the steps leading down to the walkway each have a flower on them. In the thick evening air, they call out to me like beacons, disappearing down the path.

I keep my knife in my hand, because, well, that's just good sense, and bound down the steps, following the trail of lights. There must be hundreds of the illuminated blooms leading me closer to the cabana and the beach.

The short trees sway in the gentle breeze, and the reedy grass that sprouts from the sand sways, doing its timeless dance in the Caribbean breeze.

I follow the lights, wondering what these four have planned for me, when I pause at the end of the path after making the last turn where the path disappears into the sand.

There, I find my four guys, each on bended knee, waiting.

"Who had money on a knife?" Lucas asks when he catches sight of me.

Epilogue 2

Jacob's hand rises, and Han groans. "I thought for sure she would have grabbed a gun," he mumbles.

"What's going on, guys? How long have you been down here?" I ask, drawing nearer.

"Well, we had a whole plan for dinner and then things, but someone," Noah grouses as he looks at Lucas, "got impatient and switched up the order."

Lucas just shrugs his shoulders. "I called dibs and I'm sick of sitting on them."

"Dibs? What the hell? You're not making me choose, right?" My voice quivers as I look down at the four men before me, kneeling as if they're waiting to be knighted. Fuck that, I am not Queen anymore. Plus, that wasn't a thing, anyway.

"No, Buttercup, a different kind of dibs."

With a flick of my wrist, I send the knife into the sand, embedding the blade into the soft grains. Clearly no one is under attack and accidents happen, so I'd rather be safe and unarmed because my hands are shaking with uncertainty.

I drop to my knees before the guys, so we're all on the same level. Standing above them felt odd, and I'd rather look them in the eyes without getting a cramp in my neck. The granules dig into my knees, but the discomfort is nothing when faced with the adoration in each of my guys' eyes.

Lucas reaches forward and takes my hands in his. "Buttercup, I've felt for you since you first held a knife to my cock, loved you since we sat on that beach and talked about our lives. I don't see a future unless you're in it. I love you." His eyes well, and I remove a hand from his to run a thumb along his cheek, clearing the escaped tear.

"I'm not going anywhere, Red." My words are clear and firm, assuring him. "I can't imagine my life without you either, and I love you too, so much."

"Good," he whispers and kisses me softly. He transfers my hands to Noah's. "Trouble, the best nickname I could have ever given you." I laugh at his words, reminding me of our first solo date. "You are a light in the darkness. A woman I want to cherish, and spoil rotten, and strive to always be better for. You deserve everything the world offers, and I want to be one of the men to offer it to you. I want you to always challenge me, to keep me from becoming stagnant. You are a firework in a starless sky—a riot of color and endless wonder—I love you."

Epilogue 2

His words have me on the verge of tears. First, Lucas. Now, me. Taking a shaky breath through trembling lips, I lean forward, kissing him gently. My Captain. "I love you too, you steadfast, constant man. You keep us level, and we desperately need you—no, want you—to do that. You are our Dear Leader, our calm port in the storm."

Noah sighs against my lips when my words trail off. There are not enough expressions, words, phrases in the dictionary to explain the love I have for these men. The sheer overwhelming rising tide in my chest is proof enough of that.

Han takes hold of my hands, passing one to Jacob, and they link their hands so we form a triangle between us.

"Ivy, my first love, and one of my last." Han smirks as he shoots a glance at Jacob, who smiles in encouragement. "You are my biggest support, my constant friend, and my love for you knows no bounds. You encourage us to be who we are, and love who we love. I've been lucky enough to have one of my loves lead me to the other."

Jacob speaks before I can even respond to Han. His grip on my hand is warm, and his dark-rimmed glasses reflect the lights of the flowers that brought me here. "Han is right. It takes a rare woman to bring any one of us to our knees, and here you have four of us. I love you and your competitive nature. Your drive. Your heart. Darling Mine, I'm glad we finally settled on a nickname, but I think it's time we change it again."

My brows raise in confusion. I cannot go back to Snuggle Muffin. I can't do it.

"I love you, too. And I love you, Han." My eyes bounce between them as their words all wash over me. This is either the most misleading break up in history or something big is coming.

I glance between my four men, my guys who have stood with me and supported me in everything. Never once stepping in to take over, but trusting that I could handle myself in the myriad of situations I've found myself in over the last eighteen months.

Jacob and Han release my hands, and as one, they all dig into their pockets, each pulling out a square box.

I resist the urge to bring my hands up to my quivering chin like they do in the movies, but it's damn hard. I clasp my hands in front of me, watching. Waiting. It feels as if I've been waiting for this my whole life and at the same time, as if no time at all has passed since we met.

In unison, they open their boxes.

Four rings glint back at me, each band inlaid with stones in the colors of

Epilogue 2

their flowers. There is no showy rock, no clunky band, both of which I appreciate, as it would make it difficult to do a job with an iceberg on my finger.

Lucas is the one who speaks up. "Buttercup, will you marry us? I know we can't do the whole legal part because four isn't exactly a legal number of husbands, but would you marry us in a commitment ceremony? All of us?"

My head was nodding even before he finished speaking. Noah laughs at my enthusiasm, but his grin is just as big as mine.

"Yes. YES!" I shout.

As one, we stand, embracing in the cool sand, the breeze cooling my heated skin and flushed face. One by one, the guys slip their rings onto my finger. Stacked together, they resemble the bouquet sitting on our kitchen table. My heart, my once icy and untrusting heart, swells in my chest, and I rub a palm over it, trying to hold on to the sensation for as long as possible.

I hear shouting behind us, and I turn to find Mrs. M running toward us from the cabana. "No sex on the beach! I'm still filming!" Dick is strolling after her, shaking his head and laughing at her antics.

"From way over there? I doubt you picked up anything at that distance. It might have been safer to stay there," I warn her. My body is hyped up on adrenaline, and there's nothing more I want currently than my guys curled around me in every possible way.

"Uh, Trouble..." Noah drags my attention to him. He unbuttons his shirt, and I find a small microphone taped to his chest. The others show that they were all wired, as well. Then he points out the cameras stationed around us, hidden in the darkness.

I hang my head. "Fucking feds."

They all laugh and I'm swept up in congratulatory hugs and kisses from my men and Mrs. M.

"Come on, dinner is ready. Lucas, honey, why did you switch the order?" Mrs. M asks, grumbling about how the food will be cold by now.

"I had a feeling that proposing would make me hungry. I was right." He shrugs as he rubs his stomach. "By the way, Buttercup, did you ever notice the ring in the painting I did when you showed me the art room?" he asks.

"You painted a ring on me all those months ago?" I ask, cursing myself for not noticing the tiny detail. I mean, the thing hangs in our hidden sex room, so it's not like it's out of sight with how often we sneak down there. Clearly, that room is distracting.

"I knew I wanted to marry you almost as soon as I saw you. I just had to

Epilogue 2

wait for you to catch up." His sly smile is addicting as he leads me to the table.

We stroll to the dinner they arranged, a large table set in the sand so we can watch the stars and celebrate in peace. Mrs. M and Dick join us for the food, but make their excuses early, giving us time to revel in the new chapter we're about to begin. Together.

We may not get married tomorrow, or even next year, but our commitment to each other will remain unchanged whether it's official or not. I used to imagine having a normal life, coming home to a normal husband, ordering pizza, and talking about our days.

How much better is it to have an extraordinary life with extraordinary men?

Afterword

This series brings so much joy to my heart. It was my first attempt at writing, and while looking back at it now has me aching to edit it to high heaven, I've mostly left it alone because it is where I started and the words managed to grip so many of you. It is the series that got me into the author world and has allowed me to continue on my journey. I am so grateful for each and every one of you who picked up one of my books and gave me a chance. *You* are the reason I do this. I want to hear your reactions, see the edits, and chat on Insta about fan theories. Thank you from the bottom of my heart.
    Thank you.
    Thank you.
    Thank you.
    Xoxo
    Mila

Made in the USA
Columbia, SC
02 October 2024